STALKING GINEVRA

GIGI STYX

AUTHOR'S NOTE

This dark romance book romanticizes morally black and machiavellian behavior for entertainment. If you're offended by gaslighting, controlling psychopathic exploits and other reprehensible acts, do not continue reading.

TRIGGER WARNINGS

This is a dark romance that includes dub-con, graphic depictions of torture and violence, and sexually explicit scenes. If any of this content is triggering for you, please do not read this book.

Abduction
Alcoholism
Attempted rape (villain)
Blackmail
Blindfolds
Bombing
Bondage
Breeding kink
Butt plugs
Cannibalism (rumored)
Cesare slander
Choking
Costumes
Decapitation
Degradation
Denigration
Domestic violence
Dubious consent
Ephebophilia (villain backstory)
Evisceration
Facials
Femicide
Forced exhibitionism (backstory)
Forced marriage
Forced shaving
Foster care (backstory)
Fraud
Gaslighting
Grooming (secondary character backstory)
Hidden cameras

Humiliation
Immolation
Imprisonment
Improper use of catgirl cosplay
Incest (between consenting adult villains)
Isolation
Kitten play
Knife play
Masked man
Montesano brother slander
Murder
Nihonophilia
Old man peen
Panty play
Parentification
Pearl necklace
Pit traps
Primal kink
PTSD
Rape (backstory)
Seppuku
Seraphine slander
Shibari
Spanking
Stalking
Stockholm syndrome
Surveillance
Teenage pregnancy (secondary character backstory)
Toys
Verbal abuse
Violence
Virgin hero
Whipping
Wild hunt

Reader discretion is advised. If you find any of these topics distressing, please proceed with caution or consider choosing a different book. Your mental health matters.

*For every girl who ever wanted an unhinged stalker
to tear out a man's heart for touching you.*

SUMMARY OF CHARACTERS

Characters:

Montesano family - the oldest crime family in the state of New Alderney, once run by Enzo Montesano. Five years before the novel, he was betrayed by his lawyer and most trusted lieutenant, who embezzled several assets, arranged his murder, stole this businesses, and framed his eldest son, Roman for murder.

Capello family - an up-and-coming crime family once loyal to the Montesano family until their leader, Frederic Capello, decided to betray his boss. At the beginning of the series, Leroi Montesano murders the entire Capello family after Frederic's 60th birthday.

Galliano family - the largest crime family in New Jersey, run by Tommy Galliano and his brother, Matty. The Galliano brothers financed Capello's betrayal and rise to power and stole the Montesano family meth lab.

Enzo Montesano - the former Montesano boss who was murdered in his own nightclub. Father of the Montesano brothers.

Lucia Montesano - his wife, who left the family after Enzo's murder to marry Tommy Galliano, but died during a breast augmentation. Mother of the Montesano brothers.

Roman Montesano - the eldest brother who was released from death row for a murder he didn't commit. In Snaring

Emberly, he embezzles his family's stolen assets back from Capello's illegitimate daughter.

Benito Montesano - the middle brother who dropped out of law school when his father Enzo was murdered and worked hard to keep the family together. In Stalking Ginevra, he punishes his ex-fiancée for breaking his heart and for her father's role in his family's downfall.

Cesare Montesano - the youngest brother who dropped out of medical school after his father's murder and became addicted to drugs. After rehab, he runs the nightclub and doubles up as the family torturer. In Breaking Rosalind, he tortures an assassin sent to spy on his family.

Leroi Montesano - the brothers' first cousin who lived separately from the age of ten when his father died. He is the assassin who wiped out the Capello family and found the evidence to free Roman. In Taming Seraphine, he rescues a girl chained in Capello's basement.

Frederic Capello - the leader of the Capello family who worked closely with Enzo Montesano's allies to embezzle his assets and steal his business. He also has multiple mistresses and illegitimate children and was murdered by Leroi at the beginning of the series.

Samson Capello - Frederic's eldest son, who survives the massacre when his cousin slept on his bed, only to send assassins after Leroi. He's ruthless, psychopathic, and twisted.

Gregor Capello - Samson's saner, more calculating twin brother. Murdered by Leroi at the beginning of the series.

Seraphine Capello - the daughter of Samson's favorite mistress Evangeline. When a blood test revealed she was the bodyguard's daughter, Frederic moved Seraphine into his basement to pay him back for the money he spent. After holding her brother hostage, the twins trained Seraphine to become an assassin.

Gabriel Capello - Evangeline's son and Seraphine's older brother, whom Frederic Capello used as a liver donor

Emberly Kay - Frederic Capello's daughter with a mistress who escaped during pregnancy and spent her life on the run with Emberly. She inherits the Montesano stolen assets after the fall of the Capello family, but has no idea about the identity of her father.

Joseph Di Marco - Frederic Capello's lawyer who helped transfer the Montesano assets to his client. He was the father of Ginevra and husband of Losanna and was murdered by Leroi while in bed with his mistress.

Ginevra Di Marco - Joseph's daughter from a relationship with an underage girl prior to his marriage. She has been in a relationship with Benito Montesano since they were eight but was forced to break their engagement when Joseph joined forces with Capello to steal Enzo Montesano's business.

Losanna Di Marco - married Joseph after her underage cousin abandoned Ginevra as a baby with her family and was later murdered by serial wife murderer, Gianni Bossanova.

Martina Mancini - Ginevra's childhood friend, law school study buddy, best friend, and colleague, who works for the Di Marco Law Group. She is the attorney who gave Emberly vital information about her inheritance.

Myra Mancini - Martina's younger sister, who works in Cesare's fetish store. She's the sales clerk who helped Seraphine with her purchases.

Tommy Galliano - blackmailed Lucia Montesano for decades when he and his brother drugged and impregnated her. Forced Lucia to marry him after the death of her husband, Enzo.

Matty Galliano - the biological father of Lucia's youngest son, Cesare. After his children are murdered during the Capello massacre, he becomes obsessed with making Cesare acknowledge their relationship.

Rosalind Galliano - Matty Galliano's step daughter who he groomed and impregnated when she was fourteen. She trains as an assassin with the Moirai Group to storm the Galliano mansion to get her baby back but becomes trapped in a contract she can't escape.

Miranda Galliano - the daughter of Matty and Rosalind Galliano. After being abducted by Rosalind in a brutal shootout, she spends the rest of her childhood in boarding schools, believing Rosalind is a cruel older sister who murdered her parents.

Gianni Bossanova - another prisoner on death row who gave Roman advice on women.

The Moirai Group - the largest firm of assassins who recruit and train children to be killers. Hired by Samson Capello and Tommy Galliano to take out the Montesano men.

Isabella Cortese - Cesare's chemistry professor who ran the meth lab. She, her team, and her son were abducted by Tommy Galliano and forced to produce meth.

Reaper Cortese - Isabella's younger brother, Benito's former law professor and right hand man, who teamed up with Benito to search for Isabella and set up Mortis House, a fraternity of mafia boys they're grooming for success.

Gil Agostini - former boxer and loyal lieutenant who once took a bullet for Enzo Montesano. Currently Roman's right-hand man.

Sofia Veccio - the Montesano family housekeeper, who stepped in as a mother figure for the boys when Lucia Montesano fell into a depression.

Elania Salentino - close cousins of the Montesano brothers, who run the Newtown Crematorium and occasionally dispose of corpses.

Aria Salentino - Elania's kinder, friendlier, tomboy twin sister.

Amethyst Salentino - daughter of the twins' older brother, Giorgi. Also known as Amethyst Crowley, who is best friends with Martina's younger sister and also wrote to a serial killer and became his obsession in I Will Break You.

Xero Greaves - serial killer, former Moirai assassin, and associate of Rosalind, who helps Cesare blow up the Moirai Group's headquarters. He stalks Amethyst in I Will Break You.

ONE

GINEVRA

Samson's hideout has erupted into World War Three. The Montesano family is attacking, and we're all going to die. I should be using this chance to escape my psycho fiancé, but he's tossed me in a closet.

Instead, I'm kneeling, naked, knotted in shibari... numb with a sense of inevitable doom.

I wish this was the punchline to a bad joke.

Ropes constrict my torso, creating a diamond pattern from my breasts down to my crotch. He calls it Japanese bondage, but it might as well be a butcher's meat trussing. The fibers tease my clit, triggering an uncontrollable surge of arousal.

I couldn't escape without help even if the mansion was on fire.

Samson wanted to show his guards how he could make me come without using his hands. Bastard didn't get a chance to finish before a small army stormed the compound with automatic weapons.

He was supposed to be dead weeks ago—shot down by the lone gunman who infiltrated his father's sixtieth birthday party and massacred the entire Capello family.

When Dad told me the Capellos had been murdered, I was relieved—even happy. I never asked to be engaged to the world's angriest and most abusive asshole, never asked to endure rejection, degradation, and insults.

Dad broke my engagement with my soulmate and childhood best friend to join forces with an up-and-coming mafia family. I was the collateral he sacrificed to become the Capello consigliere. While he reveled in power and prestige, I paid with my dignity.

The relief at losing my fiancé only lasted the hours it took for Samson to stumble through our door, still high from whatever shit he took at his dad's party. After driving me home the night before, he'd crashed into a lamp post and spent the night unconscious at the wheel.

The man has the luck of the devil, but it's about to run out.

Gunfire thunders from the grounds, accompanied by the panicked shouts of Samson's men. Vibrations travel through the floorboards into my bare skin, making me tremble.

They're coming closer.

It won't be long before bullets rip through the cupboard door inches from my face, scattering wood chips and dust over my naked body. I squeeze my eyes shut, my heart pounding so desperately against its cage that I swear it's about to burst.

Sweat trickles down the valley between my breasts and soaks into the rope. At the sound of bullets shattering glass, I whimper.

They're here.

Terror grips my senses, and the acrid scent of gunpowder sears my nostrils. Fear coats my tongue, metallic and bitter, making me want to gag. This reminds be so much of the time Samson forced me to deep throat his gun. I breathe hard, holding down a surge of panic as the voices reach a crescendo.

I'm going to die. Die before I even got a chance to apologize to Benito for breaking our engagement. Life with him was simple. I was the center of his attention—he catered to my every whim.

Benito placed me on a pedestal, treating me like a princess. It was impossible not to love him when his entire personality revolved around being at my side. When I enrolled in law school to follow in Dad's footsteps, he did the same to keep me company.

Instead of living in a sorority house with my best friend, Martina, I stayed in an apartment by the campus with Benito. He insisted on separate bedrooms because he was saving us for our wedding night.

Our love was so pure that sometimes, I felt like one of his anime figurines—lined up on a shelf, pristine and untouched. He never let his hands wander beneath my clothes.

It's funny how my final thoughts center on the man I wronged. Despite the chaos beyond the closet door, I would give my soul to be engaged to Benito again instead of Samson.

He isn't just a monster, he's obsessed with a little blonde girl he kept in his basement, and even placed a chip under her skin. I only found out about this an hour ago, when a red-headed boy brought her to Samson as collateral for a negotiation.

The girl explains why Samson only had sex with me once during the five years we were engaged. It was never about my supposedly loose pussy or off-putting red pubes. At twenty-eight, I was simply too old.

I need him to die. The world is a better place with one less child predator.

The closet door creaks open, flooding my vision with harsh light, making me squint. A large figure fills the doorway, clad in full body armor. Shivering, I tilt my head, peeking up at him through a gap in the ropes Samson wrapped around my eyes.

His face is hidden behind a black helmet, the tinted visor concealing his eyes. He raises a gloved hand, pointing a pistol directly at my face.

My stomach lurches. I can't let him blow my brains across the closet wall. My soul will be forever tainted with the guilt of breaking Benito's heart.

"Please," I rasp, my throat so dry the sound comes out a strangled whisper.

The figure remains silent, his aim unwavering from the space between my eyes. My heart pounds so hard and fast that my ears fill with its echoes. I can't let this be my last moment.

"Let me live, and I'll give you anything," I croak.

He stares down at me for several tense heartbeats, and my life flashes before my eyes. Memories of a childhood spent accompanying Dad to the Montesano mansion surface—where the housekeeper would take me to the kitchen and teach me to make cookies. Benito would linger in the doorway, watching from a distance.

My mind fills with a kaleidoscope of snapshots, each one featuring the same bookish guy: buying me tiger lilies because they reminded him of my hair, surprising me with first-edition copies of my favorite novels, making me yuzu tea because I love everything citrus. Benito wasn't like other sons of mafia bosses. He was lanky, awkward, meek—but endearing.

The memories are warm. Comforting. And for a moment, I'm transported to the happiest years of my life. Then, they fade, and I'm pulled back into the present, facing the barrel of this stranger's gun.

After what feels like an eternity, the man in the doorway places his weapon in a holster and draws a knife.

I shudder, bracing for the cold bite of his blade. Warm blood will trickle down my skin, soaking into the ropes. I'll still be trussed up like a Thanksgiving turkey when the police bring Mom to identify my body.

Rage heats my blood. I don't deserve any of this, yet here I am, staring into the cold visor of death. Gritting my teeth, I force down the emotion, focussing only on my survival. Dad should have lived long enough to witness how his choices led to my destruction.

The man reaches a gloved hand and grabs my shoulder, making me whimper. He forces my torso downward, pressing my lower body against my thighs, and cuts the ropes binding my arms.

My heart pounds a deafening drumbeat as my hands flop to the side. Circulation floods back to my upper limbs in an explosion of pins and needles. I wince at the prickling sensation, hoping he'll withdraw the knife and leave. Instead, he grabs the ropes around the back of my head and forces me upright.

I stare at the finger tapping the padded triangle of fabric protecting his groin. It's attached to the rest of his tactical gear with reinforced straps and buckles, but more importantly, misshapen by the bulge of his erection.

Dread rolls through my stomach like thunder, bringing it with a burst of suppressed fury.

"What do you want?" I whisper.

The fingers in my hair tighten as if the answer is obvious. Pain slices across my scalp, making me wince but also sharpening my memory.

I offered him anything to save my life. As if I had the choice.

Now, he wants me to suck his cock.

"F-Fellatio?" I whisper.

With a curt nod, he loosens his grip on my hair. A shiver runs down my spine, but I shove away the fear and focus on survival. Because if I get through this ordeal, I'll be sure to apologize to Benito.

I raise trembling fingers to the quick-release buckles and unstrap the groin guard. The bulge in his pants expands, making my breath catch.

He looks well-endowed—impossibly large. I've only done this once before on a real penis. It was humiliating, painful, and unpleasant. Afterward, Samson shoved me aside, calling me talentless.

My stomach dips. What if I fail to please this man and he retaliates?

Swallowing the lump in my throat, I pull down his zipper and groan at the monstrously thick cock straining against his silk underwear.

It's thicker than the dildos Samson forced me to practice on, bigger than anything I've ever seen or imagined. Heart pounding, I ease down the fabric and release his length.

His hips shift—his only indication of impatience—before he yanks my hair by the roots. Hissing through my teeth at the pain, I drift forward, positioning my mouth so close to his erection that its heat radiates against my lips.

As I run my tongue along the flat of his veiny flesh, his grip loosens, and he exhales a long, deep moan. The primal sound shoots straight to my pussy. Breathing hard, I trace a line up his shaft, slowing at his thick crown.

My nostrils fill with the intimidating musk of his arousal, accompanied by the taste of salt. His heat pulses against my tongue, and in a perverse way, it's pleasurable, and takes the edge off my anger.

Stifling a jolt of unwanted desire, I focus on making him come. I suck the head between my lips, working the underside with my tongue. The man rocks his hips back and forth, sliding his shaft in and out of my mouth.

I shift uncomfortably on the floor, the ropes separating my labia rubbing against my swollen clit.

His breath quickens, and I suppress a surge of pride at moving this powerful being. Switching my thinking, I imagine the stranger is Benito—only he's dominant, dangerous, and demanding.

Arousal builds in my core at the thought of controlling his pleasure. I hollow my cheeks, taking him deep into my throat.

Every vein, every contour, every ridge presses against the membranes of my mouth as I swallow him whole. Thanks to Samson and his stupid toys, I've lost my gag reflex, and the man I'm pleasuring seems impressed.

My gaze flicks up, eager to meet his eyes, maybe hear a little praise, but all I see is my reflection in his helmet's visor. The woman staring back at me looks like a flame-haired porn star, with lips stretched around a thick shaft.

I force myself to breathe as he thrusts forward, sliding his entire length down my gullet. His generous girth crushes my windpipe, cutting off my air. Tears well in the corners of my eyes. My lungs burn for oxygen, yet I can't explain why the thought of choking on him makes my clit throb and my nipples tingle.

The rope splitting open my pussy no longer chafes, becoming slick with my arousal. It's the first time I've reacted this way to my own debasement.

Gulping around his shaft hard enough to make him groan, I pull back and gasp for breath. My eyes water, vision blurring until I blink away the tears. They gather on the rope encasing my head, making the fibers expand.

I barely get the chance to inhale another breath before he snaps his hips, burying himself back down my throat. The unexpected force has me seeing stars, but he doesn't pause to give me time to adjust.

Groaning, he pounds in and out of my mouth, using me ruthlessly for his pleasure. I roll my hips against the ropes, creating delicious friction.

By now, I can't stop the tears. They seep through my binding, stream down my cheeks, and drip onto my breasts. I'm moaning through my mouthful, gasping, choking, bucking my hips, trying to match his rhythm.

My pussy throbs in sync with his thrusts. Every time he pushes deep, he ignites a fire in my core that grows hotter. I reach down between my thighs, unable to withstand the urge to touch my clit. My fingers slide along the soaked ropes then brush against my aching center.

Sparks of pleasure jolt through my system at the barest touch. I've never felt so excited at being at a man's mercy. Never felt this level of euphoria.

The stranger quickens his movement, indicating that he's close. I rub circles over my clit, timing them with his strokes. I want to make him come. I want to swallow his release. I want to please this man because my life depends on his satisfaction.

In this moment, he becomes my world, my entire universe, and I revolve around his axis of pleasure.

His grunts become harsher, filled with lust and anticipation, the sound resonating through my core.

After years of Samson's abuse, I never thought degradation would get me so aroused, but here I am, allowing a strange man to use my throat as his fleshlight. Maybe it's because I have a choice, even though it was limited. Maybe it's because this stranger has proven Samson wrong. I'm not frigid, talentless, or undesirable. If that were true, I'd be dead.

Pressure builds up around my clit, a thrumming sensation close to unbearable. Sharp bursts of ecstasy radiate from my core, lighting up my nerves with every thrust.

A growl rumbles in his chest, and his grip on my hair tightens. This time, my body interprets that pain as pleasure. Shuddering, I increase the suction and quicken my strokes over my clit.

When he growls, something inside me snaps. My body tenses for a heartbeat before releasing a deluge of pleasure, coursing through my system and crashing through every nerve.

I groan around the shaft in my mouth, my pussy spasming

and clenching in blissful climax. It's like diving into the ocean and being tossed around by powerful waves.

His cock throbs before pulsing once, twice, three times down my throat. Warm cum fills my mouth, making my taste buds sing.

Stroking myself through the climax, I ride out the pleasure as the man above me exerts his final thrusts. He's spurting faster than I can swallow, making cum dribble down my chin and settle on my breasts.

Without a word or a grunt or a pat on the head, he drops the knife, letting it fall to the floor with a clatter. Then he pulls out, tucks himself in, and walks out without a backward glance, leaving me utterly destroyed.

TWO

BENITO

I came here to kill her. Instead, I came down her throat.

Stepping back from the closet door, I stuff my cock back into my pants and turn to face the rest of the room. Everyone is dead, from the red-haired boy with a bullet through his head to the guards lying face-down on the floor.

Ginevra was... I shake my head.

Her death was supposed to end my obsession, but when I saw her displayed so prettily, begging me for her life, it was hard to do anything else but spare it.

After five years apart, I'm still the simp who caters to her every whim. Case in point. I'm now walking around the room, looking for her clothes so she won't have to leave here naked once she's cut herself free.

My heart pounds so hard that my fingers tremble as I step over Samson Capello's carcass to reach a chair draped with her purse, her size seven shoes, and a stack of feminine garments. That was my first blow job, and I'm already yearning for a second.

After lifting my visor, I pick up her lace panties, bring them to my nose, and inhale the heavenly scent of her pussy. My cock stirs, making me light-headed. The greedy bastard urges me to carry Ginevra away, confine her in my treehouse, and never let her see the light of day.

I shake off that thought. Our family is in turmoil, and I'm the only brother capable of taking control. Roman just got released from death row, and Cesare is still interrogating the assassin who came to murder us in our beds. We need to retrieve the assets Capello stole from Dad, handle the threat of the Galliano brothers, and deal with potential unrest within our ranks.

Then there's the scholarships, the fraternity house, the bastards we're tracking at the casino, and negotiating the cremators with the Salentino sisters...

There's no time to reignite my obsession.

I slip the panties in my pocket for later perusal, gather Ginevra's clothes in my arms, circle back to the closet, and lay them down by the door.

A soft groan has me whirling around to the source of the sound. Samson Capello spasms within a pool of blood, looking like he's in the final throes of death.

He's still alive. How the hell could I have missed that?

Because Ginevra Di Marco has always been a distraction. In a matter of days, she's now become available, having lost her father and fiancé. And I won't be able to clear my mind of her until she's finally dead.

Heart pounding, I reach into my holster for my handgun. By now, she'll have removed the ropes from around her head. I'll shoot her between those beautiful gray eyes and end her hold on my psyche.

Footsteps approach from the direction of the stairs, accompanied by Cesare's voice. Hackles rising, I turn around to find him walking into the room with a tiny blonde.

"What are you doing out of the triage truck?" I ask.

My brother pauses in the doorway, his eyes narrowing. "Why are you still here?"

"I'm asking the questions," I say.

"We're here to finish Samson."

My eyes narrow. I glance from my youngest sibling to his even younger companion, recognizing her as Seraphine, the woman whose abduction triggered this entire battle.

Our cousin Leroi called hours ago to tell us he'd located Samson, hiding right under our noses in a compound halfway down Alderney Hill. After Leroi killed Samson's family, his right-hand man traded an innocent girl to spare him from Samson's assassins. Based on the bullet lodged in his skull, I'd say his plan backfired.

Leroi must be in love. Why else would he waste such a good hacker?

Cesare tosses a doctor bag on the floor, narrowly missing Samson's head, and crouches in the dying bastard's pool of blood. Seraphine kneels beside him, trying to press her fingers into the gunshot wound on Samson's stomach.

Grabbing her wrist, my brother lectures her on the importance of not contaminating a victim's wound. I tune him out, retreat to the corner of the room, and wait for Cesare to complete his triage.

I trust my brother to give Samson a slow death. He's the family torturer, and a genius at reviving victims over and over to prolong their agony. As a boy, he was so fixated with eviscerating that Mother and Dr. Brunelli thought he would become a serial killer. To put his urges to better use, they encouraged him to be a surgeon.

If Cesare discovers Ginevra in the closet, he'll dissect her as punishment for leaving me for Samson—never mind that she's the daughter of the man who helped Capello steal our family's assets from Dad.

An hour after sitting through the world's most gruesome bullet removal surgery, Cesare drags Samson out of the room and down the stairs. Seraphine, whose hands and face are covered in blood, gives him a standing ovation, making me wonder if Leroi knows he's fallen in love with a psychopath.

Shaking off that thought, I turn my attention to the closet. While my brother and his unhinged little friend were toying with Samson's insides, Ginevra slipped her clothes through a chink in the door, as they've disappeared.

I slide the gun back into the holster. Killing Ginevra tonight would only give me a moment's satisfaction. Keeping her alive and giving back all the pain she's inflicted on me will be a sweet, drawn-out pleasure.

Besides, Roman has Capello's daughter, Cesare has the

assassin he's slowly torturing, and Leroi has Seraphine. Why shouldn't I have something too?

I hurry down the stairs, finding the mansion empty, save for Capello's deceased guards. Outside, the first streams of sunlight seep through the evergreens, and I inhale a burst of juniper-scented air.

After ordering our men to clear the courtyard, I remove my bullet proof jacket and helmet, don a baseball cap and face mask, and drive a car to the front steps.

At some point, Ginevra will pluck up the courage to call an Uber, and I intend to be the man behind the wheel. Sitting in the driver's seat, I wait for her to emerge.

Hours pass. Eventually, Ginevra pokes her head through the mansion's double doors, the faint light coloring her auburn hair an iridescent shade of copper. The modest, green shift she wears hides her curves, making her look like the sweet girl who held my heart for twenty years.

She's so shaken by tonight's carnage and cock sucking that she fails to check her app.

Winding down the window, I lean across the back seat, making sure to stay concealed beneath the visor of my cap. Her face is pale and drawn, her eyes puffy and red, and it takes every effort not to pull her into a hug.

In a thick, nondescript accent, I ask, "Uber for Di Marco?"

"Yes." She opens the back door and sits inside.

My cock hardens at the thought of the game that's just begun. As I pull away from Capello's ravaged hideout, I glance at her through the rearview mirror. She sits clutching her purse with white-knuckled fingers.

"Nice evening, Ma'am?" I ask.

When her features tighten, I smirk beneath my mask. She might act affronted but I know she brought herself to climax. All from sucking my cock.

Samson must have trained her extensively during the five years she was his fiancée, because we never did more than kiss. She was my pure little goddess, my future wife. I didn't want to besmirch her honor before marriage.

If I'd known she would leave me for a bastard like Capello, I would have fucked her at every opportunity. Maybe then, I would have moved onto another woman, and been more like Cesare, who has a roster of beautiful employees with benefits.

I navigate the hair-pin turns of Alderney Hill, reveling in her discomfort. When she wipes away a tear, I wonder if it's for her soon-to-be dead fiancé or for her recent degradation.

"Where to, Ma'am?" I ask.

"Don't you have my address in your system?" she asks back, her voice tight with impatience.

"32, Willow Lane, Queen's Gardens?"

"Yes," she hisses.

I suppress a chuckle. "Rough night?"

She doesn't answer.

"Only you look a little disheveled."

"Would you mind driving faster?" she asks, her pretty lips tightening with distaste.

"Of course, Ma'am," I answer, taking my foot off the gas.

Ginevra inserts wireless earbuds into her ears and stares out through the window, determined to avoid my probing questions. With a smile, I leave Alderney Hill and turn the vehicle onto a longer route.

Silence stretches across the back seat of the car, filled only by the soft purr of the engine. When she brings her trembling fingers to her mouth, I can't help but think she's still tasting my cum.

It's light by the time I deposit her outside the front doors of her family home, a sprawling McMansion set within a quarter acre of lawns and manicured hedges.

Opening the door, she steps out without so much as a thank you. Her movements are hurried, frantic. I smirk, watching her stumble up the steps to her family home.

She fumbles with her keys and drops them on the welcome mat. When she bends to pick them up, her dress rides up just enough for me to catch a glimpse of her gorgeous thighs. I lean across the driver's seat and groan. Finally, she unlocks the door, throws a glance over her shoulder, and she slips inside before closing it shut.

"See you sooner than you think, little Ginny."

I drive around the block and park just outside the tall hedges bordering the Di Marco property. After slipping on my helmet and bulletproof jacket, I stay low, weaving between the trees and shrubs of their garden. I reach the house's rear, clock the narrow ledges and windowsills just wide enough to grip. After a quick glance around to make sure no one's watching, I grab hold of a ledge and haul myself up toward the upper floors.

Using a knife, I wedge open her dressing room window and slip inside. The morning sun streams through the gaps in the door leading to her bedroom. Crossing the narrow space, I peek in to find Ginevra standing with her back to me, undressing.

My breath catches as she slips out of her shift, revealing delicate skin marred with rope marks. The diagonal patterns catch the light, and I'm entranced at how they shift and stretch as she moves to her nightstand and extracts an eye mask. After slipping under the covers, she slides the silk blindfold over her head and sobs.

"Are you crying for me, little Ginny?" I whisper. "Or for him?"

At the soft sounds of her misery, my cock hardens. I press the heel of my hand into my groin, waiting for my little obsession to cry herself to sleep. Once her breathing evens, I slip out of my hiding place and creep across the room.

I stop at her bedside, my gaze fixed on her serene face. Beneath that innocent, peaceful exterior is a woman trained to satisfy Samson's depravity. My fingers itch to touch her, to claim her, but I hold back.

With the entirety of my sexual experience limited to that single blow job and jerking off in her name, what could I possibly offer a woman like Ginevra Di Marco?

Revenge.

I will terrorize her from the shadows, unravel her perfect life, and make her regret the day she left. She'll pay for the wound she inflicted on my soul—that's a pleasure I intend to draw out until she breaks.

And when she shatters, I will pick up her pretty little pieces and make them mine.

"Enjoy the slumber while you can," I murmur. "The game has only just begun."

THREE

My head pounds as though I've had too many sleeping pills, but I didn't take even one.

I only meant to sleep three hours, but I was out like a stubbed cigarette. By the time I crack open an eye, all traces of sunlight have gone, as has the rest of the work day.

My only saving grace is that I now own Dad's law firm.

Pain lances through my chest. He's been gone for five days. Murdered in the master suite. For reasons I can't fathom, Mom moved back in the moment the police completed their investigation.

They said it was the work of a professional, who left no traces, save for the long, blonde hair on the pillow. Mom said Dad was having an affair with one of the lawyers at the firm, but it's ridiculous. He'd been busy with Capello business. The only other people he consorted with were Martina, Julian, and a few male legal assistants.

Memories from last night rise from the dregs of my mind.

Samson is as good as dead.

When I peeped through the closet door, Cesare Montesano was removing a bullet from his stomach and stitching him together for further torture. It's only a matter of time before my psycho ex succumbs to his revenge. After last week's massacre, Samson is the only Capello left standing.

Another memory shoves itself forward. The masked man whose cock I had to suck to avoid getting shot. He didn't see my face through the ropes encasing my eyes. All I was to him was a warm mouth.

He was probably one of the small militia of men who've guarded the mansion at the top of the hill since Mr. Montesano died and Roman was framed for murder. Benito and Cesare have kept a low profile since their big brother was on death row. I'm not surprised the family is fighting back now that he's been exonerated.

Despite needing to apologize to Benito for Dad's part in his family's downfall, I plan on staying out of their way—at least until the dust settles.

My mind drifts back to that blow job. The way he moaned as his thick erection slid down my throat. Samson never let me near his cock after that first time. I've spent five years being forced to humiliate myself with toys for his amusement.

He used to force me to prove myself worthy of his supposedly huge dick, but I can't even remember it from the first time.

Maybe the rumors are right and some hooker bit it clean off then chewed the pieces and swallowed them so there was nothing to sew back. It's far-fetched and stretches the realms of reality, but would explain a hell of a lot.

"Ginny?" Mom calls from downstairs.

"What?" I shout back.

She remains silent. That's her way of telling me to come down and find out.

Shoulders sagging, I drag myself out of bed, slip on a robe, and exit the room. This is probably about Dad's funeral. She wants to leave him in the morgue to rot, even though our family has a mausoleum in the Parisii Cemetery. Every time I suggest cremating him, she scoffs.

"Mom?"

More silence.

Rolling my eyes, I continue down the hallway and descend the stairs. Each tread creaks under foot because our mansion only looks grand in a brochure. Everything is fake and in need of repair, from the linoleum floors pretending to be marble, to the peeling faucets. What they say about all things glittering not being gold is true.

We moved from a perfectly nice townhouse a five-minute walk from the subway to this monstrosity, just so Dad could be closer to Frederic Capello. Now that they're both dead, we're stranded.

When I reach the bottom of the stairs in search of Mom, a tall figure appears at an open doorway. My stomach plummets to my feet. Fake tan, salt-and-pepper hair, tailored suit, and a brilliant white smile. I'd recognize that deceptive facade anywhere.

It's Valentino Bossanova, but you may as well call him Blue-beard. Over the decades, he's collected on more multi-million dollar life insurance policies than I've collected degrees. Every few years, he marries some gullible woman, only for her to meet an unfortunate end. Then when he runs out of money, he goes sniffing for another victim.

What the hell is he doing here?

"Little Ginny Di Marco." He struts forward, his gaze raking over my silk gown. "My, how you've grown."

I shudder. He's no silver fox—he's a wolf.

"What brings you here?" I ask, my voice stiff. "Have you come to pay your respects to Dad?"

He places a hand over his heart. "Ginny, I'm truly sorry for your loss."

"It's Ginevra," I reply through clenched teeth.

Mom's footsteps resound from the stairs leading down to the kitchen. Don't ask me why a 12,000 square foot, pseudo-Georgian mansion needs industrial-sized cooking facilities in its basement.

I turn my attention away from Bossanova to where Mom emerges, holding two martini glasses.

"What's that?" I snap.

"Relax," she slurs and hands one to Bossanova. "I'm sober."

Lips tightening, I force my gaze from the cream sweater sliding down her shoulder to her eyes. They're just like mine—a mid-gray that changes color, depending on the light. Right now, they're bloodshot.

Does it count as a relapse if a person is in denial of their alcoholism and just needs a few drinks to get through the shock of finding her husband murdered while he may or may not have been in bed with another woman?

"What's going on?" I ask.

"You know Val?" she asks back. "He's come to pay his respects."

Bossanova turns to me, his handsome, leather features falling grave. "Your father was a prince among men. I'm truly sorry for your loss."

I grind my teeth. One of the downsides of working for a law firm with mafia clients is tolerating low-lives. Bossanova is related to the Bellavista family, our second-largest client outside the Capellos. Part of our customer service includes giving their relatives an occasional helping hand.

Somehow, Dad has managed to force multiple life insurance companies to pay up, even though Bossanova is a serial widower. Even though his wives all die within twelve months of marriage under suspicious circumstances. Even though his brother and fellow grifter, Gianni Bossanova, is on Death Row for being caught on camera shoving his wife down the stairs to claim the insurance money.

Dad was a great attorney but even he couldn't work miracles. With luck, Valentino will follow his brother into the electric chair.

Bossanova brings the martini glass to his lips and gives me what he probably thinks is a smoldering stare. Some people say he has bedroom eyes. Ever since I discovered what he and his brother do to innocent women, all I see is the human embodiment of the grim reaper.

"Thank you," I say, remembering he just offered his condolences.

I glance at Mom. "Should you really be drinking that?"

She offers me a boozy smile. "It's only my second."

It's probably her fourth.

Bossanova clears his throat. "Actually, Ginevra, I have something serious to ask you."

My spine stiffens. I clench my jaw, holding back a reaction. This is the moment he tells me the insurance company refused to pay out on his latest wife's accidental death. That, or the firms have finally caught up with his bullshit and decided not to sell him a policy.

"What is it?" I ask.

"Losanna and I have been friends for a while. I've always held your mother in the highest esteem."

My gaze darts to Mom, who sways on her feet, holding a now empty martini glass.

"What's this about?" I ask again, my stomach churning.

"Well, I've been waiting for the day she finally stopped tolerating Joseph's philandering—" He clutches his chest. "Forgive me for speaking ill of the dead."

Blood roars through my ears, muffling a long-winded speech about how he's always loved Mom and how she's been the object of his desire since before I was born. I can barely concentrate on the words because I know exactly where he's going.

Throughout this, Mom gazes at Bossanova as if he's the second coming of Christ. There's a second glass in her hand, which she's already emptied. I didn't notice when that slimy old bastard handed back his cocktail.

"Ginny," he says, his voice pulling me out of my horrified stupor. "Will you give me your blessing to marry your mother?

FOUR

BENITO

I would have stayed all day watching Ginevra sleep, but someone needs to take care of the family business. Instead, I observe her from the app on my phone. She's as still as death, which is understandable, considering she's under the influence of the sedative-infused patch I placed on her skin.

It was a necessary precaution to stop her from awakening when Reaper sent his best tech geek to install the cameras. They're dotted about in her bedroom, bathroom, closet, and car. Once she and her mother leave the house, we can complete the rest of the interior.

Music pumps in through the closed door, ruining my concentration. The downside to having the bulk of our assets still in the hands of the Capello family is running an empire from the back of our nightclub.

A knock on the door pulls me out of my musings. "Enter."

Nick Terranova strolls in, clad in a tired black suit that has seen better days. There are more streaks of gray in his beard, and he's lost more of his hairline each progressive year since losing his license to practice law.

He's a second cousin, once removed, and another casualty of our enemies. While Frederic Capello was scheming with

Ginevra's father to swindle Dad of his most valuable assets, Ginevra's father was also ousting Nick from their law firm.

"Benito."

Nick slopes into the office, his movements etched with exhaustion. While he's unable to practice law, I've got him working around the clock, tracing the family's stolen assets.

I wait for him to sit before asking, "How are things going with your appeal to the Supreme Court?"

"The last petition for reconsideration was denied," he replies with a sigh. "Maybe things will be different now that Di Marco is dead."

I send Reaper a text, summoning him to the office. "It's time for you to claim back your father's firm."

His brows pinch. "How?"

"As the Practice Manager. You'll run HR, admin, finances, client relations, marketing, compliance, and risk management."

The smile Nick gives me is incredulous. "Practice Manager?"

"Did Di Marco ever pay for your share of the firm?"

"No."

"Then you're owed at least a job."

Nick leans forward, resting his forearms on the table. "You're telling me I just walk in and take over?"

"You walk in with a small army of my interns and take over."

A knock sounds on the door, and Reaper enters with four young men from Mortis House. Nick rises off his seat, facing the newcomers, his posture stiffening.

"Meet Rimaldo, Bianchi, Marino, and Capri," I say. "All four of them are students at Alderney State University, majoring in law. They're armed, trained, and loyal to the firm. March in with them today, and put yourselves on the payroll."

Nick gazes at the quartet, his features slack with astonishment. "You're serious?"

I lean back in my seat. "The Montesano family is about to reclaim its assets. Who better to serve our interests than the Terranova Law Group?"

Breath quickening, he turns to me with a smile, already looking ten years younger. "This is brilliant," he says, his words choked with gratitude. "I can't thank you enough."

I nod. "This is your family's legacy. It's about time you took it back."

As he turns to the interns, giving them each a firm handshake and a look of determination I haven't seen in him for years, I rise from my seat and gesture for us to move the discussion to the bank of sofas on the other side of the room.

Reaper, Nick, and the interns follow me in silence. The boys of Mortis House are sons, nephews, and grandsons of our most loyal employees, trained from the age of eighteen to take on leadership positions within the state of New Alderney.

Dad wanted his sons to have an education before joining the family business. Roman did an MBA, I went to law school, and Cesare studied medicine. After he died and Roman was framed for murder, I knew we needed to secure the future of our family.

Many of our men defected to Capello, leaving us vulnerable. To maintain the loyalty of those who remained, I educated their sons. With Roman's approval, I used my personal funds to establish Mortis House and set up scholarships based on academic merit. Now, any of our employees can have their children groomed and educated to be influential members of society. In return, they will serve our family.

Once we're settled on the sofas, I turn to the quartet of college students. "Our objective, gentlemen, is to ensure Mr. Terranova's smooth transition to power within the firm. Take charge of communications, payroll, and client relations. Identify and remove all employees loyal to the Capello and Di Marco families."

They nod.

Bianchi clasps his hands. "What level of force is permissible, sir?"

I meet his gaze. "Diplomacy first, followed by polite levels of escalation. I don't expect a group of attorneys to offer too much resistance, but if you find yourself cornered, use any level of force to protect yourselves and Mr. Terranova."

When there are no more questions, I flip open a laptop, bringing up Ginevra's picture. "This woman is off-limits. Keep a discreet eye on her."

"Who is she?" asks Capri.

"Ginevra Di Marco," Nick says through clenched teeth. "Daughter of the man who got me disbarred and stole my law firm."

"Alienate her, exclude her from important meetings, sabotage her work, but if anyone touches her, they answer to me," I snarl. "Understood?"

A chorus of affirmatives echo around the low table.

"Dismissed." I close the laptop.

The interns stand, each man straightening his suit jacket with a quick pull at the lapels, before turning in unison to the exit. Grinning, Nick rises and follows them out.

He pauses at the door, shoots me a jaunty wave, and says, "Thanks again, Benito. I'll be in touch soon with the contracts."

By contracts, he means our strategy to extract Dad's assets from Capello's last surviving heir, Emberly Kay. Roman is holding the old man's illegitimate daughter captive and fucking her into submission.

Removing my glasses, I pinch the bridge of my nose, hoping my big brother knows what the hell he's doing. He's only four days out of Death Row and the first woman he sets his sights on is the daughter of our enemy.

"Problems?" Reaper asks.

I turn to my former law professor, Remus Cortese. "Just family bullshit. How's your nephew and sister?"

"Still under observation at the clinic." Gaze softening, he reaches across the sofa and clasps my shoulder. "Thank you for finding them."

Suppressing the urge to squirm, I shift on my seat. "It should never have taken so long."

Five years. Doctor Isabella Cortese and her son, Christian, were missing for half a decade because my brothers were hooked on a TV show. Cesare got the bright idea to set up a meth lab and even identified the perfect cook. Then he convinced Roman to charm a prestigious college professor into refining the formula and running the operation.

The laboratory was extremely lucrative until Roman went to prison and Cesare turned into an addict, leaving Capello to steal the equipment along with all the cooks.

Reaper came to me years ago, frantic about his missing family members. I agreed to help in exchange for him taking charge of Mortis House.

He shakes his head. "I'm just glad they're back."

I nod. "Everyone who ever fucked with us will pay. That's a promise."

His features harden. "In blood."

Everyone, including Ginevra Di Marco. Except, I want her tears.

"You didn't just summon me here to introduce the boys to their intern supervisor. What's up?" Reaper asks.

"Has the team completed their surveillance of the casino targets?"

He reaches into his pocket and pulls out a thumb drive. "We have car registrations, timetables, addresses, locations of their lovers, the works. Say the word. We're ready to move."

"Stand by. We strike the moment Nick confirms transfer of the casino ownership to the family." I take the drive and plug it into the laptop.

"When do you want to finish your surveillance project on the Di Marco girl?" he asks.

"When she finally makes it to the office."

"Doesn't she live with her mother?"

"I'll time your man's arrival with mine."

He smirks. "What are you planning?"

"Let's just say that Losanna Di Marco is about to discover her late husband died with so much debt, she'll have to sell her home to cover the installments."

"So, they'll be destitute?"

I meet Reaper's sharp eyes. He was our Constitutional Law professor and observed my devotion to Ginevra first hand. When she broke our engagement, it didn't just break my heart. I dropped out of law school entirely.

"The key to taking control of Ginevra is through her mother," I say. "If she's in peril, Ginevra would do anything to save her, including selling her soul."

And with enough pressure, I'll have Ginevra on her knees, exactly where she belongs.

FIVE

GINEVRA

I pull into the office parking lot the next morning, my head pounding. In between erotic daydreams about that man fucking me doggy-style, I keep freaking out about Mom.

Shouldn't there be a rule that says a woman should wait until her first husband is in the ground before marrying the next? Mom can't even make a decision on Dad's funeral, and she's already entertaining men.

Not just any man but the worst kind of mass murderer.

They laughed when I refused to give my blessing, and Bossanova scooped Mom into his arms then carried her out of the house. I spent the rest of the day off-balance, waiting for Mom to return, but she stayed out the entire night.

Someone's ostentatious convertible is parked in Dad's old space, so I drive around to find all the lots full. Something must be happening at work. We usually have at least six empty places. I drive around the block and have to park on the street, only to find that I have no change for the meter.

Making a mental note to send Pamela out later, I exit the car and walk to the office on foot. We have the nicest, most efficient receptionist. When Dad was murdered, she organized a hotel for Mom and arranged for her sobriety coach to visit so she didn't relapse.

Bossanova must have interfered and got Mom drinking again to make her susceptible to his dubious charm. Why else would she entertain someone so morally corrupt?

The Di Marco Law firm occupies the top floors of a 34-story Beaux-Arts building overlooking the park, with an arched entrance and ornate sculptures adorning the facade. The security guards incline their heads to me as I step through its grand doors into a lobby of marble floors and intricate moldings.

An ancestor of Dad's former partner, Paolo Montesano, built it in 1929 for his youngest son, who wanted to fight the prohibition law. Dad joined the firm as a junior associate and worked his way up to partner. When Paolo's great-grandson was disbarred, the firm appointed Dad as the managing partner.

Now, at the tender age of twenty-eight, it's all mine.

It's not all offices—we have the most extensive law library in the state, a fully equipped gym, a cafeteria, a rooftop garden, a media room, state-of-the-art IT facilities, and Dad's penthouse for when he works late.

The lining of my stomach flutters as I take the elevator to the 30th floor. I don't know if I should be myself or act like a managing partner.

I haven't been to work since the Capello massacre. Technically, I'm still mourning the death of my fiancé. Samson wanted everyone to think he'd died with the rest of his family, at least until the firm of assassins he hired had taken out the lone gunman. I should be at home, grieving Dad's death, but I can't be alone with my thoughts.

Before I can even contemplate that dilemma, the doors open and I step out on trembling legs. The first person I spot is Pamela at the reception desk. Raising a hand, I smile, expecting her to return the gesture, but she looks through me like I'm invisible.

Is she having a bad day? I cross the space to pause at her desk, only for her to turn her head and pick up the phone.

Dismissing her behavior as peculiar, I walk around the cubicles. No one acknowledges my presence, except for clingy Julian, who rises from his cubicle and opens his arms for a hug.

"Ginny," he says, his voice breathy with exaggerated sympathy. "Welcome back!"

His imploring gray eyes, a shade darker than mine, set within sallow features and muddy blond hair, are off-putting enough to make me pivot toward Dad's office. I don't want to be cornered so soon after being bound and shoved into a closet by one man and then freed by another in exchange for my throat.

Julian is a hardworking attorney who makes insightful contributions in client meetings, but he spends more time looking into my eyes than focusing on the discussion. Now that I'm newly single, I expect his behavior to become worse.

I open the door to Dad's office, finding it occupied. The man sitting behind his desk has his head bowed, pouring over a stack of documents. He's in his late 40's to early 50's with a receding salt-and-pepper hairline, and a matching beard. He's vaguely familiar, but I'm certain he isn't an employee.

Flanking him on his left and right are two college-aged men in sharp suits who comport themselves like soldiers.

"What are you doing here?" I fold my arms over my chest.

He raises his head, sweeps his gaze up and down my form, and rests his hands on Dad's desk. "Ginevra Di Marco, I presume?"

"Yes," I say, my spine straightening. "Who are you?"

"Niccolò Terranova. Practice Manager and true owner of this law firm."

I rear back, my breath catching. The Nick Terranova I remember from the past was younger, sharper, and handsome. The man in front of me has aged at least fifteen years.

"But you're—"

"Disbarred?" He rises from his seat, his shoulders broadening within a pale blue shirt.

"You're..." I gulp. "Forbidden to practice law."

"For now," he says, his voice cold.

"You shouldn't be here."

He smirks. "Do the rules say I can't enter a building I own?"

My mouth opens and closes, but I can't muster a counter argument. Dad once mentioned the building belonged to the firm, which Terranova had to relinquish when he lost his license to practice law.

"Do you have any proof of your claims?" I ask, trying to keep my voice from trembling.

Terranova's smile morphs into a full-on grin, his eyes sparkling with mirth. "Rimaldo, give Miss Di Marco the documents."

One of the men standing behind him walks to a bookshelf and picks up a stack of lever-arch folders. Without meeting my gaze, he asks, "Want me to take it to your desk?"

My jaw clenches. "This is my office."

"Capri," Terranova drawls. "Help the young lady out."

Capri, a man the size of a wardrobe, lumbers forward, making me step back. I won't be manhandled by these interlopers in my own law firm.

Grabbing the door handle, I step out into the bustling office space. Every attorney, paralegal, and administrative assistant in the cubicles stops work to stare.

A lump forms in my throat. What the hell is happening? Who allowed this hostile takeover?

I walk to the other private office, which Dad let me occupy, only to find it containing four desks. Two of them are occupied by college-aged men in the same sharp suits as the pair orbiting Terranova.

They glance up as I step in, their eyes flicking over my face without a hint of recognition.

"This is my office," I say.

One of them, a tall guy with spectacles perched on his nose, raises an eyebrow. He leans back in his chair, folding his arms. "Mr. Terranova assigned this room to the interns."

My heart pounds so hard that my body throbs with frustration. Fury flushes through my veins, filling my cheeks with prickly heat.

I would stay and argue, but I don't have any of the facts. Turning on my heel, I narrowly avoid bumping into Rimaldo, who flicks his head toward the cubicles.

"Your workspace is this way." He walks around the room's perimeter, leading me back toward Pamela's desk. Now, I understand why she avoided eye contact. She knew what was happening and hadn't offered a word of warning, not even a text.

My stomach clenches at the betrayal. Each person I pass seems to shrink back, avoiding my gaze. This is worse than any walk of shame.

Julian rises from his cubicle and raises a palm. "Over here. The seat next to me is empty."

Dread rolls through my insides with the force of an avalanche. I glance around for an empty place, but they're all occupied.

Rimaldo places the folders on my new desk and strolls back to Dad's corner office. I'm torn between pouring through the documents and walking out. The latter is so tempting, but I'm not about to lose Dad's legacy.

With as much dignity as I can muster, I lower myself on the seat and open the first file. It's so full of convoluted legalese that I almost forget I'm 3 years qualified.

Did Terranova kill Dad to take control of the firm?

Julian leans in from his cubicle. "Hey—"

"Could you..." My throat tightens. "Could you please give me a minute?"

"Sure thing, Ginny," he murmurs, his voice whispery and low. "Anything you want. Just know I'm here for you. If there's anything you need, don't hesitate to ask. You hear that? You can ask me. Anytime... You know that. Any. Time. Ginny."

I breathe hard, tuning out his incessant chatter. His words might be sympathetic, but he could have called or texted to warn me I was walking into an ambush. I can't trust anyone in this firm. Not a single person.

When a hand lands on my shoulder, I'm ready to scream. I whirl around and lock gazes with my best friend, Martina, who offers me a sympathetic smile.

"Let's go for brunch," she says. "I can fill you in on what's happened."

SIX

GINEVRA

I walk out of the office in dignified silence. Martina's supportive hand on my shoulder is the only thing keeping me from falling apart. How did Nick Terranova and his little enforcers get past security? Someone should have called me or at least the police.

"Ginny," Martina's voice cuts through my thoughts.

Blinking, I take in our surroundings. I was so preoccupied with my inner ranting that I didn't even notice we'd stepped out of the building. The morning traffic rumbles past, its noise filling the silence.

Martina cups my cheek. "Are you still with me?"

I finally meet her eyes. She's wearing green contacts instead of her usual blue. We haven't seen each other since Samson took me hostage, but she looks different. Her blonde hair is now chin-length instead of flowing down her shoulders, but I don't have the mental bandwidth to inquire about her altered appearance.

"What do you know about Terranova?" I ask.

"Quite a lot, unfortunately," she replies with a sigh.

"What does that mean?"

"Come on." She loops her arm through mine. "This calls for a drink."

Martina takes me to the Costosa, a ridiculously expensive

Italian restaurant that serves exquisite food in tiny plates. It used to be Dad's favorite for entertaining clients, but I found it too stuffy. The maître d' welcomes her with a handshake and a warm smile before leading us to our table.

Anticipation makes palpitations resound through my chest, and my insides twist into knots. I have no idea why she's drawing out the suspense, but the reason can't be good. Without prompting, a sommelier brings two mimosas. Martina pushes them both across the table and orders a buck's fizz.

"Tell me what's been happening," I say.

She nods toward the flutes. "Drink those."

I pick up the first one, let its contents slide down my throat, and stare at my best friend. She points a manicured finger at the second, so I choke it down.

"Ready," I say, bracing myself for the worst.

"Pamela told me she visited the firm the morning after Joseph was killed," she says, her voice thickening with grief.

I exhale a shuddering breath. The Di Marco and Mancini families go back decades. Our grandfathers were business associates, and Dad went to law school with Martina's parents. When Martina's sister dropped out of college to work for a publisher that produced porn, Mrs. Mancini came to visit Mom in floods of tears.

"She said everyone was in shock and confused about how to react," Martina continues. "I wasn't there. I couldn't leave the house for a few days because I thought the gunman would come after me."

"Why would he target you?" I ask.

She raises a hand, accepts her buck's fizz from the sommelier, and takes a long sip. "It looked like he was targeting everyone connected to Frederic Capello. Joseph and I were working on their high-profile case."

I tune out her detailed recounting, waiting for her to take a breath before bringing the conversation back to my question. "And Terranova?"

"Sorry." She shakes her head. "While I was at home, fretting for my life, he filed a petition for liquidation."

"What?" I squawk.

She nods. "The court acknowledged that Nick owned a hundred percent of the equity, having inherited it from his father and uncle. Joseph never owned the firm."

My stomach drops. "No."

"It's true." She reaches across the table and grabs my hand. "Nick had to leave after being disbarred. Joseph was supposed to buy out his share of the firm, but the money never materialized."

I shake my head. "Dad wouldn't..."

Martina gazes across the table, her eyes shining with pity. "Joseph kept you away from the worst of his dealings, but it's not difficult to imagine one of his mafia associates putting pressure on Nick to walk away empty handed."

She's right.

If Dad can help Capello steal nearly a billion dollars worth of assets from Benito's father and entertain a client like Valentino Bossanova, then robbing a man of his legacy is plausible. I reach across the table and pick up her buck's fizz.

"So, that's why nobody warned me?" I ask.

"If I'd been at the firm when the shit hit the fan, I would have tracked you down." She cocks her head. "Where have you been?"

After the waiter takes our orders, I tell her about how Samson came to us the morning after the massacre, and how he decided to hide in plain sight directly under the Montesano's noses.

More drinks arrive, along with a brunch platter containing a selection of pastries and fruits. Picking at my food, I skip over how I spent days with Samson parading me in front of his guards, using me as a shield to hide his impotence. I fast forward to the part when his enemies found the hideout and how he stuffed me in a closet while gunmen raided the house.

"That was considerate of him, I guess," she says, her brows pulling together. "Were you hurt?"

My gaze drops to the platter, but my mind is elsewhere. The gunman hadn't hurt me physically, but he left emotional scars. I'd imagined my first taste of pleasure would be with Benito—not with a masked man, bartering my life for fellatio.

She leans across the table. "What happened?"

"One of the Montesano men found me at the end of the night." I peer up at her through my lashes.

Face falling slack, she rakes her gaze over my body as if checking for bullet wounds. "Did he recognize you?"

I shake my head.

With a hand over her chest, she exhales an audible breath of relief. "I'm glad he let you go. Imagine if he dragged you up the hill to face the brothers. Roman's out of Death Row now."

I stuff a mini saccottino in my mouth and chew. Dark chocolate invades my senses, doing nothing to calm my nerves.

"Did the man hurt you?" Martina asks.

Dipping my head, I mumble, "I gave him fellatio."

She squints. "What was that?"

"I sucked him off, alright?" I pick up a fresh flute, washing down the taste of chocolate with Prosecco.

Her jaw drops, her green eyes sparkling with excitement. "No," she says, her voice breathy with disbelief. Then she furrows her brow. "But aren't you technically a virgin? I mean, it wasn't consensual that first time with Samson—"

"Hey," I snap, trying not to bristle. "We agreed never to talk about that."

Martina flinches at my sharp tone, her mouth opening like she's about to tell me to relax, but her gaze flickers over my shoulder. She makes a double take, her eyes widening.

I turn around to see what's captured her attention, and my stomach plummets.

A tall man in a suit tailored to his athletic frame strolls into the restaurant, stealing every ounce of my focus. He towers over the maître d' with an air of power that commands the room as he's led to a private booth. His eyes are hidden behind glasses, yet my pulse quickens at the sight of his sharp jawline, broad shoulders, and muscular chest, making all thoughts of Samson and the gunman drift into the ether.

At his side is an equally attractive older man, but he barely registers. Because if you take away the chiseled features, designer stubble, and sharp clothes, the man walking through the restaurant is heartbreakingly familiar.

It's Benito Montesano.

The man I betrayed to be with a psychopath like Samson.

My pulse quickens, my breath shallows, and my skin breaks

out with prickly heat. The last memory I had of Benito was him walking into the lecture theater, dejected after I'd vacated our apartment, leaving the diamond engagement ring on the table with a note.

Benito wanted to know what he had done, how he could make things better, begged, pleaded, and implored me to take him back, promising he could change, but I didn't have an answer.

Dad told me something terrible was brewing, and it was time to cut ties with the Montesano family. The only way to save us from the fallout would be aligning ourselves with the Capellos.

When I refused and asked if we could warn the Montesanos, his response was violent. It was the first time he'd ever hit me, and I'd been stunned into obedience. Before I knew it, he marched me over to Victoria Gardens, where I became engaged to Samson.

Within a week, I was begging him to give me to the less volatile Capello twin, Gregor.

"Ginny?" Martina snaps her fingers, breaking me out of my trance.

Moments after Benito takes his seat at the booth, the two men rise, their gazes fixed on an approaching woman. She's a stunning brunette in a deep red dress that hugs her perfect figure. After shaking the companion's hand, she cups one of Benito's cheeks before kissing the other.

The Benito I know would have flinched, stiffened, or stepped away. This new and improved version of him places a hand on the small of her back and gestures for her to sit between them.

My throat thickens.

Did I expect him to pine for five years? Of course, he's moved on. Both men stare at the woman like she's their own personal succubi queen, and she laps up the attention.

"Ginny!" Martina snaps.

"Sorry." I tear my gaze away from the femme fatale and face my friend.

"Isn't that your ex?" she whispers.

. Nodding, I gulp.

"What's he doing with Professor Cortese?"

My eyes drift to the older man for a millisecond before snapping back to Benito.

"I don't remember him looking so hot in law school." She shakes off the remark. "Enough about Benito. Tell me about the man who spared your life at the gunfight. Are you going to see him again?"

Ignoring how the muscles of my pussy throb at the reminder, I shake my head. "I never saw his face."

"How was it?" She wiggles her brows.

My gaze darts to the booths, where the beautiful brunette holds court. Benito is absorbed by whatever she's saying, practically entranced. I order another glass of Prosecco, wondering if I should go over there and apologize for the broken engagement.

Dad, Frederic Capello, Samson Capello, and even his quieter twin warned me not to explain my reasons. According to them, anything I said might warn Benito of the impending shitstorm, and we'd all get caught up in it, possibly facing jail.

I wasn't convinced until Dad threatened outright that the next time Mom was flat-out drunk, he'd let her aspirate on her own vomit.

By the end of the month, Benito's dad was dead, his older brother had been arrested for murder, Nick Terranova had lost his license to practice law, and his mom had run off to hole up with Tommy Galliano in New Jersey.

I continue picking at my food, trying not to glance at Benito and the woman, but it's futile. My mind is so preoccupied with why he's completely absorbed in what she's saying that I barely register my best friend's chatter. Later, when the waiter comes with the check, Martina raises her palms.

"Sorry, I left my purse at the office."

I dig into my bag, fish out the company credit card, and hand it to the waiter.

He swipes it through the reader, and turns back to me with a sharp shake of his head. "Declined, ma'am."

My stomach knots. I fumble for another card, and thrust it at him, my hands shaking. He swipes it again, and almost immediately, hands it back with an exaggerated sigh.

Panic rising, I shove two more cards his way, hoping one will clear. Each time, he swipes, waits a split second, then shoots me a look, his lips tight with impatience.

I glance at Martina for help. She grimaces. "Let me jog to the office and get my purse."

Before I can ask her to wait for me to try another card, she's gone.

I sit back in my seat, humiliated. The patrons at a nearby table snicker, their eyes gleaming with judgment. Squirming in my seat, I dip my head and wait for Martina.

"Ma'am, you need to vacate your place as it's reserved," says another waiter.

The woman at the nearby table giggles. I glance over, seeing her and her companion leering. Tears prick my eyes. They probably think I tried to dine and dash, when I've never so much as been short on cash. I've never had a card declined. Never been so socially embarrassed.

Rising, I back away from the table, the waiter guiding me toward a spot by the entrance. My thoughts spiral. What happened to my account? I was supposed to get paid last week. Martina's taking forever to return with her card.

Humiliation creeps up my neck, prickly and hot and relentless. I'm almost certain every eye in the restaurant is burning with accusation. My instincts scream at me to defend myself, to announce that I'm not a thief. But common sense and propriety take control, and I stay quiet.

I glance over to Benito's booth, but it's empty. Then I turn just in time to see him sweep past with his companions, leaving a cloud of sandalwood, engrossed in conversation, without sparing me a glance.

As the trio step into the back of a limousine, the manager approaches, his features somber.

"Ma'am, you're free to leave. The gentleman has covered your bill."

I blink, stunned. "Who?"

"The tall gentleman in the navy suit and glasses," he replies.

I whirl around, searching for Benito's vehicle, but it's already gone.

SEVEN

BENITO

Hours after witnessing Ginevra's humiliation at the restaurant, I sit in the back of the car, my eyes glued to the surveillance app. She tosses and turns in bed, tangled in her sheets. After the day she's had, I'm not surprised she can't sleep.

Nick Terranova has taken back the law firm her father stole with the help of Capello, the transfer of her salary has been reversed, with the company credit cards canceled. And Valentino Bossanova is romancing her mother like she's a billion-dollar insurance policy.

Her problems are piling on thick and fast, but they're about to become worse.

It's been a productive day. After preparing the boys from Mortis House for the upcoming casino raid, Reaper and I met my cousin, Elania, to help with waste disposal. She and her sister run the Newtown Crematorium.

Instead of giving me a price for the use of her four twin cremators, she launched into a detailed spiel about the destruction of DNA during cremation. The heat obliterates most genetic material, but some traces might linger in the bone fragments.

She lectured us on the high-tech forensic methods that could recover these remnants, but it all amounted to one thing. Elania wants an exorbitant amount for the extra work to make sure there's zero chance the cops will recover DNA from the ashes.

I offered to take the ashes to the yacht and pour them into the ocean, but she refused. The crematorium is her place of business. If she gets caught, she and Aria would be facing charges of obstruction of justice, conspiracy, tampering with evidence, and accessory to murder.

When I told her I wanted the men burned alive, she lost it, pointing out that burning live bodies would be premeditated murder, adding to the list of charges. She asked me if I wanted to replace Roman on Death Row and send her and Aria to the electric chair, then tripled her price.

On the plus side, she didn't say no.

Home is chaos. Business is carnage. Roman is allowing Capello's daughter to roam the house and grounds because she's a feral creature who can't be caged. If she's not hurling herself off balconies, she's smashing the heirlooms.

We were also the target of a female assassin. So, in between torturing betrayers, Cesare is doing unspeakable things to her in our basement. Leroi, who may or may not be the target of assassins, is also hiding out on our grounds with a stomach wound.

I recently clawed back our stolen meth lab from the Galliano brothers in New Jersey, but they're demanding the return of its cook, Isabella Cortese. She's Reaper's sister, who they tortured for half a decade. I'll be damned if she spends another hour in the company of either of those Galliano bastards.

Things are tense between us and New Jersey. Roman met with Tommy Galliano tonight at the Phoenix. I watched the door, making sure he didn't bring an army. Cesare was supposed to keep an eye on the cameras, but there's a suspicious gap in the recordings. And a female employee he was caught choking a few days ago and subsequently fired was found murdered in the alley.

I don't need to watch the deleted footage to know he's the culprit.

Roman will confront him tomorrow. Cesare was my responsibility while he was on Death Row. It's time to pass the burden to big brother before chaos becomes carnage at home, too.

Now, I'm frustrated, needing to blow off steam, with twenty years of pent-up desire to offload. And my cock still thinks she's the only woman in the world.

At least she's no longer off-limits, which is why I'm parked behind the hedge bordering her house. She's home alone, and her mother is out on another date with Bossanova. When I strike, no one will hear her scream.

Several minutes later, Ginevra finally settles. I put on my helmet, exit the car, and make the same route into her bedroom through the closet window.

I step out, finding moonlight spilling through the windows, casting a cold glow on Ginevra's sleeping form. Her auburn hair fans out on the pillow, making her look like a Pre-Raphaelite painting of Ophelia.

The sight of her is heartbreaking. Beneath that beautiful facade is a backstabber.

Crossing the room, I stand over her, my fists clenching at my sides. Hatred and desire wars within my soul. How can I still want her after she left me for Samson Capello? The broken engagement was the first of many betrayals to befall our family, all orchestrated by a false friend who resented our legacy.

She knew what was happening and didn't think to send a warning. She left my grandmother's ring with a note that said next to nothing.

"Ginevra," I hiss through the voice changer.

Her eyes flutter open. In the dim light, they're a deep gray, bordering on black.

"Who's there?" she whispers, sounding half asleep.

"Did you come?" I ask, my voice low and rough.

Her eyes dart back and forth, unable to meet mine. She shifts uncomfortably on the bed, her cheeks flushing.

"I... what?"

"It's a simple question. Did you or did you not climax from sucking my cock?"

She swallows, her lips trembling. "What are you doing here? I thought we were even."

"Then you place little value on your life," I growl. "You can be a good girl and stop evading my question or discover exactly how I punish bad girls."

She breathes hard, clutching the comforter to her chest like a shield. The sight of tears glistening in her eyes makes my cock twitch.

When she still doesn't answer, I hold a knife to her throat.

"Yes," she whispers, her breath quickening, her eyes glued to the blade. "I came."

Stifling a groan at her admission, I clench my jaw.

A single word from this woman's plump lips practically has me on my knees. I should snuff her life and end her dangerous spell, but I've loved her for so long, killing her would be like slicing open my heart.

"Show me," I demand.

When her gaze jumps from the knife to my helmet, I bark, "Now!"

Whimpering, she pushes back the covers, revealing her delectable body. Her skin is pale, almost luminescent in the moonlight, covered in a light sheen of sweat. Her breasts rise and fall with each ragged breath, her pale nipples hardening in the cool air. Every part of her quivers, vulnerable, exposed.

With trembling fingers, she trails a path down her belly to the apex of her thighs. Moisture glistens between the lips of her pussy as she spreads her legs. The sight grips me like a vise, tightening around my chest.

I swallow hard, my breath catching, intoxicated by the raw need. My pulse hammers in my ears, a deafening rhythm that drowns out every other thought.

She hesitates, her fingers hovering, and glances up at me through wide, fearful eyes.

"Do it," I command, my voice sharp enough to cut through the tension like a blade.

Her fingers part her folds, at first moving tentatively. She circles her clit with slow, deliberate strokes, her breath hitching. The sight stirs my most primal urges, releasing a part of me that snarls and claws for release, but I force it down, focusing instead on my simmering rage.

"Faster," I snap, the words striking out like a punch.

She whimpers, a soft, broken sound that hits me like a jolt of electricity, making my muscles clench.

Her movements quicken, becoming more urgent as she rolls her hips.

My hands curl into tight fists as she slips two fingers into that sweet cunt with a frantic intensity. She moves like this is her last night on earth.

The room fills with the slick sound of her digits plunging into her pussy, mingling with her desperate moans. It takes every ounce of control I have not to lose myself in the debauched sight.

As her hips lift off the bed to meet her thrusts, a groan claws its way up my throat. I bite it back, my jaw aching with the effort to stay contained.

"Did I give you permission to use your fingers?" I snarl, the words coming out harsh and rough.

Tension coils in my core, threatening to snap.

"No," she moans, her voice breathy, laced with a need that sends heat racing down my spine.

"No, what?" I deepen my voice.

"No, sir," she gasps, her eyes flickering up to meet mine.

"Call me Master."

"Yes, Master." Voice trembling, she moves her hips faster, her fingers working at a feverish pace. Her cries grow louder, more desperate, filling the room and making my cock push painfully against my zipper.

The pressure is unbearable. I want to take her, to claim her, to bend her to my will, but for now, I let the tension stretch, savoring every moment of her unraveling.

Ginevra was never like this when we were together. It's no wonder she left me for Samson. That sadistic bastard unlocked a sensuality in her I could never touch.

"Look at you, so eager to come in front of a stranger," I growl.

She cries out.

"You're nothing but a desperate slut," I sneer.

Tears slip down her cheeks, but she continues, her body shaking with the effort. I revel in her submission, in her humiliation, in her degradation. Pushing Ginevra Di Marco off her pedestal is the sweetest form of addiction.

I lean in, wishing I could remove the helmet, let her see the face of the man stripping her bare.

"You disgust me," I say. "And yet, I can't stay away."

"What do you want from me?" she sobs, her voice breaking.

"Your complete and utter ruin."

She squeezes her eyes shut as though trying to block the reality of her situation. That she loves being forced to masturbate at knifepoint.

"Do you want to come, little slut?" I drop my voice to a growl, lacing each word with menace.

"Please," she groans, her desperation making my pulse thrum harder.

Breath quickening, I pull back the knife, enjoying how she shivers in its absence. "Then take out my cock."

She scrambles to sit up, the sudden movement making her breasts bounce. Her fingers fumble with my fly, pulling down the zipper and freeing my length.

A moan escapes my throat as the pressure eases.

Her lips part, revealing a tantalizing glimpse of her tongue.

"Who gave you permission to taste my cock?" I ask with a smirk.

She stares up at me, her mouth falling slack. I hold back a chuckle. Dirty little Ginny can't get enough of me.

"Use both hands," I command. "And keep your eyes on me."

Swallowing hard, she wraps her soft fingers around my shaft and strokes. The heat of her touch spreads down to my balls, sharp and immediate, like a spark catching fire. My breath falters, and every muscle coils tight as pleasure surges up my spine. Every stroke is maddening, pulling tension through my core. My eyes roll back, and it takes everything in me to stay conscious.

"Scoop some of that wetness from your pussy," I say, forcing my voice to stay even. "Use that as lube."

Without hesitating, her hand disappears between her legs. The sight of her glistening fingers has my knees buckling. She spreads the slickness over my shaft and continues stroking.

"Good girl," I say, almost wishing I wasn't using the voice changer.

Her fingers quicken around my cock, milking it with a

desperate rhythm. A deep, guttural groan rumbles through my chest. Pleasure surges through every nerve as the tension coils, a thick band of pressure tightening low in my gut. My body tenses, my muscles contracting as the edge draws nearer, threatening to drag me into oblivion.

She's good at this—too good. That Capello bastard trained her well, but I'm not here solely for my pleasure.

"Stop."

Her fingers still.

I point the knife toward the apex of her thighs. "Sit back on your heels. Open your legs wide. Show me that pretty little cunt."

Fear flickers over her features, but she obeys and perches on the bed with her legs splayed, revealing her swollen clit and glistening pussy lips.

"Touch yourself, Ginny. Let me watch you debase yourself for a stranger."

Trembling, she reaches between her legs, her fingers sliding over the slick folds of her pussy. A gasp catches in her throat as she touches her clit, her body shivering. Eyes locked onto mine through the visor, she licks her lips.

"Faster," I command.

She increases the pace, her fingers slipping and sliding over her soaked flesh. As her beautiful, red hair spills over her glorious tits, I grab a handful and stroke my cock in time with her movements. She's so beautifully degraded, so willing to submit to my whims.

"Faster," I order, my own hand moving more urgently.

She obeys, her body trembling as she rubs her clit in frantic circles. Her ragged gasps echo through the dim room, and I wonder how it would feel to bury my cock in her cunt.

Sweat trickles down the side of my face. The muscles in my legs tense as I push forward, my grip on her hair tightening.

"Open your mouth," I growl.

Her eyes widen, but she obeys.

I guide my cock towards her open mouth, teasing her lips with the tip. "Wider."

She complies, her jaws parting to accommodate my girth. The

sight is intoxicating, her submission infusing my spirit with power.

With a grunt, I thrust into her mouth, feeling the wet heat envelop my shaft. Her tongue moves tentatively at first, then more boldly as I begin to fuck her mouth with increasing intensity. Her eyes water, but she keeps them locked on mine, tears streaming down her cheeks.

"That's it, little Ginny," I say, my voice strained. "Take it all."

Pressure builds, the tension coiling tight in my core. I pull back, withdrawing from her lips, leaving her gasping for air.

"Keep that fucking mouth open." I stroke my cock faster, the slickness from her tongue and pussy making my hand glide over my shaft like butter.

"Good girl. You're going to take every drop," I say, my voice rough with the urge to release.

She stares up at me through wide eyes, her fingers flying over her clit. The pressure behind my balls becomes unbearable, every muscle tightening as I hover on the edge. With a final, guttural moan, I switch the angle of my cock, shooting out powerful jets of cum.

It splatters across her eyes, her cheeks, and her nose. As she screams, I shoot into her parted lips. The rest lands on her breasts, streaking her pale skin with thick, white ropes.

She squeezes her eyes shut and whimpers, looking beautiful with my release dripping down her face. I step back, panting at the sight of Ginevra—utterly debased and covered in my seed.

Her body shakes with silent sobs, tears mixing with the cum on her cheeks. "Please, leave."

"Look at you," I say, my voice breathy with satisfaction. "My filthy, obedient slut."

I zip up my pants and head to the closet, my steps muffled by the sound of her defeat. Hearing her cry makes my heart soar with a twisted surge of victory. Reaching the door, I pause to spare her one last glance.

She curls into a ball, fragile and trembling—a broken, beautiful mess that's mine to destroy. My pulse quickens at the thought of what's to come. I can't wait to finish her, to watch my beautiful little obsession unravel further under my control.

"Go back to sleep, Ginevra. And be ready for me the next time I call."

She shudders, her body quaking as if she already knows our next encounter will be worse. Because she's right.

Despite the hatred, despite her betrayal, I'll never let her go. She belongs to me now, and I'll ruin her over and over until there's nothing left but her submission.

EIGHT

GINEVRA

Hours later, I'm barricaded in the guest room, my skin raw from being scrubbed clean, yet I still can't erase his touch. I can't shake the feeling of his dominating presence. I've locked every door and window, but I don't think that will deter my stalker. Nothing will.

Morning sunlight streams in through my closed eyelids, reminding me that I've stayed awake the entire night. Every creak, real or imagined, made me think he'd returned for another round.

After his footsteps retreated, I lay on my bed with cum in my eyes, not knowing if he was still watching. I replayed every moment over and over, wondering where the hell I went wrong.

What happened that night was supposed to be a one-off, but it looks like he wants a pound of flesh in exchange for sparing my life.

I should have called the police right away, but I froze. The man is tied to the Montesano family, who may or may not be connected to Dad's murder. What if he's the lone gunman who massacred the Capellos? It would make sense, since Dad was murdered in his own bed. Calling the cops on him will only get me killed.

Not to mention Mom.

She spent the night at Bossanova's apartment, and for once, I'm relieved she's found a boyfriend. That murderous old bastard won't make a move on Mom until after he's married her and placed a policy on her life. At least she's safe with him... for now.

In the meantime, I need to get rid of this sexual terrorist before he escalates.

When the alarm on my phone buzzes, I crack open an eye and force myself out of bed. The stalker is only one of my problems. I need to investigate what Martina heard about Dad. Dad always talked as if he owned the firm outright after Nick Terranova lost his license.

Movement downstairs makes my heart jump into my throat. I slide out of bed and rush to the door, pressing my ear to its surface. At the sound of a high-pitched, feminine giggle, every knot of tension in my belly melts, and I step out into the hallway.

Mom is staggering up the stairs in a red dress with its straps falling down her arms, exposing more than the appropriate amount of cleavage. Bossanova follows behind her with his hands on her hips, wearing a tuxedo and an overly bright smile.

"Have you been drinking again?" I hiss.

She stares up at me through bleary eyes, blinking as though clearing spots from her vision. Her gray eyes are bloodshot, with pupils so wide they may as well be bottomless pits.

"Ginny," she slurs. "We're celebrating."

"Celebrating what?" My gaze bounces to Bossanova.

The leathery-skinned asshole smiles so widely I can see his gold molars. "Show her, baby."

Mom raises her hand, revealing the largest, most ostentatious diamond engagement ring. It's twice the size of the stone Benito gave me, which was ten carats.

When it slips off her finger and bounces on the faux-marble stair, my eyes narrow.

"Careful, babe." Bossanova releases her hips to pick up the fallen ring. He slips it back on her fingers and plants a kiss on her lips. "We'll get it resized tomorrow."

"Which dead wife did it belong to?" I snap.

He flinches, his crocodile grin morphing into a grimace. "That's a dangerous assumption to make, Ginny."

"Ginevra."

As quickly as the grimace appeared, it melts back into a fake smile that freezes halfway to his eyes. "Come on, baby. Let's get you to bed."

Mom staggers up the stairs, wobbling from side to side, with him holding her steady. All the while, his hateful eyes try to penetrate my defenses.

"Thanks for bringing Mom home, Mr. Bossanova. I'll take care of her from now," I say, facing down the back-stabbing coward, daring him to object.

"But the fun has only just begun," he croons.

"My mother is too drunk to consent to sex," I grind out through clenched teeth.

"Ginny!" Mom says, sounding scandalized. She turns to her future murderer, her cheeks flushing. "I'm sorry, Valentino, darling. We taught her better than to be so crass."

Bossanova flashes his teeth again. "It's alright, baby. She's protective of her mama. I'll see myself out."

Mom murmurs something about wanting him to stay, but the glare I shoot is fierce enough to make Bossanova plant another kiss on her cheek and retreat downstairs.

I round the bannister, meeting Mom halfway, and help her to the landing. She blows sloppy kisses at Bossanova before he opens the front door with a jaunty salute and exits.

The moment the door clicks shut, she collapses on the top and sighs. "I thought he'd never leave."

Brow pinching, I sit beside her and ask, "Mom?"

She shakes her head from side to side, her curls bouncing. Mom's hair is almost the same shade of auburn as mine, although the henna rinse she uses to cover the gray makes it darker. She rubs her temples as if chasing away the last traces of alcohol.

"Don't interfere with Valentino, darling, he's a dangerous man," she says.

I splutter. "Of course, he's dangerous. Do you know what happened to all his wives?"

She reaches into her purse, extracts a silver cigarette holder, and flips it open. Inside are a lighter and three tightly rolled joints. My jaw drops. Since when did she smoke?

"Femicide," she finally answers.

"If you know Bossanova is a murderer, what are you doing with him?"

"Your father left us with enough debt to bankrupt a small country." She places one between her lips, lighting the end before taking a deep drag that makes the tip smolder. She offers me another, but I shake my head.

"We're screwed if we don't come up with ten million dollars." She blows out a long stream of smoke. "A loan shark tracked me down to the hotel with contracts your father signed. He spent money like a fire hydrant to keep up the appearance of a high-powered lawyer."

"Did you sign anything?"

"Loan sharks don't give a damn. I'm his widow, therefore I inherited his debt."

My throat thickens, and the knots in my stomach return, twisting so tightly that I have to stifle a groan. Having a stalker is a picnic compared to these sharks.

"Can we sell the house?" I ask.

"Have you ever noticed that no-one moves into this part of Victoria Gardens?" She doesn't wait for me to reply. "Over the past few years, the land has become riddled with subsidence. Real estate prices here have crashed and no one is stupid enough to buy a money pit."

I gulp. "So, what are you doing with Bossanova?"

She meets my gaze, looking so sober that I pull away, wondering what the hell happened to my alcoholic mom. "Your father told me how Valentino operates. The life insurance policy he places on his wives are joint, meaning if one spouse dies, the other inherits a fortune. I plan on killing him before he makes his move."

"Mom—"

"Don't talk me out of it." She places her fingers on my lips. "Valentino knows about my money problems, and he's prepared to pay off the sharks. We'll move into his penthouse overlooking the park, then he'll die of an unfortunate overdose."

"This is crazy."

"But necessary."

"Do you even have a drinking problem?"

"Not really." She raises a shoulder.

"What does that mean?"

Mom takes a long drag of her joint, holds the smoke in her lungs for several seconds before blowing it out in a long stream. "In this world, it's deadly for a woman to show her weaknesses because they'll be exploited. It's better to fabricate one you can control. Something that keeps people at a distance."

"So all those AA meetings, detox resorts, and sobriety retreats?"

"Were an excuse to get away from your father."

My heart plummets to my stomach and sinks in the acidic waters of betrayal. Tiny chunks break off, eroding piece by agonizing piece. "But I spent years worrying about you."

She turns to me, her eyes softening. "I'm sorry, sweetheart, but you're the world's worst secret-keeper. When you were little, you used to tell Benito Montesano everything, and Benito would tell his father."

"What are you saying?"

The corner of her lips lifts into a crooked smile. "You're too pure-hearted for this world. Just like your mother."

My heart skips several beats. Mom once said something about not being my biological mother when she was drunk, but she claimed not to remember about it when she was sober. When I asked Dad, he told me to forget about it, mumbling something about alcoholic dissociation. I let it slide, since our combination of hair and eye color is so unique, we have to be related.

"So, it's true?"

She brushes a lock of hair off my face. "Your father ordered me never to reveal the truth. My cousin, Jennifer, was the woman who carried you, not me."

My lips move, but I can't form words. Mom gazes into my eyes, with a look of guilt and compassion that makes my insides crumble.

"Then how did I end up with you?" I whisper.

"She was young, impressionable and in love with your father, who wouldn't leave his current wife. When she got pregnant, he ghosted her, and she moved into our family home. Something changed the moment she gave birth. She couldn't connect with you, and ended up leaving you in our care."

Mom takes another drag, her expression darkening. "She needed the kind of love she couldn't get from a baby. Another older man swept her off her feet and married her in a whirlwind romance."

I clutch my stomach, trying to hold back the sensation of sinking dread. "What happened to Jennifer?"

"She married Gianni." Mom's gaze bores into mine. "Gianni Bossanova."

Shock hits me in the gut, making me suck in a sharp breath through my teeth. My insides twist into icy knots, as if the coldness of realization is freezing me from the inside out. Gianni Bossanova is the brother on death row, who was jailed for pushing his wife down the stairs on camera.

"She was murdered," I whisper.

Mom nods.

"And you're marrying his brother for revenge?" My voice rises several octaves.

"Do you know what these loan sharks will do if I don't pay your father's debt?" Mom asks.

"Kill us?"

"They might kill me, maybe harvest my organs. A beautiful girl like you will stay alive and earn that money. I don't want you to fall into the hands of traffickers."

A heavy silence falls between us, thick with the gravity of her words. My heart races, and I force myself to think. As much as I want to scream at her, to pull her out of this twisted scheme, I know she's right. The world we live in doesn't allow or forgive mistakes. This can't be the only way to keep us both alive. There has to be another way.

Mom wraps an arm around my shoulder. "Don't interfere with Valentino. He's our only route out of this mess."

"What about the law firm?"

She chuckles, the sound bitter. "Your grandfather owned ten percent of the equity until he sold it back to the Terranova family to cover your father's gambling debts. Joseph Di Marco died worse than penniless, leaving us with nothing but a trail of liabilities and at the mercy of loan sharks."

"So, Nick Terranova was telling the truth about dad stealing his firm," I mutter.

Mom's grip on my shoulder tightens. "If he's returned, then you should update your resumé. What your father did to that man was unforgivable. I don't want you bearing the brunt of his vengeance."

NINE

BENITO

Last night was exactly what I needed to relieve the tension. Spraying cum over Ginevra's face is just as satisfying as coming down her throat.

I lean against the wall of Dad's old study, tuning out Roman's conversation with Nick Terranova. They're talking about the finer details of a convoluted plan to claw back Dad's assets. My attention is fixated on my screen, where Ginevra sits on the stairs with her drunken mother. They're having a heart-to-heart. I don't need to hear the audio to know Losanna Di Marco is falling under Bossanova's spell.

The man is a wonder with women, capable of weaving wefts of bullshit, blinding them to his obvious faults. Any quick search online will show the number of wives he and his brothers have murdered, yet this aging Casanova is as popular as ever with the ladies.

Why must a man be a sadistic asshole to gain their respect? All I ever showed Ginevra was affection, and she left our family to rot. Mother said Ginevra was the daughter she always wanted, yet she threw away years of our love and care to join forces with psychopaths.

They both did.

Mother's betrayal cuts too deep to contemplate. Roman was already arrested for a crime he didn't commit when she left us for Tommy Galliano. Because of her, Cesare fell into addiction. With one brother incarcerated and the other a junkie, someone had to be strong.

"You with us?" Roman's voice cuts through my thoughts.

I glance up from the phone, ask Nick a few pertinent questions about the contract before turning my attention back to Ginevra. She's risen from the top of the stairs and is hugging her mother as if she isn't a burdensome drunk.

Ginevra's weakness for Losanna will be her downfall.

Roman rises from behind his desk and exits through the patio doors. Now that we have the contracts to swindle his captive out of the assets she inherited from Capello, he's eager to trick her into completing a portrait of him, which he will purchase using a rigged agreement.

Thanks to Nick, we've clawed back over thirty million dollars of Dad's cash from Capello's estate. It's only a matter of days before Roman gets that woman to sign over ownership of the casino.

The older man closes his briefcase, rises off his seat, and adjusts his jacket.

As he strides to the door, I slip the phone back in my pocket and ask, "How's it going with the firm?"

He grins. "Taking back the corner office was a breeze, thanks to your interns."

"Glad to be of service. How is Ginevra?"

"Quiet," he replies. "She came in yesterday, demanding to know why I'd taken control of her father's so-called empire."

I shake my head. "Joseph Di Marco was a piece of work."

"A piece of shit and the worst kind of grifter," Nick replies, his lip curling. "His daughter seems the opposite. She spent the rest of yesterday poring over the partnership agreements and court documents. She thinks Di Marco's claim on my firm is legit."

"When are you going to fire her?" I ask.

"Want her out by close of business today?"

I rub my chin. "Keep her for longer, but make her employment at the firm intolerable. Give her the most demeaning work. I want her demoralized."

"Sure thing, Benito," Nick replies with a nod.

"Who's your plus one for tonight's party? I need to inform the guards at the gate."

"It was going to be the best friend, Martina Mancini, but she's already going with Ernest from the art gallery."

I nod. Ernest Lubelli is an important part of Roman's plan to swindle Capello's daughter. She's an impoverished artist who's ignorant of her father's identity and has no clue she's inherited a billion dollar's worth of assets.

"So, your wife?" I ask.

He flashes me a sheepish grin, implying he's either started sleeping with Martina or plans to get her into bed. Sometimes, I envy other men's ability to shrug off a woman like a worn sock and slip into another. I'm astounded at how men like the Bossanova brothers could go so far as to romance and murder them for money.

If I had even an iota of that callous indifference, then I wouldn't be so obsessed with Ginevra. Intellectually, I know other women exist, but my heart only beats for one. It's been like that since the beginning, which is why I want to see her broken.

As Nick leaves the study, Sofia enters with a tray laden with fresh coffee and a special selection of the bruttiboni she used to supply Roman on Death Row.

And she's wearing red lipstick.

Valentino Bossanova steps into the room behind her, flashing our housekeeper his brilliant smile. Blushing, Sofia dips her head and scampers to the door. He makes a show of turning around to watch her ass as she exits before blowing out a low whistle.

"What are you doing?" I snap.

He turns to me, his brow furrowing. "Benito?"

"Sofia is off-limits," I snarl. "Don't talk to her, don't whistle at her, and don't ogle her. She's ours."

Bossanova flinches. "Sure thing, Benito."

"It's Mr. Montesano to you."

Features hardening, he offers me a curt nod. This old bastard might be the same age as Dad, but he doesn't command a fraction of his respect. His tan, greasy charm, and modus operandi makes him lower than any grifter.

I walk around the desk, lowering myself into the seat and take my sweet time leaning the phone against a stack of books. Onscreen, Ginevra has moved to the shower, looking like she's scrubbing the cum that's dried on her hair.

"Report," I say.

"Losanna's drinking problem makes her an easy target," he replies, shifting on his feet. "She's eager to be Mrs. Bossanova, and everything's going to plan... More or less."

My gaze flicks to the gray regrowth on his temples and the smeared product he uses to conceal pale skin dotted with liver spots. I make a mental note to age with dignity and not cling to my youth. "Tell me more about the less part."

He sighs. "The daughter isn't nearly as easy to fool. She cock-blocks, makes barbed comments, and is overprotective of her mother. If you could just get that little bitch to—"

I shoot out of my seat, making him step back with a gasp. Before I know it, I'm swinging at his tanned, leathery face, my knuckles hitting bone. Blood explodes from his nose. He spins into the wall, clutching his face with a groan.

"Ginevra Di Marco is no bitch," I snarl.

Cowering, he glares up at me, his eyes shining with murderous intent. "My apologies," he grinds out. "I only meant to say she was tenacious."

I flash my teeth, making him flinch. "Keep working on the mother. Make her agree to a wedding date. Arrange for the most lucrative life insurance policy and find a way for it to fall into Ginevra's hands."

"How?" he asks, his eyes blazing with resentment.

"You're the conniving Casanova," I snarl. "Work it out."

"And afterward, you'll tell me how Roman escaped Death Row," he says through whitened teeth.

I nod. "That's our agreement."

"Because Gianni doesn't deserve the electric chair."

And the wives they murdered didn't deserve the accidents, poisonings, or staged suicides.

Roman walked out of Death Row because he was innocent. He'd never met the woman he was supposed to have raped and murdered. After our cousin, Leroi, massacred the Capello family, he found hard drives containing footage of the real killer. Footage that didn't just exonerate him but identified that we'd been stabbed in the back by a trusted associate.

"Roman's having a welcome home party tonight in the ballroom. Bring Losanna. Formal dress."

Face pinching, he manages to nod.

"Dismissed," I say.

Bossanova slinks out of Dad's study like a whipped dog. By the time I return to the desk, Ginevra has already moved to her dressing room, where she's dried off and slipped on cream underwear.

I watch, mesmerized, as she runs lotion over her pale skin, her fingers caressing those gentle curves. She's doing this on purpose, driving me insane with the way her hands glide over every dip and contour. Her movements are slow and deliberate, a torturous seduction I'm powerless to resist.

My breath catches, and a familiar heat stirs low in my gut. My cock lengthens and thickens until it's straining against my zipper.

I can barely breathe as her hands skim across her collarbone, down to the soft swell of her breasts, lingering on the delicate skin before sliding lower, over her abdomen. Her fingers spread the lotion at a tantalizing pace, as if she knows I'm watching and wants to light a fire under my skin that only she can extinguish.

Last night, those delicate hands stroked me almost to completion, lubricated with her arousal. Ginevra has become a dirty girl, hungering for my cum. And she'll get it—more than she can handle. I'll have it spilling from every tight, trembling hole.

The thought sends a shiver down my spine, my cock throbbing against the confines of my pants.

Groaning, I reach into my pocket and extract one of the panties I took from her laundry basket. The silk is cool against my skin, a stark contrast to the raging heat of my libido. Holding them to my nose, I inhale the sweet musk of her desire—an intoxicating scent that invades my senses, leaving me lightheaded.

My tongue darts out to lick the remnants of moisture clinging to the silk fabric. She's all-consuming, a fever burning through my veins, leaving me ravenous.

No other woman will ever have this effect on my soul—only Ginevra. She's a drug, and I'm hopelessly addicted.

As she slips on a shirt, the thought of what I'm going to do to my dirty little Ginny—how I'm going to break her—becomes more than I can bear.

My mind swarms with depraved images. I'll have her on her knees, begging for my cock, eyes wide and desperate, knowing that the only way to quench her desire is to take me beyond her limits. I'll fill that sweet pussy until it's overflowing.

Reaching beneath the desk, I pull down my zipper and my cock springs free. Its swollen head is already slick with pre-cum. I wrap her panties around my shaft, the silk gliding against my skin as I make slow, deliberate strokes.

I imagine her tongue sliding out for another taste, those pouty lips stretched wide as she struggles to take the girth of my crown, the way she'd gag and choke as I thrust deeper, holding her head in place as I pound into her throat.

Pressure builds, coiling tight in my core, a firestorm of all-consuming lust. I force myself to slow down, to prolong the agony, to savor every moment of this exquisite torture.

Onscreen, Ginevra sets down the lotion and collapses onto a bench and sobs. Tears stream down her cheeks, and her beautiful features twist with anguish.

"Are you crying for me, little Ginny?" I croon, my fingers quickening over my shaft.

She bows her head, robbing me of the sight of her destruction, her shoulders shaking with the force of her misery.

My strokes quicken at the sight of her so vulnerable and on the verge of breaking. I want to stand over my little betrayer, watch those tears mix with my cum as I shower her with my release.

The thought is too much—my control snaps, and I erupt, shooting jets of fluid on the underside of the desk. Each spurt becomes more intense than the last, making me lose track of the fact that I'm desecrating Dad's furniture. I keep stroking, riding the wave of pleasure, my body convulsing with each surge.

As the last drops fall from my cock, I collapse back in my seat, panting hard.

This woman is going to be my undoing.

TEN

GINEVRA

I sit in a bathroom stall at work with my head resting between my knees. After that conversation with Mom, I don't know what the hell to think–about myself, about her, about Dad. He got a young girl pregnant, left her heartbroken, and did nothing when she married a known wife-killer.

A suspicious part of me wonders if he even made the introduction to get her out of the way. Why else would he still defend Gianni Bossanova?

My life has turned to shit, and I don't know how to cope.

Julian won't give me a minute of peace at my desk, and I have no time to think. He keeps interrupting me when I'm investigating the mess Dad left behind. Now vultures who liquidate companies are walking around the building, taking inventory of everything down to the office paper clips.

The law firm I thought I'd inherited is in worse trouble than a ship without a captain. After consulting the court documents, I discovered that Dad really hadn't paid Nick Terranova for his equity. The man now has the right to liquidate its assets, leaving every employee jobless.

It's not surprising no one wants to look me in the eye. I'm the daughter of a scammer. Dad made everyone think their jobs were secure. Now that he and our biggest client are dead, the firm may as well be the Titanic.

I can't think straight because my pussy still throbs from last night's encounter with the masked man. It was harrowing, hot, and humiliating. He came all over my face just as I was on the verge of climax, and I'm sure he aimed the spray of cum in my eyes on purpose.

He needs to be stopped. A man like him won't be just satisfied with a blow job or masturbation. He'll escalate. He might even be a psychopath. If I don't do something about him now, I could end up pregnant. Or dead.

And then there's Mom. Who isn't actually my birth mother, but a first cousin, once removed. Knowing she took care of me when I was at my most vulnerable makes me love her even more. I can't let her carry out that harebrained scheme to murder Bossanova for the insurance money. Valentino and his brother only got away with it for so long because they're connected to the Bellavista family, who have been pulling strings for them for years.

Mom has no contacts, no influence, and no money to hire a defense attorney. Killing Valentino is a one-way ticket to the electric chair.

A knock sounds on the stall door, pulling me out of my thoughts. I jerk backward, my pulse pounding.

"Ginny," Martina says from the other side of the bathroom. "Are you in there?"

"Yeah." I rise off the toilet seat and flush.

Grabbing my purse from the coat hook, I open the door. Martina steps back, staring at me with a furrowed brow.

"You okay?" she asks.

I reach the sinks, breathing hard to stay calm. With trembling fingers, I turn on the faucet, letting cold water rush over my hands. The change in temperature only heightens my frazzled nerves. I lather them with soap, rubbing them together, desperate to wash away the anxiety crawling beneath my skin.

"Everything's fine," I mutter, my voice hollow.

"You don't scrub up like that unless something's gone wrong." She stares down at my hands and frowns.

I snatch them from the water, stride to the dryer, and shove my hands beneath the nozzle. The hot air blasts against my skin, making me flinch. I rub them together, forcing them dry with frantic motions.

"Is your OCD flaring up again?" she asks at my back.

My shoulders stiffen. "No. Why do you ask?"

"Do you remember that time at college when your dad told you to break off your engagement?"

Guilt clutches at my chest. I whirl around, meeting her artificially colored eyes. They're a deeper green today, matching the emerald pendant hanging between her breasts.

I shake my head. "I'm just under a lot of pressure."

"Let's talk about it over coffee."

Skin prickling, I glance at my feet. "The company card was canceled, and something went wrong with last month's payroll."

"Same here," she says.

My head snaps up, and I look her full in the face. "What?"

She nods. "Nobody got paid since the court froze the firm's bank accounts after your dad died. Nick is working hard trying to sort out the mess."

My throat tightens. It's no wonder the entire firm welcomed him without question. Nothing sways decades of loyalty like an empty bank account, or the bitter discovery that their dead boss's greed might threaten their livelihoods.

We walk in silence to the staff restaurant, which is crammed. I suspect no one wants to waste money outside when they can have a free lunch on the 30th floor. It's more of a cafeteria with a large serving hatch that offers a few limited gourmet dishes.

I navigate through the throng of employees, ignoring a few filthy glares. The sight of food makes my stomach churn, so I select a lemon tea with a small snack, while Martina grabs a plate of eggs Benedict.

A pair of paralegals rise from their seats, leaving trays half-filled with barely-touched meals. Sighing, I clear the clutter before returning to our table.

"Are you going to tell me why you were hiding in the ladies' bathroom?" Martina asks through a mouthful of eggs.

Where do I begin? Certainly not with Mom's plot to murder

Bossanova to avenge my birth mother and use the insurance money to clear ten million dollars in debt.

I love my best friend, but she's impulsive. In our first year of college, she called the police on a thirteen-year-old girl who pushed her abusive teacher to his death off a roof garden. He was a predator who groomed the child, got her pregnant, then brought her home for the weekend where he tricked her into taking an abortion pill.

The little girl had confided in Martina's younger sister who reached out to Martina for advice, swearing her to secrecy. One 911 phone call later, an innocent child ended up facing charges for first-degree murder.

Two days later, Mr. and Mrs. Mancini woke up in the middle of the night with a gang of armed thugs in their bedroom, threatening to throw them in a cremator if they didn't fix her daughter's mess. They shot her dad in the foot to show they weren't joking, and even set their kitchen on fire.

Martina's knee-jerk reaction could have gotten her parents killed and sent a victim of abuse to prison. In the end, Mr. and Mrs. Mancini worked with a psychiatrist to prove the girl was insane, which still ended up ruining her life.

She's dead now, murdered because she fell in love with a serial killer. I still wonder how her life would have changed if Martina had kept her mouth shut.

So, no. I won't tell her anything about Bossanova and Mom.

"Ginny?" She waves a hand over my face. "Are you still with me?"

I shake off my thoughts. She wanted to know why I was crying. "It's my stalker."

She smirks. "Are you still pining for his big dick?"

"He was in my bedroom last night."

Her jaw drops. "No."

"Yes." I bring the tea up to my lips, the warmth doing nothing to soothe my stomach's cold knot of fear.

"What did he..." She glances from side to side, checking for eavesdroppers before leaning in, her eyes narrowing. "Did you have sex?"

I shift on my seat. "Not really."

"What does that mean?"

Leaning forward, I tell her everything about last night. Martina breathes hard, her cheeks turning pink. The way she reacts, you'd think I was narrating the spicy scene of a dark romance novel. She interrupts, demanding to know if he pressed the knife to my skin or just pointed it at my throat. When she asks if his cock was leaking precum, I scowl.

"Are you even listening?" I ask.

Her features morph from excited to shocked. "Can't you see I'm on the edge of my seat?"

"He's dangerous," I snap. "What if he becomes murderous?"

"Then do what he says," she replies with a frown. "It sounds like you're enjoying his attention."

My lips tighten. "Arousal doesn't mean consent."

"Did you even say no?"

Martina doesn't understand. Her parents make their money from real estate and don't have to consort with lowlives. Mine are connected to multiple crime families. I know first-hand what happens when you're cornered without a protector and turn down a man's advances.

The first time Samson ordered me to deep-throat a dildo, I refused. He punched my stomach, cracked a rib, and then made me do it anyway. Even Dad slapped me to the ground and kicked me while I was down when I resisted breaking my engagement with Benito.

I rise from my seat. "Hard to talk back when there's a gun pointing at your face or a blade pressed into your jugular."

She grabs my wrist. "Don't go. I'm sorry. You know what I'm like... Always playing devil's advocate?"

"Don't, because I'm not in the mood." I pull my arm out of her grip.

Her features flicker with hurt. Any other time, I'd rush to apologize for being so snappish, but I can't muster up the will to sooth her feelings when I'm teetering on the edge of ruin. "Okay. I just thought you were playing along with the adventure, because you could end it with a single word."

My jaw clenches, and I narrow my eyes. "If it's that 'just say no' bullshit—"

"Benito."

I rear back. "What?"

"The stalker works for the Montesanos. Your ex is the second-in-command. If one of their men is harassing you, he could stop it in an instant," she says as if the answer is obvious.

Why on earth didn't I think of that? Because Dad is dead, Mom is about to marry a murderer, the law firm is in shambles, and I've just discovered a secret about my parentage. I couldn't think straight even if someone handed me a slide rule.

"You're welcome," Martina says, her tone flat, but I'm too frazzled to pick up on the subtext.

"Thank you." I squeeze her shoulder, walk to the exit, and let Martina's protests fade into the background.

Mind spinning, I push through the cafeteria doors and exit the building. The drive across town blurs into a haze of stoplights and sharp turns, my grip tight on the wheel. I park a block away from the place where Benito is supposed to operate.

Samson once bragged that his dad had taken all the Montesano buildings, leaving them with just the nightclub, a karaoke bar, and a store that sells dildos. Last time I checked, that's where Martina's younger sister had a part-time job.

According to Samson, Benito sometimes holds meetings in the club's back room, the same place where his dad died of a heart attack. I'd call that gruesome, but Mom and I still live in the house where Dad was murdered.

When I round a corner and spot a limousine parked outside the Phoenix, my heart skips several beats. If the car isn't for Benito, then it will be for one of his brothers. I've known all three of them since I was eight which has to count for something.

I hurry toward the nightclub, past the stores, including Wonderland, with its BDSM window display. When the Phoenix's wooden double doors open, I break into a run.

Two men step out, both wearing suits that accentuate their athletic frames. I vaguely recognize the older one as our old professor, Remus Cortese. But all my attention is on Benito. He looks like a different man in the distance—dangerous, untouchable, edgy. I only recognize him from the glasses.

When the limo driver scurries out and opens the door, I shout, "Benito!"

Both men pause to turn in my direction. A seed of longing in my chest blooms into hope. Benito was always so kind, so generous, so giving. No matter how far we've drifted apart, he still wouldn't want me defiled by his employee.

I run across the road, narrowly avoiding an oncoming car.

Benito's dark eyes lock onto mine as I approach, the distance between us a chasm. I'm desperate to cross it, aching to reconnect. Instead of moving closer, he remains by the limo, looking like the perfect mafia prince. He's tall, handsome, and exuding the kind of lethal composure that makes me feel safe.

Except his eyes don't flicker with recognition or even interest. Instead, his gaze is ice, sharp and unforgiving, slicing through my soul with a pain that cuts deeper than a knife.

With every step, the distance between us shrinks, as does my hope. I'm beginning to feel like a beggar on the street, pleading for spare change.

My heart lurches. Why would Benito give a shit about the problems of a long-dead and buried ghost from the past?

When I reach him, my pulse pounds so hard I can barely hear the sound of my panting breaths. "Benito... um... thanks for covering my check the other day. I meant to call you to ask—"

"I'm late for an engagement." His gaze flicks past me, indifferent.

The word hits like a slap, and my breath catches. Engagement? "I just..." My voice falters, and I swallow hard, fighting back a surge of guilt. "Something's happened. I need your help—"

"Set up an appointment with my assistant."

"Benito... Please," I whisper, but he's already turning away, dismissing me as if our sixteen year relationship meant nothing.

Without another glance, he climbs into the limousine. The door slams shut, sealing off any hope of getting help.

I stand frozen on the curb, watching the vehicle disappear into traffic. What the hell was I thinking—that Benito would revert back into that golden retriever, eager to fulfill my every whim? He's moved on, probably happy with that woman. I'm just a painful chapter he wants to forget.

But what the hell am I supposed to do now?

ELEVEN

BENITO

I spent the rest of the day reveling in the way Ginevra tried to get my attention. The anguish in her pretty gray eyes replays in glorious technicolor, making my heart thrum with satisfaction.

These are the first words we've exchanged since she cast me aside, like the lifetime of love I poured into her meant jack shit. Because of Ginevra, I let my guard slip at Roman's welcome-back-from-Death-Row party—an unforgivable lapse in vigilance.

Now, I'm standing on a stage with my brothers, no longer distracted. Roman just got shot, and Cesare's gone feral, firing at the scattering guests.

The only things standing between us and death are our bullet proof undershirts. If the little assassin we left Cesare to interrogate in the basement escaped to finish the job she started, I'll wring his neck.

But more concerningly, Roman's captive has disappeared, taking with her our last chance to claw back Dad's assets.

My older brother gives chase, leaving me to handle the attack on our family. To keep Cesare out of trouble, I order him to find our billion-dollar hostage while I go in search of Losanna Di Marco. She's inebriated, vulnerable, and my key to manipulating Ginevra.

I jump down from the stage, heading toward the ballroom's

exit. Guests are still streaming through the open double doors and out into the hallway. I scan the room, checking for signs of a drunken older woman. Finding none, I push my way through the crowd.

The hallway is crammed with servers, guests, guards, and staff, all streaming toward the front doors. To stop the shooters from escaping, I've ordered bottlenecks and blockades at all exits. Reaper and his boys are patrolling the grounds surrounding our property with orders to shoot anyone trying to escape on sight.

As the realization sinks in that Losanna is unprotected, a cold dread tightens around my gut, propelling me through the throng. I shove my way to the front doors, not wanting to waste another second. She could be terrified, trampled, or torn apart.

The outside courtyard is a chaotic mess of darkness and noise, with guests scattered and frantically yelling at valets for their cars. The usual juniper scent fades to the background, now thick with the stench of exhaust fumes, gunpowder, and anxiety.

Amid the confusion, I spot Valentino Bossanova trying to slither his way into someone's limousine. His white tuxedo jacket is splattered with blood, making my stomach lurch.

I rush forward and grab his arm. "Is she in there?"

He whirls around, staring at me through haunted eyes. "Who?"

"Who do you think?" I snarl.

His lips tremble. The bandaid on his broken nose quivers. "I lost her in the chaos."

"Valentino?" A gray-haired woman pokes her head through the back door. She's Donna Lewis, the new president of the New Alderney Cemetery Board. "Do you still need that ride?"

"Leave without him," I snap.

Valentino pales, despite his thick coating of fake tan. I grab his shoulders, wanting to shake him until his teeth rattle.

"Where did you abandon her?" I snarl.

"We got separated when Roman was shot."

In other words, he ditched her at the first sound of gunfire. Panic threatens to surge, but I shove it down, narrowing my focus. If Ginevra loses her mother, it will be disastrous. Not just for my plans to use her safety as leverage.

I only ever want my little betrayer to feel the pain I inflict.

Grabbing Valentino's arm, I make sure to dig my fingers into his flesh hard enough to bruise, and drag him back through the frantic crowd. We pass panicked guests shoving their way toward the exits, servers dropping trays, and guards barking orders as they attempt to regain control. As we near the side corridor, I spot a door wedged ajar by a pair of stockinged feet.

My gut tightens. How the hell did I walk past that the first time?

The sight of Ginevra's mother crumpled on the ground hits me like a bullet. Everything else—the chaos, the noise, the assassins plaguing my family—fades into the background. I ease the door open, giving myself enough space to gather her in my arms. She weighs next to nothing, as if her bones are made of air.

"Is this how you treat your dates?" I snarl, my gaze boring into the old bastard's.

Face contorting, Valentino shrinks backward like a salted slug. "I didn't mean to leave her—"

"Bullshit," I snap. "You fled at the first sign of danger."

He follows me through the hallway, away from the pandemonium of escaping guests, to a downstairs room. I lay her atop a bed and scan her for injuries. Her breathing is shallow but not labored. I press my fingers to the side of her neck, feeling for a pulse. It's weak, but there.

"Benito, please believe me, I didn't mean for this to happen," Valentino whimpers, hovering by her feet.

I grab the old buzzard by the collar and shove him toward the door. "You're going to make this up to me or our deal is off."

Eyes widening, he nods. "It will never happen again."

Ignoring him, I pull out my phone and dial Dr. Brunelli, who picks up after a few rings. "It's Benito. I need you in the downstairs guest room, now."

While I wait for our family physician, I check in with the observation team, the men at the gate, and the guards patrolling the perimeter. They've disabled the shooter and are in pursuit of his accomplices. Bossanova sits by Losanna's feet, putting on a show of fretting over the woman he just ditched.

Fingers moving on autopilot, I dial Leroi. The phone rings twice before a female voice answers. It's Seraphine, who's staying with my cousin in a cottage on the outskirts of our property.

"Where is he?" I ask, not bothering to hide my impatience.

"He's asleep," she mumbles, her voice groggy.

Of course, he is. Leroi came to the battle on Alderney Hill with a stab wound and exacerbated his injury by climbing up the side of Samson's hideout to rescue Seraphine.

"We have assassins on the property," I say.

Her breath catches. "The Moirai?"

"Probably," I reply, not giving her time to process the shock. "The windows of your cottage are equipped with bulletproof shutters. There's a remote taped to the underside of the night-stand, do you see it?"

"Um... Hold on."

As the receiver fills with the sound of scuffling, my attention turns to Dr. Brunelli bursting into the room with his brown leather bag, out of breath. He kneels beside Losanna and checks on her vital signs.

Bossanova hovers above them, muttering a string of excuses. I turn my back to the trio, forcing down a surge of fury. How the hell does this sun-ripened cockroach get women to ignore his red flags?

"Found it." Seraphine's voice slices through my thoughts. In the background, the metallic shutters clatter into place.

"There are weapons under the bed, in the closet, and in the bathroom, along with bullets," I say. "Grab some pistols and stay alert. If anyone interferes with the shutters, shoot first. Ask questions later."

There's a pause on the line, then a shaky, "Okay."

"Call or text if you need help," I say before hanging up.

After watching her stitch up Samson's injured body under Cesare's dubious guidance, I'm confident my cousin is safe in her hands. Leroi tends to gravitate toward murderous women.

I turn back to where our family doctor is tending to Losanna.

He glances up at me, his mustache stretching with the curve of his smile. "She's coming around."

"Thank you," I reply, already turning to leave. At the door, I point at Bossanova. "Ditch her again, and I'll break your fingers."

By the time I return to the hallway, the crowd has thinned. Our men march unfamiliar guests toward a holding room, having bound their arms with zip ties and duct tape. Everyone remains a suspect until we identify the assassin's accomplices.

I walk around the house's perimeter, pull out my phone, and tap on Reaper's name, needing reassurance that our boys are in position. No bastard should be able to fuck with the Montesano family. Not during what was supposed to be our biggest high point since Dad died. Not when we're on the verge of restoring our empire.

"Benito," Reaper's voice fills my bluetooth.

"What's the situation?"

"We caught two gunmen trying to escape through the trees, but there's more," he replies.

"How many?"

"Hard to say. These guys are pros."

I grind my teeth. "Sweep the entire hill. Detain or eliminate anyone suspicious."

"Understood."

I hang up, and a security alert flashes on my screen—grainy footage of someone slipping through a hatch connecting our basement distillery to an abandoned property at the bottom of the hill. She's blonde, dressed in black, and probably one of the assassins. My gut tightens. How the hell did she manage to escape our guards and Reaper's men?

Another call comes through. It's Gil, my older brother's right hand. He's our highest-ranking enforcer, loyal as hell, and a former boxer who once took a bullet for Dad.

"We've got a situation," he starts. "The society editor for the Times is leaving the grounds with a guest not on the list. The men at the gate want to take her in for questioning, but he's crying false imprisonment."

"Where are you?"

"Downstairs storage room, securing the detainees," he replies.

"All the more reason to drag his date in for questioning," I snarl. "If he doesn't like it, he can spend the night being interrogated for any connection with the shooting."

"Sure thing," Gil replies before the line goes dead.

My phone buzzes with more updates, each one demanding my attention. I spend the next half hour in an observation truck, where some Mortis House boys supervise the surveillance of the wooded areas around our property with drones.

The blonde from earlier managed to disappear into another house at the bottom of the hill. By the time we pinpointed her exact location, she'd already escaped on the back of a motorbike. We retrace her steps and discover she entered the party with the caterer, disguised as staff.

White-hot fury ignites in my chest. Somehow, the assassins know the layout of our house better than its occupants.

Later, I spot Gil by the entrance, watching over the valets helping guests into their vehicles.

"Where's Roman?" I ask.

He flicks his head toward the upper floor. "In his room with Miss Kay. A waiter tried to abduct her during the panic. She said he had a cop tattoo."

My jaw clenches at the prospect of someone stealing Capello's daughter before we claw back our assets. "So, we were infiltrated by the police, too?"

Gil shrugs. "The shooter isn't any kind of cop."

"Where's Cesare?"

"He dumped his little assassin with the guards, telling them to watch over her with the other detainees. From the looks of things, she tried to leave through the distillery."

"No doubt with that blonde who escaped," I mutter. "Where is he now?"

"Roman sent him to the basement to interrogate the shooter."

I nod. "Valentino Bossanova and Mrs. Di Marco are in a downstairs guest room. Don't allow them to leave until the morning."

Gil nods and steps away to relay the orders. I scan the courtyard, watching traumatized guests huddle in groups. Some are injured, others are splattered in blood. Armed guards stand watch, looking more menacing than the assassins.

This is a public relations nightmare.

Just as our family stands on the brink of reclaiming power, assassins transform our house into a battlefield. Tomorrow promises a shit show of media spin, damage control, and tightened security.

Once everything's under control, I plan to work through my frustrations with Ginevra.

TWELVE

GINEVRA

"Strip."

The command slices through my nightmare, jolting me awake. My eyes snap open, locking onto the visor of my stalker.

My heart slams against my chest. How the hell did he find me at Martina's apartment? I went straight there from work after Mom told me she'd be out all night with Bossanova, advising me not to wait up. Moonlight streams through the windows, illuminating his imposing form. It might be my imagination, but tonight he seems even more menacing.

"What do you want?" I whisper, trying to stop my voice from trembling.

He yanks off the comforter, leaving me exposed to the cool air. The neckline of my nightgown gapes open, baring my breasts, and the hem has ridden up to my waist. Tension coils around my throat. I may as well be naked. I thought changing locations would solve my problems, but it's backfired.

"Take off that Scrooge nightshirt and get naked," he hisses.

Heat rises to my cheeks, and a flush spreads down my neck. I would tell him this isn't my usual night attire, but why the hell do I need to impress a stalker?

When I don't immediately comply, he pulls out the knife. The light streaming through the window glints on its blade, sparking a surge of unwanted arousal. I didn't escape one abuser to succumb to another.

My pussy clenches, already flooding with moisture. If I don't resist, this man will turn me into a no-limits degradation slut. Before I know it, I'll start begging him to do worse.

"No," I reply.

He tilts his head, which would look comical if the movement wasn't accompanied by his knife slicing down the front of my nightshirt.

"What did you say, little Ginny?"

I grind my teeth, trying to stop them from chattering. "You heard me. I refuse to play your games."

He laughs through that infernal helmet with so much dark amusement that his chest heaves. I can't tell if he's bulky or thin beneath all that armor. All I've seen of him is that humongous cock.

"Very well." He withdraws the knife.

My stomach flips, and my heart sinks a little at this anticlimax. Maybe Martina was right and it really is as easy as saying no. Or maybe this is the calm before the meltdown. I stiffen, waiting for him to yank my hair by the roots, slap me across the face, or bully me into submission, but he slides the knife back into a holster on his thigh.

Every instinct itches to ask why he's given up so easily, but I clamp my mouth shut. This is what I want, isn't it? For my stalker to leave me the hell alone.

Turning his back, he retreats toward the door and places his gloved fingers on its handle. I lean forward, my pulse fluttering.

Is that all?

A small, treacherous part of me doesn't want him to leave. That dark kernel of my psyche aches for the stalker to persist. It's the same part that still stings from being perpetually rejected—first by a fiancé who placed me on an impossible pedestal, then by another who made me feel unworthy.

Not to mention Benito brushing off me yesterday like I was insignificant.

I lower my head, loathing myself for this pathetic longing. It's pitiful to want to feel desired, even if it's by a weapon-wielding maniac who revels in my degradation.

"Let's see the color of Martina's blood," he growls.

Cold shock punches me in the gut, making me scramble off the bed. I race across the room and grab his arm. Up close, he's imposing. Broader than both my former fiancés. At the thought of Benito's cold dismissal, I pluck up the courage to press my body against his side.

His deep growl reverberates through my core.

"Don't touch my friend," I say.

He stares down at me, his helmet obscuring his features. I try not to think about why he hides his face. Try not to imagine the elderly gardener or some of the older Montesano lackeys. I'm no erection expert but my stalker's dick is long and strong and powerful. And thick. It helps me imagine he's in his late twenties or early thirties.

"I see a lot of standing around but no stripping," he says.

Stepping backward, I pull off my nightgown, exposing my body to his gaze. Cool air swirls around my bare skin, making my nipples tighten.

His breath quickens, as if he likes what he sees, infusing me with a perverted sense of confidence. Samson always said my nipples were too big for my breasts, calling me a show dog, a bitch only good for display. The guards he invited to watch my degradation laughed and agreed, making me feel lower than shit.

Pushing back the memories, I snap, "There. I'm naked. Will you move away from the door?"

"Beg," he growls.

"Please," I say through clenched teeth.

"On the floor."

What's left of my pride urges me to resist, but he snarls so menacingly that I drop to my knees. His helmet follows my movement as if he's transfixed. I can't believe I'm comparing a stalker to my ex. Samson's degradation might have been bearable if he and his men thought I was hot. Most of the time, they played cards or watched TV, with me writhing in the background. The only time he'd pay attention was when I stopped.

"I'm begging now," I say, my voice wavering. "Please, don't go out there and hurt my friend."

The stalker moves away from the door and to the chair where I left yesterday's clothes. He picks up my discarded panties and brings them to where I'm kneeling.

"Open."

I rear back. "What?"

He grabs my cheeks, squeezing so hard that my jaws part. "Be a good girl and take these filthy panties."

Without warning, he stuffs the fabric into my mouth, his hand clamping down over my lips before I can protest. The panties slide over my tongue, pushing toward the back of my throat. I try to pull back, to spit them out, but his grip tightens. My breath turns shallow, each inhale a battle, my skin pricking with humiliation.

They're wetter than expected. Saltier, too. My brow furrows. Did he? Realization hits me in the solar plexus, and I flinch. That armor-clad bastard masturbated in my panties. Now, they're halfway down my throat. I gag on the semen-sodden silk, my eyes widening.

Reaching into his back pocket, he extracts a roll of tape, tears off a piece, and presses it over my lips. Then he discards the rest, pulls out a marker, and draws something on my covered mouth.

His chest shakes as if he finds my outrage amusing.

What an asshole.

"Crawl across the room and present yourself." He pushes my head down with so much force, I need to place my palms on the floor to break my fall.

Grinding my teeth, I refuse to comply. I've done everything he wants. This has gone far enough.

All thoughts of rebellion vanish the moment he steps on my hand. It's more shocking than painful, and I yelp into the gag, my eyes pricking with tears.

"Quiet," he says. "You don't want to wake Martina."

With a nod, I pull my hand free and crawl across the room. His gaze burns into me, igniting a dark, arousing sensation.

I try not to shiver, but the effort is futile. My clit swells, and arousal trickles down my thighs. My pussy hasn't yet gotten the message that this isn't a sexy game.

This masked pervert is making me unravel. My pulse pounds, and my thoughts scatter into chaos. I'm losing control—of my reaction, of the situation.

Something silver glints on the nightstand. A butt plug with a poofy orange tail. I rear back. Does he expect me to shove that up my ass?

"Bring it," he snarls.

Heat floods my veins, and my mind spirals. Body moving on autopilot, I crawl to the hideous object. Wrapping my fingers around the tip, I drag myself back to my stalker.

My gaze fixes on the misshapen crotch of his armor. He's getting off on my degradation, and there isn't a thing I can do to stop him. The moment I object, he'll threaten Martina.

With a rough grip on my shoulders, he forces me to turn. The air shifts as he moves closer to my ass and kicks my legs apart. Cool air swirls around my most intimate flesh, making me shiver. When he rubs the metal tip against my pussy, I have to swallow back a moan.

"Who needs lube when you're so soaked?" he says with a dry chuckle. "My eager little slut."

Cringing in place, I pant hard, letting the tip of that infernal plug graze my swollen clit. What the fuck is wrong with me? I hate this, but my body can't get enough.

"That's my dirty girl. Always slippery, always wet."

For the next several minutes, he teases every contour of my pussy, dragging me to the edge with filthy praise that ignites both shame and desire. My breath quickens. My thighs tremble. My heart wants to smash its way through its cage and hide in the bathroom. This torture is exquisite.

Tears stream down my cheeks as he brings the butt plug to my anus. I turn around, pleading with him to at least use a toy without this ridiculous tail.

I want to tell him I'm a nice girl. From a good family. Who stayed a virgin until my second engagement. But all my attempts to communicate fail through the panties stuffed down my throat.

"You think you're a good girl?" he asks as though reading my thoughts. "Your purity is only a facade. Degradation is your kink. Humiliation is your vice. You crave the powerlessness, yearn for the pain. And I plan on drawing out this sweet torture until you admit you're mine."

He's wrong. I would never belong to such a depraved creature. But as he pushes that metal toy through my tight ring of muscle, we both groan loud enough to wake Martina.

The plug slides into my anus, stretching its walls, making every nerve ending come alight with fire. He takes his time, drawing out the torture until my pussy clenches with hunger. It's lonely, empty, wanting his fingers, craving his cock.

"Pretty little kitten loves her tail," he says with a chuckle.

My heart twists, bleeding out the final dregs of my pride. Despite my body's betrayal, I can't deny the truth. I loathe myself for how I'm reacting, for how every nerve sparks with shameful pleasure.

When the plug is in place, he grabs a fistful of my hair and yanks me up to sitting. Pain lances through my scalp, making me wince.

My eyes are still closed when a headband slides through my hair. From the weight of it, I can tell there's something attached to the plastic. I reach up, finding fluffy ears.

I bite down on the sodden panties, my nostrils flaring. All I need is a pair of furry paws, and this masked motherfucker will turn me into a catgirl.

Shaking my head, I yank off the headband and toss it across the floor. This is where I draw the line.

"You shouldn't have done that," he snarls. "Because bad little kittens get punished."

THIRTEEN

GINEVRA

Punishment?

Staring up at the stalker, I question what the hell I did wrong. All I did was tear off a humiliating headband.

I can't endure violence.

Not again.

I'd rather die than fall under the control of another sadistic psychopath. Samson always knew how to hurt me and avoid leaving visible marks. My shoulders stiffen, bracing for the blows that left deep, invisible bruises. Tears gather in my eyes, making them sting. The memories are too recent, too raw. Will he use his hands, his tools, or worse?

He stares down at me, his expression still concealed by the visor. Pressure tightens around my ribs, making my breath hitch. He doesn't need to give out the orders—I already know what's next.

Scampering on my hands and knees, I grab the fallen headband and slide it back into place. When he doesn't react, I position my hands into paws, mimicking those anime catgirls.

He chuckles, the sound mocking and low. As he brings a hand to my face, I raise both hands to protect my face, and brace myself for the blow.

Instead of striking, he cocks his head to the side, like I'm a curiosity, and caresses my cheek. "Naughty little kitten has to do better to escape her punishment."

Humiliation burns beneath my skin, making it prickle. I can't fight this asshole, can't flee, and freezing will only escalate my torment. There's only one way he'll be appeased.

Gulping, I fumble with the fastenings of his crotch guard and lower his zipper. His thick cock springs into my face, the head swollen and slick with precum.

Warmth floods my pussy, making the muscles tighten. I wrap my fingers around the shaft, its heat pulsing against my palm. I can barely fit my hand around his girth, but I grip tight, using the slickness at the tip to lubricate my strokes.

His breath hitches, a low moan vibrating through the air as I pump him with deliberate, teasing strokes.

"Good girl," he rumbles. "You're milking me so well."

The praise goes straight to my clit, which swells to the point of aching. I quicken my movements, making his cock jerk in my hand.

He breathes hard, responding to every squeeze, every twist of my wrist. All those times Samson made me practice with the dildo are paying off because I have this horny bastard shivering under my touch.

"Fuck. Dirty kitten wants her cream. You're going to get it. All you can handle."

My chest swells with a twisted satisfaction. For once, I have the power to affect him, to bend him to my will, if only for a moment. I glance up, taking note of the tilt of his head, the only indication he's watching.

"You look so pretty on your knees, pumping me with those slender fingers."

Heat pools between my thighs, and my clit pulses with the need for friction. I roll my hips in time with my strokes, desperate for release.

I hate myself for enjoying this so much. Despise the part of me that revels in feeling wanted. Pride and self-loathing battle for dominion in my psyche, yet my body still yearns for his touch.

The whole world disappears, and the cold dread gnawing at my stomach dissipates. The humiliation of being the daughter of a man who stole an entire law firm fades under the heat of the moment. I let go of my resentment toward Dad for breaking my engagement, Mom's suicidal plan to murder Bossanova, even the ten million dollars of debt hanging over our heads.

All that matters is making this powerful man come.

His breathing quickens, his hips rocking into my fist, his thigh muscles flexing beneath his armor as he nears the edge. The shaft beneath my fingers throb, and I know he's close to losing control.

"Naughty kitten," he groans, his voice thickening with lust. "My filthy little girl is about to get her treat."

My heart flutters. If I make him come, maybe he'll spare my punishment. I move faster, my lips parting as my mind teeters over the edge between fear and submission. Squeezing my eyes shut, I pull back my shoulders, and brace myself for him to shower my face with warm fluid.

"Fuck," he roars.

Just as he's about to explode, he snatches back his shaft. My eyes snap open as he comes all over the floor. Thick, pearlescent streams shoot from his tip, splattering across the dark surface. The liquid glistens in the moonlight, each drop reflecting its glow with a shimmer, looking almost beautiful.

Rejection stabs me in the chest. I swallow back the sharp and bitter tang of disappointment. Inner shame trickles through the cracks of my mind, whispering why I wasn't worthy of a pearl necklace.

A gloved hand cups my face. I turn away from the cum to find his cock still hard, still tantalizing, still glistening. A dark part of me rises to the surface, wanting him to tear off the duct tape, rip the panties from my mouth, and force me to take him down to the root.

If I'm already degraded, why not lose myself to ruin?

Leaning down, he brings the helmet to the side of my face and rasps, "Go on, little kitten. Lick your cream."

I jerk back, my eyes wide. He wants me to do what?

Moonlight glints off his visor, and I swear he winks.

My stomach roils, the strange sensation settling in my pussy. Kneeling in front of him like a catgirl is bad enough, but licking semen off the floor? The thought makes my cheeks burn, and my throat thickens with a surge of emotion.

I hesitate, my mind racing. Do I dare defy him? Could I withstand his punishment if I refuse? The thought of what he might do terrifies me more than the act itself, but what about the consequences?

My heart clenches. One day, I'm lapping his cum off the linoleum. Next, he could make me do it before an audience of jeering men.

With a snarl, he grabs my hair, dragging me to the beginning of the stream, pushing my face into the mess. The warm, sticky fluid smears against my cheek, its scent making me moan. Gasping, I push back, but he's too strong, too heavy, too determined to break my spirit.

"Finish your treat," he growls. "Every last drop, you filthy little kitty."

I shake my head, trying to protest, but I'm silenced by the gag. My tongue pushes against the tape, but it's stuck fast. All I can do is whimper as his grip tightens in my hair, lighting up my scalp with sparks of pain.

A deep, belly laugh echoes through the helmet. My heart lifts. Maybe he was joking. Maybe all he really wanted was the hand job. Leaning down, he rips the tape from my mouth and pulls out the panties.

"Kittens can't devour their cream when they're gagged," he says, his voice full of mirth. "Go on, little Ginny. Enjoy your delicious treat."

I tilt my head to stare up at him, my vision blurring with tears. The question spills out before I can stop myself from making matters worse. "Why are you doing this?"

"Do you want me to parade you outside on a collar and leash?" he snarls.

Panic seizes my chest, my breath stuttering at the thought of being displayed like an animal in public. Without hesitating, I turned to the spilled cum and lower my head. My tongue darts out to take the first tentative taste. His release is salty, slightly bitter, but not as bad as I feared.

He crouches at my side, inspecting my progress.

I lick fast, hoping to end the humiliation. Maybe he'll be satisfied, lose interest, and leave. Each swipe of my tongue feels like a battle—pride clashing with fear—but I drag it across the floor, desperate to finish.

"What the fuck are you doing?" he snaps.

A heavy foot presses down on my back, forcing me to slow. "Savor it." His voice is dark, demanding. "Appreciate the flavor of my cum. Relish in its taste. Show me how much you love it."

A sob builds in my chest, but I force it back.

My body trembles, although I can't tell if it's out of fear or arousal twisting in my gut. Either way, the emotion is unwanted. I don't want to give him the satisfaction of seeing me shatter. I will myself to focus on anything—the coldness of the floor, the distant sound of a ticking clock—but the heat between my legs intensifies, clawing at my insides with every breath. It's a sick fire I can't extinguish. Sobs build in my chest, as heat and wetness pool between my thighs.

This is so depraved, so degrading. I hate every moment, but my traitorous body responds to the humiliation with a sick, twisted need. I've never been more aroused in my life, and the realization only deepens my shame. The wetness slicking my thighs makes me feel filthy, the heat throbbing deep inside a betrayal I can't suppress.

He leans so close that the material of his visor cools my skin. "What sweet, little noises. Are you enjoying this, kitten?"

His words heighten my shame, yet I can't hold back this forbidden desire. It courses through my veins like molten temptation. Each lick of the salty fluid brings with it a depth of arousal that makes the muscles in my pussy flutter. It isn't just the act that gets me excited. It's the way he watches me like I'm his own private show.

For the first time in years, I don't just feel degraded but desired.

I shake off that thought, swallowing back the tears threatening to spill. This is all wrong. I shouldn't enjoy being this creature's plaything. The heat between my legs intensifies, and clenching my muscles does nothing to hold back a surge of need. It's like being trapped in a vessel I can't control. Even as I complete that thought, more arousal streams down my inner thighs, making me whimper.

"You're enjoying this, aren't you?" His voice is a low growl, laced with dark amusement that sends a shiver down my spine. "Look at you, so eager to please. Such a filthy little slut."

I can't let him see how much his words stir my inner darkness —a shadowed corner of my psyche I barely understand, a place steeped in shame.

"Answer me," he growls.

"Yes." My voice trembles.

His laughter is soft, mocking, a sound that wraps around my throat like a noose. "Eager little slut probably wants more."

My breath hitches with the need to escape this torment, even for a moment. But there's no getting away from the depravity that's invaded my soul.

"Do you want to come, filthy kitten?" he asks, sounding almost tender.

Need claws at my chest, relentless and merciless, driving me to the edge of madness. There's no denying how my thighs clench, aching for release. With a desperate jerk of my head, I nod.

He closes the distance, crouching near enough that I can feel the heat radiating from his huge form. Heat and musk and the salty tang of his semen takes control of my senses. I want to come so badly that if he leaves me in this state of need, I'll die.

"Look at me."

I whimper.

He grips my chin, forcing my head up until I meet his visor's reflective surface. I can't see his eyes, but I feel them burning through what's left of my defenses, leaving me stripped and raw.

"You're pathetic," he murmurs, his gloved thumb stroking my jaw in a mockery of affection. "So desperate, so willing to debase yourself for a stranger. Is this what you've become? A whore who'll do anything to get off?"

I choke back a sob, the truth of his words cutting deeper than any insult. I should hate him. I should spit in his face. I should recoil from his cruelty. Instead, I lean into his touch.

He pulls away, leaving me wanting more. Rising, he taps his thigh with a gloved hand. "If you want that orgasm, you'll hump my leg like a good little kitten."

FOURTEEN

BENITO

She struggles, her pretty features contorting with shame and fear. My beloved Ginevra, reduced to a sexual object, humping the leg of my armor in a frenzy.

Her auburn hair hangs in wild tangles, catching the faint light like molten bronze. Humiliation darkens her pale complexion, but the orange cat ears perched on her head complete her degradation.

This is what I wanted. The woman who has haunted my dreams, vulnerable and broken.

Ginevra refused to see that I was the man for her, not Samson. But he's dead, just like her father. All that's left is me.

And it's only a matter of time before she realizes she's mine.

As she rubs against my leg, the fluffy tail sways with each frantic movement, making her look like a scene straight from anime porn. Seeing my once proud little goddess, now reduced to grinding against my shin like a cat in heat fills my cock to the point of pain.

Every jerk of her hips confirms how far she's fallen, every desperate moan goes straight to my balls. Ginevra could have been worshiped like a queen if she had stayed with me.

Tears gather in her gray eyes, and her lips tremble with stifled sobs. I don't pity little Ginny— she brought this on herself when she chose Samson Capello over me. She thought he could elevate her to power, offer her a life of riches, but here she is, at my feet right where she belongs.

"Take off the visor," she says, her voice a shaky whisper.

"Keep humping, slut." I smirk beneath the helmet. "Take what you need."

She will never know the identity of her tormentor. I'll take this secret to the grave. It's only a matter of time before this degradation gets too much and she comes running to me for help.

Her breasts bounce as she humps my legs. Her sweet cunt is probably leaving a trail of moisture on the fabric. I grip her hair, making her wince.

This is what she deserves. What I'm owed.

All those years I spent loving her from the depths of my heart, following her to law school to keep her safe. Despite this, she threw away my efforts and threw herself at Samson. This is only a fraction of what I suffered. When she comes running to me for protection, she'll discover I'm the only one who ever truly loved her.

As she continues undulating against my shin, her movements grow more frantic. Her breath catches, her muscles tightening, frustration clear in how she presses harder, trying to find relief. I won't make it easy for her—not after everything she's done. My hands tighten in her hair, twisting so hard that she gasps.

Leaning in, I drop my voice to a low whisper. "What would Daddy say if he saw you smearing your sloppy cunt on a stranger's leg?"

She flinches, her features twisting with anguish, yet those hips won't stop moving.

"Look at you, debasing yourself for a little pleasure."

Her lips part, her breath hitches. She's trying to hold it together, but she can't hide the cracks in her facade.

She's close, desperate, but I won't allow that orgasm until she understands how far she's fallen from grace. Grip tightening, I lean down, my visor brushing her ear.

"You don't get to come until you beg, kitten."

Her lips part with another whimper. I could listen to that sound all night.

"Please," she says, her voice throaty. "Let me come."

"Tell me how much you want it."

"I need it so much."

"Tell me you're my little kitten."

She sobs, her hips quickening their pace, trying to chase the pleasure.

I yank her head back. "What do you say?"

"Your little kitten needs to come," she cries, tears rolling freely down her cheeks.

Her desperate plea sends a surge of blood rushing south, making my head spin. I could never deny my little Ginevra, even when I have her on her knees.

"Go on. Help yourself."

Blinking away the tears, she moves again, desperation clear in every frantic thrust. Satisfaction rumbles in my chest as those hips chase her release.

Her hair sticks to her damp skin, her breasts bouncing with each movement, her flesh skin flushed with shame and arousal. The orange cat ears still perched on her head rock back and forth along with the tail.

My breath quickens as she clings to my thigh, holding me in place as her delectable body quivers. Then every muscle goes taut, and she cries out with the force of her orgasm. Her body convulses, and I nearly come in my pants when her wetness soaks through the fabric.

I stare down, looking forward to the aftermath when the endorphins fade, leaving behind her humiliation.

She bows her head, trembling through the aftershocks, her breath ragged. I absorb every detail. The way her body shudders, the tears that splatter to the floor, the helpless way she clings to my thigh, seeking aftercare I'll never give.

At least not until she comes to me on her knees, groveling for breaking our engagement.

As the last tremors fade, I pull back, letting her feel the absence of my touch. She pants and trembles, her skin blotchy, looking broken, spent, entirely under my control.

But I'm not done with her yet.

I reach down, cup her chin, and force her to look up. Her eyes are wide, still glistening with tears. "You're mine, little kitten."

When she shakes her head, I tighten my grip.

"Remember how easily you gave in, how quickly you broke. It's only going to get worse from here."

Her lips tremble, but she makes no sound. I expect she's overwhelmed, too lost in the extent of her descent to filth. Her eyes swirl with fear and confusion, and my chest inflates as she realizes this is only the beginning of her new reality.

I'm the one who controls every aspect of her life, just as she once controlled mine. She's caught in my web, and there's no escape.

Releasing her chin, I step back, letting her slump forward onto her hands and knees. The fluffy tail still sways, powered by a battery charged with kinetic movements.

She convulses with silent sobs, and I wonder if she regrets leaving me for him. She's no longer the proud, independent Ginevra who could bend me to her whim. And that's exactly how I want her.

I pull out my cock, making lengthy strokes, reveling in the degradation I made her endure. The pleasure in seeing her brought low, in taking another piece of her dignity, is intoxicating.

"Look at me," I say, my strokes quickening.

She shakes her head.

A smile tugs at my lips. She might feel broken right now, but there's so much more I can take from my little Ginevra. So much more I can strip away until there's nothing left of her but me.

Pressure builds behind my balls, threatening to spill.

"Raise your fucking head unless you want me to drag you up by the hair," I snarl.

She lifts her chin, staring up at me with a hatred so fierce that tips me over the edge. Ropes of cum spurt from my cock, showering her face and neck in thick fluid.

"I hate you," she screams.

"Lick my cock head clean."

Ginevra lurches, looking like she might bite off my cock. I grip her jaw so tightly that she whimpers.

"Stick out your tongue."

She obeys.

I rub my cock's wet tip over her velvety flesh, feeling every little taste bud. She squeezes her eyes shut, and I wonder what she's plotting. Once I'm clean, I shove her backward, allowing her to scamper into the corner.

"Until next time, kitten," I murmur, reveling in the way she trembles.

I slip out of the door, letting it close behind me with a soft click, and cross her friend's hallway. Triumph soars in my chest, mingling with the anticipation of what's to come.

There will be a next time. I'll savor it more than this. Now I know just how far she can fall—I will make sure she plummets even further.

Soon, there will be nothing left of the woman who once dared to think she could leave me.

FIFTEEN

BENITO

Hours later, I walk through the grounds after watching the sun rise from my old treehouse. The morning sun filters through the juniper trees, warming my skin. The Bluetooths in my ears buzz with a barrage of calls. Roman has confined us to the grounds until we eliminate the threat of the assassins. According to Cesare, their client ordered a triple hit.

Last night was a public relations catastrophe. Everyone who mattered in the state of New Alderney was at the party, from the governor to the police chief.

The Mortis House boys I sent to watch over Nick Terranova are managing most of the fallout, while I focus on smoothing over last night's disaster with the press and the highest echelons of New Alderney.

Whoever commissioned that public attack on Roman made the Montesano family look weak. I know what the underworld used to call Cesare and me—the princes in the tower.

Roman ordered us not to retaliate against Capello or even Galliano, who lured our mother into marriage. I couldn't even take back Ginevra. He told us to play small, focus on fighting his unjust imprisonment, and help Leroi plan the elimination of the entire Capello bloodline.

For five years, we lay low, plotted, waited for the right time to rise from the ashes of our ruin, only for some bastard to piss on our kindling.

"Yes, Governor Johnson," I say, barely listening to his rant. "We've handed all the evidence to the authorities. Police Chief Reed assures me he will investigate the matter personally."

He won't.

Every official holding any measure of power within the state of New Alderney is neck-deep in corruption. If we're not paying them off, then they're accepting kickbacks from the Orazi family. Or the Capellos. Now that they're dead, I expect the officials will switch loyalties to the Galliano brothers.

"I'm sorry to hear your wife sprained her ankle in the rush to exit," I reply to whatever he just said. "Please send her my fondest regards."

Governor Johnson rejected Roman's multiple pleas for clemency because he was so indebted to Capello that his breath stank of the dead man's balls.

But today, Johnson's out of excuses, and I hang up on him without a shred of regret, switching to the call waiting from the mayor. It's the usual whiny bullshit, only this time, he's complaining about the escort we detained. She'll continue staying with us until we determine she isn't an assassin.

I tune out his diatribe. Men like him are susceptible to the allure of a pretty young thing, so blinded by her tight skirt and fake smiles that he won't notice her red flags. Just like Leroi with Rosalind. And Cesare with Rosalind. Neither of them realized she was dangerous until it was too late.

This is why I would rather be alone than under a woman's thumb. All they ever do is take what they want and leave a man in ruins.

The hour I spent degrading my darling Ginevra was exactly what I needed to face this shitstorm. Everything's now under control. Mostly. Roman has confined Capello's daughter to the master suite, and Cesare is interrogating the assassins who failed to escape.

I've sent Reaper and his team after the blonde who fled down the chute, but I'm not hopeful. She's a trained professional, who will likely lead us into a wild goose chase.

Leroi is safe in his hiding spot. I made the mistake of walking across the grounds to check on his recovery. Even after calling ahead to tell Seraphine that the house and grounds were no longer on lockdown and to open the shutters, she still tried to shoot me in the face.

Maybe my cousin was high on painkillers, but he didn't even register her behavior as unhinged. He just gazed at her like she was a broken masterpiece, a Picasso in human form, failing to even notice he's taken in a deranged little hellcat. I told them there's a new hit on the three of us and advised him to leave the house and convalesce in the mansion. Leroi glanced at Seraphine and refused.

My phone buzzes. It's a message from someone at the door, telling me Losanna Di Marco and Valentino Bossanova are ready to leave. Cutting off the mayor mid-sentence, I burst out of the trees, passing the pool house, and sprint across the lawn.

Sunlight beats down on my back, powering my stride as I round the side of the house. The muffled sounds of conversation from the front grow louder with each step, and I falter, catching sight of Losanna at the front steps, bickering with my men.

Her eye is bruised from being trampled in last night's stampede. My lips tighten. She's either disorientated or still drunk. Her green dress, now more like a rag than a gown, hangs off her like a crumpled leaf, the fabric clinging to her pale skin, reminding me of all her wasted trips to rehab.

Handing my phone to a nearby gardener, I order him to shoot footage. The moment he starts to record, I slow my steps, making sure to clear my throat. At the sound of my approach, the men restraining her draw back, giving Losanna a clear line of sight.

Straightening, Losanna smooths her hair off her face. "Benito, you're looking well."

I can't say the same for her. Losing a husband and a future son-in-law appears to have taken a toll on her sobriety. I wouldn't be surprised if she didn't order a liquid breakfast.

"Good morning, Mrs. Di Marco," I say. "I trust you're feeling better after last night."

"After being trampled?" she replies, swaying on her stockinged feet.

Bossanova stands beside her with his jacket slung over his shoulder, and her shoes dangling from his fingers. He looks equally as wrecked, but not from the booze. One eye is swollen shut, his lip split, and bruises mottle his once-handsome face, the kind that'll take weeks to fade. I would almost regret ruining his looks if he wasn't such a murderous asshole.

"Apologies for that," I say to Ginevra's mother. "It looks like allies of Capello and your late husband are determined to destroy what's left of the Montesano family."

My barb cuts through her drunken haze, and she flinches. All traces of belligerence bleed into bitter regret, and she looks like she's trying to shrink into herself.

She stumbles, nearly dropping her clutch as she grasps at what's left of her dignity, her body swaying like a sapling in a strong breeze. "If I'd known Joe was plotting against your family, I would have warned you."

I wave off the apology. "Karma got to them in the end."

And by karma, I mean Leroi and his gun.

She sighs. "May we leave? Your men refuse to call us a cab, and the signal up here is terrible."

I hide a smirk. After Cesare's little assassin sent megabytes of intel using our WIFI, the IT nerds at Mortis House have pulled the plug on anything more than basic connectivity. When you live in a mafia fortress at the top of the hill, it pays to have loyal employees with a range of skills wider than thuggery.

One of our enforcers pulls up outside the house in a bullet-proof car. It's what we're reduced to using until we've handled the assassins.

Sweeping an arm toward its back seat, I offer her a tight smile. "Tony will drive you home."

I stand back, letting Bossanova half-lift, half-shove her into the backseat. Her legs flail, her dignity dropping somewhere on the gravel. The car rounds the courtyard and disappears. I stay still until they're out of sight, my mind already turning to the next steps in my plan.

"Mr. Benito," says the voice of an elderly man. "Do you still want me to keep filming?"

I take the phone from the gardener and replay the footage,

capturing my interaction with Losanna. When Ginevra sees it, she'll understand the message: her stalker holds a trusted place within the Montesano family, and the only man powerful enough to protect her is me.

This is exactly what I need to herd Ginevra into my arms.

SIXTEEN

GINEVRA

The shower's hot spray washes away the sweat and semen, but nothing can scrub away the shame. That masked bastard went too far, making me lick his cum off the floor. I've more than compensated him for sparing my life. The next time he comes to me for entertainment, I'll make him bleed.

Minutes after the stalker left, I called a cab from Martina's apartment, not wanting to endanger my friend. I was too shaken to operate a vehicle and needed to go home.

I turn off the water, step out of the shower, and wrap my hair in a towel. How the hell did he track me down to my best friend's place when I left directly from work?

The only plausible explanation is a tracker.

If he inserted one beneath my skin, then wouldn't I feel the difference? Even if he did it while I was asleep, I'd wake up with itching or inflammation. I stand in front of the mirror, checking my body for marks. Twisting around, I run my hands down my back, but it's smooth.

Apart from the circles under my eyes, and the throbbing around my asshole, I look perfectly untouched.

After getting dry, I move to my walk-in closet. The morning sun streams in through the window, reminding me that I've barely had three hours' sleep. Mom wasn't in her bedroom when I knocked. She must have listened to my advice about moving in with Bossanova. I don't want her to be home alone until I can get this pervert off my back.

The phone buzzes as I pull open my lingerie drawer. It's probably Martina, wondering where the hell I disappeared to in the middle of the night. Walking over to where I left it on the counter, I check my message.

Unknown: *Skip the panties.*

My breath hitches. It's him. The sexual terrorist. How does he know I'm about to put on my underwear? My gaze darts around the open closets. When there's no sign of a large lurker, I rush into my room and check beneath the bed.

Is he watching me from inside the house or from a distance? Either way, he needs to go to hell.

Ignoring him, I rifle through my drawer and pick up a pair of period pants. They're the largest pair I own, more like boy shorts, and are so bulky that I only wear them in bed. This asshole can go fuck himself, preferably with the butt plug he left up my rectum.

As I slide on the thick panties, the phone buzzes again. Determined not to give him the satisfaction of my attention, I slip on a bra and walk to the wardrobe to select a shift.

He messages over and over, presumably with threats of what he plans to do tonight. I continue dressing, acting like he and his phone don't exist, until it rings.

My spine stiffens. What if it's Martina? Or Mom?

I turn back to the phone, finding it lit up with a number that isn't in my contacts. Chewing my lip, I contemplate whether it could be Bossanova regretfully informing me that Mom has fallen down the stairs.

Fuck it.

I answer. "Hello?"

"Ignore me at your peril, little kitten," says the dreadful voice from last night.

Panic spikes at the confirmation that he's watching. I glance around, looking for where he might have hidden the cameras, but they could be anywhere.

"Don't call me that," I hiss.

"Would you prefer cum licker or dirty slut?"

I grind my teeth. Maybe kitten isn't so bad. "What do you want?"

"Take off those panties."

"Or what?"

He falls silent, making me wonder if he's hung up. I pull the phone away from my ear, only for it to buzz with an incoming message.

It's a photo. Of Mom. Lying in a bed, clad in her new green cocktail dress. My breath catches, and dread coils in my gut.

"This is fake," I whisper.

"There was a shooting at the boss's welcome-back-from-prison party. Your mother was injured, and she's staying in the mansion overnight."

My stomach plummets. "You're lying."

He sends another picture, this one of a wider shot of her in bed with Valentino Bossanova. A tight fist of alarm squeezes my heart, making me fight back a sob. Why the hell did that decrepit old bastard transport her into the jaws of our enemy?

I want to scream. Tell him I used to be engaged to his boss. Tell him Benito will fire him the moment he discovers he's harassing his former fiancée, but the memory of his cold dismissal forces me into silence.

Benito hates my guts. Despises me for breaking his heart. And he's moved on to another woman— the type who appreciates his devotion.

"What the hell do you want?" I hiss.

"Put me on speaker."

With a trembling hand, I comply.

"Good girl," he says. "Now, slide off those oversized panties."

Gulping, I obey.

"I left some gifts for you in the back of your lingerie drawer. Find them."

Dread seeps into my bones as I obey his command. My fingers close around another butt plug. It's smaller than last night's monstrosity, with a heart-shaped jewel set within its base.

It would be beautiful, even touching, if I didn't need to shove it up my ass. Without waiting to be ordered, I run its bulbous tip under warm water, rest my foot on a stool, and slip it into my anus. The stretch is uncomfortable, but a pulse of unwelcome heat flickers low in my belly, igniting a sensation I refuse to acknowledge.

"Feels good, doesn't it? Now pull out your second gift."

Grinding my teeth, I extract a silicone U-shaped device with a rounded body. One end is bulbous, and the other is elongated and thin.

"Slip it in your pussy," he says, his voice breathy.

I grind my teeth, hating this sadistic, controlling bastard. "Don't you think two toys are overkill?"

"Speaking of killing—"

"Alright," I snap, and shove the thicker part of the toy into my pussy. My muscles grip around the thick object, creating a teasing pressure. It swells into a heat that coils deep in my core.

"Adjust it so the thinner part covers your clit."

Resentment burns through my veins like acid. I can't allow this to continue. He doesn't get to sneak in the shadows, threatening the people I love to obtain sexual favors. What kind of desperate sicko goes so far? He probably has no teeth or an unfortunate-looking face.

Shifting the object in place, I shoot my phone a glare. "Anything else?"

"Keep that toy where it belongs until I give you permission to remove it."

My lips tighten. He doesn't need to voice the unspoken threat. Before I can even complete that thought, the sex toy rumbles. Of course, it does. Because he's determined to dominate every aspect of my life.

The sensation is maddening, a slow, insidious pleasure that's subtle, almost bearable. But with each pulse, the vibration creeps deeper, sending a humiliating warmth pooling between my legs, no matter how fiercely I resist. The thought of his control makes my jaw tighten. I loathe how my thighs clench, craving more, even as my mind twists with horror.

"I have a question," I say, my voice wavering. "Did you murder my father?"

There's no answer.

An hour later, I head to work, feeling like everyone knows my secret. The toy seems sound-sensitive, buzzing with every spoken word. My talkative Uber driver, with his endless chatter, nearly drove me to the brink of climax.

Mom won't answer her phone, and I don't have Bossanova's number. On the journey downtown, I messaged my stalker, demanding an update on her situation, but he went silent.

He only replied when I tampered with the toy in the bathroom. The bastard sent a photo of Mom speaking to Benito at the mansion's double doors along with a message about following her home.

I can't concentrate. Not on the court documents, not on client phone calls, not even in the privacy of my cubicle. Julian won't stop chattering. Every time he leans over to offer his condolences, the toy vibrates.

Nick Terranova calls me into Dad's old office for a meeting with Salvatore Bellavista, the owner of the largest casino equipment manufacturing company in North East America.

He's a jowly, corpulent man, resembling a bloated version of an old-school mobster.

Dad used to manage the Bellavista account with Julian, Martina and his trusted team. Now that he's dead, Mr. Bellavista wants to work with me. I can barely concentrate on the meeting because their raised voices keep aggravating the toy. Each word spoken seems to sync with the pulsing between my legs, the buzzing more insistent.

Sweat breaks out across my skin and trickles down my back. I shift in the seat, my fingers tightening around my pen. Its plastic bites into my palm, grounding me for just a moment the sensation becomes overwhelming. The room disappears as the buzzing intensifies, blurring my vision and scattering my thoughts.

"Loyalty is very important to me, Mr. Terranova," says the old man. "As such, I would like to continue my relationship with your firm, working with Joseph's heir."

Biting my lip, I stifle a moan. This conversation is relentless. As is that fucking toy. My hips shift, trying to avoid the protrusion vibrating against my clit. Heat surges up my spine, making it impossible to stay still, as every small movement heightens the maddening sensation. I roll my eyes, my body teetering on a dangerous precipice. Martina gives me a hard shove, forcing my attention back to the meeting.

Terranova's lips tighten. "Miss Di Marco is a capable attorney, but her expertise is in research. Possibly even drafting. May I suggest Miss Mancini?" He gestures at Julian. "Or Mr. Riva?"

Bellavista's gaze lands on me. "Do you think you can handle my account, Ginevra?"

I clear my throat. "Um... Yes, sir. I'm... Oh..." I blow out a breath, trying to disguise a moan. But the vibration is unforgiving, and I can barely remember what I was about to say. "I'm fully versed in contract law. Taking on your account with the help of my colleagues... Ah... Won't be a problem."

The old man frowns, his jowly features wrinkling with concern. "Are you okay?"

"Yes." I give him a trembling nod.

The heat crawling up my neck is unbearable, every second drawing me closer to the edge. This is insane. I need to get a grip. Working closely with Bellavista might be the answer to at least one of my problems. The man is related to the Bossanova brothers. He could tell Valentino to stop sniffing around Mom.

"Miss Di Marco is under a lot of stress," Terranova says. "She lost her father and fiancé within a space of days."

I swallow. Not to mention the law firm I thought I would inherit. The toy ramps up its vibrations, making me moan out loud.

All eyes turn to me. My heart pounds as heat crawls up my neck, my face burning under their confused stares. The unending thrum drowns out their words, and all I can feel is the mounting pressure. I can't breathe. Can't speak. Can't do anything but will my body not to react to the thing terrorizing my clit.

Terranova clears his throat. "Mr. Bellavista, I implore you not to pressure my employee at her most vulnerable. Julian Riva worked closely with Mr. Di Marco. He's more than capable of taking on the work."

"Fine," Bellavista says, casting me a concerned glance.

The toy hums, pushing me to the verge of orgasm. I bolt from my seat and dash out of the room. Footsteps pound behind me, but I sprint to the bathroom, my vision blurring with tears, desperate to escape before climaxing in front of my colleagues.

The hallway stretches ahead, and it feels like everyone's eyes are boring into my back. Each step drags me closer to disaster, the tension coiling so tight I can't hold it together much longer. Every passing glance, every whispered conversation, seems to be about the fact that I have a sex toy buzzing inside my pussy.

Just as I reach the bathroom door, a large hand clamps down on my shoulder. I whirl around to find Julian staring down at me, his features pinched with worry, which only amplifies my humiliation.

"Let go of me." I shove against his chest.

"Ginny, you've got to believe me, I didn't steal your client," he says. "You must think I'm a backstabber, but I'm not. I value you too much as a colleague and a friend. I didn't... I would never. Please, listen to me, Ginny."

Blood roars through my ears, drowning out his incessant chatter. I throw myself backward, but his grip on my shoulder holds firm. The toy pulses again, pushing me to the precipice. Every nerve battles to fight the inevitable, but the sensations are too intense. My face twists, muscles locking, but it's useless. The pleasure overwhelms what's left of my resolve, rippling through my body like an unstoppable wave.

I slide down the door, the orgasm reducing me to a shuddering heap.

"Ginny!"

I can't believe it's happening here. In front of him. Not like this...

Humiliation scorches my entire being with searing shame. I come hard, my body trembling with the force of this unwanted pleasure, my lips releasing breathless moans.

When I finally look up, there's a tent in Julian's pants.

SEVENTEEN

GINEVRA

I kick open a stall door, wanting to escape the bathroom's overhead fluorescent lights. It swings shut, nearly hitting my ass, and I slide its lock into place before collapsing onto the toilet seat.

My head drops into my trembling hands, and I exhale a shuddering breath. Every inch of my body still quivers from that humiliating orgasm, and endorphins run riot through my veins. How the hell did I allow that bastard to make me climax at work?

I clench my thighs, forcing back the toy's residual buzz. It's a sickening reminder of how easily he manipulated me into wrecking my career.

This has to end. Now.

He's crossed a line. I keep saying that but my chest tightens at the reminder of how he made me crumble like a broken puppet.

Scooting forward, I reach between my legs with trembling hands and grip the vibrating rod. I rip it out with a hiss, my inner muscles fluttering.

Every instinct screams at me to toss it into the sanitary bin, but that would only backfire. I glare at the object glistening with my juices, wishing I could bring him this vibrating piece of mayhem and shove it down his visor.

Instead, I wrap it in toilet paper and stuff it in my bag. Then I scrub at the moisture clinging to my thighs wanting to wipe away more than just the physical evidence.

After flushing, I unlock the door and walk to the sink. The mirror reflects a woman trapped in her own personal hell. The eyes staring back are mine, but they're colder, harder, filled with something dark.

Pure, seething rage.

That bastard also didn't answer when I asked if he'd murdered Dad.

This twisted little game of his is over.

As I turn on my heel and head toward the door, Julian's face floats to the forefront of my mind. That sick hunger on his sallow features made me shudder, but the erection straining against his pants made me heave.

Shame burns my cheeks almost as hot as the fury searing my chest. I can't believe I came right in front of him. He'll never let me live this down.

Shoving away those thoughts, I cast one last hard look in the mirror, straighten my clothes, smooth down my hair, and fling open the bathroom door.

Julian topples forward as though he's been leaning against it the entire time I hid from his prying eyes. He gazes down at my mouth and licks his lips.

"Hey, Ginny—"

"Not. Now," I growls.

He rears back a little and blinks, but still blocks my path. I shove past him, my hackles rising. First thing I need to do is speak to the police.

I stride down the hall, my cheeks still heating from my embarrassing display. My colleagues cast me cold glances, but I'm too furious to cower. Just as I'm about to reach my cubicle, a hand lands on my shoulder.

"Ginny—"

"When will you get the message," I snap. "Back off!"

His grip only tightens. "You sure? I'm here if you need anything. Anything at all." His voice dips lower and he leans so close that his breath warms my ear. "Just say the word."

Skin crawling, I round on Julian and look him square in his

face. Concern creases his features, although I can't fathom why. When Dad was alive, I never gave him so much of a scrap of attention. Now that Dad is dead, he seems to think he can exploit my grief.

"Congratulations on getting the Bellavista account. There's no hard feelings, but not leaving me alone when I ask is harassment."

His face falls. "Sure, Ginny. Whatever you say."

I leave him standing at the cubicle, staring after me as I walk the long way out of the office. Right now, I can't muster up the strength to deal with anything else but my stalker.

———

Several minutes later, I'm standing outside the glass doors of a police precinct, wondering if I'm about to make matters worse. In this world, we don't report to the cops, but the rules about unwanted sexual advances are murky.

As long as I don't mention my suspicions about Dad's murder, I won't be crossing any lines.

Sucking in lungfuls of courage, I step inside, inhaling the mingled scents of stale coffee, desperation, and sweat. The detective who handled the homicide said to come right away, so I take a seat in the waiting area. Staring at the grimy floor tiles, I practice the words in my mind and remind myself not to mention that my stalker works for the Montesano family.

After what feels like an eternity, Detective Douglas calls me into his office. Today, his suit is rumpled, and the collar of his shirt is stained with sweat.

"Do you remember anything else about your Dad's situation?" He gestures to a chair across from his cluttered desk.

I lower myself into a worn leather seat and grimace. "I'm here about a stalker, remember?"

He leans back in his chair, making its springs squeak under his weight. "He's the killer?"

"No," I reply, forcing my voice to stay even. "He's been following me, sending messages, and making me do things against my will."

His eyes narrow. "How long has this been going on?"

My mind flashes back to the shootout at Samson's hideout. The last thing I want to do is admit to any connection to him or the Montesano family.

"A few days ago," I say, skipping over the first time I met my stalker. "He broke into my bedroom and forced me to..." I gulp. "To touch myself."

"And?" Douglas leans forward, his eyes sharpening.

I shift in my seat. "He...well. He made me pleasure him...then he finished on my face."

His eyebrows shoot up to his thinning hairline. "Finished?"

I grit my teeth. He's only feigning ignorance because he wants me to say it in plain English. This asshole is enjoying every second of my discomfort.

"He made me masturbate," I enunciate, each word tasting like acid. "First myself, and then him. Afterward, he ejaculated on my face."

The corner of Douglas's mouth twitches. He leans across the desk, his beady eyes gleaming with a predatory interest. "How do I know this wasn't something consensual? Some kind of role play that got out of hand?"

My stomach churns, the back of my throat thickening with disgust. "He had a knife."

"Did he threaten to cut you?" His gaze drifts down to my breasts.

"He didn't need to," I say through clenched teeth. "The blade at my throat did all the talking."

"Did you climax?" he asks, his tone laced with amusement.

"Why the hell are you asking?" I snap. "He's a stalker who breaks into my house."

Leaning back, he picks up his pen again and taps it against his notepad. "Why didn't you report him after the first time?"

My jaw drops.

I don't have an answer that won't incriminate the Montesano family. My gaze drops to my lap. "He's a very frightening man."

"Because you sure don't look like a woman scared for her life."

Recoiling at his insinuation, I ball my fists. This bastard doesn't want to help. He just wants cheap entertainment.

I rise from my seat. "If you won't take this seriously, I may as well leave."

Douglas leans back with a smirk that makes my skin crawl. "Next time he comes for a little something, be sure to give me a call. But don't wait too long—things like this can escalate."

I rush out, my cheeks flaming. The cool air does nothing to calm my burning skin. Contacting the police was stupid. They're useless and half of them are taking bribes.

It's time to swallow my pride and speak to a man more powerful than any stalker—Benito Montesano.

EIGHTEEN

GINEVRA

I barely make it back to the office before my lunch break ends, my head buzzing with my fruitless encounter at the precinct. Julian's eyes bore into the side of my face as I slip into my cubicle, but I can't muster up the energy to tell him to get lost.

Pulling out my phone, I call Benito's number and hold it to my ear. The flat, disconnected tone makes my stomach twist into painful knots. It's dead.

"Damn it," I mutter under my breath and scroll down to another contact—the Montesano mansion.

Maybe someone there can get him on the line. The phone rings and rings, each tone stretching out my nerves until someone finally answers. A formal voice says he's not home. Instead of leaving a message, I call their nightclub, letting it ring for over a minute. It's a long shot, but I'm low on choices.

"Phoenix. Who's this?" says a woman's sharp voice.

"I need to speak to Benito Montesano. It's urgent."

She snorts, and I can practically hear the eye roll. "Benito's busy. What's this about?"

"Tell him it's Ginevra Di Marco, and it's personal."

There's a beat of silence, and I can almost hear her considering whether to blow me off. Finally, she sighs, and the line goes silent.

I stare into my cubicle, wondering if she's hung up. Julian hovers somewhere on my periphery, trying to catch my eye, but I pretend to be engrossed in a client call.

After what feels like an eternity, the receiver resounds with a click.

"Ginevra."

After five years, I'm still reeling at this cold, distant version of a man whose love for me was all-consuming. But desperation has me pushing past the hurt.

"Benito, I...I need your help."

He pauses, leaving a silence so heavy it's almost suffocating. I can already picture him standing in the back office of the club, reviewing its accounts with his new woman.

"What kind of help?" His tone is void of warmth, stripped of any trace of the man I once adored. Now, he's nothing but a stranger.

"Someone's stalking me. He's dangerous. I tried going to the police, but they were useless. I don't know where else to turn."

When he doesn't reply, I press on, hoping to break through Benito's barrier.

"I really need your help. He's threatening my mom. Please, Benito. I wouldn't call if it wasn't serious."

The line goes quiet, and I hold my breath, waiting for his response. Just as I think he's going to hang up, he asks, "Where are you?"

"At work."

"I'll send someone to pick you up."

He hangs up before I can respond, leaving me staring at my phone. Relief hits so fast, I collapse into my laptop. Maybe if we're face to face, I can finally explain that I was forced to break our engagement.

———

The moment the car pulls up outside a high-rise on the other side of town, I know something's wrong. This isn't the Phoenix. The driver stays silent, nodding toward the entrance.

I hesitate, waiting for instructions. When none come, I step out. The glass doors slide open, revealing a lobby of polished floors, towering ceilings, and abstract paintings.

The elevator ride is suffocating, tension thickening with each floor. Strange that Benito chose this place when the club is closer to my office. As the doors open to a sprawling penthouse, all the air vanishes from my lungs. The front wall is all glass, overlooking the casino Dad helped steal from Benito's family.

Did he choose this place to remind me of that betrayal?

My gaze settles on Benito sitting in an armchair by the window, bathed in golden light. He looks otherworldly, untouchable, like a deity.

His dark hair is slicked back, accentuating his sharp cheekbones and strong jawline shadowed with stubble. A tailored navy suit clings to his broad shoulders and tapers down to his narrow waist, emphasizing his athletic build.

Even seated, he exudes a quiet menace I never noticed while we were together. This version of Benito radiates authority and a kind of ruthlessness that demands respect.

I step out of the elevator on shaky legs, waiting for him to acknowledge my presence. When we were together and even before then, his gaze always followed me across the room. That unwavering attention warmed my spirit, stirred my soul, but all I'm getting from him now is indifference.

He doesn't look up from his papers, even as my heels click on the marble floor. I clear my throat, but he doesn't even twitch.

My chest tightens. Should I interrupt him or should I wait? I slow down, not knowing how to act. It's like I don't know Benito at all.

"Thanks for agreeing to see me..."

He turns the page as though absorbed in his reading materials.

"Benito?"

He glances up, making my steps falter. His eyes are darker than I remember, maybe because of the glasses. They're stormy and impatient, making me feel like an intruder.

My heart pounds at the intensity of his gaze. There's no warmth, no recognition of the woman he once loved. All I see is a ruthless mafia prince staring down an enemy.

Forcing one foot forward then the other, I continue toward what could be my last hope. There's no way in hell I'll allow his coldness to stop me from getting help, but when I try to speak, the words tangle in my throat.

"Benito, I'm sorry—"

His hand cuts through the air like a scythe, making me fall silent. "Spare me the apologies. I'm not interested."

My explanation dies in my throat, leaving only another sting of rejection. Benito didn't bring me here for closure or reconciliation. He's probably just curious.

"Tell me about this stalker." He leans back, his expression unreadable.

The command snaps me to attention. "Someone working for you broke into my house and made threats. The police won't help."

Benito's eyes narrow. I squirm under the heavy silence, feeling small and painfully exposed. When he picks up his paperwork, I almost see the thoughts flickering in his mind. I'm wasting his time. It's all my fault. If I'd stayed with him, I'd be treated like a princess, not some pervert's pawn.

"The things he makes me do are degrading," I say with a shiver. "He comes to my room at night, demands sexual favors, and he nearly got me fired at work."

When he glances at his watch then frowns at his document, the words shrivel once again on my tongue.

The Benito I knew would have flown into a rage at the thought of a man trying to get too close. Instead, he's more interested in his work. This indifferent version of him may as well be a stranger.

"He's dangerous," I add, my chest tightening, my voice wavering with desperation. "And depraved. It's only a matter of time before he escalates and somebody gets killed."

That finally captures his attention, and he glances up from his document. He leans forward, making me hold my breath in anticipation of his response.

My heart flutters in its cage like a trapped bird. This is more nerve-wracking than waiting for the verdict of a judge.

"What do you want me to do about it?"

His question hurts worse than a gut-punch. When he picks up his phone and glances at its screen, my stomach drops to my feet. Benito once lashed out when some guy bumped me in a hallway at college. Drove his face into a door then made him apologize to me on his belly.

This lack of reaction is... uncharacteristic.

I expected anger or assurances—not this apathy. Pride tells me to walk away, but I stay rooted in place, determined to get his help with my stalker.

As the moments drag on, my lungs tighten with frustration. I want to snatch those papers and tell him my life is at risk. But I'm in no position to make demands. Sucking in a deep breath, I gather the last shreds of my dignity.

"I was hoping you could help, tell him to back off, or assign someone to watch over me," I mutter.

His eyebrow arches, and my confidence unravels. My heart shrivels along with my courage. What gave me the nerve to come to the man I betrayed for help?

My gaze darts to the exit. "Sorry. I know I'm asking a lot considering... I shouldn't have come—"

"Ginevra."

I freeze, my chest expanding with a flicker of hope. Maybe part of him still cares.

"You're asking for my protection?"

"Yes," I rasp.

"Protection to the level you're demanding isn't as easy as assigning you a few of our men. I don't need to explain why our ranks are diminished."

I flinch, my chest caving into my stomach. Over half the Montesano organization defected to Samson's father after Uncle Enzo died, taking with them about a billion dollars worth of assets. Holding Benito's gaze, I force myself not to fidget. This is the moment he confronts me outright about how Dad helped steal from his family.

After what feels like an eternity of silent accusation, he adds, "That sort of protection comes with a price. It's the only way I can guarantee your safety."

Relief loosens my muscles, and I give him a hesitant nod. "What is it?"

"You said your stalker works for my family?"

"Yes."

"As my wife, you'll be untouchable. No one would dare cross me, let alone this character."

The words land like a slap. Marry him after everything I did? With no demands for an apology or even answers? My mind reels, struggling to process the enormity of his proposal.

He can't still want the children we talked about years ago in our tree house. He can't ignore my role in his family's downfall and live happily ever after with me? If he did, he wouldn't brush me off so callously.

No, this has to be a trap.

I came here for help, not to submit to his vengeance.

"Benito, you can't—"

"Either marry me or handle the stalker yourself." His icy glare chills my bones to the marrow.

NINETEEN

BENITO

I hoped for begging, tears, maybe even a little groveling, but Ginevra strides to the elevator, her hips swaying. Heat tightens low in my gut, my instinct pulling taut against the leash. In the visor, I would tackle her to the floor and take what I need.

As myself, I'm restrained.

The refusal was disappointing but no surprise. I didn't expect her to fall at my feet, but I also didn't expect her to walk away with a dignified silence.

Instead of humbling herself, she stabs the elevator button, her movements jerky with impatience. I sit back, wondering what it will take for her to show me the same deference she gives her stalker.

The elevator doors slide open. Reaper steps out, clad in a black overcoat that barely hides the blood on his shirt. Ginevra brushes past him, oblivious to being in the presence of a killer.

As the doors close, a smirk tugs at my lips. Reaper catches it and lifts a brow.

"Why the change in venue?" he asks.

"Wanted her to see the view."

Reaper glances at the Capello Casino, then back at me. "So, what's next?"

I rise from my seat, move to the security control panel on the wall, and switch to the live feed. The screen flickers to Ginevra leaning against the elevator wall, her eyes wide, her chest rising and falling with panicked breaths.

Reaper crosses the room and stops beside me to watch Ginevra's mini breakdown.

"How's your little project progressing?" he asks.

"Not as quickly as I hoped, but she's an endless source of entertainment."

He chuckles. "That's because you're drawing it out."

"Pressure unlocks fascinating aspects of her personality," I say with a smile. "Besides, she's not ready to show me the appropriate level of deference."

Reaper nods. He knows how well I treated her in his lectures. Taking her back before she's broken will just repeat the same dynamic. I want Ginevra desperate, humbled, and appreciative. I'll keep on the pressure until she folds.

"Ready to speak to the boys?" he asks.

As we walk across the penthouse to the low tables, my phone buzzes. Elania's name flashes on the screen. With a swipe, I answer, and her office fills the display. She's seated behind a desk with Aria, both looking like they've been at each other's throats.

"Report," I say.

Elania leans back in her seat. "Everything's set for tomorrow, but we need 50% of the payment upfront."

Frustration tightens in my chest, but I sit in an armchair, keeping my expression neutral. What happened to family loyalty? Leroi never once mentioned prices, even though he cut through an entire bloodline of Capellos. We rewarded him handsomely without him whining about advance payments, yet her fixation with business is grating.

"You'll get your money after the raid. I'll send someone with the briefcase as soon as the cash is in hand."

Elania's eyes narrow. "We've been in this business long enough to know promises don't pay bills. We want half up front."

My jaw tightens. "Fine," I say through clenched teeth. "You'll have it first thing in the morning."

Elania exchanges a glance with Aria. They might dress differently, but they still wear the same sour expression. Elania leans forward, her lips tightening. "Make sure it's on time. Neither of us is playing games."

"It will be there."

The call ends. I place the phone on my chair's arm and exhale. Reaper shifts on the sofa but remains silent. He knows better not to comment on family squabbles.

"We've already run through the plans, but we should go over the details again," he suggests.

"Let's get it over with," I mutter.

He picks up a computer tablet and makes a call. Onscreen, the boys at the fraternity house are tense. They're team leaders, young men in their early twenties, sitting around a large table. I gaze at the future of the Montesano family.

They've proven themselves with the successful raid on the meth lab and the rescue of Reaper's sister. But that was a small operation compared to a billion-dollar enterprise guarded by a professional security team.

"Tomorrow night, we're taking back what's ours," I say. "My father's casino has been in enemy hands for too long, and it's time this city remembered its true owner."

The room falls silent, their expressions hardening with determination.

"This is about respect," I continue. "It's about sending a message to every backstabbing motherfucker that the Montesano family is back. We go in hard and fast—no mercy, no hesitation. Reaper and I will coordinate from the penthouse. Follow orders without question."

Reaper leans forward. "The bomb threats we've set up at the governor's residence, mayor's house, and across multiple police precincts around town are in place. Cell Phone blockers around the building will leave the casino exposed and without backup."

"Each of you knows your role," I add. "Keep your subordinates in line. Don't let them lose focus, and don't hesitate to remind them what's at stake if they do."

My phone buzzes. The driver is broadcasting the feed from

the limo. Ginevra now sits in the back seat with her head in her hands. As her shoulders shake with sobs, my veins thrum with satisfaction. She's breaking. Her submission is only a matter of time.

Reaper clears his throat, pulling me back. Onscreen, the team leaders sit up straight, their eyes sharp with anticipation, their bodies tense. Our boys are ready.

"Have an early night. I want you all refreshed tomorrow to wipe out the last trace of that Capello bastard. Dismissed."

The screen goes dark, leaving me staring at my reflection. We're so close to victory, I can almost smell the metallic tang of blood.

Another message pops up on the phone, indicating that dinner has arrived. I unlock the elevator and allow a staff member from the mansion to enter, bringing in the scent of roasted lamb and garlic.

Reaper crosses the room and settles at the dinner table, taking the seat opposite mine. We wait in silence as the server lays out the plates and pours the wine. When the elevator doors slide shut behind him, we continue.

"Has Roman taken ownership of the casino?" Reaper asks.

Satisfaction settles in my chest at the thought of Capello's empire slipping from his daughter's grasp. "Everything's in place. The deed was signed this morning. By tomorrow night, the Capello Casino will be nothing more than a memory."

Reaper nods, his features tense.

Brows furrowing, I tilt my head. "Problems?"

"Isabella still insists on helping with the new meth lab," he replies with a sigh.

I stab the meat, bitterness coating my tongue at the thought of Reaper's sister falling into Tommy Galliano's clutches again. "You'd think she would've had enough of cooking."

"She's lost the will to teach," he says, his voice heavy with resignation. "Christian has no interest in school either. Cooking is all they have now."

"Did she ever open up about what happened while she was under Galliano's control?"

Reaper shakes his head and grimaces. "Never spoke a word."

My gut twists. I wonder if Mother was ever happy with that bastard. Or if he coerced her into the breast augmentation that ended her life. Cesare killed the surgeon before I could investigate. Frustration presses down on my lungs, turning my breath shallow. Why do women leave good men to consort with demons?

Reaper narrows his eyes. "Why aren't you at home, enjoying time with the family?"

I wipe my mouth with a napkin. "I can't focus on anything but tomorrow's raid." His brow lifts, so I add with a smirk, "And her, I suppose."

His smirk matches mine. He knows better than to pry, but he understands why Ginevra is always on my mind. Her betrayal has been a dagger in my side for years, and I'll make sure she pays for every moment.

We finish the meal in silence, the weight of tomorrow's operation hanging over us like storm clouds. We've studied the casino for years, planning the takeover with obsessive precision. We know the management team's routines better than our own bowel movements. Despite our meticulous preparation, anything can still go wrong.

Reaper sets aside his plate and stands. "Get some rest. Tomorrow's going to be long."

I nod, watching him leave. The moment he's gone, I pull out my phone and bring up the feed. My pulse quickens as the car pulls up outside her home. I switch to the cameras I set up around her house, sit back, and enjoy the show.

Her movements are frantic, unsteady, as she exits the vehicle and rushes up the steps. She fumbles with her keys, and drops them once before finally unlocking the door.

Inside, Ginevra moves like a nervous bird, flitting between windows to lock them. She rummages through a kitchen drawer, her hands shaking as if preparing for a storm. When she extracts several tubes, my brows pinch.

Back in the bedroom, she squeezes the contents of one tube on the window sill before pulling it shut. It's probably superglue. Over the next several minutes, she moves around the house, sealing every window. Once they're secured, she takes a knife from the kitchen and slides it beneath her pillow.

I lean back and smirk. She thinks she's safe, that she's kept the monsters at bay. But she's wrong. I'm the one she should fear. I'll let her sleep tonight, because tomorrow, the real nightmare begins.

TWENTY

BENITO

The next day, I stand at the penthouse window, looking out over Dad's casino. The twelve-story, crescent-shaped building dominates the skyline, its design echoing the grandeur of the Colosseum. The lights below pulse, casting the fountains in a deep, golden glow.

Dad always called it his greatest achievement. He took a run-down hotel—a relic from our great-grandfather Paolo—and turned it into what it is today. A larger, more opulent version of our mansion on Alderney Hill, with that same timeless architecture.

This place was more than just a casino. It was his headquarters, the nerve center of our operations, and our primary hub for laundering money. Which is why it's hard to believe his supposed heart attack happened at the Phoenix.

Sometimes, I wonder if he knew Capello had taken it from him but was too proud to tell us. If Dad wasn't at home, he was there. This casino was his reason for living.

Now that ownership of the casino and its attached hotels have returned to the Montesano family, we can finally take back Dad's legacy.

Reaper places a hand on my shoulder, pulling me out of my thoughts. He's wearing the same body armor as the rest of the crew, but has yet to strap on his helmet. His sharp eyes reflect the tension we've both been holding in check.

"Where's your brother?" he asks.

My lips tighten. That's an excellent question. Roman was supposed to be with us tonight, taking back what was ours. He used to joke about the three Montesano brothers, strolling through the lobby with assault rifles, gunning down every treacherous bastard involved in Dad's downfall.

Roman is out celebrating our victory with the same woman he stole it from—Capello's daughter. I didn't invite Cesare because he's busy. The bulk of Dad's men are protecting the house and Roman from assassins, so I only took a skeleton crew.

Thank the saints for Reaper and the boys of Mortis House. Their tech nerds have already set half the city into chaos with numerous bomb threats on the other side of town, giving us free reign to act.

"Don't worry about Roman," I mutter, my gaze fixed on the casino. "Are the boys in place?"

"Twelve teams of three stationed outside the homes of each target," he replies. "We're waiting for your command."

"And the power outage?"

"Ready whenever you are."

I nod. Seconds later, the casino's lights flicker off, indicating that stage one of our plan is underway. By now, one of the hackers from Mortis House will have set off the fire alarms, forcing the casino staff to evacuate to their assembly points.

"Begin extraction," I command.

Reaper confirms that all teams are on the move.

"Let's go."

We take the elevator down to the basement. At my side, Reaper checks his rifle. We've trained for this—every move, every shot. Beneath the parking garage lies a lower level, connecting the apartment building directly to our target. Our great-grandfather built hidden passageways during Prohibition when it was the Salerno Casino. His son made sure to connect them during the construction of these condos, continuing the tradition.

Contrary to the movies, the leadership team isn't always located in the basement. The managers we're after—Esposito, De

Luca, Napolitano, and Delucci—have their offices upstairs, giving them a clear view and easy access to the gaming floors.

They won't leave the casino until they see flames. I hope to resolve that by the end of the night.

We continue in silence through the dim corridor, the distant rumble of fountains above barely masking our footsteps. If we had all the Montesano men at our disposal, I would have managed the hostile takeover from the penthouse. But our ongoing issues with the assassins have turned that plan to shit. With our forces stretched thin, we have to rely on precision, strategy, and the boys of Mortis House.

The hallway widens as we approach a steel door with a glowing keypad. Reaper enters the code, and it slides open with a soft hiss.

We grab our rifles from the lockers hidden in the walls. The boys I sent to watch over the Di Marco Law Group are already armed, waiting at the security hub—a setup of monitors patched into the casino's system. The screens flicker with live feeds showing each part of the building: lobbies, gaming floors, emergency exits—every possible escape route under surveillance.

Most patrons and staff have evacuated to the fire assembly points, leaving behind only the die-hards and security forces—those too stubborn to abandon their posts.

Before I can issue the next order, an alert flashes on the central monitor: security forces are moving, not toward the fire exits but deeper into the casino.

"Benito," says a voice through the Bluetooth. "We've got a situation. Looks like the security teams got tipped off about the plan. They're not evacuating. They're preparing for a fight."

"Don't tell me we have a mole," Reaper snarls.

I grind my teeth. Every organization has its betrayers, especially the one Dad ran when he was alive. Capello was his most loyal enforcer until he poured poison into the men's ears and convinced a large proportion of them to defect.

This is why I wanted to recruit them young. Train them in discipline, loyalty, and ruthlessness, so they were too committed to their brothers-in-arms and accustomed to our ways to be anything but loyal.

"We'll soon find out," I growl. "Rimaldo, Capri. You're with us."

The pair snap to attention, grabbing their rifles from the racks. We move toward the service passages and enter the casino through an old security door, making our way up through narrow, dimly lit corridors that still carry the scent of cleaning chemicals.

Tension thickens as we approach the doors. The familiar scent of the casino hangs in the air—stale smoke, spilled spirits, and sin. We burst through, tossing smoke bombs onto the main floor.

Thick, gray plumes swallow the flashing lights and chaos. Alarms blare, lights flicker, and the distant crack of gunfire echoes from deeper in the casino.

We storm through the smoke-filled room and open fire on the security forces in our way. The main gaming floor is a battlefield of overturned tables, shattered glass, and fallen bodies. I move through it with Rimaldo and Capri, cutting down anyone in our path.

"Benito," says another voice in the Bluetooth headset. "We've captured the management team."

Relief floods my system, but that doesn't mean we won't stop until every last one of these bastards is in chains.

Reaper returns, hauling an injured guard by the collar. Streams of blood trail from his shattered leg, and his face contorts with agony. Reaper slams him against the wall, making his head hit the brick with a satisfying thud.

"Who warned you?" Reaper growls.

The guard trembles, his breath coming in short, panicked gasps. "Giovanni Romano," he chokes out. "He sent a text... warned us about the attack."

I turn to Reaper. "Send some boys to Romano's house. Find out who the hell leaked the raid."

"Consider it done," Reaper replies.

Another voice fills the Bluetooth. "Boss, we've got a problem. The woman at Newtown Crematorium is refusing to allow any of our men inside without full payment upfront."

"Fuck," I hiss through gritted teeth.

————

Several minutes later, the casino is locked down. No one gets in or out. Reinforcements arrive, securing the perimeter while I leave Reaper in charge of finishing the raid. I should be inside, overseeing the final sweep, but instead, I'm in the front seat of a bulletproof truck with a briefcase full of cash, heading to the crematorium.

I can't believe Elania Salentino would hold up such an important operation over money. That's why I wanted to deal with Aria —she's the more reasonable twin. While Aria will punch a man in the face for disrespect, Elania once took a hatchet to a man's balls without warning.

Newtown Crematorium is a simple brick building that backs onto the Parisii Cemetery flower gardens. Its architecture is more like a modernist mausoleum than a place for the dead, with tall chimneys rising to the sky.

The parking lot is filled with trucks. My Mortis House boys stand scattered around the lot in tense clusters, their hands hovering near their weapons. They've formed a loose perimeter around the building, facing down the crematorium's guards at the entrances. The air is thick with anticipation, every man here knowing that this standoff could erupt into violence.

I step out of the truck with the briefcase, cutting through the crowd of men. The Mortis House boys part to let me through, their gazes fixed forward, not daring to make eye contact. It's not their fault my cousin won't let them access the crematorium, but they've been trained to resent failure.

As I approach the entrance, the crematorium's doors swing open. Elania steps out, dressed like a gothic queen in something far too tight and low-cut for a tense standoff.

Her gaze drops to the case. "Is it all there?"

"Count it." I thrust it into her arms, making her stagger under the weight.

The door behind her opens, and she disappears. I grind my teeth, wanting to wring her scrawny neck. A side door opens. Aria steps out dressed in the blue overalls of the crematorium's head cremator, Marco. His name is stitched in neat letters over her chest, but her scowl is pure Aria.

"Come on in, guys," she says with a grimace.

Her lackeys swing open both doors, and Aria steps aside, prompting my boys to disperse. They return to their trucks, unloading them with dozens of familiar faces. Men and women, once loyal to Dad, who helped Capello steal his empire.

I walk around to the side, where my cousin offers me an apologetic smile. "Sorry about Elania. That was strictly business."

My brows rise. "Does she know you're letting us in?"

"She ain't the boss. We own this place fifty-fifty. If it were up to me, I'd burn those motherfuckers for free."

I'm about to answer when my phone rings. "It's Rimaldo," says a voice on the other end of the line. "We've found the leak. Giovanni Romano's cousin told him to call in sick tonight because something big would go down at the casino."

"His name?" I ask.

"Leo Salvatore."

Shit.

That's one of Roman's men. Time to drag big brother out from between Capello's daughter's legs.

TWENTY-ONE

GINEVRA

I was ready to maim him, but he didn't come.

Instead, I spent the night lying awake, with one hand beneath my pillow gripping the knife, the other drifting between my legs while I imagined overpowering my masked molester.

That's why I look like shit. My skin is so pale and thin that the vessels beneath them stand out like veins in blue cheese. Dark circles ring my eyes, and my hair lies flat against my sallow features like melted wax.

Fuck my life.

I can't believe Benito proposed. As if I'd be stupid enough to marry a man Dad forced me to stab through the heart.

Just when I'm free from one abusive relationship, I'm not about to stumble into another. Samson had no reason to treat me like shit, other than his sexual hangups. Benito, however, has several.

I knew at the time that breaking our engagement would ruin his family, yet I did it anyway because Dad threatened Mom's life. That decision to protect her meant that I failed to warn Benito and his family that one of their most trusted lieutenants was plotting their demise.

With a sigh, I loosen my robe and prepare myself for another day of work. My life feels like that *Shirley Temple* movie where her dad died and couldn't pay the boarding school fees, so she was forced to scrub the floors.

A crack of gunfire jolts me out of my self pity, turning my blood to ice. At the second shot, I'm racing down the stairs, reaching the bottom before the echoes die. Blood roars between my ears, drowning out the frantic beat of my heart. I burst through the front door, my lungs burning.

The morning air hits me like a slap. Mom stands frozen in the courtyard, surrounded by men who look like they've crawled out of the gutter. They crowd around her like wolves surrounding a trembling cat. She's barefoot and clad in a dress that's slipping down her cleavage.

Bossanova slopes behind her, squirming like someone set fire to his crabs. The old bastard looks like he's hiding something—or maybe just trying to disappear.

The leader steps out of the throng of thugs, all broad shoulders and dead eyes. He's a brick shithouse of a man who looks fresh from a cage fight.

"Where's the money, Mrs. Di Marco?" His voice is a low growl.

Mom's lips tremble, too frozen by fear to speak. Behind her, Bossanova stiffens.

Fury pounds through my temples. Fury at the unknown killer who murdered Dad. Fury at Dad, for dying in debt and leaving us to pick up the pieces. Fury at these goons for harassing a widow still reeling from the murder of her husband. Fury at Valentino fucking Bosssanova for using a frail woman as a shield.

I step forward, my hands curling so tightly into fists that the nails bite into my palms.

"My father is dead!" The words explode from my throat. "Get the fuck out of here!"

When the leader's gaze shifts from mom to me, I stiffen. What happened to the caution I used when dealing with Dad, or Samson, or any of the underworld lowlives?

It evaporated the moment someone threatened Mom.

The man's eyes are so dark that his pupils and irises meld together to create twin voids—voids attempting to suck my soul.

He sneers, the curl of his lips slow and deliberate, as if he's savoring the sight of me quaking in my robe.

"Debt doesn't die, sweetheart. And if you can't pay..."

He doesn't finish. Doesn't need to. I can see it in his eyes, the way they rake over my body like I'm merchandise he can carve up and sell to the highest bidder. My stomach lurches, and I draw in a sharp breath. From the way his thick tongue slides across his lips, I can tell he's already sizing me up for a brothel.

As the last shred of hope evaporates in the morning sun, I turn to Bossanova. Someone has punched him so hard in the face that bruises ring both eyes. The band aid fluttering on the bridge of its nose looks like it's failing to conceal a fracture.

"Do something!" I hiss. "You said you'd help us!"

The old bastard's gaze drops to the ground. He takes a step back, shoulders hunching as if the weight of his cowardice is too much to bear.

"I—I... Your mother..." His words are a pitiful murmur, barely more than a breath. "It's complicated."

Fucking useless.

Mom and I are alone, facing the mouths of six hungry sharks. There's no help coming. Not from Bossanova. Not from Benito. Not from divine intervention. Not from anyone.

My gaze darts back to the leader, who smirks. "If you can't make the first payment, we'll find a way to take what's owed."

Bile rises to my throat. I swallow hard, which does nothing to push back the encroaching dread. "We have furniture. Cars. Jewelry."

He scoffs. "That won't even make a dent."

Before I can counter with anything else, he shoots out a hand. His thick fingers close around my arm with a grip tight enough to send lightning bolts of pain across my shoulder.

"Let go of me." I try to yank free, but his hold is iron.

The men part as he marches me toward a grimy truck. It's the kind of vehicle that's almost certainly held captives. He'll toss me in the back with his buddies, and they'll take turns softening me up for a life of sex slavery. I'll service lowlife after lowlife in a world of degradation and pain. Then, when I'm too old or beaten down to appeal to clients, they'll harvest my organs.

Stomach churning, I throw myself backward, desperate to escape his grip. No matter how much I fight, it's futile, and dread tightens like a vice around my chest.

With a scream, Mom hurls herself at the man, but he shoves her to the ground. She drops to her ass, her breasts falling free from her neckline. The men surrounding us snicker. Bossanova helps her off the driveway, his leathery fingers fumbling with her nipples.

My heart races, the familiar clutch of fear morphing into something darker, harder. Rage surges, hot and blinding, burning away my panic. My fists clench, and the edges of my vision turn black.

Nobody humiliates my mother.

"Get the fuck out of here," I scream, my voice cracking. "I belong to Benito Montesano."

Stiffening, his grip around my arm relaxes. "What the fuck did you say?"

Dread plummets through my stomach. I said those words in the heat of the moment. The last person I want to drag into this mess is an ex with a grudge, but backing down will earn me a one-way trip into that truck.

"Montesano?" he asks, his heavy features flickering with suspicion.

Sharp claws of fear rake through my chest. "He proposed to me yesterday," I croak. "Took me to his penthouse in a limo and demanded my hand in marriage."

His eyes narrow. "Benito Montesano. The same man who seized control of the Capello Casino last night and made its entire leadership team disappear? *That* Benito Montesano?"

My breath catches. What the hell is he talking about? Benito took back the casino? He didn't mention anything like that to me. My heart sinks into my stomach. Why the hell would he confide in the woman who stabbed him so deeply in the back that his heart shattered?

The leader flashes his teeth. They're stained with nicotine, each one ground down so badly that they resemble rings of a tree.

He chuckles. "You're telling me a bad-ass motherfucker like him had time during this casino heist to get down on one knee?"

My jaw clenches. "Call him. It's the truth."

His gaze darts to one of his companions, who no longer looks so arrogant. Then the grip on my arm loosens a little more.

Buoyed by a surge of confidence, I lift my chin and shoot him my most defiant glower. "What do you think a man capable of taking over a casino will do to you when he discovers you touched what belongs to him?"

Doubt crosses his eyes, which are no longer an impenetrable black. I finally see wide pupils and shades of dark brown. Benito's name never used to carry so much weight. At least not with me. Now, I'll wield it like a club.

"Let go of me," I snap.

His fingers loosen a little more, making my chest rumble with satisfaction.

That's right. I pull back my shoulders, my eyes hardening. Then I sweep a malevolent gaze across the courtyard and revel in the way the men shrink.

"Unless you're starting trouble with the Montesanos, I suggest you all fuck off," I say, making my voice venomous and low.

The leader finally releases his grip on my arm and his men exchange uneasy glances. Their confidence seems to waver, but they still hang around waiting for his command. No one seems to know how to act.

If I wasn't obscuring the truth, I would snatch a phone and call Benito. But I walked out on the man without even answering. His proposal of marriage wasn't a declaration of war but a promise of retribution.

Now I know why he brought me to that penthouse. It wasn't just to make a point about the casino Dad helped Frederic Capello to steal. Benito was about to take it back. Until this moment, I didn't know he was such a major player in this world.

"Leave," I say.

As the men back toward their vehicle, I know our troubles aren't over. In minutes, he'll contact his boss, who will reach out to someone in the Montesano family. They'll ask Benito if we're engaged again, and he'll say no.

I need to make sure Mom won't be there when they return.

TWENTY-TWO

BENITO

I pound on Roman's bedroom door, working through my frustration on the wood.

He's late.

Again.

I didn't expect him to join us for the casino raid, although I would have appreciated his help with handling Elania. However, I sure as hell thought he'd at least grace us with his presence after we'd done all the work.

The door creaks open. Roman steps out, fresh from a night of fucking. Bloodshot eyes, sluggish movements, and a crooked grin that speaks of zero regrets.

I keep my expression neutral, holding back a surge of envy, not wanting to begrudge him some action. Five years without a woman must be brutal. But nothing compared to my lifetime of virginity.

But that doesn't stop me from raising concerns about Roman's choice of bedmate. He's getting attached to Capello's daughter, when he should be plotting more efficient ways to make her sign over the rest of Dad's assets.

After he brushes me off, we walk in silence through the hallways and into the waiting car. Once we're far from prying ears, I drop the news of Leo Salvatore's betrayal. If that asshole wanted to warn his relative to avoid the casino, he could've done it without exposing our plans.

Less than half an hour later, we reach the crematorium. We've been burning betrayers through the night, thickening the air with the scent of charred wood and something darker. I expect it's the stench of souls being dispatched to hell.

We enter the cremation room, which is crammed full of our men, who surround a quartet of assholes I saved for Roman.

Aria stands by the control panel, dressed in a set of overalls and elbow-length gloves beneath a fire-resistant apron. Hearing our footsteps, she turns, takes off her safety goggles and grins.

Her smile widens the moment she spots Roman. "Well, look who it is," she says, her voice bright ."The prodigal brother returns!"

Roman's lips twitch, and the tension in his shoulders eases. "Good to see you, Aria."

"Damn right it is," she says, striding over to pull him into a fierce hug. "You had us all worried. But look at you, back from death row and ready to kick ass."

"Something like that," Roman mutters.

She pulls back, clapping him on the shoulder before turning to me, her grin still in place. "Now, let's get down to business. We're running these babies hotter than usual. Flames will burn longer too—no bone left when we're done. Nothing for the cops to find, even with a microscope."

My brows rise. Elania made it sound like they'd have to sift through the ashes with forensic tools, but she's the more dramatic of the pair.

While Aria details the process, Roman continues into the room to address a quartet of casino managers. I tune out his speech. De Luca, Dellucci, Esposito, and Napolitano know what's happening next. They already pissed their pants watching their underlings getting burned alive.

A knock sounds on the door. One of the Mortis House boys steps forward, his head down. "Reaper says the clothes are ready at the penthouse."

Thanking him, I take my place beside Roman to share a few

parting words. A variation on the speech I plan on giving later, when I stroll through the casino as its new boss.

After our men load the quartet into cardboard coffins and introduce them to the flames, Roman calls forward Leo Salvatore. He's a bulky man whose hairline has receded to the midpoint of his scalp. Salvatore glances toward the cremator, his face breaking out in a sweat.

"I know what this is about, Roman," he says, his voice wavering. "I swore my cousin to secrecy. He should never have told his buddies at the casino of your plans."

Roman's plans?

My lips tighten.

It's petty to bristle that Roman's getting all the credit when his role in clawing back Dad's assets is the most pleasant. Seduce an attractive woman and trick her to sign on the dotted line. Cesare has to drag bodies to the basement and interrogate threats to the family, which I admit, he enjoys, but he's still getting his hands dirty.

Roman's just getting down and dirty and loving every moment of it.

I'm the one who hired the detectives to find the woman. I'm the one who set up Mortis House and recruited Reaper to help me nurture the boys. I'm the one who helped Leroi plan the Capello family massacre. I'm also the one who sifted through Capello's hard drives to find the blackmail material that secured Roman's release.

And I led the battle to take back the meth lab.

Fuck, am I really whining about not getting credit from a backstabber?

I'm snippy because I skipped a night with Ginevra.

Shit. I'm screwed.

A gunshot pulls me out of my self pity. Salvatore drops to the tiled floor, having avoided a fiery fate.

We dismiss the men, who continue toward the casino to prepare for our entrance. I text Cesare, hoping he can tear himself away from interrogating the assassins, but I'm not optimistic. My little brother is more concerned about eliminating threats to the family than reclaiming our stolen legacy.

I'm still wearing last night's armor and Roman could use a second chance to wake up, so we head for the penthouse.

Roman gets ready in a guest room, while I stand in front of the mirror, fastening the last button on my shirt. Reaper, who caught a few hours sleep in the master suite, now leans against the wardrobe, watching me straighten my tie.

"Are you ready?" he asks.

I blow out a long breath. "We've been working toward this for years."

He nods. "This will be a place where the boys can practice their skills before we unleash them to the outside world."

The corner of my lips lift. "All I need to do now is convince those hardened casino employees to follow the lead of a man who dropped out of law school."

Reaper pushes away from the wardrobe, closing the distance until he's standing at my back. "Having doubts?"

"Of course, not," I say. "But the casino was Dad's. Everyone expected it to go to Roman."

"He trusts you."

I swallow. "He had no choice."

We lock gazes for a second, leaving so much unspoken. We all had our ways of coping during the years Roman was on Death Row. Cesare lost himself in women and drugs. I had Mortis House. And Reaper.

Together, we transformed those boys from misfits to loyal soldiers, ready to kill for the cause. Now, it's my turn to provide them and the Montesano family with a future.

He clears his throat. "Your speech should hit them with what they need to hear, then stop. Let the silence hang."

I glance at his reflection in the mirror. He's talking about showing them that I'm not just Roman's brother but a force in my own right. "Any suggestions?"

"Make it clear they're either with us or against us. No middle ground."

Nodding, I tighten my tie, the silk sliding under my fingers. The knot settles on the base of my throat like a noose. All I ever wanted was Ginevra. If she hadn't been so blinded by power, I'd have her instead of needing to take this bloody, convoluted path to greatness.

"And if they push back?" I ask, though I already know the answer.

Reaper's smile is cold, a flash of teeth that doesn't reach his eyes. "Then our boys will be ready to cut them out. The first to step out of line will be an example of what we do to dissenters."

With a smile, I turn to meet Reaper's gaze, mirroring his resolve.

"You look the part," he says. "Make Mortis House proud."

I take a deep breath, the weight of what's to come settling on my shoulders. "I'll deliver."

Nodding, he follows me out to where Roman awaits by the exit in a sharp suit, looking every bit like Dad's heir. A tiny kernel of doubt creeps in that he'll change his mind and take the casino for himself, but I shove down that thought. He promised it to me. Besides, he's too distracted by that woman to wrestle me for power.

The three of us exit the elevator into the basement, where our vehicle awaits. Cool air clings to my skin, and I savor a final moment of calm before what might be a shitstorm. We've weeded out the worst of the betrayers, but roots have a way of resurfacing as choking vines.

Roman rides at my side, with Reaper sitting in front with Gil and the driver. The journey to the casino is mercifully short, giving me little time to succumb to nerves.

When we step out, the sun beats down with the heat of twin cremators, tempered by the fountains' cold spray. A building crew at the entrance strips down Capello's vulgar sign. By tonight, it will be the Casino Montesano.

Pride tightens my chest. This is ours. It's finally back where it belongs.

Roman and I walk through the grand entrance, which is exactly as Dad designed. Marble, gold accents, the ceiling a burst of color from the glass installations.

Applause echos from staff lining the path toward a podium. I keep my gaze ahead, moving shoulder to shoulder with my brother. When we reach the stage, he gestures for me to step forward.

A hush falls across the crowd, followed by quiet muttering. They were expecting *him* to take control. Not me. Ignoring a burst of nerves, I place both hands on the lectern and glare at their confused faces.

"When my great-grandfather built this place," I begin, my voice slicing through the chatter, "he had a vision. A vision of unparalleled luxury, steady employment for the community, and a legacy to pass down to his descendants. That vision was taken from us. But today, we take it back."

Chatter breaks out, punctuated by a few gasps. If they didn't know we executed last night's attacks, they do now. I let the words settle, tighten the tension. I fix my gaze on each member of the management team, examining their masked features. Anyone still loyal to Capello will join him in hell.

"This casino—this empire—was built by our family. From this moment forward, it's under new management." My voice reverberates through the silence. "If you're with us, you'll be part of something unstoppable. If you're not, then you're in the way."

Reaper, who's standing at Roman's side, offers me an encouraging nod. I square my shoulders, stand straighter. "Your loyalty, your dedication, is what will keep this place running, what will make it stronger than ever. But make no mistake—there will be no room for weakness, no tolerance for betrayal."

The silence is absolute, every eye on me. I don't need to spell it out. They understand.

Finally, the employees applaud, hesitant at first, then stronger. As the applause swells, I turn toward Roman, catching his eye. He smiles, letting me know I have his full approval.

I've finally taken control of the casino.

Now, it's time to take control of Ginevra.

TWENTY-THREE

GINEVRA

I ride the elevator, still on a high from subduing the loan sharks. Mom has agreed to stay with Bossanova until we can work out how to keep them away. I'm hoping Benito's name will be enough to deter those bastards, but I'm not about to take any chances.

The doors open at the 30th floor, breaking me out of my thoughts. I step out, spotting a crowd gathered around Pamela's desk. They're too close, leaning in, murmuring like something's happened.

My breath catches. Don't tell me there's been another disaster? I continue toward the receptionist's desk, forcing down a surge of concern. Maybe it's just gossip. There's no need to assume the worst.

"Can you imagine?" Pamela's voice rises from the chatter. "Finding out your own father is a casino thief?"

I stop dead, my stomach churning. They're talking about me. My pulse quickens. My blood heats, anger simmering in my veins, threatening to break free. I should turn around, walk away, act like I didn't hear a thing, but my feet propel me to the crowd of gossiping hyenas.

"She completely lost it yesterday," says a male voice I recognize as one of the junior associates. "Made herself come in front of Julian as if he would give her back the Bellavista account."

Pamela snorts. "Desperate."

Fury and shame burn through my throat, making me swallow hard. I clench my fists. Is this what they're saying about me behind my back?

Keeping my heels from striking the polished floor, I reach the edge of the crowd. Pamela is the first to spot me through the throng. She pauses mid-sentence, her smile freezing, her cheeks draining of color.

"Is there something you'd like to say to me?" I keep my voice controlled, imagining it to be a blade wrapped in silk.

The crowd parts, and the associates back away from her desk. Some of them cast apologetic glances. Others grimace. I'm more concerned with the woman who was supposed to be a friend.

Pamela has always been there for our family. In turn, we've given her support. Dad allowed her to stay in his penthouse when she was hiding from her abusive ex. Mom and I visited her in the hospital when she had that miscarriage. I thought she was more to us than just a colleague.

Her smile wavers. "Oh, Ginny, we were just—"

"Gossiping?" I place my hands on my hips. "Speculating? Or just making things up for attention?"

"We were just concerned." Her gaze darts from side to side as if looking to gain support. "After everything with your father... and yesterday..."

Her voice trails off, leaving me squirming. I focus my attention away from the incident with the toy, not wanting my confidence to waver. Instead, I look her dead in the eye.

"What happened yesterday?" I ask, daring her or any of those bastards to repeat those filthy words.

An ugly flush blooms across her cheeks. It spreads down her throat before disappearing into the neckline of her shirt. Her eyes flicker again for backup, but everyone falls silent.

They're watching, waiting. I step closer, savoring her crumbling bravado. Her mouth opens and closes, struggling to find the words. The remaining stragglers shift behind her, none daring to look me in the eye.

Good.

"Slander isn't the kind of offense you should commit against an attorney," I say through clenched teeth. "Keep my name out of your fucking mouth."

When she drops her gaze to the desk, I turn to the nearest asshole, who averts his eyes. The others follow suit and dissipate toward their cubicles.

But I'm not satisfied.

I glance around for the male associate who made that sexual innuendo, but the rat already found a hiding spot.

This can't stop with Pamela. I need to deal with them all.

Pulse drumming in my ears, I walk to the center of the office, where there's a water cooler. Everyone stops working as if I'm the most interesting thing that's happened since Dad's downfall.

I grab a chair, move it toward the wall, and stand on its seat. When all my colleagues are paying attention, I start.

"I had no idea my father was involved in fraud," I say, letting my voice carry. "His actions didn't just affect you. I'm also under threat."

Chatter spreads across the office. Some of their features flicker with surprise, making me wonder if they thought I was sitting on a pile of his ill-gotten gains.

"Because of him, we're drowning in debt. This morning, loan sharks came after my mother. They attacked her. If I hadn't been there, anything could have happened. He's put us in the worst kind of danger, and you stand here laughing about us like hyenas."

The room falls dead silent. No one moves. No one breathes. I don't care that I'm laying out all my problems to a bunch of assholes who will use it as fodder. They need to know we're not profiting—we're suffering.

"All I ask is for a little courtesy. To be treated the same as everyone else in this firm." My voice tightens. "I'm just trying to survive."

The weight of judgment presses on my chest, thick and suffocating. I withstand the scrutiny. That masked man has made me endure worse.

Movement in my periphery turns my attention to the corner

office, where one of Nick's goons stands in the doorway, filming. I no longer give a shit. Let him record. Let the world see that I'm innocent.

Silence drags on, making my insides churn. I withstand the scrutiny until Julian shoots out of his seat with an awkward round of applause. My stomach twists. I glance away from him, only to lock gazes with Nick Terranova.

He steps forward, his lips tightening. "Come to my office when you're finished."

So much for making a stand. It looks like I've talked myself out of a job.

Heart sinking, I step down from the chair and trudge past the cubicles. Each step becomes heavier with the weight of their stares, but I force my head high. If this is my last day at the law firm, then I'll leave with my dignity.

I step into Terranova's office, the door clicking shut behind me like a prison gate. He's already seated at the desk, his silhouette backlit by the window. He sits straighter than last time, his hair slicked back, his features sharper.

Guilt tightens in my chest. Whatever confidence he lost when Dad stole his firm is flooding back to him.

"Sit," he commands, not even glancing my way.

I take the chair in front of his desk, my spine stiff, bracing for the blow.

"You're a problem, Miss Di Marco," he says, his voice cutting like a razor. "A distraction. Your presence here disrupts the office. What you did yesterday in front of a client was unacceptable."

A flush burns at the base of my throat, but I force my face into a mask of calm. I've faced worse. This man won't see me crack.

Terranova rises from his desk, towering over me like a judge about to smash a gavel on my fate. "Your performance has been underwhelming. I've wondered if nepotism is the only reason you're here."

The accusation hits like a slap. My jaw tightens, but I stay silent. Defending myself won't help. He's already made up his mind.

He steps back. "I was thinking of firing you today."

The world shifts, and for a second, I feel like I might shatter. I grip the chair, forcing my features to harden. I won't give in to despair. Not here. Not now.

"But that little speech showed me you've got some fight."

My heart slams against my chest. Blood roars in my ears, but I stay still. I don't blink. I won't let him see the flicker of hope.

"I'm giving you one last chance. Bob Brisket at the Meat Show is having legal issues. Go fix them." He lowers himself back into his seat.

"I'll handle it," I rasp.

His eyes stay locked on mine, unmoving. "See that you do."

I push to my feet and walk to the exit on trembling legs. It's time to get my career back on track.

TWENTY-FOUR

BENITO

I shove the door open with enough force to cut through the low murmur of voices. As I step into the meeting room, its occupants fall silent.

Eight Mortis House boys march in behind me, armed with files and firearms. Fear lingers in the air, mingling with the stale scent of sweat. I sweep my gaze over the casino's department heads, who seem more concerned that I've entered with backup.

Good. Let them sweat.

Roman and I hosted a lunch with the new leadership team—twelve men and women who sat around him like it was the last fucking supper. They're about to discover their messiah went home, leaving me in charge.

"This casino's future depends on us accounting for every dollar." I stride to the head of the boardroom table and take a seat. My boys flank me on my left and right like sentinels. "Before you take on your new positions, understand that financial transparency is non-negotiable."

In other words, mistakes will be punished.

I let the words hang, my gaze sweeping the room. Most of my new employees nod, eager to show they're on board. But there's always one.

The head of security sits back in his chair with his arms

crossed, his greasy lips pulling into a smirk. He thinks he's untouchable because my brother shook his hand. "Thought Roman would be the boss. The heir, not the spare."

My jaw ticks but I don't flinch. A chill settles over my skin, and tension thickens in my gut, threatening to burst. The other department heads shift in their seats, their gazes darting everywhere but at me. I meet the asshole's eyes, letting the silence stretch until his smirk falters.

"Roman is the head of the Montesano family," I say, my voice even. "And I'm the head of this casino."

He holds my gaze, likely thinking he can push my limits.

Fool.

Rising off my seat, I close the distance between us, timing my footsteps to the pounding of my pulse. "Tell me something, Mr. Malfi," I murmur, leaning in just enough that my breath brushes his cheek. "How did you get your sudden promotion?"

Smirk fading, his shoulders stiffen. "Hard work."

What a comedian. I place a hand on his shoulder. "And your predecessor?" I whisper. "Would you like to know where he is right now?"

Malfi swallows hard, his breath quickening. He and the others know what happened last night, even if they don't have the details. An entire casino management team doesn't just disappear into thin air without a mass murder. Mass murder is how we clawed our way back into power.

"Do you want to keep your job, Mr. Malfi?" I ask, my voice low.

His jaw clenches, his features flickering between fight or surrender. I maintain the pressure, my fingers tightening around his shoulders hard enough to bruise.

"Yes, I want to keep my job," he grits out through clenched teeth.

"Then stop acting like an asshole, or you'll end up like the others."

He lowers his gaze, muttering an apology that barely passes for sincere. I'll watch Malfi carefully. Assholes serve their purpose, but at the first sign of treachery, he'll burn like the rest.

As I ease off, his shoulders sag, and his breath finally evens. I let my hand linger a moment longer, and turn my gaze to the rest of the management. "If you're not up to the task, there's the door."

I release Malfi's shoulder and take my seat, leaving the room heavy with silence. They've seen what happens when someone pushes back. Now, it's time to remind them who's in control.

With a click of my fingers, I order one of the Mortis House boys to toss a thick file onto the table. The thud echoes across the room, cutting through the tension. My men close in, each occupying a space between the department heads.

I steeple my fingers. "Last night, we reviewed the financials. Each section has varying amounts of discrepancies."

Their eyes flick to the file, then back to me. Nobody needs to see the numbers to know what's inside. Direct theft, embezzlement, or incompetence. I don't care if it's a mistake or intentional. The result will be the same.

"These could be innocent errors," I say, letting the words hang. "Or they could be evidence of a casino-wide attempt at grand theft."

Some department heads flush. Others heads break into a sweat. Some even shift in their seats. One thing is for certain. No one wants to be the first to speak.

I let them squirm, building the pressure until someone finally breaks. Seconds later, the head of hospitality shoots out from his seat. He's a bald, round-faced man, whose cheeks glow with the force of his anger.

"You're setting us up," he yells. "I've been here for years and never been accused of stealing."

I let him continue, let the words tumble out in a belligerent rant. While he protests his innocence, I survey the room, finding others nodding. Malfi, however, sits as still as death.

With a flick of my head, I signal to the Mortis boy stationed on the man's right. He steps forward, reaches into his jacket and extracts a gun. It hits the table with a dull thud, ending his diatribe.

The head of hospitality's eyes widen. He glances at the pistol, then back at me. The flush in his features pales, losing all traces of righteous anger.

"What do you know about seppuku?" I ask, keeping my voice light.

He shakes his head, his jowls quivering.

"Seppuku is a ritual suicide." I lean in, resting my weight on my arms. "An honorable death for those who've failed in their duties. Since you're so concerned about your honor, show it in a blaze of gunfire. Alternatively, sit the fuck down and listen."

Knees buckling, he drops back into his chair, his features slack. The others glance at him, then at me, but maintain their silence.

I turn my gaze across the table, locking eyes with each employee. "I don't expect perfection, but I demand honesty. Loyalty. Dedication. If you can't give me that, you are free to leave."

They nod, their earlier defiance snuffed out.

"Starting today, my interns will be auditing your departments," I say. "Cooperate with them fully or there will be consequences."

Still silent, the department heads nod, their expressions set in stone. I take in each of their faces, noting the tension in their jaws, the flicker of unease in their eyes.

Good. They're starting to understand what's at stake.

I push back my chair and stand, reveling in the way they shift under my gaze. If they're intelligent, they'll know who holds the power. Not Capello. Not Dad. Not Roman.

Me.

Without another word, I walk around the table and leave the room. My Mortis House boys stay behind, already moving in to set up appointments to review each department. I know I've asserted my authority, but I also know this is just the beginning.

Fear alone won't keep them in line forever. I'll need to employ every method at my disposal to keep ahead of these bastards.

But first, I have an appointment with Ginevra at the Meat Show.

TWENTY-FIVE

GINEVRA

I pull up to The Meat Show and cut the engine. Buildings loom ahead, their neon signs flickering in the overcast daylight. Thick clouds hang low, muting the sun and draping the area in a somber gray. The air is heavy, thick with the stench of rot and grease, clinging to my clothes as I step out onto the cracked pavement.

The street is unnaturally still. No cars, no people—just the distant hum of traffic. I glance around, my skin prickling with unease. The Meat Show squats at the edge of a deserted block, its windows dark with walls streaked with grime.

If my job wasn't dependent on impressing Mr. Brisket, I would turn back and arrange to meet him in the office.

Tightening my grip on my bag, I head for the entrance. The door is old, covered in peeling paint, with a tarnished handle. I hesitate, wondering if Terranova has sent me to the right place, but then press the doorbell anyway.

The buzz is loud, cutting through the silence like a blade.

I wait with my ear close to the wood surface, straining to hear any sign of life behind those dark windows. But there's nothing.

Frustration simmers beneath my unease. I step back, glance up at The Meat Show's blinking sign, just to make sure I'm in the right place.

When I press the bell again, harder this time, nobody answers.

My pulse quickens, a dull throb that echoes in my chest. Something isn't right. I should return to the car. But what if this is a set up? Terranova is looking for any excuse to put me out on the street.

I pull out my phone and dial the office. It rings twice before Pamela's voice cuts through. "What now, Ginny?"

I swallow down a surge of bitterness, refusing to let her hear how much she's gotten under my skin. "Can I speak to Mr. Terranova? He sent me out to meet a client but no one's answering."

"After what you did today, you should be the last person making demands," she snaps. "Do you have any idea how humiliating that was for me? Getting insulted like that in front of the entire office?"

My patience frays, each word grating against my nerves. "I don't have time for this. I'm in the middle of nowhere. Get him on the line. Now."

She pauses, and I can almost hear the smirk in the quickening of her breath. "Mr. Terranova is in a meeting and can't be disturbed."

The line goes dead.

Fuck that bitch. I shove the phone back into my bag, turn back to the doorbell and press it again. The buzz is louder, more urgent, but the response is the same—nothing.

The unease that's been simmering now starts to boil. I pull out my phone again, searching online for a contact number. The internet connection in this abandoned district is slower than shit, and my stomach tightens with stress.

Just as the number pops up on screen, a shadow shifts at the edge of my vision. I barely have time to react before an arm locks around my waist, yanking me off balance.

My phone slips from my grasp, hitting the pavement with a sharp crack as I'm pulled through the door that slams shut behind us.

"Hey!" I twist in my attacker's grip, but his hold is like iron.

He pins me against rough brick, grinding his larger body into mine. "Miss me, little Ginny?"

His voice is low, calm, sending a shiver down my spine. Panic claws at my insides, but I force it down. I turn my head and dart my eyes around the dim room. We're in some kind of strip club, with a darkened bar and a fire exit beside the stage.

"Let go of me," I say from between clenched teeth.

The moment he steps back, I bolt toward the fire door, powered by a surge of adrenaline. I make half a dozen steps on the sticky floor before he wraps an arm around my waist again and yanks me back with brutal force.

The scream tears from my throat before I can stop it, raw and desperate, echoing off the walls and swallowed by the darkness.

"I have an appointment," I say, my voice rising with panic. "With Bob Brisket."

His dark chuckle rumbles at my back. "That's me, and you're mine for the rest of the day."

My stomach plummets. "What legal advice could I possibly give a deranged stalker?"

He laughs, the sound low and menacing. Before I can wriggle free, his palm cracks down on my ass, the sting of it making me freeze. The shock of pain reverberates through my nervous system, bringing everything into sharp focus.

The abandoned strip club in the middle of nowhere. My missing phone. *Him.*

My heart batters against my ribs, but I refuse to show fear, even when he turns me around so we're standing face to face. His broad frame, encased in dark tactical armor, fills the space, with the visor concealing his eyes. I can't see an inch of skin yet I still quail under the intensity in his stare.

He steps back, giving me just enough space to breathe, but not enough to run. Since this bastard can call my boss and even pay the firm a retainer, he can also report me for walking out on a client.

I lick my dry lips, making him draw forward, seeming to track the movement.

"Mr. Brisket," I say, keeping my voice even. "How can I help you?"

"I've got all sorts of problems, little Ginny. But right now, you're the only one that matters."

He wraps an arm around my waist again, moving us to the bar, where a bucket of champagne awaits. With a flick of his gloved hand, he pops the cork, and I force myself not to flinch.

"Celebrating something?" I ask.

"Our new association." He fills the flutes with bubbling liquid, then hands me a glass. His gloved fingers brush mine, sending a jolt of electricity to my core. "You and me, working together."

I take the glass but don't bring it to my lips. "And what exactly is this work?"

"I'm a man obsessed. There's this particular little lawyer I can't get out of my head."

My breath quickens. "I'm engaged."

"Samson Capello is dead," he growls.

I flinch. Of course, he'd know about Samson. He would have walked past my ex's carcass when he found me in the closet. "I'm engaged to Benito Montesano, the new owner of the biggest casino in town."

His posture stiffens, and his shoulders hunch. He stares down at me as if I just claimed to be connected to Scarface or Don Corleone. Breathing hard, he finally utters, "You're bluffing."

I suppress a smirk. Invoking Benito's name is getting me out of all kinds of trouble. Straightening, I raise my chin. "He proposed to me last night. The only reason I don't have a ring is because he's been busy taking back his casino."

He studies me, his gaze dropping on my empty hand before returning to my face. The silence stretches, making the air crackle with tension. My stalker was probably out last night, helping Benito. That explains why he failed to appear in my room.

As he shifts on his feet, I force back a pang of regret. Maybe it was too heavy handed of me to hint that I could get him into trouble with his boss. I shake off that thought. Why am I sympathizing with this bastard?

"So, it's not official yet," he rumbles. "Until you can prove it is, you belong to me."

He wraps his fingers around the hand holding the glass and brings it to my lips. The liquid bubbles on my tongue, washing away the taste of fear.

"Benito is a dangerous man," I murmur. "Your boss won't take kindly to you touching what belongs to him."

"Let me handle Mr. Montesano," he growls.

"Why am I here?"

"To give me a show."

I set down the glass and look him straight in the visor. "This is completely inappropriate. I'm an attorney, not an adult entertainer."

His arm whips out, and he grabs my throat. "I bought and paid for you, little Ginny. Now, you perform."

Breath catching, a dangerous thrill surges through my veins, battling the fear. Anger flares at Terranova for not vetting this client and at Brisket for hiring me like I'm available for services. I pull back, resisting the urge to submit.

"No," I whisper, more to myself than to him.

But it's a battle I'm not sure I'll win.

TWENTY-SIX

BENITO

I glare down at Ginevra, my jaw clenching. How typical of her to walk out on my proposal of marriage, yet use it to escape trouble. The sharks I sent to her doorstep didn't know what to do when she mentioned my name.

It's time to escalate. If she thinks Bob Brisket will back down, she's mistaken. I'll leave her so broken and humiliated that she has no choice but to come to me for protection.

I tighten my grip around her throat, making those pretty features twist with anguish. Her skin reddens, becoming nearly as vibrant as her hair.

She shoves at my chest, but she may as well be trying to fell a tree barehanded. My disdain for her has roots as deep as my desire.

"Let go of me," she says through clenched teeth. "If Benito finds out—"

"That you love to suck my cock?" I growl through the voice changer.

Whimpering, she squeezes her eyes shut. The sight of her so conflicted sends a rush of heat to my groin, making my shaft lengthen and thicken. There's a part of her that loves my attention almost as much as I love making her grovel.

If I had satisfied her urges in the past, maybe she wouldn't have stabbed me in the back.

"Will you strip for me, little Ginny, or will I have to strip you with my knife?"

She shivers. "Don't destroy my clothes. I need them for driving back."

I smirk. "Then you'd better give me a show."

Releasing my grip on her throat, I step back, lean against the bar, and sweep an arm toward the stage. Tonight, Ginevra will be my private dancer, my pretty little slut.

Standing on trembling legs, she clutches the lapels of her jacket together as if they're holding her last shreds of dignity. "But Benito..."

I wait for her to complete that sentence. When she doesn't, I reach into my pocket and pull out a burner phone. "Call Mr. Montesano. Tell him all the filthy things we've done together. If he still wants you, I'll walk out of this door and leave you alone."

Her lips tighten. "I'm not lying. Benito really did propose."

And she walked out without a reply. I don't voice that in case she mistakes me for Reaper, who she passed at the elevator. The last thing I need is for her to become obsessed with my right hand.

I cock my head. "Who are you trying to convince, little liar? Yourself or me? Strip!"

With trembling fingers, she fumbles at her suit jacket, peeling it off to reveal nipples protruding through her shirt. I let out a low growl of approval, the sound reverberating to my cock.

"You love degradation," I say, holding back a surge of contempt.

"I don't," she whispers.

"What was that?" I cup my hand behind the part of the visor concealing my ear. "I didn't catch what you said."

"Nothing," she spits, hurling the jacket in my face.

Chuckling, I fold it in half, place it on a stool, and gesture for her to go up on stage. Thank fuck this visor conceals my smile. Her venomous glare feeds my inner darkness.

Ginevra was never so entertaining when we were together. I spent my time running around, catering to her every whim just to earn a fleeting smile.

Five years apart has cleared my head of that unhealthy obsession. I've grown from that little boy who spotted her in our kitchens and made her my idol. She became the center of my universe, my reason for breathing. She was my deity, and I was her number one acolyte.

Now, my little goddess is about to fall off her pedestal.

She storms across the club, every step fueled by resentment, before ascending the stairs to the stage.

I reach behind the bar and pick up the remote that activates the lighting. A press of the button bathes her in crimson, accentuating her rage and lust. Then, I hit the switch that starts the music.

Ginevra begins to move, awkward at first, her limbs uncoordinated and stiff. I never knew she was so clumsy. It's almost endearing. Then she kicks off her shoes, shooting me a furious glower. I'm too busy fixating on her nipples, which harden to betray her arousal.

Picking up the bucket of champagne and her flute, I cross the room and stand at the foot of the stage. This was one of many private members' clubs Dad ran when he was alive. We had to shut it down shortly after Roman's conviction when Capello lured away our workers.

I don't blame the lower-level employees who moved on to work for the backstabber. They had families to feed. With Roman out of action and us confined to Alderney Hill, the Montesano empire was crumbling. But Dad's lieutenants left in a stampede, having arranged their defection before Capello even engineered his death.

Our family still owns this useless piece of real estate, along with many others in this run-down part of town. For now, it serves my purposes. I can continue hiring her as Bob Brisket until she either quits her job or comes running into my arms.

The music stops, as do Ginevra's movements.

"There," she snaps. "I've given you a private dance. Now, may I return to the office?"

As the next track fills the speakers, I slide the champagne flute across the stage. "You're wearing too many clothes."

She picks up the glass, downs its contents, and hurls it at my helmet. "Fuck you!"

Broken glass flies everywhere, making me chuckle. I reach down, pick up a piece, and hold it like a shank. "Are you offering?"

With a shriek, she skitters back and resumes her dance. This time, her movements are fluid, as if she's done this before. My gut tightens, jealousy twisting like a knife. Did she dance like this for Samson Capello?

All thoughts of that bastard evaporate when she loosens the button of her shirt, giving me a tantalizing peek of cleavage.

Groaning, I shift on my feet, my cock lengthening and thickening to the point of pain. It's not like I haven't already seen her naked. This is the first time she's taken off her clothes for me without the encouragement of a knife.

Tossing aside the shank, I focus on the rest of the show. Ginevra unbuttons her shirt, revealing a lace bra, black against her pale skin, a pretty contrast that makes my pulse quicken. Her flat stomach draws my attention, each taut little muscle quivering with strain.

She turns around, giving me a view of the curve of her ass. My breath catches. From the front, she's the goddess of flames and fury. From the back, she's my dirty little girl.

When she glances at me over her shoulder, my knees buckle. I brace a palm on the stage, wondering if I'll ever grow out of being her simp. This version of Ginevra tantalizes me even more than the groveling girl I haunt at night.

But when she's powerful, she's beyond my control.

She unzips her skirt, revealing black silk panties that stretch over the most perfect ass in the universe. Those cheeks are the eighth wonder of the world, but her pussy is the ninth.

I want that sweet cunt. Up close and without a visor. I want to bury my face into those wet folds and drown in a sea of her arousal.

My jaw clenches, and I grind my teeth. Why must I be so weak for this little betrayer?

"Get naked," I growl loud enough to make her flinch.

With a tremor, she unhooks her bra, revealing those glorious breasts. They're B-cups, with pale nipples that stand erect, begging for my touch. I want to pinch them until they darken, twist them until her face contorts and tears leak from her eyes.

She slides off the panties, revealing a trimmed patch of fiery red curls.

Scratch that. I'm back to needing her pussy.

I reach into my pocket and extract some rope, my heart pounding with anticipation. "Come here."

She approaches the edge of the stage, her steps hesitant. I pull her down, binding her wrists together with a few quick loops and a knot. Then I extract a blindfold and wrap it around her eyes.

"B-Brisket?" she asks with a whimper.

"Silence," I snap, laying her on the stage with her legs dangling off the sides.

I lift my visor, finally seeing her nudity with my own eyes. The sight of her, exposed and vulnerable, makes me lightheaded as blood rushes to my cock.

Positioning myself between her spread legs, I part her pussy with two fingers. Her labia is reddened and slick. Her clit is so swollen, I could snap it between my teeth. The exquisite tableau makes me groan.

"You're ready for me," I growl, mimicking my voice changer. "Wet and wanting."

She shakes her head, a feeble attempt at denial. My little Ginny is so aroused she can't even form words.

"You might lie, but your body screams the truth. You love being my slut."

"Shut up," she screams. "I hate you!"

I run the flat of my tongue up her slit, silencing her protests. Her body falls limp under my touch.

Chuckling, I swirl my tongue around her swollen clit, marveling at her body's responsiveness.

Ginevra acts like this is the first time a man has licked her pussy when I'm almost certain this is the method Samson used to lure her away. My little Ginny doesn't want to be a goddess—she enjoys playing the slut.

Nerves flutter in my stomach, but I swallow back the surge of anxiety. I've watched countless videos on how to do this, studied every technique in detail, but theory doesn't always translate to reality. What if I'm clumsy? What if I fail to make her come?

TWENTY-SEVEN

GINEVRA

I lie on the cold stage, blindfolded, wrists bound, waiting for him to make his move. My heart pounds loud enough to muffle the music, and my breath comes in shallow bursts.

He's been silent for too long.

Anticipation gnaws at my insides, twisting them into knots. He stopped touching me, and I have no idea why. What if he hated the taste of my pussy? What if he took a closer look at my red pubes and decided I'm not worth pleasuring?

After the first time we were together, Samson said my body was so unpleasant to look at that he couldn't muster an erection. What if he was right?

Tears sting my eyes, threatening to soak my blindfold. I can't bear the thought of Brisket walking away, leaving me aching for a release he's too disgusted to give. Humiliation burns my chest, filling my veins with fire.

His breath, hot and ragged, hovers inches from my skin. He's so close I can feel the heat radiating from his mouth, which feels almost like a caress. I shiver, waiting for more.

"Scared no one will make you come harder than he ever did?" His voice is a low growl, vibrating through the air, taunting, and cruel.

I swallow, my throat dry. Is he talking about Benito? Samson never gave me a measure of satisfaction—only pain. At least Benito strove to make me happy. I keep my mouth shut, not wanting to give him the satisfaction of the truth that no man has ever excited me more than him.

His gloved fingers brush my inner thigh with feather-light touches that make my breath hitch. I hate him for making me want him. He drags his fingers higher, so close to the outer lips of my pussy. I arch my back, needing more.

"Your body is begging for me, Ginny," he murmurs, his voice decadent and dark. "You've become even wetter."

He's right. I've never needed him more. I can't stand how easily he's breaking me down, how my body won't cooperate with my need for control. I feel it slipping with every shallow breath, and I'm powerless to stop it. I bite back a whimper, refusing to give him a reaction. Men like Bob Brisket feed on a woman's desperation.

Just as I expect him to move away, he presses a single finger to my entrance. Every nerve ending sets alight. I squirm against his touch, then he pulls back.

"And you say you don't want this. Little liar."

"Fuck you," I snap.

He chuckles, the sound so menacing and dark that shivers skitter up my spine. "Oh, I plan to. But first, you're going to beg for it."

My stomach plummets. What the hell am I saying? Gritting my teeth, I hold onto a semblance of my crumbling restraint. The heat between my legs is unbearable, the need eating away at my resolve. His breath, hot and heavy against my aching pussy, makes it impossible. My self-control is slipping, sliding out of my grasp with each passing second.

I hate how easily he can unravel my restraint and how my body betrays my dignity. I need to stay strong, but I'm already falling apart.

His tongue flicks out, circling my clit, slow, deliberate. Sparks of pleasure detonate across my nerves, and my back arches off the stage. I cry out, desperate for more.

"Tell me," he says, his voice laced with amusement. "Tell me how much you want it."

I shake my head, refusing to give in. "You're the one who lured me here. Seems like you want this even more."

He pulls back again, leaving me trembling, teetering on the edge of something dangerous. My heart lurches. If he stops now, I'll die.

"I'm not touching you until you beg," he says, his voice hardening. "So be a good girl and ask nicely."

Tears of frustration sting my eyes. This bastard is breaking me down, and I can't stand that he's winning.

"Please," I whisper, despising how my voice wavers.

"Louder, Little Ginny. And be specific."

"Please," I say through clenched teeth, trying to curb the desperation. "Please, lick my pussy. Make me come."

He hums in approval, finally pressing his tongue to my clit, flicking it with just the right amount of pressure. I gasp, my hips bucking, my lips parting with a gasp.

"There you go," he murmurs, his voice a dark caress. "That's my good girl."

Before I know it, he's circling my clit with unrelenting focus, flicking, sucking, each movement infusing me with shockwaves. I writhe under his control, every nerve ablaze, every breath a ragged gasp.

I can't think, can't breathe. My entire world narrows down to the sensation of his mouth on my pussy, the way he plays my body like his own personal instrument.

My eyes roll to the back of my head, my muscles trembling with the need for release. Pressure builds up in my core, threatening to explode. Just as I'm on the brink of climax, he pulls back, leaving me aching.

"You don't get to come until I say so."

Any other time, I would tell him to get fucked. Now, he's stripped away what's left of my pride. I need this. Need him. Besides, it doesn't count if I'm blindfolded. I can pretend to be someone else. A sexy stripper entertaining a besotted client.

"Please," I say through panting breaths. "Please, let me climax."

His low, cruel laugh rings with satisfaction, making me shiver and squirm. "You'll come when I give you permission, little Ginny."

My body is afire, every nerve ending screaming for release, but he's in control, seeming to relish every second of my torment.

His hands find my hips, gripping hard enough to leave bruises as he moves some of my wetness to my ass. I shudder as something cold presses against my entrance, and I know what's coming next.

It's that fucking tail again.

The headband slides on next, and I clench my jaw.

He's turning me into a fucking catgirl.

Again.

"Who's my pretty little kitten?" he says, his voice a pleased rumble.

I grind my molars.

He blows a stream of warm air on my aching clit, making me shudder.

"It's me," I say through gritted teeth. "I'm your pretty little kitten. Now, please, will you let me come?"

Chuckling, he gives in, his mouth returning to my clit with a renewed intensity. He slips his fingers in my pussy, curling around until he hits a spot that makes me gasp.

All thoughts of being a catgirl disappear into the ether as the pressure rebuilds. I writhe against his eager tongue, chasing my pleasure. Every nerve in my body screams for release, the pressure building to a fever pitch.

"Good little kitten," he mumbles around my clit. "I'm going to make you come so hard, you'll be purring for more."

At his words, something inside me snaps. An orgasm crashes through my core, making every muscle tighten and convulse. Wave after wave of pleasure consumes my senses, and I fall adrift in a sea of bliss.

Brisket doesn't stop—his clever tongue keeps stroking my clit until I'm reduced to a shuddering, sobbing mess. The finger deep in my pussy pumps back and forth, teasing out a second climax.

Only when my throat becomes hoarse from screaming does he pull away, leaving me gasping for breath. My body falls limp against the stage, shivering and spent.

"That's my filthy little kitten," he says, sounding almost proud. "You came apart so beautifully."

My breath comes in ragged gasps, and I can't even respond. I'm too exhausted, too broken, too furious with myself for allowing this to happen.

I hate him, but most of all, I hate myself for wanting him.

Trembling through the aftershocks, with my veins still pulsing with the bliss of my orgasm, I wait for the sound of retreating footsteps. Tension coils low in my belly, telling me this is far from over.

Since when did Brisket ever leave without coming?

The air shifts with the unmistakable weight of his presence. My pussy clenches, needing more than just his fingers. I brace myself, expecting him to take whatever satisfaction he needs, but instead, he loosens the ropes confining my wrists.

I meet him halfway, wriggling out of the bindings to free my hands. He doesn't stop me when I reach up to the blindfold, so I peel it off. Harsh light floods my eyes, making me blink against the glare.

When my vision clears, I find Brisket on the stage, towering over me with his cock out. It's long and thick and glistening with precum.

My breath catches in my throat. He doesn't need to voice a command—I already know what he wants.

Scrambling up to my knees, I open my mouth, ready to take him down to the hilt. But just as I lean forward, he stops me with a hand on my shoulder.

"No," he growls.

Panic grips my chest. If he doesn't want my mouth, then... I try to push away the thought, but it digs into my psyche, relentless. He's going to fuck me. Stick that massive cock in my pussy and pound into me until he fills me with cum.

"Brisket," I whisper. "I'm not on birth control."

He chuckles, a dark rumble that sends a shiver down my spine. "What would Mr. Montesano say if you carried the child of Bob Brisket?"

My heart pounds, the panic mixing with excitement. I

scramble to my feet, ready to bolt, but he shoves me down onto the cold, hard stage.

"Don't do this," I scream, my voice still hoarse from climaxing.

He ignores my plea, his hands finding my breasts, his fingers pinching my nipples with a cruel twist that sends a shock of pain radiating to my aching core. I cry out, the sound escaping before I can stop it, but that only seems to excite him more.

"You love it, little Ginny," he says, his voice thick with lust.

I shake my head, not wanting to admit that the pain makes my clit throb. I clamp my thighs together, not wanting this stranger fuck me without a condom. Instead of forcing my legs apart, he shoves me down, moves further up my body, resting his hot, heavy cock between my breasts.

Relief floods my system, and I exhale a long breath.

He grips my tits, pushing them together around his shaft, before rocking back and forth. I'm drenched in sweat, and slick with precum sliding against my skin. With each thrust, he twists my nipples, sending a surge of sensation that makes my hips buck.

My body reacts against my will, a low moan slipping past my lips. He's taking what he wants, and my own treacherous body can't help but respond.

As he fucks my breasts, I reach down between my legs, finding myself aching and wet. My fingers press against my clit, circling in sync with the rhythm of his movements.

"Touching yourself, little Ginny?" he grunts, his voice thick with arousal.

I shake my head, which only makes him laugh.

"Since you get off on degradation so much, I will become your master."

I can't answer, too lost in the sensation, my mind succumbing to this twisted pleasure. His cock slides faster between my breasts, his grunts quickening with every stroke.

The tension coils tighter and tighter in my core, and I know I'm close. My hips buck, seeking more friction. I press harder against my clit, pushing my body back to that delicious edge.

With a roar, he shoves forward, his cock pulsing between my

breasts, and then he comes with thick, hot spurts painting my chest and throat.

I screech at the warm mess splattering against my skin, but his movements don't falter. Through panting breaths, he asks, "You like it when I mark you as mine?"

After his final spurt, he grabs the champagne bottle from earlier and shoves it into my pussy. I'm so wet that it glides in without friction. My muscles spasm at the sudden intrusion, making me forget I'm covered in his cooling cum. He jostles the bottle, aggravating the liquid. It's like a carbonated rush, hitting my walls and cervix. I clench my teeth, bucking and straining against the unusual sensations.

"That's my greedy little slut," he rumbles, sliding it in and out. "Taking this champagne bottle like my good girl."

"How dare you," I say through clenched teeth, holding back my third orgasm. It's bad enough that this bastard stuck a plug up my ass with an attached tail, now he's making me climax with a bottle?

He moves the infernal glass object in and out of my pussy, stretching it beyond the point of pleasure. I jerk my head from side to side, not wanting to give him the satisfaction of seeing me come apart. But one twist of the bottle sends its cold edge grazing against a spot that sends me over the edge.

Another orgasm hits me like a popped cork, making me scream. As I'm panting through the spasms, he yanks out the bottle and pours the champagne over my chest. Cold liquid hits my skin, washing away the cum in a deluge of icy bubbles.

He stares down at me through that impenetrable visor. "You're my favorite toy, and I will never let you go."

My body quakes both from the cold and a surge of fury. No one has ever treated me with such disrespect and made me enjoy every minute. I despise my stalker from the depths of my soul, but deep down, buried beneath all the bullshit, there's something darker, something I can't deny.

I want more.

TWENTY-EIGHT

BENITO

Hours later, I sit in my office, perched high above the casino's VIP section. Below, the floor is alive with activity—gamblers huddling around poker tables, while others hover over roulette wheels and blackjack games.

The constant murmur of voices and clinking of chips rises like a chorus, layered with the soft hum of slot machines and the distant sound of laughter. Cocktail waitresses glide between the tables, balancing trays of top-shelf liquor, their smiles calculated to loosen wallets.

From up here, I see everything. And everything is mine.

A smirk pulls at my lips as I lean back in my leather chair, savoring the afterglow of my date with Ginevra. The footage from the cameras I installed at the stage plays on my phone, capturing every twitch of her body, every gasp and moan.

I rewind to the moment she came undone, her body arching off the stage. A wave of satisfaction surges straight to my core, my cock stirring at the memory. My first attempt at eating pussy was a success. All that time spent watching porn, studying every move, every technique, paid off.

My hand drifts toward my belt, ready to indulge in a replay of the pleasure I took in marking her as mine. Next time, I'll make her suck me off while I drown in her juices, time our climaxes so we both come in a simultaneous rush. I make a mental note to buy a set of orange paws to match her ears and tail.

A sharp knock on the door pulls me from my thoughts. My smirk fades, replaced by a scowl. Who the hell would dare interrupt my private time with Ginevra?

Forcing back a surge of annoyance, I pause the video.

"What?" I bark.

The door opens, and Enzo Vitale steps inside, carrying a thick folder. He's one of the more promising boys from Mortis House, with a knack for spotting patterns others miss.

Sitting straighter, I smooth out my features. He wouldn't interrupt unless it was important.

"We've got a problem," he says with a gulp.

I lean forward, all thoughts of Ginevra receding. The boys have spent the entire morning performing audits on the departments. We already analyzed the data our hackers extracted from the casino's financial systems months before the raid. This has to be something new.

"What is it?" I demand.

Vitale drops the folder onto my desk. "Counterfeit chips. It's the biggest financial drain on the casino. They're flooding the floor."

Cold fury explodes in my gut. I rise, pushing the chair back with enough force to make it squeal against the floor. "Show me."

Nodding, Vitale turns on his heel, leading the way out of the office. As we walk, Franco Lorenzo joins us. Lorenzo is another from Mortis House, also majoring in accountancy.

We descend from my office, taking the private elevator that drops us onto the ground floor. The noise and lights hit like a wall, but I push through, my focus honed on the financial drain.

Lorenzo outlines how the counterfeit chips have slipped past our security checks. "They've been mixed in with the legitimate ones, swapped during busy hours when the floor is packed. We traced the flow, and it's been happening for months, maybe years."

The more he talks, the colder my rage burns. Every time a scammer cashes one of those chips, the casino bleeds cash. What I don't understand is how Capello allowed that to happen. Or was the theft his way of rewarding those who defected from Dad?

We exit the staff door and step into the public area, steeped in the clamor of the casino, but I'm only focused on finding the source of this theft.

We pass the main bar, and I spot Carla Romano, a cocktail waitress on my personal payroll. Reaper planted her here years ago to keep an eye on the casino. She's a petite brunette, whose sharp eyes miss nothing, and has a way of blending in that makes her invisible to the untrained eye.

I signal for Carla to follow, leading us to a quieter corner away from prying ears, and more importantly, the cameras.

"What do you know about counterfeit chips?" I ask.

Carla hesitates, her eyes flicking between me and the boys. "The old head of security knew about them. From the way he talked, it was just a few thousand bucks leaving the casino. He said it was under investigation."

I scoff.

Her brows furrow. "That was a lie?"

The boys flanking me both nod.

She rubs her chin. "I didn't realize it was this big. I guess he was hiding his scam in plain sight."

Eyes narrowing, I turn my thoughts to the arrogant fucker I had to subdue. "And the new guy?"

She shifts on her feet, her gaze dropping to the floor. "Malfi? He worked closely with the old boss. He had to know."

I nod. "Back to work."

Carla deflates with relief and scurries away. But this isn't over. Not by a long shot.

Hours later, after gathering more intel, we head out to the home of Albert Malfi, a modest apartment a mile away from the casino. The four of us—Vitale, Lorenzo, and two others from Mortis House—approach the building in a bulletproof vehicle. I still need to take precautions, since Cesare and Roman still haven't resolved that bullshit with the assassins.

The street is quiet, but my mind is a storm. If I don't fix this shit with the chips, I may as well hand the casino back to Roman.

Breaking in is easy. The door barely creaks as Vitale jimmies open the lock. Malfi's apartment is small, cluttered with cheap furniture and the smell of stale cigarettes. We move through the narrow hallway, finding him passed out in bed, his mouth open, his stubbled chin glistening with drool.

With the stuffed animal cradled in his arms, he looks nothing like this morning's cocky bastard.

I press the barrel of my gun against his temple and cock the hammer. At the sound, his eyes snap open, and he sucks in a terrified gasp.

"Boss... I—"

"Quiet."

He clamps his mouth shut, his breath quickening. Sweat beads on his forehead, and his gaze darts around the room like a trapped animal searching for an escape.

"Tell me everything you know about the counterfeit chips," I growl.

Panic flashes across his features as his lips flap, scrambling for a response. "I was just following orders. My old boss was the one running the operation from the inside. I swear, I didn't make a dime of profit!"

"Prove it."

Lorenzo steps forward, snatching Malfi's phone from the bedside table. He thrusts it in front of his face. "Unlock it."

Shivering, Malfi swipes his fingers across the screen. Lorenzo digs through the apps, using his Mortis House training to track any trace of offshore accounts or hidden assets. While he runs through emails, messaging apps, and whatever else he can find, the other boys search the apartment.

Minutes pass, and tension mounts as we wait. I glare at Malfi, daring him to move. He's clever enough to remain silent, yet sweat rolls down his face in rivulets.

Finally, Lorenzo breaks the silence. "All I'm seeing is his personal account. Nine hundred bucks and change. No offshore holdings, no big transfers."

Malfi collapses, his fear morphing into relief. "I would have said something, but I didn't want to be a snitch. That sort of talk can get a man killed."

"Who else was involved?" I demand.

He rattles off a list of names, his gaze locked on mine, too terrified to look away. Vitale makes notes with the occasional question.

When he's finished, I ask, "Anything else?"

The man hesitates, his eyes darting to the stuffed bear beside him before he blurts, "My old boss had a contact at BV Holdings. Maybe he knows something about the chips."

BV Holdings. The name rings through my mind like a warning bell. Salvatore Bellavista's company. If he's involved, this scam is much bigger than I thought.

I motion to Vitale. "Dig into the Bellavista family tree. I want to know if any of their members are employed at the casino."

Nodding, Vitale jots down my command. I spare the stuffed animal a glance before turning to leave the room.

"What about me?" Malfi asks.

I pause, my lips tightening. Contrary to my actions, I'm not a monster. I understand how power works in this world. Going against one's boss might get a person killed. I should have set up one-to-one meetings with every department head. Given them the opportunity to inform me of the corruption within their ranks.

But I'm the last person to trust what anyone says. Two people I loved and trusted the most, Ginevra and Mother, said they loved me one day and were gone the next. Despite this lack of trust, I regret skipping the private sessions. Maybe we could have sifted through the bullshit faster.

"You'll submit to a beating. If you survive, you can keep your job."

He nods, his face streaming with tears. "When?"

I smirk. "At a time of my choosing."

"Thank you, boss." He exhales a shuddering breath. "I swear, I'll be loyal."

Leaving him alive might be a mistake, but the casino is already desperately short-staffed. Its entire management team are now ashes scraped off the corners of my cousins' cremators. Besides, I have more pressing concerns than Albert Malfi.

Salvatore Bellavista is powerful and connected to families across the United States. If he's involved in this counterfeiting ring, it could be the tip of a festering pile of shit.

TWENTY-NINE

GINEVRA

My nipples still ache from yesterday's encounter with Bob Brisket. The muscles in my pussy still spasm with need.

That masked bastard is corrupting my spirit.

I lean against the elevator wall, gripping the handrail so tightly that my knuckles ache. My gaze fixes on the numbers above, watching them ascend toward the thirtieth floor. No matter how much I try to force back those memories, they rise to the surface, bringing with them a festering mix of anger and humiliation.

And an unquenchable desire.

The doors slide open, revealing the office thick with hostility. What was once a second home now feels more like a trap. Pressure builds in my chest, ready to explode. Mom has a point. It's time for me to find another job.

I step out into the reception area, only to hear, "Did you find The Meat Show okay?"

My gaze snaps to Pamela's smug face, and a question slices through my already frayed nerves. Did she know what was waiting for me yesterday?

Heart hammering, I breathe hard, forcing my features to stay neutral. I won't let her see me rattled. But that smirk pulling at her lips heats my blood. Anger and humiliation coil through my gut, ready to snap at the barest provocation. My muscles twitch, wanting to lash out, and my lungs burn with the urge to scream at this duplicitous bitch for sending me into a trap.

But despite that knowing smirk, it's not Pamela who handles client relations. That's the remit of our new office manager.

Holding my tongue, I storm past her, my heels clacking against the marble floor. I can feel her eyes burning into my back as I weave around the cubicles and head toward the corner office.

I should have known something was wrong. It didn't make sense to pull me from a lucrative account like Bellavista only to send me to a strip club. I wouldn't be surprised if he was in cahoots with Bob Brisket.

If Terranova wants revenge so badly, why doesn't he just fire me? Or is he making me suffer in Dad's place? Curling my hands into fists, I tighten my abs, ready to confront the bastard who's been pulling my strings.

As I near the corner office, Julian rises from his seat like a jack in the box. "Ginny?"

My spine stiffens. He's been hovering close ever since that humiliating climax. Don't think I didn't notice that half-assed erection straining through his pants. My jaw clenches. I don't have time to deal with his feelings, and I sure as hell don't want to rehash the incident with the sex toy.

He grabs my arm, but I shrug him off without breaking my stride. "Not now."

"This is important," he whines, trailing after me like a lost dog.

I don't turn around. If this is his attempt to explain that he didn't steal Bellavista, he can save it. Terranova hasn't been in the firm long enough to gauge either of our abilities. We both know our boss handed the work to Julian out of spite.

Two of Terranova's goons step in my path, standing like statues in front of the office door. The sight of their broad shoulders blocking my path is like gasoline on the flames of my fury.

"I need to see Mr. Terranova," I say.

Neither of them budge. They stare down at me, their eyes cold and unblinking.

The muscles in my jaw tighten, and the frustration that's

been welling up in my gut since I reached the Meat Show boils over.

"Are you going to let me in?" I ask.

The larger of the pair smirks as if my situation is a joke.

"That client meeting was a set-up," I snap. "You bastards sent me into a trap!"

The office falls into a dead silence, the open-plan space suddenly feeling too small, too crowded. Every head turns or rises from the cubicles, their eyes on me. Yesterday's humiliation crashes over my ego in a wave, turning my anger into something sharper.

I'm about to cite a dozen sexual harassment statutes when Terranova's voice sounds from behind the door. "Let her in."

The goons exchange smirks, confirming my every suspicion. They probably all laughed about sending me to meet a sexual predator.

Heart pounding, I shove open the door, bracing myself to unleash a storm.

Then my entire world stops.

Terranova stands bent over his desk, his body pressed against a woman's back. Blonde hair spills across the polished wood as he drives into her with hard, relentless thrusts. Nausea churns in my gut, freezing me in place.

Dad's office is no longer the place I knew. It's been defiled, transformed into something grotesque. No wonder the goons were snickering. They knew their boss was having sex.

Not wanting to stick around for Terranova's tryst, I spin on my heel and reach for the door. Sweat breaks out across my fingers, making them slip over the handle. When the door won't budge, I tug harder.

Panic grips my throat as the truth slaps me upside the head. Terranova's goons have either locked the door or are holding it shut. Grunts and gasps and groans fill the small space, each hard thrust making me shudder. The air is thick with the scent of sex, making me sway on my feet.

"Let me out of here," I yell.

The assholes on the other side of the door snicker.

"Nick..." says a female voice, breathy with the sound of pleasure.

"Tell Miss Di Marco about her father," Terranova growls.

The words slice through my consciousness like a blade. My skin prickles, and cold dread tightens in my chest. The mere mention of Dad hangs in the air, ready to detonate. Despite every instinct screaming at me to leave, I force my gaze back to that disgusting scene.

The woman splayed out on the desk like a perverted picnic is Martina. Lust contorts her pretty features but her eyes burn with malice. The moment our gazes meet, my stomach plummets with dread.

Lips trembling, she tries to speak, but the words are caught in her throat. She moans and pants with each of his thrusts, but Terranova won't pause long enough for her to catch a breath.

"If you want to come, you'll tell her." He punctuates every word with another snap of the hips, as though his dick is forcing out the truth.

"I... was having an affair with your dad." The words spill out, jagged and broken. "I was also.... Oh... in bed with him... Ah... when the gunman blew out his brains."

The confession hits like a punch to the gut. I stagger back, my ass hitting the wooden door, my world spinning out of control.

Everything I thought I knew about Martina and Dad shatters into a thousand tiny shards of confusion. My mind reels, flipping through memories like a frantic slideshow. I don't remember them being particularly close.

"Why would you sleep with my dad?" The question tumbles from my lips a breathy whisper.

Martina's eyes flash with malevolence, before she releases a breathless laugh. "Because I was too young to realize he was a predator."

Her words hang in the air, but they can't penetrate the fog of disbelief. This can't be right—it doesn't make sense. My pulse races, hammering in my ears, drowning out a reality too painful to face.

"How?" I rasp.

Terranova picks up his strokes, pounding into Martina hard enough to break her in half.

"My parents... Oh, God," she says with a moan. "They used to send me over to your place." She shivers as he reaches between their bodies. "You were always... Aaah... Fuck!"

I clench my jaw, trying to follow her train of thought.

"You were always...."

I'm about to tune out when Terranova eases off, allowing Martina to say, "You were always out with the Montesanos, leaving me alone with your dad." Her voice drips with resentment, and her eyes glint with feral hatred. "You were too preoccupied with Benito to notice me."

The mention of Benito jolts me out of my shock, and my mind races through old memories for signs I'd overlooked. Martina never mentioned spending time with Dad. Even when he invited her to intern at the firm, I just assumed it was because of our friendship. I spent too much time with my fiancés to notice what was happening.

But Mom did.

She kept insisting that Dad was having an affair with a blonde. I was stupid enough to tell her that he spent all his time with Julian and Martina.

"Is that why you're sleeping with our boss now? What's your excuse this time?" I cringe as I say the words, barely able to look at her reddened face. She pants and moans like a mockery of a porn star.

What the hell am I saying? She's a victim, not a vixen. Dad probably groomed her to submit to his authority.

Her face hardens, her breath hitching as Terranova continues his ruthless pace. "Not everyone... Aaah!"

"What?" I snap.

"Not everyone has a life handed to them by rich daddies." She pauses, her eyes rolling to the back of her head. "Oh, fuck... Rich dads and even richer fiancés," she says through heavy, panting breaths. "Some of us... Oooh... Some. Of. Us. Have. To. work. For a living."

The venom in her words slashes through my last defense,

ripping open fresh wounds. I stare at her, disbelief mingling with hurt. "Why didn't you say something?"

"You stupid bitch," she screeches. "Why didn't you notice?"

Terranova reaches beneath her and does something to cut off her rant with a moan.

"Nick," she says through a gasp. "I'm coming."

"Good girl."

This time, when I try the door, it opens. I rush through the office, my vision blinded with tears. How is every secret rising to the surface? How could I have never noticed Martina's burning resentment?

I run to the elevator, ignoring Julian's cries for me to stop. Only one person can straighten things out, and it's time to speak to Mom.

THIRTY

BENITO

I bring only two boys to the breakfast meeting with Salvatore Bellavista because any more would be a declaration of war. He lives in a mansion within a walled compound, its smaller buildings housing his extended family. It may as well be a fortress.

A butler leads us through a marble hallway and out through patio doors into a lush garden, where Bellavista lounges in a gazebo.

He's grown fat over the years, his gut spilling over his belt. His hair, once thick and dark, is now a thinning silver, slicked to the side to hide a retreating hairline. His face is rounder, with sagging jowls, but his eyes remain predatory and calculating, like a wolf who's learned to enjoy the comforts of an easy life.

Two young women in skimpy maid outfits fawn over him, dropping sugar cubes into his coffee with silver tongs. One of them giggles as he slides his hand down her back and cups her ass with a self-congratulatory chuckle.

Disgust curdles in my gut. Forcing my expression to remain neutral, I step into the gazebo, flanked by Vitale and Lorenzo.

"Benito," Bellavista says, reclining in his seat with a smirk. "Condolences about your father. Such a tragedy. And your mother... Lucia was a fine woman."

My jaw tightens, but I keep my voice steady. "I'm not here to reminisce."

Smirk fading, he gulps down the contents of his cup. "Of course. So, what's the reason for this morning's visit?"

I let the silence hang, watching the maids top up his coffee, adding another two sugar cubes. The way they linger, their fingers brushing against his, makes me want to put a bullet through his head. Bellavista never took sides during our family's downfall, but he didn't hesitate to supply Capello with everything he needed to expand his empire while ours crumbled.

He's like Switzerland during World War Two—ever neutral, loyal only to himself.

"Duplicates of the chips your company makes for us are flooding my casino. How is that possible?" I slide the counterfeit chip across the table toward Bellavista.

His fingers close around it, turning it over, inspecting it like it's a diamond riddled with flaws. "How do you know it's counterfeit?"

Vitale steps forward. "Each chip has an embedded RFID tag with a unique encrypted ID number for authenticity. When a chip is issued by the casino's cashier, the ID is logged in the system. RFID tags allow us to track every movement while they're used for play and when cashed out—"

"I've been in the casino business longer than your parents have been alive," Bellavista snarls with a wave of his hand. Get to the point."

Vitale sniffs. "The counterfeit chips are perfect duplicates, mimicking the originals down to the RFID tags. Someone's been cashing them while the originals are still in play. It's a large-scale operation."

Bellavista's expression darkens. "That's impossible. No one could replicate our chips without access to the molds or the codes."

"Someone did," I snarl. "And it's happening right under your nose."

Bellavista falls silent, turning the chip over again in his hand, as though the answer might reveal itself in the details.

"You have cameras," he mutters. "Shouldn't your security team catch the culprits?"

"If it were that simple, I'd have lined them up at the parking lot and put them out of their misery," I snap. "This isn't a few idiots slipping past security. It's a large-scale operation, with a small army of people coming in and out of the casino. It's only possible because these chips contain your proprietary security measures."

Bellavista clicks his fingers. "Phone!"

One of the maids scurries forward with a handset. The old man snatches it from her grasp, dials a number and mutters something I don't catch. Then a second maid brings a stack of pancakes, topped with thick slices of pineapple and ham then slathers it with syrup.

This silence is a power play. A weaker man would rise off his seat and demand answers. A nervous man would fill the void with threats. I have Reaper and a small militia waiting at the gates, ready to shed blood.

As Bellavista plows through his breakfast, the boys and I refuse the maids' offer of refreshment. Just as the old man drains his coffee cup, a slimmer, younger version of him scuttles in, wiping his hands with a cloth.

His gaze darts to us before he turns to Bellavista and says, "Yes, Dad?"

Bellavista sets down his cup. "Antonio, how did counterfeit chips end up in Casino Montesano?"

The younger man's eyes widen, his brow glistening with a sheen of sweat. "I... I don't know. I swear. What are you talking about?"

I recline in my chair watching the back and forth. It continues until Bellavista slams his fist on the table, upending his half-eaten stack of pancakes.

"You're embarrassing me, boy!"

A maid rushes forward to clear the mess, but the old man shoves her back. She stumbles to the side, only to be caught by a colleague.

Antonio clears his throat. "I sold a few duplicate chips to a woman named Beatrice."

"Beatrice what?" Bellavista spits.

The younger man swallows hard. "I don't know her last name. She approached me a few years ago, saying she needed chips for a private game. I didn't think—"

"You didn't think, this stranger would take the chips to bleed a casino dry?"

My jaw clenches. This is a charade. The only part about it that's unclear is whether Bellavista is working with his son.

Antonio shifts on his feet, avoiding his father's glare. "I can pass on her information... All I did was sell her a few chips. Blame her."

I lean forward, my fingers steepling, and add, "I blame you."

He flinches, but the old man only scowls.

"BV Holdings guarantees these chips." I strike the table with my index finger to emphasize the point. "You will neutralize the counterfeits immediately, refund every cent stolen from this scam, and punish the perpetrators."

Bellavista nods, his features pinching. "Consider it done."

I turn to the son, my gaze hardening. "Starting with the bastard who helped steal from my casino using your name."

Panic dances across Antonio's features, his eyes darting as he opens his mouth to speak.

But before a single syllable can escape his lips, his father extracts a gun from beneath the table.

Alarm punches me in the chest. I hold still, despite the surge of adrenaline. My heart pounds against the bulletproof under-shirt, reminding me that our heads are unprotected.

The boys on either side of me draw their weapons. I, however, remain unmoving. I grew up in a mafia stronghold, where hot-headed bastards flashed their guns at every opportunity. Every-thing is bullshit until someone pulls the trigger.

"Benito," Reaper's voice infiltrates my earpiece. "Give me the go-ahead to launch the grenades."

Ignoring him, I focus on the old man with the gun. The cameras in my glasses are broadcasting Bellavista's movements. Reaper will launch into action if any of us get shot.

"Dad?" Antonio croaks.

"You heard the man." Bellavista aims at his son's chest and fires.

A gunshot echoes through the gazebo, and the younger Bellavista stumbles back, collapsing onto a side table.

My stomach plummets, and my fingers twitch toward my weapon, but I keep them on the table. The boys I brought with me gasp. I grew up with assholes pulling out guns at the dinner table, but nobody who mattered ever got shot.

Screaming, the maids flee into the garden.

Bellavista sets the gun on the table and turns back to me, acting like he didn't just shoot his own flesh and blood over a few million dollars. "Is this to your satisfaction, Benito?"

My brows rise. I sure as fuck didn't ask for this.

"The counterfeit chips will be neutralized by the close of business tonight," he adds.

I incline my head, acting like I see this kind of shit every day. "My team will send a breakdown of our losses. I expect the money in our account within twenty-four hours."

THIRTY-ONE

GINEVRA

I drive through town, gripping the steering wheel tight enough to break through the leather. The city blurs around my periphery into gray buildings, shadowy trees, and people moving like ghosts.

All I can see is Martina beneath Terranova, her betrayal burning a hole through my soul.

Or is it *my* betrayal?

I should have noticed something—anything happening between my father and best friend. Instead, my life was consumed by men. Benito was my everything. I lost myself in his protection, his love, his unwavering devotion. Then Samson was demanding and abusive. There was little left over for Martina.

How I wish I could turn back time.

My navigation app directs me to Bossanova's building, one of the exclusive apartment blocks overlooking the park. As I walk through the marble lobby on autopilot, my mind spins with her parting words.

The elevator chimes, breaking me out of my musings. Its doors slide open, revealing Bossanova's penthouse, which looks like a trip back to 1974.

I glance at the dark wall panels, wondering why on earth

someone would sacrifice the light. Crossing the large living space, I cringe at the shaggy, burnt-orange carpet muffling my steps.

Scattered light dances from a disco ball hanging from the ceiling, casting tiny reflections across the dark walls. I shake my head, my lip curling at how this place mirrors its owner's faded decadence and his desperate attempts to cling to his youth.

"Mom?" I call out.

"Balcony."

Pushing aside my unease, I move through a bank of leather couches, and pass a perspex coffee table cluttered with old magazines and crystal ashtrays.

Beyond a set of floor-to-ceiling windows, I spot Mom reclining on a chaise with a martini glass. For reasons I can't fathom, she's wearing a white bikini.

I step out onto the balcony, my gaze dropping to what's in her drink. From the bottle resting within a bucket filled with ice, I'm guessing it's champagne.

She turns to me, her eyes glassy. "Ginny, darling, What's wrong?"

My lips purse. Mom said she wasn't an alcoholic. Was that another lie, because she's playing the part like a seasoned actress.

I suck in a deep breath, pushing past the accusation clawing at my throat. "Did you know?"

Mom's brow furrows. "Know what?"

"That Dad was having an affair with Martina."

She stares at me for several heartbeats, as if trying to piece together what I've said. Then, her expression shifts and confusion gives way to fury. Hand trembling, she sets the glass down on a low table.

"What did you say?" she whispers.

"Martina was sleeping with Dad. I found out today."

Color drains from her face. She jerks her head away, staring out at the park as if she can find the answers among the trees. "I knew he was having an affair," she murmurs, the words weighted with resignation. "But Martina... I didn't know it was her."

I wait for Mom to elaborate. Wait for her to bring up any encounters she might have noticed while I was away visiting

Benito. Martina said Dad groomed her during the times I wasn't home. Where the hell was Mom?

"Aren't you shocked?"

She shakes her head. "Not particularly."

My blood simmers. "How can you be so calm about this?"

Mom finally turns to face me, her eyes softening. It's rare to see her lucid. Even rarer for her to show emotion. I straighten, bracing myself for what she might say next.

"Ginny, you forget that he targeted my cousin. Jennifer was sixteen when they first met. I doubt she was his first underage girl, or the last."

Her words hit me like a punch to the gut. It's easy to forget that the woman who raised me isn't my birth mother. I tear my gaze away, staring at my feet, unable to withstand the intensity of her eyes.

"Everything in my life has been a lie," I mutter.

Mom reaches out and grabs my hand. "My love for you has always been true."

I meet her gaze again, allowing myself to sink into the comfort of her touch. Mom is one of the few people in the world who doesn't resent me. Years ago, I would have included Benito. Now, there's no mistaking his contempt.

"How can you just accept it?" I ask.

Sighing, she pulls me down to her chaise. "When you've been hurt so much, you learn to bury it deep."

We sit together in silence, leaning on each other for support. I stare out across the balcony at the treetops swaying in the breeze. So much has changed since Dad's murder, only I can't tell if it's for the worse.

We're broke, but that's no better than living off stolen money. Instead of a violent fiancé, I have Bob Brisket, and Martina has finally shown her true face. At least she's no longer holding back her seething resentment.

I could also say the same for Benito.

She releases my hand to pick up her glass. "Have you found another job yet?"

I cock my head, trying to process the abrupt change in

subject. Of all the things going wrong in our lives, she's worried about my career? "I have bigger concerns."

Mom sets down the glass, her gaze sharpening to study my face. "What do you mean?"

My brows rise. Has she already forgotten the loan sharks? We both know I lied about my engagement. They'll return the moment they realize the truth. But talking about them will only bring up her suicidal plan to marry Bossanova.

"I have a stalker."

She downs her glass, her brow furrowing. "Who?"

"He calls himself Bob Brisket," I mutter.

"Has he hurt you?"

The question lands like a punch to the gut, knocking out lungfuls of air. I picture the day I opened up about the forced engagement. How Mom looked sober on the sofa, looking sober, only for her eyes to droop.

Where was this concern when I complained to her about Samson or tried to show her my bruises? Memories flood back, hot and sharp, of times she was too drunk for my complaints to register. I learned to hide my pain because having it brushed off hurt worse than any type of abuse.

Was that another act? Her way of evading confrontation? Old resentments rise to the surface, propelling me off the chaise.

Needing space to breathe, I place a hand over my chest. "Nobody ever hurt me worse than Samson."

Mom flinches, her features flickering with guilt. She turns her gaze away from mine and stares down at her manicured fingers. "I'm sorry, Ginny. I thought I was protecting us by letting you handle it on your own."

My lips part with a gasp. "What the hell does that mean?"

"Celebrating without me?"

Bossanova steps out onto the balcony, dressed in a burgundy smoking jacket and a silk cravat. He saunters toward the ice bucket and picks up the bottle.

"Celebrating what?" I pull away from them, my hackles rising.

Chuckling, he refreshes Mom's glass. "We've got all the paperwork in place to set a date."

My stomach heaves, bringing up a wave of nausea that hits the back of my throat. I reel on my feet, my vision flickering with a wedding, a murder, a life-insurance payout, and the electric chair. My gaze swings to Mom, who beams up at Bossanova like he's skinny Santa.

Panic claws at the edges of my mind, and my heart pounds faster than a drumroll. I need to stop this wedding, end this madness before one of these two get killed.

Mom sips her glass with a demure smile and flutters her lashes at the old leathery bastard who grins back with teeth sharper than any crocodile's.

He raises the bottle in a mock toast, his gaze never leaving mine. "To new beginnings. And to prosperity."

Mom clinks her glass against his bottle, oblivious that she's out of her depth. Bossanova is an efficient killing machine, and Mom is too drunk to see the sword of Damocles hanging over her head.

It's time for me to do something to save her from herself.

Maybe I can get help from Bob Brisket?

THIRTY-TWO

BENITO

The moment I step through the front doors of our house, the weight of the day hits me with a kick to the balls.

My deadly encounter with Bellavista fades, as does the clamor of the casino. Back home, I'm the prince in the tower, the spare who takes second place to Roman. I shake off that treacherous thought. He's handed me an empire I intend to restore to greatness.

I stride through the marble hallway, passing staff who offer polite nods. Roman called a family dinner tonight, and I'm obligated to bring a date. I would have brought Reaper, but my brothers would jump to the wrong conclusions. Cesare already calls me a eunuch.

Before I can even shrug off my jacket and mount the stairs, Gil appears from the dining room and steps in my path. Since Roman left prison, Gil has become his right hand and seems more focused on the family business than either of our brothers.

"We've got a problem," he mutters.

I resist the urge to pinch the bridge of my nose. "What is it now?"

"Allegra Visconti was found stabbed to death in her car."

The name doesn't ring any kind of bell. I stare at Gil, waiting for him to elaborate.

"Cesare's ex who ran the karaoke bar," he adds.

I flinch, my stomach plummeting. Roman mentioned that another of Cesare's women was murdered last week, but a second? I bite back a curse, forcing down a wave of alarm. "Where was he when it happened?"

Gil leans close enough for me to smell his cologne. "That's the problem." He lowers his voice. "Nobody knows. I would confront him, but that's something best left to a brother."

Right. Because Cesare has a temper. Some poor bastard struck his little assassin, and Cesare shot him in front of the men. It took Gil and Sofia forming a human shield to stop him from tearing through the ranks. Bullshit like that is what leads to families getting stabbed in the back.

"What about Roman?" I ask.

Gil shrugs. "He confronted Cesare the last time."

The implication is clear: it's my turn to deal with our potential serial killer. Before I can work out the best way to accuse him of murdering another ex, a shrill voice cuts through the hallway.

"Giiil!"

I turn to see a large-breasted blonde teetering out of the dining room, clinging to the doorframe like it's the only thing keeping her upright. Her eyes land on Gil, who shoots me a sheepish grin.

"Is that your date?" I ask with a smirk.

Gil chuckles. "Where's yours?"

Gilberto is sounding too much like Cesare. That little bastard is always the first to taunt me about never getting laid. If he knew my sexual experience until recently consisted of internet clips and my hand, he'd never shut the hell up.

I walk past him, heading for the kitchen, nearly colliding with Sofia. I place a hand on our housekeeper's shoulder, holding her steady.

"You're my date for tonight," I say before continuing down the hall.

After getting changed, I step into the dining room, pull out my phone, and check on the surveillance app. Ginevra lies in bed, beautifully naked. Her auburn hair fans across the pillow, forming a halo of sin. She would look like a work of art if you ignore what she's doing with her hands.

Her fingers slide down her belly, gliding between her folds in a way that makes my blood heat. I slip in an earpiece, listening to the sounds of her pleasure. Every soft moan, every gasp is like gasoline on a fire.

I send her a message: *Did you get my gift?*

Seconds later, her reply comes through: *Fuck off.*

Smirking, I text back: *Continue like that and I'll fuck your ass tonight with no lube.*

An exasperated sigh fills my ear. She opens the box beside her bed and pulls out the toys I sent, along with a maid's costume. My breath quickens as she hesitates, her fingers hovering over the black fabric.

Put it on.

She stares at the screen, her lips tight. I message her again, making her rise off the bed and slip into the costume. Her movements are jerky, almost reluctant, but I'm transfixed by the way the outfit clings to her curves, the way the silk accentuates every contour. Heat floods my cock, and I shift on my seat.

"Benito." Roman's voice cuts through my evening's entertainment. "Where's Cesare?"

I shrug, barely registering the question, too focused on Ginevra fastening the last button. She's waiting, her posture unsure, her fingers shivering with anticipation.

Get on the bed. Kneel.

Gil answers Roman's question and poses another about the empty seat on my left. Ginevra positions herself for me on the bed, her head bowed, that glorious hair falling around her shoulders.

I text again: *Spank yourself five times. Count them.*

She hesitates for several heartbeats, and I wonder if she'll say no. But then she bends over and delivers the first slap.

"One," she whispers through my earpiece, her voice breathy.

My cock stirs. She continues, her voice breaking with every slap. The sound of each spank sends heat through my veins. I take a bite of my bruschetta, immersing myself in the beauty of her obedience, the way she submits.

When she reaches the fifth, her skin flushes, her breath becomes ragged, and her nipples stand out like bullets. I shift on my seat, stifling a groan. My dirty little Ginny wants more.

Choose a toy.

She hesitates, her fingers hovering over the open box. That sweet reluctance makes the game all the more satisfying.

I send another message: *Start with the largest one.*

With trembling fingers, Ginevra selects a dildo the size of my cock. She runs her fingers over its veiny shaft and waits for my next command.

Just as I'm about to tap an order, my phone buzzes with another message, only this time it's not from Ginevra. Gil sends a text from the other side of the table, reminding me to confront Cesare about Allegra.

I'll do it in my own time.

By now, Ginevra is glancing around the room, perhaps searching for hidden cameras. Or does she miss me?

I message her with: *Stick it in your cunt.*

She lies back on the bed and obeys, sliding the silicone into that wet little pussy. Her back arches, and her hips rock as she takes the toy deeper, her thighs trembling with every push. As my cock presses against my zipper, my gaze darts between Gil and Roman. They're both too preoccupied with the family dinner to notice.

I send another message to Ginevra: *Deeper.*

Her breath comes in ragged gasps as she obeys, pushing the toy deeper, her body tensing with every inch. The sight of her splayed out for me is beyond intoxicating. My grip tightens around the phone as she squirms against the mounting pleasure and struggles to maintain control. I breathe harder, waiting for the moment she shatters.

Insert the butt plug, I text, my breath hitching with anticipation.

She reaches into the box and extracts another toy, this one attached to a fluffy, stripy orange tail. Annoyance flickers across her pretty features, but I revel in the sight of her discomfort.

Do it, I command.

Ginevra takes a bottle of lube from the box, her hands trembling as she coats the plug with the slick substance.

Squeezing her eyes shut, she pushes the toy into her ass with a soft whimper that makes my heart skip.

Her submission sends a thrill down my spine that settles in my balls. The power I hold over her, the way she bends to my will —it's everything this treacherous beauty deserves.

At some point, a clink and rattle of metal becomes too distracting to ignore. I glance up from my important business to find Cesare leading in his little assassin, only he's dressed her in lingerie, heels high enough to break both ankles, and a leather skirt that looks sprayed onto her skin. My gaze drops down to the source of the sound: each ankle is connected by chains.

He isn't just playing with fire, but with flaming swords. The woman's eyes are sharp enough to slice my brother's throat. My lip curls. Is this how he wastes valuable stock from his fetish store?

After a pointless back and forth with my brother, I make a mental note to obtain a few similar items for Ginevra.

By now, she's inserted the plug, along with a pair of matching ears. Without prompting, she slips on some furry gloves, and lies on the bed, waiting for my next order.

I stifle a groan.

The only thing distracting from this perfect moment is that she's debasing herself for a masked stranger and not for me.

Dismissing Cesare's antics with a grunt, I focus on Ginevra's struggles with the toy.

Lick it clean, I order, wondering how far she'll go.

Seconds later, Roman smashes his fist on the table, making my head snap up. Since everyone, including Cesare's little assassin, are glaring at Gil's date, I turn my attention back to the phone.

The dining room is a blur, the sounds of clinking silverware and murmured conversations fading into the background. All that matters is the scene playing out on my phone, the way Ginevra debases herself for the camera.

Her body trembles as she fights against the pleasure, but there's no denying the intensity of her arousal. She loves my attention. Loves these filthy orders.

Ginevra's breath hitches, her body arching off the bed as she teeters on the edge of release. I tighten my grip on the phone, my own pulse quickening in response.

Don't come until I tell you, I text, knowing it'll push her even further. The thrill of control, the power I hold over my Ginny— it's a rush like no other.

But just as she's about to break, someone calls my name.

When I glance up, Roman and Capello's daughter are gone. So is Sofia. As is the noisy blonde. All that's left are Cesare, his assassin, and an annoyed-looking Gil.

It's time to ask my little brother if he's a serial killer.

THIRTY-THREE

GINEVRA

Was I a good girl for Brisket?

After tonight's performance, I'm sure he'll visit, wanting more.

I lie on the bed, staring at the ceiling, every nerve on edge as I wait for his arrival. The cat ear headband digs into my scalp, but I ignore the discomfort.

My mind is so scrambled, I can almost feel the tail swishing between my legs, but the soft paws rest on my thighs, making me feel ridiculous. And vulnerable.

But this is what he enjoys, and tonight, I need him to like me. I need to transform him from my stalker to my willing devotee. It happened once with Benito. I'm sure I can do it again with Brisket.

My bedside lamp casts long shadows across the walls. Maybe it's the subsidence, but I swear the house creaks in the breeze.

I close my eyes, forcing my breath to slow, but my thoughts refuse to settle. How will Brisket react to my proposal? He's dangerous, unpredictable—one wrong word, and everything could spiral out of control.

My fingers curl within these furry paws. What I'm about to do next is for Mom. Brisket is the only man who can take care of Bossanova.

Doubt gnaws at the edges of my mind. Last time we met, I told him about my engagement to Benito, but that didn't stop him from taking what he wanted. My rectum clenches around the plug. How can I gain control of a man who makes me so weak?

Uncertainty tightens in my chest, each second stretching longer than the last. I push away my doubts and focus on the goal. Figure out a way to lure him to my side. Then convince him to protect Mom.

An hour later, a faint noise pulls me from my thoughts. I freeze, straining my ears. The sound is coming from the closet— someone is trying to enter through the window.

My heart pounds in double time to the grating of metal against wood. I breathe fast, waiting for the sound of approaching footsteps. The sounds grow more insistent before making an abrupt stop.

That's when I remember I superglued every window in the house shut.

Panic tightens around my chest. What if he leaves? Hurling myself off the bed, I rush to the closet. Breath quickening, I pass through racks of hanging clothes. There's no one at the window.

With trembling paws, I fumble at the lock, trying to wedge it open. The glue is set like stone.

"Come on," I mutter, shoving with all my strength.

The stubborn window refuses to give. The thought of Brisket giving up makes me sway with a wave of despair. I jerk harder at the handle, but the window remains sealed shut.

"Fuck," I hiss.

Why does everything I touch seem to turn to shit?

With a sigh, I let go and step back. The band around my chest tightens as I turn and head back to the bedroom, my heart sinking with every step.

But when I reach the door, Brisket is already entering my room.

His imposing frame, clad in the usual dark tactical gear, fills the room with an ominous presence. The visor reflects the dim light, making him look like a faceless specter.

Relief and terror crash through my insides, making me grip

the wall. Relief that he hasn't left. Terror at the realization that he found a way to defeat the superglued windows.

My pulse quickens, a frantic rhythm that overtakes my conflicting thoughts. This is what I wanted, isn't it? To have him here, eager to do my bidding. But now that he's looming in my bedroom like a punisher, I can barely keep myself upright.

I try to suck in a breath, but it hitches in my chest. The room tilts on its axis and shrinks, and the air thickens with his presence.

"How did you get in?" I rasp.

Without answering, he slinks through the dark with the grace of an apex predator. My heart skips several beats, and every instinct screams at me to run. I can't tear my eyes away as he reaches an arm toward the bed. When he pulls back the pillow, revealing the knife I'd hidden there earlier, I swallow back a scream.

"Is that for me, little Ginny?" His dark voice sends a shiver down my spine.

My mouth opens and closes, but my lips form no answer.

His question hangs in the air like a noose. My heart pounds so hard I can feel it trying to burst out of my throat. He thinks I planned to kill him. And part of me wanted him dead, but that was before.

"Answer my question," he growls, making me flinch.

My mind races. The thought of losing him terrifies me more than the knife.

"No, I swear, it was a mistake," I blurt, my voice trembling. The words spill out faster than I can control my thoughts. "It was for knife play... In case you forgot yours. Don't you think it's pretty? I'm sorry, Mr. Brisket. Can we start again?"

I close the distance between us, my steps driven by raw desperation. This isn't just about Mom. I've grown fond of his attentiveness. Even the silly gifts. No man has ever combined sexiness with such raw devotion.

Memories of our encounters flash through my mind, focusing on our time at the strip club. He forced me into submission, made me enjoy things I didn't know were possible. The darkest parts of me enjoy his visits. Craves the power he holds over me, just as much as the dangerous thrills.

I force down my thoughts, trying to focus on the immediate threat: Brisket standing over me, still clutching the knife.

"The truth is that I've grown to look forward to your visits," I add, my voice a breathy whisper. "You're the most exciting thing that's ever happened in my life."

He doesn't move, doesn't speak, doesn't even flinch. The visor hides his face, leaving me wondering how he's reacting. I can't tell if he believes me, if he's amused or enraged, and the uncertainty is suffocating.

"Punish me, Bob. But please... don't leave."

I drop to my knees in front of him, clutching at his legs.

"Can we start again?" I ask. "I mean, have a real relationship? I need you so much."

I stare at the cold, reflective surface of his visor, meeting a mirror of my own desperation.

The silence between us stretches, thick and suffocating. Then Brisket steps back, pulling away from my grasp. I freeze, my breath catching, trying to understand what's happening. His shoulders tense, and his broad chest heaves.

My throat tightens. Is this anger or excitement?

"You need me?" His voice simmers with rage.

Flinching, I shuffle back, but he follows, looming over me like a specter. There's a dangerous energy to him now, a dark fury that seeps into the room, making the air so thick I can barely breathe.

His breath hisses between clenched teeth, the only sound breaking the heavy silence. He lifts the knife, the blade catching the light as he steps closer.

My stomach plummets to the floorboards. I've crossed a line, and now I'm at his mercy.

Brisket waves the knife in my face.

"Get on the bed," he growls. "I'm going to slice you into sashimi."

THIRTY-FOUR

BENITO

I've faced down enemies, survived betrayals, navigated the treacherous waters of family loyalty. But nothing feels as convoluted as this spate of murders.

Allegra Reggio's death shouldn't matter to me, but it reeks of Cesare.

The photo Gil sent sears into my memory—her lifeless body lying in the back seat, covered in blood and puncture wounds. And that goddamn knife left in her was unmistakable. I've seen Cesare brandish it countless times.

I close my eyes, trying to force my mind into clarity, but the images keep returning. My gut churns to think of how she suffered, but more disturbing is the gnawing suspicion that my brother is responsible.

Cesare claims the Galliano family murdered his ex, which makes no sense. They stole our meth lab, and Tommy Galliano stole our mother, but why would they kill Allegra? Why now? And how the hell would they have gotten their hands on Cesare's knife?

My fists clench at my sides, frustration and doubt swirling together into a potent mix of anger. Cesare's story doesn't add up, not with the way he's been spiraling out of control. He's always been reckless, but this is different. It feels deliberate, like he's testing the limits of our loyalty, seeing how far he can push before something snaps.

I can't turn a blind eye.

Not this time.

Allegra is the second of Cesare's ex-girlfriends to die since the night Galliano met with Roman, but I can't see why he would frame my youngest brother.

Every clue points to Cesare being the killer. He had the motive, the opportunity, and no alibi. But why the hell would he murder innocent women when he can play with three female assassins in the basement?

The questions gnaw at my conscience, the uncertainty biting deep. But it's not just Cesare weighing on my mind tonight.

Ginevra kneels before me in her skimpy costume, cosplaying a catgirl maid, ready to submit to Brisket, rather than to me.

Seeing her like this, her defiance replaced with a willingness to play along with Brisket's twisted games, ignites a fury in my chest that burns bright.

She's supposed to resist, to fight, to be so desperate and broken that she has no choice but to run to me for help. Instead, she's kneeling, ready to submit, and it feels like everything I've been working toward is falling down the toilet.

I want her needing Benito—not Brisket—to be her savior. Instead, she's turning to my disrespectful alter ego for help.

With a snarl, I grab her by the throat. Anger surges through my veins, overpowering the frustration that's been building all day. I lift her off her knees, walk her backward, and shove her down onto the bed.

She lands with a creak. I follow her down, pressing my weight against her body, pinning her to the mattress.

Eyes widening, she wriggles beneath me but doesn't fight back. Her flushed, parted lips, and the lust shining in her eyes only fuels my anger.

She's supposed to resist. To fight. To run to her brave Benito and beg for protection.

Frustration from Cesare's murders and from my failure to herd this stubborn woman blends into impotent rage.

"You think I want you groveling like this?" I hiss.

Her breath hitches, but she doesn't answer. I tighten my fingers around her throat, making her eyes flicker with panic.

Good. Let her feel a fraction of my exasperation.

"Why the sudden change?" I growl. "Why are you so eager to submit?"

Her lips part, but she makes no sound. I loosen my grip just enough for her to breathe.

"I want you," she whispers, her voice trembling.

A fresh wave of fury crashes through my chest, knocking my heart from its resting place. She wants Brisket, not me? I can't tell if she's fucking around or truly broken.

I run the knife over her throat, letting the cold metal leave a trail of goosebumps on her unmarked skin. The little temptress shivers but doesn't resist.

"You like cruelty, don't you?" I hiss, bringing the blade up to her face. "The degradation?"

Squeezing her eyes shut, she nods.

No matter how much I hate this woman, I couldn't mark her skin.

I need to push her further, to see if this desire to submit is real or an attempt at manipulation. I reach for the bottle of lube on the bedside table, and flip its lid with a click.

Her eyes snap open, her features flickering with panic. Through panting breaths, she asks, "What are you doing?"

Ignoring her, I squeeze a large quantity of lube onto my gloved fingers. "My little kitten has too much fur."

When she tries to squirm away, I pin her with my forearm and smear the liquid over her pubic hair. She trembles beneath my touch, her breath coming in short, panicked gasps.

"Please..." she whispers, but I cut her off with a low growl.

"Please what, little Ginny? Use your words."

She shivers, her body tensing under my hold. I bring the knife to her pussy and glide the blade at the base of her pubic hair, watching it fall away to reveal smooth skin. I shave away the last shreds of her dignity, wondering if this is what will break her spirit. Shuddering, she forces her body still.

Silence stretches out, broken by the rasp of her breathing and the scrape of my makeshift razor. Her fear, her humiliation, and her reluctant surrender stir my darker instincts.

This is almost what I wanted—to see her stripped bare, exposed.

But at Benito's mercy and in my fucking casino.

I continue shaving that sweet pussy until all that's left is a tiny strip. Then I place the flat of the blade over her clit and growl, "What do you want from me?"

She breathes hard, her body freezing. Her legs tremble the harder I press the metal to her swollen bud.

"Talk unless you want to bleed," I order, my patience wearing thin.

She whispers, "I need you to kill a man for me."

My jaw drops. Cold betrayal twists in my gut, but I force it down, keeping my grip on the knife. The Ginevra I loved was gentle and sweet until she plunged a dagger into my heart.

"Who do you want me to kill?" I ask, keeping my voice even.

She hesitates, her breath quickening. "Not until you agree."

I flash a bitter smile. She dares to bargain with me now? Drawing back, I kick her legs open, holding them in place with my knees. I flip the knife, pressing the hilt at her soaking entrance.

Her body tenses once more, and she gasps. "Torture me all you want, but I won't talk."

I push the hilt into her pussy, watching the way she writhes beneath my control, the mixture of pleasure and shame contorting her face. Ginevra is a dirty girl, but I'm prepared to go lower.

"You want me to murder Mr. Montesano?"

"No," she says through clenched teeth.

My chest loosens at not being the target of her animosity. I move the hilt in and out, the slick sound of it filling the room as she bucks against my grip, her body betraying her resolve. Her breath hitches, her moans growing louder, more desperate.

"Then tell me who."

Her eyes flutter closed, her body arching off the bed as she tries to resist the inevitable. But she's lost in the sensation, in this twisted pleasure.

"Say the name," I roar. "Who do you want dead?"

Sweat drips down my forehead, soaking into the collar of my armor. My breathing labors, and my chest tightens with the effort of holding back. I need Ginevra so badly it hurts, but I need her submission even more.

"Say it."

Her body jerks as she reaches the breaking point, and with a final burst of desperation, she screams, "You, you fucking asshole. Bob Brisket!"

THIRTY-FIVE

GINEVRA

I'm aching the next morning. It's a dull throb that sharpens every time I shift in the driver's seat. Morning light streams through the windshield, making me squint, but the glare pierces my eyes. I grind my teeth, trying to keep my focus on the road. But Brisket's touch lingers like a stain I can't scrub clean.

What the hell is his obsession? The question twists in my mind like a knife. I thought I could play him, use his fixation to my advantage. Instead, I'm left with an aching pussy to remind me I'm still caught in his web.

The streets are a blur. No one else is awake yet, the city still sleeping off the night. But I can't rest. Not while Mom is in peril. She called early this morning to announce they've set a date for Friday and are buying a dress.

Over my dead body.

I speed through a yellow light, too lost in thought to care. Mom's waiting for me to help pick her outfit, and Bossanova is probably already sizing her up for a coffin. I can't let her go through with this ridiculous scheme.

After pulling into a spot outside the Dolce Vita Boutique, I kill the engine and step out. It's time to shake some sense into Mom.

The boutique reeks of money—soft lighting, plush carpets,

and racks of dresses that scream excess. I push through the door, and the bell overhead chimes, turning everyone's heads. Mom sits up from where she's perched on a velvet settee, with Bossanova breathing down her neck.

She's already tipsy. That leathery bastard is feeding her champagne, no doubt to make her pliable. Today, he's dressed in a navy blue captain's jacket, complete with a gold emblem on its chest. His gaze is flat, disinterested, but there's a flicker of something in his eyes when he sees me—a glint of calculation.

I cross the boutique, waving off the owner's offer of champagne.

Bossanova leaps to his feet, his crocodile smile fading into something sour. "What are you doing here?"

"Mom invited me," I say through clenched teeth.

He glances over at Mom, meeting her glassy smile. "I thought we were going to fuck in the fitting rooms," he says, his words tight. "That's going to be awkward with Ginny listening on the other side of the wall."

My jaw drops.

Mom giggles, the high-pitched sound ridiculous and fake. "Stop making me blush."

"Ladies, have fun," he says, his voice slippery as slime. He strides past me, leaving a cloud of expensive cologne.

I glare at his back, wanting to fill him with bullets, especially as he pauses at the door, and turns back to spare Mom a mournful glance. "What a pity, baby. I would have taken you all day long."

My stomach churns. I curl my lip, holding back a wave of disgust. The man is half-vulture, half-leech, all decrepit predator.

He gives her one last smile, all teeth and no warmth, before slipping out the door. As soon as he's gone, Mom reaches for another glass, but I move faster, intercepting it before it touches her lips.

"Mom, we need to talk." I pluck the flute from her fingers.

The sales assistants hover nearby, eager to push more alcohol — anything to keep the cash flowing. But this isn't a conversation we can have in front of an audience. I need her sober, and I need her to listen.

I sit next to her and lean in close. "You need to push back this wedding."

Mom's hands curl into fists. "That's impossible. We've already set a date and paid for the venue in full."

"You're walking into a death sentence," I whisper. "If he doesn't kill you, they'll fry you for taking him out."

Her gaze meets mine, losing all traces of drunkenness. "It's him or us."

My throat tightens, and I swallow hard. "There has to be another way. Give me time to find it. Please."

She shakes her head. "Those sharks came knocking at Valentino's penthouse. Marrying him is the only way to keep you safe."

I grab her hand, my insides crawling with desperation. "But you're going to die."

She pulls me close and whispers, "Better me than you."

The words slice through me like a bullet. I rear back, my mind reeling with a pulse of shock. It settles so deep in my gut that I suck in a shuddering breath. Before I can recover, the door swings open, activating a bell.

Benito steps in, dressed in a black suit and a shirt that skims the lines of his muscular physique.

The sight steals the breath I just managed to catch. He's with that same stunning brunette who had him wrapped around her finger at the restaurant. She's flawless, elegant, dressed in red. The kind of woman who wouldn't let anyone, least of all her father, break off an engagement.

And she clings to him like they've just spent the night making love.

Our eyes meet, and something inside me tightens. Benito's expression is unreadable, his eyes sliding past me like I'm insignificant.

The dismissal is a knife to my gut.

I snatch away my gaze. Seeing them so happy together makes me convinced Benito's proposal was a twisted game. Why would he want me when he has her?

Out of the corner of my eye, I spot the proprietor rushing up to them with a broad smile. Benito used to be a regular here—this was where he purchased me gifts.

I shut down that thought. He has someone else now. He's happy. The only thing he wants from me is petty revenge.

While I'm processing Benito's indifference, Mom seizes a champagne flute from a passing tray and sways toward him.

"Benito, darling," she calls out, her voice carrying across the boutique. "Thank you for arranging the doctor after the shooting."

My heart lurches. Shooting?

I push past an associate holding a tray, catching up with her just as Benito's eyes flicker with mild acknowledgment. His focus shifts immediately back to his new woman, who watches us with cool detachment.

"What shooting?" I ask, trying to keep the tremor out of my voice.

Mom waves a hand. "Oh, it was just a little thing at Roman's party. Some gunshots, a bit of chaos, and I got trampled in the mess. But Benito had me stay over at this house. Even got the family doctor to check me over."

My stomach plummets through the floor. I knew Bossanova took Mom to the Montesano mansion, knew they spent the night there, but this is a whole level of negligence. I search Benito's face for any hint of a reaction, but his eyes slide right past us, landing on the woman holding up a set of red lingerie.

"What do you think, baby?" she purrs. "Should I try this on?"

The tension in my chest tightens, sharp as a wire. I manage to force out the words, "Thank you for helping my mom."

Without looking in my direction, he inclines his head, as if I'm beneath his notice. The woman beside him flashes a dazzling smile, enjoying every second of my discomfort.

Benito leans into her, murmurs something low before leading her toward the fitting rooms. She glances back at me, her eyes gleaming with smug satisfaction, before disappearing behind the door.

Nausea twists in my gut.

They're going to fuck. Fill the boutique with the sounds of their pleasure.

Whatever love he had for me is gone. The Benito I knew was a gentleman, one who would never sink so low as to flaunt another woman to carve open my heart. But I guess that man no longer exists.

Mom places a hand on my shoulder. "Ginny?"

"Can we go somewhere else?" I ask, trying to hold back a well of tears. "I'm not sure how much more of this I can take."

THIRTY-SIX

BENITO

Hours after that farce with my cousin in the Dolce Vita changing room, I'm parked outside the Di Marco Group's building. My eyes are glued to the footage of Nick Terranova's office.

I'm surprised Elania even agreed to the charade after that bullshit she pulled at the crematorium. Aria refused on the grounds that she wasn't 'wearing no fucking wig to fuck with a relationship that could be fixed with a conversation,' while her less pleasant twin jumped at the chance to cause mayhem. I needed to remind Ginevra she had an option better than Brisket, yet she failed to fall onto her knees.

Ginevra sits across the desk from Nick, her shoulders tense, her expression wavering between exhaustion and suspicion. She's about to regret ever answering his call on a Saturday.

I made sure Nick knew exactly what to say to twist the knife. Since she tried to drag Brisket into solving her problems, it's time to escalate. The feed flickers as Nick leans back, his lips curling into a smug grin.

He's about to drop a pile of shit on her pretty little head, and I'm here for the fallout.

I lean forward, the anticipation a dark thrill. This is where the pressure builds, where she starts to realize there's no one willing to help her but me.

Onscreen, Nick steeples his fingers. "There's a tape of you at the Meat Show, with Mr. Brisket."

Gasping, Ginevra tightens her grip on the chair. I smirk. The footage only exists in the privacy of my phone. No one gets to see Ginevra but me. However, I want her to believe Brisket would expose her to the world.

"I didn't make a tape," she rasps.

"The recording says otherwise. You were supposed to help Mr. Brisket with his legal issue, not fuck him."

She stiffens, her eyes wide with shock. I breathe hard, savoring her discomfort, loving how those pretty lips tremble. In ten minutes, she'll be crawling to me, begging on her knees where she belongs.

Nick leans forward, his smile chilling. "Care to watch it? See for yourself?"

When she doesn't answer, he clicks a remote. The sounds of our conversation at the Meat Show filters through the speakers. She recoils, her gaze snapping to the screen behind him. Fear flickers across her face, and I savor my victory.

It's just the opening moments of the recording before things get exciting. In a minute, the screen will go dead, but she's not to know.

"Turn it off!" she cries.

Nick pauses the replay and stares at her across the table, letting the silence stretch. She squirms in her seat, her pretty features twisting with anguish. I tilt my head, wondering what's going through her mind.

Will she continue turning to Brisket for help or finally realize he's a villain bent on her destruction? Just as it looks like she's about to make up an excuse, Nick finally speaks.

"These antics go against our firm's code of conduct and the ethics of an attorney. You could lose your license."

She whimpers.

I lean in closer, relishing her reaction. She's teetering on the edge, and the threat of losing everything she's worked for is exactly the push she needs.

Nick launches into a lecture about her shitty performance and how her presence is a distraction to her colleagues. It's all true. Nick, the receptionist, and Martina Mancini have kept alive rumors about what Joseph Di Marco might have done with the firm's missing millions.

Di Marco ran the organization to the ground, since the majority of his work centered on non-paying clients. He protected Frederic Capello's illegal operations from the law, never sending out a single invoice.

Pro bono work for a demanding client and his cohorts is the quickest way to go broke. Bellavista also never paid a dime in legal fees for the five years Di Marco took control. The firm also defended relatives of the old man, such as Gianni and Valentino Bossanova, for free.

With all this shit uncovered, everyone in the organization can't help but ask if Ginevra knew about her father's fraudulent dealings.

She didn't. According to Martina, Joseph kept her far from his schemes. She wasn't even allowed to work with the firm's gangster clients.

But Martina knows Di Marco's dirty secrets. She thinks fucking her new boss will make her immune from the fallout. Nick only keeps her around because he wants to know if Di Marco has any hidden accounts.

"What about you?" Ginevra snaps, her voice pulling me out of my musings. "Screwing Martina over a desk doesn't exactly scream ethics."

"Your father had me struck off, remember? Don't deflect the conversation away from how you fucked a client."

Her breath hitches, and I can almost see the anger giving way to desperation.

"It wasn't my fault," she says, her voice cracking.

Nick leans in, his expression darkening. "Are you accusing Mr. Brisket of sexual assault?"

She freezes, her eyes widening, her mouth opening and closing but making no sound.

Nick doesn't give her a moment to recover. "No? Then what do you have to say for yourself?"

The room falls back into silence.

"Give me something," Nick growls. "Your performance is

shit. You're distracting my staff, and you're bringing the firm to further disrepute. You're a dead weight—just like your father."

When her face crumples, my nostrils flare.

Nick didn't need to go so hard.

"Miss Di Marco," he says over her sobs. "I have no other option but to let you go. Leave the building. You're no longer an employee of this firm. One of my interns will pack your things and deliver them to your home."

She's crumbling, her armor falling away. This is the downfall I engineered, but the part of me that still loves Ginevra wants to rush out and protect her from the world.

The meltdown lasts less than a minute before she forces her features into a mask of composure. Without a word, she rises from her seat and walks to the door. I lean back in my seat, torn between guilt and satisfaction. This never would have escalated if she hadn't refused my proposal.

I'm a bastard, but still determined to make her mine.

As she walks out of the office, I make a quick call to the loan sharks. "Be outside the Di Marco house in thirty minutes. Offer her twenty-four hours to find the money or she will be trafficked. If she invokes my name, tell her you checked, and she isn't engaged."

"Sure thing, Mr. Montesano," says the foreman.

Ending the call, I glance at the firm's double doors, wondering when she'll exit, when my phone rings. Nick's number flashes on the screen, and I answer.

"It's done," Nick says. "But something's off. Martina was supposed to take her out of the office to talk, but Miss Di Marco shoved her against the wall."

"Shit," I hiss, my plans to coincide with her shattering.

"Yeah. Last I saw of her, she was followed into the elevator by a male colleague."

"Who?"

"Julian Riva. He's harmless—a bit of a leech, but nothing more."

"What does that mean?" I snarl.

Nick hesitates, and I can practically hear him choosing his words. "The little asshole has a crush on Miss Di Marco."

My jaw tightens. I have no doubt that this Julian Riva character will take this opportunity to swoop in and make a move on my Ginevra.

"Send the interns after them," I snap, hanging up before Nick can respond.

My gaze returns to the window, where there's no sign of Ginevra or Julian exiting the building. I grind my teeth.

Julian Riva wasn't part of any plan.

THIRTY-SEVEN

GINEVRA

Tears blur my vision as I stumble through the office, each step a struggle to keep from breaking into pieces. Everyone working the weekend rises from the seats, their eyes boring into my back.

I reach the elevator, pressing the call button over and over, needing to get out. Mom was right. I should have left with my dignity when I discovered the truth. Nothing good could have come from staying in a firm Dad stole from the Terranova family.

The doors open, and I step inside, squirming at the sight of my tear-streaked face. I've become so pathetic, it hurts. Before I can press the button to go down, the doors slide open again, and Julian steps in.

Stomach plummeting, I reach for the control panel but he presses the button for the penthouse. Annoyance surges, burning through the haze of despair.

"What are you doing?" I say as the elevator ascends.

"I've been trying to talk to you for days," he says. "This might be my last chance."

Before I can lunge for the control panel, the doors slide open, revealing the penthouse. The familiar scent of old leather and aged whiskey hits me with a hit of nostalgia. I stare at Dad's desk, which backs onto a floor-to-ceiling view of the city.

Julian grabs my arm and yanks me out of the elevator. I try to pull free, but his grip tightens, leaving me no choice but to follow.

The doors close behind us, and the elevator descends, along with the lurch in my stomach, leaving me trapped with no way out.

"Let go!" I shout, the drop in my gut twisting into panic.

He releases my arm and turns to face me with an earnestness in his gaze that makes my skin crawl. "Your dad was funneling money out of the firm."

My jaw drops. "He was?"

He nods. "He squirreled away Fifty, maybe a hundred million."

I stare up at him, not knowing what the hell to think. As if reading my mind, Julian adds, "Sometimes when we worked late up here, I saw the transactions."

"But how?" I ask, my voice breathy with shock.

"Everyone thought he was helping the mafia for free, but he was getting paid off the books."

His words seep into my mind, stealing my breath. It makes a twisted sort of sense, considering there wasn't enough cash for the firm to cover payroll. But those amounts are ridiculous.

"Are you sure about this? How did no one else see those transactions?"

"Your dad never let anyone come up here but me and Martina." He flicks his head toward Dad's desk. "And let's just say they left me alone a few times to give me the chance to snoop."

Unease twists in my gut. Dad brought Martina up here for sex? The mental image threatens to derail my thoughts, but I shove it aside. There are bigger problems now, with our lives hanging in the balance. The missing millions could pay off the loan sharks, move Mom out of Victoria Gardens, and keep her away from lowlifes.

"Does Terranova know?" I ask.

He shakes his head. "I wanted to run it by you first."

"Why didn't you say something sooner?"

Julian's gaze hardens. "Every day, I tried to get your attention, but you were too stuck up to even notice."

The bitterness in his words stings because they're true. I

treated Julian like he was the biggest nuisance since the mosquito. Still, a part of me wonders why he went to such lengths to tell me in person when he could have written a note. What does he stand to gain now by telling me this?

Folding my arms, I look him full in the face. "Maybe I was. But this money could help us all. So, what can you tell me about these accounts?"

He cocks his head, studying me with narrowed eyes. The tension between us thickens, making me shift on my feet. There's a reason why I avoid Julian. The way he looks at me is disconcerting. It's the kind of desperate longing that makes my skin itch, as if he's waiting for me to finally recognize we were always meant to be together.

"Don't think I'm going to hand it over for free," he finally says, his voice a low growl.

My stomach dips at the implication. The hopeful part of me assumes he wants a cut of the money. Maybe a twenty-five percent finder's fee that I'll have to negotiate down to ten. But the way his breath quickens, while those gray eyes devour mine, makes my flesh want to crawl off my bones.

"What do you want?" I ask, forcing my voice to stay even.

He pauses, his gaze sharpening.

"A relationship."

The room feels smaller, the air thicker, making my skin break out in a cold sweat. I step back, my breath shallowing, my head shaking from side to side.

"Is this blackmail?" I whisper.

Julian advances, his gaze darkening. "You know, I used to see you as flawless. Thought you were untouchable, my dream girl."

He looms over me, his shoulders broadening, like a polar bear about to strike. My pulse accelerates, and every fine hair on the back of my neck stands on end.

"But after what you did with that client in a filthy strip club, you can get on your knees and earn that information."

The words slam into my chest, freezing me on the spot. I recall every reason I kept Julian at arm's length. The way he always pushed my boundaries with his words or his presence, the way his eyes always found me across the office. I never bought into that nice-guy act, and I was right to trust my instincts.

Heart pounding, I force my legs to move, turn on my heel and stride back to the elevator. I jab the button, but nothing happens. No light, no flicker. Just silence.

His low, mocking chuckle sends a shiver down my spine. "It won't come."

My shoulders rise to my ears. "What do you mean?"

"I've overridden the lock," he says, sounding gleeful. "You're not leaving until I'm satisfied."

The horror of the situation tightens around my neck like a noose. I don't turn around. I couldn't stand to look at his smug face. "How did you—this was my dad's apartment. You can't—"

"Do you know how many times your dad and I worked late here?" he taunts, drawing closer. "How many times Martina was under the table, sucking him off while we talked business?"

My stomach churns at the image, my throat thickening with bile. I don't want to believe what I'm hearing, but after Martina's confession, I can't dismiss it as a lie.

"You want proof?" he asks.

"Of course not," I snap. "Why the hell would I want to see something like that?"

"Not about your dad and Martina. The accounts."

When his voice drifts to the other side of the penthouse, I finally turn around. Julian walks over to the desk and pulls open a drawer. He extracts a file and waves it like a flag. "Do you want it?"

My breath catches. I want to snatch the papers, to end this nightmare, but I'm powerless against a man his size. Every instinct screams at me to keep pressing that damned button, to somehow override the lock, even though I know it's futile.

"What do you want?" My voice trembles.

He grins. "Get on your knees and crawl for it."

Disgust churns in my stomach. There's no way I'm debasing myself again. It will only backfire like it did with Brisket.

"Do you even have the information?" I snap.

"It's right here."

"Then why didn't you take it to Terranova?"

His eyes narrow. "I told you why."

"Let me guess? You tried to claim the money for yourself, but you hit a dead end because you're not my dad's heir?"

He stiffens, his nostrils flaring, but he doesn't reply. Because I've struck a nerve. He needs me to extract that money. Instead of telling me about it and demanding a finder's fee, he wants to make me submit.

Because a cowed and humiliated Ginevra is more likely to share that ill-gotten wealth than one who's stuck up.

"Release the lock on the elevator, then we'll go to a coffee shop and talk."

I have no intention of discussing anything with this asshole. Not when I finally have some leverage with the loan sharks. They can retrieve Dad's stolen money and squabble over the rest with Terranova. All I care about is getting the hell out.

Julian walks around the desk with the files tucked under his arm. I don't believe for a minute that they contain anything of substance. Anyone with a lick of sense wouldn't keep that kind of information where Martina or Nick Terranova have their little trysts.

I step aside as he closes the distance between us, but he drops the files to the floor. Heart lurching, I stagger back, but he yanks me into his arms.

"Why do you only love violent lowlives like Benito Montesano and Samson Capello?" he asks, his breath hot against my ear. "Why not me? Am I too good for you? Too blond? Too clean-cut?"

His large hands close around my head in a vice-like grip, holding me in place. Panic punches me in the chest, making my body stiffen. Then he crushes his lips to mine, the kiss rough and forceful. Gagging, I struggle against his grip, but he's too strong.

My heart pounds, pumping blood to my extremities. If I don't get out of this, I'm screwed. I reach down between our bodies, take hold of the erection straining through his pants, and twist.

"Bitch!" he howls and stumbles to the side, only to backhand me across the face.

Stars explode in my eyes, the blow bringing with it the sharp taste of blood. I stumble, trying to recover, but he crashes into my side.

I topple to the carpeted floor, his weight on my back crushing all the air from my lungs. He grabs at the edge of my skirt, his erection digging into my back.

"Is this what you want, Ginny?" he sneers.

"Get off me," I scream and elbow him in the gut.

Julian's body goes rigid, and he hisses through his teeth. My breath quickens. Did I break a rib? He falls to the side, revealing a masked figure looming over us, holding a curved knife. Blood drips from its tip, answering a hundred unasked questions.

It's Bob Brisket.

But is he here to kill us both?

THIRTY-EIGHT

BENITO

The helmet traps the heat, turning each breath into a slow burn, but it only sharpens my senses. I dismiss the sweat gathering beneath the padding, focusing on the bastard sprawled on the floor. He's gasping, with a dark pool of blood spreading beneath his carcass and inching toward Ginevra.

She's crouched a few feet away, her eyes locked onto the scene. Horror twists her features, her breath coming in short, uneven bursts.

I drop to my knees beside him, gripping the knife. Julian's gaze locks onto mine, frozen in a rictus of terror. After slicing through his shirt, I press the blade against his abdomen, savoring the way he shudders, the way those eyes widen with dread.

The same eyes that dared to lust after my Ginevra.

"Thought you could have her?" I say through the voice changer.

Blood bubbles between his lips. "Who are you?"

"The man whose property you touched." I drag the knife across his belly, feeling the resistance as it slices through skin and muscle. Blood spurts, warm and thick, soaking my gloves before falling in rivulets down his sides.

The asshole beneath me convulses, his breath coming in

ragged gasps. This is just a fraction of the torment he inflicted on my Ginevra.

Leaning closer, I bring my helmet to his ear, reveling in the way he chokes on his own panic. "You thought you could touch what's mine?"

I jab the blade into his side, twisting it deep, making his body jerk with a pained sob. Each stab I deliver is a punishment for every twisted thought he had about my property. He's paying for that pathetic attempt at blackmail, his hands on her precious body, his sick obsession.

Crouching just feet away, Ginevra lets out a strangled cry, but she doesn't move, seeming frozen in horror. I continue slashing, filling the room with the satisfying sound of tearing flesh and the wet gurgle of Julian's desperate attempts to breathe.

The blood spreads, reaching her feet, staining the hem of her skirt. Her terror is a living thing, feeding my need to make this bastard suffer.

This isn't just about punishing him— it's about sending a message. No one touches her. No one scares her but me.

Not wanting her to view Brisket as a hero, I slice into his abdomen, and the skin parts like wet paper. Then I plunge my hand into the wound, curling my fingers around his intestines. He convulses with a garbled scream as I yank out a length of his guts, letting them spill across the floor. But it's not enough. I dig deeper, encountering the barrier of muscle, and slice through it with the blade. I work my fingers into his chest cavity, until I feel the slowing beats of his heart. With a sharp yank, I tear it free.

Screaming, she scrambles backward and slips in the blood. Then she rounds the corner, filling the air with the sound of retching.

Good. She should be afraid. She should be disgusted.

As the scents of blood and bile seep through my helmet, Ginevra's footsteps disappear further into the apartment. She's going the wrong way if she wants to escape.

Julian's twitching slows, his breath turning into a wet rattle. I yank my blade free and wipe off the blood on his ruined shirt. The light flickers out of his eyes, leaving behind a broken carcass.

Rising, I step over his body, my attention shifting to where she disappeared. As I round the corner, I find her doubled over, stumbling into the bathroom. In a few rapid steps, I wedge the door open before it shuts.

"Get away from me," she screams.

I shove into the marble-tiled room, pleased at how she skitters backward. She presses herself against the wall, her eyes wild, searching for an escape that doesn't exist. Her breath hitches in uneven gasps, her body locked in a rigid stance, as if caught between fight and flight.

"This is what you wanted. I murdered that man for you." Raising a hand, I offer her his still-twitching heart.

Horror flashes in her eyes, and I wonder if she blames herself for the man's death. She shakes her head, trying to form words, but they catch in her throat.

"B-Bob," she whispers. "I didn't... I wouldn't. You don't understand."

I grab her wrist and shove the organ into her palm. "I have paid your price with his blood. Now, you're mine."

She flinches, letting the heart drop to her feet.

I reach for the bottom of my helmet, pretending to unfasten it. Eyes widening, she grabs my hands.

"Stop!" she cries.

The corner of my lips lifts into a smile. She no longer sees Brisket as a savior.

My hand falls away, and I step back.

Her screams weaken to breathless sobs, leaving only revulsion and fear. With a sudden burst of panic, she tries to dart past me toward the bathroom door. I pull her into my chest.

"Where's the appreciation, little Ginny?" I growl into her ear.

She wriggles in my grasp. "Let go of me... Please."

"Are you an ungrateful little cunt? Or are you ashamed to admit your pussy is wet? I killed at your command, and I will do it again. Say the word, and I'll deliver you another heart."

She stiffens.

"Now, get on your knees and thank me."

Ginevra hesitates, her features flickering with realization. The man she once thought would save her is bent on tearing away the last shred of her dignity. She opens her mouth but fails to produce words. What can she say when her nighttime hero has turned into a monster?

"What's wrong, little Ginny? Have you forgotten how to play?"

She falls to her knees and bows her head, as if submitting might shield her from more cruelty. I thread my bloody fingers through her hair and yank her head back so I can look her full in the face. Tears stream down her cheeks, her pretty features contorted with agony.

She clamps her mouth shut as if holding back a scream, but I tighten my grip on her hair until she hisses. "Please... Stop."

I release her with a shove hard enough to make her sprawl across the floor. "Next time I see you..." I pause, letting her anticipate the threat. "I'm taking that pussy."

She crumples into herself, hugging her knees in a tight ball of sobs.

Satisfaction thrums through my insides, and I nod. My message is clear. She's seen what Brisket can do, and the terror in her eyes confirms that this masked man is no longer her savior. Now that I've shattered that illusion, she'll have no choice but to come to me.

Without a word, I step over her, out of the bathroom, and down the hallway leading to where I left Riva's corpse. I exit through the roof garden and head toward the service elevator.

My work is done. If this isn't enough to have her running into my arms, then the loan sharks I've stationed outside her house will do the job.

Soon, Ginevra will be mine.

THIRTY-NINE

GINEVRA

This is a nightmare.

A hell of my own making.

The marble floor feels cold against my flesh, but it's nothing compared to the chill seeping through my bones. Brisket's touch crawls under my skin, making my muscles tighten, as though trying to shake off the memory of ever enjoying anything about him. I clutch my knees to my chest, squeezing my eyes shut as if that will erase the memory of him forcing that organ into my hands.

I never want to see that black-hearted bastard again.

The silence in the bathroom is suffocating. I edge toward the door, straining to listen for any signs he might be lurking outside. But all I hear is the rapid thud of my heart. It pounds through my eardrums, barely drowning out his final words.

Time loses meaning. Minutes or hours, I can't tell—every second drags out, my limbs frozen in place while his words echo in my mind. I'm still trembling, still fucked up from being the cause of a man's brutal death. Common sense reminds me that I can't stay here forever. What if Terranova unlocks the elevator and finds a corpse? I'll be suspect number one.

With a shuddering breath, I uncurl my muscles, pull the door open a crack, and peer down the corridor. It's empty, save for a few bloody footprints.

Each step down the hallway feels like dragging myself through mud. My legs grow heavy, and my lungs tighten, struggling to pull in air. I round the corner, finding Julian's lifeless body sprawled by the elevators. The sight of his intestines spilling into a pool of congealed blood makes me heave.

I force myself to walk around the corpse, careful not to look too closely, not to let the horror seep into my bones. Hell will turn to a holiday camp before I grieve a man who tried to assault me in my own Dad's penthouse.

My gaze lands on the dossier he tossed aside. I reach down and pick it up with trembling fingers, only to find the papers all blank. I huff a bitter laugh. The offshore accounts, the promise of hidden money—it was all bullshit he made up to steal my attention.

I turn back to his corpse, this time looking directly into the face frozen with terror. "Idiot," I hiss, my voice thick with disgust. "You would still be alive if you'd taken a fucking hint. Not even a hundred million dollars would make me give you the time of day. Go straight to hell."

Tossing the papers aside, I crouch beside Julian's corpse and search his pockets. My fingers close around a small key. "What kind of man traps a woman who doesn't want him?"

I unlock the elevator and step inside, my mind racing with a single, urgent thought: escape. The ride down feels endless, the walls closing in with the weight of Brisket's parting words.

He thinks the man I wanted dead was Julian. With this murder, he thinks he's bought my soul. What if he turns that deadly violence toward me? Or Mom?

The second the doors open, I rush out through the building and to my car, and check the back seat before starting the engine.

My drive home is tense, every shadow on the road twisting into the shape of Brisket and the way he tore through another human's insides like a butcher. His words continue to resound in my mind, a constant reminder that he thinks I'm his property.

Gripping the wheel, I force myself to stay alert. To plan how I'll protect my hide.

But I can't do this alone. As much as my dignity protests at the thought, I might need Benito. The bitterness of his rejection claws at my chest, and my pride screams at me to leave him alone. He could help, but would he even care? He was so cold and dismissive at the boutique, having moved onto the type of woman who wouldn't stab him in the back.

But does that matter if Brisket comes after me tonight?

I pull into my driveway, still debating whether to call Benito, when headlights flood my rearview mirror. It's a truck pulling in from behind.

Men pour out of its doors, circling my car like predators. My stomach twists into painful knots. I already know who they are—the loan sharks.

The leader, the same bastard from before, strides toward the driver's side door with a broad grin. Breath catching, I tighten my fingers into fists.

My body tenses, my mind races for a way out, but I'm trapped.

His eyes rake over the car, like he's already decided I'm his. Negotiation isn't on the table.

I keep my eyes forward, not wanting to meet his gaze. He taps on the glass, daring me to face him.

"Guess what, sweetheart? Turns out Benito Montesano isn't engaged, so you're not under his protection."

A chill runs down my spine. I hoped to have resolved the situation with the loan sharks before they returned.

"Open up. We need to have a little chat."

My heart slams against its cage. I force myself to breathe, but my chest tightens with rising panic. The doors are locked. They can say whatever the hell they want then leave.

When I don't answer his attempts to get my attention, the leader draws back his fist and slams it into the window, shattering my hopes of survival. Flinching, I scoot to the other side, but another man is already in place, smashing his fist into the front passenger window.

Shit.

Shit.

Shit!

Fractures spread across the glass. These bastards aren't playing around. I glance from side to side, the beginnings of a heart attack twisting every muscle in my chest.

Before I can grab the phone and call 911, the leader punches through the cracked window, sending cubes of glass flying across my lap. His hand snakes in and yanks the door open.

The next thing I know, he's grabbing my arm and dragging me out of the car.

A cold breeze swirls around my damp skin, its bite seeping through to my bones. Eyes fixed on his leering face, I pull my body into the car's frame as if trying to vanish into the metal.

He looms over me, flanked by at least a dozen goons whose bulks form a wall. My nostrils fill with the mingled scents of spirits and sweat and semen, making my stomach lurch.

"Twenty-four hours, princess." He slams my back against the side of the car, the force tearing my blouse.

Pain explodes across my spine, making me wince.

He draws forward, his breath reeking, hot against my face, the stench of cigarettes and cheap cologne making me gag. "That's all the time you've got to come up with the cash."

My pulse hammers in my throat. "I don't have it. You know I don't—"

His hand shoots out, aiming for my throat. I twist away, but my foot slips on the gravel, sending me crashing to the ground. The sudden motion rips my skirt, exposing my thighs.

Laughter cuts through the night, sharp and cruel. My limbs lock on the floor, frozen in place, every nerve numb with shock.

"Look at her squirm!" one of them shouts, his voice thick with mirth.

The others snicker.

Their leader crouches down, his eyes boring into mine. "Fail to produce the cash and we'll take you as payment. Right here, in this fucking driveway. And I'll be the first to break you in."

As he thrusts his hips, I snatch my gaze away from his rancid crotch, only to find the others making the same movement. The men close in, jeering and taunting, filling my ears with their crude laughter.

One of them yells out, "Don't forget the MILF!"

Bile burns the back of my throat, but I choke it down. They won't just take me—they'll come for Mom too. I can't let that happen. I can't let her get dragged into this hell.

I force down the terror, the revulsion, the shame. All my options have dwindled to nothing, and my back is up against a proverbial wall. It's time to swallow my pride and throw myself at Benito's feet.

FORTY

BENITO

Ginevra should have come straight to me.

I lean forward in my seat, my eyes fixed on the screen. Her driveway fills the display, but I can barely see her through the crowd of sharks.

They have permission to speak to her, but with minimal touching. Because her body is mine. I control every inch of her skin, every breath she takes. But one question still burns through my mind.

How far will I have to go to force her to seek my help? The Brisket persona should have been repulsive enough to send her running into my arms, yet she's returned home.

By now, my sharks will have communicated the extent of the threat hanging over her pretty head.

If she continues dismissing me as an option, I'll be forced to stage an auction, hire frightened-looking girls and leering predators. An organ trafficker will win the girl before her, making Ginevra cry out for a savior.

I'll arrange for the vilest looking man to bid on her body, shouting out obscenities that will make her heart lurch. Then at the last minute, I'll step in, outbid the bastard, and make her collapse with relief.

What an ordeal.

All for a woman I should have shot in the head.

Her death might have freed me from this addiction—my cock's relentless need for only one woman in the entire world. Ginevra Di Marco bewitched me from the moment we met. Now, no other individual in the world, real or imagined, will satisfy my needs. My body only wants her.

A knock on the door pulls me out of my thoughts. I don't turn around. The casino floor can go to hell for all I care right now. Whoever's out in the hallway knocks again and again until I roar at them to enter.

Albert Malfi lumbers inside, out of breath, knowing better than to interrupt.

My teeth grind, and I tear my gaze from the screen just long enough to shoot a glare at my security chief. "This had better be important."

"There's a guy trying to cash in counterfeit chips worth a hundred grand. Eighth one tonight."

"Handle it," I snap. "Search through their devices. Get names, addresses, specifics."

He hesitates, his bulky form hovering in the corner like a bad smell. "We think it's a syndicate."

I exhale lungfuls of frustration through clenched teeth. "Of course, it is. Get out there and get those details. Don't interrupt me unless you find their leader."

The door clicks shut behind him. I turn back to the footage, my focus snapping to Ginevra. The pressure in my chest builds, hardening into a knot. What the fuck will happen next?

Onscreen, the men back off, their figures retreating toward the truck. Ginevra remains sitting on her ass, trembling and too paralyzed to act.

I give her a count of ten to move, but she doesn't. I drum my fingers against the desk to the beat of my frustration. She should be up by now, getting in the car, driving straight to my casino.

I exhale through clenched teeth, my patience fraying with each second. She's testing the limits of my patience. If this doesn't push her into my arms, will I need to stage that fucking auction?

"Come on, Ginevra. Get up."

She doesn't budge. The truck's tail lights flicker as they vanish into the night, leaving her alone in the driveway. It takes every effort not to rise off my seat, drive down to Victoria Gardens, and take control.

Her hesitation grates on my nerves, sharpening my anger to a razor point. If this isn't enough to light a fire under her delectable ass, I'll have to switch tactics.

My fingers twitch toward the phone. Bossanova could marry her mother tonight if I give the order. I could arrange the whole thing within hours—a quick, casino ceremony with a courier sending her a polaroid attached to a slice of wedding cake.

Then she'll come running, begging for my protection. And I won't even need to stage the auction.

At last, she stirs. My eyes narrow as she rises, moving like she's dragging herself out of a nightmare. She walks to the car, and for a moment, I think she's finally going to drive straight to me. But then she stops, opens the door, and grabs her purse.

Frustration surges, my fingers clenching around the table. She's still stalling, still refusing to do what I expect. That car should be on its way here, not sitting idle in that driveway. She's wasting time, and my patience is wearing thin.

A second knock, harder this time, drags my attention from the screen.

"What?" I yell.

The door opens, and the security chief stands in the doorway, his face set in a grim line. "We've caught another one trying to cash in counterfeit chips. It's a woman who says she got them from Bellavista."

I leap to my feet, unable to ignore the opportunity to meet the ringleader.

"Fine." I snap and follow him out, my thoughts remaining with Ginevra.

She has the next three hours to reach the casino or I'll take action.

———

As we step into the elevator, Malfi's voice cuts through my

thoughts. "Bellavista must be more involved in the counterfeit chips than you thought."

I bristle, barely suppressing a snarl. "Is this your way of telling me Bellavista is making me run around in circles?"

He flinches. "No, sir. I just—"

"You let your predecessor flood the casino with counterfeit chips and didn't gather a shred of intel?"

The elevator doors slide shut with a metallic thud, leaving Malfi shuffling on his feet. He stares at the floor, muttering something about needing to keep his job. He will, until one of my Mortis House boys grows into the role. I make a mental note to ask Reaper if any of them would be interested.

"Any leads on his crew?" I ask.

"Not yet. We haven't yet interrogated the last woman we detained for trying to cash the chips."

The doors open, letting in flashing lights, clinking chips, jumbled conversation and laughter. Normally, the casino is invigorating. Tonight, it barely registers.

We weave through the crowd toward the back offices, and it takes every effort to keep my thoughts away from Ginevra. Whatever she decides to do tonight, I'll counter with a contingency plan. It's only a matter of time before she becomes mine.

Malfi leads me into the interrogation room where a pale, jittery woman awaits. A black curtain of hair hides her features, but she's dressed in a low-cut cocktail gown that showcases her assets.

Not bothering with pleasantries, I slam my fist on the table, making her startle.

Her head snaps up, and she stares at me through wide eyes smudged with mascara.

"Start talking." I snarl.

She stammers, her words tumbling over each other in a desperate scramble. I catch snippets—promises of easy money, threats from unseen figures—but my thoughts keep drifting back to Ginevra. That wretched woman won't even allow me to focus on the casino's biggest financial drain.

"Names. Locations," I snap, cutting through her babble.

She flinches, swallowing hard before spilling more details. As Malfi scribbles notes, it takes every effort to remain focussed.

I glare down at the woman, unimpressed. "Who sold you the chips?"

Her throat bobs. "He said he'd kill me—"

"Which is better than what I'll do to you if you don't talk." I flick my head to Malfi. "Did you scan her phone?"

"Of course."

"Send out a team to drag in her family. I want parents, siblings, lovers, kids—"

"Wait," she shrieks. "It was Victor. Victor Bellavista."

My brows rise. "Which one is he?"

"Salvatore's brother? He said it would be okay, since the chief of security uses the same chips."

I whirl around to glare at Malfi, who raises his palms. "She isn't talking about me!"

"What else?" I ask the woman.

"That's everything," she rasps, her eyes shiny with unshed tears.

I nod to Malfi. "Turn her over to Lorenzo. He'll verify her story."

Malfi crosses the room to grip her arm, and I walk out into the hallway. Once the door closes, I allow myself a moment to breathe, rolling my shoulders to ease the tension.

Salvatore Bellavista's younger brother?

Since the man he shot was his son, then either Salvatore is trying to protect Victor, or Victor is an impostor. That would make sense, considering Salvatore went to great measures to reimburse the casino's losses. He wouldn't allow the scammer to continue targeting my establishment, but then the only person capable of creating those chips has to be connected to BV Holdings.

Only further interrogation will uncover the truth.

I should be back in my office, watching the feed from Ginevra's driveway. I should be drinking whiskey, enjoying the sight of my future wife battling through her options.

Instead, I have a conspiracy to uncover. That will mean

talking to every asshole we capture tonight who even touches one
of those counterfeit chips.

FORTY-ONE

GINEVRA

I pull up at the casino. Its neon lights illuminate the street, casting an unforgiving glow on my reflection. Panic claws at my insides. My hair's a mess, my makeup's smudged, and my clothes are smeared with fuck knows what.

God, I look like I've crawled out of hell.

The thought of Benito seeing me like this makes my intestines twist into painful knots, but there's no time to fix my appearance. No point. Not when my insides are shredded. Not when every vein courses with hopelessness. Not when sharks are circling me like I'm filling the water with blood.

I drag myself out of the car and force each trembling step toward the entrance.

Inside, the noise hits me like a tsunami—clinking chips, murmured voices, bursts of laughter. It's all too loud, too bright. I want to curl up and die. Instead, I push through the unease because I need Benito more than I need to breathe.

The air here is thick with the scent of expensive cologne and desperation, and not just mine. It's the kind that clings to the gamblers hunched over slot machines, hoping for a miracle. I weave through a crowd of sharp suits and glittering gowns to reach the reception desk.

The woman behind it looks up from her computer, her cold

gaze sweeping over the suspicious stains on my clothes. Her lips curl into a sneer but she doesn't voice her contempt.

"I need to see Mr. Montesano," I rasp.

She arches a brow. "Do you have an appointment?"

"No, but—"

"Call in the morning," she snaps, dismissing me to turn her attention to a man on my left.

Humiliation burns under my skin like firecrackers, and desperation claws at my throat. The sensation tightens with each second I'm kept away from Benito.

But I can't back down. I can't wait. After all the shit I've escaped, this woman doesn't get to brush me off. As the crowd closes in around my personal space, the words burst from my chest. "I'm Benito Montesano's fiancée!"

Heads turn, eyes narrow. Whispers rise like a hiss.

The receptionist's smile falters, and her fingers freeze above the keyboard. She sweeps her gaze down my disheveled form, her lips tightening with disbelief.

"Excuse me?" she says.

"You heard me." I raise my chin. "Now, get my fiancé."

The reception falls into a hush, and eyes bore into my skin like blunt daggers. My stomach twists, and every instinct screams to crawl into a ball, but I straighten my spine.

The woman picks up the phone, her gaze never leaving mine, and whispers something into the receiver. Seconds drag until a security guard appears at my side. He grips my arm like I've been caught counting cards.

Hope flickers in my chest as we thread through the casino, passing the glittering lights and glamorous patrons. The further we go, the dimmer the atmosphere, the more the plush carpets give way to cold tile.

My pulse quickens, unease gnawing at the edges of my mind. I stare at the man's profile. "Where are you taking me?"

"Waiting room," he mutters, not meeting my eyes.

We reach an unmarked door at the end of a narrow hallway. He opens it and shoves me inside. I stumble forward, catching myself on the edge of a metal table. Then the door slams shut, sealing my fate.

Turning, I take in my surroundings—bare walls, no windows, a single chair, and a table bolted to the floor. This isn't a waiting room. It's a cell.

I rush back to the door and pound my fist against the cold metal. "Let me out! I need to see Benito!"

Silence answers. No footsteps, no voices—just the suffocating quiet and the thunder of my pulse.

I slump into the chair, my mind reeling. It's all too much—Mom marrying a murderer, the cold detachment Benito showed me at the boutique, getting fired, Julian's grabbing hands, Brisket ripping him into bloody shreds. My stomach churns at the memory of his lifeless eyes, his blood pooling across the floor.

Then there's those fucking sharks.

Tears burn behind my eyelids, threatening to blur my vision. I'm in the worst trouble of my life, utterly alone, and it's entirely my fault. I walked away from Benito to avoid pain, but all I found was trauma.

Chest tightening, the fear, the regret, the horror of today bubbles from the pit of my stomach until I can no longer hold back. Wet trails streak down my face, but I don't bother to wipe them away. For the first time in years, I let myself break.

My chest heaves with sobs I can't control. I've lost everything —my job, my dignity, and now, my last shred of hope. The pain is too much, the regret too sharp.

Benito used to make me French toast and strawberries every morning before class. He'd carry my books, take my notes, and draw lavender-scented baths every night. I can't believe I allowed Dad to tear us apart.

Now, I'd give my soul to be his again. To be safe in the warmth of his love.

My sobs turn into wails, and I collapse to the table, wishing I could disappear. Every breath hurts, every thought is a knife twisting in my gut.

This is what I deserve for betraying him.

As if summoned by my guilt, the door creaks open. Benito stands in the doorway, looking like a Roman god. I scramble to my knees, every instinct driving me to beg for forgiveness.

But my words come as sobbing gibberish. I can't form a

coherent sentence, but I tell him about everything that's happened since someone murdered Dad in his bed. The words spill out in a mad rush. How I met Bob Brisket, his late night visits, Valentino Bossanova's plan to murder Mom for the insurance money.

Between wracking sobs, I confess my stupid plan to manipulate Brisket into murdering Bossanova. And how it backfired. I tell him about the sharks who will return tomorrow to collect me as payment for their debt.

Throughout this, Benito remains quiet. I don't know if he's processing my words or is too horrified to speak.

All I can do is look up at him, hoping for a flicker of something in those dead eyes.

But there's nothing.

"Benito," I wail, my fingers tightening around the fabric of his tailored pants. "Say something."

The man I once knew would demand to know who dared hurt his Ginevra and swear bloody vengeance. He would gather me into his arms, pull me onto his lap and rock me until I slept. Instead, he gazes down at me with a face carved from stone, unreadable and unmoved.

My heart shatters all over again, and I cry, "Didn't you hear me?"

There's still no response—no anger, no pity, no disgust—just cold.

The last thread of my strength snaps. This is it. He's going to cast me out, leave me to the sharks. I can't let that happen. I can't let them drag Mom into this mess.

I cling to his muscular thigh, rest my head against his hip, and gibber out a string of pleas. Eventually, he places a hand on my head, pulling me out of my spiral.

"You know my terms." His words slice through my haze, cold and sharp as ice.

I blink up at him, the words barely sinking through my skull. "What?"

"This isn't the kind of mess I can clear up in a night. The cost of rescuing you and your mother will be steep."

"Please, Benito..." I exhale a shuddering breath. "I'll do anything. Just save us. Please."

His eyes narrow, and for a moment, I'm sure I see emotion flicker in them, but it's gone before I can grasp it. With a nod, he pulls his gaze toward the door.

"An assistant will bring a dress. He will escort you to the casino chapel for an immediate ceremony."

Dread coils in my gut. I swallow, trying to digest his words. Marrying a man I've wronged is like begging for punishment, but I nod, the motion jerky, robotic. It's not like I have any other choice.

My life in exchange for him to clear ten million dollars in debt, the threat of Valentino Bossanova, Julian's dead body, and Bob Brisket.

FORTY-TWO

BENITO

Striding through the casino, I pull out my phone and call Reaper, adrenaline spiking with the thrill of victory. Lights flash off polished floors, catching on the high-rollers drifting from table to table, but none of it registers. My mind is already on the chapel, and on the moment I finally claim what's mine.

When he picks up on the second ring, I say, "Get your ass to the casino. You're going to be my best man."

There's a beat of silence, then he splutters, "What? You're kidding."

"You heard me." I let out a low chuckle, imagining his shock.

I hang up before he can respond and tuck the phone into my pocket. Each step toward the chapel heightens my anticipation. It's finally happening, just as I intended.

My plans have come together, all the pieces falling into place. Before the hour is up, Ginevra will be mine.

She looked so beautiful, offering me the raw desperation she only reserved for Brisket. This is the Ginevra I've craved. Primal. Submissive. Needing only me. She's no longer the austere goddess who dismissed my offerings, but exactly where I want her. Groveling to me on her pretty little knees.

The casino fades into a blur. I push open the doors to the

chapel, ready to seal the deal. But the room is empty—no Reverend Johnson, no witnesses, just rows of empty pews.

My nostrils flare. That old bastard was supposed to be on standby.

An assistant rushes in, tripping over his own feet. His borrowed Elvis wig slips over his brow, breaking away from the painted-on sideburns.

"Where the hell is Reverend Johnson?" I snarl.

He flinches. "He's in the private dining room performing a ceremony for Mr. Montesano."

"Cesare?" I snap, my eyes flashing.

The assistant's face pales. "Mr. Roman, sir."

I rear back. Roman is getting married, tonight of all nights? What happened to his plan to kill Capello's daughter after fleecing her inheritance?

Shaking off that thought, I dial the hotel manager, who picks up before the first ring finishes.

"Strawberries and chocolate in the honeymoon suite," I say.

Silence stretches, the kind that makes my jaw tighten. The kind that makes the pulse between my ears pound.

"What?" I snap.

"The suite's occupied, sir. Mr. Roman Montesano has it," the manager replies.

I grind my teeth. "I reserved that suite the day I took control of the casino."

He clears his throat. "Sorry, sir. I thought you reserved it for Mr. Roman."

Heat surges through my veins, burning away any patience. Roman just poached my wedding. I ought to wring his neck.

Just as I'm griping over my big brother, the phone in my pocket buzzes. I yank it out, barely glancing at the screen before answering.

"What?" I snap.

There's another uncomfortable silence before a voice says. "Sir, it's Vitale. Miss Di Marco refuses to wear the dress."

My lips curl into a sneer. What happened to the submissive little Ginny who wept on her knees for help? Or the desperate little kitten who humped my leg? If she's expecting goddess treatment, she's about to get a shock.

"Tell her this isn't a fashion show," I snarl. "If she doesn't like the dress, she can march across the casino naked."

Vitale stammers his acknowledgment before hanging up. I shove the phone back into my pocket, my mood darkening. She wanted my protection. In exchange, she'll give me her submission.

Clenching my fists, I will myself to stay focused. This perfect night is morphing into a series of irritations. I turn to the chapel assistant, who flinches.

"I'll be in my office. Call me the second Reverend Johnson shows his face."

"Yes, sir." He backs away like I'm about to explode.

I stalk out of the chapel and down a hallway lined with wedding photos. The casino's noise bleeds back in as I push through the doors, but it barely registers. All I can muster are thoughts of damage control.

Ginevra needs to understand that becoming Mrs. Montesano won't revert our relationship to where it began. I'm no longer that obsessive boy who needed her more than oxygen. She's insignificant—no more a possession than the anime figurines I keep on my shelf.

Just as I round a corner, I collide into a large figure. I step back, ready to release a barrage, until I discover it's Reaper. He's already dressed in a tuxedo and arrived quicker than I expected.

I cock my head, my brows rising. "You got here fast."

Smirking, he shrugs. "The girl I'm stalking was already in the casino with her little friends."

"That student?" I ask.

He dismisses the question with a wave of his hand. "You know what it's like to be fixated on a single woman."

A bitter laugh escapes my lungs. "Unfortunately, I do."

The irony isn't lost on me—both of us are obsessed, willing to burn the world down for women who don't deserve our loyalty. It's not surprising we get along so well.

He glances over my shoulder. "So, where's the blushing bride?"

I blow out a long breath. "The officiant is playing musical

chairs with my wedding plans, Roman's hijacked my honeymoon suite, and now Ginevra's throwing a fit over a dress. If that isn't enough to ruin a man's night, I don't know what is."

Reaper's smirk fades. "Sounds like you've got your hands full."

"That's an understatement." I mutter and steer us both back toward the casino's main floor. The air fills with the sound of chatter, clinking chips, and bursts of laughter, but the noise fades into nothing, drowned by the fury simmering in my gut.

Lights flash across the tables, surrounded by bustling crowds. I don't have the mental bandwidth to consider how many of these patrons are using counterfeit chips. Now that they're deactivated, my security people will round up whoever tries to exchange them for cash.

We push through the crowd, shoulder to shoulder, cutting a path through the gamblers and waitstaff who step aside. Tension tightens as we approach a security door leading to a private section of the casino.

Where the hell will I put Ginevra tonight?

Back in her cell? A sleepless night might establish her place and teach her not to fuss over a dress.

Reverend Johnson stumbles through the doorway, out of breath, covered in sweat, and dressed in an ill-fitting hotel uniform.

"Where's the Elvis costume?" I snap.

He tries to straighten, but the old man sways on his feet. "Apologies for the delay, sir. I just checked Mr. Roman Montesano into the hotel."

My jaw tightens. "Do I even want to know?"

Reverend Johnson hesitates, then shakes his head. "It's best not to ask."

Reaper claps him hard on the shoulder and lets out a dark chuckle. "Let's get this wedding started."

FORTY-THREE

GINEVRA

I walk through the casino, the dress clinging to my body tighter than dried blood. With each step, its tight fabric cuts into my flesh like a blunt knife.

Heads turn as Benito's goon marches me through the crowd, their eyes raking over my exposed cleavage, fueling the fire of my humiliation.

My skin prickles under the gamblers' scrutiny. Can they tell I'm fresh from a murder scene? Benito's goon didn't even allow me to wash off Julian's coppery scent.

I drop my gaze to the floor, focus on the click of my heels against the marble, but it's futile. The air is thick with cologne and cigar smoke, mingling with the sharp scent of fear.

My fear.

Everything is wrong. The Benito I loved wouldn't force me into a Jessica Rabbit-style contraption covered in red sequins, but then he wouldn't also be so cold.

Every step toward the chapel feels like a march toward the gallows, and an invisible noose tightens around my throat.

The rough hand gripping my arm steers me around a corner. The lights blur, and the voices blend into a muffled roar as we approach the chapel doors.

"Ready, Miss Di Marco?" asks the goon.

No. Not by a long shot, but I force a nod.

He shoves open the door, and we step into a room reeking of old wood and something that churns my stomach, but I only have eyes for Benito. He stands near the altar in his navy suit, his gaze sweeping down the front of my dress.

Maybe I should have come here naked.

A microphone screeches. I turn to the altar and find an Elvis impersonator fumbling with its stand. His wig slips over his sweaty brow, and I swear he painted on his sideburns without a mirror.

I tear my gaze from him and meet the smirk of my old law professor, Remus Cortese. What's he doing here?

My heart pounds against the sequins digging into my ribs. The walls close in, and I squint against the bright lights. I would scream or even run, but the alternative to marrying a man who hates me is a hundred times worse.

The Elvis impersonator clears his throat, making me flinch. "We are gathered here today..."

His voice is a caricatured Southern drawl. Any other day, it would be comical, but Benito's gaze locks onto the side of my face like a hungry predator.

Every bone in this dress crushes my lungs, stealing my air. Black dots appear on the edges of my vision. I blink them away, trying to focus on the impersonator, but his words blend into the background noise of my pounding heart.

My legs threaten to collapse, but I lock my knees, refusing to fall.

"Do you, Benito Montesano, take this woman..."

The words dissipate into a fog of panic, only broken when Benito says, "I do."

When it's my turn, the words stick in my throat, but I manage to choke out, "I do."

Elvis grins, his wig slipping to the side. I'm so entranced by how it seems to have a life of its own that I don't notice Benito's hand until it's gripping mine, and he stares into my eyes with an intensity that could reduce me to ash.

The air thickens until every molecule smacks me in the face. There's no escape now that I've sealed my fate.

"You may now kiss the bride."

Benito's eyes darken to molten pools of black, making my heart skip several beats. He grips my waist and pulls me against his larger body with a force that steals my breath. Blood roars between my ears, and my nostrils fill with the heady scent of his sandalwood cologne.

All traces of his cold indifference evaporates in the heat of his gaze, and my muscles relax with relief. Exhaling away my tension, I wonder if we can finally make something work.

Before I can even complete that thought, his lips crash down on mine with a fervor that leaves my mind reeling. The room tilts, the lights spinning like a carousel.

All sensations rush south, and I squeeze my eyes shut to keep from fainting.

This kiss is wild, overwhelming, all-consuming. It floods my senses with heat and drowns out my terror. I'm swept up in his passion, unable to resist the feel of his mouth, which devours mine as though staking his claim.

He parts my lips with his tongue, making my heart somersault. My knees buckle, and I collapse against his chest, but his arm keeps me anchored within the storm.

I'm lost in Benito. Every rational thought washes away with his intensity. My world narrows to the feel of his lips, the mint on his tongue, the way he dominates me so completely.

My body can't tell if it's thrilled or terrified.

But when his erection presses into my belly, hot and thick and insistent, my panic ratchets to eleven. He's aroused. He's going to expect sex. I can't face the demands of yet another man.

When he finally pulls back, I'm swaying on my feet, gasping and half-blinded by a lack of oxygen. Sparks of sensation crackle along my lips, and my mind won't stop spinning.

This isn't the Benito I knew. He was patient. Gentle. This man and his kiss has shattered every expectation, leaving me weak.

"Thank you, thank you very much," Elvis says, his voice barely registering over the roar of my blood.

The moment Benito draws back to meet my eyes, my knees

buckle. I grip his jacket, trying to stay upright, but the dark spots spinning in my vision overwhelm the glaring lights.

His arm locks around my shoulders, pulling me back to his chest like I'm his prize. My lungs burn, and panic flares in my chest like a caged bird beating against my ribs.

Professor Cortese slides a pen into my fingers, and Benito guides my hand toward the marriage license. I sign, my handwriting shaky. The ink is barely dry when Benito snatches the paper, his eyes glinting with something dark.

I belong to the man whose heart I broke, and there's no turning back.

Professor Cortese takes the license from Benito. He writes his signature with a flourish and turns back to us with an innuendo-laden congratulations.

I manage a nod, my throat tight, the weight of the day pressing on every nerve. Every fine hair on my body stands on end, and I feel like the world's dumbest prey animal, especially since I'm caught in Benito's gaze.

Without warning, Benito scoops me into his arms. The world shifts on its axis like I've stepped into another dimension. Breath catching, I dig my fingers into his lapels.

As he carries me toward the chapel doors, my gut twists with a knot of dread. When we were together, Benito was always so gentlemanly when we kissed. I never once felt a trace of any erection. Today, he made me feel the full extent of his passion.

It was long and thick, surpassing the dildos Samson forced me to fuck. Maybe even bigger than Bob Brisket. The thought of that psychopath makes me shudder.

Placing a hand on Benito's chest, I whisper, "What are you going to do about my stalker?"

"He won't bother you anymore," Benito growls.

"Do you know him?"

"He won't be difficult to weed out."

"And Bossanova?"

"I won't let that bastard near your mother."

My throat tightens. "And the loan sharks?"

"I'll pay them off in the morning."

Exhaling, I force myself to relax, but my muscles remain taut.

My body can't forget the press of Benito's penis. I can't let this go any further—I have to say something, anything to stop him from taking me to bed.

"It's been a traumatic day. I'm too exhausted to consummate this marriage."

He doesn't slow, doesn't even acknowledge my plea. His face remains set in stone, his focus on the path ahead. When he turns away from the casino and through a staff hallway, my chest seizes.

"Just give me time, Benito. Please."

His jaw tightens, but his pace remains steady. I may as well plead with a marble statue.

Before I can protest further, Benito shoves open a heavy door, releasing a rush of cool air. He steps inside a concrete room almost identical to the one from before. Without a word, he deposits me onto the floor.

"Benito?" I scramble to sit up, my fingers splaying against the cold tiles.

He walks out, slams the door shut, encasing me in the dark.

FORTY-FOUR

BENITO

The next morning, I stand in the hallway outside the honeymoon suite, my nerves snapping with impatience. Roman and his new wife have finally vacated it, but Housekeeping is dragging their feet.

It doesn't help that my surveillance team spent an hour installing cameras to capture every corner. Ginevra's new cell must be perfect. Every angle must be visible, every inch inescapable.

Last night, I watched her cry herself to sleep on the concrete floor, feeling only a fraction of my five years of anguish. Now, it's time for her to learn her place.

Malfi shifts his bulk from side to side, twitching at these new arrangements. My security chief should have saved that discomfort for when his predecessor flooded the casino with chips. Wringing her hands beside him is the cocktail waitress I installed to watch the casino.

"Carla, you're on room service. Be there to provide my wife with anything she needs except clothes and her freedom." I flick my head to the room opposite. "Malfi, you're across the hall. I want you in the corridors, doing whatever's needed to scare her out of escaping."

The man's frown deepens, the doubt in his eyes making me itch.

"Something wrong?" I snarl, daring him to utter a word in defiance.

He snatches away his gaze. "No, sir."

"Good." I glare into his face a beat longer, daring him to question me again. When he doesn't, I turn to Carla. "Get changed. Both of you. Be in place within ten minutes."

I stride down the hallway, leaving Malfi and Carla to their roles. In the elevator, I pull out my phone, watching the feed from Ginevra's cell. She sits in the corner, still clad in the sequined dress.

Tousled hair frames a face I've committed a thousand nights to memory. She's a beautiful cryer, even with red-rimmed eyes and tears streaming down her cheeks. Her misery no longer tugs at my heart, except with a brief flicker of annoyance. I should be offended that she sobbed harder at the prospect of marrying me than she did for Bob Brisket's degrading assaults.

The elevator doors slide open, and I step into the low murmur of the casino. Morning dulls the noise, leaving only the die-hards clinging to their games, chasing lost causes. Eyes flick to me, recognition sparking before they quickly drop back to their bets. No one dares meet my gaze.

Valentino Bossanova stumbles into view, looking like a half-polished turd. Bloody bandages encase one side of his face and wrap around his hand.

My steps falter. He looks like he's been run over by a bus. "What the hell happened to you?"

Wincing, the old man raises the bandaged hand like it's a trophy. "Losanna," he snarls. "I broke it off, just like you ordered. She came at me with a carving knife, trying to take my balls."

I arch a brow, masking my surprise. Ginevra's mother was always a docile drunk. Bossanova must have handled her wrong.

As we cut through the tables, he casts me a sullen glare. "I did what you wanted—got involved with the mother and rubbed it in Ginevra's face."

His words grate with resentment, but I ignore his whining. A man who marries women for financial gain should get used to a few cuts and scrapes. Nobody, not even a lush like Losanna Di Marco, appreciates a deadly user.

When we reach the bar, I motion for the tender to pour him a drink, but Bossanova only glares at the glass like it's poison.

My patience thins. "Where is she, now?"

"Back in Victoria Gardens," he mutters, his eyes snapping to mine. "I did my part. Now, I want to know how Roman walked off death row."

Amusement flickers through my insides. When a letter from Gianni Bossanova arrived at our doorstep, postmarked from Alderney State Penitentiary, I became intrigued. Even more so, when the inmate introduced himself as a buddy of Roman's, also framed for a crime he didn't commit.

Valentino's condemned brother offered me five million for the secret. I considered tossing the letter in the trash until I went online and looked up the Bossanova brothers. Their involvement with the Di Marco Law Group made them a potential route to winning back my Ginevra. Turns out that it took more than the threat of Valentino Bossanova to make her run to me for help.

I lean into the old bastard, dropping my voice to a growl. "Roman was innocent all along."

He flinches, his craggy features twisting with disbelief. "Bullshit."

The corner of my lips lifts into a smirk. I pull back, cross my arms, and let the tension build. "We found footage of the real killer. That's our secret."

A flush blooms across his tanned skin, and the veins visible around the bandages pulse. Fist clenching around the glass, he snaps,. "You played me."

"With the truth?"

He flashes his overly white teeth. "I wasted my time on that drunken old whore for nothing—"

My fist slams into his face, sending him across the bar. Bottles clatter to the floor, shattering on impact, the air filling with the sharp scent of spilled liquor.

I close the distance before he can straighten, and drive my fist into his jaw. His head snaps back, but I don't stop. Another punch sends blood spraying across my knuckles, and his nose crumples under the impact.

Grabbing him by the collar, I slam my fist into his gut, folding him in half with a rusty wheeze. An uppercut makes him hit the floor, and I stomp on his throat, crushing his windpipe underfoot. Leaning in close, I shift my weight, savoring how his eyes widen with terror.

"You ever speak about Ginevra or her mother again—or even think about them—you'll be shitting teeth. If you so much as look at them, you'll lose your eyes."

Bossanova gasps, his hands scrabbling at my leg, his eyes bulging with the effort to breathe. His choked gasps mingle with the faint hum of distant slot machines. Security draws closer, their hands hovering near their weapons, unsure if they should intervene.

I ease the pressure a fraction, giving him a chance to respond, but he chokes on his own fear, unable to force out the words. When that doesn't work, I grind my heel into his windpipe. "Say it."

"Alright," he finally wheezes out, his voice cracking. "I won't go near them again!"

I flick my head toward the security hovering nearby. "Get this piece of shit out of my casino. He's barred from all Montesano properties."

They drag him away, his curses barely audible over the pounding in my ears. I smooth down my shirt, keeping the rage in check as my man Vitale approaches. He waits until the last of the security team drags Bossanova out of sight before speaking.

"Sir, we've got twenty more names associated with the counterfeit chips. Everyone we questioned either mentioned Luna Bianchi, the woman we caught last night, or Victor Bellavista."

My lips tighten. "How's he connected to the old man?"

Vitale shuffles on his feet. "That's the thing. We've combed through the family tree. Salvatore Bellavista doesn't have any sons, brothers, or cousins named Victor."

The implications hit hard. If there's no Victor Bellavista, then someone's using the name as a cover. Understandable, considering Salvatore would shoot his own blood for messing with his business.

The low murmur of the casino blends with the hum of the air conditioning, the scent of cigar smoke hanging in the air. This so-called Victor Bellavista has to be connected to the factory, otherwise he wouldn't be able to obtain the chips.

"Did you show them photos of his son?"

"We printed out pictures of every known Bellavista male, young and old. None of the people we caught with the chips recognized them as Victor."

My teeth grind. "Summon Bellavista to the casino. Make sure he knows this isn't a request."

Nodding, Vitale pulls out his phone and walks around the bar, his voice low as he relays the order.

I glance at my watch, realizing half an hour has already passed.

It's time to retrieve my wife and remind her exactly who holds the reins.

FORTY-FIVE

GINEVRA

Darkness presses down on my chest, heavy and suffocating. It squeezes the air from my lungs, making each breath a struggle. The cell feels smaller with every frantic heartbeat, the concrete walls creeping closer to trap me in this tomb.

I curl up tighter in the corner, pulling my knees to my chest. The cold floor leeches the warmth from my skin, but it's the dread that makes me shiver. The thought of life with Benito—locked away, powerless, until he wrings every drop of revenge—tightens a knot of fear deep in my gut.

How long will he keep me here? How long before I break?

Each second in this concrete box erodes my resolve, grinding down my will. I press harder against the wall as if I could slip into the cracks and disappear out of his reach. The thought of being his prisoner sends my pulse pounding against my skull.

The door creaks open, flooding the cell with artificial light. Squinting against the glare, I raise a hand to shield my eyes, but there's no mistaking the figure that fills the doorway.

Benito.

He stands immaculate in a dark suit that clings to his broad shoulders. Light pours in behind him, giving him an air of power and control. Shadows cut across his chiseled features, turning his beauty dark and dangerous. The man I loved is now a stranger.

His presence fills the room, overwhelming and oppressive. I'm pinned to the bricks, my heart pounding with sharp, painful beats. Every muscle coils, braced for whatever comes next.

There's no trace of the old Benito, only a man who could crush me without a second thought. I can't read his expression, but the weight of his gaze pins me to my corner.

I shrink into the bricks, wondering what the hell he's going to do. Is this where he demands my body? Fear claws at my throat, tightening it until my lungs scream for air. I want to close my eyes, but I can't look away.

Not from him.

Not from my husband.

Benito enters the cell, his footsteps heavy on the concrete floor. Flinching, I brace for his next move, expecting him to grab my arm, force me up, demand something I can't give.

Instead, he extends a hand.

I stare at those manicured fingers, my brow furrowing, and meet his eyes. Eyes that once melted in my presence. Eyes that once bathed me in security and love. His face gives nothing away —only an unnerving calm.

Instinct screams to pull back, to keep my distance. But that gesture stirs something buried deep inside, something that wants to believe in the boy I once knew.

"What about my mom?" Voice shaking, I force out the words. "Where is she?"

"She left Bossanova's apartment this morning."

Skepticism twists in my gut. "I don't believe you."

Without a word, he pulls out his phone, taps the screen, and holds it out for me to see. The footage is distant, taken from a security camera. It shows one of the casino's bars. Benito punches Bossanova in the face, following him as he stumbles back. In the next moment, there's a flurry of strikes, followed by him crushing the old man's throat.

I don't need sound to understand the message. Benito's made sure Bossanova won't come near Mom or me again.

The sight of Benito overpowering Bossanova releases some of the fear tightening around my chest, making it easier to breathe.

Benito tucks the phone away and offers me his hand again,

but now, my mind dredges up that spine-tingling kiss. Knowing Mom is safe gives me the courage to accept his offer.

With a gentle grip, he pulls me to my feet. My legs buckle, but Benito catches me, his hand steady on the small of my back.

"Can you walk?" His voice is unusually soft.

I nod, even though the edges of my vision blur and blacken from exhaustion and the relentless gnaw of hunger. The last thing I want is to show more weakness.

Forcing one foot in front of the other, I walk to the door, even though every step feels like I'm wading through molasses. Benito guides me out of the cell with an arm around my waist as if he's worried I'll collapse. We move through a narrow service corridor, avoiding the bright lights and prying eyes of the casino floor.

The quiet hum of the hallway soothes my senses, broken only by the distant clatter of dishes and the muffled voices of staff. It's a relief not to be paraded past the gamblers, avoiding their judgmental eyes. Benito keeps his pace slow, matching my faltering steps, and I'm grateful for the small mercy.

Eventually, we reach the hotel and take an elevator to the top floor. Benito leads me into a room that reeks of cold luxury. Floor-to-ceiling windows flood the space with daylight, reflecting off the mirrored furniture. A king-sized bed dominates the center, complete with a headboard made of silver bars. The mirrored ceiling above it makes the space feel surreal, like a stage set for a porno shoot.

I glance at the glass table, laden with fresh pastries, chopped fruit, and coffee. The sight of it makes my stomach churn.

The sweet smell turns my stomach further, mixing with the coppery stench of dried blood still clinging to my fingers, and the filth stuck to my skin. The room's polished luxury feels like a cruel joke, mocking the horror of last night.

But I can't forget. Not with blood still encrusted beneath my nails.

My mind dredges up Brisket tearing through Julian's guts, the twitching weight of his heart shoved into my hands, my fingers slick with warm blood.

Breath catching, I tear my gaze away from the breakfast and meet Benito's eyes.

"What happened to the body?" My voice comes out tight, almost strangled.

"I sent a cleaning crew to the penthouse. They took care of everything. No trace of the blond man remains."

His detached tone is jarring, as if Julian's death were just another task on his to-do list. I don't know what I expected—some horror, a flicker of remorse, maybe even a promise to handle Brisket.

Shaking off those thoughts, I focus on my filthy hands. "I need to wash."

Benito gives a sharp nod, my cue to escape. I rush to the bathroom, desperate to scrub away the blood, the memories, the fear that clings to my skin.

Inside, I close the door and finally let out a breath. The bathroom gleams under the harsh lights—white marble and chrome, spotless and sterile. Too perfect. Too clean. I feel like a stain.

Not daring to look in the mirror, I fumble with the boned dress, struggling with the zipper until it gives. The fabric pools at my feet, a glittering heap of humiliation.

I turn on the shower, scalding hot, and step under the spray. The water burns, but it's exactly what I need. Grabbing the shampoo, I lather it into my hair, scrubbing hard enough to wash away the blood, the shame, the fear. Conditioner follows, then enough shower gel to make my skin as slippery as a baby seal.

Steam clouds the cubicle, and the hot water pounds against my flesh, making my head spin. I grab the loofah and scrub every inch until my skin burns. But no matter how hard I wash, I can't purge the memories.

The water runs red at my feet, but it's not enough. I can still feel Julian, the loan sharks, and Bob Brisket. Only this time, he's forcing his cock down my throat and making me hold the pulsing heart to my pussy.

My hips move with every imagined thrust, and my fingers slide down to rub my clit. I'm slick with arousal, twitching with need, empty and desperate to be filled. I press harder, circling faster, chasing that sharp edge as my breath shudders. Heat coils low, a knot of tension winding tighter. Then I double over, coming in a hot rush, my fingers still working frantic circles.

A sob catches in my throat. Has Bob Brisket warped my mind so badly?

I stumble out of the shower, my skin stinging and raw. After turning off the hot spray, I scramble into a robe hanging by the door.

The rest of the suite is empty. Benito's gone, and so is my appetite. I can't stomach more than a few bites of croissant, so I move away from the table and head for the closet. Hopefully, Benito had yesterday's clothes laundered, but when I pull open the door, it's empty.

A chill creeps down my spine. I hurry across the suite and into the bathroom, hoping to find my red wedding dress. But when I open the door, it's gone.

All I'm left with is this robe.

I clutch it tighter, but it does nothing to shield me from the terrifying truth. Benito may have moved me from a concrete cell to a luxury suite, but I'm still his prisoner.

Different walls, different chains, same fucking trap.

FORTY-SIX

BENITO

I should be upstairs, watching Ginevra eat. Instead, I'm in a secluded parking lot beneath the casino, flanked by two armed guards. I'm still wearing this morning's suit, only reinforced by a bulletproof undershirt. Strength doesn't need to hide behind armor.

This place is hardly used, yet the air thrums with the mingled scents of oil and exhaust fumes, and of course, the approaching truck. Its headlights cut through the dim light, illuminating the empty space.

My men tense, their hands hovering near their weapons, but I remain in place.

The truck pulls up in front of us and stops its engine. Its back doors swing open, and one of my men steps down. The second drags out Salvatore Bellavista like a sack of meat.

His silk smoking jacket hangs off one fleshy shoulder, and his cravat wraps around his neck like a noose. Both men march the old man to my feet and force him onto his knees, shoving his face into the oil-streaked concrete.

"Release him."

They step back.

Bellavista raises his head to stare up at me through wide eyes. When he realizes it's me, his mouth falls slack.

He should be afraid.

"Did you get the compensation I sent?" His voice wavers, his bravado betraying desperation.

I stare down at him, unblinking, allowing the silence to stretch as the weight of the situation settles into his thick skull. Tension mounts, and I savor every moment of his fear.

"The money came through," I finally say, "but your problems go deeper than a prodigal son releasing counterfeit chips."

Bellavista shifts on his knees, his eyes darting between me and my men. "What's this about, Benito?"

"Every scumbag we've rounded up in the last twenty-four hours with those deactivated chips mentioned two people. A woman and an old man named Victor Bellavista."

Confusion flickers across his jowls. "I don't know any Victor."

"This Victor knows you well enough to infiltrate your factory and steal chips." I cock my head, studying him for signs of deception, but all I see is terror. "Funny, how you shot your own son over the fraud. Almost like you were covering up something bigger. Something bad enough to take down your whole family."

Sweat beads on his forehead, trailing down his temples and sliding down his pale cheeks. His eyes dart to the gun holstered at my side, and he shudders.

"Everyone knows your family wiped out the Capellos," Bellavista says, his voice cracking. "You waited five years for the right moment to take out their entire bloodline."

My brows rise. Turns out the outside world doesn't see us as weak.

"My son was a liability," he adds, his voice wavering. "An addict making stupid mistakes and drawing unwanted attention. I couldn't let his recklessness bring your wrath down on my family. I did what I had to do."

He drops his gaze, his shoulders sagging, his spine sloping to the oil-stained floor.

I crouch down to look Bellavista in the eye. "Is your son still alive?"

He hesitates, then offers a tight nod.

"Then you'll question him. Between the two of you, you'll

uncover this 'Victor' and bring him to me alive. Fail, and the Bellavista name will be wiped out of existence."

His lips tighten. "Over counterfeit chips?"

"Over the conspiracy I'm yet to uncover," I say.

Bellavista breathes hard through flared nostrils. An outsider looking into this situation would call me unreasonable. After all, the man shot his son over the fraud and covered our losses.

But giving people the benefit of the doubt is what led to Dad dying, and our mother defecting to the Galliano family only to get killed. Everything started with Ginevra breaking our engagement and taking up with Samson Capello.

Dad brushed it off as just a young woman not wanting to marry a simp. I knew it was a symptom of something insidious. Ginevra needed to pull away before her father and Capello ruined our family.

"There's no conspiracy," Bellavista says from between clenched teeth.

"Why would I believe the word of a man who continued doing business with the bastards who stole my father's casino?"

His eyes flicker with regret. The neutrality that kept him wealthy while we were down has turned around and bitten him on the ass. After a moment of tension, he nods, the motion stiff. "I'll investigate it."

"Good." I stand and gesture to my men.

They move in, bundling the old man back into the armored truck. As its engine roars to life and pulls away, the phone in my pocket vibrates. I pull it out and see Reaper's name flashing on the screen.

"Everything okay?" I ask.

"What do you know about a massive crater on the other side of town?" Reaper asks.

Brow furrowing, I gaze out at the disappearing tail lights. "What crater?"

"One of our surveillance units tracked a truck leaving the scene of a massive explosion. The damn thing backed straight into the Montesano armory."

"When?" I snap.

"Fifteen minutes ago."

My grip tightens on the phone. "Was anyone hurt?"

"No one who matters. The truck reached a destination on the edge of town, then reversed out of it before getting swallowed into an expanding crater. Then it arrived safely into Montesano territory."

I take a step toward the elevator, deciding to call Roman before heading upstairs to check on Ginevra. Vitale bursts through the doors, his face twisted with urgency.

"Boss," he says, barely catching his breath. "Someone's rigged the slot machines."

My gaze sharpens, even though my mind still lingers on Roman and the crater. "What do you mean?"

"Payouts have been boosted. A woman just won half a million. She looks almost identical to someone who won six months ago."

I grind my teeth, my pulse quickening as the bulletproof undershirt grates against my skin, making me want to scratch. This morning has already been too full of surprises, and the thought of another scam running under my nose sets my nerves on edge.

Frustration builds under my skin like a pressure cooker ready to explode, but I blow out a long breath. "Where is she now?"

Vitale points upstairs, the direction I'd planned to go anyway. "In one of the VIP lounges enjoying complimentary champagne, but it won't be long before she bolts."

"Keep her there. I'll deal with the woman myself."

Problems pile up on my chest like lead weights—Ginevra, Roman, the crater, the scams—the pressure's reaching a breaking point. I need to seize control before every fucker who doubted my right to the casino laughs in my face.

FORTY-SEVEN

GINEVRA

I move from one side of the suite to the other, pulling open empty drawers. Harsh sunlight slices through the wall of windows, reflecting off the polished furniture.

Benito's taken my clothes, but he's also seized my purse and phone.

My gaze darts around the suite, taking in its gleaming surfaces, mirrored walls, and the massive four-poster. I pull the robe tighter around my chest, the soft fabric feeling like a shackle.

I eye the phone on the nightstand. It's an old-fashioned rotary, the kind you see in old movies, but it can't just be there as an ornament.

Dialing Mom's number on this old-fashioned contraption is near impossible. I fumble with the clunky dial, my fingers slipping over the numbers. When it finally rings, the tension in my muscles releases, and I sit on the edge of the mattress.

Benito has never lied to me before. If he says Mom went home, then I'm sure she's safe, but I still need to hear her voice. I also need her to send me a change of clothes so I no longer feel so trapped.

On the fourth ring, the line clicks. Instead of Mom's familiar voice, a robotic tone fills my ear: "We're sorry, but this call cannot be completed as dialed."

My heart stutters. I try again, dialing slower this time, as if it might change the outcome. The same mechanical voice cuts through the silence, reminding me there's no connection. No way out.

Shit.

I slam the phone back onto the receiver, my breath coming in shallow gasps. This place is only an upgrade from last night's cell, but I'm still more or less trapped. I clench my fingers on the silk comforter, my nails digging into the smooth fabric.

Benito can't treat me like a prisoner.

A second glance at the phone reveals two buttons: one for the reception, the other for room service. Desperate for answers, I pick up the receiver and try again. The line rings twice before it connects.

"Room service, how may I assist you, Mrs. Montesano?" asks a chipper female voice.

"My bag and clothes are somewhere in the casino. Can you send someone to bring them up?"

There's a pause on the other end. "I'm sorry, ma'am. We don't handle personal belongings. Would you like to order breakfast instead?"

Frustration bubbles in my chest, and my grip tightens on the receiver. "If you can't get my things, can you at least send up some fresh clothes?"

The next pause is even longer. "I can send someone up with fresh towels or a robe, if that helps."

"Can you at least check with lost property or housekeeping?"

"I'm afraid that's outside my scope, ma'am. You could try contacting the front desk."

The line clicks off before I can respond, leaving me grinding my teeth. Anger simmers under my skin, and my pulse pounds between my ears. I'm wasting time with the staff when I need to call Benito.

I stab the button for reception, my pulse quickening as the line connects.

"Reception, how may I assist you?"

"This is Mrs. Benito Montesano," I say through clenched teeth. "Please put me through to my husband."

"Mr. Montesano is unavailable at the moment."

"Can you at least try his office?"

The line goes quiet again for a second before the phone on the other end rings and rings. I stare into space, wondering if I should streak through the hotel in my robe.

Each ring stabs deeper until the receptionist interrupts with, "Would you like to leave a message?"

I swallow hard, the words catching in my throat. "Tell him his wife called."

The line clicks dead.

Determination propels me off the bed. Fuck this. I stride across the suite to the door and yank it open. A woman in a hotel uniform strides toward me through the marble hallway, holding a silver bucket of ice.

"Excuse me." I raise a hand.

Pausing, she sweeps her gaze down my robe and bare feet before meeting my eyes. My hair hangs in wet clumps around my face, which is probably still reddened from the hot shower.

"Yes, ma'am?" she says.

"I need your help—"

"One moment, ma'am. I just need to deliver this ice."

She continues to the door opposite mine and knocks. It swings open, revealing a gorilla of a man in a black suit. His gaze lands on me, lingering a beat too long for comfort.

Suppressing a shiver, I step back into my room and pull the robe tighter around my neck. Even though the woman hands the man the ice, his eyes don't leave mine until I dip behind the door.

What a creep.

The woman turns back to me with a faint smile. "How can I assist you, ma'am?"

"Can you come inside for a moment?" Not wanting that man to overhear our conversation, I step aside to let her in.

She hesitates, then nods and enters the suite. Her gaze darts around the room as if taking it in for the first time. She's several inches shorter, with huge brown eyes and petite features.

"I just married Benito Montesano but I have no clothes— nothing but this robe."

Her brows furrow. "Did you send them to housekeeping, ma'am?"

"No, I didn't send anything anywhere," I say, my voice tightening. "They were here this morning, and now they're gone."

She looks even more puzzled. "That's strange. Sometimes guests send their clothes to be pressed or cleaned. Maybe that's what happened?"

Frustration builds in my chest. I try to keep it from seeping into my voice, but it's a losing battle. "Can you please find me something to wear? Anything."

The woman's eyes dart toward the door, and she swallows before taking a step back. "I'm really sorry, ma'am. But I don't have access to any clothes. You might want to ask Mr. Montesano."

"I've been trying to reach him but he's not answering. Can't you just find a hotel T-shirt and sweatpants so I don't have to keep wearing this robe?"

She grips the door handle, looking ready to bolt. "I'm sorry, ma'am. I really can't help with that."

I lurch forward before she slips out. "What's your name?"

The woman flinches, her eyes widening. "It's Carla."

Fear flashes across her face, and I take a deep breath. I need to calm the hell down. She isn't my jailor—that's Benito fucking Montesano.

"Carla, I'm sorry," I say, my voice softer. "I didn't mean to scare you. This whole situation is overwhelming."

Hesitating, she nods. "Would you like me to pass on a message to Mr. Montesano?"

When I nod back, she adds, "If you need anything else, just call room service and ask for me by name. I'll do my best to help."

"Thank you," I say, forcing a weak smile. "I appreciate that."

Carla slips out the door, leaving me alone with my swirling thoughts. My gaze drifts to the barely touched breakfast table laden with pastries, fruit, and eggs. My stomach churns with a protest, but I need my strength for whatever comes next.

With a sigh, I cross the suite, drop into a chair, and grab a fork. I take a tentative bite of the eggs, then a piece of fruit, barely registering the flavors. Each mouthful feels like a struggle, but it's the only way to reclaim some control.

I won't be weak when Benito finally comes to visit—I'll be ready.

FORTY-EIGHT

BENITO

I walk around the table, circling the jackpot winner. Debbie Clark is a middle-aged woman with a baseball cap obscuring her graying curls. She sways back and forth on the chair, her chest rising and falling with rapid breaths.

Her first mistake was stealing from my casino. The second was drinking all that champagne. By the time we escorted her out of the VIP lounge, she and her friend had already finished an entire bottle, complete with a box of liqueurs.

For a terrified woman, alcohol works better than any truth serum.

Dim light flickers across stained concrete, casting shadows on her face. Vitale stands silent in the corner with his arms crossed, adding on the pressure. For propriety's sake, we've allowed two female security officers to assist with the interrogation.

The Casino Montesano is ruthless to its enemies, but we're not predators.

Mascara streaks down her cheeks, mixing with the tears that won't stop. "Please, Mr. Montesano," she gasps, her voice cracking. "I didn't mean to—"

I raise a hand, cutting her off. "You've seen the footage. The woman who collected that last jackpot was you. Stop wasting our time and tell the truth."

Her breath hitches, and she stares up at me through wide, desperate eyes. "It wasn't my idea. Someone else rigged the machine and said it would be okay. I only get ten percent, I swear."

More words spill out in a jumbled rush. I tune out the pitiful attempt to save her hide.

Holding her gaze, I let her talk herself hoarse. When the excuses run dry, I lean across the table and place both palms on its plastic surface.

"His name," I say.

"Larry Zambino," she blurts. "It was his idea. If it wasn't me collecting the winnings, it would have been someone else."

The taller security officer steps forward. "Larry Zambino is still on the job, sir. Should we put him in a cell?"

I nod. "Do it."

My lips tighten with distaste. Capello allowed every hungry cockroach who wanted a bite to consume the casino's profits. He didn't give a shit because he obtained it so easily. Now that it's back with the Montesano family, I intend to exterminate the vermin, even if it means filling my cousin's crematorium with corpses.

As she leaves, the phone in my pocket buzzes. I pull it out, finding Carla's name flashing on the screen.

"Report," I say.

"Your wife is asking for clothes."

I smirk. "Did you show her the toy box?"

She pauses. "Sir?"

"Go back and tell her each room on her floor comes with a complimentary box containing necessities. She might find what she's looking for beside the mini bar." I hang up, sliding the phone back into my pocket.

The thought of Ginevra encountering another box of sex toys sends a surge of arousal to my cock. I shake off the excitement, wishing I didn't have to contend with these grifters. My blushing bride can wait. I have another casino conspiracy to uncover.

I turn back to the woman. Her shoulders shake, and her eyes dart between me and the door like she's calculating an escape. I slide a pen across the table toward her clenched fists.

"Write down every name. Every detail. Dates, locations, and the bank accounts where you transferred the money."

Nodding, she reaches for the pen with trembling fingers. "Are you going to call the police?"

I lean in, looking her straight in the eyes. "Only if the money isn't returned with interest."

Her pained whimper only gives me a measure of satisfaction, as I'm aching to see the princess I left in her tower.

My phone buzzes again. I pull it out to find a call from reception.

"What?"

"Losanna Di Marco is here. She said she has an appointment."

A breath catches in my throat. It takes every effort to suppress my excitement. If Ginevra's mother attacked Bossanova with a knife, how would she react to discovering I could be corrupting her precious daughter?

I turn my attention to Vitale. "Finish this up."

He steps forward, towering over the older woman, who shivers.

Without waiting for a reply, I stride out of the cell and head to the casino, letting the hum of chatter and clinking chips fade in the background. Ginevra likes to think of her mother as an innocent victim to the ravages of alcohol, but all I see is weakness.

The woman was always in and out of retreats, trying out different therapies to curb her addiction, but she never once seemed to make much of an effort. Ginevra wasted half her life trying to rescue Losanna. Even her marriage to me is another attempt to protect her mother.

As I round the blackjack table, I can't help thinking about Cesare. After our mother abandoned us to marry Tommy Galliano, my younger brother became addicted to his own crystal meth. Gil and I locked him in a room with Sofia and Dr. Moretti taking care of his needs.

His detox was brutal, painful, yet he hasn't relapsed once.

Unless he's swapped drugs for serial killing.

Shaking off that intrusive thought, I reach the reception area. Losanna Di Marco sits on a sofa with a clutch. Strangely, she's brushed her hair, straightened her clothes, and is showing no traces of her infamous cleavage. When she rises off her seat and glares into my eyes, I wonder if Bossanova's rejection was what it took to get her sober.

Tension ripples through her posture as I approach. She puffs out her chest and asks, "What's this about you marrying my daughter?"

My lips curl into a slow smile. "Want to see Ginevra?"

"Naturally," she clips.

I offer her my arm and smirk. "Should I start calling you 'Mother' now?"

Features tightening, she slips her hand into the crook of my arm. Her face might display annoyance and strength, but there's no mistaking how her fingers tremble.

I could elaborate by explaining that the machinations of her husband killed Dad and drove my mother into the arms of a maniac, who coerced her into undergoing unnecessary cosmetic surgery. Surgery she would never have contemplated if she'd stayed with her sons.

But why use words when I can show my displeasure with actions?

Savoring the fear she's trying to hide, I steer her out of the reception and through the hallway.

This reunion will be delicious.

FORTY-NINE

GINEVRA

I move from one side of the suite to the other, gripping the edges of the cotton robe. Sunlight heats one side of my face, trying to sap my strength. Every step is a fight to gather much-needed courage. Benito has taken everything—my clothes, my freedom, my sense of control—but he won't take my dignity.

When I stop in front of the mirror, the woman reflecting on its surface looks unhinged. My hair is still damp from the shower, settling into tangled waves from all the times I clutched at my scalp.

Unease gnaws at my gut with razor-sharp teeth, but I shrug off the sensations. I've faced worse and survived. Benito might think he's in control, but I can't allow him to think of me as weak. The moment he returns, I'll demand to know why he's treating me like a prisoner, and tell him this stops now.

After all, I'm his fucking wife.

The door bursts open. Mom stumbles into the room, her features twisting with anguish. My heart leaps to my throat. What the hell?

"Mom?" I step forward, ready to tell her everything until Benito fills the doorway.

Freezing, I clutch my chest. His gaze sweeps the room before locking on my eyes, making my pulse stutter under the weight of his stare.

Mom rushes forward and grips my shoulders with trembling fingers. "Ginny, oh my God, are you alright?"

My throat dries to the consistency of legal parchment. I'm far from okay. A part of me still reels from seeing Julian murdered. My fingers still feel the twitch of the heart Brisket pushed into my hands and no amount of showering could wash the sensation of that warm, sticky blood.

Hell, even if I wanted to tell her everything, I couldn't with Benito watching over us like a jailor. Instead, I force a smile.

"I'm fine, Mom. Really."

Eyes narrowing, she leans in and whispers, "What's he done to you?"

I lower my voice to a rasp. "Benito paid off the sharks and got rid of my stalker. Thanks to him, we're safe."

Brow furrowing, She tightens her grip on my shoulders. "Ginny, I already had a plan," she whispers. "Everything was in place—"

"Stop," I hiss. My gaze darts to Benito, whose dark eyes narrow. I'll be damned if I let Mom incriminate herself with him watching our every move. "It's over."

I pull her close, trying to draw some comfort from her presence. Mom relaxes in my embrace, finally seeming to understand. Over her shoulder, I meet Benito's gaze. His eyes bore into my soul with a cold intensity that sends shivers racing down my spine.

Dread coils around my gut like a constrictor. What does he plan to do now that he's got me under his control?

His gaze is relentless, peeling away every layer of my defenses, searching for truths that don't exist. Every instinct screams at me to look away, grab Mom, and run, but it's like being locked in the gaze of an Indian cobra. Mesmerizing and hypnotic, it anchors me in place, the intensity making my knees want to buckle. Mom's grip loosens, and I sense her hesitation, as if she feels something is wrong.

"Ginny..." she whispers, her voice tinged with fear.

But I don't respond. I can't. Not with Benito here, a constant reminder of my powerlessness. Coming to him feels like accepting punishment for breaking our engagement, but I've run out of choices.

I force myself to swallow the rising panic, keeping my expression neutral even as my heart hammers like a warning bell. This isn't the time to show fear, not in front of him. Not when he's waiting for me to crack.

"Ginny, is he hurting you?"

My heart skips, making space for recent resentments. Mom's concern is too late—I'm already damaged. Screaming this would be futile because I'm torn about where to vent my frustration. Toward Mom for pretending all those years to be incoherent, or to Benito for trapping me in this marriage. Or to myself, for my contribution to this mess.

When Mom whimpers, I give my head a frantic shake. "He's been a perfect gentleman."

It's a half-truth at best. Benito hasn't laid a hand on me yet, but he did make me spend our wedding night in a concrete cell. His eyes burn into the side of my face, daring me to spill the truth.

Despite everything, a small part of me clings to the hope that beneath his cold exterior is the boy I loved. The boy who treated me like his queen. I just need to find a way to reach him, to coax out that tiny kernel of the past.

Mom pulls back, her eyes welling with tears. "Come home with me."

My stomach churns at the prospect of stepping out of this suite and facing Bob Brisket. His parting words thud through my ears, making me shudder. I don't want to have sex with a man capable of such unbridled violence. Benito's protection is the only thing keeping us safe.

He hasn't moved from the doorway, yet his presence fills the room, making it hard to inhale. I swallow, trying to stay upright when the weight of his stare presses down on my bones.

"We can leave right now," Mom adds. "You don't have to stay here."

Benito steps forward, closing the distance between us in an instant. "This is our honeymoon. Ginevra isn't leaving."

The word hits like a blow, cold and paralyzing. *Honeymoon.* I can't imagine anything more terrifying. Benito and me, alone, with nothing to shield me from his intentions. My stomach knots at the thought. I'm so painfully inexperienced, yet he's been with that beautiful woman and possibly several more in the years we've been apart.

My pulse races, and my chest tightens to the point of pain. It takes every effort to hold a neutral expression, to hide how much his words shake me to the bone. But the thought of being so vulnerable with the man I betrayed turns my insides to ice.

Mom releases me to glare at Benito. "Thank you for paying off our debts, but was it necessary to demand Ginevra's hand in marriage?"

"Yes, it was," he replies, his voice flat.

Silence mounts until the tension becomes heavy and thick. Mom shifts on her heels, her eyes darting between us, but even she quails beneath his stare. Sweat beads at my temples, and the robe's toweling fibers aggravate my skin.

"Why don't we have lunch together?" Mom says, her voice artificially bright. "The three of us, at the restaurant downstairs."

"No."

Benito's sharp reply slices through the air like a blade. He steps closer with a bone-chilling smile. "I want quality time with my wife to catch up on the five years we've lost."

His words tighten the knot in my stomach. Mom's fingers twitch around my shoulders, but she has no reply. How could either of us explain how we failed to warn him about what would happen to his family?

Mom's eyes linger on my face, searching for some sign that I'm under distress. I force a smile, but it feels like a mask, fragile and on the verge of cracking.

"It's okay." I cut her off before she can speak. "Benito's right. We need some time alone."

She hesitates, her gaze fixed on me, searching for reassurance. I force another smile, pleading with her to understand. "Don't worry. We'll be fine."

Mom pulls me into a tight hug, her arms wrapping around my middle with a desperate kind of protectiveness. "Call me if you need help," she whispers, her voice trembling. "I mean it."

Benito stands close enough to hear my racing heart. I nod against her shoulder, urging her to go, even though every instinct screams for her to take me out of this gilded cage.

Finally, she pulls back, her eyes scanning my face again as if trying to memorize every detail. With a reluctant sigh, she releases her grip and walks toward the door. Her steps are slow as if giving me the chance to change my mind.

I swallow back the urge to beg her not to leave, forcing myself to stay strong. This is my burden, not hers.

When Mom reaches the door, she lingers for several heartbeats. I glance at Benito, who smirks. "Ginevra is safest with me."

Mom freezes, her features flickering with confusion.

Before she can ask what he means, Benito strides to the door and opens it, guiding her out with a gentle hand on the small of her back.

As she tumbles into the hallway, the door closes with a soft click, sealing me in the room with my captor.

My throat thickens. Is this the moment he demands his conjugal rights?

FIFTY

BENITO

Ginevra storms across the suite, her eyes blazing. I would believe in her righteous fury if her fists weren't clenched so tightly around the collar of the robe. She stops out of arm's reach, panting hard, and I can practically see a complaint bubbling up inside her chest.

"You're treating me like a prisoner."

I raise a brow, daring her to elaborate.

"Well, you've left me with nothing but this robe!"

A smirk tugs at the corner of my lips. I take a slow step forward, enjoying the way she stiffens.

"If you have complaints about the robe, I could always take it away." I drawl.

She flinches, her arms crossing over her chest. Sunlight streams through the floor-to-ceiling windows, coloring her flyways a vibrant shade of amber. I stare down at my beautiful Ginevra, letting her anger feed my satisfaction. Is my little princess dissatisfied? Her torment hasn't even begun.

With another step, I close the gap until our bodies mingle, the air crackling with tension. She stiffens but doesn't retreat. Her breaths come in shallow, uneven bursts, and the resistance in her eyes flickers like a dying candle. She fights to hold on to her courage, but the way her gaze flits away before snapping back tells me it's waning.

I lean in, just enough for her to feel the heat of my breath against her skin, and I savor the fine cracks in her composure.

She's trying so hard to stay strong, to stand her ground, but there's no hiding her helplessness. Ginevra is a trapped queen in a game I've already won. Watching her struggle to keep control is almost as satisfying as the victory itself.

"Having second thoughts?" I ask, lowering my voice an octave.

Her breath quickens, her lips press into a thin line. I let the silence linger, enjoying her barely concealed frustration.

"I never wanted to leave you, but my dad forced me to break our engagement," she finally says.

Her words reverberate through my skull, and everything freezes. I stare into those defiant gray eyes, my mind racing. Why the hell would I believe the words of a woman who would try to manipulate an unknown stalker into committing murder?

Anger, sharp and consuming, flares in my chest, and my vision narrows to my treacherous little siren. Even if she's telling the truth, she still let her father tear us apart.

She knew trouble was coming to the Montesano family, yet she kept her mouth shut.

My anger sharpens to a blade, slicing through any remaining doubts. I reach out, closing my fingers around her throat with a speed that makes her gasp.

Eyes widening, she stares up at me as if I'm a monster like Brisket.

"You should have come to me," I growl. "We could have protected you, hidden you away. Instead, you chose to leave."

Her breath hitches as I pull her closer until our bodies touch. Every primal urge screams at me to squeeze harder, cut off her air, but I fight to contain the boiling fury.

"You chose to be with him," I hiss, my breath coming in harsh, controlled bursts.

"Benito—"

"No more excuses," I snarl.

She whimpers, her eyes squeezing shut.

My mind snaps back to that day in the lecture theater, when she stood before me cold and composed as she dismantled my world. I asked what I did wrong, begged her for another chance, but she said she was happy with Samson.

Now, with her pulse quickening beneath my fingers, all I can think about is how easily she discarded a lifetime. My grip tightens, and I pull her so close that we're sharing the same air.

I lean in, my lips brushing her ear. "No more secrets. No defiance. Absolute loyalty."

She jerks back, but I tighten my grip around her throat, my fingers pressing into the soft skin. "Don't forget," I whisper, my voice a low growl, "Your life hangs by a thread, and I'm the only one keeping you from falling."

Ginevra tenses but doesn't break free, but I don't let go. Her breath quickens to a staccato rhythm that echoes the pounding of her heart. Ginevra needs to understand she's in no position to make demands.

Finally, she nods, and I walk her back toward the bed. With a gentle shove, she stumbles backward, collapsing into the mattress like a perfect little wife. Face flushing, she opens her mouth to protest, but I turn on my heel and head toward the door.

Moments later, she grabs my arm. "Where are my clothes?"

I pause, letting her stew before sparing her a glance. She glares up at me, trembling like a soaked kitten, desperate and defiant in nothing but that robe. The sight of her fills the darkest parts of my soul with a sick satisfaction.

Arching a brow, I lean in just enough that she can't escape the intensity of my stare. "Why do you want them, Ginevra? Planning to leave?"

She blinks, her face falling slack, as if she finds my question confusing. Her mouth opens, then closes, her eyes flickering as she struggles to find the words.

"You can't keep me caged forever," she says.

My lips twitch. I lean closer, my gaze locking onto hers, until her eyes flicker with doubt. "Good wives earn the privilege of clothing."

Her lips part with a gasp, and those pretty eyes widen with

shock. The anger in her features gives way to something vulnerable. But just as quickly, the fire returns.

"Are you demanding sex?" she snaps.

My mind fills with memories of her on her knees for Brisket, those pretty pink lips wrapped around my shaft. Ginevra might think she's fooling me with this false sense of propriety, but I've seen first hand that she's a dirty girl.

When I grab her throat again, my thumb brushes over her pulse point. Her breath hitches, and her eyes glaze.

"Is that what you want?" I murmur against her lips.

She shakes her head, her face flushed, her lips darkening with lust. Heat rushes to my cock. My body thrums with tension, desire coiled tight. I could take her now, make her enjoy every moment of her submission, but that would be too easy.

Ginevra Di Marco needs to realize just how completely she belongs to me.

Wrong.

She's Ginevra Montesano.

Warmth fills my chest at the reminder that I've made her my wife. No matter how much she protests, she's mine until death. With no fiancé to tie her into kinky knots and no stalker to satisfy her urges, it's only a matter of time before little Ginny begs for my cock.

Releasing her throat, I step back before I lose control. Without another word of acknowledgment, I turn on my heel and stride toward the door.

The moment I step into the hallway, the cool air slaps against my overheated skin, but it's powerless against the inferno raging in my core. My muscles coil tight, every fiber of my being thrumming with unspent desire. It's a raw ache that refuses to subside. I was a breath away from claiming her, from unleashing everything I've held back, and the restraint it took has left me on the edge of madness.

I limp down the hallway, my cock pressing painfully against my zipper. I need release, and fast. But for now, I let the desire simmer, let the anticipation build.

She'll come around, and when she does, it'll be worth every second of this agony.

FIFTY-ONE

GINEVRA

I lie on my back, staring into the mirror above the mattress, every muscle in my body trembling with a cocktail of rage and something far more unsettling. My clit swells, and the pulse behind it pounds so hard its vibrations reverberate against my thighs.

When the door clicks shut, the sound breaks me out of my spell.

Benito has no right to make my body react to his hand around my throat. No right to make me so aroused. For a moment, I hoped he would throw me against the wall and consummate our marriage, but instead, he left me in this needy state.

My pussy clenches, and I grind my teeth, forcing back another surge of arousal. How dare he strip me of my dignity and walk away? How dare he talk like I'm his fucking property? How dare he offer me clothes as an incentive for being a good wife?

I clutch the edges of the robe tighter until my knuckles feel like they're about to crack. The soft fabric only aggravates my heated skin.

Benito has no right to be so arrogant.

His audacity ignites a fire that burns through what's left of my confusion. When did he become this cruel, controlling figure? I'm almost certain he got off on seeing me squirm. He doesn't get to have the last word. I need to confront him again, demand answers, and claw back a semblance of control.

I push myself off the bed, land on my feet, and march across the suite to the door. Grabbing the handle, I yank it open with maximum force.

Fury propels my feet into the hallway, but the door to the suite swings shut. Its locking mechanism whirrs, freezing me in place. Breath catching, my throat tightens with panic. I whirl around, gaping at the locked door, realizing I'm trapped out in public with nothing but this robe.

The hallway stretches out to my left and right, a long, empty expanse that may as well be the desert. I glance toward the elevator, which closes shut.

"Benito?"

He can't hear me. Shit.

Fury fades, replaced by the sensation of being exposed. Cold sweat prickles at the back of my neck, making me shiver. I need to find a phone.

The door opposite mine creaks open. That brute from earlier —the one who leered at me with the ice bucket, emerges, grinning like he's just won a prize. He fills the doorway like a troll, his gaze sweeping up and down my body, lingering on the swell of my breasts.

"Need help, sweetheart?" he rumbles with a wink that makes my skin crawl.

Revulsion ripples down my spine and settles in my gut. I force up my chin, mustering every ounce of self confidence. "My husband is around the corner, getting ice."

The tremor in my voice betrays the fear coiling in my gut, and his grin widens.

"You just got married?"

"To Mr. Benito Montesano. The casino's new owner."

"So I should leave you alone because you're a mafia wife?" Chuckling, he swaggers forward, the door to his room propped open behind him like a portal to hell.

Shit. Shit. Shit. Should I run? That would only trigger his predator instincts and make him think I'm lying.

I take a step back, the soft carpet doing nothing to muffle the thudding of my heart. The brute continues advancing, his bulk filling the corridor and sucking up all the air. My breath quickens, each inhale sharp and shallow as my lungs squeeze with alarm. I can't run, but I also can't let him close that distance.

"What are you wearing under that robe," he growls.

"Benito?" I say.

His gaze lifts toward the end of the corridor as though someone just rounded the corner. Just as I'm about to dart forward, he lunges.

I scream but a massive paw clamps over my mouth, muffling the sound. My elbow lands in his side, but he barely grunts. I kick at his shin with my bare foot, but a meaty arm wraps around my waist and lifts me off my feet.

Panic crashes over my senses, drowning out all rational thought. My mind spins, scrambling for a way out, but all I can see is his leering grin as he drags me into his room.

The moment we cross the threshold, he throws me onto the bed with a force that knocks the breath from my chest. I gasp, trying to fill my burning lungs, but terror grips them tighter.

"Get away from me!" I scream at the advancing bastard.

The suite we're in is dark, its windows obscured by blinds. The brute looms over me, his broad silhouette blocking out the light from the hallway.

"Put her down!" screams a shrill voice.

Carla, the room service woman, rushes inside with an empty bucket. Hope flickers in my chest, until the man whirls around and throws a punch toward her head.

"Wait your turn, bitch," he roars.

Carla skitters backward, the bucket slipping from her fingers with a clang. She fumbles for her walkie-talkie with trembling fingers and holds it up like a shield. "I'll call security!"

The brute's fist connects with her jaw with a sickening thud. Carla spins across the suite, hits the wall, and crumples to the floor.

My jaw drops. What the hell am I doing still on the bed, waiting my fucking turn?

Something inside me snaps, pushing away the terror, replacing it with a rush of adrenaline. I lunge for the nearest object—a glass bottle of water—and clutch it so tight my knuckles ache. Heart pounding, I scramble off the bed and raise the weapon just as the man turns around.

Hunger gleams in his dark eyes, and he bares his teeth into a sadistic grin that makes my stomach lurch.

"Nice tits." He advances on me with slow, deliberate steps, his gaze flicking down to the front of my gaping robe.

Desperation claws at my throat. I scream, but that only makes him lick his lips.

"Do you want the bottle first, or me?"

Before I can even react, he slams into my front, crushing me onto the mattress. Pain explodes across my ribs, and the air rushes from my lungs. As he pins me to the bed, I swing the bottle at his head, but he catches my wrist before the strike can land.

"I love it when they fight," he growls, his hot breath making my skin crawl.

Terror surges through my veins, powering my limbs. I thrash beneath his bulk, but he's too heavy, too strong, too determined to trap me to this bed. With my free hand, I claw at his face, but his other hand clamps down on my throat and cuts off my air.

"That's it, baby." He rocks back and forth, the movement making my stomach heave. "Lie back and enjoy the ride."

I suck in a breath but it's stuck in my crushed windpipe. I jerk my head to the side, trying to dislodge the hand gripping my throat, but his fingers only tighten. Stars dance at the edges of my vision, and my lungs burn with the need for oxygen.

If I can't muster up a surge of strength, I'll die.

Just as the world starts to fade, Carla's voice breaks through the haze. With a cry, she throws herself at my attacker and clings to his back with her arms wrapped around his thick neck. She tries to choke him, but it's like wrestling a beluga whale.

The man's head jerks to the side. "What the fuck?"

Carla's teeth clamp down on his ear. Roaring, the man lurches backward, leaving enough space for me to reach the fallen bottle.

It's time to fight back.

Fingers tightening around its glass neck, I swing the bottle on his temple with all my strength just as Carla turns her head to avoid the impact. It lands with a satisfying crack, sending a jolt up my arms.

With a pained bellow, the brute reels back, his grip on my throat loosening just enough for me to gasp for air.

"You're dead, both of you." He rises off the mattress, his hand shooting out to grab Carla by the neck.

My heart lurches as he lifts her off the floor, her feet dangling, her face turning red as she struggles to breathe. Every instinct screams at me to do something, anything, but I'm paralyzed by the sight of Carla's life slipping away.

The smaller woman's eyes meet mine, her features twisting with a silent plea for help. I can't continue being a victim. I can't let her die risking her life to save mine.

My gaze snaps to the nightstand, where he dumped his jacket. Half-hidden in the fabric and shadows is a gun. Without thinking, I dart toward the weapon and extract it from its holster, my fingers closing around its grip. By the time I turn back, Carla hangs like a limp doll, her eyes rolling as she teeters on the edge of consciousness.

"Put her down!" I scream and point the pistol at his head.

The man turns to me and laughs, his eyes dancing. "You like gunplay, baby?" He tightens his grip around Carla's throat and shakes her like a ragdoll. "When I've finished with this little bitch, that barrel is going up your pussy."

His words slam into my gut with an explosion of revulsion, but I clench my teeth and snarl, "Let go of her, or I'll shoot."

Snickering, he shifts, holding Carla in front of his head and chest like a shield.

My stomach plummets. The room spins, and the walls close in as my heart races out of control. What the fuck am I going to do now?

FIFTY-TWO

BENITO

I'm still erect as a dog from my encounter with Ginevra. My cock won't stop raging until I'm watching her through those cameras, fucking my hand as she strokes her ginger pussy.

The elevator hums in sync with the thrum of my blood, a low mechanical whir that aggravates my shaft. Need coils tighter with each passing second, every floor dragging me closer to the breaking point.

My phone vibrates, snapping my focus. I pull it out, finding a message from Malfi:

Your wife is on the move.

Adrenaline spikes. Nostrils flaring, my fingers fly across the screen, firing off instructions to Carla. She needs to be in position, ready to escalate the upcoming confrontation between my security chief and my wife.

The elevator reaches the ground floor. Before its doors even think of opening, I slam my thumb against the panel, sending it back to the top. Impatience gnaws at my gut as the metallic bastard takes its sweet time ascending.

All traces of arousal escape my cock, morphing into impending dread. The ride feels like an eternity, each second a slow torture.

Malfi had better not hurt Ginevra. He's an arrogant asshole, but how much damage can a man really do who sleeps alone with a stuffed animal? The thought would be amusing if the woman I love wasn't at stake.

My fists clench, and I glare at the polished chrome walls, which reflect a distorted image. I've never looked so feral with these sharp eyes, clenched jaw, and prominent veins.

As the elevator inches upward, my thoughts churn. What the hell am I thinking? I've been without Ginevra for five years, and now I'll resort to any method—no matter how depraved or cruel—to make her mine. Malfi's frustration has to go somewhere. He might tear her apart.

Even thinking about that bastard burns through my veins like acid. I make a mental note to myself to stop using third parties to keep her in line. No men can be trusted around her but me.

Finally, the elevator dings its arrival. The doors slide open, and I explode into the hallway in a sprint. Doors whizz past in a desperate blur. My pulse hammers, anticipation tightening every muscle.

Halfway down the corridor, the sharp crack of a gunshot shatters the air. Panic freezes my blood, making my steps falter.

Ginevra.

I charge the rest of the way, my mind a blur of worst-case scenarios. What if she's shot? What if she's dead? My entire life isn't worth living without the woman I love. With a burst of adrenaline, I slam into the door of Malfi's suite.

Ginevra stands in the middle of the room, clutching a gun. Her face is pale, her eyes wide with shock. Malfi, the dumb bastard, holds Carla's limp body in front of him like a shield.

My gaze snaps back to my wife. Her robe hangs off one shoulder, exposing darkening bruises. The hand gripping the gun shakes so hard, her fingers are at risk of pulling the trigger once more.

The sight of her beaten down, vulnerable, yet still standing, makes my heart twist. I turn to Malfi and snarl, "Nobody touches my wife!"

He drops Carla's limp body. "Boss—"

My fist connects with his mouth before he can finish that

sentence. Rage explodes in my chest, burning away any semblance of control.

Malfi was supposed to be a random creep, someone Ginevra could dismiss. But the bastard just called me boss. My fists land blow after blow, fueled by the fear that everything I've worked for is about to unravel.

I can't let her see me as a puppet master pulling strings. I need her to view me as her savior.

Each punch drives that desperation deeper, my knuckles splitting as they collide with his face. Blood spatters, but I don't care. Malfi just jeopardized Ginevra's trust in me, my plans, our future. He needs to die.

A voice screams at the edge of my consciousness, but I'm too deep in the rhythm of violence to care. The impact of the blows sends shockwaves up my arms, and my knuckles become slick with blood. The pain only fuels my anger. I pour everything into each punch—the frustration, the fear, the panic when I heard that gunshot.

"Benito!" The voice screams my name again, louder, cutting through the haze of my rage.

I freeze mid-swing, my breath ragged. Blinking through the haze of fury, I glance up to find Ginevra standing close, her pretty face streaked with tears.

"Benito, stop it. You're killing him!"

Her anguish cuts through the remnants of my anger. I stagger back, my chest heaving. Did she hear Malfi's slip up?

I stare into those wide, gray eyes, forgetting how to breathe. My mind clears, leaving only gut-churning dread. Breath hitching, I freeze, wondering if this is the moment she asks if Malfi was a plant to keep her under my control.

My eyes snap to the pistol she's still holding, its barrel pointing down at my feet.

"Give me the gun," I say, keeping my voice steady.

She hesitates, her eyes flickering between Malfi's fallen body and my bloody fists. "You can't..." Her voice trembles. "Don't kill him."

Relief surges through my system, and I exhale lungfuls of tension. Holding my features into a mask of impatience, I stretch out a palm. "Death is too good for this bastard. He needs to go to jail."

Her shoulders sag, and she steps forward, finally handing me the gun. Then she collapses against my chest. I wrap my arms around her shoulders, pulling her close. Honeysuckle invades my senses, reminding me of better days, when she was my sun, and I was her most ardent acolyte.

She sobs against my chest, trembling, and I hold her tighter, murmuring vague reassurances. Congratulating myself, I rock her from side to side, luxuriating in the moment I've orchestrated.

Ginevra now knows I'm nothing like Brisket, who would carve through a man's insides to extract his heart. I'm the man who stopped. The man she can cling to when everything falls apart.

As she cries, I allow myself a small, inward smile. Finally, I'm the hero she needs.

Just as I'm about to scoop her off her feet, she pulls back and points to Carla, who lies unmoving on the floor.

"She tried to save me," she whispers, her voice still trembling. "Please, help her."

My brows rise. This isn't the self-absorbed goddess I once knew. She's just been through hell, but her first thought is for the woman from room service?

Masking my reaction, I nod and slide the key card from my pocket.

"Go to our suite." I press it into her hand. "Get cleaned up."

She hesitates, searching my eyes. For what, I'm unsure. I offer a kind smile, the sort that conveys that I still have a heart.

"Go, so I can call the police. We don't want your name mixed up in this mess."

Features relaxing, she gives me a trusting smile before drawing back. I watch her disappear through the exit and wait until I hear the click of the suite door.

Once she's gone, I drop my mask, secure the door, pull out my phone, and dial Officer Rizzo.

He picks up on the second ring. "Benito?"

"Where are you?" I ask.

"Precinct."

"Bring Barzelli. Get a team to the Hotel Montesano. I want the police swarming the upstairs hallway."

"For what?" Rizzo asks.

"Put my head of security in handcuffs, knock on the honeymoon suite door, and demand to see Mrs. Montesano."

"Your mom?" Rizzo asks.

"Don't ask dumb questions," I snarl. "Just do it."

I hang up, shoving the phone back into my pocket just as Carla rises off the floor and scowls.

"You okay?" I ask.

She rubs her throat with one hand and crosses the fingers of another. "After this, she and I will be inseparable."

I nod. "Good work."

My gaze shifts to Malfi, still crumpled on the floor. Blood trickles from his split lip, which only ignites my fury.

"Get the fuck up," I growl.

Wincing, Malfi struggles to his feet. That beat-down is only the beginning. He's going to pay for almost jeopardizing my plans.

FIFTY-THREE

GINEVRA

I exhale the moment the door clicks shut behind me, muffling the outside chaos, but my heart thinks we're still under attack. The sunlight streaming in through the windows burns my retinas, making me squint against the glare.

Half blinded, I stumble into the bathroom. Each step is shaky as if the marble floor might give way beneath my feet. My pulse pounds hard enough to drown out all but the wet thud of Benito's fists against the brute's face.

The scene replays in my mind over and over like a horror film I can't escape.

With a shuddering breath, I grip the edge of the sink, and stare into the mirror. The woman staring back is wild with crazy eyes, a blood-streaked face, and hair matted to her pasty skin. Red finger marks stain my throat like a macabre choker.

My stomach lurches. This time yesterday, I was an attorney. Now, I've become a monster's punching bag.

That man could have—

No. I can't voice that thought.

Stripping off the remnants of my robe, I turn to the shower and twist the spigot. Water cascades from the oversized head, soothing, hypnotic, captivating, and glimmering.

I want more. I want to lose myself in its flow. Wash away the day in a scalding torrent.

Shivering, I step into the cubicle, letting the hot spray pound against my skin. The physical pain is almost a relief, giving me something to focus on other than this relentless revulsion.

Water streams down my skin, but it isn't nearly enough. This is the second time in twenty-four hours I've found myself covered in a man's blood.

I snatch the shower gel off the shelf, pour a large dollop into my fingers, and rub my palms into a thick lather. The honeysuckle scent overwhelms my senses, but nothing can chase away the tang of metal.

Steam fogs the shower walls, thick and suffocating as I scrub at my skin, trying to erase the grime, the blood, the disgust. No matter how hard I try, it's not enough. I can still feel the brute's hands around my neck, his eyes on my breasts. My ears still ring with his lascivious comments, but more than that, I see Benito's face.

His cold, detached fury as he beat that man to a pulp almost reminded me of Brisket.

At least Benito knew when to stop.

Bowing my head, I breathe hard through my relief, but I can't shake off a creeping dread. I'm safe now, but at what cost? Benito rescued me but what will he want in return?

As the water flows over my head, washing away the filth, my thoughts drift to Carla. Guilt gnaws at my chest, more relentless than the scalding water. Is she okay? Did Benito call 911 or did he just leave her on the floor to handle that bastard?

I should have done more to help her, but my mind froze with fear. I hate feeling so powerless, but in a world full of monsters, the best hope a woman has for survival is to ally herself with the strongest of them all.

"I hope she's alright," I whisper.

Benito wouldn't fire her for attacking a guest... Would he?

He was never so irrational except when it came to me.

My arms fall limp at my sides and I rest my head against the tiles. Benito is cold, calculating, even terrifying, but he's not a monster. Not like Brisket. That realization offers a small comfort, but it's not enough to silence the screaming doubts.

I rinse off the soap, turn off the shower, and shiver in the sudden silence. It's almost deafening in the steam-filled cubicle. My fingers grope for a towel, and I wrap one around myself and step into the rest of the bathroom.

The robe I left on the counter is gone.

As are all the others that were hanging on the wall.

Realization hits like a slap—Benito must have taken it. Why the hell has he stripped me of even the simplest of coverings? Anger flares across my chest, but it's swallowed by the cold reminder that I'm still at his mercy. Still trapped in this game where I don't know the rules.

I tighten the towel around my chest, every nerve on edge as I step back into the main room. The fabric feels too thin, a flimsy barrier over my dignity.

Benito stands by the bed, holding a green kimono. The sight of him, so undisturbed after beating a man half to death, makes my breath catch. He's a bronze statue with high cheekbones, a slight Roman nose, and the same well-shaped lips I once loved to kiss. The navy suit clings to his athletic frame, every fiber perfectly in place. If I hadn't witnessed it myself, I would think another man had laid into that brute.

Every instinct screams at me to keep my distance, but I force my feet forward. My pulse quickens with each step, filling my ears with a frantic drumbeat. I reach out for the proffered kimono. Its smooth fabric glides against my fingers, doing nothing to ease my stomach's twisting sense of unease. I slip it on over the towel, feeling its weight settle around my shoulders as Benito secures it with a matching belt.

He steps back, his gaze never leaving mine, his eyes tracking every movement as I pull down the towel and let it drop to the floor. It's as if he's stripping away my defenses one by one, leaving me bare and vulnerable.

Those dark eyes penetrate my soul, without a trace of the boy, or even the young man who once catered to my every whim.

Silence stretches, thick and suffocating. He keeps staring me down until pressure mounts like a tea kettle, ready to shriek. What does he want from me, an apology for leaving this gilded cage?

The words burst out before I can catch them. "Why are you keeping me here like a prisoner?"

Benito cocks his head to the side, his expression so detached I wonder if he's snapped. I search his dark eyes for a flicker of humanity, but they reveal nothing.

How can he stand there so composed while I'm falling apart?

The room spins, and my vision blurs. I sway on my feet, my strength crumbling under the weight of his unyielding stare.

"Please, Benito, say something!" My words come out desperate and raw.

Just as he's about to respond, someone pounds on the door. I jump, my hand flying to my chest, wondering if that monster has resurrected.

Benito strides over and cracks it open, blocking my view.

"This is Officer Barzelli. I'm here to speak to Mrs. Montesano."

My heart somersaults. I inch closer, peeking through the tiny gap in the door, spotting two officers dragging the brute from earlier into the hallway. He's handcuffed and swaying on his feet as if drugged.

"Mrs. Montesano died a long time ago." Benito's voice is like ice, cold and cutting.

"The young lady said that guy attacked Mrs. Montesano," the policeman snarls. "Where is she?"

Benito pauses a beat before replying. "Ask Tommy Galliano for the location of her final resting place."

The words send a chill down my spine, colder than the water still dripping from my hair. I knew Mrs. Montesano died a few years ago, but the thought that Benito and his brothers haven't found her grave is heartbreaking. Guilt clutches my chest. This is yet another reminder of everything I was forced to cause Benito to lose.

He shoves the officer back, slams the door, and turns to meet my gaze. The suite's walls close in around us, making the space too small, the air too thick. As he closes the distance, my heart gallops around my chest like a bolting horse.

"You left me once," he says, his voice glacial. "How can I be sure you won't leave me again?"

My lips part with a gasp, and my mind races a hundred miles an hour, struggling to catch up with his mood swings. Before I can muster up a reply, he turns on his heel and leaves.

FIFTY-FOUR

GINEVRA

The next morning, I sit cross-legged on the sofa overlooking the casino's fountains. At this time of the day, sunlight streaming through the clouds colors the spray a pale shade of gold.

One good thing has come from marrying Benito, apart from the obvious protection. It looks like I've made a friend. Carla, the woman from room service, stayed for breakfast and let me rub ointment on her neck. She's actually quite fun when nobody's strangling us to death.

She's a refreshing change from Martina, who hid her resentment for me behind a veneer of friendship. If she had even hinted something was going on between her and Dad, I would have intervened.

Carla bounds across the suite to the small closet beside the minibar. After flinging it open, she extracts a black box large enough to hold a birthday cake.

"Did you ever open it?" she asks with a smirk.

My lips twitch. "That toy box?"

She brings it to the low table and opens it with a faint pop, releasing the faint scent of leather and plastic. Chuckling, she sifts through its contents and pulls out a box containing a dildo.

"That's so unhygienic," I say with a shake of my head.

Her laughter fills the suite. "They come to us sealed, and housekeeping replaces these after every stay."

I snort. "Even if they're unused?"

She nods. "If you open the box, the room gets charged."

I shake my head, remembering how I rifled through its contents, looking for something to wear and finding a peephole bra and panties. The only thing I found useful was the silk blindfold, which helps block out the light.

Lunch arrives, and it's the largest, most ostentatious charcuterie board. The man from room service sets it up on the dining table, filling the air with the rich scent of cured meats and cheeses. I rise off the sofa, my jaw dropping.

"Told you it was good," Carla says with a proud smile.

I shake my head, marveling at the selection. Half the items are new to me, but I recognize prosciutto, soppressata, brie, manchego, gouda, and cheddar. Breaking up the display of cheeses and meat are tiny bowls of figs, dates, grapes, sliced apple, olives, cornichons, and sun-dried tomatoes. They've even provided condiments, a selection of nuts, crackers and baguette slices.

My hands land on my chest. This is a work of art.

"What are you waiting for?" Carla asks. "Eat!"

"You first." I sweep my arm toward the display.

Carla takes a plate and picks through the selection, careful not to disturb its symmetry. I follow after her, not wanting to make a mess. You'd think I'd be used to fine dining, but Dad kept me out most of corporate dinners. Benito's family always sat around the table and passed around bowls. Even though the food was top-tier, their style was always informal.

Once our plates are full, we take our seats, and Carla pops open a bottle of prosecco and pours us each a glass.

Watching her place a slice of gouda on a cracker without a care in the world, I blurt, "How did you do that yesterday?"

Carla looks up at me with a frown. "What are you talking about?"

I sit back, pushing a grape around my plate with the tip of my finger. "I mean, you jumped on that brute like it was nothing."

Carla shrugs, her eyes hardening. "You do what you have to."

"But he was huge," I press. "You didn't even hesitate."

She leans back in her chair, popping a pickle into her mouth and chews. For a second, I think she's going to ignore my question until she speaks. "I grew up in foster care. You either fight or get eaten alive. I guess I've had a lot of practice at not letting guys like that scare me."

Throat tightening, I freeze, waiting for her to elaborate, but she doesn't. Her gaze stays fixed on the charcuterie board, and she reaches for a slice of brie and places it on a cracker. Silence between us stretches, the weight of what she's said pressing down on my chest.

"Sometimes, fighting like an animal is the only way to survive."

She states this brutal truth as if it's the most natural thing in the world, leaving me gaping, not knowing how to respond. What the hell can I add? My problems feel so trivial compared to her childhood when mine was so idyllic.

I open my mouth to say something—anything—but Carla shifts in her seat and asks, "Have you ever tried brie with fig jam?"

"No," I murmur.

Smiling, she picks up a knife, spreads a dark substance on top of the brie, and passes it to me on a slice of bread. I take it, biting into the sweetness of the jam and the creamy cheese. After such a heavy subject, talking about food seems so strange.

"Good, right?" she asks with a wink, like we're just talking about flavors, not how she learned to fight for her life.

We sit in silence for a while, picking at the board and sipping prosecco. I can't stop thinking about how much of Carla's life must have centered on survival. Sure, mine took a nosedive when I broke off my engagement with Benito, but before that, I was a princess. I had my father's protection, his wealth, his connections.

Now, I'm tangled up in something darker than I ever imagined. And Carla's been living under that shadow for years.

I should feel guilty for even trying to compare our situations, but something in me feels connected to her. I know what it's like to feel trapped, to have to fight to protect yourself. It's primal, desperate, all consuming.

We spend the rest of the meal picking at the food and talking about lighter things—movies, books, stupid celebrity gossip. It's a welcome distraction, and for a little while, I almost forget I'm a prisoner.

Eventually, Carla glances at the leftovers and nods toward a plastic container. "Mind if I stash away some of this for my old man?"

I glance down at her left hand, finding a slender band. Curiosity scratches at the edges of my mind, wanting to know when she got married. My throat constricts. Asking nosy questions about her husband will only lead to a conversation about mine.

"Take whatever you want," I say, waving her off.

As she packs up the food, my gaze flickers to the black box on the sofa, which reminds me a little of the one Bob Brisket sent to the house. I shift on my seat, trying to push away thoughts of that monster, but they linger.

I'm trapped in this suite, married to a man who holds my life in his iron fist. Everything about my world feels out of control, like I'm teetering on the edge of something I can't escape. Even now, a part of me misses Brisket's twisted sense of pleasure.

Shit. I can't be pining for a psychopath.

"Well, thanks for the company." Carla pulls me from my thoughts and stands, clutching a tupperware box crammed with leftovers.

I smile back, though my mind is still swirling. "Thank you for everything, and for saving me."

As she reaches the exit, she turns to me, her eyes softening. "It was my pleasure. Anytime."

The door clicks shut behind her, leaving me once again alone in this suite. Forcing myself to move, I stand up and stretch, wandering over to the black box. My pussy clenches, and my fingers twitch toward the dildo still encased in cardboard.

No.

Tearing my gaze away from the offending item, I snatch the

newspaper off the coffee table and skim through the headlines. Ignoring the report about an explosion across town, I flip straight to the business section.

There's an article on the Di Marco Law Firm, reporting Nick Terranova's appeal. It says that his chances of being reinstated look good, and my heart sinks. The moment he's back in charge, he'll change its name, erasing everything Dad built. We'll lose the last remnants of our legacy.

Maybe it's for the best.

Sighing, I toss the paper onto the floor and scrub a hand over my face. Why am I sympathizing over a predator and crook? Because he's the only father I know? I shake off the frustration and roll my shoulders. Every corner of this suite feels suffocating.

I need a distraction, anything to pull me out of this downward spiral.

Grabbing the remote, I flip on the TV, hoping to catch something to give me a sense of what's going on in the world outside these walls. But all I see is the hotel's room service menu. No channels, no connection, no escape.

Fury simmers beneath my skin. They've even cut off the internet.

Stomach churning, I toss the remote. Isn't it enough for Benito to keep me cooped up in this room? Now, he has to imprison my mind?

Grinding my teeth, I yank the silk blindfold off the bed and pull it over my eyes, trying to block out my predicament. But the darkness only amplifies my thoughts, sending me careening back to yesterday.

My throat tightens at the remembered touch of the brute's hands, my lungs struggling under his crushing weight. I'm about to tear off the blindfold when my mind dredges up Benito's face.

Saved by my jailor husband. I should be furious that I'm still under his thumb, but the thought of him makes my muscles melt into the mattress. Maybe it's because I've always associated him with something pleasant—the warm, chewed-up blanket that's always there to offer comfort.

Sleep finally comes, pulling me under, but it's not a peaceful escape. In my dream, I've found my way to Brisket's lair, giving him a slow, sensual lap dance. The music is sultry, my hips swaying to the rhythm. His helmet looms in front of me, hiding his face, but his hands linger on my thighs.

Arching my back, I press my body closer to his, feeling his grip tighten. There's something intoxicating about his touch—about the way he controls me, even in my dreams.

His breath rasps beneath the helmet, harsh and ragged. The sound of his excitement sends a shiver of anticipation down my spine. Just as he pulls me onto his erection, a knock on the door jerks me awake.

Heart racing, I rip off the blindfold and sit up. By now, it's gone dark, and the view outside my window is the night skyline. The dream still clings to my senses, wrapping around my mind like a collar.

"Come in," I call, my breath coming out in shallow gasps.

The door opens, and Carla walks in, this time wheeling a tray stacked with beautiful boxes. "Another gift from the boss."

I shake off the last vestiges of sleep. Benito already took my clothes, confiscated my phone, and won't let me communicate with the outside world. He doesn't get to smooth over keeping me prisoner with gifts.

"Take it away," I rasp and wave my hand toward the door.

Carla's smile falters, her eyes flickering with concern. "You okay?"

I shake my head, hating myself for snapping at a friend. "All I want is the internet."

She shifts on her feet, her gaze dropping to the floor. That silence screams everything I need to know.

"Did my husband order you to keep me cut off?" I ask.

Carla mutters an apology, making me grind my teeth. It's not her fault. I shouldn't take out my anger on her. She sets the boxes down on the dresser and slopes to the door. "I'll leave a message with Mr. Montesano."

The moment she's gone, I launch myself off the bed, grab the boxes, and dump them in the hallway. I close the door, return to the bed, and slide on the blindfold.

Just as my mind transports me back to sexy time with Bob Brisket, the door creaks open again.

A male voice calls my name, sending my heart leaping to the back of my throat. I yank off the blindfold and sit up.

Benito stands at the foot of the bed, holding the discarded boxes. He stares at me through the dark with cold eyes. "Do you want these clothes or not?"

FIFTY-FIVE

BENITO

Ginevra lies on the four-poster bed, her kimono parting to expose legs I want to wrap around my waist. Half-asleep, she grumbles about the lack of internet, telephone connection, and underwear.

The irritation would be cute if she wasn't such a backstabber, but there's no denial that she looks adorable. Her gaping neckline reveals an expanse of creamy skin I ache to lap up like a starving tomcat, but I keep my expression detached.

After yesterday's slip-up, there's no need for me to add to her suspicions that she makes me weak.

When her complaints slow, I cut in. "Put on the clothes."

She blinks, crinkling her pert little nose, her gray eyes flickering with suspicion. "Why?"

"Can't I take out my wife for the evening?"

Her jaw drops, cutting off her complaints. Then she scrambles out of bed in a flurry of green silks, rifling through the boxes scattered on the mattress.

Maria from the Dolce Vita boutique packed all Ginevra could need for the night. She's taken care of everything from makeup to her gown to accessories. I lean against the wall, enjoying the sight of Ginevra gathering the items into the larger box before disappearing into the bathroom to get ready.

The door clicks shut behind her, and my phone rings. Since it's Gil's name flashing on the screen, I don't allow the call to go to voicemail. My brothers are both missing, and he and Reaper are leading separate search parties.

"We found your father's vintage Mercedes," he says from a noisy background. "It's the last thing Roman was seen driving. We tracked it down to a scrap yard."

My stomach drops. "What's it doing there?"

"It's been cubed."

Anxiety punches me in the chest. Glad to have the wall at my back, I ask, "Any human remains?"

"None."

Hearing that should be a comfort, but it feels hollow. What the hell happened to Roman? And to Cesare? I knew nothing good would come of turning an entire firm of assassins into a crater. Did either of them send out a follow-up crew to track down the survivors? Did either of them care?

We have so many enemies, from the Galliano family to the assassins. The thought of any of them going after Roman and Cesare sets my blood to ice. After telling Gil to double his efforts in locating Roman, I dial Reaper.

"Pull back all the men from Bellavista," I say, my voice tight. "Focus on finding my brothers."

Reaper hesitates. "What happened?"

I breathe hard, trying to stave off a surge of panic. "I don't know yet, but something's off."

Over the next several minutes, we deploy teams around key sites within New Alderney. Some of them interrogate informants, others employ drones to search wooded areas. Even our friendly cops, Rizzo and Barzelli, expand their patrols.

There's a chance that it's nothing—my brothers might be holed up with their women, too obsessed with their whirlwind affairs to care that I'm turning the world upside down to find their irresponsible asses. But they could be in any amount of peril, including dead.

Who the hell could be behind their disappearances?

The bathroom door opens, and Ginevra emerges, dressed in a deep emerald gown that clings to her curves. Her auburn hair falls in loose waves around her shoulders, and her eyes shine with a brightness I haven't seen in years. The sight is enough to stir a sense of longing deep in my chest.

Her bright smile reminds me of the girl who stole my heart. I should tell her to change back into the kimono and order room service. I should explain that something important has come up. But when she spins around, showing off that perfect ass, my pulse quickens to the point of insanity.

All thoughts of my missing brothers crumble to dust.

Then she crosses the room, encasing me in her honeysuckle and vanilla scent. It wraps around my senses, making it impossible to think straight.

"Where are we going?" she asks, that soft voice a siren's cry.

As my gaze drifts down to the nipples protruding through the green silk, I decide that Reaper and Gil can handle the search parties. In my current state, I'd only get in the way.

"Casino," I say, fighting to keep my tone steady.

I can't afford to let her sense the way my pulse races, the way my thoughts scatter with her so close. Keeping my face in a mask of iron, I hold out my arm.

She loops hers through mine the same way she did when we were younger. At one point, Ginevra knew me better than anyone. The thought of her slipping past my boundaries is dangerous.

We step out of the suite and head toward the elevator in silence. She clings to my arm on the ride down, her touch amplifying the tension coiled in my balls.

I should be thinking about Roman and Cesare, should be worrying about that cubed Mercedes, but my mind keeps slipping back to Ginevra. I've had this woman on her hands and knees, wearing cat ears and a fluffy tail, yet seeing her dressed like a lady erases everything. My entire world condenses to the way her body brushes against mine, and how her fingers graze my forearm.

The doors open into the lobby connecting the hotel to the casino. Lights glitter from the ceiling, reflecting off the polished floors and bouncing off the wall's gold embellishments.

Distant chatter beckons us forward, along with the tinkling notes of a grand piano playing Sinatra. As we continue through to a walkway above the casino floor, the air fills with a buzz of excitement, and not just from the tables.

Ginevra glances from side to side, taking in all the sights. In my periphery, I spot several men casting me envious glances, while their female companions stare at Ginevra's dress.

She's intoxicating, a vision in the midst of sin. In a world filled with nearly four billion women, my eyes see only one.

Her bright chuckle breaks the silence. "Remember when we snuck in here all those years ago?"

She nudges me with her elbow, her laugh infectious, and for a moment, it feels like old times. The two of us against the world. The weight of the years we've spent apart slips away, replaced by a fleeting memory of simpler days.

I don't let the nostalgia settle. Falling into this trap and reverting to her loyal acolyte will only get me discarded again for the type of man who would stomp over her dignity.

After all, Ginevra couldn't get enough of Bob Brisket.

Or Samson Capello.

She leans in, her lips brushing my ear, and whispers, "I used our winnings to buy that ridiculous fake diamond necklace. You were furious, but you let me keep it."

Her breath, warm against my skin, sends a shiver down my spine. My jaw clenches in a desperate attempt to keep my focus on the present. She's trying to rebuild our connection, but I know better. She will never get inside my head again.

"You were happy," I reply, my voice tight. "That's all I cared about."

Her laughter softens into something more intimate, the kind of sound that wraps around a man's neck like a garotte. She gazes up at me with those siren's eyes, dredging up the memory of her betrayal.

Despite all that, she's no less captivating.

We reach the main floor, greeted by the casino's cacophony. Lights flash from the slot machines, cards slap against tables, mingling with the murmur of voices. The casino has been reborn, becoming sleek, powerful, untouchable. Just like me. And just like this place, Ginevra will be mine again, refashioned to fit my world, whether she wants it or not.

But everything fades into background noise when she slides her hand down my arm, her finger tips caressing my skin.

"You don't have to keep me at a distance forever. We were good once, weren't we?" she murmurs, her voice coaxing.

She stops, pulling me to a halt. Her wide, earnest eyes search my face, the vulnerability in them twisting my fraying heartstrings, making me want to believe she's still the woman who once loved me with all her soul.

But she's not. She never was.

I tilt my head, my lips tightening. "We were young and stupid. You made sure to remind me of that when you left."

Her lips part as if to argue, but she can't drum up a quick enough excuse. Hurt flickers across those beautiful features as she lowers her lashes. "I tried to explain, but you wouldn't listen."

My jaw clenches, and the air thickens. We're surrounded by the opulence of the casino, but all I can focus on is Ginevra. She's right. I cut her off earlier when she raised the subject of our breakup. But the more she speaks, the more I want to open up my veins and bleed for her.

Emotions swirl in my chest—longing, nostalgia, love. My fingers twitch, itching to touch that creamy skin, to pull her close and erase that distance.

But I resist. Barely.

"Your engagement to Capello was in the papers within days of our breakup," I grind out.

Her pretty features flash with guilt before she hardens her eyes and squares her shoulders. "Do you really think I would walk away from you if I had the choice?"

I don't answer. Nothing should separate twin souls.

Remembering us means remembering everything—how her body felt against mine, how she used to kiss me with the kind of passion that could burn down the world, how she whispered that she loved me before tearing out my heart.

Before I can stop her, Ginevra steps closer, her scent—a mix of honeysuckle and temptation—curling around my senses, suffocating my resolve. She places a hand on my chest, her fingers splayed over my heart as if she's activating its rapid, uneven beat.

My blood roars, drowning out the chatter, the click of roulette wheels, and the shuffle of cards. I stiffen, every muscle tightening in defense.

"You're still in there," she whispers, her breath ghosting over my lips, close enough that I can feel the warmth of her skin. "The man who loved me."

I grab her wrist, needing to push her away. Instead, I'm suspended in this infernal tension. My grip tightens just enough to remind her—and myself—that I'm still the one in control.

"Do not mistake me for the same man," I snarl, even though every cell in my body screams for me to pull her in, to claim her mouth.

Her lips tilt into the smallest, most dangerous smile. "Good. Because I don't want the man you were. I want the one you are now."

And that's when she leans in, closing the last few inches. Her lips brush mine, a feather-light touch that sparks a fire so intense it threatens to consume us both. I want to pull back, to stop this before it goes too far—but the truth is, it's already too late.

I crush my mouth to hers, all the pent-up frustration, anger, and desire I've been holding back crashing into that kiss. Her fingers dig into my chest, and her body molds to mine, every curve igniting a thousand memories I've tried to bury. The heat of her skin seeps through the silk of her dress, searing through my suit like a brand.

She tastes like sin—dangerous, forbidden, and utterly addictive.

I let myself drown in Ginevra's warmth and scent, remembering how perfectly we fit together. It's like I'm back with the girl I fell in love with—the one who used to steal my sweatshirts, curl up in my lap, and laugh like I was her entire world.

But then reality slams back into my senses, and I tear away, my breath ragged and my heart pounding like it's trying to escape my chest. That girl I loved no longer exists.

"Don't think this changes anything," I rasp.

Ginevra gazes up at me, unmoving, her lips swollen, her eyes gleaming with satisfaction.

She thinks she's won, but she hasn't.

Not even close.

FIFTY-SIX

GINEVRA

I reel on my feet, breathless from Benito's kiss. It's been years since any lips last touched mine, and now I'm tingling for more.

No one kisses like Benito. Hell, no one's ever kissed me at all apart from him. I might have slept with Samson once and fooled around with Bob Brisket, but at least one part of me has always been faithful to Benito.

I hoped that kiss would bring something back, that it would reignite our old connection. But he avoids my gaze. His arm returns to the small of my back as if what we just shared meant nothing.

He walks me through the heart of the casino, passing workers in red uniforms mingling with gamblers in evening wear. They're a welcome distraction from the mess of my swirling emotions.

Regardless of the cold front, Benito holds me close, his grip possessive. His touch is both comforting and suffocating. How can one man offer me safety at the cost of my freedom? With the men casting him approving glances, it feels like he's parading me around as a trophy.

I glance at Benito from the corner of my eye. His jaw is set with those cold eyes scanning the casino floor. I can't shake the image of the boy who once loved me so desperately.

That kiss replays in my mind—soft at first, then fierce. My lips still burn from our connection, but the coldness in Benito's eyes snuffs out any lingering warmth. A knot tightens in my chest. Is this how it's going to be now? Him pulling the strings, keeping me close but never letting me in?

This hot and cold act is leaving me aching.

As we pass the poker tables, a small group of gamblers shoots us looks—some envious, others curious. I'm not blind to the way women eye Benito. With his athletic physique, he's even more commanding. I barely recognize him now that he owns the casino and its attached hotels.

Passing a pair of security guards built like trolls, we ascend a crystal staircase. It leads to a private dining room with a wall of glass overlooking the casino floor. The waiter guides us to a table lit with candles. It's all too intimate, too much like the past.

Benito pulls out my chair like a gentleman, and I sink into my seat. Memories flood in from dinners at our student apartment, in restaurants, at the Montesano mansion, where we were the only people in the world. Now, there's a distance between us I can't bridge.

He takes his seat, his face a mask of control, but I know Benito better than that. He's wrestling with something. I can see it in the tension in his shoulders, the way his fingers tighten around the napkin.

Pressure builds up around my chest. I should break the silence. If I don't speak now, we'll keep circling each other like this forever.

"How long are we going to stay angry at each other?" My voice is soft, but the question cuts deep from the flicker of emotion that crosses his handsome features.

When he clenches his jaw, I press on. "We were friends once, weren't we?"

His eyes darken, and his mouth pulls into a tight line. Shit. That was the wrong thing to say. He's always hated that word, preferring to call ourselves soulmates, even when we were ten.

"Is that what I ever was to you? A friend?"

The accusation lands like a slap, making me flinch. "Every good relationship is built on a foundation of friendship."

When his nostrils flare, I push back my chair and stand. My

instincts want to tell him the truth, but getting him to listen is harder than climbing a mountain. Benito sits up, his eyes narrowing. I walk around the table, place my hands on his shoulders and demand his attention.

His muscles bunch beneath my fingers, and he keeps his eyes straight ahead. Even without him looking at me, I press on, needing him to listen. The words I've rehearsed a thousand times catch in my throat. What if he looks up, and all I see is disbelief?

"My dad forced me to end our engagement," I say, my voice hoarse. "I didn't want to leave you. I never did."

Silence.

My throat tightens. "Benito. We've been together since we were eight. Who walks away from a lifetime of happiness?"

Finally, he looks up, his dark eyes piercing mine, searching for the truth. "Explain."

His voice is low, dangerous, sharp as a blade.

The truth spills from my lips. I tell him how Dad slapped and kicked me when I refused to break it off, and how he threatened to do the same to Mom. Benito's lips part, and I already know what he's going to ask. I speak first, before he can hurl the accusation. "You want to know why I didn't come to you for help?"

He nods.

"That would mean leaving Mom. I couldn't let her take the brunt of his rage. All it would take was him plying her with drink, ignoring her when she was passed out, and letting her choke on her vomit. Someone needed to make sure she didn't self-destruct."

His gaze hardens, and for a moment, I think I've lost him.

"That week, Mom was at a twenty-eight day detox retreat in Switzerland. The staff wouldn't put me through to her. I was frantic. Not thinking straight. They were all putting pressure on me—"

"Who?" he asks.

"Dad. Frederic Capello. Samson. Even Gregor."

His lips twist at the mention of the Capello twins.

"It was five years of hell," I say. "And I regretted every minute, but that engagement was the only thing keeping my mom alive."

When he glances away, my heart flips like a crepe. "Benito,

I'm sorry. I'm so grateful for everything you've done to help us, but please, stop keeping me a prisoner. I'm not going anywhere."

Something shifts in his eyes—a flicker of understanding, of the old Benito, the one who would have done anything to make me happy.

He sighs. "Go back to your seat, Ginevra."

Gulping, I retreat to the other side of the table, just as the waiter arrives with a domed tray that smells so familiar that I melt. He lifts the lid, revealing chateaubriand.

Happy memories rise to the surface like steam, making my chest swell with warmth. I glance across the table at Benito, wondering if there's meaning behind his choice of dish. "This is just like my 21st birthday. Do you remember?"

His eyes soften, and for an instant, he looks like the eager young man who bent down on one knee and asked me to make him the happiest man on earth. I resist the urge to glance at my ring finger.

Before he can answer, the phone on the table buzzes .

He glances at the screen, his face hardening. "I have to take this."

My chest deflates at the sudden distance, but I nod.

I strain to hear his conversation with Cesare. There's something about the Galliano brothers and a sister. When Cesare mentions Roman being held hostage at a BDSM hotel, my heart sinks. Whatever's happening on the other side of the line is more urgent than the moment I'm trying to salvage.

Benito ends the call, his jaw clenched. He doesn't need to speak for me to know something's wrong. When he turns to me, his face is unreadable. "Something has come up. Can I trust you to finish your meal and return to the suite?"

"Go," I say, waving him away. "Take care of your brothers."

He hesitates for a second, his eyes lingering on my face as if he's trying to catch me in a lie. I hold my breath, trying to convey my intentions to be an obedient little wife. When his phone rings again, he turns and walks away, leaving me alone at the table.

I'll finish my steak, drink my wine, and return to my luxury cage.

But first, I'm going home to pick up some clothes.

FIFTY-SEVEN

BENITO

Less than thirty minutes after leaving Ginevra, I'm racing through the Atlantic on a jet ski. The ocean's roar mingles with the engine humming beneath my feet, drowning out all thoughts of her confession.

Cesare's little assassin accelerates past, stopping at a large cruiser. Waves crash against its hull like Poseidon is awakening, but my focus hones in on a gray-haired figure standing on its swimming platform, pointing an automatic weapon into its interior. I grind my teeth. It's Matty Galliano, who was supposed to be dying or dead. Cesare must have revived him to serve as bait.

It turns out Cesare was innocent. The youngest Galliano brother murdered Cesare's ex-girlfriends to drive a wedge in the family—all because of some belief that Cesare is his biological son. I always knew my brother was different, but I'm still reeling from the story he just told me over the phone.

I don't want to dwell on how Matty Galliano became my brother's biological father. The bastard also impregnated poor Rosalind, who gave birth to Cesare's sister. She's family, even if her blood is tainted by Galliano's.

Regardless of Cesare's parentage, he's still my sibling. By extension, so is the girl he's rescuing... even if she's the daughter of Galliano and that little assassin.

She speeds ahead, just as Cesare fills his biological father with bullets. As the old bastard falls into the water with a well-deserved smack, I throttle down and steer away from the vessel. Cesare and Rosalind can handle the extraction.

This is his fight to finish, not mine.

Keeping my eyes on my brother and his assassin as they secure the cruiser, I tap my earpiece, calling Reaper on the yacht. "Keep an eye on Cesare. Make sure no one sneaks on them from behind."

"Copy that," he replies.

I reach into my life jacket, extract a pair of binoculars and place them over my eyes. Moments before we jumped on the jet skis, Tommy Galliano tried to attack from a helicopter. Rosalind took down the aircraft with one of our missile launchers, but there's no telling if the old snake escaped before the explosion.

My gaze scans the burning wreckage. The mess of twisted metal bobs up and down on the waves, threatening to sink. One of my men is en route to confirm that the bastard is finished, but I won't hold my breath.

The jet ski hums beneath my feet, but my mind is already ticking forward. I won't rest until we've confirmed his carcass. Loose ends have a habit of re-forming over time to wrap around a man's neck like a noose. Even if the elder Galliano is clinging onto life, he still needs to be neutralized. Permanently.

My phone buzzes against my thigh. I tap my earpiece again, maintaining my focus on Cesare and the boat.

"Talk to me," I mutter.

"We've found Roman," Gil says on the other side of the line.

"Where?"

"BDSM Hotel, just like you said."

My chest tightens. Cesare was right. Capello's daughter locked up my older brother and left him to rot.

"Is he okay?"

"Dehydrated but alive."

Relief surges through my system, and I squeeze my eyes shut. "Where is he now?"

"Home."

"Good," I say through clenched teeth. "Make sure he doesn't leave."

I end the call and exhale, but there's no time to bask in the relief. My gaze shifts back to Cesare and Rosalind on the cruiser. They're in a group hug with the little girl. That part of the plan is going smoothly, but I can't see the wreckage as the yacht is in the way.

Throttling down the jet ski, I let the roar of the engine fade as the Bella Lucia looms ahead. Dad's yacht cuts a powerful silhouette in the dark, its lights illuminating the Atlantic. I steer around its side toward the rear platform and guide the jet ski alongside its boarding ramp.

A crew member is already waiting, throwing a rope to secure the ski as I step onto the deck. The firm surface beneath my feet is a welcome shift from the waves.

Nodding my thanks, I turn to the steward, who greets me without a word.

"Prepare for Cesare," I say. "He might be hurt. There's a woman and a young girl with him. See to their needs."

She spins on her heel and hurries off to make the arrangements.

Taking a shortcut to the deck, I pull out my phone and call the house, still curious about Roman's condition. He already got Capello's daughter to sign over Dad's assets. For reasons I still can't fathom, he married her at the casino, then left her in the honeymoon suite to blow up those assassins. There's a chunk missing from his story, and I'm determined to uncover all the facts.

"Montesano residence, what do you want?" Sofia answers, her voice tighter than usual.

"It's Benito. Where's Roman?"

"Dr. Brunelli had to sedate him. He's on an IV."

My stomach churns. Sedation? That's not like Roman, who survived nearly five years on Death Row. Something's wrong.

"What happened?"

Sofia hesitates before responding. "He was there for days without food or water. He's disoriented, weak, and needs his rest."

I grit my teeth. "What did Brunelli say?"

"He's sleeping on Roman's sofa, just in case."

My breath hitches. Sofia ends the call, not elaborating on whether my brother's condition is completely physical or mental.

The yacht's engines thrum beneath my feet as I wait on deck, my eyes fixed on the approaching skiff. Cesare emerges from the lightweight boat cradling the dark-haired girl in his arms as if she's made of glass. She's thin, and can't be more than fourteen, but my brother gazes down at her with wonder like she's a newborn.

Rosalind emerges right behind him, scanning the deck like she's ready for another fight. My gaze flicks between the two women. The girl could be a younger version of Rosalind with the same sharp features, but something in the curve of the girl's jaw, and the set of her eyes is all Cesare.

I shake my head, wishing my brother had kept Galliano alive long enough to explain his actions. As well as what happened to Mom.

Reaper strides over, his features grave. "Drones are over the wreckage. No bodies found."

My jaw clenches. "Shit."

"Yes," he replies with a sigh. "I've got my men patching into surveillance feeds from around the marina. We don't have any footage of the helicopter's explosion."

"I was looking right at it and didn't see a parachute."

"He could have worn black," Reaper mutters. "Or just jumped."

"Or he was broadcasting from somewhere else."

"Anything is possible," Reaper growls.

It takes a split second to remember the extent of Reaper's burning hatred for Galliano. That old bastard kept his sister hostage for five years. "Keep searching. When Cesare gets a minute, he might give us a few places to look."

Reaper walks back toward the bridge.

There are too many moving parts: Roman's condition, Cesare's newfound paternity, Galliano potentially alive. Not to mention a casino riddled with scammers.

I pull out my tablet and flip through the surveillance feeds. The camera monitoring the honeymoon suite displays an empty room. No Ginevra in bed, no trace of her in the bathroom. A muscle ticks in my jaw, and I switch to the camera at her old house.

She's in the dressing room, yanking clothes off hangers, shoving dresses and shoes into a suitcase with frantic urgency. My breath stills as the image tightens around my heart, each click of the hangers echoing like a countdown.

Cold realization kicks me in the gut. Ginevra is leaving me.

Again.

A slow, burning fury coils through my insides, filling my veins with liquid outrage. I shove down the surge, molding it into something more controlled.

Turning on my heel, I head straight for the yacht's armory, my pulse pounding in my ears. Inside, I search for bulletproof armor in my size. I pull it on, one piece at a time until I'm no longer recognizable as the man who loved that little traitor.

Tonight isn't just about stopping Ginevra from leaving. It's about making sure she never escapes me again.

By the time the last strap clicks into place, the man who loved her has burned to ash. I roll my shoulders, testing the weight of the gear. It's familiar. Comforting.

Brisket is the part of me she thought she could escape. The part I discarded when she agreed to be my wife.

And there's no time for hesitation. I've already lost too much. I'm not about to lose her again.

She's about to face Bob Brisket.

And Bob Brisket doesn't lose.

FIFTY-EIGHT

GINEVRA

Hours later, after the waiter packed dinner to go and Mom picks me up from the casino, I'm back home, tossing essential items into a case. There's enough here to keep me going for at least a week.

Benito will eventually want me back at the mansion or in his penthouse, but I don't plan on following him there naked.

Our love is complicated, messy, but after tonight, I know it still exists. Benito isn't perfect. He's still hurt and with a wall of ice around his heart, but I'll keep trying.

I wasn't lying when I told him no one walks away from a lifetime of happiness. Part of him still believes in us, otherwise he would have allowed Mom and me to rot.

After zipping up my case with a sharp tug, I inhale a deep breath, brush off the remnants of doubt, and wheel it through my bedroom.

As I step into the hallway, the air feels heavy, like the weight of my past is pressing down on the back of my neck. Maybe it's because I associate this place with deception. Maybe it's because I no longer recognize it as home.

My footsteps creak on the fake marble floors, the sound reminding me of a ticking clock. I need to return to the suite before Benito realizes I'm missing. He's no longer the young man I could coax into forgiveness. This version of him is colder, harsher, brittle. He'd rather snap than wrap around my fingers.

I turn the corner and almost collide with Mom. She blocks my path, her eyes dropping to my case. "Where are you going?"

My grip tightens on the handle. "Back to the hotel."

Her expression sharpens. "To Benito Montesano?"

I stiffen. Since when did she refer to him by his full name? "Yes."

"Why?" she asks, her voice breathy with disbelief.

"Because we're married," I say. "Because he still loves me. Because he's given us a second chance."

Mom scoffs, the sound cold and bitter. "You're walking into a trap. Men aren't capable of love."

"Benito saved us from the mess Dad left behind. I want to hold up my end of our bargain."

As much as I want to tell her about Julian's death, my protective instincts rear up to stay quiet. She doesn't need to know Benito helped me cover up a murder. She'd only see that as a moral failing.

Mom shakes her head and retreats down the hallway. "Men only see women as possessions, nothing more. He saved you from the sharks because he wants to do the biting."

Her words hit like a slap because they ring with truth. Benito locked me in a concrete room on our wedding night out of spite, and I don't believe he lost my clothes.

I stare at her back, my jaw tightening. "Hey, Mom?" When she continues walking, I add, "Don't forget that Benito saved you from murdering Valentino Bossanova. That sort of thing can get a woman thrown into the electric chair."

Mom continues down the stairs, her light footsteps making them groan. I wouldn't be surprised if they weren't infested with wood worm. I'm beginning to think they're a reflection of her secretive personality.

Dismissing me with a wave of her hand, she mutters, "Like mother, like daughter."

My stomach drops.

"What does that mean?" I call after her, heat rising in my chest, frustration bubbling in my gut. It isn't like her to make cryptic remarks or passive-aggressive digs, but then she hides her true personality behind an alcoholic haze.

She doesn't answer.

"Mom," I say, my voice sharper. "What do you mean by that?"

She reaches the ground floor, saunters down the hallway and descends to the basement kitchen. It's as if she's accustomed to throwing barbs and not backing them up with words.

Leaving the case behind, I rush after down the stairs. After all the sacrifices I've made for her, I won't let this go. I reach the bottom, which is dark, save for a stream of light filtering through the front door window.

By the time I catch up with her in the basement, she's already disappearing into the pantry. I use that word loosely because it's a tall closet with shelves filled with unused appliances. She reaches behind the snow cone maker and extracts a bottle of gin.

My lip curls. I thought she said she wasn't an alcoholic.

Mom shuffles across the kitchen to the counter and opens another cupboard. Before she selects a glass, I snatch the bottle from her loose fingers.

"What do you mean, 'like mother, like daughter'?"

She whirls around, her gaze falling to the gin. "Jennifer also thought she had it all figured out. She thought Joseph loved her... but look where that got her."

The name stings. Jennifer. My birth mother. A woman I don't even remember, reduced to a cautionary tale.

"Wasn't she just a child?" I ask.

She walks to the refrigerator as if I haven't spoken, and opens it to pull out a jug of iced tea. After pouring herself a glass, she finally makes eye contact with me and brings it to her lips.

"What are you talking about?" I step closer, the pulse between my ears pounding.

She downs her glass and sighs. "Jennifer was grown when she took up with Gianni Bossanova. She thought he would give her a better life and look where she ended up."

"Murdered," I rasp.

Inclining her head, she fills her glass again. Something tells me there's more to that concoction than just sugar and tea, but she parts her lips to speak. "Men in that world don't love. They use women. Just like your father did to me. Just like he did to you and your little friend, Martina."

I stumble backward, my head spinning. "So, you knew?"

She shakes her head. "First I heard of Martina and your father was from you."

"But Benito isn't like the Bossanova brothers or Dad," I rasp. "He wouldn't hurt me."

Her gaze sharpens, her lips curling into something between pity and scorn. "Who killed Samson? Or the Capellos? Or your father? You really think those deaths came from nowhere?"

I shake my head, trying to block out her words. "It wasn't Benito."

"Someone from the Montesano family did it," she says, her voice as cold as her beverage. "Don't fool yourself into thinking he's different."

My throat tightens, the kitchen cabinets spinning with the truth of her words. "But the Capellos started the war when they killed Uncle Enzo and stole his—"

"How can you call that man your uncle?" she snaps.

Every ounce of frustration I've held in my heart from the moment Mom admitted to faking her alcoholic episodes cracks. "Where were you when Dad dragged me into criminal households, setting up arranged marriages with mafia princes?"

She rears back, hissing, "What?"

"You heard me. You didn't do anything! Didn't lift a finger to protect me! But now, you have the nerve to stand there and spew out lectures?"

The overhead lights flicker, casting shadows across the kitchen walls, making us both freeze. It feels like the house's shitty electrics can't withstand the tension.

But then the power cuts, enveloping the room in darkness.

My stomach plummets. "Mom?"

Less than a heartbeat later, a large hand clamps over my mouth from behind, yanking me backward into a solid chest. Panic slams through my heart, and I release a scream.

The gloved hand tightens, muffling the sound. I kick and thrash, but the grip is too strong.

"You owe me, sweetheart," growls a garbled voice. "It's time to pay up."

That low familiar sound sends ice down my spine.

It's Bob Brisket, and I know exactly what he's about to claim.

FIFTY-NINE

GINEVRA

Ice floods my veins, turning my insides to sludge. I freeze, my body going cold despite the heat of Brisket's chest against my back.

How the hell did he know I'd gone home?

Same way he commanded me to play with those toys. The hidden cameras. My mind spins, every instinct screaming at me to fight, to escape his grip. But he's overpowering, and I'm too weak to resist.

Anticipation skitters down my spine, making me nauseous. Have I already forgotten the way he tore out Julian's heart?

My lips part to scream again, but it comes out as a muffled whimper beneath his gloved hand. His fingers press harder against my lips, his other arm tightening around my waist.

"Shhh," he whispers, his breath quickening as if he's feeding on my terror. "You know I like it when you struggle."

"Ginny?" Mom says in the dark. "Are you okay?"

Brisket carries me across the kitchen into the landing before the basement stairs and slams the door. Its locking mechanism whirrs, making my stomach drop.

With a scream, Mom's footsteps patter closer, and she rattles the kitchen door. "Ginny?" her voice breaks through the dark, confused and frantic. "What's happening? Why aren't the lights on?"

She has no idea we're in the presence of a killer. Or that she's better off trapped behind a locked door. She doesn't have a clue we're both in the worst kind of danger.

"Ginevra Di Marco!" She pounds on the door, her voice rising with panic. "Answer me! What's happening?"

"Mom, hide!" I try to scream through his hand, but it comes out a garbled mess.

I thrash harder, using my whole body to fight against his grip. My foot connects with something solid, but Brisket's armor absorbs the blow. My nostrils fill with the mingled scents of leather and sea water, confusing my senses as he presses his visor to my ear.

"Warn her and the old bitch dies," he says in that infernal voice.

Cold panic punches me in the heart, making me jolt. He wouldn't? I shiver. What the hell do I know about Brisket except that he's a psychopath?

He chuckles, the sound menacing and low. "She can't help you now, little Ginny. It's just you and me."

His fingers loosen enough for me to take a ragged breath. I push against his arms, trying to twist out of his grasp, but he's not ready to let me go. Instead, he slides a hand down my waist, over my belly, his touch slow, deliberate, possessive.

Breath hitching, I stiffen, my entire body trembling.

"Ginny?" Mom's voice cracks, the door handle rattling again. "Say something... Please. Open the door."

Even if I could, I wouldn't. Brisket's body is a wall behind my back, his hand sliding lower, slipping beneath the waistband of my leggings. My stomach wants to churn, my mind urges me to feel disgust, but my body won't cooperate. Instead of shivering with revulsion, my skin burns under his touch, a mix of anticipation and something I refuse to name.

"Fight all you want," he murmurs, his fingers inching lower, "But Bob Brisket knows what you need."

I shake my head, squeezing my eyes shut, biting back a

protest. "Go away," I manage to choke out, but my voice cracks, broken and weak. "You're a murderer."

"But you wanted a man dead, so I killed him on your command," His fingers slide over my pubic area, the sensation making me gasp and shudder. "Doesn't that make you a murderer as well?"

My heart slams against my chest. He's twisting my words, making it sound like I ordered him to kill Julian. I can barely think straight when his gloved digit circles my clit.

Biting down on my bottom lip, I swallow back the moan, but there's no mistaking the way my body trembles at his command. Without meaning to, I relax into his grip.

"You bastard," I say. "I'm married to your boss. He'll kill you."

"Ginevra?" Mom's voice trembles. "Who are you talking to? Who's out there with you?"

"Tell her," he rasps through the helmet. "Tell her you've moved on from a mafia prince to a predator."

I stay silent, my breath coming in ragged gasps as I fight the tears pricking the backs of my eyes. My mind races. I need to break free. Need to fight. Need to stay faithful to my new husband. But all I can focus on is the way those relentless fingers continue circling my swollen clit, the heat building in my core despite the shame.

His hand tightens on my waist, holding me upright as my legs buckle. My hips—those wretched traitors— shift backward into the hard bulge pressing into my ass. I swallow back a whimper, but the sound escapes my lips.

"That's it," he growls, his voice dripping with satisfaction. "I can feel how much you want me."

I hate him. I hate him for twisting my emotions, for coaxing my body into this heinous betrayal, for knowing how to play on my weaknesses. I hate him for making me crave his touch despite the loathing that churns in my gut. I hate him for making me betray my vows.

Most of all, I hate myself even more for wanting him. For needing his touch.

His gloved thumb presses harder on my clit and a shiver of pleasure skitters up my spine.

Behind the door, Mom screeches, "Ginevra, what's happening?"

Tears sting my eyes as Bob's relentless fingers push me closer to the edge. My chest heaves, my breath coming in shallow gasps. Pleasure coils tight in my belly, hot and overwhelming.

I shake my head from side to side, trying to fight it, trying to focus on the sound of Mom's voice, but Bob's touch is all-consuming.

"You've always been mine," he whispers, his voice thick with triumph. "No one else can make you feel this way. Not even Mr. Montesano."

A sob catches in my throat because he's right. Things were never like this with Benito. He was my childhood friend, my warm blanket, my prince charming. What we had was family, love, companionship. But it was never this all-consuming passion.

The pressure builds, and my entire body trembles under his insistent touch. One hand tightens on my waist, while the other continues these torturous caresses.

My pulse pounds, and every nerve in my body thrums with pleasure. I claw at Bob's wrist, fingers digging into his thick armor. I should push him away, tell him to stop, scream for help. But it's as if rational thought has fled my mind, replaced by this all-consuming need.

I bite down on my lip, the sweet pain a futile attempt to stave off the rapid onslaught of pleasure that threatens to consume me from within.

Through the misery and the guilt, Bob's ragged breath rasps against my ear, his need mirroring my own. "Admit it, little Ginny. You want this. You want me."

"Benito," I cry. "I want my husband."

He chuckles, a mocking sound that reverberates through my ears. "Your lips say one thing, but your body screams another."

My eyes squeeze shut, the muscles of my pussy spasm and clench. Returning home was a mistake. I should have obeyed Benito, stayed at the hotel, and been satisfied with the kimono. I should have given us a chance.

"You lie so sweetly," he murmurs, his voice weaving through the fog of my resistance. "But it's time to let go."

Every muscle in my body coils like a spring ready to snap from this unbearable tension. My consciousness blurs as I teeter on the precipice of unspeakable pleasure. Mom's cries, her frantic knocking, her entire existence becomes distant.

I can no longer resist. The fingers teasing my clit quicken, becoming the epicenter of my existence. All I can think about is the man pushing me to the brink of ruin.

Then something inside me ruptures. Gasping, my head falls back against his shoulder as my body convulses with bursts of ecstasy. It rips through my core like an electric storm. With each shuddering moan that escapes my lips, I surrender deeper into this rapture.

Brisket's mocking laughter drowns out the sound of my sweet betrayal. He holds me through the aftershocks, his fingers still teasing my clit.

"You're mine, Ginevra," he says, his voice dark and possessive. "And I will destroy anyone who gets in my way."

I sag against his larger form, the last of my strength leaving my veins, the shame curling around my neck like a constrictor. Tears spill down my cheeks, hot and bitter, but I can't bring myself to move, can't bring myself to fight.

Behind the door, my mom's voice trembles. "Ginevra, please… what's going on in there?"

But I can't answer her. I can't say a word.

Brisket arranges my body on the stairs so I'm lying on my back with each tread digging into my spine. A tiny stream of light reflects off his helmet, but I turn my head, not wanting him to see my face.

"Just leave," I rasp.

His cackles echo through the stairwell.

"Did you think we finished?" he asks. "We've only just begun."

My heart leaps to the back of my throat.

I'll never escape this maniac.

SIXTY

BENITO

The helmet feels heavier tonight, trapping the heat of my body and the weight of my thoughts. But I keep it on because I need to remind myself that no matter how much I desire Ginevra, she's the worst traitor since Jezebel.

She lies on the stairs, her chest heaving, her body limp and trembling from her release. She doesn't realize it yet, but what I'm about to do isn't just for her. It's for me.

What's the point of pining over someone so fickle or treating her like my goddess when she would so easily come apart at the touch of another man?

She's so accustomed to chasing pleasure that I could never satisfy her as Benito, the virgin she discarded. I need to practice on her... as Brisket.

The air between us thickens with the sweet scent of her arousal, but my body thrums with something more. Anticipation. Hunger. Fear.

My heart pounds so hard it throbs in my throat, and for a second, I wonder if I can even go through with Brisket's demand.

Can I take her?

I swallow hard, trying to steady my breath. I've waited years for Ginevra. Years of watching her from close and afar. Years of loving her, even as she lost herself in other men. Years of imagining this exact moment.

She's mine, now. Mine via marriage. Mine via seduction. Mine via deceit. She's always been mine, even after she left.

But this is different.

I crouch beside her, my gloved hand grazing her thigh, testing the feel of her skin beneath my fingers. I've touched her before. I've felt those lips around my cock. I've felt her body tremble under my hands. But this time, I'm claiming her in every way.

Ginevra flinches at the contact, but it's not out of fear. It's a need I sense humming just beneath the surface of her skin. She won't admit it, but she yearns for Brisket. Yearns for any man except her Benito.

"You still want me," I murmur, my voice distorted by the helmet. "Even now."

A small whimper escapes her lips, but she doesn't deny it.

She can't.

I pull out my knife, which feels heavier in my grip than usual. Then I hesitate, my hand hovering over her waistband.

This is it—the point where everything changes. Once I cross this line, there's no return. The thought clings to my psyche, but I shove it aside. I need to do this. I need her. With a slash, I cut through her leggings, exposing her skin, piece by piece, watching her shiver beneath the blade.

When the fabric lies on the stairs in tatters, and all that's left of her are creamy thighs and a glistening pussy, my heart stutters.

I have to pause, to take in the evidence of her arousal. My gaze bounces to her face. She looks up at me through half-lidded eyes, her lips parted and red. Is this a freeze response? Have I frightened her into submission, or is this a silent surrender?

"You look so beautiful, lying there, trying not to beg for my cock."

"Fuck you, Brisket," she whispers.

What the hell does that mean?

"Is that an invitation?" I growl.

Hips rocking, breath quickening, she licks her lips, each movement telling me what words don't. Her need burns as hot as mine, undeniable and raw. Sensation hits me so fast, I drop the knife. It's all the justification I need for what comes next.

This is real. She wants it. This is happening.

My cock throbs painfully against my groin protector, straining to be freed. But as I unclip its fastenings, my fingers falter for a second. I've never done this before.

Realization trickles through my skull, unsettling and heavy. This is my first time. My first moment of truly being with her. Of being with anyone.

After this, nothing will ever be the same.

The weight of losing my virginity hits me harder than I expected. I wanted our first time to be on our wedding night, with me peeling off her white gown, making professions of love.

But she's no longer that Ginevra. She belongs to Brisket. To Capello. To any other edgy bastard she finds exciting.

Need outweighs my jealousy. I have to be inside Ginevra, to claim her, to finally have what I've been denied for so long. My breath hitches as I free my cock, exposing it to the cool air.

Positioning myself between her spread legs, I rub my tip against her slick, heated folds. She shivers at the contact, gasps when my crown grazes her swollen clit, and her hips rise for more.

Her eyes are on mine, wide and scared and full of anticipation. I can't help but groan.

"Is this what you want, little Ginny?" I growl. "Bob Brisket's cock?"

"Shut up," she snaps.

I chuckle, the sound bitter. "That doesn't sound like a no."

When I press my cock head against her entrance, skimming her warmth and her wetness, she rocks into my touch.

Fuck. She's slick, inviting, and so ready for me, that I can't help but let out a grunt of approval.

I swallow hard, my throat dry. Heart racing, my fingers tighten on her hips. Will she notice I've never done this before? Will she laugh?

When she makes an impatient noise in the back of her throat, I thrust forward, hard and fast, burying myself deep inside her sweet cunt in one rapid motion.

She cries out, her body arching off the stairs, her heat enveloping my cock, those walls clamping down in a way that's so tight, so perfect, that I can barely breathe. A groan rips from my throat. The sensation is overwhelming. It's more than I imagined.

I stay still for several rapid heartbeats, my cock buried deep, savoring the feeling of finally being inside her, reveling in the overwhelming bliss. My first time, and it's with the only woman in my existence. Ginevra thought she could run, but she always belonged to me.

The satisfaction of that thought falls flat, because now that I've tasted Ginevra, I would give my soul to have her again and again. I've spent years building walls, staying untouchable, yet this taste of heaven leaves me vulnerable.

Ginevra's breath hitches. Her body tightens and trembles around me as if she's resisting the urge to move. She grips the banister like it's an anchor keeping her from being swept into the waters of infidelity, but she's already drowning.

I pull back and thrust into her again, harder this time, trying to chase this incessant longing. She gasps, her body jerking beneath mine, and I keep going. We build a rhythm, each thrust delivering shockwaves of unbridled pleasure.

As I work myself toward a climax, my self-control slips.

"Who do you belong to," I growl, my voice thick with desperation. I need her to say it. To make a decision. To let me know if I'm wasting my time being fixated on a woman so fickle.

Either she doesn't want to answer or she can't. Her breath comes in ragged gasps, her body jerking with each snap of my hips.

I fuck her harder, faster, losing myself in the whirlpool of her heat, her scent, the way she fits so perfectly around my shaft. My mind tumbles, my thoughts crashing into each other like waves on a stormy sea. I lose sight of everything but Ginevra.

Through gritted teeth, I groan out once more, "Who do you belong to, little Ginny?"

Her body arches, her pleasured cry fills the air. But just as I think she won't answer, won't give me the satisfaction, she gasps out between ragged breaths.

"Benito... I belong to Benito Montesano."

Pride swells in my chest, even though it shouldn't. My wife might be unfaithful, but there's a part of her that still clings to me. Pressure builds in my core, my veins coursing with white heat. Her words are a sweet concoction that tip me right over the edge.

"Bob Brisket," I demand, my voice a ragged whisper. My hand snakes around to her clit, fingers rubbing in tight, fast circles, pushing her to the edge. "Say it."

"My husband, Benito."

Her head falls back, a strangled cry tearing from her throat as her walls milk my cock with brutal precision. She cries out with another powerful orgasm, the sound and sensation pushing me over the edge.

I follow my wife, my hips slamming into hers as I come hard, shooting jets and jets of hot cum. My entire body shudders, the release so violent and all-consuming that every nerve in my body sets on fire.

Coming down from the high, I collapse against her, but the satisfaction I expected doesn't follow. My cock twitches, but the thrill is fading fast, leaving behind a strange hollowness. I balance my weight on the stairs, my heart still pounding in my ears.

This was supposed to be perfect—what I've waited for, fantasized about for years. But instead, there's this gnawing emptiness, like I've lost something I'll never get back. My first time, and I'm no longer sure if I've claimed her or if I've given away a part of myself I can't claw back.

"Get off me," she snarls, her hands pushing on my shoulders.

I pull out, my breath ragged, my eyes fixed on Ginevra's face. Her cheeks are flushed pink, her lips swollen, but I've never seen her look so disdainful. For a second, I wonder if my helmet has come loose, but I still have night vision.

"No matter what you do, I will never want a man like you," she spits.

Even though she's talking to Brisket, I can't help but flinch. Pushing my cock back into my pants, I swallow hard, wondering what the hell I've just done.

Ginevra curls into herself as if hiding from what just happened. "You've taken what you want. Now, leave."

I stand up, adjust my pants, unable to prolong the charade.

My first time was everything I thought it would be, yet there's too much to process.

All I know is that I'm no longer the same. In taking her, I've changed. There's a part of me that feels raw, exposed, in ways I didn't expect. Like my soul is torn open, corrupted beyond repair.

But it doesn't matter.

She will belong to me by any means necessary, even if I have to burn everything else to the ground. If this is what it takes to keep her, then so be it.

"Get out," she screams.

My jaw clenches, and reality trickles back. She doesn't get to paint herself as the innocent victim, taken against her will. Despite her words, a part of her still wanted Brisket.

I crouch beside Ginevra, grabbing her chin and forcing our gazes to meet. Her eyes are distant, her breath still unsteady, and I know she's thinking about what just happened. She's replaying our first time together and hating herself for how much she enjoyed it.

"You'll never be free of me," I whisper. "Never."

I let go and step away, leaving her trembling and broken on the stairs. If Ginevra thinks she'll be able to slip back to the hotel and resume our marriage like nothing's happened, she's in for a cold, hard awakening.

Tomorrow morning, Brisket will deliver a surprise that will tie Ginevra to me forever.

SIXTY-ONE

BENITO

I step out of the car, letting the cold breeze hit me like a slap, but the burst of juniper-scented air does nothing to clear the mess of my thoughts.

My mind won't stop reeling from my first time with Ginevra. Her tight heat still clings to my shaft, and no amount of menthol can shift her aroma. I'm haunted by her moans, her gasps, the sight of her beneath me on the staircase.

Shit. It wasn't supposed to be like this—in the dark, on concrete steps, with me pretending to be someone else, taking her like some damn thief.

But she gave me no choice.

It looked like we'd reached a breakthrough after I rescued her from the brink of multiple disasters and after a pleasant evening at the casino where we'd connected. But The moment I turned my back, she left.

It was wrong, but I couldn't stop. Not when my heart only beats for her. Not when my blood only flows for one treacherous woman.

I pass a pair of gardeners at the flowerbeds, who nod a greeting. As I ascend the steps leading to the double doors, the morning sun shines down through the clouds, soaking through my armor. I press my palm into the warm wood, and it strikes me that this will be the first time I enter the house, no longer a virgin.

But I'm entering without my bride.

Last time I checked the app, she was still sobbing on the steps. I could pull out my phone and see if she's skipped town, but what's the point? Ginevra fucked another man, even after vowing to be faithful.

Granted, that other man was me in disguise, but my adulterous wife thinks he's Bob Brisket.

With a snarl, I push open the door and step into the marble hallway. Coming here alone makes the weight of Ginevra's betrayal settle deeper in my chest. I was supposed to carry her over the threshold.

Desire, dejection, disappointment churn together in a knot that tightens with each passing moment. After last night, I don't even know if I can ever look her in the eye.

Gil emerges from around the corner, his face a stoic mask. At the sight of me, he frowns but doesn't ask what's wrong.

"Roman's awake. He's in his study."

Stomach clenching at the reminder of my brother, I shove thoughts of Ginevra aside. Now isn't the time to dwell on my adulterous wife. Not when Roman is going through hell and Tommy Galliano might still be alive.

I walk toward the study, my steps dragging on the marble floor tiles. Gil follows at a distance but pauses before I reach the door. Turning back to him, I say, "Send for Cesare."

With a nod, Gil disappears around the corner, leaving me to step inside. My gaze lands on the portrait above Roman's desk. Emberly captured his commanding presence down to the sharp angles of his face.

The man in the picture looks powerful, in control... deadly.

The man slouched on the sofa in the far right of the room is a mere shell.

Roman's head hangs like he's carrying the weight of the world. He continues staring into his tumbler of whiskey even when I cross the room. A black shirt hangs off his frame like he's been on a hunger strike, and his gaunt features hang beneath three days of stubble.

The contrast between the man in the painting and the one sitting before me is like a punch to the balls.

I fold my arms, watching him swirl the glass as if the amber liquid contains the answers to his problems. The Roman who spent half a decade on death row never looked so broken.

"She locked me in that room," he mutters, his voice cracking. "No phone. No clothes. Left me tied to the furniture like a fucking dog."

My eyes narrow. "Emberly?"

Fingers tightening around the tumbler, he nods. I expect the crystal to shatter any second.

"Didn't think she had it in her," he mutters.

I step closer. "Where is she, now?"

Roman lets out a short, humorless laugh. "Probably pregnant."

My jaw drops. "How would you know?"

Leaning back, Roman drags a hand through his hair and stares up at me through red-rimmed eyes. "I tampered with her birth control."

"Why?" I rasp.

"Figured it'd give me some leverage for when she discovered the truth."

His words hang in the air, thickening the tension. I study my big brother, my mind working through the implications. That was bold, reckless even, but in desperate times, even the lowest of measures are justifiable...

Even if she was Capello's daughter.

"What made you think it would stop her from retaliating?" I rasp.

He raises his head, finally meeting my gaze. His eyes are so bloodshot, I wonder if it's more than just the booze.

"Wouldn't you have done the same if it meant keeping Ginny Di Marco?"

Throat thickening, I swallow, my thoughts shifting back to Ginevra. If I'd made her pregnant five years ago, then she wouldn't have left me for Samson. Her desire to protect that child would have been stronger than her desire to protect her mother.

Would a baby tie her to me, now? My fingers flex at the possibility.

"It's not the worst idea," I murmur.

Scoffing, Roman tosses back the rest of his drink. "My timing was fucked. She was supposed to discover the pregnancy before the revelation, but she figured it all out. Then she locked me in that fucking dungeon before I could explain why I stole her inheritance."

"You only took back Dad's assets," I mutter.

Roman sets down the glass with a clink, his features tight with regret. After several beats of silence, I cross the room, lower myself into an armchair and pick up the decanter. After topping up Roman's glass, I pour myself a shot.

Ginevra needs someone to fixate on other than her mother... or her libido. She would give her all to a helpless baby. If she can't commit to me, then she will to our child.

That's if she hasn't already skipped town. She would think about leaving, but that would leave Losanna exposed. Shaking my head, I shove aside the thought. There's more to deal with than the mess I've made of my marriage.

"You think she'll forgive you for that?" I ask, already suspecting the answer.

He leans back against the sofa, rubbing his face with both hands like he's trying to erase the memory. "Would you?"

I shake my head, not wanting to add to his misery, and keep my mouth shut. My thoughts drift back to Ginevra, the way her body surrendered to mine—to Brisket's. How she came around another man's cock, milking me to the point of insanity.

Arousal surges to my groin, making me stiffen.

What the fuck? Does that make me a cuck?

I shove away the image. Not now. I have to focus.

Roman's gaze burns the side of my face, his bloodshot eyes sharpening. No one knows I'm back with Ginevra, except maybe my cousin, since I needed a woman at my side to give the appearance of moving on. Elania mocked me relentlessly. She was the worst choice of wingwoman, but there's no way I could get Aria into a dress.

My brother's idea wasn't bad. His execution was off, but I might be able to improve on his manipulation. Pregnancy could anchor Ginevra to me for at least another two decades. That, and a touch of financial control.

But I push those thoughts aside. "Gil found Dad's Mercedes," I say, watching him from the corner of my eye. "Cubed."

His body tenses. "Where?"

"Scrapyard."

Roman sighs, his grip tightening on the glass. For a second, I think he's going to throw it against the wall. "I told her how much the car meant to me. That was probably her last fuck you."

My jaw tightens. "That was low, even for a Capello."

He shakes his head. "Don't."

"What?"

"Emberly isn't like them," he rasps. "She's good and sweet and kind. I should have explained the situation to her from the start."

"And have her run into her cousin Galliano's arms?" I ask.

"She wouldn't."

"Cesare and his little assassin were held hostage by the Galliano brothers. She told them how she left you to die. That's how he knew where to find you."

Roman sits up, his eyes widening. "She went to them?"

"They have bigger things to worry about than a penniless cousin with a grudge."

"What do you mean?"

I tell Roman everything, from Cesare's frantic phone call to what we found last night at the Marina. My men fished Matty Galliano from the water after my brother finished harpooning him to death. The old bastard's corpse is now at the crematorium, where Elania will preserve it to serve as bait for Tommy... that's if he survived the helicopter crash.

"Fuck," Roman mutters, shaking his head with disbelief.

I lean back, exhaling away the weight of our conversation. "What do we do about Cesare?"

Roman's gaze sharpens. "How does he even know the Gallianos were telling the truth about his parentage?"

"He seemed pretty convinced last night, and it explains the murders."

Roman blinks. "What?"

I recap how Leroi murdered Matty Galliano's offspring, who had stayed the night during the Capello massacre, which had made Matty Galliano desperate for a new heir. "When Cesare didn't defect, Matty tried to create a wedge between us with the murders."

Roman slumps back, his eyes squeezing shut. "But Matty?" His voice tightens, disbelief coloring every word. "How the hell, when Mom married Tommy?"

"No idea," I say with a sigh.

"Where is he, now?"

"Sleeping it off with the assassin and his new little sister."

Roman cocks his head, glaring at me for an explanation, but I shrug. There wasn't enough time last night to demand answers when we had to deploy two search parties. One for Roman, who we thought might be heavily guarded or dead, and the second for Cesare.

I wanted to ask my little brother last night when he boarded with his girls, but my concentration went to shit when I discovered Ginevra had gone home. All I cared about was intercepting her before she skipped town. After leaving Reaper in charge of the clean up, I returned to the marina via jet ski.

"When did Cesare find out?"

"We'll have to ask him when he comes."

Roman rubs his temples, the weight of the revelation sinking through all that whiskey. "So... what the hell does that mean for us?"

"He's still Mom's son," I say.

Nodding, my big brother releases a low breath, probably still reeling from the news. Neither of us speaks for a while, the silence growing heavier with every second.

"What's the situation with Tommy Galliano?" Roman finally asks.

I knock back my whiskey and grimace. "After Rosalind shot down his helicopter, we scoured the waters but found no bodies."

Roman lets out a harsh breath, shaking his head as if trying to clear the fog. "And if he's alive?"

"If Tommy survived, we'll deal with him and the rest of those Galliano bastards."

A knock on the door cuts through the tension. Gil pokes his head through. "Cesare's coming down."

I sit up. Maybe our little brother can shed light on why Mom left. It might give me an insight into the mystery that is Ginevra.

SIXTY-TWO

GINEVRA

I gaze at the bubbling fondue pot, my vision blurring.

The rich scent of melted cheese fills my nostrils, making me queasy. Steam rises off the surface, intensifying the nausea. I dip my crouton into the mix, forcing myself to take another bite, but it might as well be a hot brick. With trembling fingers, I lower the fork.

Last night, I rushed back to the hotel, leaving behind the suitcase. I couldn't sleep, wondering if Brisket would reappear.

I skipped breakfast, but now I can barely stomach lunch.

"Don't you like it?" Carla's voice is bright, oblivious to the storm churning in my gut. She dips a piece of bread into the fondue and pops it into her mouth. "You've hardly touched your plate."

I manage a smile, but it's tight and brittle with the weight of guilt pressing down on my chest. How can anything not taste like ash when all I can think of is last night? Things went too far with Bob Brisket. I can't believe my body gave into him so easily.

"Not hungry," I mutter, turning my gaze away from the platter of dippers.

Cara frowns. "You've been like this since breakfast. Are you okay?"

How the hell do I explain I just cheated on my husband? I

part my lips to respond, but the door creaks open, and Benito steps into the room.

The words wither on my tongue.

His presence invades the room like a gust of winter. In his black suit and matching shirt, he might as well be the grim reaper. He sweeps his cold gaze across the table, his features unreadable. My heart slams against my ribs, every muscle stiffening under the weight of his stare.

"Leave us," he says, his voice flat.

Cara hesitates, her eyes darting between Benito and me. Her concern lingers for a second, but she's in no position to question her boss. Without a word, she hurries to the exit.

The door clicks shut behind her, leaving me alone with Benito, and my stomach twists into knots. Silence stretches tighter than a noose, and the air becomes too thick to breathe.

My gaze drops to what he's holding—a manilla envelope—and my heart drops.

Did someone send him photos of me with Brisket?

Benito crosses the room, stopping at my table, still clutching the envelope. My pulse quickens. Every instinct in my body yells at me to ask what it contains, but I bite my tongue. I want to scream, to explain, to say something before it's too late. But my throat dries, the words caught in the web of guilt that tangles around my heart.

He knows. He has to know. And yet... he hasn't said a word.

I peer up at him through my lashes, not daring to raise my head. His face is impassive, but his eyes are sharp, watching me with close scrutiny. Curling my hands into fists on my lap, I dig my fingers into my palms to keep from trembling.

Finally, after what feels like an eternity, Benito speaks.

"How was dinner last night?"

My chest tightens. Tears prick my eyes, but I blink them back.

"Ginevra?" he asks.

"I..." My throat spasms. "I asked the waiter to pack it up."

"To eat in your room?"

His voice is calm, but the weight of his question makes my blood run cold. He knows. Knows I didn't return to the hotel. Knows I disobeyed his orders. But does he know about Brisket?

The envelope lands on the dining table with a gentle thud that may as well be the strike of a gong. Panic claws at my throat, desperate to escape, but I choke it back. My mind races, scrambling for words that might cushion the truth.

"I went home," I blurt. "To pick up some clothes. And to share the Chateaubriand with Mom. Then the lights went out and my stalker appeared from nowhere."

Benito doesn't move. He doesn't even blink. His eyes remain locked on the side of my face, waiting for my confession.

"He abducted me from the kitchen and made me," I say, the words tumbling out in a rush. "I didn't have a choice."

The silence stretches again, thick and heavy, pressing down on my lungs, urging me to spill the truth. When I don't elaborate, Benito says, "The stalker forced himself on you?"

"Yes." I shake my head. "Kind of. He seduced me, made me weak. I... I didn't know how to say no."

I can't finish. The words evaporate like the steam rolling off the cheese, as my excuses have more holes than the bread. Benito's expression doesn't change, even though I swear something flickers in his eyes. It's so dark and wounded, it might be a projection of my own heart.

He bows his head, his posture sagging. With a sigh, he picks up the manilla envelope.

"I'll annul the marriage," he says, the words sounding like a death sentence.

Without elaborating, he turns toward the door, making my heart lurch.

Panic surges through my chest. I scramble off the dining chair so fast that it falls to the marble floor with a thud. I chase after him on bare feet and grab his arm. "Wait! Where are you going?"

He turns back to me, his eyes like ice. "To file a petition with the court."

The words land harder than any blow. My heart falters. My blood runs cold. No. This can't be happening. Benito and I are forever. I tighten my grip on his bicep, forcing him to stay.

"What about the loan sharks?" I ask, my voice breaking. "And you promised to protect me from Brisket."

Benito stares down at me with hardened eyes, his gaze incredulous. "It sounded like you enjoyed his attention."

I flinch, his words cutting deep. My mouth opens, but I produce no sound. I can't argue because it's all true. I couldn't resist Bob Brisket. The man has a way of taking control until I don't know what I'm doing is wrong until it's too late.

"Benito, I don't want him. He's a psychopath. He's evil. I wouldn't..." I stumble over my words, my mind scrambling for something—anything—to convince him not to cut me loose.

His eyes narrow. "Why would I believe the word of a woman who couldn't wait to run into another man's arms the moment I turned my back?"

The accusation hangs in the air like a knife poised to strike.

After an agonizing pause, Benito breaks the silence. "I won't demand the money back from the sharks. That would leave you and your mother vulnerable. But you're free to go. Be with Brisket if that's what you want."

His rejection punches through my ribcage and snatches my heart, squeezing tight until it bleeds. Before I can stop myself, tears spill down my cheeks and land on my kimono. I drop to my knees, clutching at his pants.

"But I don't want him!" I say, my voice breaking. "Please, don't throw me away like this. I'll do anything."

Benito stares down at me, his face expressionless, but I can feel the tension in his thighs. This is no different from the time I saw him with Professor Cortese outside the Phoenix. Back then, I felt like a beggar. Now, I'm pleading for a second chance.

He snatches his gaze away from mine, as though he can't stand to look in my direction.

"Don't leave," I rasp.

"How can I keep you around when you can't stop fucking other men?" His voice is sharp, biting, each word slicing into my chest like scalpels.

I shake my head from side to side, my vision blurring with tears. "I'll never do it again. I'll be good, I swear on my life. Just give me another chance, please!"

He sucks in a sharp breath, and I take my chance. I reach for his fly, my fingers trembling as I fumble with the zipper, offering him the only thing I have left. "I'll give you anything—anything you want."

Grabbing my wrists, Benito crouches down, his scandalized face inches from mine. "Are you serious?"

"Yes!" I sob, my chest heaving. "I'll do anything."

His eyes darken, his grip tightening around my wrists. "I want fidelity. No more secrets. No more lies. No more disobedience. No more leaving."

Nodding, I choke on my sobs. "I swear it. I'll do everything you say. I'll never leave again."

But his gaze sharpens, and if anything, the intensity of his stare grows colder, more calculating. He lets the silence linger, stretching the tension between us until it feels unbearable.

"You will tell me everything about your relationship with Samson Capello... and all the others."

A lump lodges in my throat. "Alright."

"And I want the family you promised me when we were younger," he says, his voice dangerously low.

My breath catches, and I blink away the tears. "What... what do you mean?"

Benito leans closer, his lips brushing against my ear. "You're going to let me breed you again and again until you're pregnant."

SIXTY-THREE

BENITO

Ginevra is too intelligent to lie when the envelope I brought in might contain evidence of her infidelity. She won't buy my mercy with the truth.

I stare down at my wife, reveling in the way she trembles at my feet. Crocodile tears roll down her cheeks and drip on her pretty green kimono, but the sight of her misery no longer touches my heart.

This moment has been a long time coming. After watching her slither and sidestep my traps, she's finally ready to submit. I love the way she kneels before me. My once untouchable goddess, now reduced to begging.

I force down a surge of triumph, even though I can already taste the victory, and ask, "Do you agree to my terms?"

Her lips quiver, and her gaze flickers with a thought that remains unvoiced. She knows better not to speak—knows I won't tolerate another lie so soon after her admission of yet another infidelity.

"Answer me," I demand, leaning closer, savoring how her breath catches.

She nods. "Yes, Benito. Anything."

"Be specific," I hiss.

"B-breed me," she rasps, her cheeks flushing. "Get me pregnant."

Heat surges to my cock, leaving me light-headed. She's perfect like this—broken, at my mercy, her pride shattered and scattered at my feet.

But I'm not done. Not yet.

"Stand."

Relief relaxes her pretty features. Exhaling, she offers me a hand but I step back. Five minutes of begging and weeping won't erase her manipulation and deceit. Her hand falls back limp on her lap, and those vibrant gray eyes flicker with rejection.

I would smirk if my cock wasn't in so much pain.

She wobbles to her feet, stumbling before she regains her balance. The kimono slips to the side to reveal a tantalizing peek of shoulder.

"Strip," I command.

Breath quickening, she clutches its collar tighter around her neck. "Benito?"

My brows rise. "Changed your mind already?"

She shakes her head, lowers her lashes, and releases the fabric. Her petite fingers fumble with the knot at her waist before untangling the obi.

The silk kimono falls open, making my breath catch. Every urge screams at me to step forward, unwrap my traitorous bride, but I resist.

Ginevra must submit to me of her own free will.

She peels the kimono off her slender shoulders, exposing an expanse of creamy skin. I've seen her nude multiple times over the past weeks, both through the visor and on camera, but this is the first time she's stripped for me and not Brisket.

The silk slides down her body, revealing breasts tipped with pale, pink nipples I long to caress, a slender waist, a gently curved belly, and a tiny patch of auburn pubes.

Ginevra stares up at me, studying my features for a reaction. I've called her beautiful every day since she was eight and that level of simping only got me rejected. I meet her gaze with the only expression she deserves—my indifference.

"Crawl to the rug," I growl.

Her eyes widen, and red splotches of shames spread down her throat and over those luscious breasts. She hesitates for several seconds as if she can't believe I could be so demeaning, but I square my shoulders, letting her know there's no room for argument.

With a shaky breath, she kneels on the floor, her palms flat on the marble. Her auburn hair spills down as she crawls. Every movement accentuates her gentle curves, making me swallow back a moan.

Ginevra is gorgeous in her submission, and her humiliation is delicious. My gaze roves over her exposed flesh, taking in the curves doused in the afternoon light. Despite the suite's even temperature, her skin has erupted into goosebumps.

My breath quickens, and I savor every movement of her exquisite form—the arch of her back the way her hips sway only for me. The sound of her shallow breaths fills the air, drowning out the roar of my blood.

Ginevra is everything a man could desire, and she'll soon be mine in every sense.

She reaches the rug, her fingers sinking into its thick, gray pile. Her shoulders tense, her head hanging low like a dog trained to heel.

I cross the distance, taking my time, letting the anticipation mount.

Does she feel the heat building in her core? Does it burn as brightly as the blush staining her cheeks?

Pausing behind her, I place my boots inches from her bare feet, towering over her like her true master.

"Stay," I say with a smirk.

With a sob, she trembles, not daring to glance back. The fear wracking her form is more intoxicating than whiskey. I step closer, reveling in the way her body tenses at the approach of a predator.

I graze the back of her neck with my fingertips, tracing the delicate line of her spine. She shudders beneath my touch but doesn't pull away.

"If you think I'll allow you to stay without retribution, you're sorely mistaken," I growl, my hand moving lower until my fingers brush over the curve of her hips.

She whimpers.

I kneel beside Ginevra and grip her shoulder, holding her in place. "You're a traitor, and as such, will be punished."

She sucks in a breath, her body stiffening. Tension builds in her muscles, pulling them taut, and her skin prickles into tiny peaks. I let the moment stretch out, enjoying the way her breath shallows and quickens as my fingers linger on her skin.

"The next man you touch will die slowly, and I'll force you to watch, is that understood?"

"Benito—"

"Yes, or no?"

"Yes," she says with a gasp.

Without warning, I bring my hand down hard, the sharp crack of my palm against her ass reverberating through the room. She jerks forward, her lips parting with a gasp. I tighten my grip on her shoulder, not letting her escape.

"Don't move without permission," I snap.

She trembles under my hands, her pale ass cheek reddening with my mark. There's something delightful about the way her body responds to my touch.

I bring my hand down again, harder this time, drawing out a harsh cry.

"Thank me," I snarl.

She hesitates a moment before managing a strangled, "Thank you."

"Good," I whisper, my hand moving across her smooth skin with an almost gentle touch. Her back arches at the contrast of sensations, but she remains still.

I slide the hand on her shoulder down to cup her breast, enjoying the weight of it in my palm. Her nipple hardens beneath my touch, and I brush my thumb over its peak, eliciting a sharp gasp.

She squirms, trying to resist the pleasure, but I know her better than she thinks.

"Stay still." I deliver another hard spank that makes her moan. "Look at me, Ginevra."

She turns her head to the side, her eyes meeting mine. Fear shines from their gray depths, tinged with something darker. I wonder if that's because the lines between Benito and Bob Brisket are starting to blur.

"Do you understand your punishment?"

She swallows hard and nods, loosening a fresh set of tears.

"Are you sure about that?"

My hand trails lower, and I slip my fingers between her pussy lips. They're slick with arousal, even as she trembles. I drag the digits across her wet folds, making her sob.

"Why are you so wet?" I growl. "It's like you enjoy being chastised."

She shakes her head, trying to deny it, but it's useless. Her body is mine. As is her mind. I spank her again and again, harder this time, savoring the way she jerks into my side, her cries mingling with the sharp crack of my hand.

Leaning in close, I growl into her ear, "Tell me what you want."

Her body shivers, her sobs growing louder, each one a melody that fuels the heat coiling in my core. But it's not enough. I want more than her tears. I want her absolute submission. I want her to beg for me.

I rub her clit in slow circles. She shudders, her hips moving against my hand, the rhythm of her need betraying her shame. She's helpless against my touch, and I savor every second of her weakness, every inch of control.

"Speak, or I'll stop."

"Forgive me," she bursts.

"Forgiveness must be earned, Ginevra. Tell me how."

Her breath comes in short, ragged gasps, her hips convulsing with need. Without the freedom of being Bob Brisket, I might never have learned to play Ginevra's body like an instrument.

When she doesn't answer, I stop circling and withdraw my hand.

"Benito," she says, meeting my eyes once again, "Please!"

"Tell me what you want," I snarl. "Beg me."

She shivers. "Breed me."

"Tell me you want me to fuck you on this rug like an animal."

Another sob bursts from her throat. "Benito—"

"Now," I snap.

"Please," she cries, her words guttural. . "Breed me. Fuck me on the rug like an animal."

"Dirty girl," I snarl. "I'm going to pound into you until you bear my child."

SIXTY-FOUR

GINEVRA

I try to steady my breathing, but it's futile when my heart won't stop pounding like it wants to break through my chest.

Benito pulls me back into his larger body, making me feel every inch of his control. The man I loved was never so sexual or commanding, but I suspect he lost his inhibitions with that beautiful woman.

As he slides down his zipper, I ask why the hell I'm thinking of her. My clit throbs with need, and my skin becomes more sensitive with each beat of my pulse, making me acutely aware of the burn in my knees from kneeling on the rug.

I hate degrading myself in front of the only man who placed me on a pedestal. Even more, I hate how desperately I need to come.

"Please," I rasp, my hips moving from side to side.

Benito's cruel laugh hits like a slap, and the blunt tip of his crown presses against my entrance. "Are you going to take this cock like a good wife?"

"Yes." I bite my lip to stifle a moan.

Our first time together, and he's breeding me like I'm a prize bitch, yet I've never been so wet.

"Good girl," he growls, his voice rough and low. "And you're going to fucking love it."

Before I can catch my breath, he thrusts inside with a snap of his hips that knocks the air out of my lungs. The pressure is unbearable. My walls stretch to accommodate him, but the thickness of his cock leaves me gasping. It feels like he's splitting me open. I jerk forward at the sudden invasion, my nerves processing the intoxicating cocktail of pleasure and pain.

I've never felt so full, so stretched. Benito is even longer and thicker than Bob Brisket. My walls flutter, adjusting to his unreasonable girth.

"Oh, god," I moan, my fingers gripping the rug's pile.

"I prefer Benito," he growls. "But feel free to speak in tongues."

Before my body can get used to his size, he grips my hip tighter, pulls back and slams into me again, setting a punishing rhythm that has me crying out with each thrust.

He pounds into me from behind at a relentless pace, delivering equal amounts of pleasure and friction. Each thrust sends shockwaves through my core, each brutal snap of his hips pushing me to the edge of insanity.

The air around me thickens, becoming suffocating to the point where I can barely draw in oxygen. My head swims. I can't even think.

"Fuck," he groans, his voice dark and dripping with satisfaction. "You're soaking my cock. You love this, don't you?"

I shake my head, trying to deny it, but my body betrays me again, my hips moving back to meet his thrusts, desperate for the release that's just out of reach.

"Liar," he growls, slapping my ass hard. The sting radiates through my skin, but the sharp pain only heightens the unbearable pleasure building in my core.

"Say it," he commands, his thrusts growing harder, deeper. His crown grazes a spot that makes me pant and tremble. "Say you're looking forward to taking my cum. Tell me how much you love being bred."

"I don't," I manage to gasp, even as my body trembles beneath him, my pussy clenching tight around his cock with every snap of his hips.

Pressure builds in my core, threatening to burst. I clench my teeth, not wanting to give him the satisfaction of knowing I'm out of control.

"Liar," he snarls, his hand coming down on my ass, delivering a burst of sensation and sting.

I cry out, but the sound is closer to a moan.

Benito continues thrusting, his cock grazing my g-spot with devastating accuracy. My arms tremble, barely holding up my upper body, and I'm teetering on the edge, about to fall apart.

"You're going to take my seed like a dirty little slut," he growls, his voice a dark, filthy promise.

My body is trembling, and I can feel the orgasm building, my muscles tightening around his shaft. I'm so close that my eyes roll to the back of my head. The pleasure is unbearable, and I want to fight it, want to hold on to the last shred of control, but the muscles of my pussy clamp tight.

Benito's hot breath warms my neck as he continues pounding into me with violent thrusts. "Fuck, Ginevra, you're going to come."

I bite down hard on my lip, trying to hold back the overwhelming flood. Benito can't know how much I enjoy this degradation. He'll never return to treating me like a queen.

"Admit it," he hisses. "Tell me how much you love this cock."

I clench my teeth, shake my head again, trying to deny his accusation, but the sensation is too overwhelming, too intense. The muscles of my pussy tighten around his shaft with so much force that his movements slow.

Just as the first wave of climax threatens to hit, Benito pulls out, leaving me collapsing forward on the rug.

"What?" I cry out, my breath coming in ragged pants. Every inch of my body still screams with need.

"You were close, weren't you?" His voice is lower, almost mocking.

"Benito, why?"

Chuckling, he grabs me by the waist, yanking me upright, and forcing me onto his lap. I straddle him, my back pressed against his clothed chest, his erection poised at my entrance again.

He grips my hips, holding me into position. "Now, you're

going to ride this cock," he growls, his voice thick with lust. "Fuck yourself on my shaft until you come."

"Why are you doing this?" I ask.

"Because you're my wife," he snarls, positioning the crown back to my entrance. "Because you need to understand you belong to me. Because I plan on ruining you for other men."

He thrusts up into me, hard and deep, making my eyes water. I gasp, my vision blurring with tears.

Both his hands tighten on my hips, forcing me to sink lower. Each time I slide down, his cock hits something deep inside me, sending a wave of sensation that blurs the line between pleasure and pain. My thighs quiver, struggling to keep the pace with this new angle as every nerve lights up like fireworks.

"Why can't we make love like a normal couple?" I say with a gasp.

I hate that he can turn my body into something unrecognizable, but I can't stop myself. I'm already his. I always was. My body moves on its own, grinding up and down that thick cock, the pleasure too intense to resist.

"You fucking love this," he snarls. "You're dripping all over my balls."

I shake my head, refusing to acknowledge his filthy words. My sweet, dependable Benito is gone. In his place is this cold-hearted villain who revels in my degradation.

His hand lands on my ass with a sharp crack, making me jolt.

"Faster," he growls. "Ride me harder. Take everything you need, little wife."

I sob, my body trembling, but I can't stop. I'm grinding against him, desperate for the release I was denied. "Touch me… Please."

His hand moves between my legs again, rubbing my clit with brutal intensity. I can't hold back anymore. I'm falling apart. I throw my head back, resting it on his shoulder, as my hips move against my will.

"Look at you," he growls in my ear. "You're going to come all over my cock while I breed you like a dirty little wife."

I try to shake my head, try to deny him one last time, but my body betrays my will. The pleasure he delivers is like a drug, addictive, potent, rendering me powerless. My hips move faster, harder, chasing the release I can't stop. I'm so close.

"You're going to take my cum" he growls, his hand moving faster on my clit. "Soak up every drop as I breed that sweet little cunt."

His words are too much. My body shatters, the orgasm ripping through my system with brutal intensity. I scream, my walls clenching around his thick shaft, my body shaking as pleasure crashes over me in violent waves.

"Fuck, yes," he groans, slamming into me one last time.

His cock pulses in my pussy, filling me with his warm, thick cum. His arm clamps around my waist, holding me in place as he pounds upward into my twitching walls.

"Good girl. Take every fucking drop."

My ears ring. I'm still trembling, still reeling from the intensity of that climax, and he continues to fill me with his release.

"You're mine, now," he snarls, his breath ragged in my ear. "And we're going to breed like this every day until you're pregnant with my child."

I don't respond. I can't. I'm broken, convulsing in his arms, my mind still foggy with endorphins. But beneath the mist is the creeping dread that I might have sold myself to another tyrant to save a woman who might not deserve my sacrifices.

His cum leaks from my pussy, a constant reminder that I'll never escape my fate. Benito's revenge for leaving him is becoming his prisoner. Instead of shackles, I'll be tied down with children.

Shit. I don't know if I'll ever be the same again.

SIXTY-FIVE

BENITO

I ease Ginevra off my cock and back onto the rug, rise to my feet, and adjust my clothing.

She lies on her side, bathed in the sunlight pouring through the floor-to-ceiling windows. It highlights the gold in her auburn hair, illuminating her skin like she's something to be worshiped.

But she's not. Not now that I have her completely under my control.

She's ignoring my presence, a final act of defiance even as she catches her breath, stripped bare on the floor.

Silence stretches for several heartbeats, and I wait for her to speak. She doesn't look in my direction, doesn't even flinch when I shift closer. She closes her eyes, as though trying to escape from the reality of her new life.

Isn't this what she wanted? To stay married to me by any means?

I should order her to open her eyes, command her to speak. What would be the point? She's made her choice. Now, she can stew in the aftermath of her submission.

A sharp knock at the door turns my attention away from my wife. Annoyance flashes through my veins like acid. Ginevra tenses, but she doesn't move.

"Stay here," I say.

Without waiting for her reaction, I stride to the door and ease it open, coming face to face with Vitale. He stands as stiff as a soldier, his features tight.

"What?" I snap and step out into the hallway, making sure to close the door.

"Debbie Clark's daughter is here." Vitale rubs the back of his neck. "She brought some cops."

"Who the fuck is Debbie Clark?"

He grimaces. "The slot machine jackpot winner."

A sharp breath whistles through my teeth. We've had that woman locked up for days, along with the husband who made the first police report. Not to mention that maintenance man who rigged the machines, Larry Zambino. It was a problem I've been meaning to deal with before my brothers went missing.

"What does she want?" I ask with a frown.

"She claims her mother came to the casino and never returned home. She's also saying her father's missing." Vitale's gaze flicks to the side, back toward the elevator. "Now, the cops are asking questions."

I grind my teeth. Of course, they are. "Send her to one of the waiting rooms. I'll deal with her myself."

Vitale nods, but his eyes flicker with uncertainty. "And the officers?"

"Keep them busy," I reply. "Let them tour the casino floor, offer them drinks. Whatever it takes to keep them out of my way."

Vitale gives a tight nod, but he lingers in the hallway, seeming to wait for further instructions. When I raise a brow, he flinches.

"Right.... I'll make sure everything stays quiet," he says before turning on his heel and heading toward the elevator.

Once he's gone, I take a deep breath, trying to shove down a surge of irritation. It gnaws at my gut, reminding me that managing a casino is rife with bullshit. If the employees aren't running scams, then it's the patrons. Or the suppliers. It will take time to weed out the corruption but I need to remember this isn't the underworld, where relatives know not to call the police.

I glance back at the door of our suite, where Ginevra lies inside. A good husband would stay behind to administer aftercare, but Ginevra was technically unfaithful. I can't revert back to that simp she dumped without an ounce of consideration.

Turning away, I head down the corridor to handle the situation with Debbie Clark's daughter. First, I need to see how her mother is connected to Larry Zambino.

I navigate the maze of hallways, my thoughts turning back to my game plan with Ginevra. It's an improvement on Roman's attempt to ensnare Capello's daughter. My brother defrauded her of assets she didn't know she inherited. He also married her without her consent and tried to impregnate her without her knowledge.

Apart from the Brisket situation, I'm operating out in the open. Everything that's happened so far has been with Ginevra's enthusiastic consent.

Granted, my agents brought her to my doorstep. The loan sharks invented Di Marco's outstanding debt, and Valentino Bossanova had no intentions of marrying Losanna. The situation with Nick Terranova wasn't entirely manufactured. He only kept Ginevra employed at my request.

By the time I reach the back offices, the irritation curling through my gut has sharpened into anger. Anger at a bunch of assholes thinking they can steal from my casino and still have human rights.

The guard at the door stands to attention. My gaze drops to the water bottle on his belt, and I hold out my palm. Puzzled, he unclips it and hands it over.

I push open the door to the cell where we've been keeping Larry Zambino, and grimace at a burst of body odor. My brows rise. He's younger than I imagined, a weasel-faced man in his early thirties with at least three days of stubble.

Zambino jerks up from where he's laid his head on the table, rattling the shackles keeping his wrists attached to the arms of his chair. The thieving bastard stares up at me through lifeless eyes, looking like he's spent the week stumbling through the desert.

I cross the room, my gaze fixed on his trembling form, and settle into the chair opposite. When I place the water bottle on the table, his eyes widen.

"Mr. Montesano," Zambino says, his tongue darting out to lick his cracked lips. "I've told your people everything I know."

"What's your relationship with Debbie Clark?"

His brows crease. "What do you mean?"

"Why was she picked to win? Why not your mother, a cousin, a girlfriend?"

Larry hesitates, his gaze darting to the wall. I don't need to be a psychologist to know he's stalling. He's likely protecting someone because I can't see a coward like this masterminding such an audacious, multi-million dollar scam.

My jaw clenches. "Someone in this scheme will die to warn others about the dangers of fucking with the Montesano family. If you want that to be you, I suggest you continue holding your silence."

"Bellavista picked her," Larry blurts, his voice hoarse. "Said she fit the profile. Middle-aged, struggling, desperate for a win. Easy to manipulate."

"Which Bellavista?" I snap.

"Victor."

The name hits like a punch to the gut, and I inhale through flared nostrils. This man's fingerprints are all over this casino's rot, yet he's as elusive as a ghost. If I don't find him soon, then Salvatore Bellavista will bear the brunt of my anger.

But first, I need to deal with the Debbie Clark problem before it explodes in my face.

"Are you in contact with Bellavista?" I ask.

Larry swallows hard. "Of course."

With a nod, I rise from my seat. "Give us his number. You're going to set up a meeting with that slimy bastard."

I signal to the guard by the door, who steps forward to stand watch over Larry. With that handled, I make my way to the waiting room, ready to face Debbie Clark's daughter. She's a loose end I plan on tying up fast.

Minutes later, I'm at the other end of the casino—the public facing area that doesn't resemble death row. I push open the door to the waiting room and step into a watered down version of our VIP lounge.

Ceiling lights cast dim illumination over the beige decor, and the strains of Sinatra muffle my steps as I walk toward the bar. The mirror-lined walls reflect me as I continue through the narrow space, passing patrons nursing their drinks.

I spot the officers first, sitting at a table by the bar beside a blonde woman with a high ponytail. She stares at me, her eyes wide with anxiety, while her companions rise from their seats.

Neither of them are Rizzo, Barzelli, or any friendly cops who might smooth out the situation.

"Is that him?" the daughter asks a blond officer with a Village People mustache, who nods.

"Mr. Montesano," Her voice is shaky, but her pale face is set with determination. "My dad reported my mother missing. She didn't come home after visiting your casino. And now my dad's gone, too."

I lock gazes with her, keeping my expression flat. "I understand your concern. We take the safety of our guests very seriously."

She steps forward, not buying my rehearsed lines. "Don't you think it's a strange coincidence that they both vanished?"

The cops shift, their gazes sharpening. I lean forward, just enough to let them feel the weight of my presence. She might suspect I'm holding Mr. and Mrs. Clark and might even know why. If she brings up the slot machines, then she'll be the next to disappear.

"Did your father mention which date and time he came to the casino?" I ask.

Her face falls. "He went missing at home."

I glance at the dark-haired officer, my brows rising in a silent question.

He clears his throat. "Miss Clark thinks the two disappearances are connected."

"We can release the security footage from Mrs. Clark's visit, but there's nothing I can do to help with a missing person who never stepped foot in my casino."

The officers shift on their feet, at least having the decency to break eye contact. The daughter's lips tighten, but she doesn't voice a rebuttal. I suspect she knows her mother has stolen from the casino but doesn't want to admit to being part of a scam.

I make a mental note to ask both Mr. and Mrs. Clark about Victor Bellavista. If the daughter is in any way connected to the slot machines, I will use her as bait.

SIXTY-SIX

GINEVRA

I lie on the rug, my breath shallow, my body still trembling through the aftermath. The orgasm Benito gave me was powerful enough, but my soul is shaken.

A dull ache radiates between my thighs, but it's nothing compared to my spirit. Two men in the space of eight hours. Both harsh in equal measures, but only one of them is my husband.

And I cheated on him.

The thought slams into my heart like a poisoned dagger, filling my chest with an ache worse than the one in my core. My first time with Benito was supposed to be tender, warm, filled with love, not demanding, degrading, and devoid of affection.

How did I let his love for me crumble?

His kisses were like sunshine. I loved the way he'd cup my face in his hands like I was the most precious thing in the world. His touch was always so soft, so patient, never intrusive like the way it felt today. But back then, it left me sexually frustrated. This new Benito leaves me aching for his love, his warmth, the part of him beneath the layers of cold control.

Maybe his love for me is gone. I probably killed it the day I left.

The soreness between my legs flares, and I push myself up, wincing as my muscles protest. My pussy throbs, feeling raw, exposed, thoroughly ravished. With shaking fingers, I reach for my fallen kimono and pull it over my shoulders. The cool silk clings to my damp skin, doing nothing to soothe the fire burning beneath my flesh.

Cum slides down my inner thighs, sticky and warm. I swallow the lump rising in my throat. This is what I wanted, isn't it? I begged him to breed me, to keep me as his wife. Now, I have to live with the consequences.

With a sigh, I limp to the bathroom, each step bringing with it a delicious ache. Benito wasn't as rough as Brisket, and he even gave me a semblance of control. But those filthy words... I shiver, my nipples tightening. Did he have to make me feel like some kind of animal? Benito wanted me to savor every inch. To make me moan like a bitch. To make me understand that no man could satisfy me like my husband.

It was almost as humiliating as the cat ears and that awful plug.

Why the hell am I thinking of that psychopath? I need to forget Brisket ever existed.

When I reach the bathroom, I turn on the faucet and splash my face with cold water. I avoid my reflection. The woman staring back has long fallen off her pedestal. I'm exhausted from having two men in one night. Two hard, thrusting cocks. Two very different but very powerful men.

"Will you please shut the fuck up?" I say out loud and place my cold fingers on my pussy.

It's hot and wet, still sensitive from two orgasms and a hard pounding. More, if I count last night, which never happened. That's right. It was just a fever dream.

A knock at the door breaks through my thoughts. It has to be Carla, returning to clear away the tray. I barely touched the fondue. How could I, knowing I'd cheated on Benito?

I step out of the bathroom, just as the suite's door opens, and Carla slips inside. She glances at me, her brows pulling together into the slightest frown as she notices my disheveled state.

"Are you okay, Mrs. Montesano?" Her voice is soft, careful, as if she's ready for an explosion.

I swallow hard, my throat tight. No, I'm not okay. I'm barely clinging onto sanity, but what the hell can I say? How do I even begin to explain? I force a smile, but I'm certain my eyes remain haunted.

"Sure, I'm fine," I say, the words sounding distant and flat.

The muscles of my pussy spasm, making me wince. In the five years I was engaged to Samson, he tortured me with toys, dildos, all manner of objects. But nothing compares to an erect penis powered by a man's punishing thrusts.

Carla's gaze lingers on me for a second too long for comfort, but she doesn't push. When she turns back to the table and clears the dishes, I finally exhale. The silence between us hangs overhead like a storm cloud, ready to burst.

I'm aching to talk to Martina, but we're no longer friends. Hell, we never were. She blames me for Dad being a disgusting predator. And Mom wouldn't understand. She acts like my marriage to Benito is worse than murdering Valentino Bossanova or falling prey to loan sharks.

My gaze drifts to the gold band on Carla's finger, and I remember what she said the day before. I can't talk to her about Benito because he's her boss, but the words escape my mouth before I can stop them.

"Did your husband enjoy yesterday's charcuterie board ?"

She freezes, her hand hovering over the tray. For a heartbeat, she doesn't respond, and I wonder if I've crossed some unspoken line. Then she turns to me with a small smile. It's polite, but edged with discomfort.

"I'm not married," she replies.

Heat rises to my cheeks. I saw the ring and assumed like an idiot and thought we could connect. Lowering my gaze to my bare feet, I lean against the bathroom door frame.

"Sorry," I mutter, still cringing with awkwardness. "I thought the ring meant something."

"It was my grandmother's," she says, her lashes lowering. "My father gave it to me when I turned twenty-one."

"Didn't you grow up in foster care?"

She smiles. "I did, but he tracked me down."

I nod, my mind drifting to Dad, the sole reason my life is a mess. If he hadn't insisted I join his law firm with a view to inheriting it, I'd still have a job. If he hadn't bullied me into breaking my engagement, Benito would still treat me like his queen. Thoughts like this swirl through my mind, reminding me how out of touch I am with normality. Everything feels broken, wrong.

Carla finishes packing up the food, occasionally sparing me a glance. There's a hint of something in her eyes, which wavers from guilt to concern, but she remains silent.

"Mind if I take some of this for my father?" she asks, her voice light. "He's a big fan of cheese."

I give her an absent nod. "Take whatever you want."

She carries the trays to the door and pauses. "If you need anything else, don't hesitate to call room service."

"Thanks." I force a smile, but it's hollow.

Maybe I should go to bed.

Hours later, I'm in the throes of an unsettling nightmare where Brisket is pounding into me from behind. Benito watches us with cold eyes before unzipping his pants. My lips part, and my throat spasms, ready to take his cock. As he reaches into his fly, a noise from outside jolts me awake.

My eyes snap open, just in time for me to catch the door opening. Benito steps inside, still dressed in that black suit. His presence fills the room, making my pulse quicken. Stiffening, I sit up, not knowing what to expect.

He steps toward the bed, his sharp gaze slicing through my defenses. I can't tell if he's still angry or he's changed his mind about keeping me as his wife. When he sits on the edge of the mattress, my breath catches in my throat.

"How are you feeling?" he murmurs, his voice the kind of calm that makes the hair on the back of my neck stand alert.

My lips part, but I hesitate, not sure how to respond. How do I convey my tangled mess of emotions? Or the way my body still aches from being bred like a beast? Or that burning resentment of how he made me beg for more?

"I'm..." My voice falters, and I glance down at my lap, my cheeks warming. "I'm sore."

When he doesn't answer, I peer up at Benito through my lashes.

His brow lifts just enough to make me feel even more exposed. "Where?"

The question goes straight to my clit. The aching muscles of my pussy spasm, and I exhale a silent moan. Benito continues staring at me as if my life depends on this answer. Heat flares across my face, trickling down my neck and over my chest.

I don't want to reply. I don't want to admit where, or why, but the silence feels like a whip.

With a shaky finger, I point down at the fabric between my legs. My entire body is on fire, but I keep my eyes down, too humiliated to meet his gaze. "Over there."

"Then I'll kiss it better," he replies, his voice dropping several octaves.

My heart stutters, my breath quickening. I glance at Benito, expecting him to smile, look lascivious, or even hungry. All I see is that mask of stone.

Shit. What if this is another punishment? I can't see any trace of the old Benito.

"No, thank you," I rasp and glance away.

He cups my chin, and tilts my face up to meet his eyes. His thumb brushes over my lips, slow, deliberate, sending a tingle across my skin. I blink, and almost miss a flicker of the man I used to love. The gentle, kind boy who would hold me like I was his entire world.

His lips press against the side of my mouth with a tenderness that makes me gasp. He moves lower, trailing soft kisses along my jaw, down my neck, igniting every inch of skin with sensation.

My body relaxes into his touch, and I melt against the pillows. Despite the hurt, despite the fear, I let myself imagine that this is the man I've known most of my life. The one who captured my heart.

But as his fingers unravel the belt of my kimono, I know that man is gone.

SIXTY-SEVEN

BENITO

Twelve hours have passed since I walked out on Ginevra, but she lingers in my thoughts like an open wound. Her pleading eyes, the way her fingers traced my chest, the desperation in her voice—it claws at the edges of my mind.

I shouldn't let her seep under my skin, but it's already too late.

The drive to the casino did nothing to shake her hold, though I focused on every bend in the road, every turn of the wheel. But now, seated in the heart of my empire, I reinforce my defenses. Ginevra will not manipulate me with her beauty, her body, or her broken tears.

I control the progression of our marriage. I control everything, including this conference room.

Teresa Carlini, the head of procurement, sits across from me, her eyes darting between the documents spread across the table. Her son, Leo, and his fiancée, Bianca, are beside her, visibly uncomfortable. They know what's coming, though they try to hide it behind weak facades of professionalism.

I allow the silence to stretch. It gives me time to focus, to push aside thoughts of Ginevra, even if just for a few moments.

Vitale and Lorenzo stand ready with evidence of their

betrayal. My forensic accountants uncovered a kickback scheme, another drain on the casino. The guilty party's silence stretches, and I let the pressure rise, savoring their mounting terror.

But my mind drifts to Ginevra, trembling under me last night, completely undone. Blowing hot and cold worked because now I have her pleading for a connection.

Focus. There's no room for weakness—not here, not now.

"You've been generous with my money, Teresa," I say.

Shoulders tensing, her fingers tighten around the armrests. She twitches her lips but doesn't speak. A bead of sweat trickles down from her hairline, betraying her mounting anxiety.

Locking gazes, I continue until she trembles. "Five years. Four million dollars. A steady stream of funds siphoned out of my businesses, under the guise of procurement."

Her son is the first to flinch. He's younger, less practiced in the art of hiding guilt. His eyes bore into my profile, darting between his mother and my men, seeming to wonder how much of their scam I've uncovered.

"Mr. Montesano," Teresa begins, "I don't know what you've heard, but I didn't—"

I hold up a hand, making her mouth shut with a click of her teeth.

She's just like Ginevra. Full of words and emotions and raw vulnerability, wanting to talk herself out of trouble. But I'm not the same man I was five years ago. That man had his heart trampled in the dust, his family broken into pieces. That man learned from his mistakes.

"Vitale," I say.

He slides a stack of invoices across the table. "We've analyzed your procurement records. Inflated orders for premium alcohol and luxury food supplies, yet only half the goods ever arrive."

Teresa's breath hitches, even though the rest of her body remains still. "I'm..." She blows out a long breath. "I'm horrified that our vendors failed to deliver our orders. This has to be an oversight. Let me take care of it."

She thinks she can talk her way out of a multi-million dollar fraud. It's laughable.

"Four vendors under delivered large orders and you failed to notice?" I lean back, folding my arms across my chest.

Her lips move, but she fails to speak. Wise of her to remain silent. In her position, I would have left the country the moment the casino changed ownership.

Lorenzo takes over, flipping another page to show stock receipts. "Here's a specific example. A shipment of a hundred cases of premium wine, each worth $2,000. The invoice billed you for two hundred grand. The actual delivery is only fifty cases."

Leo pales. He's been quiet so far, hoping to keep his head down, but his composure is slipping. Teresa clenches her jaw, her lips pressed tight.

"Let me call the vendor," she says, her voice wavering.

"My men already had that conversation, and he admitted to the procurement fraud."

Teresa's eyes dart toward the door, as if she's thinking of running. The desperation in her eyes mirrors Ginevra's. She wanted me to stay and talk as if words might smooth over a betrayal of this magnitude.

I nod to the man guarding the exit to get the door. He swings it open, and Leonard Napoli stumbles into the conference room with a grunt. He's a beaten, bloodied man whose toupée hangs at the crown of his head like a lid.

Napoli's face is a mess of bruises and cuts, and he sways on his feet, panting and punch drunk. I don't spare him a second glance, not when Teresa's paling features are so satisfying.

"He'll tell you himself," I say, my eyes never leaving hers. "Go ahead."

"Mrs. Carlini and I have been splitting the difference on the orders," Napoli stammers, his voice thick with pain. "Half the goods delivered, full payment collected. I... I couldn't refuse. She and her son were—"

"Enough." I raise a hand. "The circumstances are irrelevant. What I want to know is how you plan to reimburse the casino."

The CEO winces, clutching his chest as if one lousy interrogation is enough to give him a heart attack. "Do you take installments, Mr. Montesano?"

"No."

He splutters. "I don't have that kind of cash. All my assets are tied up—"

"Then I'll take your assets." I snap my fingers.

Vitale pushes forward a contract Nick Terranova drew to transfer ownership of Napoli Food and Drink to the casino. "Sign this, and we'll consider your debt cleared."

He stares at the page, his lips moving as he subvocalizes the terms. The moment realization sinks through his bald head, he rears back, his eyes wide. "But my company is worth over ten million—"

I pull the trigger, the shot ringing out and making everybody flinch. Blood splatters across the table, and his scream cuts the air like a blade. Napoli grabs his hand, now a mangled mess, and staggers back toward the wall. The trio of fraudsters scatter across the room like burning rats.

My gaze fixes on Napoli, who stares back, his eyes bulging with shock. Agony twists his sallow features, his breath coming in ragged bursts.

Beneath the pandemonium, the printer whirrs, churning out a fresh contract. Vitale rises off his seat, places it on a clipboard, and presses a pen into Napoli's uninjured hand.

"Sign it," I repeat.

With shaking fingers, he grips the pen and scrawls his name. When he's finished, Vitale takes the clipboard with the attached contract and nods.

I flick my head again, ordering the man at the door to drag the whimpering CEO out of the room, most likely leaving a trail of blood across my marble floor. I don't watch them go. My focus is on Teresa and her accomplices.

Her face contorts with anguish. The expression is identical to the horror on Ginevra's pretty features when I tore through Julian's entrails. If all women are the same, why am I so fixated on Ginevra?

Despite the corporate chaos, part of me is still in the honeymoon suite, watching my wife crumble. The memory of her begging for my touch, then pleading for me to stay lingers like it's tattooed on my soul. I walked away because I needed control, but how much control do I have when I see Ginevra in the face of every woman?

"Mr. Montesano," Teresa cries. "Please, don't shoot me or my son."

The little fiancée squawks at her mother-in-law's willingness to make her the sacrifice. Suppressing a smile, I focus on my head of procurement. She's trembling, her face paling, her breath shallow. Good. She's starting to understand I won't swallow her bullshit.

"You still owe me," I say.

"Please, Mr. Montesano..." Leo tries to speak up, but I shut him down with a glower.

"Take her," I say to the man at the door.

He grabs Teresa by the arms, hauling her to the exit. One of my forensic accountants will take stock of her net assets and see what they can extract. I have no doubt she's already spent the bulk of the money she's embezzled, but no one cheats a Montesano and lives to encourage others to do the same.

She screams, pleading for mercy. Her cries bounce off the walls, but she's no Ginevra. Teresa's pain only hardens my resolve. As she disappears through the door, I gesture for Leo and Sofia to take their seats.

Trembling like a pair of junkies, they return to the table and sit. Neither of them dares to speak. I'm still holding the gun.

I lock eyes with Leo and snarl, "My accountants will calculate your share of the debt. You have until tonight to get my money, or you'll follow your mother."

He nods, his throat bobbing with a gulp, even though he doesn't stand a chance of gathering the funds. When he fails, Bianca will infiltrate the Bellavista household and sniff out Victor or lose her fiancé.

I stand, smooth down my jacket, and round the table, leaving the pair in the hands of my men. As I step into the marble hallway, my mind shifts to the next task.

No matter how far I walk, I can't escape Ginevra. Her tears, her trembling, the way she pleaded beneath my touch. She seeps into my mind like smoke, filling every breath, invading every thought. I can't shake her, can't outrun the need she's branded into my soul.

In business, I never lose.

But Ginevra could be my downfall.

SIXTY-EIGHT

GINEVRA

The next morning after Benito's rejection, I sit at the dining table by the window, staring at my breakfast. I'm wrapped in a toweling gown, since Carla took away my green kimono for cleaning.

It won't be as silky once it's back. Nothing feels the same anymore.

I give up pushing around the eggs with my fork. My appetite has turned to shit. As I trace my fingers over the rim of the porcelain cup, my mind drifts to last night.

What will it take to fix us when Benito still controls everything? He gets to walk away and toss me aside like yesterday's trash. I'm trapped here, clinging onto the last vestiges of his pity.

Sunlight bathes the honeymoon suite, but all I feel is the weight of last night's silence. I can't shake the image of Benito, fully dressed, walking out the door without a backward glance. The emptiness he left behind claws at my chest, making it near impossible to breathe.

A knock at the door interrupts my thoughts. Carla enters, carrying a garment draped over her arm.

"Good morning, Mrs. Montesano," she says, her voice bright. She places a folded kimono on the bed. It's a deep sapphire blue that shimmers in the sunlight.

My gaze drifts to the garment. It's even more beautiful than the green one from last night, but I can't muster the energy to care.

"Thanks," I mutter.

"You don't like it?" she asks.

"I do," I reply, trying to inject my voice with warmth. "I just..."

My shoulders sag, dragged down by my stormy thoughts. What's the point of getting excited about a gift from Benito when it's not given with love?

Her smile falters again, but she picks up the breakfast tray, careful not to meet my eyes. "If you need anything, just call room service, alright?"

"Thanks, Carla," I mutter.

As she turns to leave, something catches my eye—a piece of tissue paper, folded beneath my coffee cup. It wasn't there before, and I know I didn't leave it. Pulse quickening, I unfold it, revealing a single line written in hurried handwriting:

It's not safe to talk here. If you need help, order ultra glide tampons.

Freezing, I stare down at the note. My mind races with rapid-fire questions. Carla must have slipped this to me while clearing the breakfast tray. But is she talking about hidden cameras? Panic prickles at the thought of someone watching.

I stand so quickly, the chair tumbles to the floor with a crash. Pulse pounding, I head for the bathroom and sit down on the toilet.

After tearing the paper into small pieces, I drop the scraps into the bowl and flush. As the remnants of the note swirl down the drain with a rush of water, one name rises to the surface.

Benito.

He must have installed cameras in this suite.

Carla means well, but I don't need her help. Involving her in my relationship could make things worse. If I'm going to get Benito back—I need to face him.

Alone.

My thoughts sharpen with a sudden clarity. If there's one

thing I know about Benito, it's that he's cautious. He's probably watching me right now, wondering if I'm cheating.

That's something I can use to my advantage.

Steeling myself, I walk out of the bathroom and over to the mini bar, where housekeeping packed the black box of toys. I crack it open and remove the largest dildo from its cardboard casting. After tearing off its plastic wrapper with my teeth, I hold it like a club.

If Benito is watching, then I'll give him a show.

I strip off the robe, letting it fall to the floor, and walk over to the bed. My body is still sensitive from last night, still aching for him in ways I'm not ready to admit.

Lying back on the bed, I close my eyes and trail my fingers down my belly, imagining it to be his lips. I spread my legs, letting the cool air brush against my heated skin.

Wetness already gathers in my pussy, and I rub my clit, imagining my fingertip is his tongue. The bundle of nerves swell under my touch, and I shiver.

"Benito," I say out loud, my voice throaty.

With my other hand, I guide the dildo at my entrance, making sure to part my knees as far as they'll go. Picturing Benito, sitting in some kind of control room, magnifying the image, I glide the silicone object deep in my pussy.

The pleasure is immediate, sharp and all-consuming. My back arches off the bed as I slide the toy in and out, my breath coming in soft pants. Crying out, I buck my hips in counterpoint to the dildo's thrusts, wanting him to watch.

Faster, harder—I ride the edge of pleasure, feeling the tension coil in my belly, tighter and tighter until it snaps. My orgasm rips through my core, and I moan his name through the spasms.

Before I can catch my breath, the door creaks open. My heart skips a beat, but I don't dare lift my head. Benito stands at the foot of the bed, his eyes dark, predatory, and furious.

"Speak of the devil," I say with a groan.

"What the hell do you think you're doing?" His gaze flicks to the new silk kimono hanging on the closet door, untouched.

"You walked out on me last night without leaving me a forwarding number. We haven't finished talking."

He crosses his arms, his eyes narrowing. "So, this is how you start a conversation? Naked and waiting?"

"How else would I get your attention?" I sit up, drawing my knees to my chest, my confidence wavering.

Benito shakes his head, his lips tightening. He turns like he's about to leave, and panic spikes through my chest. I can't let him go—not again. I leap off the bed, my feet hitting the cold marble, and launch myself at his back.

The last time I did that, he stumbled forward. Admittedly, we were twelve. Now, he's as immovable as an iceberg, except he's still heading toward the door.

"Don't tell me you're walking away from this morning's breeding," I say, my legs wrapping around his broad back.

Benito stops.

Shoulders stiffening, a muscle on the side of his jaw ticks. With a snarl, he peels me off his back and sets me on the floor. But at least he isn't moving. Instead, he glares down at me with those cold, calculating eyes that once shone with warmth .

I meet his gaze, forcing myself not to shiver.

"Return to the bed on all fours," he orders.

"No. I want it face to face." My fingers grab the waistband of his pants, and I tug him backward toward the bed. "We do this like a married couple."

His eyes flash with fury, but he lets me drag him closer. When the backs of my knees hit the edge of the mattress, I place my hands on his shoulders and push him down to sit. He stares up at me, those hard eyes burning into mine, but I refuse to back down.

I kneel between his legs and gaze up into his stony features, reminding myself this is my Benito. Beneath that cold exterior is a man who doesn't want to see me hurt. A man who wants me to bear his children. I just need to make more of an effort to draw out the love.

My fingers work to unbutton his fly, but his hand shoots out and seizes my wrist.

"Straddle me."

My brow pinches. That's the second time he's stopped me from pulling out his cock. Is it scarred or is he shy? A lump forms in my throat as another possibility floats to the front of my mind. What if my affair with Bob Brisket has made Benito insecure?

Pushing back a surge of guilt, I rise to my feet, swinging a leg over his hips, followed by the next, and straddle his lap. My lips are so close to his that we're sharing the same air, and I lean forward for a kiss.

"No."

My stomach dips. I force my gaze to remain on his, even through the sting of yet another rejection.

Benito reaches between our bodies, unzips his fly, and pulls out his cock. Its tip rests against my inner thigh, long and thick and hard, radiating a surge of heat that makes me pant.

He holds my hips, positioning me just above his crown, and grips his length at its base. Anticipation sizzles between us like static electricity, making the muscles of my pussy convulse. Holding onto his shoulders, I lower myself down on his shaft, inch by thickening inch, until he's fully sheathed.

The stretch is incredible, and I can't help but moan. Benito remains poker faced, until my muscles clamp down on his length.

His eyes flicker with emotion, and I track every infinitesimal shift in his expression. He's furious, I can feel it, but he won't shove me off. At least not until he's come.

"I've been waiting for this," I whisper against his lips. "Ever since you proposed, I've wanted you. Fucking you is like winning the jackpot."

His jaw tightens, as does his grip on my hip. He grinds into my pussy and snarls, "We're married. You were always going to get sex."

I lean in, pressing my forehead to his, my hands cupping his jaw and forcing our eyes to meet. "I don't just want to be your wife. I want to be your best friend, the way we were before I ruined everything."

His thrusts falter for a second, his breath coming out harsher, and I know I've struck a nerve. But he recovers, his eyes hardening once more as he grips my waist and drives into me with more force.

Ecstasy explodes across my core, drawing out a gasp. I throw my head backward, just as he finally begins to speak.

"You can't fix this with words." His voice is like gravel, rough and unforgiving.

"I know I betrayed you, but I want us back. I never stopped loving you."

He scoffs, his hands tightening around my waist as he holds me steady, thrusting up into me with a controlled frenzy that leaves me breathless. "How can I believe a word you say?" His words are a snarl, his breath hot against my skin. "Less than forty-eight hours after you fucked another man?"

Tears prick at the corners of my eyes, but I blink them away. "It was a mistake. I'm sorry."

He pounds up harder, his body tense beneath mine, as if trying to punish me for every word. But I don't back down. I meet his gaze, my hands still cradling his face, my body trembling with every movement.

"I love how you make me feel," I continue, my voice hoarse. "Even when you're cold and cruel... you always make me feel alive."

His breath quickens, and I see something flicker in his eyes, but it's gone just as quickly, replaced by that familiar hard shell.

"What the hell do you want from me, Ginevra?" he grinds out, his body tight with tension.

"Remember who we were, what we had," I whisper, running my trembling fingers over his chest. "That future we imagined when we were kids. I don't care what it takes. I'll fight for it. Fight for us."

His eyes narrow, his grip tightening on my waist as he thrusts into me one last time, hard enough to knock the breath from my lungs. He doesn't say anything, doesn't make any promises. He just stares at me, his gaze burning with something I can't quite name.

But I know I've gotten through to him. I can feel it in the way his body responds to mine, in the way his grip around my hips softens, so it's no longer punishing.

"You're mine," he growls, his voice low and dangerous.

"Yours," I whisper back, my heart pounding against his. "Always."

SIXTY-NINE

BENITO

Hours later, I'm crouched behind an abandoned brick building, hidden in the dark. Larry Zambino is pacing beneath a flickering streetlight at the other end of the alley. The slot-machine-tampering bastard is waiting for Victor Bellavista.

Reaper kneels at my side, scanning the street. The rest of the crew is scattered, tucked away behind dumpsters, corners, and abandoned cars, waiting for the moment to strike.

So far, Victor Bellavista has been a ghost. Counterfeit chips, rigged slots, and a host of scams we've yet to uncover. The man has had his hands in my business for too long, and I'll make him bleed out every stolen cent.

Despite the urgency of tonight, I can't stop thinking about Ginevra, and how she lured me into that ambush. She kept me hostage with her tight cunt, squeezing the life out of my cock while she filled my ears with honeyed words. Words I've longed to hear the entire time we were apart. Words that went straight to my heart.

By the time I climaxed, I was ready to fall to my knees and beg for her forgiveness. My jaw tightens. I'm powerless against that wretched woman.

Reaper claps a hand on my shoulder, breaking me out of my thoughts. "Married life getting to you?"

"Not now," I snap.

He snorts, but the fact he noticed means I'm already slipping. "Zambino looks like he's about to piss his pants."

I grunt, my hand tightening on my pistol. It's not just Zambino's nerves—it's the whole setup. The air feels too still, too quiet, like the city is holding its breath.

A car rumbles, and I turn just in time to see headlights slicing through the darkness. It pulls up to Zambino, the low hum of the engine growing louder, more menacing. Relaxing, Zambino steps toward the passenger window.

As it rolls down, his features slacken with shock. Before he can even utter a word, gunfire erupts, filling the street with a staccato crack of bullets. Zambino drops to the pavement, bleeding through multiple wounds.

"Shit!" I sprint to my car, my boots slamming against the pavement as I bark orders into my earpiece. "After them! Don't let that car leave the city."

I slide behind the wheel as Reaper dives into the passenger seat. The engine snarls awake, and my men emerge from the shadows, their tires screaming as they tear through the alley. I hit the gas, reveling in the surge of power. That bastard isn't escaping. Not tonight.

My grip tightens on the wheel as I give chase, navigating each turn, my tires spitting sparks on the asphalt. Adrenaline hums through my system, but it's the cold burn of rage that keeps me focused.

The flash of confusion in Zambino's eyes tells me Victor sent someone else. Someone who wasn't planning on Zambino the rendezvous leaving alive.

I yank the wheel hard, swerving the car around a corner, narrowly missing a heap of trash. The car ahead fishtails, clipping a dumpster, sending out explosions of debris. They're panicking. But every wild swerve, every mistake, only brings me closer. The noose is tightening.

Reaper pulls out a control pad and taps on its screen. "Deploying drones," he says. Seconds later, I catch sight of the aerial hunters pursuing the fleeing car. "They're ready to fire on your command."

The killer's vehicle takes another sharp turn, scraping against a brick wall with a metallic squeal. Jaw clenching, I lean forward. They're getting reckless. Desperate.

On the next bend, the driver's tires screech against wet asphalt. The car fishtails before slamming into a wall with a satisfying crunch. Its hood crumples like an accordion, billowing clouds of steam.

I slam on the brakes. Before the engine stops sputtering, I'm out, gun drawn, and heading to the wreckage. Heart pounding, I approach the car, my boots crunching over the broken glass, my eyes locked on the driver's door.

"Secure the area!" I snap, gesturing at my men to fan out and cover every angle.

Reaper moves in first, yanking open the driver's door. A middle-aged woman collapses onto the pavement, her bruised face hitting the ground with a thud.

Not what I expected.

Reaper crouches down to check her pulse. "She's alive."

"Who the fuck is she?" I mutter, my gaze flicking to a half-packed duffle bag on the front passenger seat.

"Makes no sense," Reaper mutters.

I clench my jaw, my patience close to snapping. This wasn't the plan. Victor was supposed to be here, and now we're left with a half-dead woman and no answers.

"Get her in a van," I snap and step back to scan the area for any more surprises. "Search every inch of that car. I don't care if it's a gum wrapper. I want to know everything."

As my men move in to lift the woman, a streetwalker steps out from around the corner. Clad in a leopard-print mini skirt and a fake fur jacket, her heels click against the pavement, and her hips sway like she's still on the clock. Her sharp eyes flick between the wrecked car and the unconscious woman.

"Rough night, huh?" she says with a sly grin. "I could call the cops, or you could make it worth my time to forget what I saw."

"Get the hell out of here," I snap.

Her gaze flickers to my chest as if she can see through the armor. Before I can deal with her, Reaper staggers backward with a shout.

"We've got a problem!"

I turn just in time to see him pull a digital device out of the woman's purse, resembling a bomb. The countdown is already ticking with thirty seconds left on the clock.

"Everyone, move!" I yell. "Reaper, get her out of here!"

Reaper scoops up the unconscious woman and runs with the other men. The streetwalker stands rooted to the spot, her eyes wide and paralyzed with fear.

"Move!" I grab her arm, but she's frozen.

With a curse, I throw her over my shoulder and charge to the end of the alley. She screams, but it's drowned out by the roar of the explosion.

We barely make it to safety when another blast tears through the night like it's Armageddon. Flames and debris rain down, lighting up the sky. I duck behind a wall, releasing the streetwalker who gasps and tries to escape.

"Stay down," I growl, stopping her from scrambling back toward danger.

Her earlier confidence is gone, replaced with wide-eyed terror. She says nothing—just nods, her knees buckling, her chest heaving like she's about to give birth.

I pull out a handful of bills from my pocket and shove them into her trembling hands. "Breathe a word about this and I'll blow you to pieces. Now, get the fuck out of here."

She sprints around the corner like there's another explosion on her back. Smart woman.

By the time I reach Reaper and the others, the wreckage is still burning in the distance, casting an eerie glow over the street. The middle-aged woman Reaper rescued is laid out on a stretcher, unconscious but breathing, her clothes stained with blood. Medics work on stabilizing her under his supervision.

This is no contract killer. Every assassin I know has mastered the fine art of escape. I turn to the medic. "Can you wake her?"

"This stimulant will do it." He pulls out a syringe and injects clear fluid into her arm.

A few tense seconds pass before she stirs, her face contorting with agony. Her eyes flutter open, and she stares up at us, confused and disoriented.

Reaper holds her steady as she tries to sit up, and I crouch down, forcing our gazes to meet.

"Who are you? Why the hell was there a bomb in your car?"

Blinking rapidly, she breathes hard. Fear flashes across her eyes, which only sharpens when she sees my gun.

"Victor Bellavista took my daughter." She chokes out a sob. "He said if I didn't do what he asked, he'd kill her."

I signal to Reaper. "See if she can identify him."

Reaper digs into his jacket pocket, pulling out a tablet. He swipes until a photo of Salvatore Bellavista fills the screen and turns it toward her.

She shakes her head. "I've never met Victor. He's just a voice on a phone who orders me about."

"You're sure?" I ask, my voice tight.

She squeezes her eyes shut, loosening tears. "Yes, I swear."

I grit my teeth. Victor's been one step ahead the whole time, and we're still no closer to uncovering his identity.

"Get her out of here," I growl.

As my men move into action, I pace outside a triage truck, my fists clenched, my veins coursing with fury. Victor Bellavista is a coward operating from the shadows, using regular people to do his bidding. Tonight's bomb tells me how far he's willing to go to conceal his identity.

Reaper joins me, his features grim. "What's next?"

"We pay Salvatore another visit. If he's protecting Victor, I'll burn his entire empire to the ground."

Reaper grunts. "You still think he's hiding the man?"

"He's hiding something." I mutter.

I stride toward the car, my mind already working through the next move. It's time to take a tougher approach—both with the bastards threatening my casino, and with my wife.

SEVENTY

GINEVRA

My days blur together in this gilded cage, a rhythm I can't escape. Every morning before breakfast, Benito arrives for the breeding sessions. After that last time, he won't allow me to fuck him face to face, instead, taking me on the rug or bent over the bed.

The lack of eye contact still doesn't stop me from talking, hoping my words will reach his heart. I remind him of our past, the nights we used to spend in our treehouse as kids, lying beneath the stars, the conversations we had about the future.

He never responds. Sometimes, his hands falter, or he changes the rhythm of his strokes, and I wonder if what I'm saying to him is working.

Kimonos in every color of the rainbow hang in the wardrobe—silks so soft they glide over my skin like a whisper. Nightgowns too, delicate and sheer, wrapped in ribboned boxes like gifts. I can't tell if they're rewards or if Benito's trying to make my captivity more comfortable in his own strange way.

He's filled my golden cage with the things I love: the books I used to read before bed, boxes of Turkish delight, and even my favorite honeysuckle perfume. But none of it matters. None of it is him.

All I want is him.

This morning, after Carla clears away the breakfast things, she returns with a pack of cards and chocolate fondue. She sets it up at the dining table by the window, and invites me over with a warm smile.

I toss aside my copy of *Dracula,* deciding I can read it later.

"What would you like to play today?" Carla asks.

"What's the most popular game at the casino right now?"

"Poker," she replies, her brown eyes sparkling. "Would you like me to teach you?"

I walk over to the dining table, my heart swelling with gratitude. Without her, I probably would have gone insane. The flame beneath the fondue pot flickers, filling the air with the scent of melted chocolate. My mouth waters and the appetite I lost at breakfast returns.

"Are you assigned to this floor, or just me?" I ask as she shuffles the cards. They're a heavy looking deck, with gold-embossed edges, embroidered with the Casino Montesano logo.

Pausing mid-shuffle, she gazes up at me through wide eyes. Her mouth opens then closes before she presses her lips into a thin line. The silence that follows is awkward. I already know what she's leaving unspoken.

"You don't have to answer," I say, forcing a weak smile. "Benito probably told you to keep me company."

Carla glances down, her cheeks flushing. "He probably doesn't want you feeling isolated."

Warmth blooms in my chest. He's keeping me here, but he hasn't completely cut me off. A small, irrational part of me holds onto that like a lifeline. Maybe I'm not so alone after all.

I gaze at Carla, marveling at the way the light streaming through the windows turns the flyaways in her dark hair a vibrant shade of umber. Outside, the sun glints off the casino fountains far below, creating dozens of tiny rainbows.

This almost feels like home.

Carla dips a strawberry into the melted chocolate, sets it on a side plate, and pushes it across the table like a peace offering.

"Thanks," I say, trying to break the tension.

She smiles, but the expression is tight as though bringing up her connection with Benito has soured the mood.

I take a bite of the strawberry, humming my approval at the delicious mix of sweetness against the decadence of milk chocolate. "Have some."

Carla shifts on her seat and picks at a loose thread on her sleeve. Shit. I've ruined everything.

I take another bite of strawberry, already forgetting about the cards. "What do you do outside of work?"

She hesitates again, but then her shoulders relax, as if she's relieved to talk about something normal. Finally, she takes a fresh strawberry and dips it in the chocolate fondue.

"Mostly, I take care of my dad," she says, glancing at me with a gentle smile. "He was in an accident and needs help."

"Is he in the hospital?" I ask.

Chuckling, she shakes her head. "At home. I only make sure he eats properly, gets to his appointments. The usual stuff."

I tilt my head. "How old is he?"

"He never said," she replies with a laugh.

"What? Didn't he mention his age when you were younger?"

Eyes flickering with regret, she shakes her head. "I didn't even know who he was until after I left foster care."

I nod, remembering the background she shared after fighting that brute. Curiosity burns in my chest about what she might have endured living with foster parents, but I clamp my mouth shut. Her trauma isn't my entertainment.

"How did you find him?" I ask, picturing her hiring a private detective.

Carla shrugs, a small smile tugging at the corner of her mouth. "He came to the door of my foster home on my eighteenth birthday, bearing gifts."

"Really?" I ask with a frown.

She nods, her cheeks turning pink. "It was like that scene in *Annie*, where she's adopted by Daddy Warbucks. It's so nice getting to know my roots."

There's something in her tone—a mix of hope and nostalgia— that makes me think of Dad. I saw him every day of my life, but I only really knew him after he was gone.

I thought the worst of him was the violence that erupted when I refused his request to get engaged to Samson. Then I found out he'd gotten an underage girl pregnant, groomed another, and stole an entire law firm.

Carla licks the chocolate off her fingers and re-shuffles the cards. I reach for a strawberry and dip it in the chocolate. It's hard to feel self-pity when others' lives are so much worse.

As she deals a new hand, a loud bang shatters the quiet, followed by the shrill ring of the fire alarms.

I shoot out of my seat, my heart hammering hard enough to break through my ribs. Carla gets up and rushes to the exit, while I stand at the floor-to-ceiling windows.

Below, people pour out through the casino's front doors and gather around the fountains, their bodies small and frantic from this great height.

"What the hell?" I whisper, my breath fogging the glass.

"Nothing in here," Carla shouts over the alarms.

"Something's happening downstairs," I say from the window.

Her gaze darts around the room, landing on a pair of sandals I left by the bed. "Put them on. We're leaving."

Before I can respond, the door bursts open, and a young man rushes in with a gun. His face is pale, his eyes wide with urgency. "Mrs. Montesano, we need to go."

Throat tightening, I press myself against the glass. "Who are you?"

"Lorenzo," he replies, his voice low. "There's been an explosion at the back of the hotel. The casino is under attack. We need to get you to safety."

A chill runs down my spine, cold fear sinking into the marrow of my bones. I don't recognize this man. How the fuck do I know he isn't the face of Bob Brisket?

Anyone deranged enough to break into a penthouse to carve out another man's heart is capable of planting a bomb in the casino to abduct me to his lair. My mind races, trying to connect the dots, but all I feel is dread. It settles into my gut, rooting my feet to the marble.

"I'm not going anywhere until I speak to Benito," I say over the shrill of the alarms.

Carla steps forward, placing a hand on my arm. "Lorenzo works for Mr. Montesano. He's one of his men."

My stomach twists into painful knots. I trust Carla, but I don't trust Brisket not to hold her father hostage. They could be working together.

Before I can argue further, Lorenzo pulls out his phone and dials. It rings beneath the alarm's incessant screech, but after a few tense seconds, Benito's face appears on the screen.

He's in the back seat of a car, his tense features softening when he sees me.

"The casino is under attack," Benito says. "You and Carla should go with Lorenzo and Vitale. They'll keep you safe."

His face disappears. I feel the loss of his presence like a punch to the gut. Lorenzo tucks the phone into his jacket, and sweeps his arm toward the door. "We need to move now, Ma'am."

I slide my feet into the slippers, my stomach lurching. If Brisket is behind the explosion, I doubt whether two young men are strong enough to keep me safe.

SEVENTY-ONE

BENITO

The city rushes past in a blur of muted lights and steel-gray shadows, but my focus isn't on the road. My phone buzzes on my lap with Ginevra's location. The little dot representing her green kimono speeds around Alderney Hill.

Relief pulses through my muscles as she nears the entrance of our family home. She'll soon be secure behind those walls, safe from whatever shitstorm Bellavista just unleashed at my casino.

A tightness in my chest eases as I turn my gaze back to the windshield. Once she's in the pool house, surrounded by my best men, I might be able to breathe.

Thoughts of Ginevra fade into the background, and my mind returns to the attack on my casino. This was no petty grudge. It was a message. I don't need to see the aftermath to know the culprit is Victor Bellavista.

The name rattles in my mind like a loose bullet. I've been closing in on him for days, following every thread of his network, every bastard who brought a counterfeit chip to my casino. He was desperate enough last week to murder Larry Zambino in cold blood.

Today's explosion proves that I'm getting close.

I grit my teeth, forcing myself to focus on the road ahead as the driver navigates through traffic. Bellavista has been pushing my limits, testing me with grand-scale fraud, rigged machines, his little minions playing their games behind the scenes. And a bomb at the back of the casino.

His pathetic attempt to slow me down won't work as long as I draw breath. I rub a hand over my face, failing to wipe off a layer of frustration. Ginevra is a constant pull on my thoughts, as are the constant drains on the casino. Over half of what's wrong with the operation leads to Bellavista.

My phone vibrates, breaking through the tension. I glance down, finding Roman's name flashing on screen. Putting him on speaker, I lean back into the seat, forcing my features into a semblance of control.

"Roman."

"You heard about the explosion?" His voice comes through, low and rough, as if he's been drinking the entire night.

"I'm on my way."

There's a pause, long enough that I can almost hear him rubbing a hand over his stubble. "It has to be Tommy Galliano. Makes sense after what we did to his brother."

My brow furrows. "We don't even know if Galliano survived the helicopter. Besides, he would've gone for Cesare or the house for revenge. Or hit the meth lab."

Roman grunts. "The house is a fortress, and the meth lab is hidden. And don't forget that Galliano was supposed to inherit the casino before we took it. He'd burn it to the ground out of spite."

I grind my teeth, feeling the tension settle between my shoulders. Roman has a point, but Galliano is too hot headed to set off a small explosion. He's more likely to rush in with guns blazing, like Scarface. Or Cesare.

"This is something else," I mutter. "A man calling himself Victor Bellavista has siphoned cash from the casino for years. Now that I'm cutting him off, he's pissed."

Roman goes quiet on the other end. I can hear the doubt in his silence. I also imagine him slumped in his chair, his eyes bloodshot and unfocused, sinking further into depression.

Five years on Death Row is enough to break any man. Falling in love with the woman he was supposed to murder, only for her to discover the truth? If he only feels a fraction of my devotion to Ginevra, I don't know how he's still alive.

Finally, he exhales, the sound heavy with resignation. "You really think it's Bellavista?"

"I would bet my life. Over the past week, people connected to his scams have disappeared, including members of staff. He's killing everyone who might talk."

"Have you spoken to Salvatore?"

"I've done more than speak to him," I mutter. "The old man either knows nothing, or Victor's got him by the balls."

Roman falls quiet again with a sigh that makes my stomach plummet. If he wants that woman, he should drag her back home. She owes him for locking him up in that dark room. And for turning Dad's classic Mercedes into scrap metal.

"I've made some calls," I say, trying to steer the conversation from his dark thoughts. "Another casino's been hit. Same counterfeit chip scam. The owner wants to meet in two days."

"Which one?" Roman asks, sounding more alert.

"Casino Demartini," I reply. "Emmanuel Demartini wants to meet in two days to discuss the threat."

"You need backup?"

"It's not that kind of meeting. He wants me to bring a date."

"Sofia?" Roman asks, his voice tilting with curiosity.

I smirk. "No. My wife."

Before he can berate me for sleeping with the enemy, I hang up. I didn't announce my marriage, but Roman knows only one woman exists for me. Regardless of what she's done, Ginevra has been mine since she stepped into our home. It's just a matter of time before she's too trapped and pregnant to consider leaving.

We bypass the chaos at the front of the casino, where evacuees are gathered under the flashing lights of emergency vehicles. The car stops at the back entrance, and I step out into the sharp tang of burnt metal and smoke. The blackened brickwork by the rear entrance makes me shudder. I can't begin to calculate the structural damage.

Malfi and three guards emerge from around the corner. His eye is still swollen from when I beat the hell out of him for manhandling Ginevra, and I swear his nose didn't bend so sharply to the left. The sight of that bastard grates under my skin, but I focus on what's at stake.

"Report," I snap.

"It was two minor bombs," Malfi starts, falling into step at my side. "They went off in the back with no major casualties. But there's something else."

I follow him around the corner, where we keep the trash. The smell of burnt debris sears my nostrils with broken glass crunching underfoot. Malfi hobbles like a man who knows he's about to get another beating but wants to delay the inevitable.

He gestures at the ground where a small safe lies on its side among the smoking debris.

"It contained a note."

My eyes narrow. "Did you open it?"

Malfi twitches. "Sorry, sir. But it burned. I didn't have time to—"

"What did it say?" I clench my jaw, biting back a string of curses.

He swallows. "It was a warning from the bomber. He said the name Victor Bellavista is just an alias and we should leave the Bellavista family alone."

A sharp breath escapes my lungs, amusement laced with anger. "Spoken like someone who wants to protect the Bellavista family."

"Get the security footage," I snarl. "I want eyes on every inch of this place before, during, and after the explosion."

Malfi scrambles away to carry out the orders. I turn on my heel and head back toward the car. This fight with Bellavista is far from over. And I won't stop until I've crushed every last person standing in my way.

SEVENTY-TWO

GINEVRA

I enter the Montesano mansion's pool house. Its architecture mirrors the big white house, complete with its columns, and its entire front wall has floor-to-ceiling windows overlooking the water.

When I used to come here with Benito, it had a nice space with an indoor barbecue. But now, it's set up like an art studio. Huge canvases hang on the walls, on easels, and stand on the marble floors. Some of them are abstract paintings with splashes of vibrant color, the others depict a man with a god-like body. Sunlight filters through the patio windows, bathing my skin in a way that would be soothing if my pulse wasn't thudding in my throat.

I glance at the far right corner toward a fully stocked kitchenette. It's as if the artist who created these beautiful works might return at any minute. My gaze drifts to the back, where a door leads to a bedroom. When I explored earlier, the clothes in the closet were close to my size, except the lingerie was a cup too small.

It obviously belongs to this mystery artist. My mind conjures up that devastatingly beautiful brunette, but she's far too curvaceous to fit in those garments. Whoever occupies this space seems tall and wiry, which I'm not.

Benito's emerald kimono now feels too tight, too voluminous, too ridiculous for this pool house, but it's all he's permitted me to wear. It's a constant reminder that I'm his possession. His doll to dress however he pleases.

Rubbing my arms, I try to erase the unease crawling under my skin. I thought Lorenzo and Vitale would send me to a safe house or even the penthouse overlooking the casino. I didn't know they were taking me to the Montesano mansion until we were halfway up Alderney Hill.

My two protectors sit outside on the pool deck, their backs to the glass doors. They're pretending to be relaxed, trying to look like they're battle-hardened soldiers. But neither of them seem old enough to have graduated college.

Bob Brisket could be nearby. He works for the Montesano family, after all. If he's watching me, if he knows where I am...

That thought spirals into panic.

Are these two enough to protect me?

The gnawing fear in my chest tightens, squeezing the breath from my lungs. I pace across the studio, needing the movement to burn off the tension. The soles of my feet are cool across the tile floor, but it does nothing to quell this mounting unease.

Movement from outside makes me freeze. Lorenzo and Vitale shoot to their feet, stiffening like hounds catching the scent of danger.

A large figure emerges from the gardens at the other end of the pool, moving toward us with powerful strides. He's clad in a burgundy robe and black pants, but even from the distance, I can tell he's a predator.

My heart lurches, pounding painfully in my chest. The man is tall, muscular, and broad, making Lorenzo and Vitale look like boys playing dress-up. A drumroll resounds through my ears, drowning out all rational thought.

It can only be Bob Brisket.

Every instinct screams at me to run. I bolt toward the end of the studio, past the half-finished canvases, toward the kitchenette. Fingers trembling, I pull open drawers, trying to find a weapon to keep him at bay, but the most dangerous item there is a steak knife.

Then the door to the pool house swings open.

I whirl around, my back to the wall, my breath coming in ragged gasps.

My stomach drops as the figure steps inside, his presence filling the room like a storm. He pauses, his gaze sweeping from one side of the space to the other, before landing on me. My legs tremble, ready to collapse on the stone tiles.

Panic cloaks my senses like a shroud, yet I brace myself to fight. Bob Brisket will have to kill me before I cheat on Benito again. I wait for him to rush across the room and order me onto my knees, but then I see his face.

The man standing in the studio is Roman. Benito's older brother. The one who just got released from Death Row for murder.

I don't remember him being so massive, or so terrifying, but the energy he radiates isn't seductive like Brisket's. It's pure, cold menace. The kind that sends a bone-deep shiver down my spine.

Roman's dark eyes narrow, his brows drawing together as he closes the distance. My back hits the wall, and every instinct screams at me to disappear. Terror claws up my throat, and my thoughts lurch to a horrifying possibility.

What if Bob Brisket isn't really Benito's employee? What if Bob Brisket is Roman?

That would explain everything. The way he knew my name. How he was able to take a photo of Benito and Mom from the mansion's grounds. The reason why he isn't afraid to cross Benito.

Because he's Benito's more dangerous, older brother.

Roman stops a few feet away, towering over me like a specter. His gaze is cold and sharp, as if I'm nothing more than filth that's slithered between his toes.

"What the hell are you doing in my pool house?" he growls in a low rumble that shakes my bones to the marrow.

My mind scrambles for something to say, but all I can feel is the crushing weight of his presence. Every membrane in my mouth turns dry, and I part my lips to speak, but all that comes out is a squeak.

"I... Benito moved me out of the hotel. There was a bomb," I manage to stammer.

Roman glares down at me for longer than I can bear, making me squirm like a worm on a hook. The knots in my stomach twist in sympathy, but all I want is to vanish.

Then his lips curl in a sneer. "You're the one my brother moved into the honeymoon suite."

It's not a question.

I nod, my body trembling as I try to hold back tears. Roman's gaze travels the length of my body, down to my bare feet. For a terrifying moment, I think he'll grab my neck and smash my brains against the wall.

Instead, he leans in, filling my nostrils with the scent of whiskey. "Break my brother's heart again," he growls, his voice dangerous and low, "And I'll kill you myself."

The threat wraps around my throat, squeezing until I hold my breath, too terrified to move. He draws back, those cold, dark eyes boring into mine, unblinking. My heart sputters, my lungs burn. It takes every ounce of willpower to remain upright, to not crumble into a pillar of salt, every ounce of strength I have not to collapse at his feet.

Finally, Roman draws back, still maintaining eye contact. Without another word, he turns and strides toward the patio door. In the absence of his overwhelming presence, I exhale a shaky breath.

When Roman pauses at the exit, I flinch, my body tensing. Has he changed his mind? Will he pull out a gun?

"Don't touch the paintings. Or the art supplies," he snaps over his shoulder, not bothering to look back.

Then he leaves.

The moment the door clicks shut behind him, my legs buckle, and I collapse against the wall, gasping for air. I press my palm to my chest, willing my heart to stop racing, but fear still fills my veins with adrenaline.

Roman is frightening. But the raw terror he inspires is cold and unpleasant.

It's not like Bob Brisket.

Brisket's danger seeps into my core, leaving me weak and sending heat straight to my clit. He makes me crave things I shouldn't. He's dark, compelling, and awakens a part of me I thought was dead, even when I'm scared out of my mind.

But all I feel with Roman is dread. Nothing more.

So my theory that Roman can be Bob Brisket is bullshit.

He has to be someone else.

SEVENTY-THREE

BENITO

My people and I spent the day scouring the security feeds from both inside and outside the casino. Whoever attacked my business knew what they were doing. They knew the positioning of the cameras, the timing of the waste disposal trucks, and how to position themselves to plant both the bomb and the safe without being seen.

To say it's an inside job would be an understatement, since Bellavista already compromised one maintenance worker. He could have dozens of them in his pocket.

I park the car at the side of the house, wanting to avoid a conversation with Roman until I can present him with Bellavista's head. After opening the door, I step out into a gust of fragrance from the climbing roses covering the wall that mingles with the ever-present scent of juniper.

Crossing the lawn, I cast my sights on the pool house. Its glass walls reflect the last traces of the setting sun, and I wonder if Ginevra is having another nap.

Lorenzo and Vitale sit outside, playing cards on the patio table amongst remnants of their evening meal. Reaper has honed those boys to become loyal soldiers. I send Sofia a silent word of thanks for feeding them.

They stand as I approach, and I dismiss them for the evening.

I wait for the pair to reach the other side of the pool before I open the patio door.

I step inside, only for Ginevra to rush at me, her kimono billowing. In three desperate steps, she throws herself into my arms, her body trembling against mine.

My muscles stiffen from the way her hands grip me like a life-line. She's usually composed, calculating, in control. Seeing her shaking and barely able to stand is disconcerting.

"Benito," she whispers, her voice frail. "I've been so scared."

She clutches at the fabric of my jacket, her grip tight enough to leave indentations. Every breath she takes shudders through her body, with her pulse pounding hard enough to reach through my suit. The fear radiating from my wife is so jarring that I cup her face with both hands.

"What happened?" I ask, my chest tightening.

"Roman was here," she says through panting breaths. "He was so frightening."

Her trembling body presses harder against mine, as though seeking refuge from the memory of my brother. I tighten my arms around her shoulders, wondering what the hell she'll say next. Ginevra has known Roman nearly as long as she's known me. They were never friends, but surely she knows he isn't capable of murdering an innocent woman?

"What did he say?"

She doesn't look up. Her head presses against my chest, as though if she holds tight enough, it will make Roman disappear.

"I've been on edge the whole day, thinking he would break in and force me to have sex," she chokes out, her voice cracking.

Her words hit like a punch to the gut, filling my veins with a surge of white-hot rage. My grip on her arms tightens, the muscles in my chest coiling with tension as I tilt her chin up to lock gazes.

"Who are you talking about?" I growl.

She shudders, her breath hitching, her eyes welling with tears. "Bob Brisket," she wails. "He's going to track me down. He'll find me and make me—"

She sobs, clinging to me like I'm the only thing tethering her to life.

Tension drains from my muscles as understanding trickles through my skull. She's not talking about sex with my brother.

"Brisket won't come near you," I murmur, rubbing her back with gentle strokes. The heat of her body against mine is comforting, and her dependence on me fills my heart with a soft ache. "I'm here now. You're safe."

Her fingers press harder into my chest, her breaths coming out in shallow, uneven gasps. "You don't understand. He's a psychopath. He tore out a man's heart and presented it to me as a gift. He's capable of anything."

The fear in her voice is real. I can feel it in the way her body tenses, the way she shakes with every word. She's reliving that moment—seeing it, feeling it all over again.

"And he's the worst kind of pervert," she says with a shudder.

My hand stills on her back as I force down a dark chuckle. Ginevra acts like she hated the filthy things I made her do as Brisket. I remembered how she would beg. In fact, she responded to me with a fire I hadn't seen in the time we've been together.

But I can't let her spiral further. Not now. Not when she's finally falling into place. Not when she's needing me in a way she never has before.

I continue to stroke her back, press a kiss on her temple, and rock her from side to side. "That bastard won't touch you again."

"How can you be so sure?" she asks, pulling back just for her tear-filled eyes to search mine. "Do you know him?"

The question hangs in the air, making my heart spasm. My mind races through the possibilities. If I say yes, she'll demand more answers. If I say no, she'll cling to this paranoia. If I say he's dead, she'll take advantage of her freedom and leave me in the dust.

Exhaling, I settle on a middle ground. "A couple of men disappeared last week with a suitcase of cash. I'm sure one of them was Brisket."

Her brows knit together. "Did you catch them?"

"Working on it." I examine her features for signs of relief or hope, but find only fear. "But right now, I have to deal with the casino being under attack."

Her frown deepens. "What happened today?"

"There's a man named Victor Bellavista," I snarl. "He's been draining money from the casino for months with counterfeit chips, rigged machines, and that's only half of what we've uncovered."

She cocks her head to the side. "Is he related to Salvatore?"

My heart skips a beat. "How do you know that name?"

She blinks, seeming surprised by my reaction. "Salvatore wanted to work with me after Dad died, but my old boss gave the account to someone else. He and his family used to come over to the house for dinner all the time. He's practically an uncle."

I step back, my breath catching, my pulse racing at the implication. "You know the Bellavista family?"

She nods, oblivious that she could be the key to finding the elusive Victor. "Of course. Salvatore always invited Dad to parties at his house and to all the family vacations. You remember how much Dad liked photos? He has a whole shelf of albums full of memories."

"Where?" I growl.

"In his study. Do you want to see them?"

My mind snaps back into focus. Pulling her into my arms, I kiss the top of her head. "Put on your shoes. We're going to your old house."

Ginevra has inroads with Salvatore Bellavista.

This changes everything.

SEVENTY-FOUR

GINEVRA

After an evening of identifying every Bellavista in Dad's photo album, we spend the night in my old bedroom. In the morning, Benito takes me to buy a gown for dinner with Emmanuel Demartini.

We enter the Dolce Vista Boutique, which still drips with the kind of luxury that used to make me giddy.

My footsteps squeak over polished floors gleaming under the light of opulent chandeliers. The air is thick with the scent of expensive perfume and the faint fragrance of leather. I glance at the gowns displayed on the racks, feeling underdressed in my leggings and tank top.

Benito walks beside me in his black suit, his hand resting on the small of my back, but all I can think about is coming here to meet Mom. She was with Bossanova, picking out a wedding dress, and that leathery old bastard tried to fuck her in the changing room. I shudder, the image of him slobbering over her sickening enough to regurgitate my French toast.

Maria, the boutique's owner, bustles over, flanked by girls holding trays of champagne and canapés. My back stiffens, my gut tightening with tension.

Last time I was here, Benito came in with that dark-haired woman to buy lingerie. I left before he could take her to the changing room, but imagining them together still grates on my nerves.

"Pick anything you want." Benito says, his voice pulling me back to the present.

His words hit me like a slap. Wasn't that what he said to her? I spin around, my mouth moving before I can stop myself. "Did you fuck her here?"

"Who?" he asks with a frown.

"You know exactly who I'm talking about," I snap, my heart racing. "The femme fatale you've been parading around town."

Benito's features remain infuriatingly neutral until something flickers in his eyes. It's a micro-expression but all the confirmation I need to know they're still together. My heart sinks into my stomach like a ball and chain.

What on earth made me think he would end their relationship? Benito never spends the night with me. Yesterday was an exception because I was still panicked about Bob Brisket and refused to let Benito go. He probably returns to his lover every evening for a night of passion before coming to breed me like a mare.

"Did you bring me here to rub her in my face?" I glare into his dark eyes, watching every flicker, every clue behind his impenetrable mask.

Benito's lips twitch with the barest hint of a smirk. I'm right. This is his idea of petty revenge.

"What's so funny?" I snap, my hands clenching into fists.

"She's Elania," he says.

I blink, the name not registering. "Who?"

"Elania Salentino," he replies, the corners of his eyes crinkling.

It takes me a second to process the name, but when I do, it's like the ground shifts beneath my feet. The Salentino twins are Benito's cousins, but they're Roman's age. They sometimes visited with their older brother, Giorgi, a lumbering brute even more psychotic than Samson.

"Oh... I didn't recognize her without Aria."

"They're not so identical anymore," Benito replies, his eyes never leaving mine.

My anger fizzles under a rush of hot embarrassment. Why hadn't I noticed she was Elania? Cringing, I peek up at him through my lashes. "Sorry. I didn't realize."

"Were you jealous?"

"No," I say, my cheeks heating.

Benito's lips curl into a smirk, the one that always makes me feel like he's two steps ahead of me, like he can read every thought running through my head. My stomach twists with equal parts frustration and nostalgia. I want to crawl under a clothes rail and hide, but his dark gaze pins me in place.

"Shut up." I shove him on the chest.

"I didn't say anything," he replies, his poker face gone. Now he looks like he's barely holding back laughter.

"You don't need to say it," I shoot back. "I can read your mind."

All he does is smile again, that infuriating, knowing smirk, and it makes my insides flutter. I tear my gaze away, looking anywhere but him.. "Stop it."

He steps closer, wraps an arm around my waist, and leans down to kiss my temple. "Pick out a dress."

Still overheated, I snatch a flute of champagne from the tray and take a long sip, hoping the bubbles might douse the flames of my embarrassment. Turning to Maria, I mutter, "Something in green."

Maria and the girls disappear in a flurry of activity, finding me every green evening gown. Dinner with Emmanuel Demartini is the closest thing to getting invited to see the King of England. Not only is he from a cadet family of the House of Borgia, but he owns the oldest and largest casino in New Alderney.

I select a Grecian style gown in emerald green, with a jeweled shoulder strap and matching waistband. It's elegant, timeless, without being too revealing. Maria takes me into the changing room, where she pins up my hair with strands of pearls and jewels. One of her girls applies makeup, making me unrecognizable.

The woman gazing back at me through the mirror is sophisticated. Untouchable. She would never submit to a brute like Bob Brisket, let alone Samson.

"You've made an excellent choice, Mrs. Montesano." Maria says as she exits.

I glance from left to right, taking in my surroundings. The changing room feels like a boudoir with mirrors taking up an entire wall reflecting a chaise lounge against the far wall wide enough for two.

Nerves flutter in my belly. This dress, the heels, the perfection of it all feels like I'm playing a role. Benito's going to take one look at me and laugh.

The door opens with a soft creak.

I catch his reflection in the mirror before I even turn around. Benito steps inside, his dark gaze sweeping over my body with an intensity that makes my heart skip a beat. The door closes behind him, his presence making the air crackle with electricity. Flames lick up my spine, setting my skin alight.

"Beautiful," he murmurs, his voice low and rough. "But you haven't been bred yet."

A shiver of anticipation settles between my legs as he closes the distance, towering over me from behind. As he reaches for the straps of the dress, I pull back and raise a palm.

"Not like this. I want you naked," I say, my voice breathy.

When we were together, the most I'd ever seen of him was in a bathing suit back before he became so muscular. After we married, through all those daily breeding sessions, I still never saw him undressed.

He pauses, considering my request for several heartbeats, then nods. His fingers move to his tie, loosening it with deliberate slowness, his gaze never leaving mine.

Breath catching, my throat tightens as the fabric of his jacket whispers to the floor. Benito's body radiates heat, even across the few inches that separate us, pulling me closer like gravity.

He moves onto his belt and then drops his pants. I glance down at the cock straining through his silk boxers and moan. Benito toes off his shoes, climbs out of his pants, his muscles shifting beneath his skin. All I can do is stare. The raw power in his body, the way his confidence radiates with every step closer to being bare—it's intoxicating.

Then he stops.

I step forward, reaching for the placket of his shirt, wanting to be the one to reveal what's beneath. My fingers tremble as I undo each button, my heart pounding harder with every exposed inch of olive skin.

When the shirt falls open, I find a tattoo over his heart. The name, GINEVRA, written in elaborate, flowing script, is surrounded by green vines and roses the exact shade of my hair.

Tears sting my eyes, and a fist clenches my heart. I trace the intricate lines of my name across his skin, over the vines and roses weaving together like the life we always planned. This tattoo is more than just ink. It represents the years we lost, the pain I caused when I left.

"When did you get it?" I whisper, my heart splitting open, wondering if he was in agony the day he sat down to brand his skin with my memory.

He remains silent, his gaze unreadable, and the weight of his stare hits me like a punch. I thought I'd destroyed us. I thought the love we had was gone, replaced by resentment. But he's carried me over his heart, through every moment of our separation. He's marked himself with my name, a reminder of what I threw away.

My vision blurs. Guilt and regret gather at the base of my throat, and I swallow. Hot tears spill down my cheeks, and I press my palm to his chest.

"I'm so sorry for hurting you," I say, my voice cracking.

Memories of our life together flood my mind—the nights we spent on the sofa, talking until dawn, the quiet mornings with his arms wrapped around my waist, his gentle laugh, the way he looked at me like I was his entire world.

The air feels too thick to breathe, my chest tightening with emotions I can't name. Words jam in my throat, useless against the flood of feelings breaking loose. My fingers still resting over his heart twitch in sync with the rhythm of my pulse—desperate, frantic, erratic.

I can't convey the storm raging beneath my skin. The love, the loss, the longing—it's all tangled up in a knot I can't untie. I want to tell him everything, but all I manage is a shaky breath, my body trembling with the weight of everything I've left unsaid. It's overwhelming, unbearable, and yet I can't pull away from him. I never want to let him go.

"Benito, I missed you every day. Every single day," I say.

All the letters I never sent, the times I nearly called him but didn't. I thought a clean break would be kinder, but standing here, seeing evidence of his love, proves me wrong.

"Benito," I rasp. "You've got to believe me. I regretted it the moment I left."

He leans down and silences me with a kiss.

SEVENTY-FIVE

GINEVRA

The kiss pulls me under, drowning out every thought I had in a rush of heat. There's no room for apologies, no space for the past—only the feel of Benito's lips, his hands sliding down my back. My heart races with the overwhelming intensity of his touch.

Finally, he's returning to the man I've always craved.

His grip tightens around my waist, possessive, like he's staking his claim. I moan against his lips, earning a deep groan that sends a ripple of desire straight to my clit. We're not just kissing anymore—we're consuming each other like we're making up for lost time.

My hands roam over the hard lines of his chest, memorizing the way his muscles shift beneath my fingertips. The heat between us is unbearable, yet I can't get enough. Legs trembling, I cling to him, wordlessly begging him for more.

He pulls back just enough for me to catch a glimpse of eyes that burn with hunger. His breath is ragged, and the restraint he keeps over his features slips, yet he doesn't speak.

"Benito," I whisper, my voice trembling. "Can we go back to how we were?"

Without a word, he lifts me off my feet. Heart lurching, I clutch at his shoulders, my legs wrapping around his waist. He holds me like I'm something precious, and the world shrinks to the tiny space separating me from Benito.

"Exactly as we were?" he murmurs, his breath hot against my neck. His palms trace the dip of my waist and the curve of my back. "Is that all you want?"

The implication of his words ignite something deep inside my core, and I shake my head. "I meant spending time together." I slide my fingers through his hair, gripping the dark strands. "Laughing over silly jokes, sharing our dreams for the future. Loving you and being loved back."

His eyes are a well of emotions too complex for me to decipher. He cradles my face in his hands, his fingers drawing circles over my cheekbones.

My stomach tightens as he studies my features, his brows creasing with an unspoken question. A part of me shrivels on the inside, wondering if there's too much betrayal between us to return to simpler times.

He steps forward, presses my back against the wall, his hips grinding against mine. The fabric of the gown I'd just been admiring moments ago feels like an impenetrable barrier, a thick layer keeping us apart.

"I'll do anything," I say through panting breaths, the words barely audible over the roar of my pulse. "All I want is this. Us."

His lips find my neck, trailing molten heat as his teeth graze the sensitive skin just below my ear. My thoughts scatter, consumed by the intensity of our combined need. Every kiss, every touch is a demand—one I'm desperate to meet, yet my words never reach past Benito's outer shell.

"You want this," he growls, his hard cock grinding against my swollen clit, the friction sending shockwaves through my core. "You want me?"

"More than anything," I say with a gasp, my legs tightening around his waist. "It's always been you."

His hands slide lower, gripping my hips, holding me in place as he continues this sweet torture. His lips trace the spot below my collarbone, nipping and sucking the tender skin.

"Why should I believe anything you say?" he mutters, his

breath hot and uneven on my skin. "How do I know you won't run off with the next man?"

The accusation cuts deep, but I cling to him harder, my legs tightening, desperate to show him what words can't. "Because I'm here now. I chose you. It will always be you."

Silence stretches between us, heavy with unspoken thoughts, but his body keeps moving, his hands gripping my thighs, his cock grinding against me in steady, punishing thrusts.

"Benito, I never wanted anyone else but you. I swear—"

His mouth crashes against mine, a wild, consuming kiss that steals the air from my lungs. It's like he's testing me, pushing me to prove that I'm telling the truth. I kiss back with equal intensity, my hips moving in rhythm with his. I pour every ounce of my love and longing for him into the kiss, hoping it's enough to convince him there will be no other men.

"Say it again," he orders, breaking the kiss just long enough to meet my eyes, his dark gaze burning with a raw desperate need.

"I'll say it a thousand times if you want," I reply, my hands moving over his muscular shoulders. "It's you, Benito. Only you."

His grip on my body tightens, and he lifts me higher, his fingers reaching between my legs. The fabric of my panties is soaked, and he growls at the discovery. With trembling fingers, he pushes the wet material aside and explores my slick folds.

"Tell me it's real," he whispers against my lips, his voice husky with desire.

"I love you, Benito. It's only you that I want."

With a snarl, he lines the blunt head of his cock against my entrance and pauses. I can barely breathe, every nerve in my body trembling with fear and desire.

"Is this what you want?" he asks, his crown teasing my clit.

"More than that," I say through clenched teeth. "I want your heart again. I want the man who planned to grow old with me. I want my lover, my best friend. I want my husband, Benito. I want you."

He enters me in a hard thrust, slamming us back into the wall.

Gasping, I dig my nails into his shoulders. He's never bred me at this angle before and it's raw, relentless. Everything I didn't realize I was missing. His rhythm is brutal, every thrust infusing me with a shock of pleasure. But it's more than just physical.

He isn't just fucking me hard enough to erase Samson and Bob Brisket—it feels like he's leaving his brand and marking me as his.

Tears blur my vision, but not from pain. It's the weight of it all, the second chance I thought I'd lost forever. "I'll do anything," I say through panting breaths. "Give you all of me. I want you, Benito. I want this family. I want our future."

His pace falters for a split second, but he doesn't stop. But something shifts between us, and what's happening doesn't feel like possession or even breeding. It's deeper.

Maybe Benito finally believes my words. Or maybe he's tired of fighting. With each stroke, I feel him unraveling, his movements growing unsteady, his breathing uneven. Then his lips crash against mine again, and I know he's finally listening.

I kiss back, pouring all my love and longing and regret. It's as if our bodies are finally merging back into a single soul.

"I missed you," I whisper into his mouth. "Open your heart for me, and I'll never leave."

He pulls back again, his breath heavy against my lips, his eyes searching mine like he's trying to gauge if what I'm saying is real.

All the while, his hand grips my thigh, anchoring my body against the wall as he pounds into my pussy with deeper, more deliberate thrusts. The raw intensity of it steals my breath. I've never felt so connected to another human being. He looks so deeply into my eyes that our souls connect, and I seize my chance to make him understand.

"That time we spent apart was like hell," I say, my vision blurring with tears. "It was like living without a heart."

He doesn't respond, but his pace changes, becoming slower, more controlled, like he's trying to hold back. But I don't want his restraint, I want the sheer force of his desire.

"Punish me. Imprison me. Call me names," I whisper, running my fingers through the back of his hair, trying to pull him closer. "But don't shut me out."

His body presses harder against mine, his lips brushing over my neck, sending a shiver down my spine. "What if the only way I believe you'll stay with me is if you're pregnant?"

My heart skips a beat, but I don't falter. If having our child is the way to mend what's been broken, I'll do it. "Then fill me with cum and give me a baby."

He presses his lips against mine in another hard, possessive kiss. Before I can even process what's happening, he's pulling me away from the wall and carrying me to the chaise.

Lowering me onto the plush fabric, he takes a step back, his eyes scanning my body in the grecian dress as if he's trying to memorize every inch. I reach out, but he grabs my wrists and holds them above my head as he straddles the chaise.

"Beg for it," he murmurs against my neck, his voice low and rough. "Let the ladies in the other room hear how much you want my cum."

"What?" I whisper.

"You heard me," he growls.

His mouth travels lower, making my lips part with a moan. He peppers kisses down the neckline of my dress, his hands slipping beneath the fabric gathered around my thighs. I arch my back, trying to press closer, but he keeps his pace torturously slow.

"Please, Benito, don't make me wait anymore. I'll do anything —be anyone. Just don't pull away from me again." My voice cracks, breaking under the weight of all the hurt and guilt that's been festering for far too long.

But he remains silent, his gaze dark and unmoved as his fingers tease my entrance, torturing me with that unbearable friction.

I try to grab his wrist to guide him, but he pins my hands above my head again, leaving me completely at his mercy. "I'm begging," I whisper, my voice trembling. "I can't lose you. Not again."

Tears stream down my cheeks. My throat tightens, but the words pour out before I can stop them. "If you want me on my knees, I'll fall at your feet. If you want me broken, I'll shatter. I'll be anything you need me to be, just please... give me another chance. Show me I'm enough for you."

When his mouth finally finds the spot between my legs, I can't hold back a throaty gasp. My fingers tangle in his hair, my hips bucking against him as his tongue flicks against my clit.

Pleasure swirls through my senses, making my eyes roll to the back of my head. I'm panting, begging for more, but he takes his time, drawing out the sensations until I'm shaking. Every moan, every gasp is like he's drinking in my desperation, reveling over his absolute control.

"Benito, please," I whimper, my voice breaking with need.

He pauses, looking up at me from between my thighs, his lips glistening, and growls, "Not until I say."

I moan louder, my body trembling as he continues, his fingers sliding into my pussy, teasing a spot that makes me see stars. Those clever digits work in tandem with his tongue, pushing me closer and closer to that delicious precipice.

Benito keeps me suspended in pleasure. I lose track of the past, present, and future, babbling strings of nonsense until he finally allows me to come. Heat coils deep in my core, radiating down my limbs. My heartbeat thunders in my ears, and the world falls away, leaving only the dizzying sensation of pure, uncontrollable bliss.

Shuddering with release, I cry out his name, my fingers curling into his hair as I lose myself to the overwhelming sensations.

Before I can even catch my breath, he flips me onto my stomach, positioning my body so I'm clinging onto the arm of the chaise. Eyes widening, I catch our reflection in the mirror.

Behind me, Benito stands naked, lips parted and red. His defined muscles ripple as he holds my hip steady with one hand, and grips his cock with the other.

My jaw drops. Long and menacing and thick, it's no wonder he always leaves me aching.

He strokes his shaft, those dark eyes never leaving mine. Then a predatory smile twitches on his lips, triggering a shiver of anticipation.

No woman in her right mind would ever want to leave a man so captivating.

Arousal drips down my inner thighs as he positions his cock

at my entrance once more before thrusting so deeply that every molecule of air escapes my lungs.

"Fuck!" I barely have room to inhale before he pulls back and slams forward again.

He grabs a handful of my hair like it's a leash and pounds my pussy like he's racing toward a finish line. His thrusts are hard, punishing, each one driving me closer to the glass.

"Look at yourself," he growls, his voice rough, his fingers digging into my flesh. "Watch how you take this cock."

My gaze snaps back to the mirror. My face is flushed, twisting with pleasure, breath escaping through parted lips as I meet his thrusts. There's nothing gentle about it—it's raw, primal. His cock drives into me again and again, his eyes locked on mine through the reflection.

"You like watching me fuck you?" he growls, his eyes blazing. "You like seeing me making you come?"

I can barely speak, my body trembling under the weight of the sensations, but I manage to gasp, "I love it."

His muscles tighten with every movement, the force pushing me harder against the chaise. I can't look away from the mirror, from the sight of his muscular body dominating mine, his cock buried deep inside my pussy. Shit. I've been with three men, yet only one of them has ever allowed me to see him so completely.

"Good," he grits out, punctuating his words with another snap of his hips. "Because I won't stop fucking this sweet little cunt until all you can think about is me."

I moan, my fingers clawing at the fabric, my back arching as I try to take him deeper. The slap of our bodies echoes across the fitting room, and I swear I hear a distant giggle.

My body stiffens, but a thick finger slips between my folds and teases my clit with tight circles. All thoughts of Maria and the girls listening on the other side of the door vanish under a lusty moan, and I keep my eyes locked on Benito, watching him claim me all over again.

"I'm yours," I gasp out, meaning every word. "Only yours, Benito."

His gaze stays locked on mine in the reflection, watching me fall apart beneath him. "Say it again."

"I'm yours. Only yours," I repeat, my voice breaking as he drives deeper.

He pushes harder, his pace rougher, more desperate. I moan into the velvet arm rest, feeling every vein, every ridge, every contour of his beautiful cock. His rhythm never falters, each thrust delivering shockwaves of ecstasy. I can barely hold myself up, my body shaking with the intensity, but I don't want him to stop.

He's everywhere—in my pussy, over my back, in my spirit. I'm lost in Benito Montesano, and it's exactly where I need to be.

As his body tenses, his thrusts grow more erratic. "You'll never leave me," he growls, his fingers moving faster over my clit. "Say it."

"I'll never leave you," I cry from the depths of my soul.

Just as he rewards me with a second orgasm, his body shudders with release. He stays deep inside me, releasing spurts and spurts of hot cum. His forehead rests against my back, his breath hot on my skin as he shivers through his climax.

My pussy clamps and spasms around his twitching shaft, milking his release. His fingers slow their circles before he finally drops his hand.

"I want us to work, too," he finally says with a sigh.

SEVENTY-SIX

BENITO

Hours later, I sit in the back of the limousine, still cringing at my revelation. It's bad enough that she lingered on my tattoo, even worse that she got me begging for crumbs of reassurance.

One simultaneous orgasm with Ginevra was enough for me to spill my guts. I've fucked up the balance of power. What's next? Do I tell her Bob Brisket is really me?

The engine's hum does nothing to ease my tension. With Ginevra staring at me like I owe her an explanation, it mounts with every passing second.

I glance out of the darkened window at the city rolling past, forcing my thoughts to stay fixed on the dinner ahead—on meeting the mysterious Emmanuel Demartini, on smoking out Victor Bellavista.

On anything but Ginevra.

She drifts closer on the back seat, her honeysuckle and vanilla scent curling into my nostrils, impossible to ignore. I clench my jaw, forcing myself to remain strong.

"It's a beautiful night," she murmurs. "I'll bet the Demartini estate looks incredible under this full moon."

I don't answer. My grip tightens on the armrest, making the leather creak under my fingers. She's trying to rebuild that connection we established at the boutique, and part of me wants to respond, but I can't let her in. Not now.

"Benito, are you going to keep this up all night?" she asks, her voice tight with frustration. You haven't said a word since we left the Dolce Vita."

Chest squeezing, I force my gaze from the window and meet her eyes.

She's breathtaking with her auburn hair piled atop her head with stray tendrils curling to frame her porcelain face. Makeup enhances the stormy depths of her gray eyes, accentuating her round cheekbones and luscious lips.

A frown pinches those beautiful features, and she searches my face for cracks in my façade, but I cling to the last shreds of my dignity. Every instinct wants to throw myself at her feet and assure her of my unwavering love, but she would only relegate me to being her doormat.

"Benito?"

"We're nearly there. Focus on the meeting." I turn back to the window as the limo veers off the highway and down a country lane.

In her reflection, she purses her lips but doesn't push further. After a beat, she looks away. Shutting her out is a shitty thing to do and borderline abusive. But stonewalling is a misdemeanor compared to the heinous crimes I've committed to make Ginevra mine.

My sins against this woman are piling higher than the Tower of Babel. One day, they'll equal the sin she committed when she withheld information that could have saved our family.

The limo slows at the Demartini estate, their wrought iron gates looming in the moonlight like the entrance to another time. My great-grandfather Paolo might have built our mansion along the lines of a Roman villa back in Italy, but Demartini is the real deal.

His coat of arms dates back to the fourteenth century, containing four gold bulls, each in a separate quadrant on a red background with a detailed gold border.

"Did you hear that he moved his family mansion from Valencia, brick by brick?" Ginevra asks, her voice breathy with excitement.

"You think it's true?" I ask, my gaze meeting hers.

She shrugs. "Well, London Bridge was moved to Arizona in the sixties."

The limousine stops in front of a stone building that looks as if it's been lifted straight out of Venice. It isn't as grand as our home's Roman architecture, but the weathered facade makes me wonder if it's truly centuries old. Green shutters flank each window, except for the portico at its center, where a trio of arched French doors stretch up to a balustrade.

A silver-haired man in a white tuxedo jacket stands at the balcony, his hands resting on its stone railing. I exit the limo, help Ginevra out, and crane my neck to the pediment at the very top.

My brow pinches. They don't even have a tower.

Ginevra places a hand on my shoulder, capturing my attention. I gaze down, admiring how the delicate green fabric of her dress hugs her curves. She's distracting. I would have brought Roman, but Demartini said to bring a date.

Movement behind the French doors makes us both turn toward the entrance. A butler emerges from beyond a set of heavy wooden doors concealed behind the glass.

With his white waistcoat and navy jacket adorned with gold buttons, red cuffs, and epaulets, he could work for Napoleon. I glance down to find his pants striped in red, white, and blue.

Ginevra gasps. I hide my reaction behind a mask of calm.

Far be it from me to notice a man's attire, but a lot can be learned about a family from the way they clothe their employees. Take Bellavista and his little maids, which implies he's a hedonist... And a predator.

Demartini's man, on the other hand, is dressed with a level of precision that signals a family clinging to old-world elegance. Emmanuel Demartini values control, tradition, and a rigid hierarchy—qualities that reveal his need to assert power, not through indulgence like Bellavista, but through the meticulous preservation of his nobility.

Dad armed all our people, down to the gardeners and kitchen

maids, with automatic weapons. But then, the Montesano family built itself up from nothing. As such, we've been at war since we crossed the Atlantic.

"Good evening," says the butler, who can't be younger than seventy, even with the dye job. "I'm Rinaldo. Mr. Demartini is expecting you."

I give him a curt nod, intending to keep up my guard. Rinaldo gestures for us to follow, and I place a hand on Ginevra's lower back, guiding her inside. The interior is less grand than the outside, with crystal chandeliers casting dim light on gilded portraits hanging among golden mirrors.

We trail behind Rinaldo down a vast entrance hall of uneven marble tiles, passing dark furniture that has seen better days. Ginevra keeps her gaze forward, her frame fraught with tension. People describe us as old money, but this place and its relics make us look nouveau riche.

"Mr. Demartini appreciates the information you've shared thus far," Rinaldo says over his shoulder. "He is looking forward to discussing your mutual concerns."

Ginevra and I exchange a glance, though neither of us speaks. Emmanuel Demartini has always been a myth who looms large over New Alderney's elite. Our grandfather, Giovanni, met him in person in the eighties when he was less of a recluse and more of a power player. Demartini refused multiple offers of partnership, dismissing them with the quiet arrogance of an aristocrat. He claimed that power rooted in bloodlines endures far longer than anything built on fear.

We stop in front of a set of heavy wooden doors, which Rinaldo pulls open with a creak.

He steps into a candle-lit dining room. At the head of a table large enough for six sits an elderly man dressed in a white tuxedo jacket. I can only assume he's Emmanuel Demartini.

He doesn't rise, but the younger man beside him stands. He's in his mid thirties—about Roman's age, with a slender build that reminds me of Cesare.

"Welcome." The old man's voice is gravelly, as though years of fine cigars have eroded his vocal cords. "Benito Montesano, I presume. Who is your lovely date?"

"My wife, Ginevra Montesano," I reply.

His white brows lift. "I wasn't aware you had married." He gestures at the younger man. "This is my son, Marcello."

"Mars," he says and offers me his hand.

I shake with the son, who then kisses Ginevra's knuckles, but Demartini only clasps his hands. A man that age probably has a compromised immune system, so I don't take offense.

Rinaldo seats us near Demartini and his son, pouring red wine from a crystal decanter before departing with a bow.

"But I didn't ask you here for pleasantries." The old man takes a sip of wine, his eyes sharpening. "There's trouble brewing in our world, particularly at our casinos."

Mars sits straighter. "Victor has plagued our casino for years, but no one from our end ever tied him to the Bellavista name."

"Our security staff have ways of making people talk." I pick up my glass.

The two men exchange glances. Emmanuel Demartini never wanted to associate with a known gangster like Grandfather Giovanni. I expect they're having second thoughts about letting me into their family home.

Mars chuckles. "Does breaking bones always get answers?"

"It works. And after that, no one wants to come back for more." I offer the smug bastard a tight smile. Just for that sarcastic remark, I won't bother to share how we've already recouped over half our losses.

"What did Salvatore tell you about this Victor character?" asks the old man.

"He claims not to have a relative of that name," I reply. "Yet the explosion behind my casino came with a note warning me to stay away from the Bellavista family."

"Why would an impostor care if you were going after Salvatore?" Mars asks.

My thoughts exactly.

"Because someone is trying to put our heads together." The old man raises a finger. "You, Salvatore Bellavista, and I have a shared enemy. The only question is who."

"You and I have nothing in common apart from our casinos," I say.

"You have BV Holdings in common," Ginevra adds.

We all turn to meet her gaze.

She sits straighter. "I've studied their financials for years since joining the Di Marco Law Group. Salvatore Bellavista funnels money through a series of shell companies."

"How did you get so close to their inner workings?" Marcello asks.

"My late father managed their account for decades," she replies. "I handled a lot of the paperwork, so I'm familiar with their entire corporate structure.

"Go on," I say, my brows rising.

She shifts in her seat. "I never understood why he funneled so much money through a convoluted network of entities and offshore accounts when he had a legitimate manufacturing business. What if those funds were stolen from your casinos?"

There's a pause, and the air thickens as her words settle. Demartini shifts forward in his seat, his attention fully on Ginevra.

Rinaldo enters with the first course, which he places on our settings. We sit in silence, waiting for him to serve more wine, before he leaves again with another bow.

"And how would you suggest we unravel the money trail?" asks the old man.

Marcello leans close as Ginevra launches into a flurry of legalese. "Your wife is a real asset."

Throat thickening, I force a nod. How the hell did I lock her away in a hotel room, degrading her into submission, when she could have reigned at my side?

As the conversation continues, Ginevra outlines how to obtain an asset freezing order to force Salvatore into being more forthcoming with information.

During the main course, the conversation drifts to history, politics, and law. I knew Ginevra was intelligent and resourceful, but watching her hold court with an aristocrat like Demartini is a revelation.

By the time Rinaldo serves dessert, I've already made my decision.

Ginevra is my equal. And I've been a fool to treat her as anything less.

Tonight, I'll let her shine. And after that, I'll treat her like my wife.

SEVENTY-SEVEN

GINEVRA

I wake to the silence of an empty room. The space beside me is cold, Benito's absence leaving a void that gnaws at my chest in the early light.

Last night, he brought me back to the pool house and made love to me until we both ached. Then he let me curl up beside him with my head resting on his shoulder.

It was the best night sleep I've had for years. Somewhere, in the pit of my heart, I felt like we'd reached a turning point. After telling me he wanted to make things between us work, then bringing me instead of Roman to the Demartini mansion to discuss business, I thought we'd grown closer.

But he's gone.

And he's taken away the warmth of yesterday's promises. Did he really mean it when he said he wanted us to work? Or was I just a pretty face to bring to the table? The way his hand lingered on my back, the way his eyes softened when I spoke... I want to believe it was real, that it wasn't just my imagination.

Chest tightening, I trace the faint impression he left on the pillow with my fingertips. No matter how much I try to hold back, I can't stop thinking about last night.

It wasn't just the business talks or Mars's admiration—it was him. Benito. The way he softened for me, his gaze unguarded for the first time in what felt like years. I saw the man I fell in love with, not the one who's kept me captive. But with him gone, it's hard to tell if that connection was real or if it was just another illusion to keep me tethered.

I felt like myself again. Professional, intelligent, independent. It was like being in a meeting when Dad was alive and having people hang on my words. But with the way I'm pining for Benito, I wonder if it was all in my head.

Sunlight streams from the back window, casting pretty patterns on the pale walls. My gaze wanders across the expanse to where a garment bag hangs on the door.

Even though it's probably another kimono, I throw back the sheets, swing my legs out of bed, and pad across the tiled floors. When I unzip it, I find a business suit.

My stomach twists. It's navy blue, sharp, tailored, and entirely out of place in this strange limbo that's become my marriage. Brows pulling together, I wonder why he wants me to get dressed.

I shake off my speculations, enter the bathroom, and take a shower. Steam fills the small space, but it does nothing to clear the tension clinging to my bones. As I work honeysuckle shampoo into my hair, my thoughts keep circling back to last night.

Benito listened to my conversation with Mr. Demartini in a way he never did whenever I talk about our relationship. Is this the reason for the suit? I work shower gel into my skin, wondering if it's just a costume for office role play.

"Shut up," I mutter, turning on the cold spray.

The shock of frigid water derails those thoughts. What's the point of torturing myself with assumptions, when I can just enjoy the morning?

After the shower, I step out into the bedroom and return to the garment bag, finding he's supplied a bra in my size, a silk blouse, heeled shoes, but no panties. I dry my hair, get dressed, stand in front of the mirror, and smooth down the lapels, feeling the weight of the fabric settle over my body like armor.

The woman reflected back no longer has dark circles under her eyes or that constant undercurrent of misery. Samson is dead, so are his men, and his humiliation rituals can follow him to the grave.

I have no idea what's next, but this outfit is an unspoken command. A subtle instruction to be ready for anything. I relax because no matter what, I'm always safe with Benito.

Dressed and ready, I step out onto the patio, where breakfast awaits by the pool. I lift the silver dome over a plate, revealing a frittata with pancetta, potatoes, and roasted onions. I sit down to eat alone, my gaze wandering past the pool and across the lawn.

Gardeners mill about the lawn, tending to the flower beds around the mansion, and a large figure in a burgundy gown moves from window to window before stopping to stare out at me.

I dip my head, focus on my breakfast, and try not to attract Roman's attention. Later, as I'm enjoying my coffee, Lorenzo and Vitale appear from around the side of the house. My stomach tightens as they approach, reminding me of my imprisonment.

"We're ready to take you back whenever you are, Mrs. Montesano," Lorenzo says from a respectful distance.

Back. As if I'm an inmate being returned to my cell. The knot in my stomach twists around my lungs until I can barely breathe.

Last night, flexing mental muscles with the Demartinis made me feel alive. My heart shrinks at the prospect of returning to being a captive broodmare.

Part of me screams to fight, to reclaim the woman I was before breaking up with Benito. But I can't remember life without him and I can't face losing my best friend.

Sucking in a deep breath, I force back those unruly thoughts, washing them away with a sip of coffee. It's hot, strong, and burns all the way down, drowning out my anxiety. My fingers tremble so I set down the cup before I make a mess.

"Let's go." I rise from the seat, square my shoulders, and act like I'm not returning to a gilded cage.

The journey back to the casino is suffocatingly silent. The hum of the engine vibrates through the car, but I barely notice it over the cacophony of my own heartbeat. Lorenzo drives, while Vitale sits in front, communicating on his tablet.

I stare out of the window, watching the city blur past, my mind racing faster than the car. What if this taste of freedom has broken my tolerance for being Benito's prisoner? What if I decide to run? Will Bob Brisket slither back from wherever he's hiding to spirit me away? Will he punish me for returning to my husband?

Shivers run down my spine at the prospect of meeting that seductive psychopath. I'd better get used to being under Benito's thumb. Brisket seems like the type of man who might groom me into becoming his homicidal helpmate.

The car rattles over potholes. The scent of the leather seats mingles with Lorenzo's aftershave from the front seat. I focus on the engine's vibrations, desperate to drown out the internal voice telling me I'm returning to my prison.

We pass the casino's grand fountains, but instead of stopping at the front door or even the hotel entrance like I expected, we park around the side. My confusion spikes as Vitale gets out and opens my door.

"This way," he says, gesturing for me to follow.

He leads me through the employee entrance, and we step into the casino's back corridors. The air is cooler here, the hallways filled with the lingering scent of cleaning products and smoke. The hum of chatter and slot machines drift through the walls, making me shiver, but I lift my chin, trying not to feel like I'm being led into the belly of the beast.

After a trip up an elevator, Vitale stops at a door, opening it to reveal a large office with a glass wall overlooking the gambling floor. I turn my attention from the flashing lights and bustling patrons below, to the two desks inside the room. One is pristine, untouched. The other is stacked with documents arranged in neat piles.

Another man enters, holding a thick folder. He's as young as Vitale and Lorenzo, yet comports himself like a soldier. "The Di Marco Group sent these over for Mr. Montesano." He places the documents on the cluttered desk. "He wants you to help trace BV Holdings' shell companies and offshore accounts."

My lips part, but I make no sound. A thousand thoughts race through my mind, each more conflicting than the last. Is this another test? Another power play? But then I push away those thoughts, choosing the small sliver of hope over my skepticism.

Is this really happening? Benito is giving me work, and trusting me with something important.

Excitement bubbles in my chest, hot and fierce , but I tamp it down. I can't afford to lose myself in the thrill of this moment even though I find myself crossing the room. My fingers itch to dive into the paperwork. It looks like I'm back in employment.

The leather chair creaks as I take my seat in this luxurious office. I crack open the laptop, my hands trembling with a mix of excitement and anxiety. For the first time in this marriage, I have a purpose beyond being Benito's possession. Ignoring the voice in the back of my mind warning me not to get too comfortable, I pick up the first document.

This work is a lifeline, and I'll cling to it for as long as I can.

SEVENTY-EIGHT

BENITO

After the events of the past few days, I'm ready to smash some heads.

The truck rumbles over the uneven road, and the bulletproof armor I'm wearing presses into my chest. This morning, I feel more like Bob Brisket than Benito Montesano, but nothing about this outfit is erotic. There's no dark excitement at the prospect of sneaking up on Ginevra, no thrill at the image of her on her knees. All that's left is me brooding in the back of an armored truck on my way to visit Salvatore Bellavista.

Across from me, Reaper sits hunched over his tablet. His gaze flicks between me and the data on his screen. I could ask him what the hell he's looking at, but I'm in no mood for a conversation. That insightful bastard is always two steps ahead, reading my mind before I've had time to catch up with my thoughts.

But last night keeps playing on repeat. Ginevra, sitting across from the Demartini men, her gray eyes sharp as blades. She looked like a flame-haired Athena with the delicate green silk clinging to her curves. They were hanging onto her every word, and so was I.

When she spoke, she wasn't the woman I'd degraded. All I saw was the girl I fell in love with all those years ago. The one who made cookies with Sofia in the kitchen, and who charmed the staff, even at the age of eight. Back then, I watched her from the shadows, feeling like I would die if I didn't make her mine.

That same need clung to my chest like smoke last night, taking me by surprise.

Ginevra controlled the dinner table with the kind of command and grace that stirred up old obsessions. In the cold light of day, I can't believe I kept my best friend under lock and key. Or bred her like a prized bitch. Or degraded her like an object to fulfill my sickest fantasies.

My throat tightens just thinking about how badly I wronged my beautiful, sweet Ginevra.

The truck rattles over another bump in the road, and Reaper glances up from his tablet. He narrows his eyes, studying my features, but has the good grace not to speak. Asshole is too observant for his own good.

"We're nearly there," he says, his voice deceptively light.

"Yeah," I grunt, trying to shake off the lingering memory of Ginevra from last night.

After dinner, I took her back to the pool house, pinned her to the bed, and pounded into her sweet cunt until she cried for mercy. It was like making up for lost time. I compensated for years of holding back, waiting for her to be my wife. Every moment was glorious, but the sweetest was afterward, when she settled into my arms.

"You alright?" Reaper asks.

I glance out of the truck's narrow window, where the Bellavista compound looms on the horizon. "Dinner with Demartini last night was disconcerting."

"It was a resounding success." Reaper sets aside his tablet. "I saw the footage. Ginevra impressed the Demartini family, made a powerful ally, and uncovered a way to get back every stolen cent. I don't see why—"

His mid-sentence pause has me turning back from the window to meet his widened eyes. When he smirks, I want to leap off my seat and wring his neck. "You're falling for her again."

"I'm not." My features harden into what I hope is an impenetrable mask.

Reaper shrugs. "Nothing wrong with that. She's beautiful, intelligent, and about to make you even richer."

I clench my jaw, not wanting to admit to an unsettling surge of guilt. Or how I haven't purged myself of the simp who catered to Ginevra's every whim. She's awoken that sappy asshole from half a decade of sleep, and he's ready to ruin our comfortable truce. With a few grandiose actions and ill-chosen words, he'll upset the balance of power. Before I know it, her dainty little foot will return to the back of my neck.

"Focus on Bellavista," I mutter, wanting this conversation to end.

The vehicle slows to a stop, and all thoughts of my wife recede to the background. Reaper and I put on our visors, ready for another confrontation with Bellavista. No matter which way I see the situation, this Victor character and him are deeply connected.

When we step out, the Bellavista compound is swarming with a mix of Mortis House boys and Montesano men. The first rays of sunlight stream in from behind the mansion, casting long shadows across the grass.

Dawn raids on families as large as Salvatore's requires an extra-large personnel. Roman is still in a semi-alcoholic stupor from losing his wife. Cesare and his little assassin are slaughtering their way through the state of New Jersey, so I'm taking charge.

I walk across the lawn with Reaper at my side toward a group of people in their nightclothes kneeling on the grass. My men went through the compound, forcing Bellavista's family and staff out of bed before sunlight. They're terrified, shivering, their wide eyes darting between us and my soldiers.

Salvatore kneels in the front with his head bowed, clad in a pair of striped pajamas. On his left are a pair of young women wrapped in towels, who I'm sure are his little maids. On his right is his son, Antonio, who he shot during that breakfast. He clutches his torso, clearly in pain.

I stop in front of the cowering old man. "Victor Bellavista attacked my casino and left a note warning me to stay away from your family. What's that about?"

Jowls tightening, Salvatore raises his head. Anger flares in his pale blue eyes, but he holds my gaze. "I already told you. I don't have a relative named Victor."

"Dig deeper," I snarl. "You also never mentioned supplying Victor with the chips."

Salvatore whirls on Antonio, his face red with fury. Bandages cover the younger man's chest, showing through the opening in his nightshirt.

"Speak up, boy," the old man snaps. "Explain to them why you gave counterfeit chips to a man as dangerous as Victor."

"I didn't." Antonio gasps, his breath shallow. "The person I dealt with was a woman."

My jaw tenses. We've been going round and round in circles with this family. The security built into each chip's production means a low-level employee couldn't steal a box without detection. Only someone with Salvatore or Antonio's access to the factory could produce this many counterfeits.

"Who?" I snap.

Antonio doubles over and clutches his chest. "I never got her real name. She was careful. Always spoke on the phone. Always paid in cash."

I crouch down in front of him and grab his chin. "Your whole family's lives depends on what you tell me next."

Tears well up in his eyes, and he squeezes them shut, letting them roll freely down his round face. "I swear, I don't know anything else! I already told Dad and your man at the hospital, but nobody will listen. It was a woman. She sounded older, or maybe she was disguising her voice."

He reels forward, collapsing onto the grass, and convulses. Salvatore rushes to his side, screaming his son's name, cradling him like a broken doll.

I step back, my lips tightening with disapproval. Why would Antonio go so far to protect this woman? My gaze darts to Salvatore's young bedmates, finding no sign of an age appropriate wife. What if she's his birth mother? It would make a sick sort of sense.

Behind me, Reaper steps closer. "What now?"

I glance around at the compound at the terrified faces. "We question everyone here. Check their bank accounts for unusual transactions. At least another one has to be connected to the woman who supplied the chips to Victor."

He nods. "And if we come up with nothing?"

"I'll wait for Ginevra to unravel Bellavista's offshore assets. Once they're identified, Salvatore will give me control. If that doesn't cover the compound interest from the amount we lost, I'll go after BV Holdings."

Reaper nods.

The old man's wails penetrate my helmet, making my ears ring. I force back a shudder. "Call an ambulance for Antonio. And while he's recovering, have one of our men go through his phone records. If there's any trace of his woman, I want her brought to me in handcuffs."

SEVENTY-NINE

GINEVRA

When Carla knocks on the office door to take me to lunch, I wonder if Benito assigned her to be my guard. Vitale and Lorenzo join us on the walk through the casino's back hallways until we reach a private dining room near the kitchens.

The chef brings us a vibrant panzanella, brimming with onions, tomatoes, cucumbers, basil, and toasted ciabatta soaked in olive oil and vinegar. When I find capers and anchovies in my salad, my breath catches. This is so typical of the old Benito—always remembering my favorites, always paying close attention to detail to make me happy.

I glance across the table, finding Carla staring at the salad with a frown. "Everything okay?"

"It's my dad." She shakes her head and sighs. "He won't eat, won't get dressed, won't leave the house. He's depressed."

"Has he seen a doctor?"

Her mouth twists. "I've set up appointments, but he's too stubborn to go."

"Keep working on him." I place a hand on her arm. "Men are like boulders. You need to wear them down, little by little. One day, you'll break through, and they'll listen."

She gives me an absent nod. "Maybe that only applies to the younger ones.

My thoughts drift to Dad and how he forced me to end my engagement to Benito with his fists, and I shudder. For five years, he did nothing—said nothing—while I suffered under Samson's abuse. He could have intervened, but his association with the Capello family was too lucrative.

It still stings, the way Dad treated me like an asset—something to be bartered and leveraged. Carla has a point. Just because Benito has stopped treating me like a caged bird, it doesn't mean all men are malleable.

Shoulders sagging, I drop my gaze to the salad. "You could be right."

We continue eating in silence, my mind still circling back to thoughts of Dad's betrayal. Later, the chef returns with a vanilla panna cotta topped with a raspberry coulis. He hovers by the door, clasping his hand, his eyes fixed on me like he's waiting for the final judgment.

I take a bite, and hum. The panna cotta melts on my tongue, a perfect contrast of silky sweetness against the tart sharpness of the raspberries.

"It's wonderful," I say with a smile.

"Thank you, Mrs. Montesano. I'm glad the dish was a success." With a quiet bow, he slips from the room, leaving behind the warm, lingering scent of vanilla and fruit.

As we continue our lunch, I wonder if this is the start of my new reality: being escorted by bodyguards, protected in even the most mundane activities.

Samson had his men, but he allowed me to go to work unaccompanied. Back then, I thought it was freedom, a twisted gesture of trust. Maybe he didn't care if I was abducted. Maybe Benito thinks I'm worth protecting. After all, he brought me to dinner with men like Emmanuel and Marcello Demartini—something Samson would never have allowed.

After lunch, Carla leaves to perform her other duties, and Lorenzo and Vitale escort me back to the office. I continue unpicking the tangle of business entities until I find a shell company with a single shareholder named Vittorio Pizzica.

Interesting.

Setting those documents aside, I wonder if this Vittorio is the same Victor who's been stealing from the casinos. A strange sense of excitement bubbles up in my chest, the kind of thrill I haven't felt in years.

I sift through more documents, my mind racing, pushing aside the haze of exhaustion. Carla breaks up the frenzy with deliveries of water, juice, and fresh coffee, helping me stay hydrated.

Hours pass. I glance through the floor-to-ceiling window at the gambling tables below. The hum of chatter and the clinking of slot machines drift up through the glass, stirring a pang of nostalgia. Benito and I used to be obsessed with this place, and now I work here with him. The casino is alive with energy, so different from the structured chaos of my old job.

I can't believe this all belongs to Benito. And more than that, I can't believe Benito belongs to me.

The door opens, and I turn to find him striding in, clad in a black suit and matching shirt. A familiar ache settles in my chest —he looks both exhausted and powerful, his hair still damp from a shower, his features set in a hard mask.

"Where have you been?" I ask.

"Cracking Bellavista heads." He walks over and presses a kiss on my temple. Instead of moving to his desk, he lingers, his arm slipping around my shoulder, pulling me into his warmth.

"Find anything?" I ask.

"My men are following a few leads," he murmurs into my ear. "How was your day?"

"Thanks to the documents you sent over, I've traced large amounts of money from Bellavista's side operations in the U.S. to offshore shell companies. It's a complex network, but I'm starting to piece it together."

"Good work," he says, his lips brushing my ear, sending a thrill down my spine. "How much are we talking about?"

"I've found twenty million so far, but I haven't finished."

He leans down, his lips ghosting over mine, his breath warm against my skin. "You're amazing."

Then his mouth claims mine in a slow, deliberate kiss. He slides his hand to the nape of my neck, his fingers curling in my hair. I gasp, my nipples tightening as he pulls me closer.

The kiss deepens, his lips moving with a controlled desperation that sends heat pooling in my core. His touch is both familiar and electrifying, and I lose myself in the moment. When he groans, the sound goes straight to my clit, but then my mind dredges up the name Vittorio Pizzica.

"Wait," I murmur into the kiss, my hands on his shoulders. "I might have another lead toward Victor."

Benito pulls away, his gaze sharpening. "Explain."

My heart is still racing from the kiss, and my thoughts stumble over one another as I stutter out an explanation. I tell him everything I discovered about the shell company and the assets Bellavista's operations funneled into its accounts.

He cups my face, his lips curving into a smile. There's something in his eyes I haven't seen for half a decade—pride. Genuine admiration.

"You're brilliant," he says.

I lower my lashes, not feeling worthy of his praise.

"Look at me."

I raise my gaze to meet his eyes. Eyes that soften only for me. Eyes framed by thick lashes, sharp cheekbones, and a strong brow. Eyes I could look into for the rest of my life and still find some new, fascinating depth.

"What?" I ask.

"I underestimated you, and I'm sorry."

"Sorry for what?"

"For not realizing what I had sooner. For not appreciating your genius earlier." Lowering his lashes, he leans in for another kiss, but I place my fingers on his lips.

"Not sorry for anything else?" My voice trembles, bracing for an apology.

His gaze hardens. "When your heart walks out on you and leaves for five years, the first thing you're going to do when it returns is put it in a cage."

A lump forms in my throat, the weight of his words pressing down on my chest. "You're comparing me to an organ?"

"You're more to me than my beating heart. More to me than the blood that runs through my veins. You're the spark that gives me life. Without you, I'm just a shell."

Emotion clogs my throat, making each breath a struggle. Tears prick my eyes, threatening to spill. I blink, forcing down a surge of guilt. I wasn't prepared for this—his vulnerability, the way he's laid everything bare. I knew leaving would make Benito miserable, but I'd selfishly hoped the hurt would fade.

"Don't tell me you were pining for me the entire time we were apart," I whisper, my voice breaking.

"Every single day." His voice is rough, the words almost strangled.

"I'm so sorry," I say, my heart lurching. "If I'd been thinking straight—"

"It's alright. You've explained yourself so many times I almost have the visuals."

A bitter laugh escapes my chest, and I rest my head against his. Every breeding session was a chance to tell my side of the story. I recounted the events of our breakup from my point of view over and over. It's a surprise he could even maintain an erection.

"I understand why you kept me imprisoned," I murmur against his lips. "But you need to understand I was also miserable."

His body tenses. "What do you mean?"

"Samson isn't anything like you."

Benito pulls back, his features creasing with concern. His eyes grow frantic, searching my face for answers. "Tell me."

I glance around the office, my gaze landing over the bustling casino below. It's too busy, too vibrant, too inappropriate for a confession of this magnitude. If he wants the sordid details, I'll need to be grounded to open up about my five years of hell.

"Can we go somewhere else?" I ask. "This isn't the sort of conversation I want to have in a casino."

He nods. "Let's leave."

EIGHTY

BENITO

I drive home in silence, with Ginevra shrinking in the front seat. Our marriage has finally reached a spot of mutual respect. Will this information shatter that fragile balance?

The setting sun dips behind the tall juniper trees lining the winding road of Alderney Hill. Occasional bursts of harsh light stream in from the gaps between the branches, making me squint.

I prefer the darkness. It's more comforting than the blinding truth. Part of me wants to gloss over the five years we were apart, but my baser instincts bellow for answers. I should tell Ginevra there's no need to speak. I've heard enough. I know why she left, but our previous relationship was based on the truth.

We held no secrets from each other between the ages of eight to twenty-three. But if I can barely handle her having feelings for Brisket, how the hell will I react to her sleeping with Samson?

Ginevra says it was unpleasant, but she also talks badly of Brisket, who pushed her limits, made her moan, gave her more pleasure than she could ever handle.

Just before the final bend, I take a turn into one of the vacant plots surrounding our family estate.

"I thought you were taking me home," Ginevra says.

My heart melts. "Do you already see it as your home?"

She shifts on her seat, hiding her features behind a curtain of auburn hair. "I spent more time at your place when we were growing up," she replies, sounding gruff. "Every time mom went on one of her retreats, Uncle Enzo and Aunt Lucia let me stay over."

I chuckle. "And Dad put you in the tower—"

"Because he wanted no funny business," we both say in unison.

Ginevra laughs, the sound reminding me of happier days. For a moment, I imagine us back at law school, coming home for one of Dad's family dinners. It's something he introduced years ago after Uncle Luca died, and his wife left with our cousins, Jennifer and Leroi. Recently, Roman tried to reintroduce the tradition, but it was a disaster.

I shake off that thought and focus on Ginevra. "You said you needed somewhere grounding."

She nods, her brows pinching.

"I'm taking you to our old hideout."

"Is it still there?" she asks, her voice rising an octave.

"Of course." I stop the car at a set of iron gates with railings covered in foliage.

The men guarding them wear full body armor and carry automatic weapons. It's been like this since Roman was framed the same week as Dad's murder. When your enemies are powerful and numerous, the only way to win is after a long retreat.

They open the gates, and we drive through a path lined with juniper trees so tall they block out the fading light. Ginevra slides a hand on my knee and squeezes.

"Shouldn't it have rotted by now?" she asks.

"Some things are worth preserving."

Gasping, she slides down the hand on my knee to intertwine our fingers. From the way her gaze burns the side of my face, it looks like she gets my second meaning.

The road ends at one of many buildings with wooden façades dotted around the empty plots surrounding our estate. They're reinforced security checkpoints where guards can rest and sleep between shifts.

I step out, walk around the front of the car, open the passenger side door, and offer Ginevra my hand. We step out together and walk past the building, moving down a narrow path winding deeper into the woods. The familiar crunch of twigs breaking underfoot brings back memories of stolen afternoons spent in our secret haven.

We stopped coming here when we started college and moved into an apartment close to Alderney State University. We had separate bedrooms because Ginevra and I were both committed to saving ourselves for marriage.

Maybe a lack of passion was our problem back then, but it sure as hell isn't now. I can't imagine myself spending a night in the same building as Ginevra and not wanting to fuck her and make her scream my name until we're both spent.

As we pass by a wall of dense shrubs, her breath hitches, and she stops in her tracks.

"Benito," she whispers. "I don't remember it being so big."

I turn to the old oak, which always looks larger at this time of the year. We chose it nearly two decades ago for its multi-lobed trunk. Dad said it would be sturdy enough to support a house and a spacious deck. The ladders we used to access it are still in place, but I built a curved staircase after the last remodel.

She grabs my arm. "This is more than just a bit of maintenance."

"Come on." I wrap an arm around her waist. "Let me show you around."

We continue toward the oak, pausing at the swing. The first version was just a plank wide enough for two. Now, it's a woven loveseat suspended by thick ropes.

Ginevra walks around the trunk's perimeter, pausing at the spot where we carved our names. She runs her fingers over the etched letters, tracing them with a sigh. "Life was simpler back then."

I run my fingers down her hair, which still feels as silky as the first day I touched her. "Things change."

She turns around, meeting my gaze with watery eyes. "Are you sure you want to know?"

"I wouldn't ask if I wasn't."

"What if you don't like what I say?" Her voice cracks, trembling as if the words alone might shatter her spirit. "What if you decide to lock me up again?"

"I won't." Exhaling, I let my hand hover near hers. She's shaking, and I don't want to rush her into accepting my touch.

Lips tightening, she fidgets with her sleeve and glances at our feet. "You say that now, but some of the things he made me do were awful."

"Ginevra," I say, softer this time. My chest tightens, and I fight the urge to reach for her again. "Trust me. Please."

Her eyes flit to mine, her throat bobbing as she nods. Shame flickers across her gaze before she turns away.

"He made you do things?" The words scrape against my throat, every syllable weighted with fear and fury.

She bobs her head.

"And you had no choice?"

"He would have hurt me," she rasps.

Rage bubbles in my chest. I clench my fists, wishing I'd been the one to murder Samson. Sucking in a breath, I force down the fury. She needs my support, not my anger.

I cup her cheek, my thumb brushing away a stray tear. "It wasn't your fault," I say, my voice wavering with the effort to stay steady. "None of it was. You hear me? Samson Capello was the worst kind of psychopath. He and Gregor kept an innocent young girl in their basement."

"What?" Her breath quickens, her eyes turning frantic and wide. "I was engaged to that bastard. How the hell didn't I know?"

"Because their father handed her to them like a party favor. What they did to you was monstrous. But not your fault. You're here, Ginevra. You survived."

Nodding, she sucks in a deep breath. "But the girl... Where is she? Is she safe, or even sane?"

My brows rise at her astute question. Something tells me Seraphine didn't emerge from the Capello basement with her mind intact, but she's sane enough to take care of Leroi's injuries.

"She's staying in one of the cottages with my cousin," I say. "It's a long story."

"Oh." She dips her head.

I slide my fingers beneath her chin and lift her head, forcing her to meet my gaze. "Nothing you tell me could ever make me abandon you. You know that?"

Ginevra nods. "Promise me you won't go into a murderous rage."

"I can't do that," I growl.

Barking a laugh, she squeezes her eyes shut, loosening tears that roll down her cheeks. "Can you at least promise not to hand me body parts?"

Pulling her into a hug, I place a kiss on her forehead. It's reassuring that she finds at least one aspect of Bob Brisket repulsive. But he's gone, and all that's left now is Benito.

"Let me take you upstairs," I murmur. "You can lie down and tell me everything."

EIGHTY-ONE

GINEVRA

I almost wish Benito had brought me to our old hideout any other time because I'm too nervous to appreciate the improvements he made to the treehouse's interior. The trunk and thickest branches still bisects its center, but it looks less like a kid's sanctuary and more like a nature retreat.

It's lighter, more airy, since most of the walls were now large windows, giving panoramic views of the forest. Benito walks me past a new kitchen area, complete with a wood-burning stove, to where we used to have our old bunk beds. He converted them into a beautiful reading nook of a deep chaise surrounded by bookshelves.

"I can't believe what you've done with the place," I say, my voice breathy with awe.

He shrugs. "While Roman was on death row, he put Cesare and me on lockdown. Instead of fighting my guards, I brought them here to help me rebuild this place and give me something to occupy my mind."

Pain gathers in my chest, rising to clog my throat. I swallow hard to dislodge it and fail. "If I'd said something earlier—"

"Did you know what your father and Capello were planning?" he asks.

I shake my head.

"Then no more apologizing." He places a hand on my shoulder and guides me down to the chaise. "I know why we broke up. Tell me what happened after."

I sink down on the cushioned seat, wriggle out of my jacket, and toss it aside. Benito does the same and places an arm around my waist.

"You need to understand I hated Samson. Even before the forced engagement."

He nods. We all moved in similar circles. Dad was Uncle Enzo's attorney, Frederic Capello was his lead enforcer, so I often met the Capello twins at family functions. They were loud, crass, and psychopathic, but they left me alone because I belonged to their boss's son.

I blow out a long breath. "Samson was polite enough in public. His father would never allow him to disrespect me if it meant jeopardizing his working relationship with Dad."

"But in private?"

Fragments flash through my senses: Samson's cold eyes boring into my soul, his grating laughter mingling with the jeers of his friends, the crack of his fist against my skull. My heart clenches, and I clutch at Benito's shirt.

"Samson... he..." Throat tightening, my voice drops to a whisper. Memories swarm my mind, splintered and unforgiving. I shove them back and concentrate on forming words. "He didn't think women were fully human. I was just an object to him. There was no conversation, only commands."

Benito pulls me into his chest, and I relax against his stronger body under a wave of nostalgia. The warmth of his hand stroking my arm anchors me to the present. Not being able to see his reaction makes it easier to speak. Bands of stress wind around my chest, urging me to offload. He needs to know what I endured so he can finally understand that leaving him was my worst mistake.

"I've never met anyone so twisted." The words come jagged and broken, as if dredging them up is tearing me apart. "He used to parade me in front of his friends."

Stiffening, his breath quickens, and his grip on my side tightens like he's bracing himself to hear the worst. "Samson shared you with other men?"

Bile rises to the back of my throat. "He told them I was too ugly to fuck and sometimes ripped off my clothes to prove his point. The others would laugh and agree with him."

"Bastard." Benito's voice shakes with restrained rage, his grip on my side tightening as if trying to hold himself back. "I should have been there. I should have stopped it."

I squeeze his hand. "There was nothing you could have done."

"If I'd known, I would have torn him apart." Benito's voice thickens with emotion. "I would have made sure he paid for every second of your humiliation."

Tears sting my eyes, blurring my vision. My chest tightens like a vise, each breath catching in my throat. A sob escapes before I can stop it, and I clutch tighter at Benito's arm, hiccupping as I force myself to continue. "Samson's family had taken everything from yours. He was unstoppable back then."

"What he did to you was unforgivable. And dangerous," he growls, his shoulders trembling, his breath coming in ragged bursts. "Did his friends give you any trouble when his back was turned?"

A bitter laugh bubbles up in my chest, bringing up a flood of tears.

"What is it?" Benito asks, his voice halting.

"I..." My voice cracks, and curl inward under the weight of shame ripping through my spirit.

Tears flow freely down my face, making my vision double. My mind dredges up the sensation of the cold floor beneath my shins and the crack of his fist against my skull. Words stick in my throat, and I battle against the urge to retreat into silence. My chest convulses with painful, suffocating sobs, making me gasp for air.

"I... I can't... I can't breathe..."

"You're safe now," Benito's voice cuts through the haze. "Take your time."

Gulping, I nod. Gather my thoughts. "Do you remember Vito Rinaldi?"

He nods. "What happened?"

The memory crashes to the front, suffocating and sharp.

"The first time Samson forced me to strip, he handed me a toy and told me to prove to his friends that I wasn't a frigid bitch." I inhale a shuddering breath, trying to block out the sounds of their laughter, the sight of Samson's sneer as he drew back his fist. "When I refused, he punched me so hard on the temple that I saw stars."

Benito's heart pounds against my ear, his body tensing, his breath coming in ragged bursts. His arms tighten around me as if he's afraid I'll slip away. I relax against the ragged rise and fall of his chest as his body trembles beneath the weight of his fury. Strangely, his rage is a comfort—a sign that I deserved to be treated better.

"I fell... Hit my head," I stammer, my words halting. My body shudders at the memory, the metallic taste of blood rising again in my throat. I can still feel the air freezing my sweat-dampened skin and shiver at the remembered snickering. "Vito picked up the toy... He tried shoving it inside me..."

Benito tenses, his heart pounding so hard that I feel the rhythm reverberate through my chest. He pulls me closer, tighter, as if shielding me from the ghosts of the past.

"And Samson let him?" he asks, the words strangled.

"No." I shake my head as the shame pours out in ragged gasps. "Samson took that as an insult and beat Vito half to death for touching his property."

"That son of a bitch should never have put you in that position," Benito growls, his breath quickening like he's barely holding back a storm.

"It was the sickest, most twisted thing I'd seen," I rasp, each word scraping against my throat, leaving it raw. "The men crowded around Samson, yelling at him to stop. No one touched him because his dad was the boss. There was blood everywhere. It was carnage."

The scene plays in my head like it's happening again: the sharp scent of sweat and blood, the crowd's jeers, and Samson's sharp grin as he wiped his knuckles. My stomach churns, making me want to gag.

"Did he hurt you any further?"

I shake my head. "Gregor shoved some clothes in my face and

told me to get dressed. I took an Uber home and ignored Samson's calls until he turned up at the house a week later."

"Did you tell anyone?"

"Mom was at one of her clinics again, and Dad only registered the part about Samson attacking Vito for touching me." Fresh rage makes my voice shake, and I can barely form the words. "In his mind, he spun what I said into some chivalrous tale where Samson protected me from a groper."

"What a bastard," Benito grits out through his teeth, his body tightening like he's trying to force himself to stay calm. "If he wasn't already dead, I would kill him for you. If I had known..." His voice breaks, the words faltering as he glances down at me, his eyes burning with helplessness. "I should have known. I can't believe I didn't see what you were suffering. I would have done something—anything—to protect you."

"Thanks," I reply, my throat thick with tears. "It was strange. Samson didn't like men leering at his property, yet he still put me on display. After that night, his men acted like I was the most uninteresting thing in the world."

"He did it again?" Benito asks.

I nod. "He didn't allow me clothes when I was in his presence, but after what happened to Vito Rinaldi, no-one dared pay me much attention."

"I'm so sorry," he says, hugging me tighter.

My eyes flutter closed. "It wasn't every day," I say with a sigh. "Samson let me live at home, go to work, have a life separate from him. He'd forget about me until there was a formal event where I had to be on his arm. The humiliation rituals usually followed."

"Shit."

"After his entire family died, he lost his mind. At first, he hid out at our house. He was too grief stricken to think of pulling any of his bullshit but everything changed when he regrouped."

"What do you mean?" he asks.

"He rented a house further down Alderney Hill and tried to gather a small army. With enough men, he planned to bypass your security and get his revenge. He dragged me along to serve as his punching bag."

"He hurt you?"

"*Emotional* punching bag," I mutter. "By then, I'd stopped resisting. What was the point of fighting someone much stronger when I'd get hurt and have to do what he wanted anyway?"

Benito rubs comforting circles on my back. His lips brush my temple, but his body remains taut with tension. "What happened?"

"By then, he'd learned Japanese bondage. While he was waiting for the right moment to attack your house, he was tying me in knots, trying to prove himself a kink master."

"What an asshole," he mutters.

Shifting, I roll my shoulders, trying to shrug off the memory of ropes digging into my skin. "He was always compensating."

"For what?"

"I heard something happened to his penis shortly after we got engaged. That's why he only raped me once."

Benito's entire body stiffens again, and his hand tightens on my back. For a moment, I think he might snap. "Ginevra, I'm sorry—"

"It was more unpleasant than painful," I say. "He was the size of a jumbo tampon. All that puffing and thrusting then a disgusting spurt."

"He shouldn't have touched you in the first place," Benito whispers, his hand trembling where it rests against my back. "I should have known something was wrong. I should have been there."

"At least that was in private. The public humiliation was the worst." Closing my eyes, I rest my face on Benito's chest. Memories press down from all directions, bitter and sharp. The words catch in my throat, each one clawing its way out. "I don't know how I endured it for so long... Maybe I thought it would hurt less, but it didn't."

Benito's fingers comb through my hair, each stroke a balm against the tension gripping my spine. I return to the present, bringing back all that remembered pain.

"So, now, you know," I say. "If I could change the past, I would have spent the last five years living here with you in this treehouse."

"If I could change the past, I wouldn't have accepted your

rejection," he replies, his voice tight with regret. "I should have known something was wrong when you broke our engagement."

"Don't." I place a hand on his chest and draw back to gaze into his eyes.

Pain etches into his paling features, his eyes darkening as if my trauma has seared into his soul. His gaze locks on mine, raw and unflinching, like he's absorbing every ounce of my agony. The sight of him so affected by my story is strangely healing. Mom always acted too drunk to understand my pain, and Martina twisted everything I told her into some exciting kink. Finally, after all these years, I feel seen.

"My dad ordered me to make our break up convincing. If I told you the truth, then your family would know mine was allying with a potential enemy."

His lips tighten.

"Everyone to blame for this is dead," I say. "Let's put the past behind us and make up for lost time."

Eyes softening, he gazes down at me with so much love that my heart flutters. The warmth in his gaze melts away the last of my defenses. Maybe losing Benito's friendship for so long was a blessing because this new version of him treats me like I'm the most alluring creature in existence.

"How can I help you feel better?" he asks, his voice lowering several octaves.

"Make me feel beautiful." I wrap my fingers around the back of his neck and pull him down for a kiss.

EIGHTY-TWO

BENITO

Ginevra's words linger in the air, haunting and raw, and her smaller frame trembles against mine. Everything she's endured slices through my chest like a dagger, each confession digging deeper into the kernels of my heart.

Rage simmers in my gut, but I swallow down the surge. She doesn't need my anger. She needs my protection, my acceptance, my strength. She needs a level of comfort that doesn't ask for anything in return.

Her breaths come ragged and uneven, like she's still trapped in those memories. I trail the pad of my thumb along her soft cheek, catching a tear before it falls.

Then she leans into my touch, desperate for my comfort.

"You're the most exquisite creature in existence," I murmur into her hair. "And the safest. No bastard will ever insult you as long as I live."

She nods, but there's a reluctance in her jerky movements as if what Samson Capello has done to her has cut too deeply to be erased with words. I weave my fingers into her hair, brushing silky strands away from her face. She squeezes her eyes shut as though she's fighting to hold herself together.

"There's no need to be strong anymore. Not with me. Not here in our sanctuary. Let it go."

Her eyes find mine, hesitant and red-rimmed. Doubt etches in every line of her expression, and I wonder if she's afraid of my judgment. I hold her gaze, trying to communicate through our decades-long connection what I can't say with words. Eventually, she lowers her lashes and releases a sigh.

"I've never felt so unwanted," she murmurs. "So worthless."

I lean in, brushing my lips against hers. "Those are the last two words I would ever use to describe you."

"How would you describe me, then?"

No matter how much I desire Ginevra, now is not the time for passion. I need to tread lightly. Her heart is wounded, fragile, and the pain of what she's endured is still raw.

"You're the flame that chases away the shadows," I say with another soft kiss on her lips. "My guiding light in a world of darkness. Samson tried to snuff you out, but a monster like him is no match for your brilliance."

She rests her head on my shoulder, her fingers fisting my shirt like I'm the only anchor in a world that's been spinning too fast.

"If that's true, then why did you keep me imprisoned without clothes?" she asks.

Knots form in my gut, twisting painfully, making me grimace. I run a hand down her side, my fingers mapping the curve of her waist, the dip of her spine.

"I'm not too different from Samson Capello," I say with a tired sigh.

She draws back to meet my eyes, her brow pulling into a frown. "What do you mean?"

"We both knew you were too good for us. Too beautiful. Too vibrant. Too innocent. Samson tried to extinguish your spark, while I tried to hoard it. I wanted to keep you hidden away where no one else could enjoy your radiance."

"Benito," she says, her breath catching.

"It's true. I was just as selfish as that bastard."

"No," she whispers.

"I'm not afraid to admit it. Nobody in this entire world is as beautiful, intelligent, or as pure as you. You deserve better. You always did, but I'm too greedy to set you free."

She raises a hand to cup my face, her thumb caressing my

stubbled cheek. Her touch is like a balm on the guilt festering in my soul.

I wanted to keep her at arm's length because coming close to her would only bring back old obsessions, those soul-deep longings I've been trying to suppress. Ginevra is my addiction, and I never want to escape.

"But I don't need to be set free, Benito. I love you too much."

"Fuck," I whisper. "I've missed you."

She shivers, not from fear, but from the icy barrier around my heart beginning to shatter.

I rest my forehead against hers, savoring her sweet, honeysuckle scent. "I used to see the world in black and white, but with you in my life, I finally see colors."

With trembling fingers, she traces my jaw, then brings her mouth to mine in a delicate kiss.

"I love your beauty," I whisper against her lips. "I love your compassion. I love your mind. I love your soul."

She kisses me again, this time, her lips more certain, her hunger mingling with mine. But I don't take control. I don't rush. I let her savor every moment, every brush of skin against skin.

"Tell me what you need," I whisper, cradling her closer. "Anything. Just tell me."

"Make me feel wanted," she says, her voice breaking.

I pull her closer, letting my lips do the talking. "I've never wanted anyone in this world, or anything more than you," I murmur into the kiss. "I want you more than I want my own life."

She melts into my chest, kissing back with equal fervor, her body now responding to mine in ways it never did before. I hold her tighter, promising through every touch that she's loved, she's cherished, she's mine.

I should have eviscerated Samson instead of leaving him to Seraphine and Cesare. Or at least demanded that they keep him alive long enough for me to strike the killing blow.

But he's dead. And rage won't fix Ginevra's trauma. All I can do is put her back together with my love.

She lifts her head, meeting my gaze with those vibrant gray eyes. The fragility in her expression cuts deep, and I'm forced to swallow the lump in my throat.

"Benito," she says, her voice breathy. "We still haven't bred today."

The words hit like a punch to the chest. Guilt winds through my broken bones and wraps around my heart like a tourniquet. My breath hitches, and my mind flashes with a kaleidoscope of sins.

I didn't just degrade Ginevra. I engineered everything that went wrong in her life to herd her back into my clutches. I dishonored her, used her as a toy, terrorized her until she became broken, desperate, fearing for her life. When that succeeded, I ambushed her with a sham wedding, followed by days of imprisonment and breeding.

Samson Capello only defiled her body. I desecrated her soul.

"No," I whisper, my voice thick with regret. "There will be no more breeding."

She rears back, her eyes widening, her pretty features clouding with confusion. "But—"

"You deserve more than being fucked like a broodmare. I want to make love to you."

Shivering, she lowers her lashes. When I kiss her temple, she relaxes her shoulders and exhales a soft sigh.

Everything about her is exquisite, from the flutter of her lashes to the faint blush on her cheeks. I can picture her naked in almost every position, but today is different.

She's no longer my possession or even my obsession. She's sacred, a goddess I will worship for the rest of my days.

"May I?" I reach for the hem of her shirt, my fingers brushing the ivory silk.

Her fingers slip over mine, giving wordless permission. I lift her shirt, unveiling inches of creamy skin until she sits before me in just her skirt and a lacy bra. Her chest rises and falls in uneven breaths, almost syncing with my heartbeat.

Maybe it's because we're back in our old treehouse, but being with Ginevra feels different. I take my time, letting my hands roam over her soft skin, cherishing her with the same reverence as when we were younger.

My lips brush her collarbone, her skin warm and delicate

against my mouth. She shivers beneath my touch, and I savor the subtle signs of her pleasure.

"You're the most beautiful woman in existence," I murmur against her flesh.

She draws in a shaky breath, her fingers tangling in my hair. "Stop exaggerating."

"You are," I whisper, trailing kisses down to her chest, feeling the rise and fall of her breath beneath my lips. Reaching behind, I unhook her bra, letting it slip from her shoulders and fall away to reveal the soft curves of her breasts.

"These are the eight and ninth wonders of the world."

She giggles. "Now, I know you're full of shit."

"Your breasts have featured in every fantasy since I was old enough to jerk off," I say, pressing a kiss to her puckered nipple. "If you had a dollar for every time I stole glances at them, you'd have enough cash to buy your own casino."

"Oh, Benito." She arches into my mouth as I swirl my tongue around the stiffened peak. "It's been so long since—"

"Since someone made you feel wanted?" Pausing around my mouthful, I glance up at her flushed face, reveling in the way her lips have reddened.

She nods. "Yes."

I smile against her skin, letting my lips travel lower to her stomach, savoring the warmth and the way her muscles twitch beneath my touch. "I'll never stop wanting you. Not for a second."

Each kiss is a whispered promise. "You're beautiful," I murmur against her skin, pressing my lips just above her navel. "You're safe. And you're mine."

She gasps, her fingers tangling in my hair, and I feel the faint tug, the quiet desperation in her touch.

"Benito..." Her voice wavers, and I know she needs more.

I shift down to the floor, kneeling between her legs. Slipping off her shoes, I reveal each delicate foot. My thumb traces her right arch, savoring the soft curve that leads up to her pedicured toes.

"You have the prettiest feet," I murmur, bringing it to my lips.

I kiss the big toe, then trail my mouth back down the arch and along her ankle, taking my time as she squirms beneath my touch.

My lips linger, worshiping her as she deserves. Then, I glance up, catching the flush blooming on her cheeks, and hold her gaze.

"Lift your hips," I growl.

She does, allowing me to slide her skirt down her legs. The fabric falls away, exposing her pretty little auburn pussy. I can't help but smirk at remembering how I didn't supply her with panties.

Brushing one thumb over her inner thigh, I trace slow kisses up her leg. She shudders, her breath hitching with each touch, and I savor every tremor, every gasp.

"Every inch of you is beautiful," I whisper, my lips grazing her soft sensitive skin.

She clutches my hair tighter, her hips arching toward my mouth, her breath hitching with anticipation. I trail my kisses higher, each press of my mouth a silent vow. She's trembling, and it's not just from pleasure—it's from allowing herself to be vulnerable, to be seen.

Our gazes meet, sparking a powerful connection. I look down into eyes filled with fire. She's no longer the broken woman who cried on my chest, she's reclaiming what was taken.

"You're my queen," I say, my voice quickening with hunger. "Ask me and I'll do whatever you command."

Her gray eyes darken. "Then let me use you as my throne."

EIGHTY-THREE

GINEVRA

I'm glad Benito brought me to our old treehouse. His cold exterior has melted away, leaving behind the man who's loved me for two decades.

He sits at my feet, his dark eyes burning with desire. "I'm yours to command."

The words go straight to my clit. Nipples tightening, I bite down on my bottom lip and pull on his lapels. "Get back here."

He scrambles up to the chaise, letting me ease him down until he's lying on his back. This is the Benito I want—the man who connects so deeply with my soul. The man willing to do anything to make me happy.

"You're wearing too many clothes again," I say with a smirk.

He smiles back, a wide grin of perfect white teeth that reaches the corners of his eyes and makes him look a decade younger. "You know what to do."

Straddling his waist, I reach for his tie, loosen the knot, and slide the silk free. After tossing it aside, my fingers find the placket of his shirt, and I loosen the button to reveal tantalizing glimpses of his olive skin. As I expose the tattoo over his heart, my breath stutters again.

Benito watches me with an intensity that makes my pulse quicken. His eyes are dark, hooded with lust, but there's something deeper—a reverence that sets my skin aflame. I can't believe this is the same man who once kept me locked away. Now, he's laid bare before me, vulnerable, willing, utterly mine.

My fingers linger over the symbol of his undying love etched over his heart, feeling its steady beat.

"Thank you for waiting for me," I say, my words thick with emotion.

"I had no choice. It was either you or nobody."

My heart flutters at the conviction in his words. "You mean you never—"

"I haven't even kissed another woman," he says.

"Oh," I reply, my voice breathy. "So your first time was in that hotel?"

An expression flashes across his features. Exasperation, maybe? It's too fast for me to process. "My first time was with you, Ginevra. It's only ever been you."

"The way you talk, I almost sound like a goddess," I whisper.

"Come here and let me worship you," he growls.

I shuffle up the chaise so I'm straddling his head. Benito's hands find my hips, gripping my flesh with a possessive need that makes me shiver.

"I love it when you take charge," he says, his voice thick with desire.

"Then you're going to love being my throne."

A low growl rumbles in his chest as I lower my hips, my pussy lips brushing the tip of his nose.

"Fuck, Ginevra," he gasps, his hot breath fanning my folds. "You'll be the death of me."

"You said I was in charge."

He moans, the sound vibrating through my pussy. "Sit on my face, woman."

I laugh, the sound giddy. "You're mine, and you're about to give me the ride of my life."

Benito's grip tightens on my hips, his fingers digging into my flesh, anchoring me in place as he pulls me down over his face. At this angle, the tip of his nose nestles against my pubic bone, and I'm staring down into his dark eyes.

It's almost a shame that other men have taken my firsts. I lost my virginity to Samson, and was forced to give him fellatio. Bob Brisket was the first man to give me oral. At least Benito is the first who's allowed me to sit on his face.

The first sweep of his tongue sends a jolt of pleasure rippling through my core, making me gasp. Thighs quivering around his head, I grab the back of the chaise to stay upright.

"God, Benito..." I murmur, my voice trembling as I lose myself in the rhythm of his tongue.

He hums as if I'm the most captivating thing he's ever tasted, the vibration infusing me with a rush of heat. I rock my hips, chasing the exquisite friction of his mouth against my swollen clit. Each movement hits with perfect precision, his tongue flicking and swirling, pushing me to the brink of madness.

"Benito..." I gasp, my fingers tightening around the fabric.

His eyes, dark and hungry, pull me deeper into his soul. The way he looks at me—like I'm the only woman who exists—is beyond addictive.

"You taste so fucking good," he mumbles against my folds. His other words are muffled, lost in the slick, messy sounds of his devotion.

I'm so sensitive that I swear I feel every taste bud, and when he swirls his tongue around my clit again, I shiver. Every nerve ignites under the intensity of his ministrations, and I lose myself in ecstasy. His stubble grazes the sensitive skin of my inner thighs, adding a delicious edge of roughness that leaves me gasping for more.

"Yes," I moan, grinding down, chasing the delicious friction.

His hands slide up my thighs, holding me steady, guiding my rhythm with a firm grip. No man has ever given me such control or surrendered to me so completely. It's almost as intoxicating as this pleasure.

"More." I tug on his hair, loving the way it makes his eyes flutter shut.

Like a good boy, he quickens his pace, lapping my clit like it's his last meal. Each flick and swirl of his tongue draws out desperate moans. It almost feels wrong to defile the tree house Uncle Enzo commissioned when we were young.

A laugh bubbles up my chest as I remember his warnings not

to engage in any funny business. Does it count now that we're married?

The thought of this beautiful, powerful protector being my husband sends a surge of euphoria that takes me to the edge.

"I'm so close," I pant, my hips rolling, my breaths coming in ragged bursts.

Benito groans, the sound vibrating through my folds, intensifying the sensations building in my core. His tongue moves faster, more insistent, and I lose myself in the delicious torment of his worship.

"Come for me," he moans, the words muffled.

The muscles of my pussy tighten as the pressure ebbs to breaking point. I've never felt so powerful, so utterly desired. Benito's fingers dig into my hips, urging me on, giving silent permission to use him. To take what I need.

I ride his face with abandon, reveling the frantic buildup of pressure, each flick of his tongue pushing me closer to the precipice.

Then something inside me snaps, and every sensation he's lavished escapes in an explosion of pleasure. My orgasm hits, crashing through my system in a rush of flames.

"Benito... fuck," I cry out, my eyes rolling to the back of my head.

My thighs clench, my torso convulses, and the muscles of my core jerk and spasm as I come undone.

His tongue works over my clit through every pulse, every wave of release, until my body becomes a raw nerve. I tighten my fingers around his hair, trying to pull each strand from the root.

Chuckling, he gets the message and eases off, finally allowing me to breathe. I gasp through the rest of the climax until the sensations become bearable.

"That was..." I say through panting breaths, my mind falling blank.

"I know, baby," he murmurs into my twitching pussy. "I know."

My heart flutters at the endearment. I meet his eyes, which soften with a smile.

With a happy sigh, I lift myself off his face, my legs still trembling from the aftershocks. Benito stills beneath me, his lips glistening with my release. His eyes shine with enough satisfaction to make me flush.

"Wow." I slide back down his bare chest and lean in to press a kiss to his swollen lips, tasting my arousal.

He returns the kiss, his hands sliding up my back and pulling me close. "You were so beautiful, coming all over my face."

Resting my forehead against his, I bask in the warmth of his devotion. "Thank you,"I whisper, surrendering the weight of my past, replacing it with the warmth of his love. "For always seeing me."

Smiling, he presses a soft kiss to my forehead. "I'll always worship you. You're my everything."

EIGHTY-FOUR

BENITO

Bringing her here was a mistake.

Even as I lie beneath her on the chaise, having come in my fucking pants, every nerve screams that I've fucked up. Ginevra's breaths are still ragged and uneven from coming all over my face, her hands running slow circles over my chest. I should be relishing this moment, savoring how I made her babble with ecstasy, but all I feel is cold terror.

Fear claws at my insides, working its way to my heart, reminding me of how badly I've lost control.

I let her in, let her see that soft kernel of me that should have stayed buried.

Her soft fingers trace my jaw, gentle, comforting, yet all I want to do is rage. Now that I've tasted true intimacy, I'd die without it because I'm weak. Weak for Ginevra, weak for her touch, weak for her connection.

She's seen through the cracks beneath my armor. Seen the hopeless idiot who worships her as the one true goddess, who would do anything to keep her at my side.

And that makes me pathetic.

I close my eyes, trying to steady my breaths, but the panic keeps spiking, refusing to settle. I've gone soft. Let her take control, let her see the man she left—that needy, desperate simp who couldn't breathe without her smile.

Now that she knows my weakness, she'll take the upper hand.

Ginevra shifts, her lips brushing my cheek in a soft kiss, but all it does is ignite another jolt of fear. Chest tightening, I fight to keep my composure, my teeth grinding together as I struggle not to shove her off.

Because she's too close, and I'm hanging by a thread.

I can't let her see what she's doing. Can't let her know that every touch, every soft word of love is stripping away my defenses. I don't want to be the man who loses control, who spills his guts the second she bats her lashes. I'm supposed to be strong. Untouchable. In charge.

But she's unmasked my façade, and now I'm back to the man I swore I'd never become: desperate, needy, terrified of losing her all over again.

A slow, shuddering breath escapes my lips, and I clench my hands into fists. I brought her here to expose her past and remind her of better times, but all I've done is expose my vulnerability. That I'm still the same fool who'd crawl on his knees, desperate for a single smile

And I can feel the shift in Ginevra—the confidence seeping back into her bones. She's reverting to that vibrant, beautiful creature worthy of worship. It's everything I've wanted for her, but it's also terrifying. Because what happens when she realizes she no longer needs me?

What happens when she remembers how to live without me?

My throat tightens, and my spine stiffens with a surge of cold panic. I can't bear to lose the one woman who makes my heart beat, but I've already lost control. I've handed her the reins, given her the power to break me, and now I'm at her mercy.

Ginevra's head shifts on my shoulder, her breath warm and steady against my neck. I dare a glance down to find her flushed with satisfaction. She's fed on my love, my praise, my devotion. Will that be enough to keep her here?

I love her too much, and that's my problem. Because love makes a man stupid, makes him weak, makes him blind to the walls around his heart. And now, I'm the one who's exposed, vulnerable, and I don't know how to claw my way back.

Ginevra shifts, her hand sliding around my neck. Her eyes flutter open, and she gazes up at me with that soft, contented smile. I should feel like the king of the motherfucking world. But my chest twists with trepidation.

Because that smile won't last forever.

Nothing good ever endures.

"What's wrong?" she asks.

I force a smile. "I'm fine."

Her brow furrows, and I can tell she knows I'm lying, but she doesn't push. Instead, she rests her head on my chest and sighs. I stiffen. Every heartbeat feels like a countdown to the moment she decides to leave.

Because it's only a matter of time.

I try to breathe, but every inhale feels like drowning. How could I be so fucking stupid? What made me think it was a good idea to let her know she's the center of my universe?

Ginevra lifts her head from my shoulder again, and she looks at me with a dazzling smile. My heart skips, and for a second, I forget my panic.

"I still can't believe how much you've changed this place," she says, her voice breathy with wonder. "It's perfect."

By now, the sun has disappeared behind the trees, leaving only the barest traces of light. I force a laugh, the sound strangled and hollow. "Yeah, well, I had help."

She tilts her head, her brow furrowing. "You don't believe me?"

"It's not that." I swallow hard, trying to focus on the present. "If I'd known you'd return, I would have kept more of your things."

Hurt flashes across her pretty features, making my heart twist. Before I can correct myself, she scrambles off my chest and gets to her feet. I sit up, watching the shadows play across her bare skin as she moves around the treehouse.

I reach for the switch and turn on the string lights so she can get a better view. Their soft glow illuminates her form, turning her into an enchanting silhouette.

"Fairy lights," she says with a giddy laugh and trails her fingers along the bookshelves and wooden beams like she's rediscovering something precious.

A lump forms in my throat. I lean forward, taking her in, committing her beautiful, naked body to memory. Because when she leaves, no force on earth will bring her back.

"It's beautiful, Benito," she says, her voice bright. "All of it."

My breath catches as she twirls around, her laughter filling the space. She means every word, and for the first time in what feels like forever, I let myself hope. Ginevra stops at the window, gazing out at the darkening forest, then she turns back to me with a shy smile that melts the last of my defenses.

"Do you think when all this trouble at the casino is over, we could stay here?" She bites her lip, looking almost bashful. "Like a honeymoon?"

I blink, her words trickling through my skull. She wants to stay. She wants to be here—with me. It's so simple, so pure that it knocks the wind out of my lungs. All the doubt, fear, and panic vanish, replaced by something warm and undeniable.

Ginevra isn't leaving. She's choosing to stay with me.

My chest tightens, but this time, not from fear. It's from the overwhelming realization that opening up to Ginevra, letting her see the real me, could never be a mistake. Perhaps this is what we've needed all along. This honesty and vulnerability has brought us closer than my machinations or control.

Rising from the chaise, I cross the space to where she stands. Her eyes meet mine, full of hope, and I cup her face between my palms.

"Anything for you," I murmur, my voice thickening with gratitude. "If this is where you want to honeymoon, we'll stay here as long as you want."

Smile widening, she throws her arms around my neck, pulling me into a kiss that feels like coming home. I hold her close, my fears dissolving in the warmth of her presence.

She wants me, and that's enough.

But she must never know what it took to get her here.

EIGHTY-FIVE

GINEVRA

When Benito's phone won't stop ringing, I break the kiss and tell him to answer in case it's urgent. One of his men calls saying he's traced the number of the woman who originally bought the counterfeit casino chips.

From what I overhear, Victor Bellavista's accomplice used a complex call forwarding chain employing virtual numbers, Voice Over Internet Protocol services, and a network of proxy servers spanning multiple regions around the world.

I walk to his side and place an arm on his shoulder. "So, where is she?"

"Right under our nose," he growls.

"Who is it?" I ask, my brows pinching.

"Our head of procurement's son's fiancée," he says through clenched teeth. "She sat through our meeting like a little mouse, letting me threaten her future husband and mother in law. I allowed her to roam free, thinking she was an innocent caught up in their fraudulent bullshit."

My shoulders sag. "Are they all working with Victor?"

Benito makes a see-sawing motion with his hand. "They're working completely different scams. My men told me both mother and son were shocked at her involvement."

"Are you leaving?" I ask.

464

His lips tighten. "I've delegated the questioning to my men."

"But you need to be down there."

Benito's features twist in that conflicted way that reminds me of when we were ten, and I begged him to let me paint his nails. Torn between pleasing me and preserving his pride, he glared at the tiny bottles of polish like they were grenades. Now, his grimace holds that same reluctance, like he's warring with himself over whether to stay.

"You need to go." I place a hand on his shoulder. "Our honeymoon starts after you've handled Victor."

Jaw tightening, he scowls and then nods. "Get dressed. I'll drop you off on the way."

Moments later, we're back in our clothes and in Benito's car. He drives in silent contemplation, so I leave him to his thoughts. My mind drifts back to that strange expression he made after I came all over his face. It was almost like regret, which I don't understand, considering he'd enjoyed pleasing me so much.

Sometimes, Benito is a puzzle. A puzzle wrapped up in prickly layers concealed in shards of ice. I thought I'd melted through them to reach the man who adored me with all his heart.

Before I know it, he pulls into an underground parking lot. Armed guards nod us through a series of metal gates and scan Benito's card with hand-held devices. Security cameras blink at us from every angle, looking like we're about to enter the pentagon.

What the hell awaits us on the other side?

"This is all connected to the casino?" I ask as Benito parks beside a row of black SUVs.

"More or less."

He cuts the engine, opens the door and exits, then walks around to help me out. We continue down a hallway, where Benito scans his card again to call an elevator.

When its doors open, I recognize its mirrored interior. "This is the penthouse overlooking the casino."

He nods. "You'll be safe here."

"Why can't I accompany you to the office?" I ask.

He presses a single button, which makes the door close. "The last woman connected to Victor came with explosives. The maintenance guy he was working with got shot in the head. I'm not taking any chances with you."

My stomach lurches as the elevator rises, and I turn to Benito with a gulp. "I didn't know Victor was that deadly."

"People will stoop to heinous levels to get what they want."

A chill runs down my spine at the thought of Victor setting up more bombs.

The doors slides open, revealing the spacious penthouse with its gleaming marble floors. Across the pale interior, through floor-to-ceiling windows, stands the casino's front façade and its luminescent fountains.

"Order whatever you want from the house or the hotel," he says. "Both will bring you food."

I grab his arm. "Does Victor know you're coming?"

"I hope not," he growls.

"Hurry back." I pull him close.

He kisses me with an intensity that makes my knees buckle. "Not even a slimy bastard like Victor can tear us apart."

The door shuts behind him, leaving me alone in the apartment. I head straight for the kitchen, needing something to calm my nerves. The fridge is stocked with bottles of wine, water, and iced tea, but none of it is sweet enough to cut through the lingering tension. I rummage through the cupboards, finding a tin of cocoa powder and a carton of milk.

It looks like I'm having hot chocolate.

I take my time, making the drink the way Sofia taught me when I used to visit the Montesano mansion with Dad. Back then, the housekeeper was a strong, maternal presence, while Benito's mother was distant.

Lucia Montesano spent all her time with her youngest son, Cesare, so it was a surprise to everyone when she left them all the moment Uncle Enzo died.

After pouring the steaming contents into a mug, I take a sip, letting the warmth spread across my tongue. The rich, creamy taste does little to soothe the uneasy flutter in my chest. What if Victor is already lurking in the casino, ready to ambush Benito?

I shouldn't be so morbid. Benito is surrounded by guards. He can take care of himself.

A few drops of liquid spill on my blouse, so I take the mug into a bedroom in search of a change of clothes. The first one I find looks like a spare, but the second is filled with the earthy scent of Benito's cologne. I step into a room decorated with ebony wood and heavy black drapes that reminds me of his bedroom at the Montesano mansion.

I slip off my blouse, letting it fall to the floor, and move toward the dresser. The drawer slides open, and I pull out a pajama top, then hold it to my nose. When all I smell is detergent, I place it back, needing something that carries his scent. Giggling at my own ridiculousness, I move to his laundry basket, and rummage through its contents for an old T-shirt.

My fingers brush against something hard, and I pull out a groin protector with thick straps. It's identical to the type Bob Brisket used to wear. Brow furrowing, I step back, wondering why Benito would possess something so specific.

I scan the room, half-expecting Brisket to emerge from the shadows. But that's ridiculous. This penthouse is secure. Benito's guards wouldn't allow an intruder to infiltrate the building.

"Then why is his codpiece in Benito's laundry basket?" I mutter under my breath.

A shiver runs down my spine, telling me the answer might be more simple than Brisket sending me cryptic messages. Ignoring every instinct screaming at me to call Benito, I walk to his closet, slide open the door to reveal rows of suits, blazers, and behind them, an identical set of body armor to Brisket's.

Stomach churning, I stagger back, my mind running in circles.

I crouch before his bedside table, searching through his books and finding everything I expect of Benito: *The Art of War* by Sun Tsu, *The Prince* by Machiavelli, *Meditations* by Marcus Aurelius, and *On War* by Carl von Clausewitz.

Beside those books is a volume of manga about catgirls. I pull open a drawer, finding a small box containing orange cat ears, fluffy orange paws, and an orange tail attached to a butt plug.

My breath hitches. This can't be real.

I fall on my ass, sending a rush of pain up my tailbone. My

head spins, pieces clicking into place with a clarity that makes my heart lurch.

Benito can't be Bob Brisket.

The brutal games. The humiliation. The degradation. The carnage. Benito wouldn't... He couldn't... could he?

My gaze lands on a tablet charging on the dresser. I stumble to my feet and stagger across the room. With trembling fingers, I try password after password, until I enter my birthday, when it unlocks. I fire up the photos app, finding it filled with hundreds of video thumbnails.

The first one I tap is footage of me on my knees, gazing up as I suck off Bob Brisket.

A lump forms in my throat. This doesn't prove anything. Benito could have found these if he raided Brisket's home.

Exhaling a shuddering breath, I scroll through the list, stopping at videos of the strip club. It's the one time Brisket might have taken off his visor, because he placed a blindfold over my eyes to eat my pussy.

I swipe past footage of my awkward strip tease to the part where he lays me on the stage and spreads my legs. When he removes the helmet, I pause the screen to catch a glimpse of Benito's face.

Benito. The man I married. The man who made me earn his forgiveness. The man who turned out to be the psychopath I was desperate to escape.

Realization hits like a punch to the gut, my insides screaming with cold horror. The tablet slips from my fingers and drops to the floor with a clatter. Bile rises in my throat, and I want to gag.

Benito is Brisket.

Brisket is Benito.

"What the hell am I going to do?" I whisper.

Benito murdered Julian, staged my terror, orchestrated every twisted scene to drive me to my knees. To make me desperate. To bend me to his will. To force me back into his arms.

If I run, he won't just find me. He'll revert into the monster who carves out men's hearts. If I leave, I need to be clever about it, and I can't involve Mom.

Carla's note floats to the top of my mind. She said she would help if I ever needed it, and even gave me a code word. Benito also said I could order room service. If I'm going to run, it has to be tonight, while he's distracted with Victor Bellavista, and before he returns to find I've discovered the truth.

My gaze darts to two phones on the dresser. I scramble to my feet, pick up the one marked *Casino*, and dial room service.

"Mr. Montesano, how may I be of assistance?" Carla's voice answers.

"It's Ginevra," I whisper. "I'm at the penthouse, and I need whatever's on the dinner menu and a pack of ultra glide tampons."

There's a pause, then a faint rustle on the other end.

"I'm on my way," she replies, her voice tight.

Squeezing my eyes shut, I inhale lungfuls of courage. Tonight might be my last chance. If Carla can't get me out, there won't be another.

Dread winds around my chest like a constrictor, tightening with every thought of what will happen if I fail. I don't know if I can survive falling into the clutches of yet another psychopath.

EIGHTY-SIX

GINEVRA

Carla drives in silence through a derelict district on the outskirts of town. Streetlights are less than plentiful here, and the few that work cast a sickly yellow glow on the cracked pavements and graffitied buildings.

I thought leaving the penthouse would be tricky, but I hid in the room service trolley, which she covered with a stained tablecloth.

Betrayal pulses through my veins like acid, along with the bitter sting of humiliation. I groveled, apologized, debased myself to earn Benito's forgiveness for... sleeping with Benito wearing a disguise?

Five years of resentment isn't something that vanishes with a few apologies. I knew I hurt him, knew what I did was unforgivable, knew he would make me pay. That's why it took so long for me to ask him for help. I knew Benito would be determined to make me suffer.

The car rumbles to a stop in front of a house that looks like Norman Bates' motel. Most pillars of its veranda are smashed, and curling strips of paint peel away from the weather-worn exterior, while the front yard has turned into a jungle of weeds.

Carla cuts the engine and spares me a nervous glance. "I know it's not much, but you'll be safe at my dad's place."

It's hard to believe this dilapidated wreck belongs to the woman who's been my closest ally. But that's exactly why Benito would never think to look for me here.

"Thank you for your help," I rasp.

We step out, the car door shutting behind us with an echoing clunk. A chill cuts through my borrowed room service uniform, making me shiver as I follow Carla towards the house.

Each step on the rickety wooden porch creaks under our weight, as if we're disturbing the worms feeding on the timber. I try not to make comparisons with the treehouse because I'm determined not to think about Benito.

Carla pulls out a rusty key from her pocket and struggles with the stubborn lock. "I've got to warn you that my dad looks messed up."

My brow creases. "You said he wasn't well."

"Car accident," she replies with a grimace. "Broken nose, fractured eye socket, missing teeth, and cracked ribs. He's in a lot of pain, so he gets cranky."

Nodding, I brace myself for what might be awaiting us inside. Carla pushes open the door, making its hinges wail in protest. Musty air wafts out from the darkened interior, carrying with it the faint scent of antiseptic and unwashed sheets.

Squaring my shoulders, I follow her into a narrow hallway, which echoes with the sound of a TV laughter track. Faded paper peels away from the walls, revealing glimpses of crumbling plaster.

At the end of the hallway, we reach a living room crammed with old furniture. I hesitate at the threshold, my breath catching as I take in the scene.

A thin man slouches in an armchair clad in striped pajamas, his features lost in the shadows. But as he turns his head towards us, the dim light from the TV illuminates a bruised face with one good eye glinting with malice.

Carla's dad bares a mouthful of broken teeth. "What the fuck is she doing here?"

I cock my head. That voice might sound familiar if it wasn't so pained. The old man places a bandaged hand on his armrest and rises off his seat with a stiffness that speaks of acute pain.

"Dad," Carla says, her voice quivering. "This is—"

"Ginevra Di Marco," he hisses.

The man approaching us is as tall as a scarecrow with a face like a smashed pumpkin. It's bruised, with one eye swollen shut, yet he moves with the unnatural determination of the living dead.

"I'm sorry... Have we met before?" I ask.

A sneer twists his lips, and I feel his disdain like a physical blow. "You don't recognize me, girl?"

My gaze darts to Carla, who rushes forward with her arms outstretched, trying to catch her father before he falls. I step backward, wondering how the hell this man could hold so much resentment toward a stranger.

Carla tries to grab his arm, only for him to shove her aside. "Do you know each other?"

"Unfortunately, yes," he snarls, his voice thick with bitterness.

My mind spins, trying to place this gray-haired scarecrow of a man, but the bruises make it hard to recognize his features.

I stare at him, struggling to fit the pieces together—the sharpness of one cheekbone, the regal line of the side of his jaw that isn't misshapen. The only man I know in that age group who isn't overweight is the one who nearly became my stepfather.

"Valentino Bossanova?" I whisper.

His glare deepens, and he flashes a mouthful of broken teeth. "I'd say it's nice to see you again, but I'd be lying."

"Dad?" Carla says, her brows knitting.

His good eye flickers back to me, narrowing with disdain. "Get her out."

My throat tightens. What on earth is Valentino Bossanova doing in a place like this when he has that ostentatious penthouse overlooking the park? And how the hell didn't I know he and Carla were father and daughter?

"Out," he barks.

"Dad, wait—Ginevra's in trouble. She's in an abusive marriage and needs somewhere to hide—"

"From Benito Montesano?" He spits the words like venom, and I recoil, my stomach twisting with dread. "Get in line. He's the bastard who messed up my face."

My throat thickens. I would ask how he knows Benito, but

one of my conditions for marrying him was to get Valentino Bossanova out of Mom's life. Then I remember Benito showing me footage of that brutal beat down. Hell, at one point, I even tried to get Bob Brisket to murder him.

The memory that they were the same man cuts into my heart like a knife, making me wince.

"How do you know each other?" Carla asks, trying to ease her father back into his armchair.

Ignoring her, Bossanova turns to me and sneers. "Montesano ordered me to court your mother."

Shock slams into my solar plexus, knocking the air from my lungs. My knees buckle, and I stagger back, grabbing at the door frame to hold steady. "What? Why?"

"Because he wanted you to come running to him, begging for help," he hisses.

My mind reels, piecing together fragments of the recent past. At the time, I didn't understand why Bossanova would try to marry the widow of the man who helped with his murderous life insurance scams.

Now, it makes perfect sense.

"He told you that?" My voice cracks, and my eyes fill with fresh tears.

I've been so blind. All these weeks, Benito's been pulling strings, controlling so many aspects of my life. "Was he behind the loan sharks, too?"

"Those thugs were there to make your mother desperate enough to marry me," he replies with a sigh.

I can't breathe. The room fades, along with the edges of my reality, replaced by a cruel maze of deception and manipulation.

Did Benito help Nick Terranova take back the law firm? His quartet of legal goons remind me so much of Vitale and Lorenzo. Their association would explain how quickly Bob Brisket reached the penthouse when Julian turned feral.

Benito—not Brisket.

"We're both victims of that manipulative bastard," Bossanova says, his sharp voice cutting through my dizzying thoughts. "Look at what he did to my good looks when I was no longer of use. You were wise to leave before he did the same to you."

Bossanova's words hang in the air like a thundercloud, heavy and oppressive. I shake my head from side to side, trying to straighten my thoughts.

Even if he's right, I'm not about to agree with a man who murders innocent women. Especially not one who's older brother killed my birth mother.

Turning away from Bossanova, I head back toward the front door. Going to Martina is out of the question, but her parents have been family friends my entire life. I could stay in one of their rental properties until I pull together enough money to leave town, or even call Mom—

Fingers tighten around my arm. "Montesano used me, just like he's using you. But I can stick it to him and set you free."

I frown, my gaze dropping to Bossanova's hand. Help me? He can't help himself. "Let go of me."

"Dad, what are you doing?" Carla says from the living room.

My gaze meets Bossanova's, whose expression hardens. "Leave this house, and he'll hunt you down with a crack team of thugs. If you haven't already noticed, Benito Montesano is the second-in-command of the most powerful crime family in the state of New Alderney."

A lump forms in my throat. "Why are you telling me this? I thought you ordered me to leave."

"Benito Montesano will pay for what he did to us."

My stomach twists. "What are you talking about?"

"Stay here, where I can keep you safe. In seven days, I'll get you enough money to start a new life with your mother wherever you want in the world."

"If this is another of your insurance scams—"

"He'll pay anything to get you back," he snaps. "I'll ask for a hundred million dollars."

His words land like a punch to the liver, sending up a wave of bile. "You want to hold me hostage?"

Valentino grins. "How else are we going to get a hundred million?"

I shake my head, my nostrils flaring. "Forget it. I'm not a bargaining chip. Let go of my arm, and I'll leave—"

A punch lands on my temple before I can wriggle free. Pain explodes across my skull, and I drop to the floorboards.

Bossanova's unfocused face swims into view, his broken teeth bared in a snarl. "You're going nowhere."

"Dad!" Carla pushes past him and rushes to my side. "I'm so sorry, Ginevra. Can you stand?"

I try to push myself to my feet, but my arms collapse under my weight. She grabs my bicep, helping me up. Legs wobbling, I rise to a half-crouch, then stand fully upright. The hallway spins, and I swear that every dust mote in the house is circling my head.

Bossanova disappears into the living room, and Carla helps me down the hallway. "I'm so sorry. I thought he was a safe space."

If I could speak over the pounding in my head and the pure, white-hot rage coursing through my veins, I would ask her whether she looked him up online. Instead all I can manage is a weak nod as we shuffle toward the exit.

Rapid footsteps creak after us. I glance over my shoulder to find Bossanova holding a hammer.

"Carla," I rasp.

She whirls around. "Dad!"

The hammer swings down, striking her head with a sickening crack. "I told you to stop fucking calling me that. It's Victor."

She collapses, her weight knocking me back onto the floor. The name hangs in the air, heavy and ominous, and my mind spins, connecting rotating dots.

I never understood why the Di Marco Law Group would help lowlives like the Bossanova brothers. Dad said they were well-connected and relatives of a valued client, Salvatore Bellavista.

If his name is really Victor, and he's connected to BV Holdings, then what if he's—

"You're Victor Bellavista," I whisper.

Bossanova raises his chin, his good eye gleaming with a sick sort of triumph. "Benito Montesano beat me like a dog, broke my counterfeit chips racket, my slot machine scam, and he's siphoning money from my offshore accounts. I finally have a way to hurt that arrogant little bastard."

EIGHTY-SEVEN

BENITO

I step into the interrogation room, a concrete box thick with the scent of tears. Bianca Tarrantino hunches over a metal table and chair bolted to the floor. She's a trembling, pleading mess, responsible for a financial drain that threatened to ruin my establishment.

Between Vitale, Lorenzo, and a team I dispatched to her mother's apartment, we've identified burner phones, bank details, and blueprints for a heist on the Demartini Casino vaults.

This woman pretending to be a victim is no innocent, but an equal participant.

The door swings shut, and I soak in the slow burn of victory. I'm so close to catching Victor Bellavista that I can almost feel the warm spray of his blood. He should have stayed in the shadows, content with the amount he scammed from my casino, but I can't forgive the stunt he pulled with the bomb.

Ginevra is safe, which is all that matters. I'll return to the penthouse the moment I've wrung Bianca of her secrets.

"Let's see how many fingers I get to amputate before you tell me what I need to know," I say.

Bianca's head jerks up, her eyes wide with terror. Mascara-colored tears stream down features twisted with anguish.

"Please, Mr. Montesano," she wheezes. "I'll tell you every-thing, but you need to protect me from Victor."

Before I can reply, the door opens, and Teresa Carlini and her son, Leo, stumble into the room. I've kept them in our basement cells since after the set of interrogations, not wanting them dead until I'd found that Bellavista bastard.

Without the makeup, Teresa's skin has turned jaundiced, her hollowed cheeks and dark circles under her eyes casting a sickly shadow. Her hair clings to her forehead in greasy clumps, making my former head of procurement barely recognizable. Leo is as pale as death, his cracked lips trembling, his bloodshot eyes darting from me to Bianca. He grips his mother's arm, as if she's the only thing keeping him upright.

"Were you working the counterfeit casino chip scam with Bianca?" I ask.

Teresa frowns. "What are you talking about? No!"

I turn to Leo who shakes his head.

"Because Bianca was his accomplice on the inside," I add.

The pair turn to the younger woman, their features etched with disbelief.

Bianca's sobs grow louder, but it looks like neither of them are in the position to give two shits about her distress.

"You were supposed to be family!" Teresa screams, her voice cracking. "How could you work with Victor behind our backs?"

"I didn't have a choice!" Bianca cries.

"What the hell does that mean?" Leo rasps, advancing on her with clenched fists. "You were in on the casino chip scam the whole time?"

I lean against the wall, watching the family drama. They confessed to the procurement scam easily enough, but swore igno-rance about the chips too quickly for my liking.

"Victor blackmailed me," Bianca stammers, her gaze flicking between Teresa and Leo. "He has a tape."

Leo's features contort, his lip curling with disgust. "With who?"

"It's complicated." Face crumpling, Bianca erupts into choked sobs.

"Enough." I step forward, pulling out my gun, and pointing it at Bianca's head. "This family has had enough grace. You, start talking. Now."

"It wasn't my fault," she says, her tongue darting out to lick her lips. "I first spoke to Victor when I had dinner with Mr. Napolitano."

I nod. Joe Napolitano was the former head of procurement and one of the traitors we burned alive in the crematorium. It doesn't surprise me that he had dealings with Bellavista.

"Wait," Leo rasps. "You were fucking Joe?"

"Focus," I snap.

Bianca takes a shuddering breath and clutches the edge of the table. "That night, he made me have a three-way with his wife. A week later, Victor sent me the footage, saying he would tell everyone if I didn't get close to Antonio at BV Holdings."

Her words dissolve into incoherent sobs. I make a slow count of ten for her to regain some composure before hurrying her along. "What were your orders?"

"To tell him I needed some chips for a private game."

"Stop crying and tell Mr. Montesano how to find Victor Bellavista!" Teresa screams.

Bianca wipes her eyes and hiccups. "Victor always emails me his latest number."

I flick my head at Lorenzo, who walks to the corner of the room and picks up a laptop. He places it on a table, flips it open and slides it in front of Bianca.

"Find it," he says. "Now."

Trembling, she taps on the keyboard, bringing up a series of emails with attachments. She double-clicks the latest one, firing up a spreadsheet filled with strings of numbers.

"What the hell is that?" I ask.

She shivers. "It isn't very sophisticated, but no one's going to look too closely at petty cash requests."

My lip curls. How many other documents are circulating the casino, communicating ways to drain us dry?

She reads out the number, which Vitale enters into his phone to send a request to the nerds at Mortis House. If we can trace the burner phone before Victor changes his number, then we have a shot at pulling him into our net.

Leaning over, I grip the back of Bianca's chair. "Call him and say you've found a stash of genuine chips you want to sell."

She flinches, swallowing hard. "What if he realizes it's a setup?"

"He will if you keep sniveling. Play it cool, and maybe you'll survive the night."

She nods, and Lorenzo slides a phone across the table. Steeling her features into a hard mask, she dials, but the call goes straight to voicemail. Hesitating, she glances up at me with pleading eyes, so I give her a curt nod to continue.

""Hey, Victor," she says, her voice steady despite her shaking hands. "I've found something you might be interested in. These chips are genuine and still activated. Get back to me."

She ends the call, placing the phone onto the table as if it might explode.

"What now?"

"Wait for him to respond, and help set up an ambush in exchange for your life," I say.

———

The walk back to the penthouse feels longer than usual, weighed down by unfinished business. Silence stretches, pressing down on my shoulders. Victor might find Bianca's proposition too good to be true and set up a counter-ambush the way he did with Larry Zambino.

I've never encountered anyone so slippery.

When the elevator doors slide open, I step into the penthouse, expecting to find Ginevra crashed out on the sofa. It's empty, and the place looks untouched, save for the faint scent of hot chocolate. My chest tightens. I hoped she would wait up.

"Ginevra?" I call out, but there's no answer.

I cross the living space, passing a spotless kitchen. The dining chairs are exactly where I left them, and across the room, the sofa cushions are still smooth and undisturbed. Everything's too still, like the whole place is holding its breath.

She's probably having an early night.

Continuing toward the bedroom, I force down a roiling sense

of dread. Ginevra and I are in a good place. We're married. In love. She wouldn't leave the moment I turned my back.

Would she?

The thought coils in my gut like a python. Its thick tail of paranoia wraps around my neck, threatening to pulverize my rational thoughts. Ignoring it, I pause at the bedroom door, telling myself I'll find her curled up under the covers.

My cock stirs at the prospect of Ginevra clad in my shirt, her auburn hair spilling across my pillow like a halo. After connecting so deeply with her at the treehouse, she has to be there, waiting.

I turn the knob, push open the door, only to find an empty bed. On its surface is a letter, scrawled in her handwriting.

Cold dread spreads across my chest, inching toward my heart. Crossing the room, I pick it up and read:

I could never love a man like Bob Brisket.

My grip tightens, crumpling the paper. Before I can fully process her words, my gaze lands on the groin protector on the bedside table, placed atop a stack of catgirl manga. Next to it, a tablet plays one of the strip club videos on repeat.

It's the one where I removed my helmet and exposed my face to the camera.

She knows. Knows I'm Bob Brisket. Knows I set her up. Knows I'm the Machiavellian bastard who engineered her fall from grace.

Dropping to my knees, I squeeze my eyes shut, collapsing in on myself with a choked gasp. My chest splinters with the weight of my betrayal, letting in a tight fist of guilt that squeezes my heart.

I've lost her forever. There's no coming back from such an elaborate stunt.

She'll be back in Victoria Gardens, crying on her mother's shoulder, telling her she was right never to get involved with a Montesano. And this time, I won't disagree.

I could have sent a bunch of flowers after her father had died, offering my condolences and support. Wormed my way back into her heart with kindness and charm. But I was so determined not to be the simp she'd left in the dust that I plotted her downfall.

Now, it's all backfired.

Winning her back will take more than groveling. It'll take something monumental.

I'm about to call Reaper, but my phone rings. I pull it out of my pocket, finding an incoming call from the casino.

"What is it?" I bark.

"Montesano," a voice says through a changer. "You have disrupted my operations for the last time."

I go still, the edges of my focus sharpening. "Victor Bellavista."

He laughs, a mocking, mechanical sound that grates on my nerves. "Correct. And you're about to compensate me for your meddling with a hundred million dollars."

A simmering heat builds under my collar, and I tighten the phone. "Or I could just kill your associates and continue draining your accounts until you're left with nothing."

"Check your email."

The line goes dead, leaving the threat hanging in the air like the blade of a guillotine.

"What the hell is he planning?" I open my email app.

An unread message sits at the top of the inbox, its subject line reading, *Evidence.*

As if a bastard like that will trick me into opening a potential virus. I would laugh at his audacity, but I'm still reeling from losing my wife. After forwarding the email to my team at Mortis House, I fire up the surveillance app. It was careless of me to leave Ginevra in a penthouse containing evidence of my misdeeds.

Making a mental note to ask Cesare for advice on initiating Stockholm Syndrome, I scrub through the security videos. Carla from room service enters the penthouse, pushing a trolley laden with silver cloches, and a bottle of champagne chilling in an ice bucket.

When the two women exchange tight hugs, my eyes narrow, and I turn up the volume. Carla encourages Ginevra to eat a grilled cheese sandwich before handing her a complete change of clothes.

"What the hell do you think you're doing?" I snarl at the screen.

My phone rings, interrupting my viewing. It's Reaper.

"Did you open the email?" he asks.

"The one I forwarded for a virus check?" I growl, my gaze still fixed on the screen where Ginevra settles inside the room service trolley. "No."

"Open it," Reaper says. "It's clean."

"What's inside?"

"Benito—"

"Fine." I pull the phone away from my ear and tap Victor's email. There's no content, just a video attachment. I press play, and freeze.

Ginevra lies unconscious on the floor of a dark room. She's wearing the room service uniform, with blood pouring down her temple.

I stare at the screen, my veins pulsing with murderous fury. Carla delivered Ginevra into the clutches of my enemy. How the hell did I not know she was working with that bastard?

Victor Bellavista can corrupt my employees, steal from my casino, and bomb my hotel, but taking my wife crosses a line he and anyone connected to him will regret.

That bastard has gone too far, and I will tear down the world and reduce it to ashes to get back my wife.

EIGHTY-EIGHT

GINEVRA

Pain splinters through my skull, dragging me from darkness. Blinking, I force the world into focus, trying to make sense of my surroundings.

Something thick and rubbery lodges in my throat, making it difficult to breathe. I'm lying on my side in a concrete basement with walls stained by water streaks and mold.

My wrists are encased in cuffs fastened so tightly that the metal bites into my skin, and a chain connecting them to the ceiling bolt forces my arms into an awkward stretch. Bindings also encircle my ankles, their cold steel pinching my bones.

Groaning, I roll onto my back, taking in my new prison. Carla lies on my other side, her body limp against the stained concrete. Blood mats her temple, but her chest isn't rising and falling with breath.

My stomach tightens. She's looking more like a fellow victim than an accomplice. I shuffle closer, wincing through the cuffs digging into my skin, and nudge her with my shoulder.

"Carla," I mumble through the gag. "Wake up."

She doesn't stir.

Panic pulses through my gut, cold and sharp, and I scan the room for inspiration. Rusted tools hang on the wall beside a pile of splintered crates, and wires snake along the ceiling. There are no windows, just a bare lightbulb that casts shadows on the grimy walls.

How the hell am I going to save us both?

Before I can even think about whether Benito can pay a hundred-million-dollar ransom, the door opens with a groan that sets my teeth on edge.

Stiffening, I peek through my lashes, pretending I'm still unconscious.

A tall figure strides in, clad head to toe in black leather from his head mask to his clunky boots. It's like something out of *Pulp Fiction*, only infinitely more sinister because I'm not watching from the comfort of a movie theater.

He glances down at me through a pair of eye slits that match the zipper over his mouth, and I hold my breath.

Is this an accomplice or Valentino Bossanova himself? No, not Valentino... Victor Bellavista.

Under his arm is a ring light on a tripod, which he sets on the floor with a clunk. He disappears through the door, returning within seconds, holding a smartphone, which he sets up on his apparatus.

Shit. Since when did this old man learn the intricacies of social media? How old is he, sixty? It's hard to tell when he's always covered in fake tan or bruises.

His movements are rough, impatient, as though this is the first time he's recorded something without help. He fiddles with the settings, grumbling under his breath, until the red light blinks to life.

With a flip of a switch, the basement floods with light, and he swaggers across the room.

"Showtime, Mrs. Montesano."

He grabs the chain attached to my wrist cuffs and yanks it taut, hoisting me up like a pulley. Pain shoots through my forearms, electric and sharp, as I'm hauled up to sitting. I swing my feet, trying to kick him off balance, but he steps out of range.

"You'll have to do better than that, Ginny," he sneers.

The bastard continues pulling me to my feet with a force that sends a searing jolt through my shoulders. I stagger to my knees, not wanting to dislocate anything, and stand.

"Here's how it's going to work," he says. "You stand there like a good girl, while I prove to your husband that I mean business."

"He'll kill you," I mumble through the gag.

Ignoring my incoherent threat, he positions me in front of the camera by the shoulders, and then grabs the neckline of my shirt. I draw in a sharp breath, inhaling the mingled scents of leather and sweat.

Revulsion ripples through the lining of my stomach. Is this where he assaults me for the camera?

His excited breath rasps through the mask as his gloved fingers slide across my skin. He wrenches my blouse apart, ripping it down the middle with a force that sends buttons scattering across the floor.

The blouse falls open, exposing my bra and bare belly to the cold, damp air. My nipples shrivel, my skin erupting with goosebumps.

"What are you doing? Stop!" I yell through the gag, my voice choked with anguish.

My panic feeds his sadistic pleasure, making his eyes gleam through the slits of the leather mask. "Don't take this personally. You're actually a useful daughter. I would have loved to have you instead of the little bitch who brings me hotel leftovers."

He tears at my room service apron with vicious jerks, ripping the fabric with a sound like the crack of a whip. Once the garment pools at my feet, he hooks his fingers under the band of my bra, yanking it up and over my shoulders.

Cold air stings my breasts. I gasp, twisting away from him, trying to shield myself, but he turns my body back toward the camera.

"Stay in the frame," he hisses, his hot breath coming in ragged huffs behind the mask.

He crouches, his fingers grazing the waistband of my skirt. Then, with a swift yank, he rips it away, leaving me naked and trembling under the blinding glare of the ring light.

"No panties?" he asks, his voice light with amusement.

Tears prick my eyes, not of terror or even shame. I've dealt with men more dangerous than an aging asshole who knocks women out with hammers. I'm furious. Furious at Benito for being a psychopath I was forced to escape. Furious at Victor-Valentino for using me as a pawn. Furious at myself for falling into their traps.

Stepping back, he glances at the smartphone, making sure it's capturing every inch of my humiliation. Then he clips a device to his mask's mouth opening.

"Benito Montesano," he snarls, his voice garbled. "You have forty-eight hours to pay a hundred million dollars, or your pretty little wife dies on camera."

I would say he's bluffing, but Valentino Bossanova has murdered women for less.

He walks back into frame, looming behind my bound form like a wraith. His gloved hands roam the front of my body, making me flinch and squirm.

"Scream for the camera," he growls in that artificial voice, his fingers closing in around my nipples.

The shock of the pinch forces out a strangled shout that makes him chuckle.

As his gloved hands release their grip to slide down my belly and cup my crotch, every instinct screams at me to fight, to run, to resist. I jerk away, but the chains pull me back.

"Forty-eight hours, or I'll start slicing off body parts, starting with her clit."

"Dad," Carla moans.

"Damn it!" Releasing me, he turns to Carla, delivering a kick in her ribs, making her jerk and sob on the floor. "Now, I'll have to edit that fucking shot."

"Stop," I yell, but the old man continues attacking his screaming daughter until she falls silent.

Heart pounding, and I stare down at the floor, where Carla lies unconscious. My blood heats, every hackle in my body bristling as I strain against my bindings. I would be shocked if this didn't remind me so much of Dad beating me to submission when I refused to break my engagement.

Now, all I want to do is tear this man into shreds.

He hobbles to the tripod, seeming exhausted from this bout of domestic violence, and turns off the recording. When he unzips his mask from around the back and pulls it off to reveal that mottled face, I stiffen.

"Don't flatter yourself," he snarls, his swollen lip curling with disgust. "I'd rather fuck Benito than get within a foot of your ginger minge."

My mind flashes to Samson, to Bob Brisket, to Julian, and all the men who have hurt or degraded my sexuality. They're all the same—using the easiest common denominator to break my spirit.

I shake my head, feeling his rejection like a small mercy. From this moment, nothing a man says or does will even knock my self esteem. All they have over me is more money or physical strength. Take that away, and they're sniveling assholes, vying for my attention.

After plucking his phone out of the ring light, Valentino strides toward the exit, his heavy footsteps echoing with each step. The door slams shut behind him, and I sag.

Forty-eight hours. That's what Victor gave Benito, but it's also what he's given me. Time to plan, time to strike. The clock is ticking, and I'll be damned if I wait to be saved. I'll find an opening and make him regret ever thinking he could use me as a pawn.

And even if Benito paid my ransom, I'm never taking him back.

EIGHTY-NINE

BENITO

Less than an hour after receiving Bellavista's emails, we traced the movements of Carla's vehicle to a run-down district at the edge of Beaumont city.

I grip my binoculars, watching the derelict at the end of the road. The place is a weather-beaten mess, its Victorian structure snapped and splintered by time. Ginevra could be in there, beaten, unconscious, and needing my help, but we can't make a move until we have confirmation.

A man like Victor Bellavista wouldn't make extracting my wife so easy. Not when he's holding her ransom for a hundred million.

Reaper stands beside me at the back of an armored truck, his eyes glued to the tablet, trying to make sense of the thermal readings flickering on the screen. We've stationed men at strategic points around the district. If Victor attempts to fight his way out, he won't get far.

"What have you got?" I ask.

"Two signatures, maybe three," Reaper replies. "Could be guards. Could be Victor himself. Could be nothing."

I lower the binoculars, my nostrils flaring. My pulse throbs, loud and relentless. Every muscle in my neck is ready to snap under this relenting pressure. "There's only one way to find out."

If it were up to me, I would storm the building, cutting through Carla and Victor to reach my wife. But my blood is running too hot and I can't afford to risk Ginevra's life, so I open the truck's door, letting out my prisoner.

Leo Carlini, my head of procurement's son and fiancé of the woman behind the counterfeit casino chips, steps out in bullet-proof armor. He fumbles with the helmet cam with trembling fingers.

I stare him down, breathing through the heat of my rage. This bastard and his family still owes me, and tonight, I'm cashing in.

"Get in there, walk around, and film every goddamn inch of that basement," I snarl. "And if you see any men, shoot."

He flinches. "Then you'll forgive our debt?"

"Yours only," I say through clenched teeth. "Screw this up, and you'll spend the rest of your life in agony."

Leo nods, a jerky movement that wobbles the oversized helmet camera.

Reaper shoves a pistol into Leo's trembling hands, tightens the equipment's straps, and claps him on the shoulder.

"Move," I bark, making him flinch.

When Leo glances down at his pistol, I can already see the thoughts running through his head. Shooting Reaper and me would solve his problems. He'd be free to start a new life.

"Don't even think about it." I push him forward, making him stumble. "We wouldn't equip you with a weapon that could penetrate our armor."

His shoulders sag, confirming my point, and he ambles down the broken sidewalk to the house. Each slow footfall grates on my nerves, every step a reminder of how many people have fucked with my family.

Ginevra and I were happy before a cohort of backstabbing bastards decided they wanted Dad's wealth for themselves. Not content with killing him and sending Roman to Death Row, they took our mother, sent my little brother into a drug-fueled despair, and ruined my Ginevra.

If anything happens to her, this entire city will burn.

By now, Leo has reached the house's front steps and is

halfway to its crumbling veranda. Reaper and I watch in tense silence, waiting for Leo to gain entry.

He pauses at the door, looking like a man with second thoughts.

"Get on with it," I growl into the comms.

Startling, he yanks open the door, making its hinges shriek, and disappears inside. I turn to Reaper's tablet, which displays a feed of the house's interior through Leo's camera.

Inside, it's worse. Cracked plaster, sagging beams, and the ceiling looks like it could come down any second. Leo's breaths rasp in my ear, amplified through the comms, each exhale stuttering with fear. His helmet cam swivels, displaying a dusty, dim hallway, with a light peeking through the gaps of a door on the far left.

"You see the basement stairs?" I ask.

"Yes," Leo whispers.

"That's where we think she's being held," Reaper says. "Get down there and scope it out."

Gulping, he heads towards the door, twists the handle with a creak, and pushes it open, revealing a steep staircase illuminated by four bulbs.

Leo's breath quickens through the comms as he descends the stairs, each creak echoing through the feed. My heart slams against its cage, every beat tightening the band of tension around my chest.

The first face Ginevra should see is mine, not Leo's. I should be the one to pull her out of this hell, yet I'm standing here, watching a coward stumble to her rescue.

"Keep your gun up," I snap.

The camera jerks as he adjusts his grip, but the gun returns to view. My fingers twitch with the urge to yank the damn thing out of his grasp and finish this myself, but I force my focus back on the screen.

At the bottom of the stairs is an expanse of stained concrete, leading to a door.

"Open it," I order.

He reaches out gloved fingers, grabs the handle, and twists. The door groans open, and I lean into the screen.

Inside is a square room with bare walls, another heavy door, and a metal chair bolted to the ground. Attached to it are leather restraints with thick metal buckles. But there's no sign of Ginevra.

My stomach still plummets. At some point during the evening, my Ginevra was in this shit hole.

"What the hell?" Reaper mutters.

"There's no one here," Leo whispers, his voice tight. "It's empty."

"If I have to come down and point out that door, it will be with a bullet through your head," I growl.

With a whimper, he continues to the next door, his breath quickening. "I don't like the sound of this place."

"Explain," Reaper says.

"I-I don't know," he replies. "Something just feels off. Like a bad vibe."

"Get a grip and move," I snap.

Leo reaches out to open the door, and the screen fills with a flash, followed by the deafening roar of an explosion.

A shockwave rips through the air, a violent roar that shatters everything. We're thrown backward, crashing into the side of the truck with bone-cracking force. Pain explodes through my shoulder as I land beside Reaper, my ears ringing with a high-pitched whine that drowns out the world. The ground tilts, and gravel bites into my palms, sharp and unforgiving.

I suck in a breath, choking on the acrid stench of smoke and burning metal, every inhale a knife to my lungs. My head spins, disoriented, my heart hammering in a frantic stutter as I scramble to my knees, searching for something, anything to ground me through the chaos.

My world is unraveling, and all I can think about is Ginevra—trapped, alone, maybe dying while I lie helpless in the dirt.

"Benito," Reaper's voice cuts through the fog, but it sounds muffled, as if I'm underwater. "You okay?"

I force my head to nod, the movement stiff. "Fine. Helmet absorbed the blow."

The lie sits heavy in my throat. I'm anything but fine. I blink, fighting to clear the mist clouding my vision, forcing my focus onto the raging inferno. Flames devour the walls, consuming the house that might have been Ginevra's prison.

Each flicker of fire feels like a personal taunt, daring me to act, to feel. I should be doing something, but all I can do is stare, my insides burning. I've never felt so powerless, so damned by my own inability to act.

Reaper barks orders I can't make out, and my vision tunnels on the wreckage, every ounce of my rage funneling into a single line of thought: Victor Bellavista lured me into a trap. The bastard just played me for a fool.

I force myself up, my legs unsteady but driven by pure adrenaline and rage. It drives me forward, even as every nerve thrums with terror. Heart pounding its way out of my chest, I stumble through the heat of the blaze searing my skin.

Squinting through the smoke, I ignore my burning eyes to search the wreckage as if I might spot some sign, some miracle that she's not in there. The fire roars, a mocking beast devouring everything in its path.

Ginevra's face flashes in my mind—every smile, every touch, every night I promised to protect her—and now, she's paying for my failure.

Bellavista's game is clear: I'm not just losing money. I'm losing my wife.

My phone buzzes again, yanking me back to this hell, and I'm filled with a new, desperate resolve. I will raze this city to the ground to save my wife.

I yank my phone from my pocket, my pulse a relentless hammer against my ribs, and find a message from an unknown number with a video thumbnail. Fear claws up my spine, making the finger hovering over it tremble before I click it.

The screen blazes to life, revealing a figure hiding his features behind a leather mask. "Benito Montesano, this is your final chance," a metallic voice taunts, slicing through my composure. "Have the ransom ready, or I'll do more than strip her naked."

The video cuts to a dank basement, where Ginevra and Carla lie motionless on a concrete floor. My heart seizes, my vision narrows, and all I see is red.

A second later, the masked figure hoists Ginevra upright and tears at her clothes until she's naked. My blood freezes. I can't breathe. Can't think. Every nightmare I've ever had about losing Ginevra plays in hideous technicolor, but this isn't a dream.

Fury and helplessness crash in my chest, releasing a tidal wave of emotions threatening to burst. The leather-clad bastard runs his filthy hands over her bare skin, threatening to slice off body parts.

Terror grips my throat, hot and suffocating, urging me to act.

Reaper's hand lands on my shoulder. "Benito."

"Pull back the men," I say, my voice breaking. "Find a way to reach this bastard. I'm ready to hear his demands."

NINETY

GINEVRA

Hours after that video shoot, I'm still in that fucking basement, yanking against the cuffs, and trying to keep the chains
from clanking. The metal grinds against my raw skin, making me
wince. Pain shoots up my arms to my shoulders, but it's nothing
compared to the agony of being held captive.

My wrists swell, raw from the steel biting into my flesh. Gritting my teeth, I push through the ache radiating through my
bones and twist my hands, testing the cuffs for weaknesses. But
there's none.

Shit. The metal is unforgiving, as solid as the frustration of
being tethered to this basement like a dog on a leash.

A soft groan floats through my concentration. I glance down
to find Carla stirring, her eyelids fluttering open.

"Hey," I say through the gag. "Are you okay?"

She touches the blood caked on her temple and winces, then
her gaze skims the moldy walls before finally landing on me.
Breath catching, she pushes herself to sit up.

Her movements are slow and pained, making me grimace at
the memory of Valentino kicking her while she was half-
conscious. And for what? If she hadn't brought me here, he'd still
be festering in front of a TV set, stewing in his failure.

I swallow hard, my throat tightening. Is Carla playing me or trapped in a cycle of abuse? My heart drums in my chest, heavy with sorrow. She brought me here. She had to know something. This situation is so messed up, I don't know what to think.

Victor didn't bother to restrain Carla like me, but could she be shackled by invisible bonds? Some men feed into a woman's deepest need and turn it into his weapon of control. Or maybe I'm projecting and giving her too much of the benefit of the doubt.

Carla's eyes meet mine, so full of fear and confusion that it stings. I can't believe this is the woman who fought that creepy oaf who dragged me into his room.

"Can you untie me?" I mumble around my gag.

Her gaze flicks down my naked body before realization hits. Eyes widening, she scoots closer, her cheeks coloring. "Oh, God." She stumbles to her feet, fumbling with the buckle behind my head with trembling fingers. "I didn't—I shouldn't have—"

Her voice cracks, and the gag drops to the floor with a soft thud. I draw in a deep breath, finally able to fill my lungs with air.

"Thanks," I rasp.

Carla's face flushes a deep shade of red, her eyes darting everywhere but at me. "I'm sorry," she mumbles, her words tumbling over each other in a rush. "I didn't know he'd do this. I thought—"

"Stop." I can't let her drown in apologies. Not when there's a chance she can help us escape. "You didn't do this on purpose, but I need you to look at me."

She flinches but turns in my direction, unable to meet my eyes. Maybe all those conversations we had about her old man were wishful thinking.

I wait for her to peer at me through her lashes before saying, "This isn't right. You know that?"

Carla's eyes flick to the floor, her shoulders curling ginward as if she's bracing herself for a scolding. Picking at the blood drying on her sleeve, she raises her shoulders to her ears.

"Dad was just cranky. He's usually really nice."

Frustration wells in my chest. The more I see of her, the more I realize she's deluded, not devious. I bite back my response, forcing myself to breathe through the frustration. She only knows him as Victor, not Valentino Bossanova, the serial wife murderer.

Pushing too hard will make her retreat. If I dropped the truth about her father, she'd either call me a liar and become defensive, or try to rationalize his behavior. Hell, she might even switch sides and allow him to groom her into becoming his accomplice.

"When did it get like this?" I ask, my voice soft.

Carla chews on the inside of her cheek. "He was the perfect dad for the first year, then I don't know. When I disappoint him, he loses control. But he has so much on his mind."

More excuses tumble out, each one bouncing off my patience like bullets on a kevlar vest. He beat the shit out of her, trussed me up like a carcass in a meat locker, and stripped me naked, yet she's still defending his actions.

Her blind loyalty to him is like a knife to the gut, but I rein in my emotions. I can't afford to say the wrong thing and upset this tenuous balance.

"Yeah," I murmur at the first pause. "But it doesn't have to be like this. No one deserves to be treated this way."

Her eyes flicker, and I sense a crack in her armor of loyalty. She glances at the bruises on my wrists with a frown.

"I thought Dad wanted to save you," she whispers, her voice breaking. "He told me Mr. Montesano was an abusive husband who would eventually cut you into pieces."

A lump forms in my throat. She must have come home every day, reporting back our interactions. A manipulative asshole like Valentino Bossanova would know exactly what to say to make her think I was an abused wife.

I huff a laugh.

What do you call a man who sends a murderer after a woman's mother, breaks into her home in disguise to demand sexual favors, and then manufactures loan sharks who threaten to sell her into a life of sexual slavery?

An abuser.

I, Ginevra Di Marco, am also a victim of abuse.

My gaze drops to Carla's and I meet her watery brown eyes with compassion.

"We're not so different," I murmur. "My dad attacked me

when I refused to break my engagement with my childhood sweetheart."

Her eyes widen, her bruised features finally reflecting a flicker of outrage. "Why?"

"Because he was part of a conspiracy to murder his father, steal their family assets, and he needed to betroth me to the son of his accomplice."

"Did you forgive him?"

I shake my head. "My new fiancé was a monster."

"What did he do?"

"It wasn't so different from what I saw your dad do to you." I pause, studying her reaction, the way her lips press into a thin line. From the way she bows her head and slumps her shoulders, my words are sinking through the mental gymnastics.

"I don't want to traumatize you with all the details, but I wanted to escape. Both my dad and fiancé saw me as nothing but a tool, and all I wanted was peace."

Tears trickle down her cheeks, slipping onto the folds of her room service shirt. "Did either of them ever change?"

"Their actions lead to them being murdered in brutal ways. The same could have happened to me, but I wasn't standing by them when they were killed."

Her breath hitches. "Sometimes, I think of leaving, but I'm all he has."

"Even if he uses you as his punching bag?" I ask. "You're more than just a tool."

She sniffles.

"Where was he while you were abused in foster care?"

She stares at the dirty floor, her fingers clenching around the fabric of her pants. "He didn't know about me."

"Did he marry your mother?"

"Yes, why?"

"And he was still married when she died?"

She nods.

"Then how did he not know his wife had a daughter if they were still together when she passed?"

A sharp breath whistles through her front teeth. "I never thought about it that way."

Triumph flares in my chest, but I school my features into an even mask. Some men have a way of shifting reality to suit their purposes. I force myself not to think of how Benito orchestrated a situation where I was in so much peril that I had to throw myself at his feet. Instead, I focus on Carla.

"Your dad is in a lot of trouble. Benito went to great lengths to secure me as his wife. If he catches up with us, he'll kill him slowly." I shudder at the memory of Brisket—no, Benito—handing me a twitching heart.

Carla makes a strangled noise in the back of her throat.

"But you can save him," I say. "And save yourself."

"How?"

"Remove these cuffs. Help me escape once more."

Her gaze flicks to the door, and I force my teeth not to grind. Breaking out of abuse isn't easy.

"I just wanted him to be proud," she murmurs. "I thought maybe if I helped him, he'd see me as a good daughter."

"But you're not just a good daughter. You're a good friend," I say, making sure every word lands. "I see a woman who fought with a man four times her size to save a stranger—"

"Malfi."

"What?"

"That was Malfi, the casino's security chief. Mr. Montesano stationed him in the room opposite to scare you into staying in the honeymoon suite."

The words land like a punch to the gut. I gulp, trying to digest this new facet to Benito's machinations. Now isn't the time to focus on his twisted games. I need to learn from that manipulative bastard and slither my way out of captivity.

"Anyway," I say through clenched teeth. "You still deserve better than to get caught up when Benito breaks in with a small army."

She looks at me, her eyes shimmering. For a heartbeat, it seems she might cry, but then she turns her gaze back to the door. "I should warn Dad."

"He already knows," I say with a sigh. "He took my mom to the Montesano mansion, where there was a brutal shootout. He's seen the army of men working for the family, yet he still decided to hold me hostage."

Pain flickers across her features. "How can I save him?"

"Release me. I'll return to Benito, take the blame, and apologize for walking out."

"But he'll lock you up again," she whispers.

It takes every ounce of self control to yell at her to look at my naked body, look around this grimy basement and compare it to a honeymoon suite with room service and silk kimonos.

"And I'll escape him eventually," I reply. "The most important thing is saving your father from himself."

Brows furrowing, she contemplates my proposal. I hold my breath, my gaze fixed on bruised features flickering with indecision. Finally, she looks me in the eyes.

"If I let you go, what will you tell Mr. Montesano?"

As I part my lips to speak, the door slams open, making my heart stutter. Valentino strides in, his movements jerky, probably from exerting himself while injured. Instead of the black leather from earlier, he's clad in a fresh set of silk pajamas.

His gaze locks onto Carla, who tenses. "Breakfast," he barks. "Now."

Carla shrinks, her head dipping. "Yes, Dad."

"Carla," I whisper, my chest flaring with panic.

Ignoring me, she scuttles to the exit, not casting me a glance. My heart sinks as she disappears around her father, letting the door close behind her with a soft thud.

Valentino turns to me, his expression smug. "Your husband triggered one of my explosive traps."

Fear punches me in the chest, but I hold my features in a mask. "My wrists hurt. I'm getting nerve damage."

"Which stings more? Your flesh or missing out on a share of the hundred mil?" he asks with a chuckle. "And I heard you trying to corrupt Carla. Next time you interfere with another of my relationships, I'll tear the skin off your back."

He disappears through the door, leaving his words hanging in the air like a bitter fog.

Valentino Bossanova, Victor Bellavista, or whatever he calls himself can get fucked. I'll find a way to break those chains—Carla's and mine.

NINETY-ONE

BENITO

The next morning, I glare at the dining table with my head buried in my hands, trying to tune out the chatter. Sunlight streams in through the patio doors, searing my skin.

My head pounds, my chest burns, and my gut churns with anxiety. I didn't sleep a fucking wink with Ginevra's torture playing through my mind on repeat. We've lost track of Bellavista, but I can handle him later. All I want now is my wife.

"You can't wire some stranger a hundred million dollars in cash," Roman growls. "How the hell do we get it back?"

"Get him on the phone," says Cesare. "We can track his location. Rosalind and I can take him out... Or bring him back alive for torture."

"Right," Rosalind adds from his side.

My head snaps up, and I glare at the dark-haired assassin dressed in black to match my little brother. "I thought you of all people would be more sympathetic to Ginevra's cause."

She purses her lips, her eyes sharpening. As a professional equally as trained as Leroi, she bristles at the reminder of being a hostage.

I caught glimpses of what Cesare made her endure, and even took notes. Any sane woman should drive a knife into his gut.

Instead, she's still deep in the throes of Stockholm syndrome and showing no signs of recovery.

"We have forty hours between now and the drop-off point," she clips. "There's no reason to spend that time not searching for your wife."

"Rosalind has a point," Leroi snarls as though agreeing with her is agonizing.

I whirl around, casting my cousin a glower. He only meets it with an even stare.

Roman called a family meeting to discuss last night's disaster. I made the mistake of asking him to lend me the thirty million he stole back from his estranged wife. Naturally, he demanded a reason for such a large transfer of cash, and I had to reveal the truth.

We're sitting in the dining room because Roman says an emergency like this calls for a family brunch. He sits at the head of the table, with the space on his right conspicuously empty. I can't linger on how much he's pining for his wife. Not when my own wife is in peril.

I'm sitting at his left, between him and Leroi, with Seraphine at the far end. Next to her sits Sofia, who looks ready to faint. She's known Ginevra even longer than me, and used to pamper her like a daughter. Rosalind and Cesare take the seats next to Emberly's empty space, with Gil sitting across from Sofia.

A knock sounds on the door, and Roman barks at them to enter. It's Reaper, looking rumpled from last night. Four of our boys were injured in the explosion and are recovering from burst eardrums, cracked ribs, and minor burns.

"Professor Cortese," Roman gestures at the place at the farthest end of the table. "Take a seat."

Reaper glances at the empty place beside my older brother but doesn't comment. After serving as my best man, he knows that Roman poached our officiant for a sneak wedding, which backfired.

My big brother's posture at the head of the table is stiff and motionless, so much like Dad that I tense in my seat. His food remains untouched, his eyes locked on me with that familiar calculating stare. He isn't just watching—he's sizing me up, and it sets my nerves on edge.

"You're sure Ginevra's a victim in all this?" Roman asks.

The words land like a slap. My blood freezes, then boils with a fury that tightens my throat. I shoot out of my seat, staring down at the skeptical bastard.

"What the fuck does that mean?" I snarl.

Roman leans back in his seat, his gaze hardening as if he's ready for a fight. My brother might be jacked from his time on death row, but I'll kick the shit out of him to defend Ginevra's honor.

"I've had nearly five years to think about what went wrong," he says. "We all know Capello didn't just waltz in and steal our fortune. He was working behind the scenes, setting up each piece before he made a move against Dad. Every step was calculated."

My pulse hammers in my ears. I clench my jaw, waiting for him to get to the fucking point.

"The first sign of trouble was Ginevra breaking your engagement," he says. "She pulled away before everything went to hell. That means she knew something was brewing but didn't say a word."

Nostrils flaring, I glance at Cesare, who meets my gaze with a steady nod. Even he agrees with Roman. Maybe my little brother was harboring doubts all along. I grit my teeth, swallowing back the urge to yell that I'm not stupid.

"Don't you think I came to the same conclusion," I grit out. "Joseph Di Marco beat Ginevra into submission and threatened her mother. She didn't have a choice."

Roman and Cesare exchange a look, their silence screaming bullshit. The distrust in the air is so suffocating, I want to smash open a window.

"If she was so scared, why didn't she come here?" Cesare leans back, mirroring Roman, and crosses his arms. "She practically lived with us. She would have been safe."

"Didn't you hear the part where I said he threatened her mother? Besides, she was young."

Cesare scoffs. "She was twenty-four. I'm twenty-four. You think I'd stab someone I loved in the back?"

His accusation is a kick to the balls, but I don't flinch. "It's easy to talk shit when you're not a defenseless woman. Don't tell me you wouldn't do anything to save Mom."

Stiffening, his mouth snaps shut. The room goes still, the tension heavy and electric. Rosalind squeezes his hand, and leans her head on his shoulder as if he's already told her about his special connection with our mother.

Leroi sighs. "We're wasting time bickering. Whatever happened in the past doesn't change the fact that some asshole is holding a Montesano woman hostage."

"Finally, a sensible thought," Sofia says, her voice sharp. Our housekeeper leans forward, turning her gaze to me. "How much money do you have?"

"Forty million in cash," I rasp. "It's all I can pull together at short notice. I need sixty more."

Silence falls over the dining table. I don't expect anyone to volunteer, since the only person more desperate to save Ginevra is Sofia. I don't expect anything but judgment.

"I have ten," Leroi says from his end of the table.

My head whips to the side.

He shrugs. "Any woman who spent time with Samson Capello doesn't deserve to become another hostage."

I glance at Seraphine, who's sitting next to him, her expression tight. Something unspoken flickers over her blue eyes that makes me suppress a shudder. One day, I might pluck up the courage to ask her what happened in Capello's basement, but this morning, all I feel is gratitude.

"Thank you," I say, my words choked.

Cesare exhales a dramatic sigh. I turn to find his head bowed, his fingers tapping against the table in a restless rhythm. When he finally looks up, his eyes meet mine with resignation.

"I've got twenty," he mutters.

All the air escapes my lungs. I blink, trying to comprehend his offer.

"Why?" I croak.

Cesare's features soften. "Because you love her," he says with a shrug. "And you're important to me."

Rosalind wraps her arms around his chest and plants a kiss on his cheek. Everything I said about the assassin's Stockholm syndrome vanishes. Her love has brought out his compassion.

All eyes shift to Roman, who sits unmoved with his fingers steepled. My big brother controls nearly a billion dollars in assets, including a loan company, and at least a hundred million in cash.

Every second he hesitates feels like a noose tightening around my neck. Victor Bellavista already bruised Ginevra's face, stripped her naked. He could be violating her in ways I can't bear to imagine. My chest tightens, with ropes of anticipation pulling every nerve as I wait for his decision.

"Alright," Roman growls.

The noose snaps, and the tension around my throat eases with a breath of relief. Emotion clogs my lungs, tears prick my eyes, and all I can do is nod.

I look across the room at my family, my heart swelling. Roman matches my nod, Cesare grins, and Rosalind beams up at me with a warm smile. Next to her is Gil, who gives me a thumbs up.

At the far end of the table, Reaper offers a tight smile. It's bitter sweet, as he's probably thinking about the five years his sister, Isabella, spent as Tommy Galliano's hostage.

Sofia wipes her tears with a handkerchief, her eyes shining with relief. Next to her, Seraphine's blue eyes are hopeful and bright. Leroi brings her hand to his lips and offers me a tight nod, making me wonder if it was Seraphine who bore the brunt of Samson's sadism.

"Thank you." My voice cracks, the words barely enough to convey the depth of my gratitude. "I'll repay you all. Every cent."

Roman glances away and grunts. I can't tell if it's out of regret or frustration that winning back his wife won't be so easy.

Silence falls across the room for several heartbeats. When this is over, I'll fall to my knees and beg Ginevra for forgiveness. This mess is completely my fault, and I'll spend a lifetime making amends.

Reaper clears his throat. "Now that we have the ransom, I think we can discuss our plans to track Bellavista."

The room erupts into a flurry of chatter, with Roman and Gil coordinating the Montesano men, and Reaper the Mortis House boys. Cesare and Rosalind are a team, as are Leroi and

Seraphine, who want to participate, even though Leroi is still injured.

I return to my seat, watching my family rally around to save Ginevra despite their reservations. Appreciation floods my heart, threatening to overflow. They've given me the lifeline I needed. Now it's up to me to make sure it's enough.

With every ounce of determination, I make a silent vow. I will bring Ginevra back and we will roast that bastard on a spit.

NINETY-TWO

GINEVRA

I blink awake, groggy and disoriented, my head pounding to the beat of my sluggish pulse. Everything aches from spending the night on the concrete floor in torn scraps of clothing.

Shivering, I pull the tattered fabric closer, but the chill still seeps into my bones. No matter how much I knotted together the remnants of what Valentino destroyed, I still can't stop feeling vulnerable and exposed.

My gaze roams around the basement's decaying walls toward the locked door. I inhale, feeling clusters of spores invade my lungs. The room presses in, dark and oppressive, squeezing out the terrifying thought that I might never leave this place alive.

Mom will be distraught and drown her grief in vodka. No one will be there to pull her out.

Benito will… Shit. I don't know.

He's just like Martina. Friendly one minute but hiding years of bottled up contempt. I can't tell if he'll rejoice at my downfall or rage that someone else got to destroy me first.

The door opens with a creak, and my head snaps up. Carla steps in with a silver tray, dressed in a tight black bodice, frilly apron, fishnet stockings, and heels.

My jaw drops. I have to blink to make sure I'm not hallucinating her dressed like a sexy maid, but she walks toward an upturned box. After moving it closer to me with her stilettoed foot, she sets down her tray.

"Room service," she says, her voice strained.

My gaze drops down to an elaborate breakfast of poached eggs drowning in hollandaise, grapefruit halves dusted with sugar, and a parfait glass filled with bright pink Jell-O topped with whipped cream and a cherry.

If I wasn't chained in a psychopath's basement and still throbbing from a physical assault, I'd think we'd traveled back to 1974.

Instead, I gaze up at Carla, taking in her split lip, the bruise blooming on her cheek, the way her shoulders slump as if she's carrying the weight of a thousand regrets. She lowers her lashes, her eyes darting everywhere but at me.

Anger rises hot in my chest, directed at Bossanova. But beneath it roils something colder—an all-encompassing dread. Dread that Carla is beyond reach. If she'd absorbed anything I told her last night, she'd be dressed to escape, not to serve.

"Thanks," I murmur. "You didn't have to make something so elaborate."

She shrugs, her gaze fixed on a spot to my left. "It's nothing. Dad likes to breakfast like a king, and there were leftovers."

My eyes drift back to the absurd costume. From the angle where I'm sitting, I can't just see her lacy stocking tops, but also the bruises spreading beneath the fishnets.

"What's with the outfit?" I ask, trying to keep my tone neutral.

She shuffles on her feet, her cheeks flushing. "Dad appreciates a full service."

My stomach drops. "What does that mean?"

Carla's blush deepens, and she glances away, her shoulders curling inward. "He says I look pretty dressed up."

Maybe it's the confinement, or even the concussion, but did she just confess to wearing sexy outfits for her dad? Silence hangs for several shocked seconds as I try to muster up a reply.

How old is she? Twenty-five, twenty-six? She caught up with her father right after leaving foster care, when she turned eighteen. Maybe I'm jumping to the wrong conclusion, but something about this situation is off.

My gaze bounces to her wedding ring, and I force in a deep breath, trying to steady my nerves. "Carla, fathers don't ask their daughters to serve them breakfast in fishnets. This isn't normal."

Annoyance flickers across her features. "You don't get it," she snaps. "He's my dad. I can't walk away from him. He needs me."

I squirm on the concrete, thinking of Martina, whom Dad had groomed to become his plaything. She didn't provide full details, but the abuse started early and continued long after she'd graduated law school and become an adult.

"Look at the bruises. This isn't a healthy relationship. It's not love."

Her eyes harden, and her nostrils flare. "And you're the expert? Mr. Montesano threw you in a cell just like this on your wedding night. He locked you up and left you without clothes for days, yet you love him, so don't pretend you're any better."

Her words are a punch to the throat. I reel back, my eyes widening. She's right. Benito caught me in a cycle of terror and manipulation. Breaking his heart changed him for the worse. All I did was cling to the memory of the boy who once loved me with all his soul.

"At least my dad is honest about what he is," she says, her voice taut with fury. "He doesn't pretend to be perfect."

Knowing that she's right fills my gut with the chilling realization that Carla isn't just trapped in this twisted form of abuse—she's committed. An ache settles in my chest, and I press my free hand into my sternum. I'm not equipped to pull her out of this delusion. No words can break through this kind of brainwashing. She's too far gone to help.

The door bursts open, and Valentino strides in, dressed only in a red silk robe. A flush spreads across his bruised face, and the eye not swollen shut glows with a manic light.

"Montesano agreed to pay up!" he bellows, his voice echoing across the basement walls. "A hundred mil. We're rich!"

My stomach drops—not just at Benito pulling together a hundred million dollars so quickly, but because he's willing to pay this much to get me back. Surely I can't mean so much to the man behind Bob Brisket?

Valentino looks me up and down, his gaze lingering over

every exposed patch of skin. "He must love you a lot to pay that kind of money," he sneers. "What's so special about that ginger minge?"

Skin crawling, I press back against the wall, every muscle tensing in anticipation for an attack. He steps closer, breathing hard and fast through his swollen lips, reaching out a pale hand, eager to claim what he's just ransomed for a fortune.

"Dad?" Carla squeaks, her voice wavering with desperation.

Valentino's head snaps to the side, making her flinch. My breath catches. Is she trying to save me?

He crosses the distance between them in two strides, wraps an arm around Carla and pulls her into his wiry frame. With a snarl, he leans down and pecks her on the lips. "You, my sweet angel, are the gift that keeps on giving."

Carla's face lights up, her cheeks flushing despite the bruises, and she gazes up at him like he's the sun.

I shrink against the wall, my hackles rising, my insides twisting into painful knots. It's like watching a car crash in slow motion. I don't know if I should cringe or scream.

"God sent me a little blessing," Valentino murmurs, his voice husky.

Carla leans into him, her eyes half-closed, drinking in the affection like it's the life that animates her veins. "You mean that, Dad?"

His lips crash onto hers in a savage kiss that makes my stomach leap to the back of my throat. Every fine hair stands on end, every nerve ending screams that I'm in danger. I want to crawl out of my skin and escape. I gag, finally realizing there's something worse than seeing Valentino Bossanova smooching with Mom.

The kiss continues, with Valentino sliding his bony thigh between her legs. A scream lodges in my windpipe, but they're oblivious to my terror, oblivious to the grime and filth of the basement, oblivious to the world that exists outside their bubble of perverse affection.

When they both exchange throaty moans, I freeze, unable to look away, unable to stop the unfolding of this horror show. As

Carla's hand disappears into that red robe, several realizations hit me at once.

She's just as twisted as her father and caught in an incestuous cycle of validation and victimization. She's beyond my paltry help. And most importantly, she must have known Valentino didn't persuade her to help the wife of the man who beat him bloody out of the goodness of his heart.

He finally breaks the kiss and turns back to me with a wide grin of missing teeth. "Why would I want you or that drunken hag you call a mother when I have my little girl?"

My lips part, but my brain can't muster up a response.

Valentino scoops Carla into his arms, making her shriek with delight, and carries her out of the room like she's his blushing bride.

Truth hits with brutal clarity: when Benito gets me back, I won't just be the woman who betrayed him, but the wife who cost him a hundred million dollars.

He'll make me repay him in a dozen humiliating ways for the rest of my miserable life.

I would rather die than entangle myself in the same cycle that's devoured Carla. I've been there before, and I won't let it happen again.

Since I can't convince Carla to set me free, then I'll have to save myself before the ransom drop.

NINETY-THREE

GINEVRA

I lean toward the door with my eyes closed, listening to the sound of the key turning in the lock. No matter how much I try, it's impossible to scrub out the image of my kissing captors.

Through ragged breaths, I wait for their footsteps to groan up the stairs. I still don't have a plan to escape, but I'll die trying. Carla's high-pitched squeal echoes down the stairwell and through the locked door, setting off waves of revulsion.

How could she? How could he? I can't understand.

Turning away, I force back a swell of anger. All that effort I wasted, trying to convince Carla to leave her father, and they're romantically involved. I was right the first time when I assumed 'her old man' was her significant other.

Stop this.

I need to focus. Need to find a way out of this hell. And dwelling on that unnatural association won't magically unlock my cuffs.

My eyes snap open, and gaze lands on the breakfast tray still sitting on the box. Ignoring the garish display, I grab a small bottle of water, twist open the cap and take a long, desperate swig.

Cold liquid rushes down my tongue, soothing and sharp, hydrating the parched membranes of my throat and jolting me back to the present. It dribbles down my lips and onto my chest, catching a draft that makes me shiver.

Once I've drained the bottle dry, I set it aside and reach for the napkin, ready to wipe the spill.

Something metallic clinks on the tray, making me freeze. I glance down at the napkin, my breath quickening as I notice something hidden beneath the smooth fabric. It's a ring of keys.

For a millisecond, I still, and my mind goes blank.

What. The. Hell?

My heart lurches, slamming against my ribs, urging me to reach down and snatch the cold metal. The first key looks small enough for the cuffs on my legs, while the second is large and rusted and could fit a door.

Carla must have left them when she set down the tray, but was it on purpose or a mistake? Does it even matter when I have everything I need?

Gripping the smaller key so tight that the edges bite into my skin, I fit it into the lock of the ankle cuff and twist. It jams, the movement digging into my raw skin. After jiggling it back and forth, the cuff clicks open, releasing my foot.

I shake my leg, letting the metal fall to the concrete with a clatter. Every muscle groans in protest as I haul my body to standing, and my breath comes in ragged bursts.

This is it—I'm free, but it's too early to celebrate. One misstep, and I'll be back in chains.

Clutching together the edges of my room service shirt, I rush across the basement. The large key between my fingers feels heavier with each frantic second as if hesitating will trap my soul in this hellhole for an eternity.

I reach the door, slip the key in its lock, and give it a tentative twist. It grinds against the door's rusty levers, creating a sound that slices through the dull roar of blood between my ears.

Turning the handle, I pull open the door and peek into a narrow stairwell. A low-wattage bulb casts dim light over the steps ascending into darkness. I creep out into a landing made of rough concrete, just as a deep groan drifts through the ceiling.

Shit.

It's accompanied by a feminine moan that makes the fine

hairs on the back of my neck stand on end. Shaking off the disgust, I grip the railing and continue upward.

The wood warps beneath my weight, filling the stairwell with a groan. In my frazzled state, it may as well be a fire alarm. I freeze, my breath catching, my eyes snapping to the top of the stairs. That's where a door looms, half open and waiting.

"One... two... three," I whisper under my breath. "Move."

I step forward, timing each footfall with Valentino's deep moans, placing my weight on the rail. The cold air thickens with every step, the house seeming alive with its own malevolent heartbeat.

Common sense says they can't hear a thing over the sounds of their pleasure, but paranoia urges me to stay cautious. My vision tunnels to the gap straight ahead, focusing on that sliver of freedom.

As I reach the top, the noises stops. My hand freezes on the doorknob. Frantic heartbeats pulse blood to my extremities, making my fingertips throb. Then Carla lets out a keening wail that echoes down the stairwell. The sound covers my exit, and I burst into the downstairs corridor.

It's late morning. I can tell as much from the slivers of bright light slicing through the cracks in the boarded-up windows. Maybe it's my PTSD, but this hallway looks entirely different from the one we entered last night.

Gritting my teeth, I stumble through the door, only to find faint beams of red illuminating the dust particles. It looks like a scene from Mission Impossible, but without the jarring sounds of sex.

My heart stalls. I glance at a camera mounted on the ceiling, its faint whirring barely audible over the drumroll of my pulse. Panic claws at my throat, but I force it back. There's no way in heaven, hell, or Hogwarts that I'll return to that basement.

Dropping to my belly, I slip the keys between my teeth, flatten my body against the floorboards, and ignore how much I ache. With bent elbows, I crawl across the rotten wood, my exposed skin catching on splinters.

I keep my head low, my chin tucked into my chest to avoid lifting even an inch too high and nicking one of those beams.

The floor shifts beneath my limbs, but I continue forward, timing my movements with the rhythmic creak of a bed and Carla's unsettling moans.

Sweat beads on my forehead, mingling with the dust and dirt, blurring my vision as I focus on the end of the hallway. My heart pounds so fiercely I swear it echoes off the walls, but it's a twisted comfort that their disgusting noises mask my clumsy escape.

The sounds from upstairs keep spilling down, louder and more frantic. Eventually, I reach the small patch of space in front of the door not covered by the sensors and ease my way up.

My chest heaves, and adrenaline courses through my veins as I pluck the keys from between my lips. I unlatch the door, ease it open, and freeze.

The deserted street is gone, replaced by a clearing of weeds, surrounded by dense woods. My mind spins, trying to piece together what's wrong.

Last night, Carla parked on a road of detached houses. How the hell did I end up in a forest?

It doesn't matter. I'm out, and I need to move. Rushing down the steps on bare feet, I reach a cracked path bisecting the untamed yard. I jog forward, just as a dog's bark shatters the silence.

A window slams open, and I whirl around to see Valentino leaning out with a gun. "Freeze!" he growls, "Or I'll deliver you to Montesano as a corpse."

NINETY-FOUR

GINEVRA

I stagger backward, my feet shuffling through weeds and loose gravel. Somewhere in my periphery, a black dog lurches in my direction, but every ounce of my attention is locked on the window above.

Valentino leans out waving his gun, his gray hair sticking to his flushed face. "How the fuck did you get past the sensors? Better still, how the hell did you escape a locked basement?"

My heart slams against its cage, trying to break through my chest. Every instinct screams at me to run, but I know he isn't bluffing. If he can murder his wives for a life insurance payout, he sure as hell can shoot me in the back.

"Girl," he barks. "Come to the fucking window!"

My blood runs cold, my gut twisting with fury and fear. Is this the moment he forces Carla to shoot me in the head as punishment for leaving the keys?

"If I have to drag you..." he says, his voice a low growl.

I can almost hear her whimper during this tense standoff. My throat tightens. What if Carla left those keys on purpose and responded to his advances to give me an opening? An opening I wasted by waking up the dog?

Options flicker across my mind like playing cards, making my brow break out in a sweat. When Valentino turns his head, I take a tentative step backward.

He yanks Carla closer, his fingers twisting into her hair. "This is your doing, cunt. How did you let her talk you into escaping?"

She squeezes her eyes shut. "Please, Dad—"

"I told you not to call me that," he snarls through broken teeth and presses the gun into her temple.

My stomach plummets. Survival instincts urge me to take advantage of this opening and run, but I can't let him murder another woman.

"Hey," I snap. "Why are you blaming her for the hatch?"

His gaze snaps to meet mine. "Which hatch?"

"What kind of abductor doesn't know the exits in his own lair?"

Confusion flickers across his features. It's just enough for him to release Carla's hair and return his attention to me. Somewhere in the back of my mind, my survival instincts are calling me an idiot, but I'm tired of being a coward.

Cowardice was what broke up my relationship with Benito and twisted his love for me into contempt. Cowardice was what kept me in an abusive engagement with Samson. I'll be damned if I allow yet another man to intimidate me into submission.

I raise my chin, glaring up into the window, where he takes the gun off her temple and points it back to me.

"Benito will want proof I'm still alive," I say.

He flashes what's left of his teeth. "He might pay more if I send a picture of your gaping bullet wounds."

My jaw clicks shut.

Bellavista presses the gun into Carla's trembling fingers. "If I find out you did something to help that ginger bitch escape, I'll make sure a bullet finds its way up your cunt."

"Dad," Carla chokes out.

He smashes his fist into her cheek. "Stop calling me that!"

She drops out of view, and Valentino disappears from the window. Without meaning to, I turn around and run toward the trees.

A gunshot cracks through the air, and the barking stops. I

whirl around, finding Carla back at the window pointing the pistol.

"Dad is on his way downstairs," she says, her voice wavering. "Don't move."

I freeze again, my heart racing in manic circles, watching Carla mishandling the gun. She's trembling so much that the barrel wobbles, looking like she might twitch and pull the trigger. Her eyes are wide, and filled with desperation, fear and a haze of something I've only ever seen on Mom.

Is he giving her drugs?

Raising my palms, I take a tentative step back. "Carla, put down the gun."

Her grip tightens, making the pistol jerk. "He'll kill me if I let you go."

"How, when you're the one who's armed?"

I inch back, my feet crunching against the loose gravel. Valentino is almost certainly on his way down. I'm not sure if I can outrun the old bastard—he's stronger than he looks. I have a better chance of talking sense into Carla.

"We're no different, you know. Both stuck with abusers."

"He isn't—"

"He just punched you in the face, and threatened to shoot you in the vagina. You just told me he'll kill you. Why not strike at him first?"

She flinches at my words, her gaze flickering from me to the room behind her, as if expecting her father to come storming back at any second.

"He's coming for you," she says, her voice flat. "You should run."

My heart plummets to my feet. Carla is too confusing to understand. A victim and an accomplice rolled into an unpredictable package. I can't afford to waste time talking sense through her skull when my life is on the line.

The dog whines from where it's tethered to the house's front post, signaling approaching danger. As I step backward toward the trees, the door slams open, and Valentino bursts out with a rope.

He's naked, with a wiry frame livid with bruises. The dog

cowers, shrinking back against its chain, whimpering as Valentino storms past. I lock gazes with it for a split second—its eyes mirroring my terror.

Not daring to catch a glimpse at the appendage swinging beneath the old man's eight pack, I spin on my heel and run.

"Don't just stand there, you stupid little bitch!" he barks at my back. "Shoot!"

The air reverberates with another gunshot, flooding my system with a surge of cold panic. It grips my gut, powering my feet. I sprint toward the trees, wincing at the twigs and gravel digging into my soles.

Valentino's footsteps slam into the ground, heavy and relentless, and Carla's alarmed cries echo in my ears. Every thud of my heartbeat is a countdown to disaster, but I don't stop. I don't dare look back.

"Carla!" he barks, his voice sharp and furious. "Keep that gun steady, or I'll put you down like the damn dog!"

Low-hanging branches whip at my face as I plunge into the forest. My breath comes in ragged gasps, each stride a battle against the uneven terrain.

I have no idea where I'm going, if I'm running toward civilization or capture, but I push harder, tripping over roots and rocks jutting up from the forest floor.

Valentino's shouts blend with the dog's panicked barks, a cacophony of fear that drowns even the thud of my pulse. Thick woodland engulfs me from every direction, punctuating the darkness with intermittent bursts of dazzling sunlight. I squint, my eyes streaming with tears.

"You can't outrun me, you red-headed whore!" he howls, sounding like he's enjoying the hunt.

Every muscle screams for mercy, and my lungs burn for oxygen, but I can't wait to catch even a single breath. Quickening my pace, I push through the underbrush as if the devil is snapping at my heels.

Valentino's breath becomes ragged and excited. Each rustle of leaves and snap of twigs amplifies my terror. He's getting closer, reveling in his sadistic pleasure. His manic laughter echoes through the dense foliage, chilling my blood to the marrow.

He's done this before.

Most likely with at least one of his murdered wives.

Just when I think I've gained some distance, my foot lands on a layer of sticks and leaves. The ground beneath me collapses. There's no time to react—just a sickening lurch as I plummet, my world spinning in a chaotic blur. I hit the bottom hard, my hip and shoulder slamming into a rough surface lined with rocks.

Pain shoots through my left side, and I gasp, choking on air filled with dust. Dirt and debris rain down on my head, and it feels like I've reached the bottom of an avalanche. When the cascade finally settles, I blink up at a jagged rim tangled with broken branches.

I've fallen into a pit trap.

My ears ring, making his insane laughter seem fainter, but I'm not about to trust my screwed-up senses. If I don't move, Valentino will catch up in minutes.

Gritting my teeth through the pain, I force myself to stand, and reach for one of the branches hanging over the pit. I pull myself up, but the wood snaps under my weight, sending me falling back on my ass.

"Shit," I hiss through clenched teeth, my eyes pricking with frustrated tears.

I claw at the walls, but they're too crumbly, too steep. Whoever dug this pit knew exactly what they were doing. When the warmth on my back vanishes, I turn my head and squint up to the sky, finding Valentino's silhouette looming at the edge of the trap.

Sunlight illuminates his gray hair like a halo, but there's nothing divine about his warped figure. He grins down like a hungry hyena, running his tongue along his jagged teeth.

"See something you like, ginger minge?"

A knot tightens around my throat.

Don't look. Don't look. Don't. Look.

Gravity pulls my eyes down his bruised chest, past the faded scars and wiry gray hair scattered across his abdominal muscles, to the hollow curve of his hips.

The penis hanging between his legs is long and thin, still glistening from sex. Revulsion spasms through my digestive system, making me gag. I tear my gaze away, double over, and retch.

He snickers. "Your mother liked it well enough."

"She didn't," I snarl through the bitter taste of bile and pull myself back to standing. "She was only with you for the money, you bastard."

Valentino just laughs, the sound echoing down into the pit. "Insult me all you like. It's the last thing you'll enjoy before I deliver your head to that arrogant bastard in a Tiffany box."

NINETY-FIVE

BENITO

Precisely forty-eight hours since Ginevra's abduction, I stalk through the construction site like I own the night. Ten agonizing seconds hearing her voice—weak, ragged, and barely coherent—was all it took to make me wire the hundred million. Now, Victor Bellavista has me chasing coordinates into this godforsaken pit.

It's a wreck of jagged beams jutting out like snapped ribs and scaffolding twisting up toward the night's sky. My boots grind against broken concrete and rusted nails, and I imagine them to be Bellavista's bones.

We've bled every lead dry, squeezed every rat in the underworld, and still come up empty. Bellavista remains a ghost, as if he's always two steps ahead. But deep down, a sickening suspicion festers that Victor might not even be a man. He could be an alias for Carla, a mastermind working through proxies and hiding in plain sight.

It would make a twisted sort of sense, since I hired her to keep an eye on the casino.

Reaper paces at my left, clad in bullet proof armor. He glances from side to side, his eyes sweeping every shadow. I need his backup. I can't think straight, still haunted by those images of the man in leather stripping and debasing Ginevra.

Disgust crawls up my throat, bitter and acidic. Both at myself for doing the same to the only woman I've ever loved, and at the rank stench of wet cement and decay that clings to the back of my throat.

How could I have been so heartless?

"Still with me?" Reaper asks, his voice cutting through my thoughts.

Forcing my guilt into the background, I lock focus on the path ahead. We're seconds away from the drop-off, and every step tightens the tension coiling around my chest.

Roman told me to stay back, that I was walking into an ambush. Cesare told me to at least wear my fucking body armor, but I refused.

The first thing Ginevra sees when Bellavista sets her free shouldn't be Bob Brisket or another faceless brute in bulletproof gear. It will be her husband—the man who will tear the world apart to keep her safe.

Rosalind and my brothers hover at the perimeter with the Mortis House boys, waiting to intercept Bellavista or his lackeys. A sick feeling in the pit of my gut whispers that no one will see Ginevra tonight. This entire building site feels like a trap waiting to spring, but I'd walk through the gates of hell to retrieve my wife.

"Up ahead," Reaper says, nodding toward a pile of twisted metal.

Bellavista threatened to deliver Ginevra gift wrapped, but I was expecting a coffin or a crate. Wedged between the rubble is a wooden box, half-swallowed by the debris. Moonlight peeks out from the clouds, illuminating it with an eerie glow.

It's barely large enough to fit a soccer ball.

The tension in my chest tightens, squeezing the air out of my lungs until I'm barely breathing. I explode into a sprint, every instinct blazing with one blistering, uncontrollable need: Ginevra. Her voice echoes through my ears, weak and desperate, begging for my help and fueling every frantic step.

Reaper grabs my arm. "Don't touch it. Could be another explosive."

The words barely register through the dull roar of blood pounding through my ears. My focus is tunneled, blackened at the edges, zeroing in on that fucking box. Cold adrenaline surges through my veins, and I shrug him off like he's an action figurine. By the time Reaper tackles me to the ground, I've already ripped off its lid.

The metallic stench of blood hits me like a punch to the throat. Something heavy and wet tumbles out—dark, slick, and glistening under the moonlight. My stomach flips. It's head-shaped, smeared with blood, with a face frozen in a rictus of shock.

Gut clenching, I hit the floor, my eyes locking on the severed head. Her face is bruised, eyes wide, hair matted with blood.

"Benito."

Reaper's voice is muffled and distant like he's calling from another dimension. The world around me cracks open, splintering into a chaos of jagged edges that cut and slice, my mind struggling to grasp what the fuck I'm looking at. Every second stretches into a slow-motion reel of horror playing on an endless loop.

"Benito."

Rough hands drag me off my feet. I swing at my best friend, wild and blind with grief. The punch lands on the helmet, but the pain on my knuckles barely registers.

"Get a hold of yourself!" he roars, grabbing my shoulders and turning me back toward the head. "Look at it again."

It takes several seconds for my mind to decipher what I'm seeing. The severed head has brown eyes instead of gray. Short dark hair instead of long auburn.

"It's not her," he yells.

"Carla," I say through panting breaths.

"Boss," says another voice. "Something else dropped out of the box."

My gaze whips back toward the fallen head, where a tablet lies on its side. Reaper releases his grip on my shoulders long enough for me to break free and snatch it off the floor.

With trembling fingers, I swipe the screen and brace myself for another horror show.

The tablet flickers to life with a view of a different room with light peeking out of its windows. Ginevra and Carla stand side by side, their wrists bound together by rope and pulled high above their heads, forcing their arms into what looks like a painful stretch.

Gagged, bruised and naked, their muscles quiver under the strain, their faces twisting with agony. Dirt cakes Ginevra's hair and stains her front, as if he's dragged her across the ground.

Fury pulses through my veins, searing away the shock, replacing it with raw, animalistic rage. It's primal, visceral, burning under my skin like napalm. Reaper's grip on my shoulder feels like a shackle, holding me back from tearing this place to the fucking ground. I want to rip the steel beams out with my bare hands, make this whole site scream the way my soul is screaming for Ginevra.

The leather-clad figure stalks into view, his face obscured by that infernal mask. My breath stutters, my fists curling with fury. After glancing around the camera, he circles the women like a predator, seeming to savor their terror, before placing a hand on Ginevra's waist.

She flinches, a whimper escaping the gag, her dirt-streaked face streaming with tears. Carla tries to turn her head, but the ropes binding her together limit the movement.

"Benito Montesano," the distorted voice sneers, dripping with mockery. "See what you have brought upon your wife?"

My throat tightens. I grip the tablet, my pulse roaring in my ears. Every instinct snarls at me to tear the screen apart, smash the device into the concrete, do anything but watch. But I can't look away. I need to know what he's done with my Ginevra. I need to know if this bastard's left her alive.

The figure steps back with a bullwhip. He unfurls it with a flick of his wrist, the leather snapping through the air like a gunshot.

Ginevra's muffled scream is a knife through my chest, her body jerking with the crack of the lash. She twists to the side, but there's nowhere to go.

Blood splatters across her pale skin, and her muscles strain against the ropes, desperate, fighting, but helpless.

"Your wife thought she could run, and this one thought she could help." He strikes Carla, who screams, her eyes widening.

Over the next agonizing minutes, he lashes both women with brutal force. The sound of leather meeting flesh resonates through the speakers as their skin blazes with red welts.

"How does it feel to be powerless, Montesano?" he snarls. "As you watch this, I could be doing anything to your wife."

Grief tightens its claws around my throat, making my eyes burn with tears of fury. This is senseless, brutal. If I ever get hold of Victor, I'll tear him into shreds.

The whipping continues until both women sag within their restraints, too exhausted to flinch. He moves behind Carla, looping the leather tail around her throat and pulling tight.

Her eyes fly open, bulging as she gasps for breath, her body convulsing.

Beside her, Ginevra thrashes, screaming into her gag, but it's no use. Victor tightens the whip, cutting off Carla's desperate gulps of air until her movements slow and then stop.

I freeze, my muscles locking, helpless to do anything but fixate on the anguish on my wife's face. Terror engulfs her eyes, and tears streak her cheeks as she screams for the other woman.

The masked man steps back, his attention shifting to the camera. "Another hundred million, Montesano. Or the next box will contain your wife's head."

Then, the screen cuts to black. My grip on the tablet tightens until I hear the plastic crack, but I can't let go. My anger roils, but there's nowhere for it to escape. The bastard just threw down the gauntlet, and all I can do is pick it up.

"What next?" Reaper asks.

My nostrils flare. "We're going back to see Salvatore Bellavista.

NINETY-SIX

BENITO

I sit in the front seat of the truck, urging Reaper to drive faster. Up ahead and further down the road, the Bellavista compound is in flames. Good. The boys have started without me. By now, every motherfucker dwelling within those gates will know I'm serious about finding my wife.

My heart lurches. Ginevra.

Images of that bastard whipping her like a dog sear through my mind, making my thoughts scatter. Her screams still ring through my ears. How dare he hurt my wife? How dare he force her to witness a brutal murder? It's only a matter of time before I catch up with Victor Bellavista, and I will make him bleed.

The truck passes what's left of the iron gates. Cesare and the others will have plowed them down the moment I gave the order to strike. As Reaper speeds down the driveway, everything from the trees to the distant buildings are alight with fire.

I open the door before he hits the breaks and step out into an atmosphere thick with smoke. Heat slaps against my skin, making me stagger back. I would say it's like walking through the entrance to hell, but my soul is already burning. Burning with vengeance. Burning for Ginevra.

The whole world will burn even more if I don't get my wife.

My heart pounds as I walk to the chaos unfolding on the

lawn. In the distance, my men pull survivors out of the flames and gather them on the only part of the compound we've left intact.

Last time, Bellavista's people knelt on the grass, stoic and tense. Now, they're frantic. They've lost everything—their homes, their possessions, loved ones who put up a fight. This is only a fraction of the anguish that's clawed through my heart since Ginevra fell into the clutches of Victor Bellavista.

Reaper catches up with me with a jerry can. Cesare and Rosalind stand up ahead, holding Salvatore and Antonio Bellavista at gunpoint. Antonio crouches on his hands and knees, coughing, gasping for air, his face streaked with soot. Salvatore sits on his ass, his aged face pale with fear.

"This is your last chance to tell me which one of you fuckers is Victor," I snarl.

"I don't know," Antonio blurts. "I swear it—"

Cesare kicks him in the side. "My brother didn't ask you what you didn't know, asshole."

Antonio collapses onto the grass, shaking, begging, but I can't even look him in the eye. All my focus is on Salvatore.

"He's taken my wife," My voice breaks, but I'm past caring about holding my emotions in check.

When he doesn't answer, I snap my fingers.

Reaper steps forward with the jerry can, unscrewing the cap and tossing it into Salvatore's face. I take the handle, the thick smell of gasoline cutting through the stench of fire.

"This is your last chance."

He squares his shoulders, breathing hard as I pour the liquid over his head. He flinches at first contact but remains in place. It's almost like he wants to die.

I kneel down, meeting his eyes. "Why are you protecting Victor?"My voice wavers, thick with rage and sorrow I can't contain. "Is the life of one man worth your family's?"

His eyes flick up to the burning mansion, reflecting the flames dancing in his pupils. Sweat beads on his brow as his jaw clenches, betraying his fear. My pulse quickens. This is the closest he's ever come to showing he knows something.

Straightening, I step back and turn my attention to Antonio, dousing him with gasoline. The liquid runs over his face, down to his chest, soaking into his pajama top. He shudders, eyes wide, his gaze darting between me and his father.

"Wait, wait, please! I would tell you if I knew anything!" Antonio's voice cracks. "Please, don't—"

Cesare smashes the butt of his gun into the back of Antonio's head, cutting him off mid-sentence. He slumps forward, coughing through the soot and gasoline clinging to his nightclothes.

"Shut the fuck up and let your old man speak," Cesare growls.

I turn to the old man, who inhales a deep breath like he's bracing himself for the end.

"Salvatore!" a female voice erupts through the commotion. "Tell them."

I glance toward the other end of the lawn and find an elderly woman in a housecoat. "Bring her here."

Reaper strides across the grass toward a group of survivors gathered beyond the reach of the burning mansion. The old woman raises her hands like a shield, her features twisting with anguish. After taking her arm, Reaper walks her to where Salvatore kneels.

When she's close enough, I turn to face her. "Who is Victor?"

She freezes, breaths coming in quick, shallow bursts. "I—I don't know who he is, but he's been blackmailing this family for over twenty—"

"Mother, stop," Salvatore hisses.

"Let her speak," I snap.

She places a hand to her chest. "Victor has been torturing this family for decades. I don't know what he has over my son, but it has to be something terrible enough to bring us all to ruin."

"Shut up!" Salvatore barks.

I kneel beside him again, my patience wearing thin. "Salvatore?"

He shakes his head, refusing to speak. Beside him, Antonio stirs, coughing up more soot and gasoline.

"Is your silence worth more than your family's lives? Because I'm about to set your son on fire, and the flames will spread to you."

Salvatore trembles, his facade cracking, but still he says nothing.

"Lighter."

Reaper presses the metal object into my palm. I flip it open, holding a flame in front of his face. "Last chance."

His eyes flicker with panic, darting from me to the flame, and back to his mother, who fills the air with sobs. He's ready to die, but will he watch his son burn in a funeral pyre? I turn the flame to Antonio, who thrashes beside him and screams.

"Your mother will be next," I whisper into Salvatore's ear.

The old man's stoic mask slips, and he squeezes his eyes shut.

"Victor has been holding my daughter hostage since she was an infant. I don't know where he's hidden her, but every time I try to cut him off, he sends a photo."

Eyes widening, I close the lighter with a snap.

"Help me find Victor," I say through clenched teeth. "I'll even help you find the girl."

He shakes his head. "He swore to deliver her head in a box if I interfered."

Reaper and I exchange glances but neither of us speak, even though the threat reminds us both about Carla.

I grind my teeth, my fingers tightening around the lighter. "I've run out of patience."

Turning back to Antonio, I pour the rest of the gasoline over his head, making sure to create a line of flammable fluid across the lawn. With a flick of my wrist, I toss the lighter at the end of the trail. The fire roars to life, racing across the lawn like dynamite to where Antonio tries to flee.

Cesare kicks him in the base of his spine, making him slump to the grass.

"No. Stop this!" the old woman sobs, collapsing onto the ground. "Salvatore. Say something. Save him!"

Salvatore lurches forward with a strangled cry, his eyes fixed on the flames closing in on his son.

"I'll tell you everything!" he blurts. "Just please, stop this madness!"

I give Reaper a sharp nod. He steps forward, stamping out the flames before they can reach Antonio. The fire hisses and dies, making Salvatore slump with relief.

"Speak," I hiss.

He stares up at me, sweat streaming down his soot-streaked face. "Victor isn't one man. He also isn't a Bellavista. They're distant cousins on my mother's side," he says, his voice hoarse. "The one still running about is Valentino. Valentino. Bossanova."

I freeze, my mind racing, blood pounding in my ears. That leather-faced lothario I hired to seduce Ginevra's mother?

"Bullshit," I growl.

Trembling, Salvatore shakes his head, his entire bulk sagging with defeat. "There are two of them. Gianni and Valentino—parasites who marry women, insure their lives, and murder them for a payout. Twenty-two years ago, Gianni was facing life in prison and didn't have money to pay for an attorney."

Fury pounds through my veins at the thought of having had that man in my grasp. I beat the shit out of him and set him free. If I had just killed him, Ginevra would no longer be in peril.

"They found out I'd had a daughter out of wedlock, and they took her." Voice cracking, he doubles over with tears. "They've held her hostage for years, using the girl to keep me in line. Every time I tried to resist, they'd send a new photo of her. I couldn't risk her life."

I glare down at him, my grip tightening on the jerry can. Questions assault my mind in quick succession: Why didn't Salvatore hire assassins or a private detective? And is her mother the woman who murdered Larry Zambino over the slot machines then nearly died in an explosion?

None of that matters when Ginevra's life still hangs in the balance.

Rage roils in my gut, violent and raw. Every ounce of pain Ginevra's endured, every second she's spent in captivity, all traces back to a man I dismissed as harmless.

"Where can I find him?"

Salvatore shakes his head. "He has a penthouse overlooking the park, but he wouldn't keep her somewhere so obvious. I've told you whatever you want. Just please, spare my family."

"If you hadn't withheld this information, I would have

stopped him before he took my wife." I reach into my pocket, extract my gun, and shoot him between the eyes.

He falls to the ground, and the old woman howls. I turn my attention away from them to lock gazes with my brother.

"Cesare," I say.

He cocks his head.

"Talk me through that harebrained scheme you had to break Roman out of prison."

"Why," he asks.

"Because we're about to abduct Gianni Bossanova from Death Row."

NINETY-SEVEN

GINEVRA

I wake up in a world of pain. Pain in my head, pain across the welts in my skin, pain in my heart. My limbs bend into an awkward fetal position, and the hard surface beneath me rumbles as if I'm crammed into the trunk of a car.

It feels like a whole day has passed since I tried to escape. The aches from falling into that pit have faded, replaced by painful welts from the whipping. The skin on my wrists burn from where Bossanova tied them too tight, but it's barely a distraction from the replay of Carla's murder. Her eyes, wide and pleading, stare out at me through the dark, begging me to do something —anything to save her life.

All I could do was scream.

Shit. I need to focus, but I can't breathe with pressure pushing down on my lungs. I exhale a choked sob at how Carla looked so pale and terrified, at the way she thrashed as the whip tightened around her neck.

Stop.

Pressing my forehead against the trunk's cold metal wall, I fumble around for a lever, a latch, a lock. Carla is gone and there isn't a thing I can do to bring her back. He strangled her like she wasn't his own flesh and blood, but lower than nothing. All because I tried to escape.

The car jerks over a pothole, jostling me against the sides of the trunk. My stomach lurches, bringing up a bellyful of bile. My lungs seize in tight bursts, the confined space constricting every ragged breath. At this rate, Valentino won't need to wrap the tail of a whip around my throat. I'll have already choked to death.

Fuck... I really need to focus on breaking free.

I turn my ear to the trunk's lid, straining to hear anything beyond the rumble of the engine. Bossanova's muffled voice seeps through the noise. I can't tell if he's talking to himself or has found an accomplice, but I try to make sense of his muttering.

He's cursing, screaming obscenities, and by the time I hear the name, Montesano, the car screeches to a halt. My body slams into the wall of the trunk, sending a fresh wave of pain down my side. I bite down on my lip, hard enough to taste blood.

The sound of a door opening snaps me back into the present. Heavy boots hit the ground, growing louder as he approaches. There's a click of the trunk, a creak, then a burst of sunlight bright enough to sear my retinas. I squint against the glare and groan.

Rough hands grab my shoulders, yanking me out of the car. I hit the gravel with a thud, the sharp stones digging into my raw skin. I clench my teeth, not wanting to give him the satisfaction of a scream.

Bossanova stands over me, dressed in a stained wife beater, his bruised chest heaving. Gray hair sticks to his flushed face, his eyes wide with desperation.

My breath hitches. Did Benito find a way to claw back the money? Last time I saw the crazy old buzzard, he was stuffing Carla's severed head into a box. He said Benito would pay another hundred million when he saw what could happen to his precious wife.

He hauls me up by my hair, slamming my head against the bumper, making me see stars.

"How the fuck did Montesano find out?" Spit flies from his mouth, hitting my cheek. Bloodshot eyes burning with insanity, he jerks my head back and forth with a grip tight enough to rip the scalp off my skull. "How?!"

Wincing through another explosion of pain, I stutter, "Wh- what are you talking about?"

"Liar!" His foot smashes into my solar plexus, knocking the wind out of my lungs. I double over, wanting to curl into a ball, but his fingers tighten around my hair. "Tell me how Montesano found Gianni," he snarls, his voice shaking with unrestrained fury. "Tell me!"

"I don't—" Another kick cuts off my words, this time to my ribs. Sharp pain radiates through my side, and dark spots swim in my vision as I try to make sense of his accusations. What's he saying? That Benito pieced together the link between Victor Bellavista and Valentino Bossanova?

He reaches into his pocket, extracts a phone, and shoves it into my face. "Look!"

The device is too close for me to focus, so I draw back, blinking over and over to clear my vision. Benito appears on screen, holding a gun to the head of a man dressed in a prison uniform. He looks so much like Valentino that he has to be Gianni.

My heart stutters, and every muscle in my chest tightens to the point of pain. That's the man who murdered my birth mother.

"You have four hours to deliver Ginevra to my gates," Benito says, sounding more like Bob Brisket than the man I married. "Or I'll send your brother back to prison in pieces."

My eyes widen. Benito must have broken into death row to hold Valentino's older brother hostage.

All to save me.

When the video loops back to the beginning, Bossanova tightens his grip around my hair, trying to pull each follicle out by the root. "This is your fault," he snarls, his voice cracking. "You must have left him a clue."

As he continues an unhinged, accusation-filled rant, my mind conjures up a dozen replies. I was escaping a manipulative husband with the help of what I thought was a friend. If I'd known Carla was the daughter of a psychopath, I would have found another way to leave Benito. How the hell was I supposed to communicate with him while tied up and held hostage?

The tirade continues, but I force my thoughts to still. This diatribe tells me only one thing: Bellavista is unraveling. If I stay alert, I might even find an opening.

He slams his phone into his pocket and drags me like a rag doll across the gravel to the car's back door.

"Get inside. We're going to rescue my brother."

After opening the door, he bundles me in the back seat and orders me to stay down. Even if I wanted to sit up and scream for help, no one would see me on this deserted road.

We pass large expanses of land, some filled with orchards, others with corn, and a few left for cattle. I coil on the back seat, readying myself for the first opportunity to escape.

After about thirty minutes, we stop at a large farmhouse. It's a nondescript building of brown bricks with clouded windows. Strangely, the land around it looks tended.

Valentino exits the car and flings open the door. Before he can drag me out again, I'm already out and on my feet. He shoves me across the courtyard and up the farmhouse's stairs, his breath hitting my bare back in ragged gasps.

If my hands weren't cuffed, I'd knock him back on his ass, but I bide my time, waiting for the right moment to strike.

Inside, the house feels like a forgotten relic from the '80s. Mirrors with gaudy gold frames reflect faded floral wallpaper. He bundles me through a living room, where a velvet couch sits with its plump cushions untouched. The air is thick with dust and the faint musk of aging fabric, giving the space an almost suffocating stillness.

We climb the stairs and reach a doorway leading to a woman's bedroom. Valentino pushes me into the edge of a vanity cluttered with cosmetics. I hit my head and grimace through another burst of pain. Before I can recover, he's already unlocked my cuffs.

"Get dressed, cover that shit on your face with makeup. We're going to trade you for my brother." He disappears through the door and turns its lock.

With a groan, I stumble to my feet, met with a wall of mirrors reflecting gaudy décor dripping with retro opulence. The bedspread is a swirl of pastel pinks and purples, with a golden chandelier hanging closer than the blade of a guillotine.

Did this belong to one of his dead wives? The thought turns my stomach, but at least it distracts me from my reflection. I look like I've spent a night battling a monster in a pit, when I've been battling through terror and grief.

A heavy fist bangs on the door. "If you're not dressed in the next ten minutes, I'll drown you in the toilet."

It sounds like a bluff, but he's not above holding my face in a dirty pan out of a sense of twisted revenge. With a groan, I get up and walk to a wardrobe filled with garish outfits, adorned with sequins, shoulder pads, and side-splits. I sift through them, trying to find something in my size.

As I pick out a safari suit, still encased in dry-cleaning plastic, a heavy object falls free, landing on the floor with a muffled thud. I glance down, finding a long item encased in leather.

A knife.

My breath catches. This is my chance.

I'll wait for the moment when he least expects it. When his guard is down.

And then I'll strike.

NINETY-EIGHT

GINEVRA

After the world's most refreshing cold shower, my mind is cooler, calmer, clearer. Stabbing is too good a death for a depraved creature like Valentino Bossanova.

He's responsible for the suffering and demise of more women than I can count. That old bastard deserves agony, and I know exactly how to deliver it.

I step out of the avocado-colored bathroom a new woman, bolstered by the shoulder pads on my safari jumpsuit and the thin covering of makeup over my bruises.

They used to call this power dressing, and I understand why: it feels like I'm channeling the strength of every 1980's vixen. Even my hair is more voluminous.

And with the knife in my pocket, I no longer feel like such a victim.

A heavy fist pounds again on the bedroom door. "Time's up," he snaps. "We're leaving."

I walk across the room, turn the handle, and step out, nearly bumping into Bossanova. With a new dark rinse covering his gray hair and a thick layer of fake tan over his bruises, he looks more like the killer Casanova I've grown to despise.

"You clean up well." He flashes his teeth, revealing a mouth full of dentures. His gaze travels down my jumpsuit, but he's too busy staring at my cleavage to notice the knife-shaped bulge in my pocket. "Are you planning on giving me any trouble on the ride back?"

"No," I rasp. "Just glad to be going home."

He snorts. "Follow me. Try anything stupid and you'll lose a kidney."

That's a bluff, but I'm not about to take any chances. I remember how he stormed the office years ago, crying tears of blood when his brother was sentenced to death. Dad told him there was nothing he could do this time because the evidence had been so damning, but Valentino swore revenge.

Maybe this is why he's treating me so badly. Because he thinks Dad could have done more to save his murderous brother from the electric chair. Or maybe it's because I looked down on him when he was pretending to be Mom's fiancé. Either way, I hope his desire to be reunited with Gianni outweighs his grudge.

I follow him down the staircase, back into the glitzy living room, and out through another exit where a black Bentley awaits beneath covered parking. My heart pounds, my hands curl into fists, and every instinct screams at me to fight, flee, or find a way to take him out. I clench my teeth, forcing myself to move forward, and slide into the back passenger seat.

The car's interior is as luxurious as it is suffocating, filled with the mingled scents of leather and expensive cologne. Nose wrinkling, I secure my seatbelt and try to stay small.

Bossanova casts me a filthy glance as he enters. "I'm not your fucking chauffeur. Sit in the front."

Grinding my teeth and unbuckling, I clamber over the console and deposit myself into the seat beside my enemy.

With a satisfied grunt, he starts the engine, making the Bentley roar to life. He pulls out from the car port and continues down a long driveway.

"I suppose you want to know why I have so many hideouts," he says.

"Not really," I mutter.

"My brother and I have specific tastes in women," he replies as if I'm interested. "We only dabble with the most beautiful, stylish, and wealthy bitches."

Is that why you fucked your own daughter?

I don't say that, of course, because I want to hurt Bossanova with more than just words. When I've finished with him, his whole world will crumble.

"Of course, your mother didn't make the grade," he continues. "Nice looking enough, but penniless."

I tune him out. This is going to be a long, hellacious drive.

We spend the rest of the day traveling through swathes of countryside, with Valentino answering the phone to give Benito updates on our progress. The old man is in unusually good spirits, even though I suspect he's walking into a trap. It's probably because he keeps stopping every couple of hours to snort cocaine.

By the time the sun dips toward the horizon, casting long shadows across dilapidated buildings on the outskirts of New Alderney, I'm so hungry, thirsty, and exhausted that I can barely keep my eyes open.

My stomach gnaws at its own walls, the membranes of my throat scrape together like sandpaper, and my head lolls back against the leather headrest.

"Wake up," he snaps.

I turn my head toward the driver's seat. "Why?"

"Because we're ten minutes away from the drop-off point. If Montesano sees you looking like the walking dead, he'll put a bullet through my brother's skull."

"You should have thought about that before starving and beating me, then," I say before I can stop myself.

His hand whips out, and he grabs my hair, sending an explosion of pain across my scalp. Screaming, I slap him away, but he shoves me to the other side of the car.

"Worthless bitch," he hisses. "I should have disposed of you alongside the other one."

"And lose your hundred-million-dollar bargaining chip?" I reply.

He returns to the steering wheel and chuckles. "That's what I like about you. Always got an answer."

My jaw clenches. He doesn't like me at all.

Ten minutes later, we approach an abandoned parking lot close to Alderney Hill. Bossanova refused to drive up to the

Montesano Mansion gates because there's only one way out. Anyone with even half a brain would predict Benito's men would block the road and rain gunfire until Valentino no longer poses a threat.

Forest land surrounds the patch of land on three sides, with the trees casting ominous shadows over a derelict truck covered in rust. We pass a few abandoned cars, stripped of their useful parts, and I wonder if this is the right place.

Bossanova parks beside the truck, using its frame as a shield. Up ahead is an exit leading to a path that cuts into the forest. He's probably positioning the car for a fast getaway.

"What now?" I rasp.

"We're thirty minutes early," he mutters, taking a flask from the glove compartment and twisting off its cap. After a long swig of its contents, he slumps back in his seat and sighs. "Montesano will bring my brother, then we'll make the swap."

I glare into the side of his face, wanting to savor his last moment of hope. "Then what?"

He smiles, revealing a mouthful of brilliant white dentures. "Then my brother and I will start a new life outside New Alderney."

Questions float to the top of my mind. Does he think Benito will let him leave this parking lot alive? Has he forgotten all the crimes he committed against the casino as Victor Bellavista? From his wistful smile, it looks like he's trapped in delusions.

I sit back, letting him enjoy this final moment of peace before everything turns to shit.

Moments later, a quartet of trucks rumble into the lot. One of them cuts off the lane ahead of the Bentley, blocking Valentino's potential escape.

"Shit," he hisses. "I told Benito to come alone."

The lining of my stomach trembles, but I don't think the sensation is connected to my hunger. My pulse quickens, and a lump forms in my throat.

"But you came back," I say.

"What the hell does that mean?" he snaps.

"You've just told Benito how much you want your brother."

"And?"

"That was a poor negotiation tactic."

"What do I do?" he asks.

My brow pinches. Is he really asking me for advice? From the way those cold eyes bore into mine, the answer has to be yes.

"Demand a simultaneous release," I reply with a sigh. "Your hostage in exchange for his."

He gives me an eager nod then darts his gaze to the trucks blocking the exits. "And then what?"

"Are you really the genius who ran circles around Benito and everyone else?"

His throat bobs. "My brother helped."

Translation: Gianni is the brains behind the operation. Valentino was just the front man.

"There's only one way to get Benito off your back," I say.

"What's that?"

"Refund the hundred million—"

"No."

"Then you can take your chances."

He pulls out a gun and points it at my head. "Or I can just kill you now."

The threat falls flat, making me purse my lips. Ignoring the icy shiver snaking down my spine, I maintain eye contact, refusing to be intimidated by a maniac high on drugs.

"Killing me will only make things worse for Gianni," I say. "I once saw Benito tear out a man's heart for doing less."

"Valentino," an unfamiliar voice says through a bullhorn.

His face drops. "Gianni?"

"Val, it's me," the voice replies. "Let the girl go. Roman's brother was good enough to send a chopper to the penitentiary this morning. We can be together, now. I'm free."

My eyes narrow at the phrasing, but I shrug off my suspicions. Now isn't the time for speculating.

Valentino winds down the window and yells, "Where are you, Gianni?"

A man steps out from behind the truck blocking the escape route. He's what Valentino would have looked like without the hard living.

Vibrant, with salt-and-pepper hair swept behind a strong

brow, and a trim beard accentuating classically handsome bone structure. He seems taller than his brother, and broader, with muscles bulging beneath his black-and-white prison uniform.

My breath catches, and strangely, so does Valentino's.

"Gianni," he whispers.

The brother raises his bullhorn. "Let the girl go, Val. I already negotiated our escape with the Montesano family."

I sit straighter in my seat, my fingers hovering over the door handle.

"What do you think?" Valentino mutters. "Is he telling the truth?"

My jaw drops. Did that cocaine come from 1980 as well as the outfit? And why the hell is he asking me? Smoothing my features into a neutral mask, I nod.

"Wasn't Roman on death row at the same time as your brother?" I ask.

He chuckles. "Of course. This is how it all began."

I don't have the mental bandwidth to ask him to explain. All I care about is leaving the car.

"Let's do the simultaneous release," I say. "Gianni walks forward at the same time. Once your brother is in the car, they'll let you go."

"They won't."

"He already secured your safety." I gesture at Gianni.

Valentino raises the gun to his temple and scratches. "If you're wrong—"

"Then I'll come back," I lie.

"Come on, Val," Gianni says. "Don't piss off the Montesano family."

He shakes his head. "Fine."

I open the door, and with a trembling breath, step out into the twilight. Cool, juniper-scented air sweeps across my face, carrying the scent of freedom. My knees buckle, but I hold onto the side of the car, forcing my body upright.

Up ahead, Gianni takes a single step forward, his gaze fixed on mine. I mirror his movements, my heart pounding hard enough to broadcast my ill intentions.

He tilts his head, gazing down at me, his eyes calculating. I wonder if he's assessing whether I'm worth the hundred million dollar ransom.

"So, you're Ginevra," he says, his voice seductively low.

"Recognize this face?" I ask with a soft smile.

His brows pinch. "Vaguely. Do I know you?"

The knife finds his gut before he can finish. "No. But you know Jennifer. I'm her daughter."

Eyes widening, he grabs my shoulders, his fingers digging in like claws. "What the—"

"That young woman you married then murdered for money." I twist the blade free, then drive it up between his ribs.

He collapses, but before I can turn, Valentino's voice booms from behind. "Gianni!"

I whirl around. Valentino is already out of the car, his pistol aimed at my head. A gunshot cracks through the night, then everything happens at once.

A blur of movement, then something slamming into my side. I fall, expecting the searing pain of the bullet, but all I feel is the crushing weight of a larger body pinning me to the ground.

Heat spreads across my chest, sticky and warm. It's blood, but not mine.

Gunfire erupts. Feet pound the earth, dragging off the weight. I draw in a noisy breath, my vision swimming, and blink away the dark spots.

When I turn to look at the face of my savior, it's Benito.

And he's gushing blood.

NINETY-NINE

BENITO

Reaper rolls me onto my back, pressing down on my neck. Sharp, burning pain flares across my throat, and I swear I feel my life slipping between his fingers.

I blink up at the twilight sky, seeing nothing but a canvas of stars. Then my vision blurs, with black creeping in the edges, dragging me toward unconsciousness.

Gunshots tear overhead, cutting through the echo of my pulse. Reaper's lips move, but I hear nothing. The sound has become distant, a dull thudding in my ears, drowned out by the rapid, weakening beat of my heart.

We were stationed in the rusty truck, using it as a hiding spot for when Valentino arrived with Ginevra. The plan was to capture him before putting a bullet through his brother's skull.

Hours after extracting Gianni Bossanova from Alderney State penitentiary, Roman's pet prison officer called. There was a sweep of his room, and inside she found documents linking Gianni to a number of scams executed at our casino.

Gianni explained that he'd only stolen from our casino after it had fallen into Capello's hands, but the evidence Officer McMurphy handed us said otherwise.

So our plan was to play along with the Bossanova brothers

until Ginevra was safe. Then they would pay for their crimes in blood.

But then Ginevra stabbed Gianni, unleashing chaos.

I moved without thinking, already knowing where Valentino's gun would strike. The bullet missed my kevlar vest and lodged in the base of my throat, but I would do it again in a heartbeat.

"Benito?" Ginevra's voice cuts through the haze, bringing me back to the present.

I try to rise, but my limbs are heavy, my body sinking deeper into the ground. Blinking the world back to focus, I meet her beautiful gray eyes. She's wearing thick makeup to cover her bruises, and her auburn hair is styled into a strange bouffant, but she's still the most beautiful woman in the world.

"Why?" she cries.

"Because I'll go to any length to keep you safe," I say, my throat burning, my eyelids heavy. "Even if it means my death."

She grabs the lapels of my shirt. "Don't you fucking dare," she growls. "You're going to stay awake. You're going to live."

"I've always loved you, Ginevra." Each word scrapes against the raw pain. "From the very start."

Her tears splatter on my face, warming my heart. If life were a fairytale, her love would be enough to bring me back. But Ginevra despises Bob Brisket, and therefore despises me. In the time she's spent with Bossanova, he'll have already told her I was behind the loan sharks, the law firm, and that scheme to endanger her mother.

I won't fool myself into believing those tears are out of love or longing or loss. They're pure, unadulterated rage.

Cold sets in my bones, spreading from my neck down into my chest. My heart sinks. This is it. I'm about to die and I didn't even get the chance to say goodbye.

Just as the edges of my vision go black, the crowd parts, and Cesare shoves his way to my side. Relief sweeps over my senses, and I exhale a rattling breath. My little brother is the patron saint of reviving torture victims from the brink of death. Maybe I'll survive this long enough to tell Ginevra I'm sorry.

———

When I regain consciousness, it's to the sound of beeping hospital monitors and not to the snap, crackle, and pop of hellfire. I inhale, filling my nostrils with the sterile scent of antiseptics, mingled with the sweet scent of honeysuckle.

The air reaching my throat is cold and sharp, each breath aggravating the dull ache radiating from the base of my neck.

I knew Cesare wouldn't let me die.

Moving my arms is a struggle, as if my body has been fused together with lead. A persistent, throbbing pain, hard to pinpoint, beats in time with my pulse. I shift on the bed, my stiff muscles protesting, and the slight movement sends a wave of soreness across my chest and shoulders.

"He's awake," Cesare says.

I crack open an eye. Light sears into my retinas, sharp and unforgiving. I squint against the glare, my vision blurring as if I'm still stuck halfway between dreams and reality.

Cesare hovers beside the bed, staring down at me like a puzzle he's still piecing together. Disheveled hair frames his bloodshot eyes, the look of someone who hasn't left my side. If the night's sky in the window behind him is any indication, then the entire day has passed.

"We almost lost you," he says, his voice tight with emotion. "The bullet lodged just below your throat, nicking the carotid artery. You were bleeding out fast. I had to clamp it myself."

"That bad?" I rasp. The words scrape out of my throat, rough and raw, like I'm trying to talk through sandpaper.

He nods. "By the time we got you on the operating table, you were seconds away from joining Dad. I had to take over and stop the surgeons from ending you with their textbook bullshit. There's no way I'd let them kill my big brother."

Heart twisting, I imagine everything he did to keep me alive. For the first time in forever, I meet his eyes, the same color as Mom's, my chest clogged with gratitude. "Thank you, Cesare," I say, the words rough in my throat. "I never doubted your talent for doing the impossible."

He blinks, exhaustion giving way to a flicker of shock, then delight. Cheeks darkening, he mutters, "The bullet did a lot of damage. You're going to be sore for a while, and your voice might never sound the same again."

A knot forms in what's left of my throat, but I manage a faint grin. "I'm just glad to be alive. Guess you didn't need that medical degree after all."

He chuckles. "Maybe not. We've got you on a lower dose of meds to avoid complications, but if the pain's too much, just say the word."

"Next time you run into a bullet, I'll shoot you myself." Roman appears from the other side of the room, his jaw tight.

"What happened with the Bossanova brothers?" I rasp.

"Filled with lead," Cesare mutters, his glare flicking to our brother.

Roman shakes his head, his lips pinching. "He wanted them for his table."

I laugh, setting off an explosion of agony that has me wincing. My big brother has snapped out of the depressed fugue that's plagued him since his wife left and now carries himself like a mafia boss.

On the subject of wives...

"Where's Ginevra?" My voice scrapes out, each syllable coated in raw fire.

Roman's features harden. "We left her in the hallway."

My heart jolts, sending a sudden spike of adrenaline that shoots pain up my neck. I grit my teeth against the sharp throb.

"What?" I hiss.

"It's her fault you got shot," Cesare snaps. "We had a plan to subdue both Bossanova bastards and keep them in the basement, but Ginevra ruined it by stabbing Gianni."

"Is she still out there?" I ask.

He glances toward the door. "Probably."

"Bring her in."

"Why?"

"I still love my wife," I grind out.

Eyes widening, his mouth falls slack with disbelief. "The same wife who got herself kidnapped, cost you a hundred million, then nearly got you killed?"

I clench my teeth, ready with a reminder of how his own

woman came to our home as an assassin. Before I can muster up a retort, Roman places a hand on Cesare's shoulder.

"Let her in," he rumbles.

Cesare's features twist with fury, but I grab his wrist. "You have no idea the depths I sank to for Ginevra. What I did to her... how I broke her... makes what you put Rosalind through look like a first date."

Curiosity gleams across his pale eyes, but he has the good sense not to ask for details. Instead, he nods and walks to the door.

Roman cups my cheek. "Don't let her slip from your fingers."

I swallow down a painful lump. "It's no longer up to me."

He nods. "Focus on getting better. Reaper and the boys are watching over the casino. Leroi, Seraphine, and Rosalind are following Bossanova's trail to take out his accomplices."

"Thanks."

He ruffles my hair, something he hasn't done since we were kids, then smooths it down when he realizes I'm about to see my wife. With a tight smile, he leaves the room.

Moments later, the door swings open, and my breath catches before I even see who's about to enter. Ginevra walks in, still clad in the same safari jumpsuit as before, stained with my blood. Her auburn hair hangs limp around her pale features, shadowed by dark circles.

Our gazes lock, and a knot forms in my gut. The relentless pull toward her amplifies every beat of my heart, every raw throb in my throat. It's as if her presence alone is a new kind of wound.

She stops, her chest rising and falling with rapid, shallow breaths. I hold mine, not knowing how she'll react to my betrayal.

Her shoulders finally slump, her beautiful features falling with relief, and she looks at me like I'm a miracle. The raw emotion in her face chases away my doubts, and my heart soars with hope.

Maybe I haven't completely shattered her love. Maybe—despite everything—we might be able to piece together our marriage.

"Are you alright?" I rasp.

Brow furrowing, she crosses the chasm between us and stops at my bedside. "You're the one who got shot."

"Bossanova hurt you."

She stiffens, as if allergic to his name. "It wasn't anything I couldn't handle."

The knot in my stomach twists tighter, making my pulse hammer. I need to know more—I need to know everything that bastard did to Ginevra while she was his captive. I part my lips to ask, but she places a hand on my shoulder.

"Don't," she says, her voice thick with an emotion I can almost taste. "Valentino Bossanova is dead. What I want to talk about is you."

I gaze up at my woman—my wife. The anguish and fury tightening her features make my chest clench. Her storm-gray eyes blaze with a raw pain that cuts deeper than anything Bossanova could inflict. Somewhere in the pit of my conscience, I know his torture is nothing compared to the wound of my own deception.

"Tell me everything you did to manipulate my life," she says, her voice trembling with restrained fury. "I want to understand how my favorite person in the world became such a despicable monster."

Her words sink in through the fraying edges of my hope. Lying by omission is no longer an option. It's already over, and she deserves the truth—even if it means she'll walk out of my life forever.

ONE HUNDRED

GINEVRA

Benito stares up at me like he's on his deathbed, his dark eyes drinking me in with the same intensity as when we first met. That gaze never fails to make me feel like the center of his universe, even though it's now etched with fear. Despite his raw vulnerability, I barely recognize what he's become.

I first noticed him hiding behind the kitchen pillar while Sofia taught me to make cookies. Back then, I had no use for boys. They were loud, annoying creatures only capable of destruction.

But Benito was different. He watched with quiet curiosity, kept his distance, never charging in with demands like Roman. Before I knew it, I was drawn to this quiet, olive-skinned boy who once said my cookies tasted like heaven. That memory feels so far away, tainted by every terrible act he's committed to keep me under his control.

We grew up together, yet I still can't understand how the hell he strayed so far from the adoring young man who once held my hands as we slept beneath the stars.

"Where do I even begin?" he rasps.

"What's the first thing you did to get me back?" I ask.

When his gaze darts to the door, I lower myself into the seat at his bedside, sensing he's about to confess something incriminating. His tongue flicks over his dry lips, and the bandages around his throat shift. I hesitate, then crack open a water bottle and bring it to his mouth.

"It was years in the making." He takes a long sip. "Dad was dead, Roman was on death row, Mom was in the clutches of Tommy Galliano. And then there was you."

I gulp, my breath shallowing. He doesn't need to elaborate, since we both know Dad forced me to be with Samson.

"We all had our reasons for taking out the entire Capello family. Mine was to get you back."

"Don't insult my intelligence," I say through clenched teeth. "That night you stormed Samson's hideout and found me in the closet, you could have taken off your visor and offered me a hand. But you didn't."

He squeezes his eyes shut, exhaling a breath so labored that I shiver. My fingers twitch toward the call button, but I resist the urge to summon help. Instead, I open the water again and give him another sip.

"Continue," I say. "Don't gloss over your actions."

Nodding, he meets my eyes again. "I hated you for leaving. I hated you for moving on with another man. I hated you for being the only woman in existence I found even remotely attractive—"

"Stop exaggerating."

"It's only ever been you," he snarls. "If I'd found a way to forget about you, I'd have taken it, but no other woman held my interest. They might as well be black-and-white cut-outs because you're the only one who's real."

My chest tightens, and his words stir up memories of when I thought he was the only man I'd ever love. No matter how much I push them down, they still flood back, bringing with them a slew of happy moments. Cooking together in our student apartment, nights we spent talking about our future until sunrise, late afternoons frolicking in the treehouse.

I was his entire world and he was mine. But our time apart turned that sweet, adorable man into a Machiavellian monster. Tears sting my eyes. I glance away, my pulse quickening with a familiar ache, but then my gaze lands on the blood staining his hands.

And just like that, reality sharpens the edges of every memory

—reminding me that Benito is capable of ripping out a man's heart.

Shit. At this rate, he'll weave a tale of an antihero driven mad with obsession, resorting to any means necessary to win back his beloved.

"Stop seeding your actions with grandiose declarations," I say from between clenched teeth. "Give me the unvarnished truth."

A muscle in his jaw clenches. "Alright."

Then he tells me how he installed four men at the law firm to help Nick Terranova take control. They spread rumors, making it look like I knew Dad had embezzled the money. They withheld my payroll and froze my company credit cards to make sure I was penniless.

"What else?" I whisper.

"Your father didn't owe money to loan sharks," he mutters, his gaze dropping to his hands. "You were supposed to come running to me when I sent those men to your house, but you were stubborn."

"So, it's my fault?"

He turns away, sighs, then shakes his head. "When you ask why I went so hard, this is the reason why. I needed you to come to me for help, but you didn't. Everything I did backfired."

"What does that mean?"

"You told the sharks we were together, so they retreated. You were supposed to come to me for help about Bossanova, but you went to him," he spits.

My jaw clenches. "By him, you mean Brisket?"

He nods.

"Who was, in fact, you."

"I couldn't have you falling in love with a masked bastard who treated you like shit."

"Because you wanted me to fall for an unmasked bastard who treated me like a pawn instead?"

His features pinch. "There's no excuse for what I did. I was insane."

"No."

He turns to meet my eyes. "What?"

"You were just being Benito," I say, my throat thickening.

"The grudges, the pride, the convoluted plots. That's all you. After Samson died, going back to you wasn't an option. We've known each other for decades. You never leave a slight unpunished."

His nostrils flare, but he doesn't reply because he knows I'm right. I glare at his handsome profile, waiting for him to deny it, but he sighs.

"When I lost you, I lost my humanity," he murmurs. "Loving you was the only thing that tethered my soul."

I shake my head. "So why didn't you fight for me? You had so many chances to reconnect. That night in the closet, you could have taken me home. I would have given you anything."

He meets my eyes again for a heartbeat before exhaling another sigh. "I wanted you humbled."

"Why?"

"To punish you for leaving," he says through clenched teeth. "To redress the balance for catering to your every whim while we were together, only for you to walk away."

My ears ring with disbelief, fuelling my mounting fury. "Let me get this straight. You stripped away everything that mattered to me during the day, and at night came to me as a stalker who coerced me into sexual depravity?"

Breath quickening, he swallows like he's trying to hold back a confession. "It was insanity. After an entire life of celibacy—"

"Don't blame this on blue balls," I hiss, already exhausted with his excuses. "You had the chance to consummate our wedding, but you wanted everything on your terms. The moment I failed to be your obedient little toy, you manufactured my adultery just so you could trap me with breeding."

"Ginevra," he says with a sigh.

"I'm not finished," I snarl. "You made me feel like a shameless slut, while setting yourself up as a benevolent husband, for what? Having sex with my own husband?"

"There's no excuse."

"Did you ever respect me?"

He jerks his head in my direction and winces. "More than anything," he says, the words breathy. "That was my trouble. I put you on a pedestal. You were my goddess. The only woman in existence. If I took you back, I'd become that hopeless simp again, then you'd get bored with me and leave."

"What's wrong with us?" I dip my head and stare at the blood splatters on my lap.

"Ginevra?"

"This relationship is toxic."

"But we connected at the treehouse," he says, his voice imploring. "And there were moments when it felt like time had never passed."

"Don't—"

"I would die for you. Kill for you. Get on my knees for you. You want me to admit I was wrong? One hundred percent. This is all absolutely, irrevocably my fault. But I was driven by love. A twisted, unhealthy love, but I can change. We can move past it."

"Our love is a prison," I whisper, my shoulders sagging.

"It won't be like that anymore," he replies, his voice choked. "I know the truth now, and you know all my secrets—"

"Who killed my dad?" I ask.

"The same assassin who killed the Capello family," he replies without missing a beat. "He was hunting Samson."

"So it wasn't you?"

"No."

"Alright."

"Ginevra?"

"While I was in captivity, I got an up-close look at an abusive relationship. Valentino Bossanova was screwing his own daughter, beating the shit out of her, and brainwashed her into believing it was love."

He swallows. "What are you saying?"

"She was trapped in a cycle of affection and abuse, pain and empty promises." My chest tightens, making me force back a wave of grief. "I saw it from the outside, and when I tried to intervene, it got her killed."

His face pales. "You can't compare us—"

"Why not?" I shoot back, my chest heaving. "Because the pain you inflict isn't physical?"

Flinching, he glances away, the sight of his agony making my chest ache.

"I'll change," he rasps.

My gaze rakes over his handsome features. Features I've loved half my childhood and my entire adult life. Despite everything, my heart still flutters at his dark brow, molten eyes, perfectly straight nose, and luxurious lips. He's perfection, the epitome of masculine beauty, the only man I've ever wanted.

The gaze boring through mine is earnest—he means every word about wanting to change. Because the Benito I know never pleaded. Hope warms my chest for a heartbeat, bringing up the future we carved for each other in the tree house.

But how can one man profess such love while ruining my life and Mom's from the shadows? Benito set all our troubles in motion to manipulate me into coming back. He's the reason we got involved with Valentino Bossanova.

I think of Mom suffering everything I endured with that crazy old bastard and shudder. Then I dredge up the horror and terror and disgust from when Brisket tore through Julian's entrails and cornered me in the bathroom.

Fingers twitching, I close my digits around an imaginary heart, still warm, still wet, still beating. My stomach lurches, and I stare into those pain-filled eyes, knowing I'm looking into the face of a monster.

"I loved you with all my heart," My voice wavers, the words both a confession and a farewell. "But the man I fell for no longer exists." Rising off my seat, I place a hand on his shoulder and gaze into that face once more, memorizing every line, every shadow. "Thank you for taking that bullet for me, but I need to end this cycle of abuse."

His lips tremble, his eyes searching mine with a desperate, pleading look I refuse to mistake for love. "Ginevra, please—"

"Goodbye, Benito," I say, the words splintering my heart. Pulling away my hand, I turn on my heel and walk toward freedom without a backward glance.

ONE HUNDRED ONE

BENITO

The door closes with a soft click, but it might as well be a gunshot. I stare at the solid piece of wood, waiting for it to open again, waiting for Ginevra to return.

But she doesn't.

Cold settles across the hospital room, the kind of chill that seeps past my chest cavity and into the chambers of my heart. I suck in a breath, but it's sharp, thin, and may as well be a knife across my throat. My chest tightens, and I lean to the edge of the bed, wanting to bury my face in my hands, wanting to stop the cresting wave of grief, but the pressure mounts in my head, my chest, my heart.

Ginevra is gone.

I should stand up, rip the IV from my veins, and chase after my wife, but my body won't move. My legs refuse to cooperate, weighed down by an unavoidable truth.

What I did was unforgivable. I broke Ginevra's trust. Hurt and disrespected her in ways I can never take back. My sins against her can't be fixed with flowers or apologies. This is the end.

Heat builds behind my eyes, threatening tears. I press my palms into my face, refusing to let them spill. Ginevra wouldn't want a weak-willed man who cries when his world falls apart. But then, she just said our love was toxic.

The beeping monitors echo my faltering heartbeat, punctuating the silence with their merciless rhythm. They may as well flatline because without Ginevra, I may as well be dead.

She's gone.

I can still hear her voice, the finality of her goodbye. Our love is a prison. The truth of it slices deeper than any bullet.

All this time, I thought I was breaking her to reform the pieces to fit my jagged edges. But Ginevra isn't an object I can mold, or a doll I can manipulate. She's my goddess, my reason for living, the air that I breathe.

I chained her down, suffocating her until she had to leave.

And now, I'm alone.

Pulling my hands away from my face, I stare down at the bandages wrapped around my neck. The bullet missed my artery, but it's lodged in my heart. I survived the gunshot, but I don't know if I'll survive losing Ginevra.

A ragged breath shudders through my chest, and I let my head fall back against the pillow. I stare up at the ceiling, trying to focus on the sterile white tiles, and let my mind go blank. It's as futile as trying to stop my own pulse.

Every thought running through my mind is in some way linked to Ginevra. Every inch of this room is filled with her absence. Every heartbeat is a reminder of what I've lost.

How do I get her back?

The door creaks open, and Roman steps inside with Cesare. At the sight of my little brother, an idea punches me in the gut. I try to ignore it, but it's already taking form, becoming too irresistible to dismiss.

"How'd it go with Ginevra?" Roman asks, his voice cautious.

The words dry in my throat. Saying them out loud only makes the loss cut deeper.

Roman frowns. "She's left you?"

My chest tightens. "She said our love was a prison."

"But you took a bullet for her." My little brother folds his arms, his eyes sharpening. "It's a fucking miracle you're not dead."

"Cesare," Roman says.

"No," he snaps. "What kind of woman watches a man sacrifice his life to save her scrawny ass, only to leave him at his most vulnerable?"

"Stop," I rasp.

Cesare glances from Roman to me. "What's wrong with you both? Someone needs to talk sense into Ginevra. She should be on her knees, kissing your feet. She can't walk out on you again!"

"It's complicated."

His eyes narrow. "How?"

I glance at Roman, who grimaces. He's the only man in the world who could understand even a fraction of my fuck up. Emberly left him because she uncovered his lies. What I did to Ginevra was far worse than taking away a stolen inheritance.

Clearing my throat, I force down the knot in my chest. "How did you make Rosalind stay?"

Cesare's eyebrow lifts. "What do you mean?"

I sit up straighter, meeting his gaze. "You're a master with women. After everything you did to her, she still hasn't left. How did you make the Stockholm syndrome stick?"

Cesare's smirks. "Sure you want my advice?"

Desperation surges in my gut. I need those secrets more than ever. "Yes."

He pushes off the wall, stepping closer to the bedside. "Abduct someone they love. That's how I got Rosalind to come back the first time she ran."

Heat ignites behind my eyes. "I'm serious."

"So am I," he says with a shrug. "The only thing Rosalind cared about was Miranda. Every time I stole her, it brought Rosalind closer."

My jaw clenches. "I don't want to be a psychopath."

All traces of amusement vanish, leaving behind a scowl. "Strange how you're asking this psychopath for advice." he says, his voice lowering. "What the hell did you do that made her leave?"

I shift on the bed, trying not to flinch at the accusation.

Roman steps closer, his brow furrowed. "Don't give Benito a hard time—"

"No," I rasp. "It's okay. Just give me a minute."

My brothers pull up seats and settle at the bedside, both wearing identical scowls. I lean back against the pillows, my gaze fixed on the ceiling, and I spill my guts.

I tell them about taking advantage of Ginevra when I found her tied up in a closet, about climbing into her house disguised as a sexual predator. I tell them about how I interfered with her job, got her fired, set up phony loan sharks, and the shit show with her mother and Valentino Bossanova.

The part about Julian is easy. That bastard deserved worse than evisceration. But my words falter at the wedding, and the days after when I kept her imprisoned and without clothes. Then tears of shame roll down my cheeks when I confess to the fake adultery and subsequent breeding.

When I finish, Cesare whistles. "Forget what I said about her earlier."

Roman clears his throat. "I can't exactly judge since I tampered with Emberly's birth control."

"There's something I don't understand," Cesare says.

"What?" I rasp, still staring at the ceiling.

"Why didn't you just show up at her doorstep with flowers?"

I jerk my head to the side, igniting an explosion of pain that makes me wince. Instead of the mockery I expect to find on his features, Cesare's blue eyes are earnest.

Frustration claws at my chest, but I don't have an answer. All the constructions I had in my head about Ginevra rejecting me for being weak crumble into dust in the light of the truth. Cesare is right, and that realization twists like a knife in my gut.

"It was a mistake."

He shakes his head. "You want to know why Rosalind stayed?"

I nod.

"I've been called a psychopath my whole life. Never pretended to be anything different. You hid in the shadows, playing games, and she left you in the dark."

His words slice through my heart, cutting so deeper that I have to squeeze my eyes shut.

"Cesare," Roman hisses.

"He asked, so I'm answering," says my little brother. "Get help. Both of you. Either become the men your wives fell in love with or leave them the fuck alone."

His chair scrapes back, and his footsteps disappear through the door and down the hallway. Silence settles in the hospital room, broken by the monitors' incessant beeping. I glance at Roman, who shifts on his seat, his arms crossed like he's holding something back.

"Do you agree with him?" I ask, my voice choked with emotion.

Roman drops his gaze to the floor. "My wife tied me to a torture rack, smashed a meat tenderizer into my balls, carved LIAR into my chest, and left me for dead. Cesare carves his initials into Rosalind and wins an instant family. Maybe he's onto something if he says we should get help."

A weak laugh escapes my throat, but it feels like swallowing glass.

Roman sighs, crossing his arms tighter. "All I can do is watch Emberly from afar. Make sure she's okay. Maybe that's all you can do for Ginny."

The weight of his words settles over my chest, crushing my lungs. I can't give up on Ginevra. Not before I can prove that I've changed—that I'm worthy of her love.

ONE HUNDRED TWO

BENITO

I didn't follow Cesare's advice right away—I sought a second opinion from Leroi, whose relationship with Seraphine seemed idyllic until he confessed that she'd stabbed him in the gut for withholding information.

Rosalind also shot Cesare in the chest and stayed, but Ginevra left without so much as slapping me across the face. Based on the small sample of men I consulted, it looks like a woman's level of violence is directly related to the depth of her love.

So what does that say about us?

Divorce papers arrived the morning the Salentino twins visited. Ginevra already signed on the dotted line. Painkillers numbed the ache on my neck but did nothing to ease the sensation of being stabbed in the heart.

I asked them for advice. Elania laughed, saying Ginevra should have cut off my balls. Aria took my hand and said I was the most twisted bastard she'd ever met and told me to seek psychological help.

So, that's how I find myself standing in front of Dr. Monica Saint's office. It's a glass front with a view of the reception area, and only a few doors down from Cesare's sex shop.

I have nerve damage, trauma to the muscles in my neck, and a reduced range of motion, but nothing means more to me than restoring my marriage.

Casting a glance over my shoulder toward the Phoenix, I check that the coast is clear before stepping inside. The receptionist's desk is vacant, but the door at the end is ajar.

My pulse quickens, but I force my features into a tight mask. Talking about what's in my heart shouldn't be so nerve-wracking, but my ears still ring with Elania's mocking laughter. I should have spoken to Aria alone, but the sisters are inseparable.

When I step inside, the smell of leather and old books hits like a slap. The office is more like a living room with its shelves, low lighting and plush velvet chairs, but the desk is set suspiciously close to the door.

Dr. Monica Saint sashays into the room, gazing up at me through her square glasses. She's tall, about the twins' age, with dark hair falling loose around her shoulders.

"Benito Montesano," she says with a sharp nod. "Have a seat."

I sit without a word, already feeling like I'm under the microscope, my fingers gripping the arms of the chair. Talking to strangers about my failed marriage is insane. I solve my problems with bullets, blackmail, or bribes. But none of that works when the problem is rooted in my psyche.

Dr. Saint moves around her desk and sits. "What can I do for you?"

"How do I make my wife come back?" I ask, the words scraping my raw throat.

"Why don't you start with why she left."

I clench my fists. "Aren't you the one supposed to give me tactics?"

Dr. Saint's patient nod grates on my last nerve. She's already dissecting me without a scalpel. "Therapy isn't about tactics. I'm here to help you understand why she left. What made her feel that staying with you wasn't an option?"

My chest tightens, and the weight of her words press down on my lungs, forcing out a response. "I thought I knew better than her. I thought I could fix what went wrong the first time she left by fixing her."

She nods. "So, the question isn't how to make her come back. It's whether you're willing to change for yourself."

The words echo Aria and Cesare's advice, tightening my gut. All this time, I've been thinking of Ginevra as something to win back, a prize I could reclaim by pushing the right levers.

That's the entire reason why she left. I'm the one who's broken, and no scheme or show of strength can salvage the side of me she finds so sickening.

"I thought I could control everything," I admit. "Even my wife."

The doctor's features soften. "That's where we start—by accepting that she isn't yours to command. Real change comes from understanding that you can't dictate her choices, but you can decide to become someone better for yourself."

A knot forms in my gut, but I force a nod. "I can change... for her."

She studies me for a moment, then shakes her head. "You need to change for you."

I slump against the seat. This is going to be one long, brutal process.

———

Days pass, and I'm still not medically fit to return to work. Reaper and the Mortis House boys take care of the casino while I recover. With both men behind Victor Bellavista dead and no longer posing a threat, they've weeded out every two-faced bastard lining their pockets with my money.

At least the casino is in safe hands.

My marriage, however, still flounders. Ginevra's silence continues to stretch. Thanks to a cash settlement from the Di Marco Law Group, she now has enough to move out from her mother's house and get her own apartment.

Nick Terranova didn't hesitate when I suggested she deserved a generous severance package. He even forwarded me a job listing at a small law firm looking for someone with Ginevra's exact skills.

I went one step further, setting up a meeting with the firm's partners and making a substantial offer: if Ginevra was the right fit, I'd pay whatever it took to secure her a place as a partner. Naturally, they'd be sworn to secrecy. She wouldn't even know she owned a portion of the firm until the timing felt natural, so as not to raise suspicions.

That was my last attempt to insert myself into her life, but I still need to keep her safe. As my wife, she remains a target for abduction, and we still haven't tracked down Tommy Galliano.

Rotations of boys from Mortis House keep a constant watch on her apartment. They have orders not to interfere in her daily life but remain close enough to intervene if necessary. I've even stationed someone to watch over her mother.

Days without Ginevra turn to weeks, and it's like going cold turkey. I resist the urge to demand footage or information on her movements. Reaper acts as go-between, relaying updates. He's cautious not to reveal too much, only verifying that she's safe.

Two months pass, and I get a message from Emmanuel Demartini, thanking me for resolving the situation with Victor Bellavista. After the prison break and before the shootout, Roman managed to convince Gianni Bossanova to refund the hundred million ransom in exchange for not returning him to death row. Thanks to Ginevra's research, we've clawed twice the amount of losses from the counterfeit chip scam.

When Demartini invites me to his establishment to ask for help with a team of lowlives running a credit scam at his tables, I bring Reaper. Mortis House is proving to be a success. We're planning on opening a sorority, where we can train young women to join the fold.

As we walk through the Demartini Casino's glittering halls, the last person I expect to find outside the meeting room is my wife.

She's standing among a group of people but there's no mistaking the way her auburn hair catches the chandeliers' low lights. It casts a glow around her like a halo, making her stand out. The black business suit she wears accentuates her curves, and my cock comes alive in the presence of his master.

Steps faltering, my heart slams against my chest.

She turns, meets my gaze, her eyes widening.

Neither of us move.

I don't step forward, don't smile, don't cross the hallway to talk. The impulse driving me to take control of her roars within its cage, but I curl my hands into fists.

If she walks over, that's her choice.

She doesn't.

But she also doesn't turn away.

"You okay?" Reaper asks.

"Did you know she'd be here?" I ask back.

"Who?" When he glances at where I'm looking, she's already disappeared inside.

"Mr. Montesano?" says a deep voice from behind.

I turn to lock gazes with a man dressed in the casino's uniform, a variation of the Demartini butler's navy jacket and epaulets.

"The Padrone will see you now."

Every urge screams at me to cross that hallway, throw open the door, and speak to my wife, but regular sessions with Dr. Saint have taught me restraint.

Swallowing back the lump in my throat, I nod to the man and turn away from my reason for living. I follow him toward the old man's office, each step dragging like lead.

But just before I disappear from the hallway, I steal another glance, wondering if she's noticed that I've changed.

ONE HUNDRED THREE

GINEVRA

I need air.

The meeting drones on, voices swirling around my head, but all I can feel is the sharp thrum of my pulse pounding at the base of my neck.

Looking at my notebook is pointless as my sight is blurred. My pen floats just above the paper, and the bullet points I scribbled down earlier might as well be hieroglyphics. I haven't taken in a single word since I saw Benito.

It's been months since I left him at the hospital. He didn't acknowledge the divorce papers I signed, instead responding via my old boss with a ridiculously generous severance package.

The sensible thing to do would have been to refuse the money, but living with Mom became unbearable. She blames herself for what happened with the Bossanova brothers. The new man she was dating wasn't much better and was always at the house. I had to get out, so I rented a studio by the park.

I could have gotten something bigger, but I've invested a large chunk of the settlement on therapy, self-defense classes, and an emergency fund. Three times a week, I see someone to process the trauma of being held captive and watching Carla die, my dysfunctional family, and everything leading up to my marriage.

All conversations inevitably lead to Benito and how I'm not ready to confront him, let alone move on.

Then an email arrived in my inbox saying Maurier and Co were hiring new attorneys. I thought it was too good to be true. But the interview was a breeze, and I was hired on the spot.

Its biggest client is the Demartini family, and the managing partner put me on the account. It means regular visits to their casino, and I've gotten close to Mr. Demartini's eldest son. Mars and I have bonded because he's also estranged from his husband.

But talking about Benito is one thing. Seeing him is another.

He looked different. Not in the way you expect after weeks apart, but his presence burned the air between us like an unspoken challenge. My traitorous heart skittered, tripped over my feet, and now won't stop racing. It presses against my ribs, wanting to connect with Benito.

I force my attention back to Mars at the head of the table, but his voice blends with the murmurs of my colleagues. My body thrums, every muscle pulled tight, my skin buzzing with a strange sense of need.

Mars catches my eye. Brow furrowing, he casts me a meaningful look. I give him a tight nod and what I hope is a reassuring smile. When he turns his attention back to the discussion, I exhale.

The meeting drags, and all I want to do is tear off my skin that craves his touch. My body aches for Benito, and not just sexually. I miss his scent, I miss his hugs, I miss the sound of his voice. But I promised not to fall back into a cycle of abuse.

Promises are slippery things, especially when it comes to him. I can't let myself forget how it felt to be shattered—not just by his actions, but by my own willingness to bend for him. That kind of love is dangerous.

"Ginevra?" A voice pulls me back to the meeting. My colleague wants an analysis of the contracts.

I stutter out a reply, but my thoughts are stuck in the hallway, tangled up in Benito's dark gaze.

The discussion lurches forward, and I let my mind drift. He was in the papers yesterday for changing the name of the second hotel attached to the casino from *Marisol* to *Lucia*. The article said he'd been involved in a lot of charitable endeavors and had even set up a new scholarship, sponsoring young women to study at Alderney State University.

He's changing. I can see that, even from a distance. But every step he takes toward redemption feels like he's moving on with his life, while I'm still stuck on him.

It's funny, since the Benito I used to know would have showered me with gifts, sent flowers, cards, apologies or commands. Instead, he's left me the hell alone. When our gazes met, I expected him to walk over. Half of me still expects him to storm inside the meeting room, demanding to speak to his wife, but one glance at the door says he's not coming.

It's what I asked for, so why am I complaining?

The meeting ends, and I shove my notebook into my bag, needing space to breathe. Rising off my seat, I follow my colleagues to the door, wondering if I'll find Benito waiting in the hallway.

"Ginevra, wait."

I glance over my shoulder, meeting Mars's handsome features. "Hey, what's up? Got time for a drink?"

My gaze darts to an empty hallway devoid of Benito. Stomach plummeting, I turn back to Mars. Concern etches his brow, his dark eyes searching mine.

"Sure." I choke out the words, forcing a smile to hide my disappointment. "That sounds nice."

Mars's office is nothing like Benito's. This room has a view of the tropical gardens, while Benito liked to oversee the gambling tables.

I drop onto one of the many cream leather couches, smoothing my skirt with sweaty palms. Mars saunters to a mahogany cabinet displaying crystal decanters filled with liquor. It's a stark contrast to Benito's cold, metallic minimalism.

After fixing us each a gin and tonic, he takes a seat across from me and leans forward. "You seemed distracted earlier. What's troubling you?"

I glance away, focusing on a painting hanging above his

leather couch. It's a muscular male form, backlit in an explosion of vivid flowers.

Swallowing hard, I choose my words, not wanting to admit any part of me is pining. "Benito was here."

"Yikes..." Mars grimaces. "Dad must have called him about the trouble we're having at the tables. He hasn't stopped talking about Benito since he got rid of the Bossanova problem."

"Of course."

The response comes out flat. Of course, it's business. Did I think Benito came here to make a grand gesture? I don't know what I wanted—maybe just proof that I still mattered to him. But then direct confrontations aren't Benito's style. He works in the shadows, manipulating everything to get what he wants.

But why does my stomach twist at the thought that it doesn't include me?

Mars doesn't push for answers, he just raises a crystal tumbler to his lips. I take a sip of my drink, the bitterness of the gin mirroring my inner turmoil.

Silence stretches between us for several heartbeats, accentuated by the distant clamor of the casino. I already told Mars the whole story, apart from Julian's murder. We've spent months exchanging traumas. Mars shared the hair raising truth about his marriage to the son of New Jersey's most powerful gangster. We're both determined not to return to our toxic relationships.

"Seeing him again brings up emotions I tried to bury," I say with a sigh. "Sometimes, all I remember are the high points, but then I think about how Victor Bellavista murdered Carla. What if she thought things would improve?"

Tears prick at the corners of my eyes, but I blink them back, refusing to let them fall. I've cried enough over Benito. Even if he's making changes, it's time to move forward.

Mars reaches across the low table and squeezes my shoulder. "I get it. He took that bullet, and you're wondering if it makes up for all his bullshit."

I release a harsh laugh. "His sacrifice complicates everything."

He releases my shoulder, reclines and swirls his gin. "That and the hundred million dollar ransom he paid to get you back."

"Whose side are you on?" I mutter.

He smirks. "Yours."

"Good, because for a minute, it sounded like you were defending him." I take a swallow of my drink, letting the alcohol burn my throat, but it does little to relieve my frustration.

"I'm the worst person to give advice," he murmurs. "The toxicity in me sees him as a morally gray hero."

"In a minute, you'll tell me he's a good man, or something."

Mars snickers. "How's it going with the self-defense classes?"

"It's good for working through my frustrations." I shake my head. "But you'd think a new place, new job, and a new bestie would make me stronger, but seeing him only brings back old feelings."

"Healing takes time."

I let out a bitter laugh. "Isn't that the last line of the *Rapunzelita* trilogy?"

"You finished it?" he asks.

"It was so good."

We talk about books for several minutes, in particular a deceased author with a suspiciously large back catalog. Mars thinks her agent hired a ghost writer to emulate her style, but I'm not convinced. Either way, we're excited for her latest book about a woman who has an inappropriate relationship with a ghost.

Mars chuckles, the sound cutting through the weight in my chest. "Some women have all the luck. My ex sure as hell wouldn't take a bullet for me."

"Has he resurfaced?"

He shrugs, giving me a half-smile that freezes partway to his eyes. "I'm over that asshole. Dad says I should stop messing around with thugs, have a lavender marriage, and start a family."

"What did you say?"

"I haven't given up on love. Neither should you."

The weight of his words settle over my heart. It's only ever beaten for one man, and part of me still pines for his toxic love. "Find me a man who isn't a controlling, manipulative bastard, and I'll consider it."

Mars tilts his head back and laughs. "Get in line, girl."

I force a smile, wishing my chest didn't feel so hollow. Mars fills the gap Martina left when she revealed she hated me for most of our friendship, but no one can replace Benito.

No matter how much time we spend apart, or how deeply I immerse myself in distractions, my heart still aches for the only man I truly loved.

ONE HUNDRED FOUR

BENITO

Months roll by, and I continue my therapy, but not a day passes without thinking of Ginevra. I didn't expect her to reach out after locking gazes at the Demartini Casino, but seeing her looking so well only ignited my longing.

She's thriving, yet I remain a shell.

Roman reunited with Emberly after rescuing her from Tommy Galliano. Cesare has already taken control of New Jersey and is blissfully content with Rosalind. Leroi and Seraphine have a perfect relationship. Even Gil has found himself a woman.

They're all happy, except me.

Lorenzo and Vitale sit across from my desk, grinning like a couple of sharks. They've got reason to be smug—our profits this quarter have exceeded projections. Since helping Demartini with the credit scam, he's guided us on how to optimize our games and maximize the casino's revenue.

He's even allowed a few interns from Mortis House into his operation to learn the intricate workings of the oldest gambling establishment in New Alderney. I'm thrilled to have broadened my boys' career paths.

"Record profits, and we're only halfway through the quarter." Lorenzo slides the reports across the table.

"Old man Demartini really knows his shit," Vitale adds.

I nod, the numbers already burned into my brain. They've been solid for weeks, and things are only getting better. "Good work," I say, leaning back in my chair. "Keep it up."

Our conversation shifts to Valeria House, the sorority I'm building with Rosalind and Reaper. It's shaping up, following the Mortis House's blueprint. Reaper's been handling the groundwork and recruitment, while Rosalind is giving us pointers on training the new girls.

They're daughters and nieces of our employees, eager for a college education. In a few years, we'll have a small army of loyal women, just like Mortis. Valeria will be a real asset.

"Any chance we'll get to train the girls?" Vitale asks with a salacious smirk.

I lean across the table. "Would you want someone like you watching over your sister?"

He grimaces. "No."

A knock sounds on the door, and my new head of security rushes inside, his jaw ticking. "Boss, we've got trouble at the tables."

"Where?"

He crosses the room, stopping at the window and points down at the casino floor. "Baccarat table seven. Some asshole is on a winning streak."

Frowning, I stare down at the table from behind the glass. A man in a tailored suit dominates the space, raking in piles of chips. He's at least sixty, with a curled black mustache and silver hair slicked back in a ponytail. It's Franco Scali, a notorious card shark who's been banned from every casino in New Alderney for his scams.

But I'm more concerned about his companion, a middle-aged woman whose red gown is slipping down her ample cleavage. She slumps at his side, barely holding herself upright. I'd recognize that auburn hair anywhere. It's Losanna Fucking Di Marco.

Scali is practically humping her, his greasy lips trailing across her jaw. My stomach clenches. I might despise the woman, but no one takes advantage of Ginevra's mother.

His kisses travel down her neckline, making my gut flare with fury. This idiot trying to scam my casino has a bounty on his head. Anyone watching would think they're working together, but I'm not about to let him drag Losanna to the grave.

"Put them both into separate interrogation rooms," I snap.

The team scrambles to obey. I stand at the window, grinding my teeth, wondering if this is my excuse to call Ginevra. She'd rush over in an instant, thank me profusely for rescuing her mother, and maybe she'll remember I'm not all bad.

No.

I will not manipulate Ginevra. She and I both know I'm no fucking knight in bullet proof armor.

I'll handle the situation, secure Losanna's safety, and let Ginevra enjoy her freedom.

Turning away from the window, I stalk across the office and out through the hallway. Heat simmers under my skin as I make my way down the elevator and through the casino's back corridors, preparing myself for a confrontation.

Losanna is Ginevra's weakest link. Her vulnerability and drunken antics were what held Ginevra back from coming to us for protection when Joseph Di Marco ordered her to break our engagement.

By the time I enter the interrogation room, Losanna is slumped on the table, her auburn hair serving as a makeshift pillow. She raises her head at my entrance, her eyes widening.

"Oh, it's you," she slurs, pushing her carcass upright.

She's a mess of smeared lipstick and smudged mascara. If I grabbed her by the shoulders and shook, she'd probably crumble into pieces.

"What the hell are you doing?" I snarl.

"Where's my friend?" she asks, blinking up at me through bleary eyes.

"That man you were with is marked for death."

Frowning, she sways in her seat. "What are you talking about?"

"Scali has a hundred-grand bounty on his head. The people about to pick him up and execute him are more likely to torture you to make him pay his debts," I say. "A weasel like him will leave you to die without a second thought."

The color drains from her face. Her mouth moves, but she makes no sound. "No, he wouldn't—"

"You criticize Ginevra for getting involved with me, yet you're no better," I snap.

She squares her shoulders, trying to muster the last dregs of her pride. "And Ginny's still waiting for you to sign the divorce papers."

The barb doesn't land with the intended blow. My therapy sessions now center on coming to terms with the fact that she doesn't want or need me, and letting her go. Anyone who said the opposite of love is hate was wrong. It's indifference.

Ginevra hasn't even filed for a default judgment, because doing so will bring us back into contact. She just wants to pretend I never even existed.

Crossing the distance, I place my palms on the table. "Here's what will happen if I set you free. Whatever enforcers, trackers, or manhunters sent after Scali will scoop you up and tell their boss to use you as collateral."

Her lips pinch.

"They won't care that you're just a reckless drunk chasing a cheap thrill. To them, you're something to use as leverage over him. Don't think for a second Scali won't let you be tortured to save his worthless hide."

"Fine," she says through clenched teeth. "Then call me a cab."

My eyes narrow. "The only way you're leaving this casino is via rehab. No more skiing vacations. No more yoga retreats or whatever else you used to tell Ginevra. She doesn't need to hold herself hostage over you."

Jaw tightening, she glares across the table, as if mustering a snide remark. Whatever she says will undoubtedly be true. I've already faced my demons. Dr. Saint diagnosed me with Obsessive Love Disorder, stemming from a sense of abandonment before Cesare was born. I was three or four when Mom got pregnant and withdrew from the family, and I must have transferred that need for female affection to Ginevra.

I meet Losanna's stare with one of my own until she finally slumps back in her seat, defeated. "Alright. I'll go."

Not wanting to give her the satisfaction of a response, I nod to the man at the door and walk out of the interrogation room, leaving Losanna behind.

She'll be safe in rehab until the shit with Scali blows over. Hopefully, when she returns, she'll no longer be a burden on Ginevra.

———

Even more weeks pass, and Losanna is still in rehab. She and her daughter haven't spoken since Ginevra moved out, making me wonder if that drunken stunt she pulled at the casino was a ploy to get Ginevra's attention.

An employee at the Demartini Casino lets me know when Ginevra's firm is scheduled to visit, so I time my trips to see the old man. We've moved from eyeing each other from opposite sides of the gambling tables to exchanging nods. Every instinct wants to close that unbearable distance, but I'm giving her time.

She needs to see that I'm a better man. The patient type who doesn't push too soon. Doesn't demand more than she's willing to give. But every time she breaks eye contact, turns away, or dismisses me with cold indifference, it hurts worse than a bullet through the jugular.

One evening, I'm seated at the center table of Chez Aquitani, Beaumont City's most exclusive French restaurant. Reaper is on my left, and we're both across from the Dean of Alderney State University.

Sweat rolls down his brow, which he blots with a napkin. Being seen out in public with a Montesano can't be good for his reputation, which is precisely why I summoned him to meet me in such a high-end establishment.

The old man clears his throat. "Your scholarship students are missing too many classes. The university has standards—"

"They're getting a real education to set them up for the business world," I say, cutting off his bullshit. "Which is better than sitting through hours of lectures."

A waiter sets down plates of foie gras with a soft clink. The

Dean shifts uncomfortably in his seat, his eyes darting around the other diners. Intimidating him won't take long.

"They need more time in lectures to balance the curriculum," he says, his voice edging on desperation.

"Let's not kid ourselves." I pick up my glass of Sauternes and take a sip of the sweet wine. "The workload you're pushing is filler. Their real work's out in the world."

His cheeks darken. "Absolutely not. The university has principles, guidelines, and expectations of its students."

Reaper reaches into his jacket and slides a folder across the table. The older man hesitates, but one glance inside and his face drains of color. We have pictures of him tangled up with his brother's wife in a situation a lot messier than skipping classes.

The Dean squirms, pulling at his collar like he's about to expire on his Michelin-star meal. "What is this?"

"Our curriculum is fine." Reaper places his palms on the table.

With trembling fingers, the old bastard closes the folder, his Adam's apple bobbing. I take another sip of wine, letting the silence do the heavy lifting.

"Where did you..." He shakes off the question. "We'll reevaluate the attendance policy for your scholarship students," he says, the words choked.

I'm about to steer the conversation back to business when the door to the restaurant opens. Marcello Demartini walks in with an auburn-haired date.

It's Ginevra.

She's too busy laughing at his witty repartee to notice me at the restaurant's center, and the sight of her happy with anyone other than me hurts like a knife to the chest.

I try to turn away but my eyes won't cooperate. She looks radiant, happy, more alive than she ever did with me, and the fibers of my heart twist.

The Maître D walks them to a cozy booth, and Demartini rests his hand on the small of her back as he settles her in. He scoots, sitting so close to her that she may as well be on his lap.

Then he leans in and whispers something that makes her

giggle. Her face lights up like the sky on New Year's Eve, and she radiates with the glow of a woman in love.

My fingers curl around the stem of the wine glass, and I force another sip, but the sweet liquid tastes as sour as fermented shit.

I turn back to the Dean, but my mind still remains in that booth, where my wife is having the time of her life with another man.

She's moved on, and here I am, forced to accept that nothing I do will bring her back.

Fuck.

My mind spins. I gave her space. I stayed back, let her make her choices. Nearly a year of therapy has taught me to respect her autonomy and to become the kind of man who sets aside his selfish desire for possession. Approaching her now would undo all that progress and only push her further away.

But now I'm watching her live a life without me. A life where she's smiling, free, where Marcello Demartini—that fucking aristocrat—is making her laugh.

I should be pleased to see her in better spirits, but the ache in my chest is a bitter reminder of the love I lost.

Reaper follows my gaze and murmurs, "She looks happy."

"Yeah," I mutter, my throat tightening. "She does."

Giving her space only pushed her into the arms of another man.

Watching her laugh with him feels like a final goodbye I wasn't ready to confront, but I've lost my wife.

And it's time to get her back.

ONE HUNDRED FIVE

GINEVRA

This hangover is kicking my ass.

My head pounds as if there are loan sharks at the door, and my throat is lined with gravel. Two separate riots break out through my insides, and the morning sun sears through my eyelids.

This is all Marcello's fault.

He has a crush on the restaurant's sommelier, so he drags us out there every other night to try their selection of wine. It's the same each time, with Marcello impressing the man with his vast knowledge of vintages, and us ending up drinking hours after the place shuts.

Groaning, I drag my carcass into the shower and wash away last night's excess. Hot water pummels my back, scalding away the regrets, and steam wraps around my senses like a forgiving embrace.

My skin tingles, the heat working its way into my muscles, loosening the ache from too much wine and too little restraint. I love my bestie. I really do, but he's such a terrible influence.

"Marcello." I huff a laugh.

We're each other's emotional support. He's one of the few people who truly understands what it's like to survive an irresistible, toxic man.

Finally, the pounding eases to a background ache. I step out of the shower, slip into a fluffy robe, and wrap a towel around my hair into a makeshift turban.

The woman staring back at me through the foggy mirror looks like a scalded cat—red eyes, red skin, red wisps of hair. I make a mental note to drink more water and step out of the bathroom, only to find a man sitting on my living room sofa.

I freeze, my mind turning to sludge. The sight of him in my space sends my pulse skittering. Benito doesn't belong in my new apartment, yet his presence dominates the room.

He's dressed in black, with the morning sun coloring his dark hair a rich shade of mahogany. With his regal features and that imposing posture, he may as well be Hades.

His molten eyes lock onto mine, boring into my soul.

Breath catching, I lose my footing and stumble backward, the lapel of my robe slipping down to expose my shoulder.

I pull the fabric together with a snap. Rage wells up in my chest, sharp and hot. I've spent months clawing my way out of a pit of heartbreak and helplessness, convincing myself that I'm stronger without him. Now he's here, and it's like nothing's changed.

"What are you doing in my living room?"

"Don't hide from me," he drawls, his dark eyes raking over my form. "I've seen it all already."

His arrogance grates against my nerves. How dare he brush off my boundaries like they don't exist? This is classic Benito. Fire burns through my veins, making my cheeks heat. I would dismiss his presence as a post-alcoholic hallucination if I wasn't so infuriated.

"Answer my question," I snap. "What the fuck are you doing here? Get out!"

He rises off the sofa, filling my small living room with the oppressive weight of his presence. I dig my heels into the linoleum, refusing to be cowed.

"What were you doing last night with Marcello Demartini?" he asks.

I cross my arms, refusing to give ground. "After everything

you've done—after the months of silence—you think you have the right to question me?"

His jaw tightens. "You are my wife—"

"You don't get to interrogate me, and you sure as hell don't get to come here, acting like I'm your possession."

He closes the distance, standing before me like the Roman god of intrusive husbands. I grind my teeth. Things were so much easier when we were both little, when I was capable of shoving him backward. Now, all I have to fight with are words.

"I gave you space to recover, not to go on dates with other men."

I laugh, the sound bitter and harsh. "Do you think ignoring me for months counts as progress? You've done nothing to fix what you broke."

He frowns. "I've been trying. Therapy, self-control—it's all for you."

"Did I ask you to see a shrink? All I wanted was honesty. No more manipulation. No more mind games. Why was that too much for you?"

His shoulders stiffen as if bracing against my words. The air between us thickens with menace before he steps ever closer. "Answer the question," he says, his voice dropping to a dangerous low, "Or I'll ask Demartini myself."

Dread clenches my stomach. Mars doesn't deserve to get dragged into this mess. "He's a friend."

"What kind?" His voice drops, low and threatening.

"The kind who can't be bought to mess with my life," I snap. "And I thought everyone knew he's gay."

His eyes widen.

The silence that follows is almost deafening. For once, Benito is caught off guard, and it feels like a small victory. But it's not enough.

"You've got your answers. Now, get out."

He doesn't move. His dark eyes search mine, and for a moment, I see something that almost looks like regret. But regret isn't change, and neither is his disappearing act.

"What about us?" he asks.

"Forgiveness must be earned, Benito," I snap, mirroring something he said months ago. "And you won't get it by bulling your way back into my life."

Leaning even closer, he inhales slow and deliberate, as if committing my scent to memory. Tingles prickle along my skin, and I suppress a shiver.

"You're mine," he growls. "And I'm yours. Whether you want me or not."

ONE HUNDRED SIX

BENITO

I leave Ginevra's apartment feeling less tense than I did earlier, but it still rankles that she spends time with another man.

Jealousy gnaws at my gut, tearing through the last shreds of my patience. It doesn't matter if Demartini is gay. It should be me taking Ginevra to restaurants, me making her laugh, me plying her with drink.

I drive home in a daze, my mind spinning with possibilities. Despite every word Dr. Saint has fed me, was it a mistake to give Ginevra so much space? Space that's now being filled by another man.

The thought is a thorn twisting in my side. Marcello might not be a threat, but who's to say the next man won't be? Someone charming enough, kind enough, patient enough to draw her away from me for good.

My hands tighten on the steering wheel as the car winds up Alderney Hill. Every instinct screams at me to intervene, to show Ginevra—and the world—that she's mine. But I force down the thought, gripping the remnants of my control. There will be no more mistakes.

Shit. I need a distraction before I spiral into old habits, undoing everything I've worked for.

As I approach the turning, my phone rings. "What?"

"Mr. Montesano, this is Frances from the Matthias Clinic. You asked me to inform you if Mrs. Di Marco skips her meeting with the sober coach. She was supposed to meet her at nine this morning—"

"I'll take care of it," I say through clenched teeth before making a U-turn.

Ginevra is finally happy, relaxed, carefree... Even if she spends an inappropriate amount of time with another man. I'll be damned if I allow her mother to spoil that peace by relapsing.

It's time to march Losanna Di Marco back into sobriety.

But first, I'll call home. Based on what I saw this morning, Ginevra might welcome a hangover recipe.

The Matthias Clinic is bright, sterile, and utterly soulless. According to Reaper's sister, it's the best addiction treatment center in the state. I stride through the stark white hallways, my anger building with each step. How dare Losanna jeopardize her recovery and make herself a burden to Ginevra again?

In between ranting about my mother-in-law I call the florist and order a bouquet of honeysuckles and roses. The man watching her apartment confirms later they were delivered, but there's no message from my wife.

My lips quirk, despite the pang of disappointment. The mere fact that she's accepted them is promising. She's lowering her defenses, opening up to my advances. It's only a matter of time before she lets me back into her life.

The door opens, and Losanna exits looking irritated but sober enough, her auburn hair catching the late-morning light. She sweeps past me with her nose in the air, pretending I don't exist.

I follow her out into the street and open the car door. "Good meeting?"

Lips tightening, she settles into the front seat. "Don't expect me to thank you for dragging me here."

"Skip another appointment with your sober coach, and the next man I send after you won't be so respectful," I reply.

Her nostrils flare, but she doesn't reply. For once, she understands her place.

When I call home, Sofia tells me she delivered Ginevra's hangover remedy herself and even encouraged her to make cookies together like they did when she was eight. Encouraged by yet another good sign, I resist the urge to send her a text.

She'll hear from me tomorrow.

———

The next morning, as I'm leaving the casino, I text:

How's the hangover?

Seconds tick by, stretching into a full minute. I sit in the back seat of the car and wait, my entire existence hinging on her response. Finally, my phone buzzes with a reply:

Better.

A single word, curt and to the point, but it fills my chest with warmth. Lips curving into a smirk, I lean back, wanting to hug my phone. It's progress.

I decide to push further:

I'd hate for you to suffer without me to bring you ginger tea.

Three dots appear then vanish. I hold my breath, hoping she'll call my bluff, issue a challenge, drop any kind of hint for me to cross town and appear at her doorstep. Seconds pass before her next message comes through:

If it's anything like the sludge you made on the campfire, then I'll pass.

Smirk widening, I recall my failed attempt at making nutmeg tea when we were fourteen and message back:

I learned my lesson. Ginger root only. No ingredients pilfered from Sofia's pantry.

Another long pause before she replies with:

Thanks for the flowers.

That's it. No invitation for more, but it's enough to keep me fueled. She's still lowering her walls, one cautious step at a time.

We continue like this for several months. I send carefully chosen gifts to remind her of better times. A first edition copy of Jane Eyre, which she once read out to me in our apartment while we were at law school. A replica of the green cashmere blanket she used to snuggle in on the sofa. Silk scarves with her favorite prints, and vinyl records of our favorite songs.

I check in on Ginevra via text and short phone calls. Sometimes she accepts my offer of a drink if I bump into her at the Demartini casino. I bring her gourmet coffee in the mornings, escort her to work, and take her out for the occasional lunch.

With the help of Dr. Saint, I'm always careful not to push her too far. Every interaction feels like a high-stakes negotiation, a delicate balance between showing her I care and avoiding the mistakes that drove her away.

It's maddening.

Every day, I fight my baser instincts, the ones screaming at me to demand more, to remind her of what we had, of what we could still be. There's no Capello organization standing in my way, no threats hanging over my brothers. I'm free to claim my wife.

Dr. Saint says I should let Ginevra come to me, but it feels more like holding my breath. I might suffocate before she remembers where she belongs.

Every passing day, another thread of my patience unravels. I'm not sure how much longer I can survive on crumbs without snapping.

One evening, as I'm watching over the casino, I get a call from the man I stationed at Ginevra's workplace. "Mrs. Di Marco worked late until eight," he says. "She's having dinner with a man at the new French bistro on Juniper and West."

My brow furrows. "Marcello Demartini?"

"No, sir."

Before I can even ask who, my phone buzzes with a message. A video arrives of Ginevra sitting in a booth with a man I don't recognize. Mousy hair, clean-cut, corporate, and very much heterosexual, he's leaning in with an intensity that turns the edges of my vision red.

Who the fuck is this man and why is he having a cozy dinner with my wife?

"Mr. Montesano?" My man's voice breaks me out of my thoughts.

"Who is he?" I snarl.

Dr. Saint's voice echoes through my mind, cautioning me

about falling back into old habits. But this isn't about controlling Ginevra—it's about protecting what's mine. Nobody but me gets to worm their way back into her life.

"We don't have a name, yet—"

"Tail him," I growl, my hands clenching into fists. "And get backup. Call when you've broken into his home and have him hog-tied."

ONE HUNDRED SEVEN

GINEVRA

At the office after a workout, I bump into my colleague, Ian. We worked late last night and finished off a productive evening with dinner.

He walks around me, avoiding eye contact, but something's wrong. Deep bruises mar the left side of his jaw, and there's a new stiffness to his movements.

"Ian, are you okay?"

"Fine." Jaw tightening, he adjusts the strap of his laptop bag. The movement shifts his sleeve, revealing wrists covered in livid red marks.

My stomach drops. I move around him to block his path. "Ian, talk to me. What happened?"

He flinches, his eyes darting toward the exit like a trapped beast. "Look, I'm really sorry about last night. I didn't mean anything by that hug. I didn't know you were married."

"Married? What are you talking about?"

Fumbling with his bag, he pulls out a piece of paper. "Here, take this." He thrusts it into my hands. "I'm resigning. Effective immediately."

I stare at the letter, my mind reeling. "What? Why? But you only just joined. How can you leave us so soon?"

With a shaky breath, he mutters, "I was attacked. Last night.

At my apartment. Your husband told me to stay away from you or else..."

All the blood drains from my face and floods my pounding heart. Benito attacked a man for taking me out for a meal? Before I can react, Ian bolts toward the door. My voice catches in my throat, and by the time I whirl around, he's gone.

Fury propels me back out of the building and down the steps. Benito Montesano doesn't get to attack my colleagues.

I drive across town in a red rage and park outside the casino's staff entrance. The pounding in my chest remains relentless, and I don't care that I'm wearing sweaty workout clothes or that my hair is a bird's nest.

A guard steps forward, blocking my path. He squares his shoulders, staring down at me like I'm crazed. "Ma'am, you can't be here."

"Step aside," I say through clenched teeth. "I need to speak to Benito Montesano."

"Do you have an appointment?" he asks with a smirk, already knowing the answer.

"I don't need one to see my husband," I snap.

He scoffs, and I can tell exactly what he's thinking. There's no way his boss would entertain a sweaty, auburn-haired banshee, but I had Benito's heart when he was just a boy.

"Ma'am, I'm gonna have to ask you to leave."

His large hand lands on my shoulder, triggering a surge of adrenaline. I drive my fist into his crotch, making him double over with a roar.

Another man rushes forward with a hand outstretched. I side-step, my heel connecting to his shin.

"Where's my husband?" I yell.

The first man grabs my shoulder again, his grip stronger. "Crazy bitch!"

"Let go!" I dip low, throw my weight forward, using his momentum to catapult him over my head. He lands on his back with a surprised grunt, just in time for the other asshole to grab me from behind and lift me off my feet.

A crowd has gathered around the employee reception, but I'm too far gone to care. All the rage boiling in my gut funnels into a primal scream, making me struggle against the man's grip. I twist and kick, my elbow connecting with his rib.

In my periphery, a figure breaks through the crowd and my heart drops into my stomach.

"Get your hands off my wife," bellows a familiar voice.

Everyone freezes.

The guard's grip around my waist loosens, and I wrench free.

It's Benito, and all I can think of is how majestic he looks in that sharp suit and black shirt, showing a peek of his muscled chest. He stalks forward, the tendons in his neck corded like steel cables. His jaw clenches, his nostrils flare, and his hands curl into fists.

I step away from the two guards, who exchange nervous glances. They don't know whether to stand their ground or cower.

The one I flipped over raises his palms. "Boss—"

"You touched my wife," Benito says, his voice icy and low. His dark eyes burn with an intensity that makes me shiver.

The guard who held me steps backward. "Mr. Montesano, she came here—"

Benito's hand shoots out, grabbing him by the throat, his grip so tight that his knuckles turn white. "I don't give a damn what she did," Benito growls, the words laced with menace. "No one lays a finger on my wife."

The guard struggles, his fingers pulling at Benito's hand. His companion steps forward, only for Lorenzo and Vitale to hold him back.

"Put them in the basement." Benito releases the man, letting him fall to his knees. His security staff springs from the crowd, yanking the guards by their collars and dragging them toward a side door.

Benito turns to me, his handsome features softening just enough to make my heart flutter. "You alright?"

My adrenaline is still high, and the concern in his eyes unleashes my pent-up frustration. I reach into the waistband of my leggings, extract the crumpled resignation letter, and wave it in his face.

"What the hell is this?" I hiss.

His brow pinches. "You tell me."

"You can't go around attacking my male colleagues and forcing them to resign!" I slam the letter into his chest.

His jaw tightens, and emotion flickers in his dark eyes. Wishful thinking says it's guilt, but it's probably impatience. Impatience at me coming here after all this time to disrupt his fine casino.

"We're not doing this here," he says.

Before I can protest, he takes my hand, his touch unlocking a floodgate of old memories. Benito leading me through the woods, eager to show me our new tree house. Those fingers curling around mine as he proposed on my twenty-first birthday.

I don't pull away, letting him guide me through the staff reception, up an elevator, and through the hallways that lead to his office.

My gaze darts to the second desk he set up for me, which still has the laptop and files I used on the day we worked together. There's even the pen I chewed, as if I haven't been gone in over a year.

When the door clicks shut behind us, I'm the first to talk. "Why the hell would you attack my colleague?"

Benito steps closer, making the air between us thicken with tension. Heart pounding, I stiffen, waiting for him to speak. "I tolerated your association with Marcello Demartini because you said it was platonic. That bastard from last night used dinner as step one in getting you into bed."

Frustration mounts in my belly as I glare into his dark eyes. "You don't get to interfere with my livelihood!"

A vein pops in his brow. "I've been working behind the scenes, trying to restore everything I took from you. I even bought you a fucking law firm."

"What?" I hiss, my blood running cold, my mind struggling to grasp the enormity of his claim. "Are you meddling with my career again?"

His hands fly up as if he has the right to be frustrated. "Of course not. I bought your partnership in secret because I didn't want to use it to lure you back."

I swaying on my feet, my mind reeling, and all thoughts of Ian evaporate under the heat of this new revelation. Does this count as Machiavellian or not?

"Believe me, I never stopped trying to be a better man for you. Not for a minute. Staying away has been agony, but I'm still working with that therapist, trying to get to the root of my need to control."

My breath stills.

Benito steps even closer, his gaze earnest. "I've changed," he says, his voice hoarse with emotion. "But every time I think of you, all I see is the abuse, the manipulation, the danger. And when I heard you were out with another man—"

"He's just a colleague," I snap.

"He set up last night's date to get into your pants," he says.

I fold my arms across my chest. "And how would you know that?"

"He admitted to planning future late nights with you to get you drunk and in his bed. I made sure he wouldn't try again."

"Did you force the confession?"

"My man cornered him in the bathroom," Benito replies. "That's where he admitted he had a plan to get you out of the friend zone. He also confirmed that when I went to his apartment."

I search his features, looking for signs of deception, but his eyes burn with the truth.

"I protect what's mine, even if that means stepping in front of a bullet or chasing off a horny asshole with my fists."

A laugh bubbles up in my chest, and I force back a smile. "What are you, my own personal superhero?"

Relief crosses his features, and he steps even closer. His gaze, dark and intense, locks onto mine as though our souls finally connect. "Your husband," he says, the words breathy. "I never stopped loving you. And I'll never stop striving to become the man who's worthy of your love."

Emotion clogs my throat, stealing my breath. I nod, unable to muster a reply. The sincerity in his words is overwhelming, but more than that, terrifying.

His fingers brush against mine, igniting a spark that races up my arm and settles in my heart. The touch is familiar, yet spine-tinglingly electric, stirring months of suppressed desire. This time, when his hand slips into mine, our fingers intertwine as if they've been starved of each other's touch.

"What do you want, Ginevra?" he asks, his voice desperate and hoarse.

"Mom miraculously stopped drinking," I say. "She called me several months ago from some rehab clinic in Ravencliff Island, apologizing for putting me through hell. Was that you?"

He jerks his head to the side, his Adam's apple bobbing.

"What did you do?"

"She came to the casino with a low-life who was about to get himself killed," he mutters, his gaze not meeting mine. "I separated her from the old bastard and gave her an ultimatum."

I gulp. "Why didn't you call me?"

He runs a hand through his hair. "I know a cheap attempt to get your attention when I see one. Besides, you were doing so well in your new job. I'd be damned if she derailed your progress."

"Benito," I whisper, my chest tightening. "You did that for me?"

"Wasn't she part of the reason our relationship fell apart?" he growls. "Even if you don't want me, I still want the best for you. Now, what do you want?"

Gratitude swells in my chest, making my pulse quicken. We've been talking almost every day since I kicked him out of my apartment. He's given me thoughtful gifts, reminded me of better times. Yet he's withheld the two most important gestures that would have me reeling with gratitude. Fixing Mom's drinking problem and making me a partner in a prestigious law firm.

Despite all his trips down memory lane, he's never once brought up risking his life to save mine. I can't believe he would do something so unselfish without even using it for leverage. This isn't the man I left.

I shake off that thought, my mind spinning. Benito has a way of altering reality so that all roads lead to him. I need to think straight. Need to protect myself from getting swept away again. Need to make sure he's truly changed.

"Did you even apologize to me?" I ask. "Are you sorry for what you did or just sorry it backfired?"

Eyes widening, he rears back as if I've demanded a slice of the moon. "That's what you want?" he asks, his words incredulous. "An apology?"

I square my shoulders. "Yes."

In the blink of an eye, he scoops me up and slings me over his shoulder like a sack of potatoes.

"Benito," I scream. "What are you doing?"

"Giving you that apology," he growls.

ONE HUNDRED EIGHT

BENITO

I tighten my grip around Ginevra's waist, holding her steady as she kicks and squirms. Her fists slam against my back, her outraged, indignant shrieks echoing through the corridor, but I don't stop. I'll endure every ounce of her fury if it means finally making this right.

"Put me down!" She twists. "Have you lost your fucking mind?"

Her anger only adds fuel to the fire already burning in my chest. I adjust her over my shoulder, ignoring her nails digging into my back through my jacket. She could claw me raw, and I'd still keep walking.

The elevator doors slide open, and I step inside to press the button. She shoves at my back with both hands, twisting with all the strength in her small, furious body.

"You're insane," she yells, her voice breaking.

I hold her tighter as the doors close, sealing us in. The desperation I've been holding in for months threatens to burst free but I clench my jaw.

"You asked for an apology," I say, the words choked. "It's not enough to tell you I'm sorry. Those are just words. The whole world needs to know I fucked up, and I'll do everything to win you back."

She freezes against my shoulder, her breaths coming fast and shallow. She probably thinks I've lost my mind, but working on myself behind the scenes isn't enough. The elevator ascends, each second stretching the anticipation in the air until it thrums.

The doors open, letting in the cacophony of the casino. I step out, carrying her past green-felt tables filled with card shuffles, clinking chips, and chatter.

"Don't make me part of some spectacle," she snaps, her voice muffled against my shoulder.

"The only one getting embarrassed here is me." I continue through the casino floor.

Staff and patrons pause from their games, stunned. Ignoring their stares, I stop in the center of the floor and set Ginevra on her feet.

Swaying, she splays out one arm and reaches for me with the other. A flush spreads across beautiful features that I want to see every day for the rest of my life. Even though her eyes blaze with fury, she doesn't shrink or bolt. Instead, she gazes up at me, breathing hard.

"Attention, everyone," I call out, still holding her gaze.

Silence sweeps across the casino like a held breath. Even the background music fades as all eyes shift to where we're standing.

Ginevra doesn't move, doesn't flinch under the stares. She just fixes her tank top and straightens.

"This beautiful, breathtaking woman," I say, letting my gaze sweep over every face in the room. "Is my wife."

Murmurs spread through the crowd, making Ginevra's breath quicken.

"I've been the worst kind of bastard," I announce, my words raw. "Lied to you on the most fundamental of levels. Manipulated you at every turn, and broke your trust. I don't deserve a second chance, but I don't run from my mistakes."

Her brows pinch, and I know she's still wondering what the hell I'm doing.

I drop down to my knees on the marble floor, eliciting gasps from the stunned crowd, but the only one that matters is Ginevra's.

"But I'm sorry, and not just because my actions drove you

away. You've always been my equal, my partner, the better half of my soul. You deserved better, yet I treated you like a pawn."

Her throat bobs, but she doesn't speak.

"I want to make things right," I continue. "And I'll spend every day of the rest of my life treating you like the goddess you truly are," I say. Emotions swell, threatening to choke off my words, but I force them down with a deep breath. "I'm also sorry for this spectacle, but the whole world needs to know how much I've wronged you, starting with this public apology and a declaration of my love."

Eyes widening, she clutches her chest, then blinks, loosening tears. The silence in the casino is deafening, but we may as well be alone, since nobody matters except my Ginevra.

"I won't ask for your forgiveness now," I say, my ribs tightening around the ache. "That's something I want the chance to earn."

A sharp, unbearable pressure grips my chest as she continues staring down at me without uttering a word.

"But while you're waiting for me to be a better man, I'll give you anything—a ring, your own house, a real wedding," I blurt. "All I ask for is the chance to be the husband you deserve."

I cling to her hips, mirroring the way she begged the day I murdered Julian Riva and the morning after I made her believe she'd been unfaithful. Pressing my forehead to her thighs, I hold on as if she's the only thing keeping me from drowning.

"I'm nothing without you, Ginevra. You were always my moral compass, and when you left, I was lost. I'm not worthy of a second chance, but I'll do anything to earn it."

An ache spreads across my chest at the admission, but I make myself continue. "I took everything good between us and destroyed it when I lied and didn't trust you, and when I tried to control your life instead of letting you live it. I see it all now, and I hate the man I became."

"Really?" she whispers.

I nod. "I'll do anything. Everything I can to improve. Not just for you, but for us."

"How?"

"I'll rebuild myself. Take more therapy. You can come with

me. Establish boundaries, whatever it takes. But I'll do it with or without you because you deserve to see me become the man I should have been."

She breathes hard as though needing more convincing, her trembling fingers hovering just above my head. I wait, feeling every agonizing second of her indecision. She wanted me to fight for her, and here I am—on my fucking knees in front of staff, security, and spectators—but the fear of her rejection rakes at my heart like claws.

"You begged me, Ginevra. You begged for trust, for love, for respect—and I didn't listen. I failed you over and over. I can never undo the damage I caused but I can devote every day of the rest of my life trying."

Her features flicker with even more of that indecision. I wait, every second stretching into an eternity. My heart hammers so loudly it drowns out the chatter, and I wonder if I've already lost her. That thought cuts deeper than anything I've ever known.

"Tell me what you need, and I'll give it to you. Tell me what I'm still doing wrong, and I'll fix it. I'll do anything, Ginevra. Just... don't walk away."

She licks her lips, finally parting them to say, "I can't forgive you. And I can't take you back."

My heart crashes into my stomach, and desperation grips me by the throat.

"Not right away," she adds.

The tension eases only a fraction. "I don't expect it to be easy. It will take however long it takes."

Her fingers finally brush my hair, a slight caress that hits like lightning. I almost break, ribs constricting, each inhale cutting like glass. I stay perfectly still, waiting for her to speak.

"Did you really make me a partner in my firm?" she murmurs.

I meet her gaze, unblinking, the answer flooding from my lips. "You earned it," I rasp. "They wouldn't have taken you on if you didn't have the skills."

"But why?" she whispers.

"I wanted to give you something that couldn't be tainted by my need to control you. Something I couldn't touch. An independent life where you could thrive away from me."

Eyes softening, she trails her fingers down to my face, and that touch alone almost makes me crack. The distance between us disappears, her warmth anchoring me in a way I haven't felt since before everything went to shit.

"You want forgiveness?"

I nod.

"Then earn it," she says.

"How?"

The corner of her lips lift. "Get off your knees and kiss me."

Heart skipping a beat, I rise, my hands sliding from her waist to the small of her back. Every wall between us crumbles as she wraps her fingers around the back of my neck, pulling me down to her mouth.

Applause breaks out across the casino floor, but I'm too cocooned in the warmth of her acceptance to care. I cup her face, my thumbs brushing over her cheeks as our lips meet in a kiss that feels like redemption.

Her arms tighten around my neck, pulling me closer until her heart thrums in sync with mine.

The world falls away, replaced by the softness of her lips and her honeysuckle scent. After all my machinations, the pain I've inflicted, the anger and regret, this moment feels like absolution.

I pour everything into that kiss. Every apology, every plea for forgiveness, every word left unsaid, it all flows in this one act of surrender. Her lips move against mine, anchoring me in the present, obliterating the darkness of our past.

A low, desperate sound catches in my aching chest. Helpless against months of pent-up need, I slide my hands down her back and pull her closer.

She breaks the kiss first, her eyes searching mine. I meet her gaze, wanting to convey the depth of my remorse, my overwhelming gratitude, my commitment to being the man she deserves.

"How was that?" I ask.

"It's a start," she murmurs.

My throat tightens, and my chest thrums with anticipation. "You'll give me a chance to redeem myself?"

She nods.

Waves of relief and gratitude make me rock back on my feet. Heart racing, palms sweating, I struggle to catch my breath. Guilt still lingers in the pit of my stomach, reminding me why I don't deserve a chance, but it's overshadowed by a glimmer of hope.

She steps back, breaking our connection. Her fingers trail down my chest, over my abs, and settle on my belt buckle.

Sensation rushes south, leaving me light headed. "Ginevra?"

"You're not forgiven yet," she says.

My jaw drops. "What do you want me to do?"

Gray eyes dilating, she leans closer and murmurs, "Work for it, Benito."

Anticipation crackles in the air like static as her fingers tighten on my belt. A shiver runs down my spine and settles in my cock. I should carry her back to my office and take her over the desk, but I'm past locking my Ginevra away.

Instead, I turn to where my security people mingle in the crowd and bellow, "Everybody out!"

ONE HUNDRED NINE

GINEVRA

What the hell did I just unleash?

I cling to the lapels of his jacket, glancing over Benito's shoulder as his men usher people toward the exits. Heart pounding, I gulp as every membrane of my throat dries. I only wanted him to be the sex object for once, but this is ridiculous.

"Are you really clearing the casino for me?"

He grabs my hips, pulling me flush against his erection. "Nothing's more important than you. The business can go to hell."

This is crazy. I wanted to return to his office. Or even a private room. Not disrupt millions of dollars worth of transactions. Before I can even protest, his lips descend on mine for another kiss.

The echoes of chatter and clinking chips fade, leaving the two of us in the hush of an emptied floor. He lifts me off my feet and sets me on a poker table, the felt brushing my fingertips. Chips and cards scatter as he lays me flat, but this may as well be another world. I'm losing my mind. Losing my resolve. Losing track of why I came here. Losing myself in Benito's embrace.

All the rage, all the hurt dissolves into the heat of this kiss, in the fire that's always burned whenever we touch. His lips devour mine like he's starving, in this moment of madness, and I forget why I ever left. My body craves the intensity, the passion I thought I could escape.

"I'm a selfish bastard," he murmurs against my mouth, his breath ragged. "But I'll do anything not to lose you."

His words ripple through my defenses, settling in the hollow ache I've carried for months. What I said earlier was on impulse. I should fight—push him away, but the pounding of his heart against mine is intoxicating.

"I don't deserve this second chance. I've hurt you, manipulated you, controlled you." This time, his admission is like he's baring his soul, laying it at my feet. "But you've always been my everything. You're the blood running through my veins, the only source of color in my world. Without you, everything is gray."

The raw need in his words sends shivers racing down my spine, and his desperation seeps into my skin. No force in the universe could pull me away from this moment, not even my shattered pieces of self-preservation.

Benito's grip tightens, pulling me closer into his orbit, his hands tracing my sides. The kiss deepens, and my fingers tangle in his thick hair, clutching as if letting go means losing him forever.

"What if I can't forgive you?" I whisper against his lips. "I can't forget everything you made me suffer."

He draws back to look me full in the face. "I don't deserve forgiveness, and I never want you to forget. But I swear to spend the rest of my life making sure no one will ever make you suffer."

Maybe I'm touch-starved. Maybe I'm awestruck that he's disrupted the casino. Maybe we're two halves of the same twisted soul, but something inside me snaps. All my restraint crumbles, giving way to fierce need.

His eyes—vulnerable and haunted—hold traces of the man I once loved buried beneath layers of control and regret. I rip open his shirt, sending buttons scattering across the green felt, tumbling off the table and clicking onto the floor.

With trembling hands, I drag my fingers over the chiseled planes of his chest, which rise and fall with each ragged breath. My touch trails lower, gliding over his abs as I crave a taste of his raw power, even though I swore to stay away.

He tears off my tank top, exposing my skin to the cool air. Overhead, the low hum of the lights casts a faint glow, outlining him in neon hues.

His dark eyes gleam. "I'll prove to you, every single day, that the man who hurt you no longer exists."

"Really?" I whisper.

"Every hour, every minute, every mother fucking second. I'll start right now by worshiping you as my goddess."

His hands slip under the waistband of my leggings, tracing lines of fire down my sides, branding me with every touch. It's familiar, yet electrifying, fueling the magnetic force of our desire.

"I won't move in with you," The words slip out, breathless, and my heart pounds as I wait for his answer.

"Don't," he murmurs, his lips brushing my jaw. "All I'm asking for is a chance to let me prove that I've changed."

Heaven help me, I'm hopelessly drawn to this sweet poison. Surrendering, even though it might end in ruin.

My hands fall back to his belt, trembling as I yank it open, the buckle clinking as I tear at the fly. I shove down his pants, exposing the rigid length of an erection pushing against his silk boxers. His breath hitches, and I groan, my fingers tracing the thick outline, feeling him pulse beneath my touch.

When he moans, the sound sends a rush of desire straight to my core. My clit aches. My folds become slick. I've missed this. Missed him.

"You're the only woman who's ever made me feel alive," he says, his voice thick with emotion. "I've spent every day without you in agony, trying to fix what I broke. And I'll keep working on myself, whether you're with me or not. But if there's any part of you that still loves me—"

"Stop talking." I ease down his boxers, freeing his beautiful cock, and wrap my fingers around his shaft, making us both groan.

I should walk away. I should tell him I need more time, but I can't. The truth is, despite everything, I still love him. I always have.

After peeling off what's left of my leggings, he slides his fingers between my folds, finding my clit with an agonizing slowness that sends a shiver down my spine. He rubs in slow, deliberate circles, each touch setting my nerve endings on fire. I part my lips and moan, my body arching into his chest, desperate for more. No one could ever unravel me like this, or play my body until I'm teetering on the edge of oblivion.

"I hate you for how you made me suffer," I whisper, my voice shaking with the weight of my emotions. "But I can't imagine a world without you in it."

He squeezes his eyes shut, as if my words are a balm to the wound of our separation. When they open again, all I find is fierce determination, a fire that mirrors the one burning in my soul.

"From now until the day I die, I'll never stop fighting," he says. "You're the only thing that gives my life meaning."

He lifts me off the tables and into his arms, and I wrap my legs around his waist. The blunt tip of his cock presses against my entrance, sending shockwaves through my core. He pauses, his dark eyes locking onto mine with an intensity that makes my heart soar.

"Are you sure about this?" His voice is a hoarse whisper, rough with need. "Because if I start, I won't be able to stop."

"Then don't," I whisper, every fiber of my being aching to connect.

With a swift, powerful thrust, he pushes into my entrance, his thick girth stimulating my nerves with a delicious stretch. Gasping, I dig my nails into his shoulders. It's been so long since I've felt this full, I almost forgot it was so intoxicating. The sensations are overwhelming, almost too much, but I've craved his touch for months.

"Fuck," Benito growls through clenched teeth, his body shaking from the effort of restraint. "You're so tight."

His words infuse me with pleasant shudders, sparking every nerve to life, igniting an insatiable ache for more. But he stills. His eyes lock onto mine, dark and brimming with emotion, as if he's fighting not just to hold back, but to reclaim what he's lost.

"What are you doing?" I ask, my grip tightening around his shoulders.

"I want to savor this moment," he says through panting

breaths. "I never thought you'd let me this close again after my selfish betrayal."

"Benito," I whisper.

His chest heaves, and every line of his face etches with regret. "You feel like heaven. Like home."

Time seems to slow, and for the next several heartbeats, we're two chambers of the same fractured heart, each yearning to heal. My walls flutter around his shaft, making him shiver.

"Come with me to therapy," he says, the words urgent. "We can do couples counseling. We can work out our differences. You can learn about all the impulses I'm trying to control."

"A-alright," I whisper.

"Ginevra."

The vulnerability in his gaze radiates gratitude, regret, and a longing for change. For the first time since he found me in that closet, I see the old Benito—the one I destroyed when I left.

I can't dwell on the past for too long because there's no denying this urgent need. It burns, deep and primal, demanding more.

"Please," I whisper, the word escaping as a desperate plea. "Move."

Breath hitching, he withdraws, then snaps his hips forward, pounding into my pussy with raw precision. As I bump against the table, his lips graze down the curve of my neck, each hot breath searing my skin, while every thrust sends waves of molten ecstasy rippling through my core.

I rake my fingers down his back, their nails digging into his flesh as I surrender to the intensity—the way he moves, the way we collide, the way he drives me to the brink of madness.

His grip tightens on my hips, pulling me closer, deeper, his pace quickening with a desperate urgency. "I need you, Ginevra," he groans against my ear, his voice rough and raw. "It's been like this since the beginning."

A shiver tears through my body at his words, the tension inside coiling tight, ready to snap. "Don't you dare stop. Not now. Not ever."

"Never," he growls, his pace quickening.

The pressure builds, every movement driving me closer to the edge, spiraling higher with each relentless snap of his hips. His breath turns ragged, the tremor in his muscles matching the tightening coil low in my belly.

"I'm so close," I say, clinging to his larger body as if I'll shatter.

"Then come with me."

His grip tightens, pulling me impossibly closer, and with one final thrust, the tension snaps, sending us both crashing over the edge in perfect sync.

Pleasure rips through my senses, pulling him into the same wild current. His cock pulses once, twice, and his groan vibrates against my skin, his grip tightening as he shudders through his release. Hot spurts of cum coat my inner walls, my muscles clenching around his shaft, milking every last drop. We tremble together, the intensity that's been building between us finally breaking free.

And for the first time in half a decade, I let myself believe that maybe we can find our way back to each other's trust.

This isn't yet forgiveness—not by a long shot.

But it's a start.

ONE HUNDRED TEN

EPILOGUE

ONE YEAR LATER

GINEVRA

I descend the treehouse steps, my feet creaking on the wood. Moonlight shines down on the forest, providing scant illumination.

Benito was supposed to return ten minutes ago with the champagne. We still live separately but spend weekends together, alternating between Alderney Hill and the penthouse. During the week, Benito brings me lunch and picks me up from work before returning to the casino. I still have my social life with Mars and a selection of colleagues, and he's careful never to overstep.

My gaze sweeps across the trees. He said he left a crate in his trunk and it wouldn't take long to pick up a few bottles, but I've been waiting for ages.

Where the hell is he?

I reach the bottom of the stairs, and my shoes sink into a thick carpet of fallen leaves. Every snap of a twig, every rustle of branches fills the eerie silence, sending shivers down my spine.

My gaze sweeps up to the treehouse's canopy, which sways with the breeze. The air is heavy, thick with the scent of damp earth and pine, clinging to my skin like cologne. Shadows flit and dance among the trees, and I swear I hear the crunch of heavy boots.

A breath catches in my throat. Is that him?

"B-Benito?" I whisper, my pulse quickening.

Maybe I should meet him halfway.

I continue walking along the worn path, forcing my legs to move forward, even though a knot of tension in my gut twists hard enough to make me clutch my middle.

The shadows between the trees shift, and I try to convince myself it's my imagination, but prickles skitter across my skin, and the hair on the back of my neck stands on end.

Someone's here.

Watching.

Stalking.

I glance over my shoulder, but there's nothing but foliage. By now, the treehouse is no longer in sight, yet I'm not even halfway toward the car.

Every primal instinct screams at me to run, but stubbornness propels me forward. My breath comes faster. Shivers crawl down my spine and settle between my legs.

Maybe the footsteps were my imagination?

Rustling from within the trees shatters that line of thought. I freeze, my body going rigid, my fight-or-flight battling with my lack of common sense. When the footsteps grow louder followed by excited, panting breaths, terror takes control and I bolt.

I crash through the undergrowth, my heart pounding in my ears. Branches whip my skin, and my breath comes in ragged gasps. The footsteps behind me quicken, snapping twigs under their relentless pursuit.

Picking up my pace, I scream, "Benito!"

Dread roils in my gut, making me groan. Benito isn't coming—he won't reach me in time. This predator will almost certainly get to me first.

His presence is overwhelming, and my skin prickles with the weight of his gaze. Primal terror grips me by the throat, cutting off my air. I stumble over roots, my arms splaying out for balance. Pushing myself off a tree trunk, I run deeper into the forest.

The footsteps pound inside my skull, heavy and relentless. Every primal instinct screams the same devastating truth:

He's playing with my fear.

I glance over my shoulder again for a glimpse of his face, but all I see is the outline of an impossibly large figure eclipsing the moonlight. My knees want to buckle, but I force my legs to keep moving. I can't let myself get caught.

My lungs burn, but it's nothing compared to my aching thigh muscles having to navigate this hostile terrain. I pick up my pace, but it's no use. He's too fast. Too strong. Too determined to run me ragged.

Frantic thoughts crash against each other as my body runs out of steam. I'm helpless. Trapped. Prey.

A strong arm encircles my waist, lifting me off the ground. I scream, but a gloved hand clamps over my mouth.

"Quiet, little Ginny," says a terrifyingly familiar voice.

It's Bob Brisket.

He's finally tracked me down. That sadistic bastard must have been waiting all these months for the perfect moment to strike. My mind spirals, and panic punches me in the chest.

Brisket's malicious chuckle grips my heart and squeezes.

"Missed me?" he croons, his grip squeezing out my breath.

"No!" I shriek, but the sound is muffled by his gloved hand. My mind races, scrambling for a way to escape his clutches.

"Shhh," Brisket's voice sends chills down my spine. "You wouldn't want Mr. Montesano to aggravate his bullet wound now, would you?"

Tears prick my eyes. What the hell did this monster do to my Benito?

Terror floods my veins, icy and sharp. I twist and wriggle, but his grip is stronger than iron.

"Don't make this harder for yourself," he growls. "All this thrashing is only stimulating my cock."

My stomach lurches, my clit swells. Brisket tosses me on the forest floor, and I land on my hands and knees. I scramble upright, but his larger body pushes me into the leaf litter. All the air leaves my lungs, and my mind spirals into panic.

"Eager little slut," he growls. "Pressing your sweet ass into my cock. Is that your way of demanding anal?"

I raise my head and scream, "No, you bastard!"

It only makes him chuckle.

Arousal simmers low in my belly, twisting with fear. Heat flushes through my veins, making my cheeks burn.

His primal growl sends a jolt of terror straight to my core. A leathery hand tightens around one wrist before shoving it to join the other. I writhe against his grip, feeling the press of his erection between my ass cheeks.

I can't breathe, can barely think. My world narrows to this hard, imposing figure pinning me to the forest floor.

"Tell me how much you want this," he growls through the helmet, his voice muffled and distorted. "Beg me for this hard cock."

Somehow, during the struggle, I lost my shoes. I kick out, my heel connecting with his shin, but the armor absorbs the blow. His free hand slides down my side, tracing the curve of my hip until he yanks up the hem of my nightshirt. With a satisfied chuckle, he kicks apart my legs, exposing my ass and pussy to the air.

"You're glistening. Wet and ready for me."

Shaking my head, I burst out a sob. It's half-terror, half-need. I hate this urgent desire, despise how much I crave this degradation, loathe this unrelenting arousal.

He spanks my ass with a sting that jolts my clit like static electricity. I moan into the leaves, my skin burning with raw, animalistic desire.

There's no denying how much I've missed the roughness of his touch, the primal dominance, the way it feeds into the dark corners of my mind. I can recognize the part of me that yearns to be used roughly by Bob Brisket.

"Don't stop," I whisper into the leaves.

Fisting a hand into my hair, he yanks my head back. Arching, I suck in a gasp of fresh air. The sound of his buttons popping open make me moan and shiver in anticipation, and the muscles of my pussy clench, desperate for release.

"I'm going to fuck you good and hard, little Ginny," he growls. "And you're going to like it."

"Fuck you!" I scream.

"Take this cock like a good girl, and I'll make your pussy purr."

"You bastard. I love my husband."

"Mr. Montesano isn't here to save you, little Ginny, but if you cry out loud enough, maybe he'll hear how much you're enjoying this fuck."

I force back a sob, but the cruel haughty laugh that follows goes straight to my needy core. He slides his hand up my inner thigh, his gloved fingertips parting my folds as if I'm his property. No matter how much I try to flinch and twist, I can't release his grip.

"That's it, little Ginny. Moan for me."

The blunt head of his cock nudges my opening, making the most obscene wet sounds. Trembling, I try to resist, but I'm drunk on terror, intoxicated by the thrill, consumed by the depravity.

With a rough thrust, he enters my pussy. I cry out, my nails clawing at the forest floor. His grip tightens on my hips, holding me in place as he deepens the penetration, pushing hard into my cervix.

The stretch is incredible, and I swallow back a groan. But Brisket laughs, seeming to hear my pleasure.

"You love this," he growls, pulling back his hips, only to thrust forward without mercy.

Pleasure explodes in my core, setting my nerves on fire. I clamp my eyes shut, trying to dismiss the sensations, but this jarring bend of agony and ecstasy is impossible to ignore.

Brisket fucks me at a relentless pace, each thrust igniting new waves of sensation. I moan, the sound ripping through my throat.

I can't believe the way I'm melting under his ministrations, can't believe I'm allowing this brute to drag me to the edge of my sanity, but with every snap of his hips, I fall deeper into an abyss of madness.

My muscles tremble. A scream builds in my chest. An agonizing crescendo of pleasure threatens to tear me apart. It's unbearable, yet I'm too stubborn to use the safe word.

Just as I'm losing myself to oblivion, Brisket pulls out and flips me onto my back. Moonlight glints on his infernal visor, making him look monstrous. I scream, turning my head to the side but he grabs my throat.

"You don't get to tune out, little Ginny," he snarls. "You're going to know you're fucking Bob Brisket."

I close my eyes. Shake my head. Refuse to give this monster the satisfaction, but his grip around my throat tightens, and he enters me from this new angle. Fireworks set off behind my closed eyelids and a rough voice echoes through my ears.

"Keep this up, and Mr. Montesano will lose his slut wife."

My eyes snap open, and I stare into the reflective surface. "Why are you doing this?"

"Because I want it. Because I've never had a cunt so sweet. Because you're my dirty little temptation, and I'll never let you go."

My mind screams for me to break away, to find some vestige of self-respect and fight. But the pleasure is too intense. Moaning, I arch my back, my hips moving in counterpoint to his thrusts.

His laughter is a deep growl, vibrating through my skull. "And you want it too."

I jerk my head to the side, unable to face this truth, but he seizes my chin, forcing our gazes to meet.

"Look at me when I'm fucking you behind your husband's back," Brisket growls. "Look into the eyes of your monster."

Shivers skitter across my skin. All I see in the visor is my reflection.

Because I never hated Brisket. He ignited a flame in me that Samson extinguished. He made me feel wanted, desired, irresistible. Without this brute, I might never have mustered up the courage to approach Benito.

Dr. Saint would call this mental gymnastics. I call it getting lost in the heat of this cock. Gathering up my strength, I shove his shoulders.

"Let me get on top."

The perverse satisfaction in his laugh makes me want to slap off the visor. "Can't get enough of Bob Brisket?"

I don't dignify that comment with an answer. He already knows how much I want him.

He pulls us up so my legs wrap around his waist, and my knees dig into the leaf litter. I ride his thick length with an intensity that borders on madness. Pleasure jolts through my veins in a frenzy that makes my head spin.

"Greedy girl," he growls. "You're taking my cock so well."

My thighs burn with the effort, and my body wants to collapse, but he grips my waist, steadying my movements.

The forest fades into a blur, and all that's left is him, our raw desire, and the steady rhythm of his hips meeting mine.

"Ginevra," he growls, his voice strained.

I drive down harder, faster, reveling the sensations. The walls of my pussy pulse around his shaft, and I swear I can feel every vein brushing against my sensitive spots. He tears off my shirt, leaving me exposed to the night air.

With trembling fingers, I reach for the helmet, release the catch, and pull it off his head. Benito gazes back at me, his eyes filled with love.

"Kiss me," I whisper, my arms wrapping around his neck.

Our lips meet, hungry and desperate, his tongue sliding against mine with a fervor that matches the rhythm of our bodies. His hands wander my back, tracing lines of sparks against my skin.

"Benito," I gasp into his mouth, riding him harder, faster. "I love you so much."

His hands grip my hips tighter, his dark eyes boring into mine. "I've always loved you," he groans, his voice thick with emotion. "And I'll never stop."

Quickening my pace, I ride him harder, each thrust sinking deeper, his thick length filling my core to the brink.

My ears fill with his ragged breath, and I'm sure I feel the strain of his muscles beneath the armor. His low groan rolls through the air, vibrating through my chest.

Pleasure builds, spiraling out of control with each relentless movement. His hands dig into my waist, urging me faster. My pulse races, and heat flares in my core, threatening to detonate.

When the tension snaps, it's more intense than an explosion, with white-hot ecstasy coursing through my veins in violent spasms. I clench around his thick shaft, my body milking his.

Benito's grip drops to my hips, and he climaxes with a bellow that startles the birds. They fly out of the trees and disappear into the night's sky.

We fall together, collapsing onto the leaves, his chest rising and falling beneath mine. I tremble against him through the orgasm, shattered and spent.

For the next several heartbeats, the only sound is our ragged breathing. I rest my head on his shoulder, my mind spinning, my fingers fumbling with the fastenings of his jacket. The leaves beneath our bodies feel softer, the night air cool against my heated flesh, grounding me after the storm of pleasure.

Benito loosens his jacket, exposing the warmth of his skin. His breath stills for a moment before he whispers, "Are you alright?"

"That was intense," I murmur, my heart still racing, my inner muscles still fluttering from the aftershocks.

"Did it help?" he asks, his voice rough.

Dr. Saint's suggestion had sounded insane at first—a primal chase to negate my recurring nightmares of being hunted by Valentino Bossanova. Benito also had concerns that I still dreaded him because of Brisket, and he wanted to turn my fear and revulsion into desire.

I close my eyes, letting the final remnants of terror fade into the night. "Yes," I whisper into his neck. "The forest doesn't feel so frightening, and I no longer think I'm about to fall into a pit."

He exhales, his frame releasing the tension. "Good," he rasps. "I didn't want to push too far."

"You could never," I murmur, lifting my head to meet his gaze. His dark eyes, often clouded with shadows of guilt, now shimmer with hope. Frowning, he asks, "Was I too rough?"

Chest lightening, I trace my fingers over his brow, smoothing out the furrow. "This was exactly what I needed."

He lets out a long breath, his chest deflating with relief. I press a soft kiss to the side of his neck, and his shoulders relax.

"I love you," I whisper.

He turns his head, bringing our brows together. "I love you too, and I'll never stop."

We lie under the stars, our hearts still beating fast, but something deep in my psyche releases. The air between us clears, and old resentments drift into the night.

The past year has been full of painful revelations, heart-wrenching truths, and forgiveness. I invited Benito for Thanksgiving, where he opened up about his early childhood, and how his friendship with me filled the void left by his mother's depression. We worked through this with his therapist and discussed alternative ways to satisfy his need for stability and connection.

Now, there's no lies, no manipulation. Just us.

I finally feel safe in Benito's arms.

Pulling back enough to see his face, I trace the lines of his jaw with my fingertips. Eyes searching mine, he tenses as if bracing for a storm.

"We're going to be okay," I whisper.

A relieved smile curves his lips. "We are."

I shift, sitting up to straddle his hips again, and rest my hands on his chest. He slides his fingers up my thighs, his gaze quizzical, his heart thudding beneath my palms.

"Benito..." I scramble for the right words. "What if I didn't just stay for the weekends?"

He freezes, his features shuttering into that neutral mask. Even his chest stops rising and falling as he waits for me to elaborate.

Heart racing, I lick my lips. "What if I moved in with you full time? No more separation. Just us. Every day."

The mask shatters, and he pulls me down, crushing me to his chest in a hug that draws out a gasp. Benito's breaths become hard and labored, and I wonder if I've said the wrong thing. But when he pulls me back, his eyes shine with disbelief.

"You—you mean it?" he asks, his voice trembling.

Chest chest flooding with warmth, I smile. "You're my home. I'm ready to return."

He buries his face in my neck, his laughter thick with tears. "You don't know how long I've waited to hear that," he whispers, his voice hoarse. "I won't stop improving myself. I won't stop striving to be the man you deserve."

Tears prick my eyes, and I stroke his hair. "You were always that guy from the beginning. Somewhere in the middle, other people warped our connection. I'm so glad we've found ourselves again."

His lips find mine, soft and slow, sealing the promise with a kiss. When he pulls away, the grin I've missed so much spreads across his handsome features.

"You're really staying?" he asks.

"Forever," I whisper, smiling back.

I'm no longer that little girl who baked those cookies, or the damsel tied in knots in that closet. Our year of therapy has fostered a new understanding, and I've emerged stronger, more self-aware, and even more in control of my destiny.

Benito has grown, too. The walls around his heart have crumbled, bringing back the man I love, but he's edgier, exciting, and enchanting. Moments with him range from soul-deep comfort to exhilaration. We've taken those pieces of ourselves and rebuilt a bond that feels unbreakable.

As we lie beneath the stars, I picture the life we'll create together: lazy Sunday mornings in bed eating pancakes, and dinners with Benito's brothers and their wives. One day soon, we'll have the family we talked about the last time we were together. It's a life I couldn't have pictured when I was with Samson—a life I regretted being forced to leave. But now it feels so real I can taste it.

For the first time in half a decade, I have a future filled with love and passion. Benito is my perfect match. Nothing, not the threat of death or even world war three could ever tear us apart.

THE END
NEXT BOOK

Dear Reader,

Thank you so much for reading Stalking Ginevra! I hope you enjoyed Benito and Ginevra's obsessive love story.

As a special thank you, I'm offering a deleted breeding scene. You can access it here:

http://gigistyx.com/breeding

Your support is everything. If you enjoyed this book, please leave a review or share it on social media. Reviews and recommendations are the lifeblood of independent authors, and your voice makes a huge difference in helping these stories reach new readers.

Thanks again for being part of this journey.

Love,

Gigi

READ MY NEXT STALKER ROMANCE

ALSO BY GIGI STYX

Morally Black Series

Taming Seraphine

Snaring Emberly

Breaking Rosalind

Stalking Ginevra

Pen Pal Duet

I Will Break You

I Will Mend You

ABOUT THE AUTHOR

Gigi lives with her husband and two cats in London. When she's not crafting twisted dark romances with feisty heroines and the morally grey villains who love them, she's cuddled up on the sofa with a cup of tea and a book.

Sign up for Gigi's updates at:
www.gigistyx.com/newsletter